THE MAN WHO LOVED THE MIDNIGHT LADY

IN THE STONE HOUSE

by Barry N. Malzberg

Stark House Press • Eureka California

THE MAN WHO LOVED THE MIDNIGHT LADY /
IN THE STONE HOUSE

Published by Stark House Press
1315 H Street
Eureka, CA 95501, USA
griffinskye3@sbcglobal.net
www.starkhousepress.com

ISBN-13: 978-1-951473-54-9

Book design by Mark Shepard, shepgraphics.com
Cover photo by Anton Darius
Proofreading by Bill Kelly

First Stark House Press Edition: October 2021

Table of Contents

THE MAN WHO LOVED THE MIDNIGHT LADY

By Barry N. Malzberg

One last time for the Editors:

Edward L. Ferman
Pat LoBrutto

And in memory of my father, Michael Malzberg
10/25/96—8/10/79

Understanding too late; forgiveness, *lachrymosa*, in time

Introduction

Originally committed to silence, exile, and cunning, those three sluggers who form the heart of the Serious Writers' lineup (I turned down all requests for interviews in the early seventies and was delighted to be told by one of the prospective interviewers that I was "science fiction's man of mystery"), I fell off the wagon circa 1974 and have engaged in perhaps the most relentless self-explanation in the history of the field. Essays here, mumbles there, introductions to collections, articles and various complaints in the magazines professional and sub-professional, anguished letters to the editor, and so on. By now at least one critic of note has suggested in print that I shut up about my career already, and I have become almost as weary of my epistolary or nonfictional voice as he.

Accordingly, L—, a *brief* introduction. (Readers seeking the Real Concordance are directed to the previous Doubleday *Down Here in the Dream Quarter*, with its three essays and twenty-two prayers; the faithful are then welcome to the Pocket Books *Best of Barry N. Malzberg*, 150,000 words of autobiography and shielded autobiography—that is, if they can find it.) Since 1976 I have written no new science fiction novels (*Chorale*, 1978, is an expansion of a novelette written in June 1976 for the original anthology *Graven Images*) but I have kept on, intermittently, with short stories for the field and fields closely allied, of which these are better examples. I still believe in the short story format. I even believe in science fiction a little (more than I believe in Temple X in town Y, New Jersey, for instance), and I believe most of all in the persistence and integrity of my fictional voice, of which I have been damned poor custodian. Nonetheless, some of this work may last a little. I hope.

I hope. The unending lesson of recent years is that there was never anything else. Silence, exile, cunning: exile batting cleanup, of course, but it is the third man in the batting order who carries the highest average and deserves the most respect.

August 1978: Teaneck, New Jersey

On the Air

—dial slow, easy to get nervous when putting it in, easy to lose the direction altogether and that is why it is important, it is important man to move the wheel slowly, not get jammed between the twos and threes, get it right, two one two, three seven six, five four *two* one, there, the first bleep sounds like a near-busy and you don't like that at all, that means all five lines are jammed and god alone knows when you'll be able to get through, how many times you'll have to sit here racketing the numbers against themselves, busies are no good man they are a bad scene ... but it goes through. that easy purring ring coming soft out of the earpiece and you know you are set. on the dial this woman she is talking about her problems with the group, just going on and on but stevie is already making the good-restless sounds you know that mean he is about to split and leave and maybe you'll be the next one in. once you get the ring-in it is just lights on the dial, stevie can push one or four oh or seventy-three for all he cares, he has explained that and it is random, call in late and get in early, call early and never get into the frame at all. it is not fair but then whoever in the words of our late great prez ever said that life is fair? ring in the earpiece, got to go, stevie says on the *rad*-io, got to take care of business and the lady burbles, burbles in stevie's ear but her voice is already soft and going. she knows when she is done, got to *go* my stevie says and then just like that he is saying hello into your ear, seven-second lag a truly great invention to keep the cursers and the funny-noisers off the air while the radio is still playing stevie saying good-bye to the woman he is saying *hello you are on the air* into your ear but this will only come out on the radio seven seconds later so if you say big f or like that stevie will hit the switch with his hand and you will be canceled into the darkness. hello stevie says again who is this ringing my bell? in ten seconds you will be *off* the air if you do not move.

—quick then, one hand flick off the switch of the radio, first thing the experienced phone talker does, second cuddle the receiver into the chest come forward then into a confidential posture, 'hello,' you say, 'stevie?' although you know it is him of course this is just what is called an instinctive nervous reaction. going on the air is an uptight-making process; stevie knows this, has warned us against it many times, let it all hang out, reel it out stevie says, forget the jet lag and the off switch or you will not be able to wing it which is the principle of free form.

'hi,' you say, 'how are you?'

—i am all right, stevie says. i am not complaining.

'the topic for this evening is drugs,' you say, 'i had a few comments on the drug situation in relation to what this previous caller said.' stevie likes you to give the calls what he says is *reference* so they do not *hang out in the open*. 'if i may continue.'

—you may continue, this is your radio.

'good,' you say. you draw yourself into it the way that you always do when you go on the air. somewhere in the hall there is the sound of movement, somewhere out on the street there is a siren which comes through the open window but these are ignored, you draw yourself into that ball of flame which is contact and going on the air. 'now i don't know about drugs,' you say, 'not really being a user but i want to say—'

—if you don't use why shoot off your mouth.

—that is stevie, he is often insulting but inside there is this core of real warmth which can be perceived and gotten hold of and despite the cynical exterior at almost any time can break down into tears if he is really moved. i have heard him in the early-morning hours near the end of his shift weeping and telling of his childhood. 'stay with me, stevie,' you say, 'and i will explain.'

—you ain't explained nothing yet. you are just calling in so that you may hear yourself on the *rad*-io.

'listen here, stevie,' i say assuming an attitude of command without which call-in live radio is nothing and you are simply at the mercy of the host who will use you for the purposes of his own moods and passions, 'you will let me explain what i have to say and then you will understand exactly why i have called in.'

—i have heard your voice before. i think that you are one of the regulars.

'everybody is a regular,' i say, 'once you call in or even try to once you are a regular. thinking about it however does not count.'

—that is the truth, he says, that is the truth.

—it may be asked why i am writing these memoirs in lower-case type without capitals that is to say and my answer is that the typewriter has a bad shift key and a poor spacer when you get into the upper-case leads. there are those who will say that this is big malarkey and the real reason for this very jazzy and self-conscious method of diction is because i am trying to reproduce typographically the feeling of anonymity of the caller in live-show radio and how oppressed and small they feel and deprived of that true sense of identification which would enable them to capitalize capitalization being a way of establishing names and identities but i say that this is a load of the selfsame malarkey as i make my points as stevie has always asked us to in my words and manner of speaking and not in any tricky methods which would only get you bleeped off on the cuts anyway. same thing with putting my dialogue in half quotes and stevie's in none and the dashes to start paragraphs that do not begin with my dialogue. it has no symbolic weight as they like to say on the heavier channels. i just feel like it and that is the truth.

—others say of live call-in radio who needs it? who needs memoirs about this stuff much less from one of the call-in creeps themselves or himself? live call-in radio shows the isolation and emptiness of modern life, lost souls in their separate shells in the city desperately trying to establish communication with the host who in his invulnerability, invisibility and assumed omnipotence can be called the only god of the end of the urban twentieth century and thus a further comment on a country which has so taken power out of the hands of its citizens to say nothing of purpose that they are reduced to call-in radio to express their humanity. this too is heavy-channel garbage of the worst sort because only a very small percentage of these so-called anonymous and frustrated citizens call in and they are not representative of citizenry in general since they are in fact as well as imagination very strong and individuated types who wish to change their lives by assuming control over them hence the call-in, one who calls in is already three quarters of the way toward being a person and from my analysis of the many people who will be on the air during the endless night you must listen as well as talk to get into the beat of the show. i would like to say that we represent a very *high* grade of intelligence and articulation well beyond most politicians for instance and do not feel at all helpless at least i do not think that they feel *completely* helpless or otherwise why would they call in at all, eh?
—now that is the question i would like to put, why they would even call in at all if they had given up?

—my name is raoul the caller; raoul the call that is how i identify myself when i talk to stevie which is every so often although he still does not recognize my voice reserving recognition for real regulars of the sort who call every night whereas i only call when i have something to say and to contribute to the discussion which in my case is no more than once or twice a week. raoul the call has a ball. 'listen up,' i say, 'about these drug problems, this situation you are talking about i have had some experience with drugs and i tell you they are a downer altogether, one does not need drugs to take the ultimate trip.' this is a lie. i have no experience with drugs.
—what is the ultimate trip?
'well there are some who say that death is the ultimate trip and others

who say sex of course but to me the ultimate trip would be actual space flight and that is what i want to say i am doing. i am going to go on a spaceship tonight. i am going to go to venus by way of the moon and i wish to tell that to everyone.'

—that is cool, stevie says, that is real cool that you are going on a spaceship, you have a spaceship in your backyard or are we talking of one now at kennedy airport which you are boarding?

'now that is ridiculous,' i say knowing how stevie can ride all over you and start to abuse unless you pull him up short at the beginning also thinking of the seven-second lag and the knowledge that if i get too clever he will cut me off. stevie as he has said calls the shots and has enough wit for all of us. 'no one has a spaceship in their backyard particularly on west ninety-third street between amsterdam and columbus avenues which is a courtyard of about two feet square and there are no commercial spaceship flights going from kennedy as far as you or i know. i am going to will myself to venus by way of the moon, inner space is a condition of validity of travel which is a proper metaphor for any external reality and one can travel if one wills oneself to do so.

—you are losing me, stevie says, inner space and external reality and validity. i do not know validity. i recognize your voice now and you are the famous raoul the call.

'that is right,' i say. i am happy because usually stevie does not recognize my voice but this proves that i have made an impression on him after all or then again that he will admit my humanity. 'i am raoul the call and inner space is the proper conjecture for the external reality. i am going to board the ship of my soul and go straight out to venus with a moon stopover.

—far out stevie says.

'i am going on a *long* trip.'

—are you carrying any messages?

'if you wish me to,' i say. 'i will carry any messages you wish. but i have been on venus and the moon many times before and assure you that they are uninhabited with conditions not conducive to life and there is no one to leave the messages *for* except maybe coliform bacteria which can make it occasionally by the gaseous light of the methane swamps of otherwise unilluminated nighttime venus.'

—oh man stevie says you are far far out you are wild. how many times before have you gone?

'i have gone to venus sixteen times and the moon eighteen and mars once, mars is so hot that there is no way you can even do any sightseeing even under glass. later on they will open the mercury shoot but this will not be for several years. there is nothing on mars or mercury either,' i add.

—you are flipped stevie says, you are freaked. raoul the call why you do this to me?

—there is a real answer to this but a fake answer is better in an entertainment medium. 'the topic was of general interest tonight,' i say, 'not limited to special subject and i thought that the discussion of drugs and trips before led naturally to this. i have been wanting to tell you for a long time of my exploits and this seemed to be a good time to do it.'

—enough stevie says you are too much. he pauses and i wonder if he is going to cut me off the way he often will do to move along if he feels the show lags but he does not want to leave this one go. i can tell this. he begins to ask me what methane gas is and i tell him giggling a little because the sheer *mention* of methane freaks.

—stevie holds me on the line after a time and takes other calls. gang calls are a technique of modern switchboard: he can bring in as many as ten talking to each other and on the air at once but he settles for just five this time. naturally they all want to talk to raoul the call about his trip to venus. some feel that raoul is crazy or being sarcastic about drugs and their effect on consciousness but at least two are very serious and want to ask further questions. how long has this been going on? how does modern technology admit of this possibility? do we have the machines and is the government, sitting on the information like it is on the ufo attacks? i reply that i do not want to get into politics or the specifics of the matter and besides the machines are not under government control. stevie cultivates callers who go into political channels but raoul the call has never taken such bait: politics acts to conceal the realities. it is at best a metaphor and dedicated to the suppression of issues and not their articulation, something which i would not get into on the air because of the general mental inferiority— although i have conceded their courage and individualism—of stevie's callers. finally i decide that it is time to go or stevie decides it is time to go the good host never letting you know when you are being manipulated unless he wants you to know, the five or six callers dropping off like apples from the old apple tree and only stevie and i are left in the singing emptiness of the invisible strand that connects us through the heart of the city from west ninety-third to east sixty-second. dead river to dead river and waste on both ends. to cavemen it would be science fiction just as my trips to venus are science fiction to stevie. i wish you a good trip, stevie says, you will call in and tell us how it was will you not?

'i have not yet,' i say. 'i have been a caller to your show for three years and two months and have made many flights during that period and have never mentioned them until now. i wish to conceal far more than i reveal.

—i can understand that, stevie says, you are freak city.

'so are you stevie,' i say with affection, 'so are you my friend my love,' and we disconnect. to put the phone down after so long is to be empty and alone my ear craving for its contact the way the cupped hand of a lover may shrivel for the beloved's body—but i will not get into the even more difficult issue of sex—and i put on the radio just in time to hear myself seven-second-lagging *so are you my friend my love*,' and a long pause even a sigh from stevie. it is too much, he says, this is some night. woodwork night full moon night. i will play a record now while i look for a record though why do we not think of what has been heard tonight and what we have learned.

—that is stevie, pedagorical. i join him in thought, thinking of what we have learned tonight and what the true sense of it all is until the thunder of the music begins to pour out of the receiver and then disconnecting it is the music itself that i allow to carry me my ship to the dark and departed spaces the incontestable fire of the planets above, mercury, mars, venus or the moon. i am carried. my voyage commences.

—there are some who will say that this story is not about actual events but is merely a clever attempt to show that traveling to mars or venus is no more absurd or strange or wonderful than talking to stevie in the night the two of us linked invisibly. there are others who will say that i have merely tied one mystery to another mystery to demonstrate that all of life is an implausibility and that i never really went to the planets at all but this would be untrue and would show that you readers are as stupid as most of stevie's listeners and missed the point.

—for i *did* indeed carried by the music began my voyage then and it is going on even now even at this moment my first and terrible and endless voyage to venus because of course i did lie to stevie. although i had had the method before i had not had the courage to use it now for the first time until at last through self-declaration on the air i found the strength to make the commitment because otherwise stevie and the listeners would have known that i was weak and carried forth by that i continue on my strange and terrible journey. in one sense i owe it all to stevie and in another i owe nothing but the resolution of this is strange and if i ever return to earth with the look of eagles in my eyes it will not matter.

June 1974: New Jersey

Afterword to "On the Air"

I wrote this story in one hour on the Sunday evening of June 23, 1974; I then drove into New York and joined Adrian Berry, author of *The Next Ten Thousand Years*, on a WABC radio talk show, which, I was assured, was heard at some point of its two and a half hours by twenty million people from Coney Island to the mysterious Mississippi. Afterward I drove home to suburban anonymity, slept, mailed in the story for Robert Silverberg's *New Dimensions* the next day, and slept some more. The story was published—here it is published again—and the talk show was heard, but for all the effect that these activities had on my inner life I might as well have been one of stevie's listeners. This is to some degree a writer's complaint, but it goes a little beyond. Stanley Elkin has some generally intelligent things to say about this at greater length and eloquence in his wonderful novel *The Dick Gibson Show*.

Live call-in radio is science fiction, of course (a point made perhaps too explicitly in the story but what the hell), and "On the Air" is a science fiction story. Initially I doubted this, but Silverberg, who (I have said before) is almost never wrong, assured me of this in his bland and civilized way and not one protest came to me. Of course it is possible that no one read the story and that the WABC transmitters went dead to the Mississippi that night.

What this story is *really* about is marriage, I think.

Here, for Just a While

ONE: You come into the room cautiously, a little tentatively, but your confidence increases as you see that the room is indeed as you have always pictured it: the ornate furniture, the religious symbols on the walls and on the bed which dominates the room (as it would have to), the woman herself naked, reaching for you. She bears a slight resemblance to the widow of a famous public figure, assassinated many years ago, and this is titillating of itself but does not obscure the aura of your feeling as you first entered the room. That feeling might be described, for lack of better, as a great earnestness. You want to do well. It has always been important for you to give a good account of yourself. You do not want to fail to measure up to anyone's expectations.

"Come here, X," she says, her arms outstretched, using that private, very personal name which you have given her in the bed, "come here and make love to me," and stumbling you take two, no three steps toward her, beginning to feel the familiar terror, and then you are upon her or she on you, hard to tell in this sudden, metallic collision of limbs. She drags you to the bed. "I want you, X!" she says and then becomes even more explicit, this language surprising from a woman so delicately attractive ... but by this time your detachment is lessened. She steals clothing from you, garments fluttering like pennants in the airless spaces of the room, and then you are on her. You know that you will do well now. You know that you will measure up to all expectations.

"Ah, X, you're wonderful," she says as if in agreement. You subside into her, caught somewhere midway between lust and confusion as your eye catches the visage of the crucified Saviour winking at you from his portrait ... and as between this union, you and the Saviour, that is to say, the woman seems almost incidental, merely a plank of wood, a board, a means to get you from her place to His ... but forget it, friend, just forget it.

TWO: At the very moment that you are engaging in the acts and thoughts described above, the man with whose wife you are locked is in another city, stretched in an uncomfortable position behind a building parapet, trying to aim a hand rifle. It is the obsession of this man for reasons which must remain in doubt (because they are not known to me at all and barely to him) that he can gain fame by assassinating three astronauts who are due to parade through the street four stories below in approximately a half an hour. The fame will allow him to express certain political ideas which he feels to be of great interest but for which, so far, he has been unable to find an audience.

Astronauts are not what they used to be before the time of this story, but the medium-sized Midwestern town in which the parade will occur is home for two of them and the parade is thus a self-celebration. Already a good crowd has gathered on Main Street and the mayor, an officious but good-natured man, is blowing into the amplifier on the reviewing stand, little wheezing, nervous breaths, waiting for review. In the heights, the man behind the parapet hears the high school band tuning, but from this very narrow vantage point he has open to him little more than an arc of avenue, a half-moon barely six yards wide through which the astronauts and their car will pass. It is ample space in which to place a killing shot. Nevertheless he is nervous. What if he misses? Even worse, what if he succeeds but finds no one interested in his ideas?

He thinks not of his wife who is committing adultery with you five hundred miles to the southeast. He is no longer romantically involved and has, regardless, much important work to do here in a small amount of time. He is under much tension and even knowledge of his wife's adultery could not change his schedule now. He is aware, of course, that his wife is an attractive, restless woman who is in need of frequent sex or at least attention, but he has not really satisfied her for several years in either way and no longer worries about that. On some level he does know that she is seeing other men. She has become accommodated to his work schedule—frequent trips out of town, weekends brooding alone in bars—all too easily.

This man, the man behind the parapet, is a psychopath. I must, sadly, state the obvious. Furthermore, his view of history is incorrect. He views history as a canvas stretched tautly on pegs of entropy between a past in which nothing existed and a future in which there will be no recollection. On this canvas a man may paint his own version of reality which will become all that is known of this time, the man has theorized, and the reality which he will exercise begins with a gun.

Already this man has murdered seventeen men, women, and children in four states. He has never been apprehended. Some of the murders were sensational. All of them so far were of obscure people or what the man chooses to think of as obscurities. This, accordingly, is his first attempt to direct the future conception of his era through the murder of some who have achieved at least a light fame. Fight entropy with entropy.

The psychopath is very nervous.

This is a bad combination, I might advise him, if he were within earshot ... these small, nervous wrenches and bubbles from the subconscious could demolish the delicate framework of his functioning psychopathology if he dwells upon them too long. Then he would be a simple, forgettable schizoid. Not that he would listen anyway. He never listened. Not to anyone. Not to his wife, certainly never to me when I tried. Now I am nothing other than a commentator and at that not first-string. A color man.

He checks the stock of his rifle, mumbles a few absent curses, pinches himself hard in the thigh for luck, and as the music grows waits patiently for the motorcade. *Oswald did this, a schmuck like that*, he murmurs, for self-confidence.

THREE: You, meanwhile, the true focus of this narrative, are now finished. All is over and you stand on the floor, slowly dressing while you give her greedy little looks. She lies there naked, her respiration deep and easy while you talk to her quickly, earnestly, drawing on your clothing with small gestures. You are satisfied and yet you are not at rest. You are sated and yet consumed with anxiety. What you seek of course is a more permanent arrangement, something on which you can depend, something from which you are not asked to go quickly. You suggest this to her.

"I'm sorry," she says. "I'm sorry, X. No commitments."

"Just once a week," you say, "or even once a month. Just something that I can count on and that is mine. That I can look forward to and stay after. It doesn't have to be frequent, just so that I know it's there."

You are frustrated. Your marriage and professional life have, in many ways, been disastrous (both of them are over) and you seek little pockets of stability in which you can, so to speak, leave your emotional small change. A liaison with this woman would help. "Please," you say. You feel humiliated yet you persist. This is your pattern from which you have never deviated.

"I'm sorry. No commitments. If we see each other again, if it happens that way, then we can do this or maybe we won't. It would be better to plan on nothing," she says. "Once you depend on something it traps you."

"I don't believe that," you say and find yourself staring again at the Saviour. He looks at you in a way wan and compassionate, consuming and detached. Ancient religious thoughts return, you think of *musaf* and the bleating of the kneeling high priest. "How about next week at eleven?"

"No, X," she says, this woman who not ten minutes ago surrounded your name with gurgles and small passionate cries, "what I said has to be. It would serve you to leave."

It would. It would definitely. Here you are, fully dressed now in this room which has turned somehow threatening and ominous, some aspect of light shifting, pouring through the downed shades, catches the crucifix at the other side of the bed and makes it glisten like the deep eye of the Rabbi pondering the congregation just before benediction. Here you are, not in a pew hungry, but nonetheless at a totally disadvantageous situation in this room in a cheap and run-down section of the city, a section into which you would normally not venture but for lust and the recommendation of a trusted friend ... and yet and yet you cannot leave. Some sense of the unfinished hangs like dust in the air. "It isn't reasonable," you say. "It's not like I'm asking so much, just to know in a week, in a month—"

"You must go, X," she says. "I have another appointment."

Her eyes flick open. She seems conscious suddenly of her nakedness and protective: she reaches for a corner of the sheet, turns it against her breast, and you see her then, one breast covered, one nipple winking, one eye open and one eye closed. It inflames. You move toward her, fondling in your pocket the point thirty-two caliber Smith & Wesson which you were given permission to carry after two street robberies some months ago. Her face assumes knowledge as you close upon her. You brace your knees against the mattress.

But you do not know exactly what you have in mind.

FOUR: The astronauts are arguing. "When do we get to the stand?" the one who is not from this town asks. "When is it going to be over?" There will be a banquet in the high school gymnasium and this astronaut looks forward to leaving as soon as possible after dinner. The others will have to stay overnight and sleep with their wives and they are, consequently, in less of a rush.

"What do you care?" one of the hometowners says, a shade bitterly. "We went through New York, we went through Chicago, we wasted a whole week debriefing, so what are a few hours in Indiana?" The car is moving at five miles an hour. Little strips of colored paper float like haze or haloes around them and like good whores (or so they think) the astronauts wave and smile as they continue talking. These public gestures are done unconsciously; it has been a long time since they thought of their personas as being at all connected to the interior. "Screw this," the first astronaut says. He is in a foul mood and the tension, high since the expedition left for Mars a year and a half ago, has been heightened by their seeming inability to get away from one another, even now. When will they be able to scatter? "I'm not a goddamned machine."

"Oh, come on," the third astronaut, who takes himself to be something of a mediator, says, "stop it, both of you. Let's be friends; we've gone through so much together and we're only here for just a while."

"I don't like him," the outsider says. "I *never* liked him. I had to listen to him for eighteen months and he still won't shut up. What does it take to make him go away?"

"Come on," the peacemaker says, skillfully catching a rose thrown by a woman. "Just a few hours and we'll be out of here. If we can give them a little pleasure, what the hell. And it's better than the Phobos run, folks."

"Shove it," the outsider says. His rage is excessive; only I know (and now you, of course) that he has had a small cerebral hemorrhage already manifesting subtle personality changes which will, through the next week, slowly escalate to unconsciousness, deep coma, and death. "I've had enough." He half stands in the open limousine and waves to the crowd, simulating gaiety although there are strain lines on his forehead, a glisten of salivation from the corners of his mouth. "It hurts," he says.

The limousine skates on. The driver is being paid a flat fee of fifty-seven dollars to move at five miles an hour in D2, not to listen to conversation. The band plays "Our Director." They are, perhaps, a tenth of a mile from the review stand.

FIVE: "Come on now," I say to the parapet man as he struggles for proper lead. "There's no excuse for this senseless violence. It only leads to chaos and besides you don't want to kill them, you only want to get your ideas across. Why don't you write science fiction novels and story collections? Why don't you write a letter to the editor? They'll pay just as much or as little attention and you can make a living at this, too. No one's interested in ideas anyway, not anymore: it's just sex or death or money or power."

Fretful, he does not listen. I doubt that he hears. I have already explained that for all the good my questions and comments do I might as well not be there at all. In this case I am not. I do not exist other than for those who will recognize me. This sense of living within a void, this realization that I have no effect whatsoever, would make a lesser spirit doubtful, lead him, perhaps, to his own breakdown, but I am of sturdier, peasant stock and do not allow this to shake my essential balance, although of course I find it disturbing. It is always disturbing to feel that you have no influence and no visibility; that you cannot affect events even when they seem to be heading toward catastrophe. Then too, judicious as always, I must admit that those who *do* attend to me almost always reach a bad end.

"This is ridiculous," I nonetheless persist. "You've already killed seventeen, which is bad enough, but here is serious trouble. The death of a public figure now is a blow to the national psyche, media makes everyone famous a relative, and anyway your wife is with another man. You had better watch yourself because this does no one any good. You didn't want it to turn out like this, no one really does, and right up to the instant of connection there is still time to back away, cut back. If you do, salvation awaits. The gates of repentance are always open. Even the Ba'al Shem cannot stand before a truly repentant sinner. For I have set before you this day the blessing and the curse, therefore choose life and live—"

No good. No good at all, really. He continues to struggle with the rifle, preparing his lead, and I can see that nothing will dissuade, nor should I try further. It would only make me crankier.

"Fool," I nonetheless say with petulance.

SIX: You stand over her and she looks back at you, you two linked into a network of connection which fuses utterly. You feel the gun within your arched hand, beating like a bird, and she stares at the hand and then at you, her look transfixed in motion, but the more deeply you look within her the more profoundly she stares at you, the more you become immersed there in the moment the more you feel that hard bright spot between the shoulder blades.

That glowing stigma created by the Saviour and the High Priest.

It expands. The blessing and the curse.

October 1973: New Jersey

Afterword to "Here, for Just a While"

Essentially a mystery, this story spoke to me powerfully when I wrote it and even more so now when I ran it through for some slight revisions. Although it was written fully five years ago it seems to address the place where I have been living consciously for the past two. And I did not know at the time what I was saying any more than I am sure I know what I am saying now.

Of all my assassination stories this may be the most deeply felt and, by that virtue, the best. It is all feeling. What fool of an interior voice helped me to go on for years and years (and years and years) by telling me I was a cold writer? A *cunning* fool, of course.

In the Stocks

I

In the tenth day of that seventh month a girl comes to the project who says that her name is Georgina and she wishes to convert me to the pleasures of heterosexuality. Whether she comes from the Capitol or is merely working this out through a painful and private sense of mission is beyond me; in any event she insinuates herself into my rooms during a period of the shift when Kenny is without and instantly divests herself of clothing, places herself on the wall in an attitude of crucifixion, and says, "Take me, take me." Her eyes are closed, her breasts palpitate like eyelids, and for a moment in the strangeness of the desire I feel I am quite paralyzed, caught somewhere between purpose and memory.

The coming of the girl is not in itself so surprising, for there have been rumors of this for months: of female stalkers through this the project who make random attempts to seduce the inhabitants. It seems to be a plot on the part of the Capitol but then again it may be no such thing; these girls may be diseased travelers, carried by the strange winds of their obsession; in any event I have given them little consideration, denying the sense of the rumors in my own heart. But the situation is now flooded with imminence; looking at her in this posture, cramped against the wall, I feel old dreads tugging at me and bolt suddenly to the door, turn the knob, find the lock bolted, and turn back to her to see her smiling at the sound. "It's quite hopeless, you see," she says, "you're sealed in here, just the two of us are sealed in, you'd better take me," and the dreads like a carnival of the animals now pour to the forefront of consciousness tumbling and shrieking. "I am going to convert you to the pleasures of heterosexuality," she says again, the phrase curiously horrifying, her tone monolithic and blank; "you can either take me or you can refuse but I will not leave until you do so. It is your choice. The choice is in your hands."

"You think I can't do it," I say, "you think that I can't do it if I really wanted to."

"I said nothing of the sort," she says. She sways on the wall, her flesh trembles. There is an unsuspected prurience to her aspect; as much as I despise myself I feel a certain pressure of response. "You were the one who said it. Whether you can or cannot is up to you; the point is that I'm staying." She leans forward, her eyes open, I see the little cords in her neck like staves in a barrel. "My name is Georgina," she says. For all the vulnerability of her position, the abruptness with which she has assumed it, the bizarre nature of the situation, she seems quite calm. "Why don't you try what I've got?"

Ridiculous, ridiculous, and yet there is no end to the cunning of the Capitol. They will try this and they will try that; then they will leave us alone for years, they will abandon us to our own lives, and then a new passel of bureaucrats with different policies and procedures will come in and all of it will start again, the same cycle. They simply will not let us live, will not trust us to our own sense of accommodation, and at this thought a new wave of despair overtakes me, that despair not unmixed with lust because looking at her in that posture against the wall I am unable to suppress more vivid, carnal images and suddenly I know that there is only one way out, one way in which to bring this preposterous situation to a close, that is to say, and therefore I divest myself of my clothing, my garments falling from me with a low rustle which yet has the sound of a gong in my head. I close the ground upon her and pin her against the wall and then rudely, rudely I enter her, taking her in one single lurch of possession.

The idea, of course, is to enter her fully, take her completely before I have had a chance to really contemplate the corruption of my act, and for an instant it seems that it will almost work, she falls around me like a gigantic insect, carrying me then to the floor as I dig my way into her, forcing myself through a flurry of strokes near climax, and she says, *ah, ah!* and then her eyes widen, she looks at me in a perfect astonishment and comprehension and says, "You can do it, you really can? Who would have ever known?" Her face has whitened with the surprise of it. "Who would have thought it?" she says. "Who would have thought that this was so?" and then she tightens around me, arms and legs fastening to me like suction cups drawing me in, taking me to the core of her—

—And that is what causes the falling away, the thought of the core, the greasy and rotten entrails into which I am plunging, and as close as I have been to a kind of qualified success, so instantly am catapulted away from it, through layers and layers of insufficiency, shrinking within her, all of my redoubling of effort contributing merely to detumescence, and I fall from her then limply, rolling onto my back, shoulder blades, looking at the pastels of the ceiling through which the distant fluorescence penetrates, not thinking, thinking nothing at all, and then beside me as if from a great distance I hear her whimpering. "You can't," she says, "you can't do it, they lied to me," and still there is nothing to say so I merely lie there, allowing my eyes to close, and after a while she has moved away from there, I can tell by the sound, and a little after that she has put on her clothing, I can hear that too, and then she does something with the door which opens it and she is gone, the door suctioning closed with a hiss, leaving me there in the spaces of the room still not thinking, not thinking, not thinking at all.

For if I were to think it would only be knowledge of how close I had come to the dead rose, the gnarled heart of corruption, and unable to bear that I would be unable to bear as well the own dank sound of my breath curling up around my ears, all of it now the only sound in the cubicle.

II

When Kenny returns I think for a moment of telling him about the girl, Georgina, and then I decide not to, not because there is a failure of trust or because I would be ashamed to tell him but only because it would hurt him ... and the important thing is that I have done nothing with her to make either of us truly ashamed. I have fallen back from the precipice. So I say nothing to him as he murmurs his way around the cubicle, telling me about the little events of his little day, say nothing to him as he chatters of events in the briefing section that have contributed to his own good spirits but simply retain an impassive exterior, and when he approaches me at the end of all his conversation I find myself prepared to respond to his touch almost as if nothing had happened with the girl, almost as if there had been no girl whatsoever ... and the touch of his fingers upon my shoulders once again starts that great gong ringing within my head, that gong ringing for the second time that day, and slowly I join him upon the floor, slowly, almost luxuriously, our clothing falls away from each of us and then we blend with each other, the old pounding, the heavy rising, and I go with him willingly, my mind funneled into that dense, stinging brightness which is always mine when I am with him, deep in the certainty of events ... but at the last moment as I feel him whine, uncoil, discharge himself into me with the thrashings of a snake there is the single image of the girl Georgina, her breasts trembling against her, which slashes itself across my consciousness as a ripped canvas would reveal some horrid form lurking behind ... and I am unable to enjoy him; for the second time that day I collapse into insufficiency, the feeling of shame pouring through me ... and then for reasons which I cannot understand I am weeping, unable to tell Kenny as he asks what is the matter, why this has happened to me, what is wrong ... until at last his questions cease and he stalks away from me; I know that in some way it will never be the same between us again, but that is not really the concern. No, that is not really the concern. The concern is whether it will be the same with me again, and, looking once again at that leaping fluorescence, I am not sure.

III

In the days ahead I see Georgina many times; I see her in the hallways at shift points, I see her on the gigantic conveyor, I see her lolling on the balconies that separate the abutments, and a few times I think that I see her as well in my cubicle itself although never at these times will she speak to me. Sometimes she will wink or nod, most of the time she will show no acknowledgment whatsoever even though I will pursue her, sometimes frantically asking questions.

"What is going on here?" I will ask her or "Is it true that you come from the Capitol?" and sometimes "Will I ever see you again?" and all that she will do, at the most, is to touch my hand in a strange, lingering caress before she moves on, vanishing so quickly that there is the possibility—there has been this possibility all along, I am not mad—that she is an apparition and never existed at all but was merely conjured up out of latency. There is precedent for such cases; I would not be the first to have reacted to certain conditions of project living in this way. "I was perfectly happy, why would anyone want to convert me?" is another one of my questions that will not be answered as well, and this is possibly the most serious and significant of all because since her appearance in my room, real or imagined, things have not been right, things have not been going well at all, and I find myself unable to climax in the familiar or normal way or, for that matter, in any way whatsoever. And Kenny will not sleep in that cubicle anymore.

At first I had resolved not to speak with her at all, ignore the entire instance, but that weak attempt at control had lapsed at once, on the second time that I had seen her, and since then the questions have been incessant. The strangeness is that she has made no attempts to avoid me; if she will not answer the questions, well, then, she will not avoid them either and I sometimes have the feeling of a man pursuing a scuttling rabid animal that has just bitten him: the horror would be to touch it again and yet there is an equivalent horror in the loss. I must find out what has happened to me. I must be able to judge the extent of the damage.

Off shift time, I take to standing alone at the parapets for hours and looking down at the city. It looks the same and yet it does not. No longer are those spaces a complex network of possibility underneath me: instead, staring from these heights, I sometimes think that they are a maze from which I will never emerge. Still, one must go on.

IV

In a dream I take myself to be with Georgina once again but this time I am able to function; I am in fact engorged with lust and as I rise far above her, looking at her features distorted to cruelty and loss in her reciprocal passion, it is as if I am looking not only at her but at the Capitol itself: that mythic construction which none of us have ever glimpsed but which all of us know to be real. "Open up!" I scream to her, to the Capitol; "open up, be merciful, let us live our lives, let us be ourselves, don't lie to us anymore, don't skulk around, don't cheat us, let us be human!" and she sinks her teeth into my shoulder until they meet, I yelp with pain and as I scream instantly come, the pain the final trigger I pour into a woman, the act is astonishing, climaxing with a woman that is to say, the first time in my life that has ever happened, and some gigantic hand seizes me by the back of the neck, yanks me all the way up through layers and layers of perfumed sleep and into the bright, gray tortured spaces of my bed where I lie alone, biting on my wrist with frantic, burning motions, not daring to look beneath me where I know I will see, still growing, the now eternal stain of implication.

V

So I am brought in front of the Group and my problem is discussed. This is standard procedure for cases such as I have become—distant, restive, unhappy, no longer bringing pleasure to the selected partner— and I should have known what would have to happen eventually. It is Kenny who brings up the issue according to procedure and then all of the others begin to question me, their questions beating at me like wings, higher and harsher, and finally it all spills out of me, dreams of the woman, the encounter with the woman, the images of her in the corridors, the failure with Kenny, the fear that the woman has come from the Capitol which will not allow us to live our lives ... all of it is spoken except for the discovery at the end of my dream. I do not think that I could bear to tell them that.

"There is no woman," they say to me then, "there is no Georgina. You have imagined all of this, it does not exist. Not even the Capitol. You have constructed all of this."

"The Capitol exists," I say. "That at least—"

"The Capitol fell a long time ago. It is merely a collection of artifacts now. Here in these projects we control our lives. There are no bureaucrats. There are no policies. There are no administrators. There is merely us."

"No," I say again, resisting this, "that is not true. I know distinctly there is a Capitol, do we not constantly receive messages—"

"The messages are distortions. The messages are created by those in other projects who wish to preserve the illusion of a Capitol just as there are those in this project who do the same to them, issue messages in the name of something that no longer exists. You must face up to the reality. It is only us. This is our life."

"Yes," Kenny adds, moving close to me, touching me, and I find his touch horrid, shrug it off, "it is only us, our lives, our decisions," and then he realizes what I have done and his face twists in pain or maybe it is merely rage. He strikes me on the back and I fall to the floor.

"No," I say again, "it is not true. For if there is no Capitol, then who would have sent her? From where does she come?"

"She comes from nowhere," the Group says, "she does not exist. You have fabricated all of this. You have created something in your mind for your own reasons. But none of it has any reality."

"If that is so," I say, lying on the floor in the same position in which I have fallen, excited obscurely by the knowledge that by looking upon my disgrace they are somehow partaking of it, "if that is so then all of this is meaningless and I have lived, been living, am being asked to continue in a lie."

"No," they say, "you are being asked to give this up and accept the truth," but I am weary, also faint, I have not been eating well, have not been doing very much at all as a matter of fact, and so I slide into a deep somnolence somewhere between exhaustion and a faint while their voices murmur on and on both above and below me. They seem to be considering my fate, what is going to be done with me now that I have proven that I am unable to function as a member of the Group. I know that I should pay attention to this and yet I am unable, somehow, to focus attention.

VI

Georgina comes into the room in the middle of this discussion, strides to my side, kneels by me, and says, "You fools, what have you done to him? What have you done? Don't you understand that of all of you he was the only one who had a chance?" and she drops her clothing, once again she is naked beside me and as the Group watches in a kind of detached fascination which merely may be shock, as Kenny stares at me from the corner with a contemptuous expression, she throws a leg over and mounts me, finds my tumescence, and I come springing into her, warm and ready, find myself rising within her and functioning perfectly, finding that I am enjoying it, I reach within a matter of seconds a wringing, gasping climax that causes me to grip her against me in little spasms and whimpers of collision as she falls away. I reach for her but she is already beyond my grasp, garbing herself again, standing. "Do you see now, you fools, what you have done?" she says. "Of all of you he was the best."

Weakly I nod, reach for her, shake my head, try to stand and justify my position—but from all parts of the room they fall upon her, surround her with their bodies, and begin to pummel. From the center of this struggle, like a bird whose wings are being stripped, I hear her terrible cries.

VII

And come from this dream to find that the Group has surrounded me, all of them very solemn, and are slowly helping me to my feet. One of them draws me closest to him, holds me against him, and in the broken lines of his face I can see the outlines of tears flowing. "You are done here," he says, "you realize that now. We cannot tolerate this. We cannot tolerate you. You are too dangerous."

There is nothing to say. I hang in his grasp, the floor slick beneath me. I would fall if I were not supported. After a time I say, "Yes."

"It is not your fault. Not really; it is simply one of those things which happen. But you must go now. You must leave us and never return. You will be moved to another part many levels below. You will be cut off from the company of men. This is necessary."

"Yes," I say, "yes," and now I feel his hands guiding me toward the door, the Group massing behind me, still glaring from those solemn, saddened faces, distended with knowledge. "She exists, you know," I say. "She is real."

"No. She is not real."

"She is real. It is all of these that are lies."

"No," he says, "no, that is not so," and after a pause, "But if you believe this then you must understand why it is necessary for you to go," and then I am in the hallway alone, the door is closed against me, I am in the blank spaces of the hallway alone, and as I slowly turn to begin the journey that will be the rest of my life, a journey and a search, I hear Georgina laughing at the end of the corridor, look up to see her naked and beckoning, spring toward her ... and as I do so she dissolves into something else, something that I cannot speak, something which I will never say ... and the knowledge of this and what they have done to me sends me to my knees and then to that fall levels and levels below where, separate from the company of men, I wait and wait for that last, great message from the Capitol.

December 1973: New Jersey

Afterword to "In the Stocks"

This was commissioned by Roger Elwood as a sequel to "Culture Lock" (appearing in the Pocket Books *Best of Barry N. Malzberg*) and is perhaps my only story of this subgenre that does not suffer from sequelitis, being all-around an extension and reordering of its painful material. Most sequels merely reiterate; this one rearranges. It appeared not in an Elwood anthology but in Silverberg's *New Dimensions 7* for complicated reasons of ancient vintage. (Elwood, it must be pointed out, did not reject the story.)

Elwood himself, who between 1971 and 1975 produced an extraordinary number (about eighty) of original anthologies and became science fiction editor for four major publishers (three simultaneously), commissioning or acquiring perhaps a hundred and fifty novels, has long since left the field in a kind of mutuality of loathing and is at this writing editing and publishing a major religious magazine on the West Coast while involved with other aspects of the religious market.* In his second incarnation (his first was as a writer of movie magazine material) I was probably his most prolific writer—six novels, a collection, and fifty-three short stories under his auspices—but rarely wrote to his order (never in the novels) and when I did so in an occasional short as in "In the Stocks" became outright subversive. At the time I thought I was sneaking material past Elwood, but that was my youth and gambling high spirits; I snuck nothing by, Elwood, a wee bit of a subversive himself, knew *exactly* what I was doing and let me alone except, of course, when he did not. The Elwood Era will not be remembered as the incarnation of science fiction's golden age, but it was an interesting time for all and should be worth a signatory chapter in the ultimate true and unwritten history of science fiction.

---

* As of 11/79, Elwood was out of the religious market, too—11/79.

The Fifties (Essay)

Harry Harrison, who himself really got going at the end, called the decade the false spring of science fiction and Robert Sheckley, whose career corresponded almost exactly with the period, shook his head when we talked about it in January 1973 and said, "Well, I squeezed a couple of happy years at the beginning, anyway." James Gunn got half his master's thesis into one of the fifty magazines that were published at some point during those years and at least twenty science fiction writers, make it forty, were making an accountant's salary from their trade. By 1960 it was all gone and it was five bleak years and another country before science fiction began to look hopeful again. Now, although many of the leading writers are still puttering around (and some like Fred Pohl and A. J. Budrys are having major second careers), it all seems at a great remove, surely as frozen in time, as historical, to the younger writers of this day as the early Gernsback era seemed to my generation. And most of the work, most of the writers need rediscovery. Many will never achieve it.

What happened? A lot of things happened. The massive International News Service, responsible for American magazine distribution, was ruled a monopoly and into forced divestiture. Twenty magazines perished immediately; the sales of the leaders (which had already been drifting) were halved. Inability to reach the audience. But the audience had diminished; it had never been large enough to support more than a few successful magazines and Sputnik in 1957 had made much science fiction appear, to its fringe audience, bizarre, arcane, irrelevant. There were dangerous matters going on now in space but the sophisticated, rather decadent form which science fiction had become paid little credence to satellites in near orbit.

Much else. Henry Kuttner and Cyril Kornbluth died within a month of one another in early 1958. Kuttner, one of the five major figures of the previous decade, had left science fiction but was constantly reprinted and was only forty-four. Kornbluth, ten years younger, was indisputably at the top rank. These sudden, shattering deaths—one from a heart attack in sleep, the other from a cerebral accident—made a number of their contemporaries question the very sense of their careers. What price any of it? "I was only twenty-three at the time," Silverberg says, "but I understood that these two men had literally died from writing science fiction and I wondered if I was going to die too." After ten or twenty years in the three to five cents a word on acceptance mills.

By 1959, Anthony Boucher, editor of *The Magazine of Fantasy & Science Fiction*, had decided to join his original co-editor, J. Francis McComas, in the semiretirement of freelancing. H. L. Gold, editor of *Galaxy*, had been literally paralyzed by war-induced agoraphobia; he had been steadily less able to function for years and a period of hospitalization (for physical cause) convinced him that he could continue editing no longer. And by 1959 too, only a few steady book markets for science fiction remained. Overproduction, the curse of the field then as ever, had resulted in many publishing catastrophes and only Ace and Doubleday (at one-thousand-dollar advances or less) remained as steady outlets for writers other than the five to ten at top rank. John Campbell had wandered from Dianetics to the Hieronymus Machine to the Finagle Factor and was just beginning to get onto the Dean Drive, meanwhile running stories by what appeared to be no more than a couple of writers under innumerable pseudonyms with the same plot and characters. An unhappy, airless time.

So emphatically so that when science fiction began to pick up again in the mid-sixties, first with the British *New Worlds* and then with the infusion of new writers/approaches in the barbarous colonies, a new audience was unaware of the dimensions of what the fifties had accomplished and talked of the field's "new literary merit," "new relevance," "new excitement," "new standards" as if nothing innovative had occurred before Ellison or J. G. Ballard. Yet, as that second and less significant false spring of the late sixties and early seventies also ebbs, the true dimensions of the accomplishments of the fifties reappear. However dimly. It is more than time to take another look at them.

Basic facts first and quickly: at the end of the nineteen forties, science fiction accounted for perhaps fifty books, hardcover and paperback, commercially published in a full year and supported perhaps seven magazines, only one of which, *Astounding*, paid decent word rates or was read by other than a juvenile audience. Five years later there were forty magazines jostling for space on the newsstands, hardcover and paperback books were coming out at the rate of two to three hundred a year, and one book editor, Donald A. Wollheim at Ace, was publishing alone more science fiction titles a month than had come out in a year in, say, 1943. *The Magazine of Fantasy & Science Fiction*, appearing first in late 1949, and *Galaxy*, whose first issue was dated 1950, were well-financed, carefully edited projects intended to offer serious competition for *Astounding* and, by the inclusion of a wider range of styles and thematic approaches, were seeking an expansion of the science fiction audience. They succeeded immediately—*Galaxy* outsold *Astounding* almost from its inception for the next five years—and behind them, publishers picking up the scent, came a host of magazines. Some like *Cosmos* or *Space Science Fiction* lasted only a short time, others like *Worlds of If* or *Science Fiction Adventures* held, through various ownerships, for many years; but through 1958 as magazines collapsed, new magazines replaced them. The growth of the field was astonishing; by 1953 there were forty or fifty times the outlets for science fiction than had existed five years before.

Writers who had struggled honorably through the bleak, building years of the forties, such as Lester del Rey, Theodore Sturgeon, James Blish, found to their astonishment that they could almost make a decent living doing what they had always wanted to do. A new generation of writers who had grown up under the influence of the Campbell decade were able to spring from late adolescence into full-time freelance writing careers: A. J. Budrys, Robert Sheckley, Philip K. Dick. The enormous expansion of the market was further signified for these people by the fact that three of the most prolific writers of the forties, Asimov, Hubbard, and Van Vogt, stopped writing science fiction completely to go into other careers and Heinlein, doing a long and profitable series of quasi-juveniles for Scribner's, was out of magazine work entirely.

It was a pretty good time for HUAC and science fiction alike. Some historians do not see these factors (sf as underground libertarian literature) as unrelated.

One has to talk, however, about what kind of work was being done to occupy the space that the audience and publishers had created. This can be said at the outset: there have been only a trickle of novels through the fifty-year history of science fiction which have consensually been accepted as masterpieces, absolute examples of what the field can be at its best. With no exception I can call to mind, all of them were published in the fifties. The jury on seventies novels is by definition still out (it looks as if *Shadrach in the Furnace, Dying Inside,* and *The Dispossessed* are going to make it) but there is virtually no novel of the sixties, however acclaimed, which does not have a substantial claque willing to argue its lack of value for that polarized decade.* Forties novels of importance, *Slan, Final Blackout, Sixth Column, World/Players of Null A, Fury,* even that non-novel *The Martian Chronicles,* look archaic now; primitive. Unfulfilled.

....

* *Bug Jack Barron, Stand on Zanzibar, The Left Hand of Darkness, Dune, The Moon Is a Harsh Mistress, The Einstein Intersection, Black Easter, Thorns,* and I rest my case.

But consider the fifties. *A Canticle for Leibowitz, More Than Human, Double Star, Rogue Moon, The Space Merchants, Gladiator-at-Law, The Stars My Destination, The Demolished Man, A Case of Conscience, Bring the Jubilee. Rogue Moon* won no awards; *Canticle* was published in that same year. Kornbluth's *The Syndic* copped no honors; *More Than Human* that year. To remember that *The Demolished Man, The Space Merchants*, and *Baby Is Three* (the central and best section of *More Than Human*) all appeared in *Galaxy* within a nine-month period in 1952 is to be awed.

Novels, of course, collect the attention, the reprints, and occasionally the money (*The Space Merchants* has probably been over the years still the most financially remunerative of all our genre novels) but science fiction, unlike other categories, lives in the short form, a structure which seems perfect to articulate and enact a single speculative conceit which (again arguably) is the task for which science fiction is most suited. The level of short-story writing during the decade in technical expertise and inventiveness has never been equaled, nor have any short stories published within the last fifteen years had the impact upon the field and its audience of what was appearing routinely in the best-of-the-year anthologies or magazine annuals. No short-story writer in two decades has sprung upon science fiction as did Mark Clifton upon *Astounding* in 1952. There is probably no way in which to teach a young audience (80 percent of science fiction readers are under twenty-one) that Mark Clifton, dead since 1962 and completely out of print, was for a period of four years the most controversial and influential writer in the magazines. No way to teach them that Floyd L. Wallace, *Galaxy's* Clifton who published novelettes of increasing inventiveness and technical clarity, now also unreprinted although happily alive, taught at least one generation of writers what the conceptual limits of the science fiction story might be.

One of the hazards and horrors of age is the reconsideration of our youthful selves, the vision of subsequent heartbreak superimposed, and the conclusion that we were, hence, fools. Perhaps it is this which has left the fifties almost bereft of significant critical reevaluation and comment because those who could best do the job were there at the time and still feel the pain. They were naïve. They know it now. But it seemed possible.

It seemed possible to remake the field. By the end of the forties Campbell and his best writers had put the technical equipment of the modern short story into the hands of those ready to begin. Hiroshima and television and the cold war had put into the hands of the new writers and editors what appeared to be an enormous audience for fiction that would truly come to terms with the potential changes in lives caused by new and inexplicable technology. It was Horace Gold's earnest belief that he could have *Galaxy* read by as many people as *The Saturday Evening Post*. Boucher and McComas, world-weary types, had less evangelistic obsession but saw no reason why the audience for literate science fiction should be any smaller than that for literate fiction, period.** These major editors and John Campbell, who never really lost his sense for a decent story, gathered about them fifty to a hundred writers who, possessed, were willing to try and take the field to the limit of their abilities, knowing that they would not be rejected for ambition. These writers could not sell the top editors everything, of course, but they could write passionately and often, and the overflow, much of high quality, was being laid off to those thirty or forty magazines which appeared and disappeared like Flying Dutchmen.

It was a period which had never occurred before mass-market fiction excepting, perhaps, the great pulp romance and detective markets of the thirties. Any writer who understood the genre and could then conjugate a sentence could find a market. Thirty magazines times eight stories a month times twelve meant close to three thousand science fiction stories needed a year to say nothing of the original anthologies, *Star Science Fiction* and *New Tales of Space and Time*. (Today, magazines and original anthologies combined accommodate perhaps three hundred new stories a year.) In 1955 there were in the United States and England perhaps two to three hundred writers familiar enough with the category and adept enough to sell it. (Today there are over a thousand.) And the book market was not negligible. Wollheim was at Ace, Doubleday had begun a program, Simon & Schuster was dabbling, Signet and Avon were toe in the water, and Ballantine, beginning a flourishing program in 1953 with *The Space Merchants*, began by offering advances of five thousand dollars.

Magazine rates were roughly equivalent to what they are now. The top magazines paid three to five cents a word, the bottom not less than a penny. In New York or anywhere at that time it was possible for one family to live poorly on five thousand a year, well on ten. One of no family perhaps half that. It was not difficult to make five hundred dollars a month writing science fiction.

Five hundred dollars a month was, perhaps, with rejects and half-finished stories, twenty-five thousand words for a professional, and

---

** The payoff which Boucher, perhaps fortunately, has not lived to see is that there is now in mass-market terms almost no audience for quality fiction whatsoever ... a fact not unnoted by science fiction editors, not, on balance, a dumb group.

twenty-five thousand words a month is one thousand a day and most weekends off. A thousand words a day is three typewritten pages: some of us bleed more than others, of course, but three pages are nevertheless but three pages. There was plenty of time for bull sessions on plans for the field, drinking sessions on ditto, and the exchanging of wives. (These were not wife swappers, these writers, they were wife *exchangers*. They would divorce and remarry. Nineteen-fifties male science fiction writers were perhaps the last to fall before the so-called new morality: nothing doing unless you were willing to follow it up with signed papers.)

The feeling in this rather insular and isolated circle of writers and their editors was that piece by piece they were remaking not so much the world (Auschwitz, Buchenwald, Hiroshima, McCarthy, Marshall had proven exactly what effect the seers and poets would have on reality) as the field itself, that science fiction was being constructed in an ideal form as it might have been a long time ago if Hugo Gernsback had not, for cynical business reasons, pocketed it into a genre of marvelous invention stories for potential engineers.

Certainly, the best of the magazine work (and it should be pointed out here that *all* of the novels mentioned above appeared originally in the magazines and most had been commissioned and directed by the editors; it was a magazine field then as it is not now) was equal technically to the best of American fiction. Kornbluth's "The Altar at Midnight," or Bester's "The Men Who Murdered Muhammed," or Wallace's "Delay in Transit," or Clifton's "Clerical Error," or Pohl's "The Day of the Boomer Dukes," or Sheckley's "Warm" (examples almost at random) were as accomplished and moving as "Seize the Day," "Franny," "The Country Husband," "In the Zoo," or "The Man Who Studied Yoga."

There was, however, a tiny little problem. Neither the stories nor the novels, outside of the field, were recognized as such at all.

This failure of science fiction to reach outside its genre audience was not of itself among the factors which blew away the false spring, but it might have been the factor that underlay everything. Science fiction remained small. It remained a small field. The audience upon which it could draw was, perhaps, half a million souls who were being asked to support their forty magazines and three hundred books and, with all their dedication, they were too small and too poor to do it. The continuing audience which perceives science fiction as important has never really increased from this half a million since the late forties, the central reason for the boom-and-bust phenomenon, as overextension has inevitably run up against a failure of the audience to expand. The only difference between the fifties and seventies is that the *fringe* audience—

those who can be induced to pay for two or three given titles a year through word of mouth or promotion or both—has expanded to several million. No science fiction novel in the fifties sold more than one hundred thousand copies. Science fiction itself was regarded with lack of interest or contempt outside of the genre walls. Its very audience was an unorganized constituency, much like the audiences for contemporary men's magazines. They might like it, buy it, need it, but they were not in the main evangelical and those who were simply increased the popular perception of science fiction as a strange field, incestuous and defensive.

The genre made no impression upon the academic/literary nexus which controls critical perception and audiences in this country. Only two stories from the decade were reprinted in the Martha Foley *Best American Short Stories* annual: Sturgeon's "The Man Who Lost the Sea" (1959) and Judith Merril's "Dead-Center" (1954). None ever appeared in the *O'Henry Prize Stories*. Not a single story from *Galaxy*, *Astounding*, or *Worlds of If* achieved even the thin gruel of the Foley roll of honor. (Some SF writers did by writing non-SF and publishing it for no payment in the quarterlies, though.) No science fiction writer other than Ray Bradbury, that non-science-fiction writer, appeared in textbooks. No science fiction novels, other than Bradbury's, were reviewed outside the genre departments of the press. Most were ignored. *The Demolished Man* was published in hardcover by Shasta, a semiprofessional press operated by thieves, presumably because no reputable publisher wanted it. *The Space Merchants* stayed in print but subsequent, possibly even finer, Pohl/Kornbluth novels disappeared.

By the time 1958, death, and divestiture rolled around, the genre was already ripe for an end. Many of its best writers were literal burnt-out cases. Aware of the anonymity of their work outside the small enclosure, aware of the necessity to go on and on, just as they had, simply to make an ever more difficult living, most either could write or would write no longer. Probably if INS had not been subdivided or Horace Gold had stayed well the field would have collapsed anyway. An entire generation of writers had been used up in the struggle to make of science fiction a respectable literary medium. They had won the struggle, and then they had learned that for all the world had cared they might not have bothered at all. Some of these writers have done no work at all for fifteen years now. Others have done no good work. A couple have reemerged as if from behind barricades, hurled one cautious story into the editorial mills, and then run for their lives again.

A very, very few, Pohl, Bester, and Budrys being the best examples, have returned to do outstanding work but only after a sabbatical of many years and then at a slow rate. Between *Rogue Moon* in 1959 and his return to science fiction writing three years ago (criticism, and he was the best in the history of the field, does not count), Budrys had published one minor novel and, maybe, two short stories. He might have been the best of them; he certainly had the most profound, subtle mind, the best insight, the deepest perspective.

Gone, then. All gone away. After the energy of the late sixties to early seventies we are in another slack period now; a return to traditional themes and approaches, editorial hostility or bewilderment at stylistic/thematic innovation, new approaches. Not to complain particularly: like Kornbluth or particularly Bester, I do not feel that my best work was cut off before fulfillment. Probably things will turn around in a while: new writers, new publishers, new editors ... most important, a different politic and a new audience.

But virtually all of the great innovators of the eighties will carry on their work, careers, and lives as if the people of the fifties had never been. They will be unaware of most of it. That work may live in the undertext of the field, influence upon influence upon influence, but these writers will not know to whom they owe what. That decade, thirty years in the past, will, for most intents and purposes, appear to have been for naught. I think it was. I do think that it was.

Each generation, Don Wollheim once said, has its own tragedy: that it must relearn, on its own, what every generation has had to learn and cannot teach. Betrayal, circumstance, injustice. The Spanish Resistance, the Cold War, Vietnam. And end broken and in silence. No answer. No answer to any of this.

And, *pace*, Gertrude Stein, I do not, anymore, even question.

January 1977: New Jersey

The Man Who Married a Beagle

I

We were civilized people and tried to keep the divorce as amicable as possible but after a while bitterness extruded. It could have been no other way. There is no such thing as a friendly divorce. I had from the start made it clear that Susan could have custody, the house, and one half of all joint property but I was insistent upon the silverware and the convertible. She gave ground on the convertible but her position on the silverware was absolute. "We need it," she said, "and besides it meant nothing to you. You never even noticed whether we were using plain forks or the specials. I spent hours polishing it. Almost all of my life, I now see, has been tied up in possessions; I won't give up this one. Etc." At a certain point the discussion broke down, took an ugly turn. After everything I had done to avoid ugliness I came to understand that in certain essential ways it would be part of our separation. Nevertheless I remained courteous. I suggested that we talk about it at some later date when we were both calmer. I left the house. Two days later I was informed that Susan had changed attorneys and had considerably upped her demands. She was going to be punitive after all. I instructed my own attorney to stand fast. I had my phone changed and delisted. For several weeks thereafter Susan and I had no contact, but when one of the boys became ill and asked for me she reached me through my attorney. I went over, of course. I retained throughout—retain to this day—the strongest ties to my family. In the sickroom I found her quite calm and reasonable.

II

Lady and I took a small furnished apartment on West Eighty-third Street in Manhattan. It had been my original intention to stay out of New York, perhaps even find quarters in another section of the suburb in which Susan and I had lived, but my attorney was very much against this and I could see his point. Throughout I had concealed our relationship from Susan; it was important to me that no indication be given of the real reasons for the divorce. The last gift I wanted to give her was that no one had intervened; our relationship, a thing of integrity, had broken down entirely on its own terms. Living in the community would have opened up the possibility of scandal. Also my attorney and friends warned about the possibility of embarrassing confrontations. We might meet in Wonder Waffles or then again at the Shlomo Meat Mart, which we both continued to patronize. Better, at least, until the separation agreement was signed, to restrict my contact to visitation.

I had never liked Manhattan even when I lived there as a bachelor many years ago, but returning under these circumstances did not prove unpleasant. Lady brought magic to our three small rooms as she had to all of the places that we had inhabited together before. To live in feeling, I know now, is the only gift. Walking her toward dusk amid the rubbish and beer cans of the West Side, pausing by the school-yard gate while she sniffed and pawed crumpled pieces of paper, going out alone late at night to pick up some cigarettes and tomorrow's *Daily News*, I felt again like a very young man, the man who had lived alone in New York in his twenties, the city resonant, the sense of connection so close that it seemed palpable; the Jersey Palisades, which I could glimpse dimly through the fumes of the dying borough, exerting upon me a sense of mystery so vast that it came close to joy, touched pain. Later in bed I would read the *Daily News*, one hand on Lady's haunches, feeling the slow and convoluted movement of her blood: only for me, only for me.

III

At length an agreement was reached through the attorneys: we would split the silverware. Not without irony I specified that Susan could have the cutting implements. On the afternoon I went to pick it up I found her strained, beaten, the harder lines of her face broken by exhaustion to reveal to me the young girl whom I had loved at a different stage of life, in another Manhattan. She had it all boxed for me, an exquisitely thoughtful touch not uncharacteristic of the woman. She was always thoughtful. She always did the proper thing. She never did anything which in any way could have been construed as wrongful. She was nice. She was a nice person. At one time I thought that this was the core of the problem—that she gave me no objective basis for my feelings of emptiness—but later, even before the separation, I came to see that this was not so. We make our own lives. Always, eternally, we live within ourselves. She wanted to talk. "Are you happy?" she said. "I worry about you."

"Yes," I said, "I'm happy. Or at least happier."

"I think about you living in Manhattan. It's such an ugly city. Do you see lots of people? Are you going out with women again? What do you do in the evenings?"

"Work," I said, "I'm working twelve hours a day." Not a breath of scandal would I bring to the divorce. How things will go after the eighteen-month formal separation and my remarriage I cannot say, but until then I will protect her as much as possible from pain. "When I come home I pick up tomorrow's *Daily News* and drink beer and read it. Weekends I rent a car and go for long drives alone and sometimes I do nothing at all."

"I don't hate you," she said. "It would be so much easier if I could, you know. But I have none of that now. Maybe at the beginning, but now, most of the time, I find that I can think of you without anger. The boys miss you, you know. They still don't understand and I can't explain it to them."

"Someday they will," I said. "I'll talk to them a little about it. I think that they do understand." Once in Burger King I explained that their mother and I did not love each other anymore or at least we loved each other in a different way but we would both always love them, but their faces became so distracted and my own voice sounded so plaintive and dull that I dropped the subject, fearing that I was becoming every male character in every story and film about divorce with children that I had ever been exposed to. "The important thing is that we will always have each other anyway," I had finished and, gesturing, had upset half a cup of Coke and an unfinished carton of french fries over my lap. When I stood the stain felt like a stain of implication. "I don't hate you either, Susan," I said. "I feel very deeply for you. Part of this comes out of love, you know. You're entitled to live with someone with whom you can have the whole range of feeling." *Like me*, I thought but did not add.

"You're a liar," she said. "You're not doing it out of love. Nothing in this place was ever done out of love by anyone for anyone." She stood, straightened the planes of her clothing. "Take your silverware and get out of here."

"I don't want to hurt you. I never meant to hurt you."

"You never meant to hurt anyone. You just spread joy where you sit. You're a really wonderful person."

"I don't want you to be bitter, Susan. I'm not bitter."

"I'm not bitter either," she said. "We had a happy marriage and we're having a wonderful divorce. I'm going away all next week. The boys will be with my parents if you want to see them but I'm sure you'll be relieved to know that you're not expected."

"Are you going away with anyone?"

"That's none of your business."

"I wouldn't mind if you were. I want you to be happy. I want your happiness and always did. It won't affect the separation agreement or anything of that nature."

"You're really a monster," she said. "Do you know that? I was packing the silverware two hours ago and even crying a little bit, but now that I see you and listen to this I know what a fool I've been. There will be no more crying. You are truly a monstrous person."

"You don't understand," I said. "You don't understand what this has done to me."

"You talk of feeling. You have no feeling. Get out of here now or I'll throw something at you."

I could see that the situation was on the verge of moving into an ugliness that I thought we had passed. "All right," I said, lifting the box and going to the door. "All right, then. Someday perhaps you will understand." I stood wavering before the door, trying to balance the heavy box with one arm while with the other reaching for the knob, but I could not reach the balance and merely stood there helplessly until I could see that Susan was not going to help me either. Grunting, I put down the box, opened the door, held it open with a foot, hefted the box, stumbled into the thin suburban dusk carrying my goods as if they were guilt.

Stumbling down the path toward the convertible, the path that I had walked ten thousand times to the metronome of my life, I waited for her to say something but she said nothing, nor did she close the door. When I came to the car, put the box in back, turned to go to the driver's side, I could see her there, standing, looking at me, and in a way her posture was as it had been many years ago on our second date as she had waited for me at the top of her stairs. It came back to me shockingly, every detail fluorescent, but of course it could not change the situation. I drove away.

My lawyer had warned me that even the coldest of divorces would be emotionally devastating. He had suggested perhaps an analyst. I had refused him—my relationship with Lady supersedes outside transactions of any sort—but now, finally, I accepted his warning. The pain, the pain! And I had thought myself to be the strongest person I knew.

IV

I knew from the first moment I saw her that it would be serious but I could not judge the extent of the involvement or the panic as I realized, early in our relationship, that I had already reached a point of no return. Being with her in the cubicle I rented by the week under a false name in the SRO hotel on Ninety-seventh Street opened me up almost immediately to what I understood aging and aging in the suburbs had done to me and perhaps all of us: we had lived in the death of feeling. Feeling had been taken away from us piece by piece in such infinitesimal bites that for most of us we might never know the difference: there are an infinite number of devices to conceal that awareness. PTA, the car pool, the temple membership, the art auction, and the Sunday summer parties; during the week a little casual adultery only to preserve the illusion of choice. But it was not only passion which we had lost, it was ourselves, and being with Lady, moving in the small and enclosed spaces which she gave to me so freely, so openly, I made that confrontation of self and from that point onward knew that I could go no further. I could not live in feeling for ten hours a week, live in death for the other one hundred and fifty-eight. I knew that I would have to make the choice and it was no choice. I had thought that I loved Susan but that was only in the negligible space which the death of feeling had left me; it was Lady who showed me, and beyond denial, what love could be.

It could not go on that way. I knew that it could not go on that way. I left with her in the room dishes of all kinds, small snacks, testimonies of my love, liquids of various flavors, little notes, confessions, my clothing, small evidences and secrets of my being which I hoped she might sniff out in the hours or days (my work was unpredictable) of our separation, and yet it was not enough, there was nothing that I could leave with her or take away from that room which would reduce the anguish of the separation. To be away from her, every separation, was to live in the death of the heart; to be with her once more was to have rekindled only for those agonizing instants what I had so long thought dead that I had not even known that I missed it.

I tried. That must be said: I tried. I am a sensible man; I had lived in commitment to that quality of sense for many years. I treasured the prerogatives of my life; living between those clean, cold instruments of my eternity I had given myself what I had been taught to believe in as a careful pleasure, and even brought to the absolute instants of self-realization I still tried to exercise a kind of control. I am a controlled man; I believe in decorousness as my ancestors might be said to have believed in the coming of the Messiah: as an abstraction, if nothing else, by which to live. A careful affair, carefully structured, that was my intention; and an affair was more to my advantage than it might have been to other men because Lady truly had no life of her own: her only life was that with me. I could keep her in the SRO cubicle, I did not have to worry about her involved with some stud down the street or making time at a kennel, leaving her odors against lampposts for crazed collies to track: no, she was all mine, and in the containment of the room it was possible for me to believe that it would continue that way.

But it could not be done. The integrity of my love, if nothing else, would not permit me to do this. It was not only knowing of her abandonment, her loneliness in the spaces of the rooms, her single yearning for me which must have consumed her just as did my own sense of loss. It was not only the realization that my marriage and my life had been a lie, that in the denial of feeling I had hid from myself the apprehension of my truest self; it was not even (although this was an important factor) that the very act of copulation with Susan, giving her those small and necessary words of love which always accompanied the act, made me feel as if I was betraying the dog on the deepest level. No, simply and ultimately I did what I must because if I had not, it would have denied, would have made a deception of the truest and deepest part of myself which, at last, had been uncovered. And so I did what I felt I must but always in the way which would bring the least amount of pain.

"It wasn't your fault," I said to Lady and I felt she understood, whimpering, turning toward me, "whatever happens, whatever comes of this you must understand, must always understand that you bear no responsibility. You bear no blame. It all came from inside me, it was my decision alone, and I know that you would never have forced me to do this. Do you see that?" I said. "Do you see it?" and in the lustrous stare of her eyes, in the slow movement of her tail, in the new softnesses that I uncovered in the touch of her ears, I knew that she did and to that degree, to the level that I knew she accepted this, I found for the first time my own tenuous passage toward sanctification.

V

Custody and the house were given to Susan along with an alimony-and-support payment of twelve hundred dollars a month, tied to my current gross earnings. The terms were very harsh and my own circumstances perilous but still I did not contest. It was important to do the right thing for Susan and the boys; it was important that all of the pain that could be minimized be so. After the settlement I would be left with an income of some ten thousand dollars yearly for myself and Lady, barely manageable for one who had been accustomed to a dignified standard of living and painful knowledge that at the age of forty-one I would be starting where I had twenty years ago with the added pain of financial obligation and terrible guilt. Still I did not protest. Harsh as the terms were, I knew in my heart that I deserved terms even harsher. I should never have married Susan; I should not have lived with her in a lie for so many years. She might have had other opportunities. She might, at the age of forty, have other opportunities yet, although I could not be optimistic about her marriageability and in no circumstances looked upon that *deus ex machina* to free me.

Not having custody (although I would not admit this to the lawyers, let alone Susan) was a relief. What would I have done with them in the first place? It is all that I can do to keep an amused, interested, suburban exterior when we are at Wonder Waffles. Too, children should remain with their mother, in settled circumstances; it would be terribly unfair, everyone knows, to uproot those who are not compelled to be uprooted. Then too, if I had had the boys it would have been difficult to have enjoyed my relationship with Lady to the fullest; sooner or later, if I wished to be honest—and I had resolved never to be dishonest again—startling admissions would have had to be made which would have been very difficult for all of us.

VI

Sometimes I wondered if any other man had been in circumstances exactly like mine and at other times I felt that it was of no consequence whatsoever. Only feeling is real; only the statement of the heart. I had learned that. Still, walking Lady on leash late at night, I would occasionally look at other men and women walking their dogs and wonder idly: Was it this way for them too? Was I in another kind of suburb: the West Side a resting place for less suburban passions? I did not know, nor would I have ever asked, I believe in the integrity now of the human spirit, but now and again I would find myself exchanging glances with some of the others, Scottish terriers or Weimaraners walking proudly at leash beside them, and think: Who knows? Who knows all of the contortions of the heart, the positions in which we may become entangled? Certainly anyone from the moon looking at Susan and me entangled in our bedroom at midnight would have regarded it as at least as strange as the behavior of us walkers and our dogs, quiet and absorbed with one another on the rubble-strewn streets of bombed-out Manhattan in the late darkness.

VII

It was my decision to get married as soon as the formal eighteen-month separation period had expired and the final papers were signed. There was no need for the contract and yet I felt that this was its beauty: that voluntarily I was making a deep commitment only because I felt within myself that the commitment was deserved. Since it was unlikely that Lady and I could be married within any of the established religions,

I found a female minister given credentials by one of the small California mail-order sects who agreed to marry us in any place we desired at a minimal fee. She stated that she would be responsible, if I liked, for bringing witnesses. Her entire attitude was so matter-of-fact, her acceptance of the situation so total, that I understood once again what self-deceit had been mine in the suburbs; I had sealed off from myself 90 percent or more of the range of human possibility or feeling as if to have it were contemptible ... only to find that what was the more contemptible was the private and unspeakable death of the heart, over and again in all of the open and closed spaces of that county.

VIII

On the day that the agreement became final Susan and I went for a drink in the cocktail lounge of Mister Bear. The boys were with a sitter and Susan said that it would have to be a short meeting; she had a date later that evening, nothing serious but someone she could not stand up. This admission, made in all shyness, opened me up, began for the first time to pry at that layer of guilt which I had had since the evening I left the house. She is finding a life of her own; she cares enough to tell me this, I thought. Looking at her in the warmth of the candles, I found myself reconstructing bit by bit her face as it had been so many years ago when we had first gone to cocktail lounges, and in this too there was no pain but only the realization that although we travel incessantly and without return, we also carry baggage as recollection. "I guess I don't hate you anymore," Susan said finally. "I don't know if I like you very much but at least I don't hate you. This must have been very hard for you also."

"It was. Harder than you can imagine. But I felt that it was best for both of us."

"No," she said, "you felt that it was better for you and I was merely carried along, whatever the price, whatever the consequences. If it had been death for me it wouldn't have stopped you." She finished her drink. "But I will say that it worked out for the best. In certain ways. In other ways, of course, it didn't."

"I'm glad for the good parts and sad for the poor ones, Susan."

"A lot of what you said makes sense," she said. "That business about the death of feeling in the suburban middle class. I didn't understand for a long time but now I'm beginning to see what you mean and even that it had happened to us."

"We didn't want it that way. It just happened."

"That's what I mean," she said, "that's exactly what I mean. It wasn't something that happened between us, it was something that happened *to* us, that was all. That was the terror." She stood, took her coat. "I'm glad we had this chance to talk," she said. "You were right. You were right all along, I didn't see the point in it but in a way it's as formal as a marriage, our last drink together before divorce."

"Yes," I said, looking at her almost in feeling. "That was what I thought."

"Are you happier now?"

"Yes."

"Have you found someone to love."

I pause, shake my head, sigh, then say, "Yes, I think so. I think so now. Have you?"

"No," she said, "not yet. But I'm glad. I'm glad for you. If it didn't kill the capacity for feeling in you then perhaps it hasn't in me as well. Someday. Someday I will."

"I very much hope so," I said and took her arm, gently, fondling the almost imperceptible bone where her joints fused. "I think you will." I went to the bar, paid the check; we walked out of Mister Bear very much like lovers pausing for a hasty, necessary meeting on the turnpike before proceeding in opposite ways toward their destiny; her kiss to mine was light and gentle and at the center of it I could sense although not really feel those darker fires which, in all of her heart and all of her courtesy, nice person that she always was, she had been unable to give me.

IX

Lady and I were married by the religious cult lady in our one room of the SRO hotel we had occupied. She brought two witnesses, bearded men who looked at us with admiration. I paid them all well and when they were gone showed Lady the lease I had just signed on a new unfurnished apartment in the West Seventies, a brownstone basement apartment with separate entrance. She squirmed against me and then her eyes turned moist.

X

We occupied the brownstone and lived in love. On alternate Tuesdays and Saturdays I took the boys to Wonder Waffles, Mister Bear, the Coconut King, and various amusement parks within the area. Once I brought along Lady to romp with them. Susan began to date a divorced dentist regularly.

XI

In April of another year I awoke, Lady beside me, and looked at her and knew (although I would not be able to verbalize this for many months thereafter) that the feeling was going and that my search, consequentially, must begin again. Life is not an ending; life is a process, I later came to understand, and it was exactly at that moment and in a way ten times worse than the first that the pain began again.

June 1976: New Jersey

Afterword to "The Man Who Married a Beagle"

I wrote this story in the spring of 1976; my old friends at *The New Yorker* rejected it by return mail ("It is an old joke and the theme is familiar") and, filled with familiar rage, I tried only one intervening market before sending it to my newer (this is in relative terms, you understand) friends at Ultimate Publications, Ted White and Sol Cohen, who did not fail me again, as they had never failed me on a submitted short story. It appeared in 1977 in *Fantastic* and elicited two comments in the letter columns, one quite approving, one superbly nasty. *Plus c'est la même chose...* I think it is one of my ten best short stories and in quality of feeling and control stands alone. Thirty years ago, in a market less cruel, restricted, and conniving, I think it might indeed have appeared in *The New Yorker*, but the culture—and this author—were nowhere near ready for this kind of stuff back in the days of "A Perfect Day for Bananafish." As has almost always been the case with my short stories I was simply glad to sell it for whatever money I could and get it into print. And again.

Big Ernie, the Royal Russian, and the Big Trapdoor

So the time comes when I am sitting in writers' heaven, which bears a striking resemblance to the set of the famous and respected Eugene O'Neill's *The Iceman Cometh*, perusing as is my wont a copy of one of the recent magazines which is imported into these environs for our reading pleasure if desired, when I come uptwixt a story by a writer whose name I will not relate which contains many character names, scenes, and stylistic references exactly identical to those of my own. It is not the first time that this has happened—it is surprising how many magazines are passed around writers' heaven and how many of them still open their pages to my imitators—but there is something about this particular manifestation that angers me. Perhaps it has to do with my relative state of inebriation so early in the day and then again it may be the matter of straws and camels' backs, which is a very preponderant cliché, even to this day. I set the magazine upon the counter and say, reasonably, "This is not right. This is absolutely not right. There should be a statute of limitations upon the plagiarization of the styles of famous dead writers, after which it is no longer permissible or the perpetrator must pay a severe penalty. I do not think it is fair, and in the bargain there is absolutely no recourse except in the matter of spectral alerts or appeals to conscience, neither of which are recognized in the technologized last quarter of the twentieth century. It is not right," I continue, "and I am deeply aggravated, but then and upon the other hand, what can be done?"

"Nothing can be done," says Big Ernie, sitting next to me in his midday stupor. "It is merely the way it is. Conditions suit. The dead can no longer address the living. The living cannot address the living. The living cannot address the dead." He looks at the empty shot glass in front of him. "Ketchum was never like this," he says.

Ernie, or Big Ernie as we call him, has had a notable career, of course, and even at this point has not fallen into total disrepute, but there is no question but that he is a bit of a bore, and even in writers' heaven, which he has occupied for half as many years as myself approximately, even by our standards, he is something of a drunk. "Something will have to be done," I say, passing the magazine across to him, "but you need not concern yourself if perhaps you believe that imitation is a form of flattery, which incidentally I do not." I look at Jimmy the Horse, who is on the morning shift in the heaven, and say, "You can pour Big Ernie another round of what he is having and you can also give me a gin straight up with no lemon. Gin is the homewrecker, as all of us know, but there is no home to wreck and I am extremely discontent even at this early hour and need to anele the pain."

Jimmy the Horse, a small guy who is on consignment from the musician quarter, shrugs and goes about his business of procuring the request, not deigning to reply. He is a phlegmatic man from years of listening to Fritz and Pablo and Gregor and the boys complain about management and has learned to ignore writers' talk, which is to his advantage and why he is now our temporarily permanent bartender. Fast Hands Willie Smith did not possess this laudable ability and after some months of taking us seriously began to show signs of latent schizophrenia and alcoholism, necessitating a swift trade, even-up, to musicians' heaven, where it is rumored he and Scott Joplin are being dried out together. "I have the rye for Big Ernie," Jimmy the Horse says, displaying it, "and I have the homewrecker for you, and I have nothing else at all. That is a very interesting cover on the magazine you are reading. One would take it to be a picture of machinery although I know that neither you nor Big Ernie are at all mechanically oriented."

This is Jimmy the Horse's idea of a joke and it is his one obligatorily humorous comment of the morning. He gives us our drinks and goes away to his secret place behind the bar where, as if from a great distance, I can hear him thinly humming passages from the greatly beloved if somewhat overrated *Pastoral* Symphony of Ludwig van Beethoven.

"It is not right," I say, not to Ernie but to the walls this time. "Something has to be done about this; our work should not be interred with our bones, of course, but our voices should be." I should point out here that Big Ernie and I are the only occupants of writers' heaven at this particular time of day. Later on they will all be here, of course: Oxford Billie and Baby Eugene and the three Johns only a sample of that great number which will come in to sing and reminisce and drink heavily until the dawn, but at this early time only the really serious drinkers, of which I am able to number Big Ernie and myself, tend to be in.

Here, in writers' heaven as in all of the other aspects of the City of God, an attempt has been made to reconstruct our rounds according to our ideals, and writers, simple creatures all despite their complaints, and assumed oddities, prefer days with a clearly defined morning, afternoon, and night, of which only the most dedicated prefer to drink through the mornings. This explains the rather sketchy nature, then, of the characterization and ambience of the bar, but on the other hand, and as I would be the first to admit, I was never too strong on heavily populated scenes or detailed stage management, and therefore it is for the best at the time of my explosion of anger that only Big Ernie, Jimmy the Horse, and I are present in the environs. "I must think of something," I say after a long sullen pause. "Perhaps I can petition the committee. I can take the matter to the committee, who would certainly approve of visitations, omens, and threats. They will understand the circumstances, and if they do not they might be able to arrange for a few premature admissions to purgatory."

"I tell you," Big Ernie says, "it is hopeless. You have no rights in life or in death. Besides, it is not so bad here. We have all we need to drink and the companionship of those who understand and now and then the possibility of tenderness. Our work is done, our good is gone. We have the rewards of finality. Dark, dark finality." He belches. "It is all nada, I must confide," he adds.

"It is not," I say. "It comes to more than that. My style is important to me; it is all that I have, really, since the cancer fund after the death of my esteemed friend the newspaper columnist now in hustlers' heaven has not been doing so good. Also no one reads my work anymore and therefore those who read the work of the plagiarists must conclude that it is a fresh and compelling style, entirely new. It is not a great style but it is not so bad," I say, draining the gin. "Considering that I was of inordinate sensitivity and wrote a lot of drip-dry sentimental stuff with great heart and handkerchief before I finally developed a different argot, it is quite good. I admit that it cancels feeling to a certain degree, but then again it is racy and its present-tense mode of narration and quick switches of gear as well as generous incorporations of the vernacular impart a sense of much energy."

"But it is dated," Big Ernie says, "it is of a world which no longer is."

I put down the gin in a bound and motion to Jimmy the Horse, who is called the Horse for no reason I can ascertain, to refill. "It is not dated," I say, "it is an artifact, a perfect recollection of a time eternal, frozen in the forever."

"That is foolish," Big Ernie says and shows the galloping Jimmy the Horse his own empty shot glass. "It is total *merde*. It is of a fantasy. It never existed."

"There is no reason for this," I say hotly, slamming the bar as the patient Horse conveys bottles to more easily accomplish his wondrous work. "To insult the style is to insult the man. Besides," I add cunningly, "you are no one to talk about the matter of dating. Your work is so dated it has ossified. No one believes in that code hero crap anymore."

Big Ernie turns upon me menacingly although the light does not nevertheless fail to glitter off his prominent if healed exit wounds. "How dare you say that," he says, "my style is pure and true. It is the truth. It is pure and good and true whereas yours is a lie."

Jimmy the Horse flicks his towel over the bar and says pacifying things. "If you don't stop it I will throw you out," he concludes.

"You will not throw us out," I say. "This is writers' heaven and we can carry ourselves as we see fit." To Big Ernie I say, "Your style is false to the bottom. It is utterly contrived and attitudinous in nature." Why I am doing this I do not know since I am not a literary critic by any standard and despise those people who are in no part of the heaven at all. Critics' heaven, mercifully, is hell. "Your style is *merde*," I say. It must have to do with my mounting sense of frustration. "He who steals your style steals *merde*."

Big Ernie looks at me. His hands tremble as he brings the rye to his teeth and then all the way down. "Let's take it outside," he says, referring to that small patch of exterior blue which lies between us and the barracks on one side, the brothel on the other. "I will deal with you in the only way that is proper."

"That is fine with me," I say. It is a terrible thing to turn on one's own, but then who else is there to turn on? "I will be happy to do so, false fisherman."

"Columnist," Big Ernie says bitterly.

"Code coward," I say in fury, "and you did lots of newspaper stuff yourself."

"*No cojones.*"

"Outside," says Jimmy the Horse definitively and we begin to move toward the doors. I think reluctantly that Big Ernie is going to be knocked unconscious yet again—this is all part of his heaven—but just as we approach the swinging doors there is a little puff of air and whisk, and through the swinging doors comes a dapper gent in European costume and high-domed forehead looking something like a breeder-owner on only slightly hard times or then again like a headwaiter in a medium-priced joint that is pushing hard for column mentions. He looks at us disdainfully and goes to the bar, struggling with his glove.

"I will have an aperitif," he says to Jimmy the Horse in haughty and measured tones, "and perhaps while sipping it I may study your wine list."

Jimmy the Horse ducks toward me, his eyes filled with awe. "I did not think he would be in so soon," he says, showing that he shares my recognition. "He must have breezed through the checkpoints."

Big Ernie tugs me by the shoulder, breathing heavily. He is not to be distracted. "Outside," he says.

"You will not want to go outside when I tell you who this is," Jimmy the Horse says. "I see that you do not know, Big Ernie." He leans forward. "That is the Russian," he says. "The Royal Russian."

"The émigré," I add.

"Your wine list, please," the Royal Russian says, seemingly oblivious to our conference, "and rapidly, steward."

Big Ernie's hand falls from me and he steps away. "Now I know who it is," he says. "Now I know it good."

Some note in his voice, some tiny note which I have never heard before, makes me glimpse the fact that I will not have to knock Big Ernie on his pins today. Although I do not know why the Royal Russian has quite this effect upon Big Ernie, I can see the aura of respect which he has generated within all the spaces of this bar, which is not otherwise characterized by its hospitality toward Salvation Army persons or the revivalist mumblings of the fundamentalist types.

"Very well," I say, returning to the bar and picking up my jigger of homewrecker as Jimmy the Horse engages the Royal Russian in vigorous conversation from which the word *Chablis* finally floats off like a balloon. I drink more homewrecker. The Royal Russian looks at me with disdain. Big Ernie to his left begins to pray loudly as Jimmy the Horse rattles bottles. Finally I decide to break, as it were, the ice.

"What do we do?" I say respectfully to the suddenly attentive Russian, "in the face of living writers stealing our styles as if they were their own and granting us no credit?"

The Russian's mask of civility breaks and becomes contemptuous. "We are all living," he says, "and we are all dead. We all have one style and to that style must return. A dance, a mask, a masque, a masquerade, a masked ball, a trip through a trapdoor." He reaches his hand for the wine. "To mask is to mock," he says and drinks.

Big Ernie sobs.

I wonder if music heaven might be a refreshing change.

July 1977: New Jersey

Ring, the Brass Ring, the Royal Russian, and I

I am standing between two famous personalities in the bar of writers' heaven at the particular time when this instance commences and, considering the relatively late hour of the day here is our temperature-adjusted heaven and the heavy imbibing which all of us have done, am in reasonably good condition until the door bangs open and comes waltzing into the bar a personage I have not seen for several months' subjective time, this personage being the well-knownst Ring of the Thousand Faces who only rarely but significantly emerges from the brothel to seek more attenuated pleasures. In what I have come to call my post-death period my opening sentences have become even longer than is my wont, but that is a natural tendency. We are all what we once were here in writers' heaven except that we are more of the same.

"I want a drink," Ring says loudly, moving to the open space at the far left. The new bartender—there is a rotating crew here, no one can take this indefinitely—makes twitching and inquiring gestures and Ring adds, "What the hell do I care as long as it comes in large quantity and makes me shudder as it goes down?" The bartender shrugs, as do all bartenders in but the very best of fictions, and begins to set up Ring a large homewrecker, neat. "That is the story," Ring says, drawing his hat down over his eyes and turning toward me. "I recognize you," he says, "and I recognize this sinister Midwestern type to your left who was extremely overrated in all things, particularly his drinking capacity, but I do not recognize this strange, highly dignified individual to your right. He radiates refinement," Ring says and takes the tumbler of gin and knocks it down in one metallic swallow, "and if there is one thing I cannot stand it is that, since refinement can only be a posture."

Little Red twitches and grasps his bourbon glass tightly. Despite his harsh kidding Ring really means no harm—he is only covering up fears that he will be rejected anyway—but Little Red has, twenty years later, yet to truly recover from the numerous shocks and insults of his life not excluding the Nobel Prize certificate when he was somewhat young and his strange last years when he switched from trying to write all the books in the world to trying to drink all the liquor. "You were overrated yourself," Little Red mumbles. "You had at best a mimetic gift. Mimetic. Hemolytic. Hemolytic euthanasia and Paul de Kruif, that impostor," he says and spills his drink all over himself. He subsides, quaking, while I work on him with napkins tenderly. One must respect a Nobel Prize certificate winner particularly in our division of writers' heaven where there are only five and each a more insistent drinker than the others. "Terribly obliged," Little Red says to me while I help him up to his normal, lurching posture. "Appreciate what you're all trying to do for me and if I had stayed away from that bitch I might have had a wonderful career."

"It is easy for you to talk of careers," Ring says, his large forehead shining, little quivers of light seeming to emanate in a precarious but dignified fashion from the gin tumbler which he similarly holds in dignified fashion, "but what did you know of life? What did you know of the true morality of your day? You did blind, cheerful morality tales and ended up trying to screw in ten languages and failing in them all."

It occurs to me reminiscently how peaceful it is when Ring is not around, which is most of the time, but is in his arena of choice, the brothel, making up for lost days on Earth. It is really a more peaceful and far friendlier drinking place without Ring, he even makes Big Ernie look tolerable, but Ring out of some sense of guilt or need for his fellow writers feels forced to come back occasionally and create scenes exactly like this. "Anyway," Ring says, toasting me, "this is the only man here who knows anything about sports which is as we all know the only thing worth talking about."

"Excuse me," the Russian says, prodding me gently. His eyes are lustrous and have the look of a $3,500 plater going to the post with allowance fillies of a higher but less predictable class, but then again, this may be only my term of reference. The Russian is quite mysterious. No one really understands him. Since his vanquishment of Big Ernie (who has not been around since the Russian's day of arrival) he has proven himself capable of drinking as much as or even more than the best of us not excluding Little Red, but in the matter of voluntary personal information or the intercourse of friendly exchange he offers none. "Who is this person?" he says to me, pointing at Ring. Apparently he has chosen me as his confidant and source of information, an odd position to be in since, even though I was at one time a gossip columnist, I have always been uneasy in the presence of those who are considered haute cuisine. "I repeat my question," the Russian says. "I wish to know who is this individual who is interrupting my consideration of eternity and the procession of the trudging weary and sinister creatures thereof."

"What kind of crap is this?" Ring says. "What is this man talking? German?"

I make a quieting gesture to him. Little Red at least is silent, muttering about his plans for Paul de Kruif when that eminent personage returns from doctors' heaven where he is apparently gathering notes. "This is Ring of the Thousand Faces," I say to the Russian. "He began by writing sports but later turned to short stories of a disturbing and most equivalent nature to humor before he did plays and musicals of a frivolous key. In between he did a few novels about sad baseball players. All of the time he was drinking and then he drank lots more and died."

"What is baseball?" the Russian says. "I mean, I know it is your national game and I made a study of some of your customs, but of what significance is it?"

"Who is this person?" Ring says. "This person is a bum in a high cocked hat. He should be denied the premises." Ring is a belligerent drunk. Sad thoughts of his missing friend Mencken are apt to come out at times like these. "Henry knew what garbage this all was," Ring says as if in confirmation. "He would throw the foreigners out. Who needs Russians? Who needs foreigners? No one has a right to pass judgment on us but us and I want another goddamned drink. Throw the bum out."

"I agree with that," Little Red says, lurching across to throw an arm around Ring's shoulder. "This is an American era; an American heaven here. No one from out of state has the right to tell us what to do."

"Get away from me," Ring says in disgust. "The trouble with you is that you have no capacity."

It is, as if one could not have already this inferred, a tense moment in writers' heaven compounded of doubt and hatred, the self-loathing of many of the occupants which persists even past death, and the very personalities of the Ring and the Russian which, as they say in the lamented and still-missed Mindy's restaurant, are created to abrade one another. The bartender has of course slid completely from view as all bartenders in writers' heaven do when either fights or credit requests are perpetrated and it falls upon me to take on the uneasy and not really sought-for role of peacemaker, a role from which I shrink even more than usual because I am rather drunk myself. One of the more decent aspects of what they have done for us is that two drinks now do the work that eight were needed to do and under the physical pressure I can feel myself begin to sway. "Come on now," Little Red says to me confidentially. "Buck up. Don't vomit. Vomiting will get you nowhere."

"Get out of this place," Ring says to the Russian. "I will not return to my other activities until I know that you no longer sully these environs."

"You are an offensive man," the Russian says. "Your offensiveness of course comes from pain—"

"Don't tell me about pain, you royalist creep."

"—and your pain from your acceptance of these circumstances; your, shall I say, *belief* that this is real, and your own sense of loss comes from the deprivation of other real objects. I will tell you what," the Russian says, "I will make things easier for you and take away your argumentative obsession. I will prove to you that none of this exists, that it is a gaiety, a façade, a construction of the ciphers of our own wishes."

"He keeps on talking like that," Little Red mutters, clutching me. "I don't understand this shit, I'm just a simple Midwesterner. A good smoker, that's all I ever wanted, a couple of jokes, some naked women, a few laughs. Some gin. He talks and talks but he says nothing."

"I will tell you," the Russian says, backing away from the bar and spreading his arms in a grandiose gesture, "I will demonstrate for you the vanity, the hollowness, the tentativeness and artful nature of these concealments, and devolving from same, you will cease your aggression. Your drunkenness comes from an infantile need to ease the pain of loss but I will prove to you that there is no loss and your pain therefore causeless. Mark ye well," the Russian says.

"I'm drunk too," Little Red sobs. "I'm not in pain. I didn't miss anything. I married that redheaded bitch and had the big prize at forty. I drink for *fun,* that's what."

But Ring, silenced for the first time in all of the years of our acquaintancing, is looking at the Russian in wonder. "What are you talking about?" he says but without animosity. "Are you saying that all of this is illusion?" His voice is gentle. Ring is not known as the Thousand Faces for nothing; he has moves like a female tag-team match in the near corner. Now all that he projects is consternation. "Are you saying that it does not exist?"

"Of course it exists," the Russian cries and gestures at the walls, "of course it exists. Everything that ever was is at this moment, not, of course," he says, pausing to make gestures on his suddenly shiny cheekbones, "that the reverse of this is not true."

And it is at that moment that something rather weirdly metaphysical happens and one beyond my own halting command of the descriptive facility. Howie the P, who is unfortunately an infrequenter of these spaces, would perhaps do a better job of explanation, but the P does not believe in the applications of drink, preferring vigorous courtyard pacing in pursuit of red snakes and flying eagles, and therefore it is left to me, remembering all of the time, of course, that even the respected and lovable P had a way of obscuring up his descriptions precisely at the point when they were most necessary, an old trick for which he narrowly missed writers' hell if last-moment pity had not been taken by the management. Suffice to say that the walls of our bar seem to dissolve to give a clear, unimpeded perspective of the other buildings, but just as we are espying some particularly random and active goings-on in the brothel that amaze us and give me an entirely new view of that aspect, in a flickering the brothel too and of itself disappears and we are looking to the clear, dead empty panels of space itself, space then parts and we see the world. I see the very world. I see the parts of the world that appealed to me.

I see, specifically, the interior of Mindy's restaurant which I happen to know has been not in existence now for a long time, it is crowded as it was in the old days and the old people are there: Carnera off in a corner with a woman looking sad and confused, the great Babe slinging quips with Mindy at the reservations desk, the sainted Winchell himself deep in consultation with two actresses whose bare shoulders I recognize. The scene is so vivid that it is as if I am there, as if I could lean forward just a critical additional space and become part of it, the old days, again, but just as I do so this too dissolves, all of the parts of this famous restaurant going away, and I find that I am looking into a saddened, wizened, enormous face which is that of the Russian itself. The face dwindles until it fills only the normal part of vision and I am once more back in writers' heaven where the Russian claps his hands together and says, "You do see now. It is all created. It is all fabricated."

Ring, his eyes enormous, says after a while, "That is a wonderful trick, a true prestidigitatory feat of wonder." Little Red, clutching at my knee, on the other hand says nothing at all. He has fallen down. He is whimpering something about Main Street to the cuff of my pants. "It was wonderful," Little Red says, "it was wonderful. It was always as I had remembered it. It is a wonderful trick."

"Thank you," the Russian says and, pleased, picks up his shot glass of neat vodka. Unwillingly pleased, he seems to beam. "It is all part of circumstance," he says and permits himself the smallest of smiles and it is at that bucolic and pastoral moment when the threads of real communication seem for the first time to have been woven from Red to Russian to Ring to me the other R that the door swings open and Tom stomps in, kicking manure loudly from his farmer's boots and belching the scent of pumpkin pie. He bellows mad laughter.

"You pulling *that* shit," Tom says and the walls shake with his enormous voice, "that *you are your world* kind of shit? Why, I pulled that swindle way back in 1929" and it is at this moment as the Russian turns to him, his regal features suffused with more than vodka, ready for a mad charge which Red and Ring and I brace to restrain ... it is at that exact and precise moment that I see that the end of another more or less normal day in writers' heaven has and not a moment too soon arrived.

July 1977: New Jersey

Of Ladies' Night Out and Otherwise

Matters being as they are here in writers' heaven, it is not often that people of the opposite gender are seen in the environs of the bar in which we, the men, pass so very much of our time. Perhaps it is gentility but I rather theorize that women writers do not tend to become drunks until at least early-late career and are never social drunks. There are women here, of course, and we get along, but for the most part they inhabit the tearooms or their own compartments or spend time picketing the brothel in an attempt to raise the consciousness of its work force but its work force, in a heaven of their own, hardly ever listen.

An environment of total masculinity can, however, become stultifying. Women are threatening to our peace but they are also an important part of it and it is therefore with great pleasure on one particular evening that I see the doors of the bar spring open as they eject into the place Carson and Wise Blood Flannery, two admirable ladies as well as sharers of the secret sorrow.

"Hello, girls," I say to them not patronizingly as they glide in, making dramatic entrance of a sort. Flannery is in the lead as always, her high forehead glistening with southern purpose. "And hello there, Carson," I say in gentler tones as that person, barely deigning to pay recognition, follows with caution. "How pleased we are to see you in this abode at present time."

I am, of course, feigning a jocularity. It is all part of this persona behind which I may hide, even unto the afterlife. Actually, as any thorough reading of my long out-of-print masterworks would demonstrate, I am actually a rather sad and sensitive man, given at earlier periods to snuffle into tissues. It was only after I learned that laugh and the world laughs with you, cry and you cry alone, as the famous and respected aphorist put it, only after I learned this that I cultivated the rhetorical devices which provided me with modest sustenance to the date of my unfortunate death.

So now, even here, I find that I must maintain this jocularity. The truth is: in the rather lugubrious spaces of the bar in writers' heaven, who would stand me otherwise? Laugh and they laugh with you. This being only in the nature of a digression, of course, but now and then I cannot resist an impulse to slip the philosophical parts in.

"May I order you ladies a drink?" I ask as they stand before the panels, looking with disapproval at the vomit stains on the walls and at the many places where Big Ernie, in one of his rages, caved his fists into the planking. "A soft drink? An aperitif? A gentle elixir such as might be sipped on the porches of southern states in faint breezes during a ripe and decaying afternoon of summer?"

"How do you stand it here?" Carson inquires. "How can you stand to be in this place? Don't you have any sense of where you are, of what this is like?"

"Please to excuse," I say. "I do not comment upon your activities and you should not bear comment upon mine."

"Seed and blood," Flannery says shrewdly to Carson. "The perpetration, the carrying forth of that one stain of implication through all of the corridors of eternity until finally it bears its stunned and withered fruit."

"I have no interest in your metaphors," Carson says impatiently. Her delicate cheekbones flush. "I merely came here at your insistence but I do not have to listen to your explanations. Yes," she says, "I think I will have a drink." She looks at me. "I think I will have a gin and tonic on the rocks with a twist of lime. If you would care to order it for me."

"I will have the same," Flannery says, "except that I will not have a twist of lime. I will have instead just the faintest suspicion of fruit, a twinkling of color at the bottom, the very most bottom, of the glass."

Put in the position of host against my will but to my necessity I signal to the bartender and make the necessary declarations. The bartender, a thin person of indeterminate years, is yet another new one; bartenders cannot stay in writers' heaven for more than a short period and therefore it is not necessary for me to grant him characterization, one of my weaknesses anyway. It is not necessary for me to grant anyone else characterization either because at the time which I am recounting I am the only drinker in the bar of writers' heaven. Big Ernie is still sulking over his encounter with the Royal Russian, the Royal Russian has learned with joy of the butterflies which frequent jungle heaven only a short distance away and has not been seen now for weeks, Baby Gene and Little Red and Ring of the Thousand Faces and Tom and the multiple Johns have altered their hours with the change of seasons so that they now lie abed until three and begin the serious drinking only when the sun sets. It is left to me to hold up the honor, as it were, of the bar of writers' heaven alone in the mornings and this I have done with resignation and a weary sense of discipline; it is not an obligation I have sought but it is one which has been conferred upon me. I will do my best. I drink not from choice in the mornings but from necessity, not that necessity does not have its own pleasures. If there were none of us in the bar in the mornings the management might, after a while, decide to economize by keeping the doors closed until afternoon and then what would happen to Big Ernie or Little Red if they stumbled from the pit of sleep with the encouragement of ten thousand red snakes? It is for reasons like this, dedication to my confreres I should say, that I find myself one leg up at this dismaying hour and entertaining Flannery and Carson, who need all the entertaining that they can get. At heart they are as morose as any of the others. This is a fact which has nothing to do with sexuality.

Their drinks in hand, the ladies move over to the far left of the bar and engage in deep, whispered conversation. Little circles of color seem to parade before my eyes as the bartender damps down the area before me with a cloth and gestures toward them. "Tell me," he says, "do they come in here often?"

"Every now and then," I say.

"How often?"

"It is hard to tell. I do not know exactly. Why do you ask?"

"I ask," the bartender says, "because it is unusual to see persons of the opposite gender persuasion in these environs. As a matter of fact these are the first such that I have seen in my term of employ."

"Your term of employ has not been very long," I say gently. "Perhaps before you engage in generalizations of this sort you would wish to be here a little longer."

"I should hope not," the bartender says, putting his cloth underneath. "This is an extremely temporary assignment and I have been promised a quick work release."

Flannery leans in my direction and says, "You know nothing of causality."

"I know more than you may think," I say.

"I'm not talking to you. I'm talking to him. You have no understanding. One moment you are alive, possessed of the force of revelation, the sinful blood rocketing toward its accustomed target, the heart. The next, a bullet is in your skull and you are dead. This is the principle of causality."

"This is the principle of death," the bartender says. "Excuse me," he adds, retrieving his towel and walking quickly to stage rear, his shoulders hunched. None of the bartenders appear to respond to us very well once the conversation becomes serious.

"Causality is death," Flannery says. "In the blood they become that awful excuse for corruption: our mortality."

"I don't know anything about that stuff," I say although I do, staring into my nearly empty glass. "I was just a simple Broadway columnist with a certain rhetorical flourish."

"Crap," Flannery says. Her cheeks are flushed; she never could hold her liquor. "You know all of the circle in the fire."

"Quiet," Carson says. "Every time you have even a weentsy drink you lose control. Show some dignity."

"Yeah," Flannery says, downing her mixed drink in a single, precarious swallow. "*Dignity*. Where did all of your dignity get you? You were wiped out at twenty-five."

"Better than not being able to write a decent novel," Carson says sweetly, "better than faking all that guilt and circumstance. You don't know *what* guilt is like until you've lived in Nyack, New York."

"At least I had a sense of form."

"You had nothing," Carson says. "A little lyrical gift, that's all."

"I don't have to take that from you."

"Ladies," I say, embarrassed by my impromptu role of peacemaker, "there is no need for these discussions. Why are you fighting so?"

"Stay out of this."

"Isn't there enough of this already?" I say. "Big Ernie wants to beat up everybody, particularly the Royal Russian. Ring thinks that Little Red was a faker and John complains about the pasture smell that comes from Tom's boots. The Royal Russian hates almost everybody and I'm just trying to keep the peace. Wouldn't we hope that the feminine element would induce a more delicate, a more gracious aspect to this place? It isn't easy you know."

"Complaints," Flannery says, "always complaints." She puts the heavy tumbler down with a crash. "I'm so sick of complaints about externals. It's the inner corruption which has created all of this, don't you understand?"

"Wordy bitch," Carson says, "can't you ever get to the point?"

"Ladies—"

"At least I died at the top of my form," Flannery says. "You didn't do a thing, not a thing for the last fifteen years. Except to drink."

"Bitch," Carson says, rising from her seat. She holds her drink before her, two-handed, like a piece of weaponry at port arms, a position with which I am very familiar from having written dispatches from the training fields in World War I. "Come here and I'll show you what I can do in the last fifteen years."

"All right," the bartender says, emerging at long last from his perch of abstinence. "Enough of this. You are both eighty-sixed. *Out*."

"What is that?" Flannery says.

"'Eighty-sixed' is bar talk for being shut off and thrown out," I say kindly. "This is writers' heaven and you are in a bar so they try to talk that way for the atmospherics."

"Do you hear that?" Flannery says. "You got us thrown out of this place."

"Don't you pin it on me," Carson says, "and besides who wants to be in this place? It is utterly disgusting. I despise bars. Private drinking in a room with flowered wallpaper, that's what I say. Transfer the pain amongst things familiar. Daffodils in the crockery, the smell of medicinal tea burbling on the stove." She walks briskly to the door. "I will never deal with you people again," she says.

"You owe a tab, lady," the bartender says.

"Isn't this writers' heaven?"

"Not for you, lady."

Carson flushes. "You pay it," she says to Flannery. "I don't carry any money with me."

"*Me* pay it? You've got a wild and blackened soul. I will pay nothing."

"It's all right," I say. "*I* will pay it." I make what I take to be a rather grandiloquent gesture but it falls upon deaf ears or perhaps it is deaf eyes as the expression does not go. "You may put it on my tab," I say to the bartender, "and it will be my pleasure."

"If you think that changes anything," Carson says, "you are wrong. You are still a dreadful and superficial man."

"With no understanding of the seed of guilt," Flannery says and sweeps ahead of Carson to the door, Carson follows her, in a clang and clutter they are both gone. Little breezes waft in their wake. I sigh and turn back to the bartender who has already retreated to his position of great distance. I cannot say that I blame him. Great distance is a reasonable necessity.

"You do not have to pay," he says. "It does not have to go on your tab, I mean. As everyone knows, the drinks are free here. It seemed merely of a necessity to get rid of them."

"I understand," I say.

"I must say that I thought the men writers are bad but the ladies are even worse."

"They are not worse," I say, "they are merely more delicate. They are better unable to stand up amongst the high rigors of the profession."

"That may be," the bartender says, "but if that is so they have no business being in that."

"They had no choice," I say. "They had no more choice than any of the rest of them excepting always for the Royal Russian who would have made a neat headwaiter or keeper of a zoo. But even he too became a purveyor of the form."

"I do not understand why this is so," the bartender says with a mystified look, coming over to set me up. "This matter of no choice. How can this be?"

"Don't ask," I say and swallow the tumbler of gin neat. Knives bite into me, easing the indeed sinful blood. "Don't ask."

August 1977: New Jersey

The Annual Once-a-year Bash and Circumstance Party

Once per annum, celestial time operating for our convenience on the same clock as earthbound time, this being another of the facilities offered by writers' heaven, there is a great drinking party in which reminiscences are exchanged, current evaluations are made, and the courses that will be taken for the next year are plotted. Those courses are always the same, we being a rather routinized and unambitious lot at the present time, but these calculations and recalculations give us a feeling of purposefulness and progress, something without which even the least of us would feel abandoned. There is nothing wrong with an eternity devoted to drunkenness, copulation, or sloth so long as there are surrounding rationalizations of a metaphysic type, and so the party serves a most important function, although of course it does not serve the ultimate function. The ultimate function is beyond the facilities of the management to offer us, although they surely would if not prohibited by tenet.

It is this evening of the once-per-annum bash and circumstance party which I accordingly recount. All of us are there except those who are too deeply incapacitated, such as Uncle Sam Clemens, to leave their quarters, but even the absentees are with us in spirit and messages of a cheerful type are relayed back and forth even to those. Ring and Little Red and Tom and Big Ernie are here, the Royal Russian himself is in a corner sipping upon aperitif and considering all of us gloomily, and in addition to these personages who have already played a part in certain descriptions of events past (the famous Carson and Flannery have consented to come but only if placed at opposite sides of the bar, interceded by many bodies which will prohibit the exchange of quips) there are many who have not been previously mentioned. No chronicler can be absolutely complete. Standing against one of the walls with a large and bright gin in my hand, occupying the role of participant observer with which I have had my many great social successes, I take note of those who are there, to say nothing of the respective statuses which they are said to occupy.

For the occasion the bartender is not one of the irregulars who pass in and out of our circumstance but is none other than the beloved Chuck the Seraphim himself. Chuck the Seraphim, a special emissary from headquarters, is rumored to have the most significant ties to management, and since he is an impressive-looking person with large mustaches and a florid complexion it would be difficult to reject this information out of hand. Chuck is seen only at special occasions on bar duty: the annual once-a-year bash as well as certain religious or sentimental occasions. His presence is always signal thus of important and meaningful events, although he is little more than a nominal bartender and has no understanding whatsoever of the important relationship between gin and vermouth in the standard martinis, thinking it to be equal. Despite this he is well liked by those who have had occasion to deal with him, mostly because of the high floridity of his person and the sense that Chuck's dislike might act in contraindicative fashion to one's continued peaceful residence within these premises.

Chuck, with only slight fumbling over difficult pronunciations during which he takes out a handkerchief to wipe his streaming but friendly visage, does the annual report. Scott is holding, Big Ernie continues to fall as fast as a twinkling star. Baby Eugene is slightly up, although there are certain weaknesses indicated. Ring is down. Flannery is down. Carson is down. I would be down if there were any position from which I could fall but I reached, as they like to say in the other regions, the absolute nadir many reports ago. As a courtesy, however, my name is included among those status *unchanged*. John M. is down, as are John S. and John O.; the three big Johns glower at one another and make threatening gestures toward Chuck the Seraphim. It is all taken as being in good fun which of course it is not.

Dashiell continues to go up. Good work being done on his behalf. Supported by the hands and elbows of a few pulp-type personages in the corner, Dashiell rises to acknowledge with a cheerless wave the polite applause. He has proven despite many humiliations to have more staying power than almost any of us. Big Bill is down. Ray is due for another revival, at least half of one, but in the meantime he continues to sink. Dashiell winks at him. The two prominent new arrivals, Corporal Jim and the Royal Russian, are greeted by name and welcomed officially to the premises. They are reminded that funeral eulogies of a praiseworthy sort cannot be said to count and that therefore their first status report cannot be given until next year. Corporal Jim grips his glass of beer more tightly and downs it with a frozen swallow, his eyes set. The Royal Russian giggles. Chuck the Seraphim pays his regards to those assembled considered too lacking in data to have a report this year. This is merely the management's way of being kind; everyone knows that these are people who have not been thought of, once, by anyone during the previous year. He asks then, in a routine way, for motions from the floor.

"I move," Big Ernie says, "that the size of the drinks be doubled. Also that in truth beds and bedding be placed inside so that those of us who would dwell may dwell. And that kindness be shown, a simple and true regard. We have purchased our peace with our souls."

Big Ernie makes this motion every year. Chuck the Seraphim shrugs. "We can double the drinks if you want," he says. "They are all free regardless so it does not matter. The respect part you have always had; that is what you are here for. Nothing on the beds and bedding, though. There are zoning laws. Can't be done."

"Truthfully you do not care," Big Ernie says. "You do not care for our dignity." He makes this response every year too, ritual being very important to Big Ernie as all of us scholars of his collected works know. "You do not care," he says, running fingers through his impressive beard. "But that is all right. I do not care either. I have seen the spiritual hole: the nada." He lifts his glass shakily, spilling a quantity of bourbon over his right shoe tip. John O., standing next to him, makes a gesture of revulsion and backs away, slapping at a stain on his country club jodhpurs. He mutters something to Big Ernie, whose face convulses with rage but as is the case with all of Big Ernie's rages it goes away quickly and his features are slack and peaceful once more. In the truth, as Big Ernie would say, he has very little ambition at the present time and he never did. All that he wants is that stasis, that nada of which he has so often and fortuitously apprised us and here in writers' heaven he is getting some although not enough. Enoughness they could not offer him without breaking all the rules of the management.

"I move that the annual reports and circumstances be discontinued," I say after a pause in the conversation indicates that there are no other motions going to be made and I wish to add a certain enlivening degree in order to justify Chuck's personal appearance at this time. "They have served their usefulness and no longer have any real purpose. We should be freed of the so-called professional rivalry here since we are all, as it were, eight to five shots who have busted out. Life is seven to five against as I have previously noted; we ought to at least get even money here."

Ring says, "The only reason you want to discontinue the rankings is because you have none. You're totally forgotten. Nobody's read your work in years."

"And yours?" I say. Ring blushes. He is belligerent but embarrasses with equal facility which is one of his charms. "No," I say, "it is not for that reason. All of us are forgotten in time. It is because the annual reports keep us from accepting our fate, which is to be forgotten, that I urge their abolition. They merely forestall the inevitable, the foreseen, the necessary. I do not have to tell you the results in the Russian and

French quarters where annual reports were abolished of necessity. Here they should be voluntarily."

"I will discuss this with the management," Chuck says. "I will present it to them as you have presented it to me."

"I do this atwixt and akin every year," I point out without rancorousness, "and every year the management in due course fails to respond."

"I have nothing to do with that," Chuck says.

"I wish you would do a better job of conveying my request."

Chuck shows me his palms flat out like a busted turf adviser. "I can do nothing better than to undertake with them to see your position," he says. "After that it is out of my hands."

"I think the management would be well advised to make a personal appearance," I say. "The management is dodging its responsibilities sending one of the emissary persuasion when it should make its own way."

"I will take that up as well with the management," Chuck says. "I will discuss with them your position."

"I wish you would convey the sensibilities of my request without my making a direct appeal."

"You cannot make a direct appeal."

"That is so," I say, "but I can create some amount of revolutionary ardor amidst the assembled here all of whom are known for their personal irascibility."

"You can create nothing," Chuck says. This happens to be quite true—our discussion, far from arousing revolutionary ardor, has resulted only in an intensified clinking of glasses, gulping, and murmurings of boredom—and I decide on the instant to accept it. It is important at the once-a-year circumstance bash, I feel, that at least one of us point out that we are persons of some independence and have more in our minds than an eternity of drink and quieter solaces, but having done that I see no reason to make an issue of it. Principle should never stand in the way of a good drink. I nod at Chuck, raise my glass on high, and take it down. He winks at me. He is not a bad personage and he is, of course, no less than anyone else simply trying to do his job. It is not an enviable position and I would not know what to do with it myself.

"Are there further comments or motions or questions from the floor?" Chuck asks and there are of course none. There would have been none a long time ago had it not been for Big Ernie and me. "I therefore," Chuck says after a reasonable and polite pause, "declare the formal annual meeting at an end. The celebrations may begin." He takes a towel from underneath the bar and wipes his hands determinedly. "I will now set up anyone who wants to be set up," and in the general rush of compliance he is completely obscured from me and, for all I know, from the world itself.

The festivities, it has been announced, may begin but except for the rush of those to refill there is really no change in the general temper of the room. It is the same as every other day except that there are many more people in attendance under compulsory statute. John O. continues to give contemptuous glances at Big Ernie, who waves his fist and calls for Scott to enter so that he can beat him up again. Scott, no dummy, is in the brothel on special dispensation and has not been out for years. Carson and Flannery, at peace for once, are listening quietly to Virginia, who off in a corner is giving them a lecture on the higher points of poetics. Every now and then a word emerges from the lecture like *waters* or *schizophrenia* or *royalties* and I feel my respect for Virginia on the rare occasions that I see her multiply; she is a sensible person. So is Emily, a lively, fluttery little woman who giggling off in a corner with Aunt Marianne and Cousin Sylvia looks exactly like a dressmaker for some of the famous Broadway musicals that in my time I have known intimately. The ladies share the men's vices but in many ways they are easier to get along with and more pleasant to know. Perhaps this is because they felt less pressure but then again and as the Royal Russian might point out it is of a mystery and not to be solved within the blunt and rusty intellectual tools which we have been given. There is certainly very little mixing of the sexes in the writers' heaven bar; this may come from simple shyness but I have a more logical explanation: the brothel, for the types who inhabit the heaven, takes care of all they care to know of the sacred male-female compact by which the world is supposed to but does not often partake.

At length I find myself in conversation with Dashiell over in an opposite corner. Dashiell, a thin type with penetrating eyes and dick's clumsiness, is one of the most companionable sort and it is a shame that I see him only at the once-a-year circumstance bash; Dashiell having gone in for heavy sleeping and meditation now while he continues on a lengthy drying-out process interrupted only occasionally by five-day drunks which destroy the cure. He is very drunk now. "It *is* heaven," Dashiell says to me, patting his mustache, "it is all that we could have asked. I was never a man of much faith, an agnostic maybe, *prove it to me*, you know, and I must say that this is better than I could have asked."

"It is a remarkable place," I agree. "It has its points. One could be happy here."

"It is writers' heaven," Dashiell says with a sigh and drinks a malt chaser. "It is writers' heaven because we do not have to write. I do not have to write anymore, do you understand?" He grasps me of the lapels, gives me his penetrating dick's stare. "Do you know what heaven that is?"

"But, Dashiell," I say, failing to disengage myself out of politeness, allowing myself to stay in position out of my genuine fondness and not to embarrass a very real person, "I accept what you are saying but in honesty a qualification must be made because you did not write for years and years before you entered these premises, about twenty by my rough count, and therefore you could be said to have achieved the heavenly state before passage. Not to write is wonderful but can be achieved on earth."

"You don't understand," Dashiell says, letting his hands drop, his eyes filled with pain and wisdom. "You are a good person and considering your background more intelligent and aware than you might be but you do not understand at all. It is not heaven because I am not writing. Any fool can achieve, as you say, that circumstance. It is heaven for another reason."

"And what," I say, eager to humor a great old trouper, one of the very best of his time and almost as much of a help to generations of plagiarists as I am, "what if I may ask is the reason if you are not writing here as on earth."

"Because," Dashiell says after a properly timed trouper's pause, "because, Damon, I don't *want* to anymore.

"I don't want to."

August 1977: New Jersey

Afterword to Four Stories About Writers' Heaven

These astonishingly bitter pieces were written in July/August 1977 and all sold to Ed Ferman except for the third in sequence, "Of Ladies' Night Out ...," which he passed, telling me that he has no more explanation for this than would I. Here is an honest man and a competent editor: a friend as well as collaborator over all these long years of my writer's decade.

As an indication of the place tenanted by my psyche that stale and brutal summer these stories raise, against my will, a question: how could a writer so seemingly at the end of all hope manage to go on? (I did.) One answer is that this is not the first time the question was in order: *Herovit's World*, finished in January 1972, reads like a Last Will &, etc., and 1972 was the year I *really* got down to work, driving through thirty-two novels to September 1974 before getting into trouble for good. I was able to go on from there, able to go on from here, wasn't easy but I managed. Although I am not inexhaustible—I wrote somewhere years ago—I am not easily exhaustible either.

Damon Runyon does deserve better, by the way. His voice indeed alive only through those of all his imitators, he has been as deeply influential as any American writer of his time. His stories had interior power and feeling, and like that other underrated and semi-forgotten artist Ring Lardner he should be in print and closely attended.

Don't book it, though, Horse.

The Appeal

But the one-time maiden special who ran in the maiden claimer proved to be there for a reason—the horse broke down on the backstretch and came home on three and a half legs—so I was down another four hundred. Incaution. One should not parlay losings. Nevertheless, convinced that the bad streak was now at its logical end, I took a limousine to the famous and relatively new casino hotel in Atlantic City and applied the principles of Martingale to roulette, driven by the fact that anyone so famous as to have a system named after him had to have something on his behalf. Seven turns of the red taught me why the professor was probably dead for so long.

Things were getting serious so I tried card-counting at blackjack but a blonde disturbed my recall and the cigarettes were hurting my eyes. Also at a certain point the dealer brought in a new deck. "You can't do that," I said to him desperately. "Is that a law?" he said with an expression so quizzical and winsome that I found myself without a comeback. Monmouth Park racetrack is not inconveniently north from the famous new hotel casino and so, knowing that matters were at a most difficult pass, I took public transportation rather than a limousine to the shore, arriving there at eleven in the A.M. which gave me two hours and fifteen minutes to work on my specialty which happens to be the daily double. Someone in the upper grandstand was rumored to have hit the three-thousand, four-hundred-dollar double which occurred on this date but I did not make the acquaintance of this person either before or after the race. With seventy-three dollars left I decided to make one of those perilous leaps into the unknown which have in the past made me known to my friends as a spirited and adventurous man, but hurdles races in the late fall are a leap into the unknown for the wretched horses who run them, let alone the horseplayers. Accordingly I presented myself in the offices of Louis the Fourteenth on the following day.

Louis is called the Fourteenth or the Quatorze as he sometimes prefers, because of the touch of class, because he is the fourteenth direct descendant of the family engaged in the same trade. At least this is what the Quatorze claims and I do not dispute with him, nor does the Quatorze tend to surround himself with those who would wish to dispute. It takes me forty-three minutes to get into his offices and it is not worth it but of course I had no choice. "I will need a little more time, Louis," I say to him. "It is a simple matter of assembling collections already due me but I am unable to settle the obligation at the present time."

The Quatorze looked at me unhappily. There is something about the unhappiness of a short, dapper man which can be peculiarly unsettling. "The tab is seven thousand dollars," he said. "And change. Not to forget the change which is three hundred and forty-three dollars and I do not mean cents."

"I know that, Louis."

"I would prefer if you would address me more formally. You promised settlement formally and for today."

"I know that."

"There have been extensions," the Quatorze said, biting his lip and looking at the paper in his hand. "*Several* extensions. The extensions as a matter of fact appear to have begun three months and fourteen days ago."

The Quatorze is a precise man with good help, an unbeatable combination. "I know about that," I repeated. "It is merely unfortunate difficulties which I am having, family illness, an aged father, difficult debts, business pressures...."

The Quatorze put the paper aside and leaned on his elbows alertly. "You have no family," he stated, "other than that which has disowned you including your aged father who lives very well on the coast of Florida. You have no business. Pressures and debts you do have."

I nod at him as gracefully as possible under the circumstances. "Your information is very good."

"In my line of work my information had better be good. I am dependent upon my sources. My sources, however, have let me down in allowing a tab of this size to accumulate. I will have to get some new sources." Louis picked a small slice of lint from the area covering his kneecap. "I will have to hit my sources over the head and drop them south of here if they do not do somewhat better than they have in your case."

"I need time," I said. "Just a little time."

"The gambler and the alcoholic do not need time," Louis said. "I have thought about this deeply. Gambling and alcoholism are an attempt to suspend time with which it is otherwise difficult to deal. I am not a simple man, you know. I am a complex person; I come to this kind of work through inheritance and I think deeply. I want the money," Louis said.

"I don't have—"

Louis put his palms flat on the desk, raised himself. In this position he had no height problem whatsoever. "I want the money," he said. "I will give you until tomorrow morning because I am a reasonable man and the banks are already closed. If the money is not here by the opening of business tomorrow I will have to consult with my sources who in turn must consult with you. I am unable to speak for them. They are not very dependable but then again they have very literal minds."

"Louis—" I said, venturing an appeal.

"Appeals are useless," he said. "Appeals will not work. Pleas for mercy, expressions of reason, mild and sensible requests for delay. All purposeless. It is a difficult world. Time passes, time pressures; it is different coin for an institution which I am than for a gambler which you are. You will please leave now."

"Now, Louis—"

"You will leave," Louis said and at my elbow appeared two assistants whose presence in the room up until that point had been masked perhaps by my own urgency. They conveyed me with stunning speed and force to an antechamber where I was permitted to wipe my forehead and adjust the cuffs of my best suit. "You hear him," one of the assistants said. "You hear him good."

"I don't have to take abuse," I said. "The fact that you work for the Quatorze does not entitle you to assume his role."

"You must be some kind of a college graduate," the other assistant said.

"On the contrary," I said, "I am self-educated."

"You are a clown."

"I am entitled to my dignity," I said and various other things while already in the process of making exit. It is useless to argue with the assistants of the Quatorze, who do not share his relative dispassion or his height problem. In the street, however, the difficulties of my situation came, so to speak, crashing upon me and fragments of my departing dialogue bubbled to my lips. "Dignity is all we have," I said and "The only way out is to make the extended reach," and "It's all metaphysical," and so on and so forth; all of this speculation, the outcome of strong self-education, carried me in a half-comatose condition through several hours and several miles of public and private transportation until I reached that place which I must have always known I would reach but of course could not have attempted had I given it conscious thought. A man after all has his pride; even maiden claimers are registered thoroughbreds. "I need seven thousand three hundred dollars, Mother," I said after we had gone through the amenities and settled in the rather large living room. "I have never seen fit to call on you like this before and have kept you well segregated from all of my activities, the Quatorze, for instance, not being aware that I *do* have a family or, more strictly speaking, I have you."

"What do you need seven thousand three hundred dollars for?" she said quietly. I twitched on my chair. My mother has always intimidated me. The only person who has ever really been able to stand up to her is my stepfather, but my stepfather is unfortunately often out of town for reasons of his own such as have sent him out of town tonight. "Sit up straight," she said. "Address the question. Don't look at your shoes."

"I have had business reverses," I said.

She laughed, a laugh that sounded oddly like the Quatorze. "You have no business," she said.

"You have no idea *what* I have. Our lives have not exactly been closely touching these many years."

"And a good thing too," she said, adjusting her glittering spectacles, little flickers of ruined light bouncing from the fluorescence off the lenses. "A very good thing. Seven thousand three hundred dollars? That is an extraordinary amount of money."

"It is half the price of a new Cadillac. It is a third of a year's income for a steelworker. It is *not—*"

"You are not a steelworker and you don't own a Cadillac. Business reverses!" she said. "I know what it is."

"I do not come to be lectured—"

"It's the wheel of fortune, that's what it is!" she said and laughed until she began to cough, quieted herself into little sobs and chuckles with a cigarette. She is not a woman of endearing habit. "You've been into all that stuff again, the horses and the dice. You probably never stopped."

"Will you help me or won't you?" I said. I paused. "This is not easy for me, you know. In fact it is rather humiliating."

"Life is a humiliation," my mother said. "The sooner you accept the fact that you *like* it that way, the better off you'll be." She took off her glasses, took a sip of coffee. "Seven thousand three hundred dollars," she said. "How very strange. How very odd that you would think that I would give it to you. Where did you get the idea?"

"*Lend* it to me. At interest."

"Lend it," she said. "Ah yes, lend it. Of course." She shook her head. "Your father was right about you. It was the only thing that man said that I agreed with but he was right. You'll never change, will you?"

"You have the money," I said. "I mean, I know you have it around. In here, in the house. You always kept twenty or thirty thousand dollars around. You said you believed in the cash on hand, that you never knew the value of money or how to respect it unless you could have it in your hands."

"That was a long time ago. Things have changed. Besides, I wouldn't keep that kind of money around with your stepfather in the house. Totally untrustworthy. Half a crook, if I must tell you the truth. I made a mistake with that man but what can I do?"

"You can lend me seven thousand three hundred dollars."

She clasped her hands. "Absolutely not," she said. "In the first place I don't have it in the house and in the second place I don't have it and in the third place I wouldn't give it to you on principle. You're twenty-nine years old. It's time that you accepted responsibility for your condition."

"You're like the Quatorze," I said.

"I don't know who you're talking about."

"Everybody knows what I should do. Everybody has the answers. But none of you know the pain."

"I know the pain," she said, looking at me keenly. "For one thing I have a son like you and you had a father like that man down in Florida now. *I* know pain, believe me."

"I'm going to be in bad trouble if I don't get the money," I said. "I have nowhere else to turn. Those people are serious. They talk in funny sentences and they kid around a lot but the Quatorze is not the fourteenth of his generation because he wears plaid jackets or talks out of the side of his mouth. The Quatorze is dead serious. And so am I."

"And so am I. No."

"I can't speak for what could happen to me."

"You can go away," she said. "You can disappear. You got here, didn't you? You say they didn't know about me, right?"

"It is different," I said. "I cannot go away, not anymore. And surely if they do not know I am with you at this moment they would have ways to find out. So you're involved whether you like it or not."

"There is nothing more to say," she said. "I was going to offer you cheesecake and coffee for old times' sake, you are my only son after all, my only child, but there is no reason for it. You are hopeless. I want you to leave now."

"I want the money. Where is the money?"

"I won't tell you. Anyway, it's not here."

"You had places," I said. "You had a few places. I used to look when I was young. I would never take, almost never anyway, but I would look. I figure I could find it here from a standing start in an hour. It isn't that big a house. And you'd keep it close to your bed. I'd find it all right."

She stood, pushed her glasses under the cushion. "This is enough," she said. "This is quite enough—"

"I'm in bad trouble, Ma. I'm in real bad trouble." I had not called her *Ma* for years but the appeal had no weight. The woman simply has very little humanity and this is the truth. She is not a humane person. Maybe if she had been different I would not have turned out this way, although of course I do not wish to look for excuses. "I'm hurting," I said, "I'm hurting badly."

"So am I."

"All you ever thought of was how *you* were being hurt. You never thought of other people at all."

"I'll make it a police matter," she said. "That's what I'll do, that's how serious I am. I want you to leave."

"You used to threaten to call the cops on me, Ma. You used to threaten all the time. When I was six, seven, you'd even go to the phone and threaten to dial. You have any idea what that kind of thing can do to a kid, a young kid growing up? The fear?"

For once she was quiet. She stood looking at me.

"You had no compassion, Ma," I said. "I looked for compassion for a long time but it was never there. Then I started to look for it elsewhere. From tote boards and the Quatorze."

She shook her head. "It's too late," she said.

"I know," I said. "I know. It's too late."

I stared at her. These people aren't clowns in rubber suits, I thought, the plaid jackets and the language does not make them unwilling to kill. It is that kind of a world. It is a killing world. Underneath the rubber masks and false noses it is murder.

My mother said, "I'll never give you the money. I'd rather die than give you the money. It's as simple as that."

"I know," I said. "I know. I know how you feel about money. You taught me the importance of it and that it was worth anything to try and get it. Anything except feeling, that is."

I stared at her. My palms were sweating lightly. Her eyes fixed.

It's six to five, I thought. Six to five and pick 'em, vigorish either way, which means that it is a 10 percent cut off the top or maybe 5 because I am a great customer, but still a losing proposition booked up all the way. Six to five. Six to five.

"You won't do it," she said. "You won't do it."

"Don't bet on it, Ma," I said quietly. "I might book it myself."

And then for a long time while I thought about a little of this and a lot of that we stood there in the house built over the swamp on the far west tip of the ruined state of New Jersey and we looked at one another.

May 1978: New Jersey

Afterword to "The Appeal"

"The Appeal" is the first of a few stories in this collection from the mystery magazines. It is no more a conventional mystery than "Final War," say, was conventional science fiction, but just as "Final War" appeared initially within genre limits, and delighted to have it there, so did this and not to its discredit. Genre fiction, even at its (oft-witnessed) worst, is *about* something; the so-called literary short story is more often than not about nothing at all. An old mumble: William Abrahams will not answer my letters about this.

"The Appeal" is a very novelistic short-short; it begins in one circumstance and voice and ends in another. Usually it took me 50,000 words to do this kind of thing. The fact that I find it here in 2,700 means either that (a) the older I get the defter my hand doth wrought, or (b) the older I get the defter my self-delusion doth weave. Or both.

Yahrzeit

February 1982: Yesterday the tenth anniversary of Leopold's death. Strange to think of the Babe gone that long, Nate under the ground and out of the world, but he must have been a frail, shambling little figure in those last years and it is useless to sentimentalize the man that he was; long gone before death. Quivering autobiography that he wrote in prison, a snivel for freedom. A participant in malaria programs: get sick for democracy. Early release. Early release! Well, he broke down at the end but it is not for that that we will remember him.

Fifty-eight years or so, call it sixty past the crime. What it must have been like to have been eighteen and rich in Chicago in that old time, plucking a small boy from the schoolyard like a chicken and carrying him off to destiny with a companion and chisel at the wheel of a new rented sedan. Great times, great deeds! But of course he would have to have been caught and repentant. Babe was ahead of his time.

Pitiable. Put him out of mind.

Nonetheless, I felt compelled to do something to honor the anniversary. The young Babe would have approved. Selected therefore a chisel from the excellent batch of weaponry I keep behind this very desk and went out into the streets. A small boy would have been best but the law is not up to that yet; will not understand for at least a few more years that it is better to catch problems at the source, not outcome. A geriatric, then. It is *always* a geriatric, I am getting so bored with them! But this would be with a chisel and in memory of the Babe; maybe I could make something special of it. I cornered the one I wanted in a bare glade in the park, having tracked him for fifteen minutes for the isolation. Seventy-five or so with liver patches all over him; a high, quivering aspect to the nostrils in motion which reminded me vaguely of my father, now unfortunately deceased. Newspapers under the arm, a brown paper bag dangling from his fingers. Ready, ready, ready to die; ten years past his time and needing release.

I backed him against a tree, raised the chisel.

"No," he said, when he finally confronted me and understood the situation. I never like to take them from behind; part of the pleasure is in seeing and sharing their knowledge of death. Some shriek, some lean to embrace, others are apathetic, but ultimately with the geriatrics it is always the same: at last an acceptance. This is why they bore me. "Please," he whimpered, "I don't want to."

"I'm sorry," I said, raising the chisel. I always say that I am sorry; in some basic sense I am. It is dull to kill one geriatric after the next, even if one must take pleasure where one can and even if it is ultimately for the sake of the government. "It's got to be done."

"Please," he said again, "you don't want to do it. Not to me. I never bothered anyone. Listen, I'm a sick man; a heart condition. The doctors told me just last week that I'm going to die soon anyway." His eyes blinked. "If I'm going to die soon, it's just such a waste," he said and I could see him try to work cunning into the proposal. "There are lots of healthy jerries around. Get one of them and it would be a service. A year from now, six months, I won't even be here, son. You remind me of my son, come to think of it. I got to write him a letter soon; I owe him a letter."

"Sorry," I said again, "you know that illness is no excuse." Most of them lie anyway, whether from fear, confusion, or genuine senility I do not know. Nor care. *For you, Babe*, I whispered, raising the chisel, *and for you too while I'm at it, Dick, you poor born-too-early, out-of-your-time sons of bitches.* I got him clean with the first shot in the forehead, cracking his skull open like the windshield of a rental car, then added another in the guts for the double tribute. *You too, Dick.* The bag fell first and the geriatric on top. I hate to call them *jerries* even though this is their own name for themselves. It deprives them of their dignity.

I left him in the glade.

Later, as usual, I phoned the local center to report. "You'll find a chisel next to the body," I added; "it's a kind of tribute."

"Surely, sir," the blank voice said, "and thank you for the service."

"Not to mention."

"If you'll give me your number we'll see that credit is properly entered to your account."

"That's all right," I said, winking at the phone. "I don't want the credit. It isn't necessary. I did it in memory of some friends of mine."

May 1972: New Jersey

Afterword to "Yahrzeit"

This was for Roger Elwood's Gold Medal anthology *Ten Tomorrows* back in early 1972, when my relationship with him was just beginning and I was doing short stories effortlessly and virtually presold. Move over, Big Ernie, *this* was writers' heaven! "I want something very short and very bitter, absolutely black and downbeat," Elwood said. Asking Malzberg to write downbeat is not unlike asking Nixon to stretch the truth a bit or asking Swifty Lazar to make them really bleed on the deal.

"Yahrzeit," for some inexplicable reason, never appeared in any of my previous collections: I just clean forgot about it on compilation. Which was a mistake I now rectify: it has a nice, sardonic H. L. Gold 1950-ish *Galaxy* feel to it, has the concision, barbed point, acidity of the quintessential *Galaxy* short of that time. It also has all the weaknesses of said quintessential short: the satire is a little too self-satisfied, the ironies hardly multileveled, the whole thing has the air of being composed by the best student in Creative Science Fiction Writing 101, smug in his technical expertise and taken with his textbook control. That there is a core of genuine (not off-the-wall either) speculation and genuine pain makes the gloss of treatment even more difficult to justify, to be sure.

But this is where I was in 1972, folks. Track me from this to, say, the 1976 title story or the 1978 "Varieties of Religious Experience" and note that there was capacity for change. Only this, nowadays, gives me comfort.... I *did* learn, I did become more than a technician; I saw the folly of my heart and thus the hearts of all the others.

Another Burnt-out Case
(with Bill Pronzini)

I was sitting in my trailer, thinking once more about the imminent collapse of Western Civilization, when the Sicilian Snare Drum and the Human Pyromaniac came in and the Snare Drum said, "Boss, we have figured a way out of all this."

"There is no way out," I said. "To die in Boca Gables, Florida, is redundant."

"Seriously," the Human Pyromaniac said. That is, I am pretty sure it was he who made that comment and the Snare Drum the first to speak. It is not easy for me at the age of sixty-one to completely individuate my employees, but then again, they sort themselves out in the long run. "Seriously," he said again, "we have figured out how to shuck the carnival racket."

I ran a small traveling carnival, called Webb Carter's Wonderama, and I should point out that it was located at this time in the very Boca Gables of which I slurringly spoke. "Indeed," I said.

The Human Pyromaniac nodded; his stage name is Giraldo and he has a certain integrity, which is to say that he has never set fire to any person other than himself. "The answer," he said, "is insurance."

"Insurance?"

"Insurance," the Sicilian Snare Drum said.

"What are you talking about? Insure who or what?"

"Ourselves," one of them said.

"Out of the basic assumption," the other one said, "that in death there is life."

I have always resisted the imitative fallacy in art coined by Ivor Winters, holding to the proposition that the employees of Webb Carter's Wonderama are as unique in their spirit as they are in their function; but I must admit that on the instinctual level I cannot accept this. Human Pyromaniac is, after all, a rather out-of-the-mainstream-of-Western-Civilization occupation, to say nothing of the Snare Drum, who flays himself nightly in place of an orchestra we cannot afford.

I said, "We already have insurance. I have always complied with all of the federal laws on the matter. We carry a large general floater with the Firehouse Fund."

Giraldo's eyes glowed reverently. "Ah," he said, "fire."

The Snare Drum said, "This general floater carries a triple-indemnity clause for loss of life during a public performance. We have checked. The total of such a triple-indemnity death would be two hundred and twenty-five thousand dollars."

I pondered this information for a time, not having previously investigated the policy to any degree. "I am beginning to see the point," I said at length. "In fact the beauty of the conception, to coin a phrase, is now unflowering in all the dense and complicated corridors of my mind."

"We knew it would," one of them said.

"But there arises a question. Who is going to die? Who is elected to perish for the greater good of us all? I cannot say that I detect a suicidal eagerness in either of your faces."

"We did not think it necessary for anyone to actually die," one of them said.

The other one said, "For the purpose of collecting on the triple-indemnity clause, it would seem that the convincing *appearance* of death would be sufficient."

"Kindly elaborate."

"Flame," the Human Pyromaniac said fervently. "We will use the flames for which I am so well known and with which I have constructed my successful if not lucrative career. Someone will appear to perish, leaving not a recognizable *corpus delicti* but little more than wisps and ashes."

I pondered further. "Which someone did you have in mind?"

"Well, it cannot be me," the Snare Drum said, "inasmuch as I must play dramatic accompaniment; otherwise, we will have no musical conviction in the performance."

"This is true," I said. "Therefore, it is obvious who the someone must be."

"We expected you would see it our way."

"I am not that person," I said. "I am not a performer, as you well know. Thus, there is only one person left in our little troupe who qualifies, and that person is Big Tiny." I smiled. "Do you not agree?"

They nodded slowly. "We agree," one of them said.

"Have you discussed the plan with him?"

"Not as yet."

"I will attend to that," I said, "and converse further with you after I have done so. I have no doubt that he will see it just as I have."

"Webb," one of them said, "we are glad that you do not consider our proposal as in any way indicative of moral corruption, but merely as a sane and wise means in which to get out of all this on our shared proceeds."

"It is not a moral failure," I said, "it is only symptomatic of the collapse of Western Civilization."

"Surely," the other one said, and both of them withdrew. The closed door of my trailer rattled in the wind.

I considered matters more carefully. After a while I stood, went outside, and walked down the small midway in the rain. Webb Carter's Wonderama takes up no more than half a city block. It is a very small show, although of course it completely lacks exceptional talent. One Human Pyromaniac, one Sicilian Snare Drum, one sixty-one-year-old proprietor, and two people of the small persuasion; our former major attraction, the Mad Ghoul, had long since departed under unfortunate circumstances.

Little drops of water flicked off my craggily distinguished features, or what I like to think of as my craggily distinguished features, as I neared the tent in which Big Tiny and Little Tiny dwelt. I knocked on the flap of the tent, which is not an easy thing to do considering the resiliency of tent flaps. Momentarily Little Tiny appeared. She is in her late twenties, weighs approximately thirty pounds, stands exactly three feet tall, and is quite striking.

"Hello, Emma," I said politely. "Is Big Tiny in?"

"Hello, Webb," she said. "Yes, he is."

When I entered the tent I saw Big Tiny sitting on his little bunk. He weighs approximately thirty-eight pounds and stands three feet two; this makes him the dominant member of the couple. I find it easier to differentiate between Big Tiny and Little Tiny than I do my other employees.

Big Tiny said, "Have you come with the paychecks, Webb?"

"I have come with something much better."

"Nothing could be better than money."

"This is true," I said. I paused. "Perhaps we should talk privately."

"Well, Emma and I are husband and wife."

"I acknowledge the legal sanctions. But it would be better if this discussion were conducted privately for the good of all concerned. Will you accept that, Emma?"

"I will accept that," she said. She is really a beautiful person. I have found her complete miniaturization of the mysteries of femininity to be some objective correlative to my own miniaturization of the world in Webb Carter's Wonderama, or at least this is one of my metaphysical speculations. "I will simply be off. I will drive our van into Boca Gables proper and in a trifle will return with a little bag of groceries." All of us in Webb Carter's Wonderama speak in roughly the same fashion, but then our rhetoric *should* be similar; we have been living together for such a long time.

When Little Tiny had slipped gracefully through the tent flap I gave my attention to Big Tiny. "You come from Bensonhurst, Brooklyn, I believe," I said.

"No, the Bushwick section."

"You would like to return there, would you not?"

"I would."

"You would like to retire in luxury and comfort?"

"Webb," he said, "are you leading up to another ploy to circumvent your financial obligations to us?"

"No," I said, "I am leading up to your death."

"My *what?*"

"Your death—or rather, your apparent death. It is, as you will soon understand, for the good of all of us in Webb Carter's Wonderama."

He stared somewhat sullenly at his feet, which was not a difficult activity under his physical circumstances. "Webb—"

"Allow me to explain," I said, and did so.

The light of knowledge appeared in his eyes. "I see. But are you sure we will be able to get away with it?"

"Certainly," I said. "Do not worry. You must think only of your share of two hundred and twenty-five thousand dollars, for with that share neither you nor Emma will have to worry about purchasing little bags of groceries for the rest of your lives."

"How am I to apparently perish?"

"In flames. You will become, along with Giraldo the Human Pyromaniac, a flaming little person; you will do this in front of a representative of the Firehouse Fund whom we will call in to witness what we will say is a new and interesting act." My mind had been working all of this time, as one may perceive. "Your death will appear to be extremely tragic, not only for the obvious reason, but because it will also bring about the ultimate demise of Webb Carter's Wonderama."

"What of the details of my flaming, ah, demise?"

"It is not up to me to handle details," I said. "You and Giraldo must work them out between you. There will, of course, be a way. There is always a way."

"This is true," Big Tiny said, and for the first time he smiled. Then he paused reflectively. "Even though you did not wish to discuss the matter in front of Emma," he said, "she must nonetheless be told."

"Naturally," I said. "Everyone must be told—except, to be sure, those who would represent the Firehouse Fund. Everyone must work together here in order that we may retire separately."

In the nature of transitions, I should now explain how contact was made with one George Feuer of the Boca Gables office of the Firehouse Fund; and of how it came to pass that Feuer came to the grounds of Webb Carter's Wonderama four mornings subsequent at precisely ten o'clock, so that he would be able to witness the initial practice performance of a new act for which, I said, we hoped to secure additional coverage. At this juncture, however, I wish to point out that I tend to dislike transitional material; I believe life itself, that one great transitional circumstance, provides all of the passage that we need ever know.

Nevertheless, I suppose it is incumbent upon me to explain how the illusion of Big Tiny's death was arranged. Thus:

The platform in the main tent, upon which the Human Pyromaniac sets fire to himself during his thrice-weekly performance, contains a well-hidden trapdoor, should he ever lose control of the fire that he allows to engulf him and therefore need to quickly escape. Below the trapdoor is a tiny cubicle filled with water. It was through this trapdoor and into this cubicle that Big Tiny would be thrust during the dual immolation of himself and Giraldo, under the protective screen of the flames, and it was in this cubicle that he would secrete himself until Feuer could be induced to leave the immediate premises. Then he would emerge and seek a more permanent hiding place somewhere on or near the grounds until the time arrived for his triumphal return to Bushwick with his share of the insurance money. (It is not difficult, naturally, for a little person of three feet two and thirty-eight pounds to locate a hiding place that cannot be detected by individuals of the larger persuasion.)

One might well note, of course, that we would need some manner of physical evidence which George Feuer would view as the remains of Big Tiny. The problem, while it may seem to have been a large one, proved quite simply soluble. The Sicilian Snare Drum (or perhaps it was the Human Pyromaniac) recalled that the Mad Ghoul had left with us—as a result of his sudden arrest on an old warrant of such an excruciatingly personal nature that I cannot to this day bear to discuss it—a large trunk that contained, among a variety of other interesting items, a collection of doubtless simulated flesh, bones, and dental remnants. These were to be appropriated and subsequently placed inside pockets in Giraldo's specially constructed asbestos uniform, the same type of uniform, I should add, that Big Tiny himself would wear.

Also in the nature of transition, I should probably discuss George Feuer a bit more. However, I do not think I will. I will say only that he was a large man with a ruddy complexion and strange highlights in his eyes. He did not speak much and seemed somehow bewildered by our proposed new and interesting act, which I had already advised him was to be billed as "The Human Pyromaniac and The Flaming Little Person."

When he arrived on this morning of which I have already spoken, I ushered him to the tent and introduced him to the other members of Webb Carter's Wonderama, who were all grouped near the Human Pyromaniac's platform. There was some dialogue, which I find unnecessary to set down here, and then the Sicilian Snare Drum took his position in our makeshift orchestra pit and commenced to flay himself with palms and knuckles in preparation for the event. Meanwhile, Giraldo and Big Tiny made advance consultations and arranged their necessary props.

Feuer and I, along with Emma, took seats in the nearby grandstand. Staring across at the platform, Feuer said to me, "Damned strange stuff, Carter, that's all I can say. No wonder you people pay such high premiums—setting each other aflame and all."

"People need entertainment," I said perfunctorily.

"*Entertainment?*"

"It is all a device, all an effect," I said, "and it is merely the illusion of pain which we give them, not pain itself. People are severely disturbed these days; they feel that they have lost essential control of their lives. Perhaps watching a little person consumed by flame along with a Human Pyromaniac will cheer them." I was merely filling in time, as you have no doubt realized; I was at that moment consumed by distraction and nervousness. What if the scheme did not work? What if something went wrong?

"Nothing will go wrong," I said to Feuer. "No one will really be hurt, least of all the little person known as Big Tiny. Rest assured that all is merely and mainly paradigm."

He nodded dubiously.

"Giraldo is inordinately competent in his pursuits, you know," I said. "He first set himself aflame in Sioux Falls at the age of fourteen. His father sent him to an orphanage."

Feuer shuddered. He seemed to be in a strange state of excitation now, I noticed; he was breathing uneasily and he continually rubbed his palms together as if he were rolling a stick between them. "Terrifying stuff," he said. "Terrifying."

"*Ad demonstrandum,*" I said. I had studied some Latin at the Rensselaer Polytechnic Institute before they threw me out during the Great Depression. "*Reductio ad absurdum.*"

"That's easy for *you* to say," Feuer said. "I never had the opportunity to learn French. I had to go straight to work when I dropped out of high school. I worked myself up in life and the company."

I said nothing in response to this. I was watching Giraldo as he and Big Tiny finished their preparations and strode to the center of the platform. When they were ready, Giraldo motioned over to me and to the Sicilian Snare Drum, who began to rhythmically thump his chest. On my left, Emma held her breath and clutched her hands together in her tiny lap; on my right, Feuer began to tremble and an odd little crackling sound came from his throat.

Almost casually, Giraldo struck a match and set his hair on fire. "Fire!" the Human Pyromaniac shouted, in the fashion of one commencing a pursuit that gives him great joy.

"Fire!" Emma shrieked, in the fashion of any frightened person of the female persuasion.

"Fire!" Big Tiny screamed, in the fashion of a little person being immolated.

"Fire!" Feuer flared, in the fashion of a man hypnotized by the sight of flame.

Orange tendrils sprang from Giraldo's hand. The Sicilian Snare Drum struck 6/8, a very difficult double-waltz time restricted normally to Johann Strauss the Elder, the third movement of Ludwig van Beethoven's Eighth Symphony, and certain fire music. Big Tiny, looking suddenly frightened, pressed in close to the Human Pyromaniac. And the flames leaped from Giraldo's right to left hand, and then there was a sheet of fire and I heard Feuer moan, and in that moment the flames engulfed both the figures on the platform.

Big Tiny wailed; then, suddenly, he was gone.

"My God," Feuer rumbled, "he's gone!"

Emma moaned terribly—and skillfully, I thought—and all of us rushed toward the platform where the Human Pyromaniac now stood alone. Just before we got there Giraldo extinguished himself in that mysterious way he has; and when all of the flames were out, there was no sign at all of Big Tiny, or of the simulated remains that had been appropriated from the Mad Ghoul's trunk.

Giraldo looked convincingly horrified; he cried, "I couldn't help it! Something must have happened to his asbestos suit!" Then he flung himself to his knees, found the secret catch on the trapdoor, released it. The opening appeared, and beneath it, the cubicle filled with water.

Only the cubicle was not, at this time, filled with water.

And it did not, at this time, contain the live form of Big Tiny. What it did contain was the remains of a charred little body—and I knew illusion had become reality after all.

Emma fainted into Feuer's quaking arms. Giraldo wept. The Sicilian Snare Drum thumped his chest softly in 4/4 dirge time. I shook my head and knelt with my shoulders slumped beside Little Tiny as Feuer lowered her to the sawdust.

Someone (I believe it was Feuer) said, "Awful. Awful. I can't believe it. How could he have been burned to nothing more than this, to a lump of smoking charcoal?"

"My clothing is specially treated," the Human Pyromaniac said tearfully, "with a highly flammable substance. When I am on fire the heat is intense—so intense I am myself sometimes burned through the asbestos. Without such an asbestos suit ..." He spread his arms in a helpless manner.

"I need some air," Feuer said. His eyes had the look of blackened cinders; all the passion within had been extinguished, much as had the flames upon Giraldo's body.

"The authorities should be summoned," I said. "There is a telephone in my trailer."

"Yes," he said. "Telephone. Yes. Authorities and telephone." He used a handkerchief to wipe his forehead and then went away.

I looked at Giraldo and the Sicilian Snare Drum; they looked at me; we all looked away. Big Tiny was dead, truly dead, terribly dead, and we could not believe it. I most of all could not believe it, just as I could not believe that Western Civilization was due for imminent collapse. But it was so.

Yes, oh yes, it was so.

There is more transitional material in order here, but once again I must repeat my dislike for it and my belief that life itself is one great transition: rapid passage from infancy to carnival to grave. Of the grief and shock of the Human Pyromaniac and the Sicilian Snare Drum and of course Emma, of the arrival of the police, and of Feuer's consternation upon coming to terms with the liability of the Firehouse Fund, nothing more need be said. Time passed. A full day passed. Life goes on.

But on the following afternoon, Feuer appeared at the door of my trailer. He no longer appeared dismayed; in fact, he looked rather grim and not a little authoritative.

"We seem to have a small problem here," he said.

"Problem?" I said.

"With your claim. The forensic people in the Boca Gables police department are not entirely satisfied with the remains of Isaac Spritzer, a.k.a. Big Tiny."

I frowned. "Does this mean you are not immediately prepared to pay us our justified triple indemnity?"

"This is what it means," Feuer said. "If forensic is not satisfied, we at the Firehouse Fund are not satisfied."

"Well, you cannot deny that you saw Big Tiny go up in flames, as did we all. Giraldo, the Human Pyromaniac, has been incommunicado ever since the unfortunate accident; he blames himself."

"Nevertheless," Feuer said.

"I do not know what more you can reasonably expect," I said. "After all, *we* cannot be expected to produce a *corpus delicti* on one who has been immolated."

"Let us discuss matters at greater length," Feuer said. "Outside, perhaps? While we stroll about the midway? The rain has stopped, and it really is a pleasant afternoon."

I sighed. "Very well," I said. "And we shall tell sad stories of the death of little people."

He gave me a strange look. "Pardon?"

"Shakespeare," I said. "Henry the Fourth? No. Richard the Three."

We left my trailer and strolled down the deserted midway. We had not had a show since yesterday's tragedy, of course, and would never have one again. But then, judging from past attendance figures, Boca Gables would almost certainly not miss us.

As we neared the main tent, I seemed able to detect little flickers of flame from within. I said, "Giraldo must have come out of his shell and begun reconstituting his act. The old trouper has not abandoned his craft."

"Why don't we go inside?" Feuer said.

We entered the tent. On the platform I saw the Human Pyromaniac and the Sicilian Snare Drum working with the requisite props of Giraldo's act. Feuer and I took seats in the grandstand, as we had the day of Big Tiny's demise. Feuer seemed disinclined to speak, contrary to what he had said in my trailer a few moments earlier; instead we watched Giraldo prepare, heard the Snare Drum begin to thump his tympanic chest. Soon flame blossomed from the Human Pyromaniac's fingertips, passing rapidly from one to the next; he spread his arms in his impressive way and created a rope of fire, then bent and brought blazing tendrils from his shoe tips to his head. Then he disappeared behind a wall of fire, and—

And incredibly, as if from the very center of the conflagration, there appeared Big Tiny: reconstructed amid the flames.

And he was pointing, pointing straight at me.

"You, Webb!" he shouted. "You did this to me!"

I jumped to my feet and hurried to the edge of the platform. "You're dead," I said. "I made sure of that—didn't I?"

"No," Big Tiny said. "Your plot to murder me did not succeed after all,

Webb. Giraldo discovered that you—it could only have been you—had exchanged my asbestos suit for a flammable cotton one, and then had emptied the water from the cubicle under the trapdoor. Immediately he effected another exchange of suits."

"But how could you have gotten out of the cubicle during the performance?"

"We created another exit, carefully concealed. Or so we thought." His voice turned sadly sardonic. "We plotted to carry through the illusion of my death only until we could collect the triple indemnity from Firehouse Fund; then I intended to confront you. Unfortunately, things have not worked out as any of us planned."

I realized Feuer was beside me. I also realized that there were several uniformed policemen nearby, and that Emma was there as well—and that Western Civilization was already, alas, in the throes of collapse.

Feuer's eyes reflected the flames surrounding Giraldo and Big Tiny, and his voice crackled as he spoke. "Extinguish yourselves," he told them.

Giraldo extinguished himself and Big Tiny; they stood smoking in the center of the platform.

Feuer released a shuddering breath. "Now then," he said, "where were we? Ah yes." He fixed me with a cindered eye. "You see, Carter, I discovered the second exit to the cubicle. I also discovered, with the help of the Boca Gables forensic people, the fact that the remains which Big Tiny placed inside the cubicle before departing were those of several different and quite ancient individuals. Thus I confronted Giraldo and the Sicilian Snare Drum, and was able to elicit their confession when I suggested you would all be charged with grave-robbing in addition to attempted extortion of the Firehouse Fund."

"He left us no choice," the Human Pyromaniac said. (Or perhaps it was the Sicilian Snare Drum.)

"No choice at all," the Snare Drum said. (Or perhaps it was the Human Pyromaniac.) "Which is the reason we have complied with this ploy of his to expose you, Webb, by forcing you into a self-admission of guilt."

Feuer looked at me. "I can understand the extortion scheme, though I do not of course condone it," he said. "What I do not understand is why you contrived to murder your employee, Big Tiny."

"Love," I said.

"Love?"

"Of dear Emma," I said. I turned to face her small, flawless self. "You never suspected how great was my reverence for your beauty, Little Tiny—how beatific and pure was my love."

Curiously, she did not seem particularly surprised by my confession of motive; none of them did.

"I really do love you," I said. "All thirty pounds and three feet of you."

"Thirty pounds and three feet?" Feuer said bewilderedly.

"Oh yes," the Snare Drum said. (Or perhaps it was the Human Pyromaniac.) "We have known all along of Webb's delusion, and have humored him because he was our employer and, we thought, our friend. Now, naturally, the masquerade cannot be continued."

"Delusion?" I said. "Masquerade?"

"Webb," one of them said, "Webb, Big Tiny and Little Tiny each stand approximately six and a half feet tall and weigh in the neighborhood of two hundred and seventy-five pounds. They are and always have been our Strong Man and Strong Lady."

"Really?" I said. "I thought they were midgets."

They took me away.

November 1975: New Jersey and San Francisco

Afterword to "Another Burnt-out Case"

Bill Pronzini (born 1943) is the best writer to enter the field of the mystery since Donald E. Westlake; he has produced thirteen novels of steadily increasing power since *The Stalker* (Random House, 1971) and has written at least two (*Blowback*, Random House, 1977, and *Games*, G. P. Putnam's, 1976) which I think will survive this last century of print if anything in print does. We have collaborated on three novels (*The Running of Beasts* and *Acts of Mercy*, both Putnam's, and *Night Screams*, Playboy Press) and somewhere between two and three dozen short stories; and that we, highly idiosyncratic writers to say nothing of people, have gone through all of this, half a million words together including three novels of ambition, and remain not only on speaking terms but actually the best of friends is a tribute to ... I don't know. Luck and the overpowering sweetness of our personalities, I suppose.

We wrote "Another Burnt-out Case" in November 1975. The last two paragraphs incite giggles to this day. No one else has giggled, to this day. The story went here and there and everywhere and snuck into *Fantastic* perhaps because of the overpowering sweetness of our personalities. We persist in finding it perhaps the funniest and most terrible of all our shorter works.

I'm Going Through the Door

Dear Mr. Baen:

While making sentimental pilgrimage to apartment 25 in premises 102 West 75th Street I found the enclosed document addressed to me in psychotic hand and wedged between the top and bottom panels of the flush mechanism in the bathroom of said premises. I cannot imagine how long its length of stay or how the author expected it to reach my hands. Perhaps he was an optimist. Perhaps he had anticipated my *nostalgie de boue*. Perhaps I dreamed all of this and wrote the letter to myself in amnesiac state, then cunningly secreted it in buried pocket until this moment of opportunity. Such judgments are beyond me. I am a simple man.

Since the letter itself (as opposed to the envelope in which it was wedged, which was incidentally disgustingly filthy) is addressed to you, I hasten to forward although with bemusement. I do not know what this W. Coyne is talking about. Do you? As always this is sent with best wishes; I have always been a great admirer of the science fiction market even though my output is often enough not quite right.

Dear Mr. Baen:

Perhaps you have heard of me. My name is William Coyne. Eight years ago or perhaps it was nine (it is increasingly difficult to keep events straight in this ruined tangle I call my mind) I wrote a letter to Frederik Pohl, who was the editor of your magazine for so many distinguished years. In this letter I described to Mr. Pohl the true and terrible plight in which I have been placed because of an endlessly multiplying time machine and asked him to write up my story in such a way that a large sum of money could be made from narrating my experiences and this sum of money used to keep me and my various selves afloat.

Well sir, well sir now, Mr. Pohl never answered my letter. Instead he published it in *Galaxy* with some kind of a house name on it. He published it as a short story. I came to understand finally that he was only trying to be kind, that when a science fiction editor receives a bizarre narration in the mail it is his business to think of it as yet another work of fiction and publish it if he can. Besides it is no small honor to think that one writes well enough to impress a top professional editor, and so after I got over my hurt and shame, I came to think well of Mr. Pohl, who I understand is no longer editing. The thirty-six dollars, although not a highly significant sum, came in handy at a difficult and terrible time of my life and although I recklessly spent it all years ago I remember it with affection. Also I came to understand that thirty-six dollars is really quite a bit of money for a science fiction story. Besides that, my situation kind of straightened itself out.

As you may recall, the time machine I invented, the machine of William Coyne, did not synchronize exactly in the present, so that every time I or one of my various selves attempted to use the machines we would, by not returning to the exact and proper time from which we departed, create yet another identity. The three hundred and eight of us who were all in occupancy of my cramped quarters at the time I wrote the letter did not get along very well and it was, all in all, only an unusual stroke of fortune that caused one of them, in a fit of despair, to twist all the dials on his portable machine to zero and vanish. Shortly after this, one by one, all the other selves began to vanish as well until there was only me, the final and original William Coyne, left who did not vanish. I have never been able to figure out exactly what the nature of this solution was but concluded after a time that what one self did eventually would happen to all since we were coexistent. This excluded the fact that I, the original William Coyne, did not vanish as well but since I know in my heart that I am indeed the one and only person of this name and gender it is only reasonable that I should remain.

It has been a quiet four years since then.

It has been quiet for longer than that: I have abandoned my experimentation for a more social existence and have, indeed, even been working at various menial jobs within the "military-industrial complex" over these times, finding that my minor engineering or mechanical skills are applicable at the fringes of this very interesting if somewhat murderous bureaucracy. I have grown a beard, added something of a wardrobe, even begun to casually date now and then, mostly the women in this very building, dislocated Upper West Side types such as I who find my nervous twitches sympathetic and understand that science fiction as the only true literature dealing with the effects of technology upon man must be the wave of the future, the cutting edge of consequence. In normal circumstances, then, my life would be so unremarkable as to make this letter unnecessary. The fact is that for the most part I have been getting along well over years recent and indeed seem close to that centrality of the simple life simply lived whose lack drove me to madness a long time ago. But I have one problem which indeed spurs this letter. Otherwise, you understand, I would never bother a professional science fiction editor again, having learned in one way or another that they tend to misinterpret.

Nevertheless, I have this problem. The problem has to do with sleep or perhaps it is only energy of which I am thinking: in any event when I take to my bed recently, over the past two months, say, I find myself being assaulted by the impression of other selves, multiplied identities, hidden doppelgangers, all of them aspects of myself and all of them coming on in waves of impulse and repudiation in those strange sliding moments just before or after true sleep. The selves (who all bear a physical and rhetorical resemblance to the undersigned W. Coyne) address me, first reproachfully and then in full accusation. What they seem to be saying—I am not quite sure that I yet fully understand their language—but what they seem to be saying is that I am somehow to blame for the fact that they are entrapped and able only to address me in moments of the subconscious. Their point seems to be that all of them yea unto the least would be living and flourishing still had it not been for my original foolishment of broadcasting our predicament to the world. Via publication in *Galaxy*.

Time and again I have tried to point out to them that this is insane, that it was their own stupidity (or a singular stupidity of one of them) which resulted in their cancellation and it was not I but one of the others who by fumbling with the devices of the machine (did I tell you that I destroyed my original model last year, finally?) resulted in his repudiation. But if I do not quite understand their language they most definitely do not understand mine. Our dialogues are invariably unsatisfactory and they do not seem to comprehend or enjoy what I have to say. They seem to feel that I am personally responsible for the repudiation of the multiplicity of W. Coynes, that were it not for me, my letter-writing, my selfishness, my haste, a million or two W. Coynes might be on the planet at this very moment and they of course would have long since put an end to war, famine, strife, etc., by a mutuality of understanding.

It is impossible for me to make them understand that my writing of the letter had nothing to do with the cancellation. All that they can suggest, time and again, in their raving, inarticulate way, is that if I had kept my mouth and typewriter shut things would have gone differently during these last disastrous years. And finally, finally—

—Well, finally I am willing to admit that they have gotten past easy repudiation, easy mockery, easily sought rationalization and have begun to afflict me with this horrid *guilt*, guilt because more and more I take myself, this modest and unassuming W. Coyne, to be sitting on more suppressed energy, more possibility, more *love* than you or for that matter I could ever conceive.

And all because of my letter to Mr. Pohl.

I was looking for help, you see, but that damned letter just about finished me off in the long run if not the short.

My question, Mr. Baen, is this. You are a modern master of science fiction and can be assumed to deal with moral questions as well as the other kinds and what I want to know is this: would I have been better off returning the check to Galaxy Publishing Corporation and refusing first world serial rights or would it have been all the same, this annihilation of my brothers, that is, and at least I have the thirty-six dollars?

That is my *basic* question and I would appreciate an answer. My other question, not so really important but nagging the hell out of me, is this: whatever happened to K. M. O'Donnell. Who *was* this person?

And why?

In equivocation and doubt,
W. Coyne

December 1966: New York

Afterword to "I'm Going Through the Door"

This was originally a straight-line sequel to my first published science fiction story, "We're Coming Through the Windows" (*Galaxy*, 8/67) and was written the same day that the latter story was sold. Fred Pohl bounced it politely, saying some very sensible words about sequelitis (see my afterword to "In the Stocks") and in one version or the next, addressed to one editor or the other, the story wandered through the underside of the field for more than eight years before I finally placed it with Jim Baen, the creditable editor of *Galaxy's* steadily sinking ship. (He got off in time and is now science fiction editor of Ace Books.) An eight-and-a-half-year gap between story and sequel may not be a record in this field, but an eight-and-a-half-year record of rejection on a story finally published might be. If so, it is one of two writing records that I hold at the difficult age of forty: that and fastest novel (65,000 words in sixteen hours, published by a paperback house in 1969 under a pseudonym I will never divulge other than to the *Guinness Book*).

"We're Coming Through the Windows" appears in my first collection; I decided after some thought not to reprint it here since the sequel stands more or less on its own, and how many readers of the 5/76 *Galaxy* would have read the 8/67 issue anyway? And what percentage of that slight fraction would remember my clever but forgettable first story? Let it be. K. M. O'Donnell was the self-selected pseudonym under which I sold my first novel and dozen stories or so.

I wish I hadn't done it and wish to apologize in print to the redoubtable Kevin M. O'Donnell, a young science fiction writer who began to publish in 1973 under the name with which he was born. I didn't know, Kevin, and I'm sorry. (The one time we spoke he told me that his middle initial was *M*. It is a hard world.)

Cornell

1. He is ordered, once again, to meet his public. Accordingly, he stands behind a lectern while a long line of people, curiously orderly, wait to speak to him one by one. "I loved your dancing," the first, a young man, says, "but essentially, you know, it was very cheap." He agrees with this. "I hated your dancing," an elderly critic points out, "but essentially I admit it was important." He agrees with this. "I both loved and hated your dancing," the third, a young woman, says, "because it was cheap and important," and he agrees with this as the line comes upon him, talking far through the night and passing, one by one, into darkness until he stands blinking in the dawn, rubbing his eyes and looking at the faint trail of litter, wondering if it is a code which somehow he could decipher.

2. He imagines himself being strangled and thrown, still alive, into a small mass of struggle at the bottom of a well. In this well he slowly explodes, balloons to enormous proportion, and as his body slowly fills the area, he perishes in his own breath. This pleases him, rather, although he is not exactly sure how he can get at it artistically.

3. In the hotel room he dreams he is watching on television a tape of his own performance. He has become a dancer and is describing great arcs of grayness while the television host smiles and a chorus of ten sings the songs he loves best. His dancing is a success, and, squinting at his own image, he notices that gaps in his technique appear to have been missed by the studio audience. At the end of his performance the television host embraces him and brings him out for another bow, before the commercial goes on. "Wonderful of you to be here with us," the host says, "and we'll have you back real soon," but although he dreams that he watches the television unsleeping for many years, he never sees himself again.

4. He receives an award from a national guild of his profession. The award is cast in the form of a finger of silver, pointing at him. No matter which which way he turns the award, the finger always points in his direction. He conceals it with small scraps of paper and hides it in his closet.

5. He is given an assignment but all that he can think of when the time comes to work is cyanosis: the way in which the facial skin will change color when strangulation ensues. It will go from the white of terror to pink to rose to deeper red to purple and finally to gentlest blue of the forgotten sea. The colors tantalize him and he is unable to work for

thinking of them, but when the time comes for his assignment to be done he is told that he has done well and is paid accordingly. He then develops a trick of thinking about cyanosis whenever the time comes for work and up to a point this functions well, although he realizes that he cannot rely on such mental tricks forever.

6. He dreams that a girl asks him for his autograph but before he can sign she walks away. Turning in his bed, he finds that this is only partially a dream and that some girl is talking to him in the sheets. He does not know what she is saying. She seems to have a speech impediment and the words are blurred. At a certain point, although he tries to be polite, he throws her out. The girl in the bed and the girl in his dream may have been the same although the question of the speech defect makes this somewhat doubtful. She has asked him very distinctly for his autograph.

7. A man in the hotel lobby asks him for an autograph. He balances the page between his knees while he signs. The man says that he grew up watching him dance and for a moment he doubts the dream until he remembers that all of them all of them all of them are liars.

8. The hotel burns to the ground. Saved, he moves to another hotel whose inscription is: WE ANNOUNCE FIRES BEFOREHAND.

9. While he sleeps something seems to seize him by the throat and he awakens gasping, but it is only the hand of one of the businessmen with whom he deals. "This can't go on indefinitely," the businessman says mildly, and he answers, "I know that very well; let me straighten it out in the morning"—and so on and so forth until the businessman finally goes away, at which point he returns to sleep until dawn. Awakening, it seems that he should remember something but there is already too much on his mind for such worthless games of recollection.

10. He is ordered, once again, to meet his public. Accordingly, he stands behind a lectern and stands behind a lectern and stands behind a lectern and stands—

Afterword to "Cornell"

Cornell Woolrich (1904-68) lived in the Sheraton Russell Hotel on Park Avenue, New York City, through the last decade of his life. He was represented by the literary agency with which I worked from 1965 to 1967, and I sought out Woolrich as an admirer of his work. I was able to do a few things for that work—Ace reissued many titles in the late sixties, *Escapade* took a story—but I was able to do nothing for the man, who was the unhappiest writer I have ever known. This is quite a statement.

Cornell is still so close and so painful to me (my younger daughter's middle name is his) that I cannot discuss him, in or out of print. This pastiche, written in July 1971 and sold to his last patron, Fred Dannay of *Ellery Queen's Mystery Magazine*, was a false attempt at purgation. No mercy, no mercy: Cornell lives within all of us.

His work of the forties was the best of his generation in his field and he will someday be recognized as one of the finest American writers. No mercy there either: such recognition in his lifetime would have made for Cornell no difference. He needed to die.

On Account of Darkness
(with Bill Pronzini)

So I took the Holographic Magnifier and the stick figures over to the Agency, talked myself past three secretaries, paid my one hour of humiliation waiting in the outside offices, and finally got into Evers' office. "I've got some terrific stuff here," I said, pulling it out of the case and laying it in front of him. "Jackie Robinson, the Duke, the Babe, the Splendid Splinter, a hundred more. A veritable Cooperstown of the mind."

"What's a Cooperstown?" he said.

"It was a famous museum where the uniforms and memorabilia of the greats were kept," I said. "Not that it matters. What matters is this: I can let you have the holographic stuff at a very reasonable price. Very reasonable."

"Football," Evers said. "There's no market for football anymore."

"This isn't football, it's baseball. Football was a contact sport of the twentieth century; baseball, purely of American origin, was played with a small round ball and a long thin piece of timber called a bat—"

"I'm not interested," Evers said. "Nothing personal, it's just that we have lots of problems here. The whole question of entertainment ..." He shrugged.

"Well, I can appreciate the range of your problems," I said. "But what I've got here is really something special. Suppose I just give you a little demonstration?"

Evers yawned.

"Oh, come on," I said. "You let me in here, you let me get this far, you know you're a little interested already." I gave him an ingratiating smile. "Did you know there was a baseball player called Evers who was very famous in the early part of the twentieth century? A second baseman for the Chicago Cubs. Tinker to Evers to Chance—that was this legendary double-play combination—"

"What's a Chicago Cub?" Evers said.

The trouble with the people at the Agency is that they are efficient but they have little historical sense. Historicity? Historicalness? They are extremely good on details, and they certainly know what will sell along the range of available techniques, but their grasp of specifics is limited. Not that I hold this against them, of course. They're only trying to do a job.

I began to set up the Magnifier, working with it until it hummed and glowed and vibrated on Evers' desk. He looked at it in a bored way and didn't look at me at all. So I said, "For that matter, there was a Hoot Evers who played for the Detroit Tigers, an outfielder in the 1950s. Hoot wasn't his real name, but that was what they called him. I think his real name was Walter."

"What's a Detroit?" Evers asked.

I concealed a sigh, setting up certain figures which I had preselected. Then I set the Magnifier for one-tenth life-size and hit the button, and the room was suddenly filled with heat and light and those strange smells that are supposed to be grass and peanuts and hot dogs. The ballplayers in their uniforms darting all over the office, like energetic little animals.

"Look at this," I said. "National League All-Stars of the middle twentieth century versus the greatest single team in baseball history, the 1927 New York Yankees. Yankees are the home team, so they're in the field first. The pitcher is Herb Pennock, Lou Gehrig is on first, Tony Lazzeri is at second...."

I went on to give him the line-ups. He didn't seem to be listening, but he had one eye cocked on Jackie Robinson striding up to the plate to lead off the game. "What's the object of all this, anyway?" he said.

"Well, the batter has to use the stick in his hands to hit the ball out of range of the fielders. If he does that, or if the pitcher misses that plate-shaped target, the batter is allowed to take one or more bases. Four bases constitute a run, and the team with the most runs at the end of the game—"

Evers raised a hand. "That's enough," he said, but he still had the one eye cocked on Robinson.

So I launched into a play-by-play, a technique which I have developed in the classic sense. Robinson hit Pennock's third pitch and grounded out to Koenig at short, and then Bobby Thomson took a called third strike. The next batter was Ted Kluszewski.

"This is pretty clever stuff," Evers said in a grudging way. He had both eyes on the game now. "I've got to admit that."

"Oh, it's very clever," I said. "You can really get absorbed in it, you know. One thing you should keep in mind is that this is only a one-tenth magnification here; you can imagine what the game is like when you lay it out in a conventionally sized stadium."

"I suppose so. But I still don't see the point of it all."

"Entertainment," I said. "Abstraction. Hundreds of years ago people used to obtain amusement watching these baseball games."

"But *why?*"

"Aesthetics," I said vaguely.

"How come you're so familiar with the subject?"

"It's my background. My great-great-grandfather worked for the last commissioner's office and this was sort of passed down through the family, a kind of heritage. And a hobby."

"A strange hobby."

"Each to his own."

"Mmm," Evers said.

Kluszewski hit a ground ball between first and second for a single; Ruth tossed the ball back into Lazzeri. "Next batter is Stan Musial," I said. "He might have been the best in his division in his time. Note the very unorthodox position he takes; that's the famous Musial Crouch. He's virtually batting on his knees, you'll notice."

Evers didn't say anything.

Musial, a first-ball hitter, sent a towering fly ball to right center that Earle Combs couldn't quite reach. The translucent ball bounced off the wall, rolled back to the infield; Lazzeri scooped it up and fired it to the catcher, Benny Bengough, holding Kluszewski at third and Musial at second.

"That was a typical Musial double," I said.

Evers said, "I think I'm losing interest. This may be clever stuff but it doesn't entertain or amuse me at all."

"You haven't seen enough yet," I said as Willie Mays came up and popped the first pitch up to Koenig at short. "Now the teams switch places and the Yankees come to bat—"

"I'm just not interested," Evers said. "Turn it off."

I hesitated but I could see that it was hopeless; sometimes you can press the point and sometimes you dare not. So much in this business is a matter of timing. I turned off the Magnifier, began to gather it and the stick figures together.

"The thing is," Evers said, "the thing is, there's no real audience for it. I can see the elements of diversion, of course, but there just aren't enough of them."

I said nothing. There is a time to talk and then there is a time not to talk, and off this great balance wheel are conducted all relationships and dealings.

"I suppose," Evers said, "that we might be able to do a little something with it in the Outlying Districts. But then again, it would hardly repay our investment. Visuals are a tricky commodity, you know."

A certain feeling of revulsion and pain began to work in me then. I had held it well down throughout this meeting, but it comes at odd moments, in little layers and surges of feeling. I seemed to see myself in ten other offices like Evers, past and present, at the mercy of people like him who understood very little and yet, somehow, controlled everything; I seemed to see myself getting older, beginning to die in stages, while the batteries in the Holographic Magnifier lost power and the figures of the great baseball players lost definition and finally faded altogether....

I had to say something then. So I said, "All right, I'll be going now; if you don't understand, I can't make you understand. You'll just never know, that's all, what a beautiful game it was." I turned and started for the door.

"Wait a minute now," Evers said.

I pivoted back toward him. "What?"

Evers cleared his throat. "I said there was very little in it, but, still and all, there might be *something* worthwhile. We might be able to convert it into an amusement for the juveniles, for example. Or there's the possibility of an exhibit over in the Central District of minor artifacts that we're planning to open." He fixed me with shrewd, veiled eyes. "We might be able to make a small bid, after all."

"How small?"

"Fifteen," he said.

"That's ridiculous. This is baseball, all of *baseball*."

"Nobody knows what baseball is. I didn't; I still don't."

"It's something beautiful, something irreplaceable...."

"Seventeen," Evers said. "That's my final offer."

"I've got to have twenty-five."

"Not from us."

"Twenty-two, then. I have expenses to cover."

"Eighteen—but that's it. Yes or no? I'll have to put it on the Terminals right away."

"Eighteen," I said. "Listen, you're talking about an entire way of life for hundreds of thousands of people—"

"Good-bye," Evers said.

"Now wait—"

"Eighteen, or good-bye."

The pain and revulsion deepened within me, but I said, "All right. All right. But I'm giving you my whole life here; I'm giving you hundreds of thousands of lives."

"We'll program the eighteen in," he said. "You can get a Verificatory from my secretary." He stood up. "It's been a pleasure having you and your quaint little pastime here, but now, if you don't mind ..."

He didn't offer his hand; he just looked away, dismissing me. So I took one last look at the Magnifier and the stick figures, and then I went out of there and took a railcab to my cubicle. Outside, the sky was just beginning to darken; night was coming on.

And the game is over, I thought. But then, if you wanted to look at it another way, they'd have called it anyway in the old days. On account of darkness. Called on account of darkness.

Then, still filled with pain, I sat down and went through my materials and tried to figure out the best places to unload hockey, basketball, and horse racing.

July 1976: San Francisco

Afterword to "On Account of Darkness"

We wrote this story in Bill's house in San Francisco in July 1976, very quickly and without undue pain. It sold on its second submission (I cannot imagine why Ben Bova rejected; twenty years and ten thousand submissions have drained all emotion from marketing for me and almost all sense of mystery, but once in a great while you still can't figure them, just as you can't figure yourself) and strikes us now as then as the best of all our collaborative stories. In fact, "On Account of Darkness" is probably as good a story as Bill or I ever wrote individually; we would as soon stand by this as "Sweet Fever" or "Final War." Utter fusion of style and vision and a story that neither could have done alone—this is the definition of successful collaboration.

I wasn't aware until I read the story in *Fantasy and Science Fiction* more than a full year later that the narrator is a crook and his operation a scam (*he* doesn't care about baseball either), but that kind of thing has happened to me before. (See my note on "A Market in Aliens" in the Ace collection *Final War & Other Fantasies*, that is if you can find it.)

Impasse

So here I am, surrounded by aliens. Aliens dangle from the ceiling, aliens loll perilously on the walls, scuttle purposefully between my feet, even drool now and then into the crevices of this typewriter, this very machine (SCM Coronamatic 2200, I would like to note) upon which, however haltingly, I am attempting some history of the difficulties.

Which are profound.

It is necessary for me to reach out periodically to slap the little buggers off the Coronamatic 2200 and send them in little clumps to the floor. Their small cries of pain are quite disconcerting although I have been assured, some time earlier, that these aliens do not have any feelings at least as you or I would define the term "feeling," and these righteous squawks as I cleave a hand through them to open up space … these righteous squawks as I called them are somewhat guilt-inducing.

I am running, I think I am running ahead of myself. Increasingly I find myself unable to lay out patiently the facts of my circumstance, relying instead upon the telegraphic condensation of material. *Telegraphic condensation of material.* But then I do not know how much time, really, I have left.

I am surrounded by aliens. Surrounded am I by aliens. The aliens are approximately the size and shape of golf balls: furry little creatures navigating or navigational by the act of rolling, bright little eyes and mouths laid into the fur like fine carving. Most of the time they are rather cheerful and their voices are deep for their dimensions: positive and positively declamatory. They speak with an accent, of course, one that seems to be vaguely Yiddish or *mittel Europa* (I am sure I would have an accent in *their* language), and not badly considering that they have been here a mere twelve months and three days.

Three months and twelve days, that is. I am sorry. To pardon. My time sense is absolutely disrupted, all is confused, the transfer of chronology from one layer of experience to the next is increasingly torturous. I am doing the best I can.

Twelve months *feels* like three in my state, three like twelve, but I am sure that it is the "shorter" period. I think. I am not so sure on second thought. I know my limitations.

I am a broken man.

Three months and twelve days, call it. I should have said that much earlier: the aliens have been in my quarters for three months and twelve days, establishing what they call a bridgehead to their eventual conquest of Earth. They are quite positive on that issue, that they will conquer the Earth I mean, but for the time being they state they are quite pleased with their conquest of my own miserable quarters. Two hundred and twenty-three of them have set up light or lighter housekeepery in these rather dismal furnished rooms, two of them plus adjoined bath on the fourth floor of a reconverted tenement on West 112th Street in Manhattan.

(My notes seem to be full of numbers, I have noticed. Three and twelve and two hundred and twenty-three and two and one hundred and twelve. This is one of the signs of insanity, I read once, the fixation on numerals as magical symbols. I do not think I am insane but there is that possibility, which in all fairness I must admit. I will not, however, discuss it.)

This is not a very amiable place I do admit, in fact it is quite cheerless, but it is the best that I was able to manage on the miserable income of a graduate student and in happier days I was rather proud of what I had been able to accomplish with it, a certain bright *je ne sais quoi* of the spirit intruding: curtains, mixed fluorescence, pink tiles in the bathroom quite personalizing these confines and making a strong impression on the trickle of women whom I was able to cajole into sharing my bed and body for the night.

"Oh, Myron, you've really made it a cozy little place here."

"Oh, Myron, you have such interesting specializing taste."

"Oh, Myron, where did you pick up that furniture?"

Well, all of that is behind me now. *Recherche du temps perdu,* Marcel, and leave me out of it, that is what I say. That part of my life is at an end. It used to be women, but now with the aliens it is obviously impossible to entertain and who is to say that my experiences with the one were not as pointless as my experiences with the others?

Metaphysical. Of all things, I am becoming metaphysical.

Not that the loss of my social life is the real problem here. It is not. It is not at all. My real problem, gentlemen, has nothing to do with the obliteration of my rather sodden and elementary sex life. Even in the best of times, alas, it did not matter that much to me and I can well dispense with the whines and inquiries of the rather unastonishing women who dwelt with me now and then. They simply did not matter that much.

Not that much at all.

Nonetheless, it is obviously impossible to *think* of consorting with women now that two hundred and twenty-three furry golf balls of aliens have come into these quarters to maintain a social life. I yield it willingly, I sacrifice without pain, with grace, it is not possible to cleave my way through the aliens to get to the corner for groceries let alone women. The aliens *themselves* are the problem. Their desires to conquer the planet is as earnest and uncomplicated as my determination in *temps perdu* to conquer these dismal women and I do not know how to handle the situation.

I simply do not know how to handle the situation anymore, I tell you.

On the one hand the problem is serious and the menace not to be ignored: these two hundred and twenty-three are the first of a vast contingent (they tell me) who intend to occupy the planet through density once the advance scouting team has sent back their report, but on the other it is very difficult, I retain enough of an objective sense here, very difficult to take these aliens quite seriously. Their appearance is somewhat ridiculous and then, too, their accents are comic, reducing everything they say (even the most colorful threats) to the laughable.

I will not try to reproduce their speech phonetically. I could if I wanted. I was—how long ago it all seems!—a doctoral candidate in political science but I studied Whorf as an undergraduate and always had an ear for languages. Of course that is all behind me now, Whorf and political science alike. The aliens would not think it wise to attend class. They have pointed that out.

"We would not think it wise, Myron," they have advised me. (Each of them speaks for all the others, a gestalt consciousness of group mind, they have told me, something like that, no leaders, no followers, merely a mass which is an extension of a single individual.) "We would not think it wise at all if you continued your studies for a doctoral degree in political science at Columbia University. Let us explicate if we may.

"In the first place," they continue with their odd but somehow compelling precision, "in the first place we will not permit you to go out alone; we would have to come after you, roll down the streets and along the very aisles of the classroom in pursuit, jump into your pockets, nestle in the crown of your hat, and so on, and this would be embarrassing, explanations would be difficult. In the second place political science is going to be worthless when we take over your planet, all two hundred billion of us. Your sociopolitical systems will collapse. Everything you have studied will be irrelevant. Geology, systems retrieval, ecology, biology, exobiology, botany, sanitation, and waste: these will be the growth studies when our invasion is complete, but political science? *Political* science? No, Myron, forget it. Far better for you to stay here and do your memoirs. Once a day you can go down to the bodega on the corner and fetch yourself a load of groceries; once a week you can go to the university bar at One Hundred and Fifteenth Street and Broadway for an hour of conversation and forgetfulness. Fair is fair. Otherwise, this is where you stay."

And so I have. And so I have.

As you may have noted (I have a certain cunning ability to feed in much information offhand) my task for these past months of isolation has indeed been to compose my memoirs. For reasons that will be obscure (which is because they are never explained) the aliens seek a rather comprehensive autobiography to be turned out on this Coronamatic 2200 with automatic carriage return. They seem to feel that documentation is important, the typical pre-invasion life history of a typical pre-invasion Earth person as they put it, and indeed as I have typed certain complicated passages dealing with, say, my sexual initiations, they have clambered upon my shoulders, run little crossing patterns up and down my arms, chattered with pleasure as they read the words pouring out of this machine and onto the paper at the rate of eighty-five per minute. (I am just shy of being a first-rate speed typist.) I do not know why they find these significant but they do. Perhaps I am revealing more than I might ever know. How would I know what strikes the fancy of a furry creature the size of a golf ball which is an extension of a gestalt consciousness and has delicate features graven upon the furred surfaces as if conveyed by an artist's brush?

How the hell would I know?

Neither do I know why I pursue this expository material. Just fifteen minutes ago I was describing practices in a boys' camp of dim and distant memory, the little creatures, seven of them, literally dancing up and down the sides of the typewriter, chittering to one another now in their birdlike language, excited indecipherable cries pouring from them, and then suddenly I found that my tolerance had been exhausted, patience had snapped, and instead of continuing in my solemn, rather portentous way to get the dreary reminiscence down in sequence, I ripped the page from the Corona and began on this instead. This direct summary starting above. I do not know why I am doing this.

I just don't.

I *know* my predicament and circumstance quite well already thank you very much and yet I cannot deny my new satisfaction. I am pleased. A sneaking, perverse, nearly *lustful* sensation overwhelms, the feeling that a child might have in seeing his parents in a compromising position. The act is valueless (and for that matter the *primal* act is valueless, so there, folks) but somewhere deep within at a place that can never be quite known is a feeling of power. Of control. It is satisfying to get all of this down on paper, satisfying at every level.

Because, you see, it is all quite hopeless.

There is no question about that. The aliens' determination to take over our planet, whatever their motivation (they refuse to discuss this), is absolute and I see no way in which we can deal with two hundred and twenty-three thousand billion of these golf balls appearing simultaneously in every crevice and palace of our power on the planet, our home, our modest Earth. They will simply overwhelm us. The ratio is disproportionate. It is also quite likely that they will first foul the machinery of self-extermination; we will not even have the dignity of mass suicide.

Not to be dramatic, but I really think we are doomed.

So here I am on the fourth floor of a tenement on the West Side of Manhattan, typing out a summary of the approaching end of the world. It has become very quiet indeed in these rooms during the last hour, since I started this. The aliens have come down from shoulders, moved away from wrists, deserted the typewriter, even left the floor surrounding and are probably at this time massing in solemn assembly in the bathroom, conferring upon the timing of dislocation. For all I know they may have chosen this moment to begin their final invasion. I have long suspected that the time was imminent and it might as well be now.

How long, after all, would I interest them sufficiently to delay their attack?

Who knows?

Who is to say, really? I continue to type in a high blaze of sweat and concentration. It has been a long time since I have been so at one with the material. There is a perfect fusion, I must say, between fingers, wrists, keyboard, paper: for the first (and for the last, I reluctantly propose) time I have a chance to explain the true and real difficulties of the present situation and at this instant it is a matter of complete indifference to me *what* the aliens do. It is quite simply—

—Well, I do not know how to put this in a way that will not sound immoral, but it is quite simply *not my problem anymore*. It is Earth's problem, the problem of the three billion of them. It is your problem, if I may indulge myself with the concept of an extrinsic readership eventually of which I probably have none. And never will.

I have lived alone with this long enough.

To repeat: I have lived alone with this long enough. Now it is time for the focus of responsibility to shift, for the moment to leap outward and into the lives of the billions who share the human if not my own private and terrible condition.

You can carry the ball now. I really have taken as much of this as I can. Even the women I brought here would capitulate after a time and cease talking about furnishings.

Typing, I can feel once again the weight of the aliens on my arms, my legs, my hands and delicately willowy wrists. They have returned. That is what it is: I see and they have returned from whatever area in which they were holding conference and are once again observing me closely with their pitiless, their remorseless little eyes, the clawed weight of them almost imperceptible on me in this new blaze of excitement in which I begin to type. I am truly excited, for something has happened.

For, as the aliens once again perch on the typewriter, reading with me hungrily these very words which pour out of the machine—ah, ah, as the aliens do this—

—An insight occurs to me that is as powerful and noble as any I have ever known and that insight not to put too fine an edge on it is this: that they are *fascinated* with my rhetoric.

They love it, they really do. They are gripped by my ability to explain this situation (otherwise why would they even have returned, I want to ask you that) and if I merely keep on typing, keep on typing and typing and typing and typing for the rest of my natural life, I may be able, somehow, to hold off single-handed and heroically at last the destruction and exculpation of Earth.

So here I am, surrounded by aliens. Aliens dangle from the ceiling, aliens loll perilously on the walls, scuttle purposefully between my feet, even drool now and then into the crevices of this typewriter, this very machine (SCM Coronamatic 2200, I would like to note) upon which, however haltingly, I am attempting some history of the difficulties.
Which are profound.
Which are profound.

Oh boy are they profound!

September 1972: New Jersey

Afterword to "Impasse"

"Impasse" appeared in Roger Elwood's very short-lived magazine *Odyssey:* two issues in 1976 (the publisher, a huge printer, was otherwise celebrated for its selection of UFO magazines) and gone forever. Filled with truss ads and full-page invitations to send in ten dollars for the secret of Mind Control, devoid of any promotion outside the publisher's domicile, this large-format magazine could not possibly have sold more than ten thousand copies an issue, none of them in the New York City area, where it was never seen. My own lone copy of Volume I, No. 1 (contributors' copies were never furnished), is in my hands courtesy of George Zebrowski, who found it in a stack of hundreds in a supermarket in Binghamton, New York. Perhaps Web Offset had a shrewd and innovative plan for distribution and perhaps Binghamton is (as George has now and then claimed) the true center of the known universe, but Web Offset crapped out after two issues, being unwilling, it would seem, to really follow up the Binghamton Plan.

It was not the worst magazine in the history of this rather junky field—in fact Elwood threw together a couple of rather creditable issues assembled largely from his inventory—although the large format, the atrocious non-art-direction, and the Binghamton Plan combined to quickly sink it. *Odyssey* did remind me of various magazines to which I've sold over the years that no longer exist—*Worlds of If, Venture, The Man from UNCLE, Eternity, Mike Shayne Annual*—and the prospect that there will be additions within the next few years. (My list is minuscule compared to that of any nineteen-fifties science fiction writer; Phil Dick, to pick a name from a hat, must have appeared in thirty-five magazines, all dead for two decades.) To be any kind of a writer of fiction but particularly to attempt to work in the short story is to try to hold on in the face of inexorable attrition ... with the exception of *Isaac Asimov's Science Fiction Magazine*, on which the books are still open, there has not been a successful new magazine in the science fiction, mystery, or literary short story fields since 1954.

This rather rambling afterword, which I note seems to be the longest in the collection, has neatly avoided saying anything at all about "Impasse," which is fine with me. If anyone would care to point out that it is yet another metaphor for the career of a science fiction writer I will hit that person, at least by proxy, very hard.

Varieties of Technological Experience

So for his various crimes against the Federation, none of which had to be explained to him (since he knew his guilt; since his entire life, he thought, was a stain of implication), they exiled Fritz to the fourth division of the Doom World which in real life was the climate-controlled sixth satellite of Neptune and there for his various crimes against the Federation explained that in order to buy his release Fritz would have to invent a universal solvent. In return for a sample they would grant him full remission and allow him to return to his old life, although of course under Federation surveillance. Fair was fair.

Fritz explained to them that the basic problem with a universal solvent was that it would dissolve any container and therefore could not be segregated. They responded that this was his problem. He asked if a formula would be sufficient with the various technicians of the Doom Planet actually preparing a batch for use. They said that this was impossible, that they already had many formulas. What they needed was proof of utility. They were very kind. Everyone on the Doom Planet was reasonable. They were not there to be punitive; it was assumed that banishment was sufficiently traumatic. What they were seeking, they explained in the most pleasant way, was results. They offered him full laboratory facilities and assistants if he desired.

Fritz, embittered, discussed the situation with his three roommates in the Dark Quarter, all of whom had been confined much longer than he. He found that he was unable to elicit much sympathy. One of them had been working on a perpetual motion device for some years, another had failed with antigravitation despite some new observations into metallurgics, and the third who thought he had had a workable disintegrator some years ago had blown out half of his laboratory facilities but in demonstration before the administrator had been unable to produce any results other than a slightly charred hand, which he claimed still gave him trouble in delicate work. "What you have to understand," the perpetual motion man said, "is that we have been handed ancient scientific paradoxes, impossibilities by definition. We have been given a life sentence, in other words, but on the other hand if we were able to defy physical laws it would be to the advantage of the Federation and they would certainly release us in gratitude. They have no shortage of potential prisoners, you know."

Fritz had become very cynical about the Federation since his detention and exile—he was beginning to suspect that it was an autocratic government interested only in self-perpetuation and any popular resistance would be defined as a "crime"—but the influence of his early technological training still sat heavy upon him and he found himself unable to accept what the perpetual motion man was saying. "They would never assign an impossible task," Fritz said. "Ultimately the Federation is a rational agency, founded upon rational principles. If there were not a way, they would not have assigned this to us. Actually, it is a test."

"It is a test, all right," the antigravity man said, "a test of our gullibility."

"A universal solvent would eat out its container," the disintegrator man said; "it could not be conveyed."

"I pointed that out to them."

"He pointed that out to them," the perpetual motion man said and poked antigravity in the ribs. "And they of course agreed and assigned you something else."

"Oh no," Fritz said, "they said that it was my problem."

"That it is," the perpetual motion man said. "And that is what they told me. I have, incidentally, been here for more than half my lifetime and until you joined us here I was the newcomer of this group. Of course there are those like you coming in all the time so I have accumulated a fair amount of seniority, haven't I, lads?"

The call to serving quarters interrupted the harsh laughter of the others and Fritz found that he had no desire to continue the discussion later. It was true what he had heard of the Doom Planet: despite the fact that the felons lived together and were exposed, almost mercilessly, to one another's personalities they tended to lead very solitary lives without much connection. Part of that came from the consuming and obsessive nature of the tasks they were assigned, of course, and another part came from the personality-set of a person foolish enough to try to overthrow the Federation. Stubborn, self-willed, monomaniacal types, Fritz had decided, never *actually* attempted overthrow. Like him, they had merely paused to consider in the interstices whether the Federation might be as benign as it pretended and that pause, it would seem, had been enough to attract the interest of the Surveyors.

In any case, it was too late for that kind of concern now. He had had a different kind of life on Mars and many associations which, if he had thought about them, he would have keenly missed, but his perspective narrowed, as perspectives on the Doom Planet tended to do, to his situation and he had decided that he would accept the conditions of his internment. He would create a universal solvent and find a container of some sort and he would present it to the Board and would be released. Once released he might carry the news of conditions far and wide to all the towns of Mars, but then again he might not. It was impossible to project that far ahead. One thing he resolved was that he would have nothing to do with his roommates or with any of his fellow felons. He considered himself to be several levels above them intellectually and he found their cynicism corrosive.

How Fritz was able to fulfill at last the conditions of his assignment and how he invented not only the universal solvent but a varying propane ring which enabled the solvent to possess other strange powers of alteration must fall without the proper scope of this history. As the various Acts & Regulations have established, the release of technological information is not only dangerous should it fall into the hands of enemies of the Federation, it is extremely boring to the majority of the populace who have no interest in the devices that manage their lives as long as these devices are workable. (Nor should they!) Sufficient to say that over a period of some time Fritz, relying heavily upon laboratory facilities and ignoring the jeers of his fellows, was able to accomplish his task and under procedure applied for an appointment with the Board to whom he presented himself in due course. When his roommates heard through the usual network of inference that Fritz had actually scheduled an appearance before the Board their contempt and amusement was virtually unbounded, but Fritz did not allow it to affect him. "You are a fool," the perpetual motion man, the harshest and most persistently abusive of his roommates, said, "you are making a mockery of their very concept of punishment. The problems are insoluble by nature."

"Not with a universal solvent," Fritz said, permitting himself the most careful of private smiles.

"You will never be welcome in these walls again."

"That is of no concern," Fritz said. "After all, I will have obtained my release."

"A fool," the perpetual motion man said, "a fool," and stalked to the doorway, attempting a dramatic exit but forgetting in his choler that exitways were barred during this period and succeeding only in causing slight but painful damage to his nose. At this the antigravitation and disintegrator men roused themselves from their quarters to laugh almost as harshly as he but Fritz, all in all a kind and thoughtful man, had already detached himself from the conversation, preferring to think of his confrontation with the Board on the morrow.

It had long since occurred to him through his period of internment and researches that the Federation was indeed a cruel and frozen regime engaging in repression at all levels of administration solely for the purpose of decadent self-perpetuation and that the Doom Planet was a fiendish means of not only interning dissidents but exploiting their very creativity, but these insights were virtually incidental to the overall element of his growth which was that he had managed to solve one of the oldest of all scientific paradoxes. Beside this accomplishment the corruption of the Federation fell away, it was of no significance whatsoever. Of course the Federation was corrupt but then again, Fritz, not a particularly introspective man, had decided that almost all of history was a matter of corruption and that ultimately only individual ends, not collective destinies, suited. He therefore presented himself to the Board in a sanguine and optimistic manner and without questioning described what he had been able to accomplish.

"That is remarkable," they said to him and indeed their expressions showed much approbation and astonishment, "but where is the solvent itself?"

"I am carrying it with me."

"You are?" the Board said. There was a slight pause. "That is even more interesting. Where is the container?"

"Ah," Fritz said, "*I* am the container."

"Pardon?"

"*I* am the container," he pointed out, "and the solvent reposes within me."

"But that is impossible."

"Certainly not."

"Of course it is," the Board said with more emotion than was its wont. "By definition you would have been dissolved. You could not be here, the solvent is a deadly poison—"

It occurred to Fritz that under pressure the Board lost its dignity, which he could have anticipated anyway if he had given the matter some thought. There was his own loss of dignity to consider; the Board was, in its lovable way, no less human than he. There was a message there, the ultimate prevailing of humanity that was to say, but he did not want to pursue the matter at this time. "But of course," he said gently, instead, "that is the point, I am in the process of being dissolved right now. There was a calculated Lag Effect."

Gently he extracted from his pockets schematics and diagrams to place before them in verification, gently he laid them in front of the gibbering old men, and then as the solvent finally reached its critical point he consequently, and with the most lingering of sighs, began to break down.

Ah, the breakdown! First the walls of molecules, then the outer edges of cells, the viscera themselves coming with relief askew the wall of self, the persona, and he became those mindless constituent atoms which under the influence of the amalgam ...

... moved out.

Moved out to dissolve the floor, the walls, the Board itself to say nothing of the planet, consuming all of it utterly as the famous prophet had pointed out concerning another matter so that all that was left of the oppressive Federation in this difficult sector was a planet-sized glob of universal solvent, hanging there in space quite unapproachable (as one might suspect) by stabilizing forces and therefore a beacon to all who would in their own way seek to assert their individuality. A planet-sized signal of Revolution to absolutely clarify, a symbol of individual human will.

But, of this glimmer of triumph from the very jaws of defeat, of the fall of the Federation, and of the heroic, brave, and finally successful efforts of the Opposition (many of whom survived in the most cunning of ways) little enough need be said at this time, the tale being part of our great and arching folklore, so we will merely pass now to our next exhibit which will depict in diorama to please all of you the history of the first and final Squaring of the Circle.

October 1977: New Jersey

Afterword to "Varieties of Technological Experience"

In a twelve-year career in science fiction encompassing twenty-five novels, seven collections, eight anthologies, and about two hundred short stories, I have appeared with fiction only four times in *Analog** (and twice with book reviews and once with an essay in the *Analog Yearbook*), always with a story of lasting inconsequence. Nonetheless the four short story sales have provided me with more emotional satisfaction than was given me by all of the other publications doubled. This has a lot to do with what *Astounding* meant to me in the early fifties (I have a long essay on the whole matter as an introduction in *The Best of Barry N. Malzberg*) and just as much to do, I suppose, with authorial perversity.

"Varieties of Technological Experience" appeared in the 10/78 issue, one of the last under Ben Bova's aegis before emotion and his own authorial persona sent him over to Robert Guccione's new *Omni* as fiction editor.

---

*"Closing the Deal," 3/74; "January 1975," 1/75; "Varieties of Technological Experience," 10/78; "The Lyrean Case" (with Bill Pronzini), 3/80.

Varieties of Religious Experience

I go by foot to Austin's Fine Used Cars & Trucks on Route Forty-six and show the obese Austin himself the point thirty-eight Smith & Wesson. "I will take the seventy-three Sedan de Ville robin's-egg blue in the second row there," I say, pointing, "and you can also fill a bag with five thousand dollars in small bills. You'd best put dealer's plates on, of course. I want to observe all of the traffic and highway regulations of the state of New Jersey."

"This is ridiculous," the obese Austin says. His face is impacted with terror or perhaps it is merely impending loss. "You are committing armed robbery. You are taking a car and money at gunpoint. That is a very serious crime."

"Don't temporize," I say briskly, "don't delay. Everything is a crime. This is a criminal civilization; we all break the statutes every day in every way. You for instance have been selling defective cars at exorbitant prices from this location for seven years, you have sold cars with faulty transmissions, cracked engine blocks, broken cylinder heads, and worn brakes; you have willingly sent hundreds to potential disaster, speeded them on their way with lies, and pointed to your as-is bills of sale if they returned, laughed in their faces. Also I have more than a suspicion that you have not turned over sales tax collected to the government. I have kept tabs on you, Austin, and your criminality is greater than mine. I have the decency, you see, to commit robbery in plain sight. This is no metaphor, this is the truth, and get those dealer plates on and start passing over the money or I will put a very neat hole into your forehead. These are serious times, this is a serious act, there is no time for conversation."

Panting, Austin does as I request, reaching to the shelf for dealer's plates; reaching into his copious pockets for bills, talking all of the time. He does not seem to understand the point of my act but I cannot blame him; armed robbery is more traumatic than simple consumer fraud. I follow him to the Sedan de Ville and watch him hinge the plates front and rear. The lot is vacant and traffic on forty-six at this late hour is very sparse. A less greedy man would have closed up shop and left for home hours ago, but Austin shows circumstances no mercy. Not for nothing does he take his own sobriquet, *Deal-a-minute Austin*, to heart. "There," he says, backing away at last, his eyes gleaming with rage. "I hope you don't get far. You won't get far; this baby's turbo-Hydra-Matic is about gone and I did a rough patching on the drive shaft. There isn't five hundred miles there without major repair. The body and paint are in good condition but the car isn't worth a damned thing. You'd be better off, you need a transportation car, with that seventy Impala over there, the red convertible. It's rusted out on the bottom but at least the engine and trans are solid; there's twenty thousand miles in that car without even an oil change. You listen to me—"

"You see what I mean?" I say sadly. I hold the gun on him, check his right pocket, and find a stray one-hundred-dollar bill, clutched to the fabric like a lost child. "The truth is not in you, Austin," I say, "and the truth is the very thing that might make you free. If you're going to be a crook, be a straightforward crook. It drains all of that ambivalence and self-hatred which make you eat so compulsively."

He stares at me astonished as I open the left front door and prepare to gracefully seat myself. "What the hell?" he says. "You Robin Hood or something?"

"Not at all," I say, "I'm just trying to make a living here. I'll keep whatever I can get my hands on. Don't call the police for fifteen minutes," I say. "Actually it's to your advantage to let me get away; you can get triple what the car cost you from the insurance and claim ten times the loss in cash. You'll look back on this and thank me, Austin," I say.

He stares at me glumly. I start the Cadillac, not without difficulty with the carburetor, and back out gracefully, stalling only twice. I crunch out of Austin's Fine Used Cars & Trucks and onto forty-six singing. The collision of truth and circumstance has always made me ecstatic.

After a while I think I might try some accompaniment on the radio, one of the easy-listening stations, but the radio of course is broken. The brakes rasp unpleasantly even at the most cautious application. Nonetheless my euphoria is unabated, I am pleased to have finally taken some direct action. There are limits to metaphysical despair after which one must act or die or so says, at least, the immortal Immanuel Kant.

Considering further the criminal mind, its alleys and corridors, the dull streaking light of its rationalizations, I drive the Cadillac seventy-five miles west and alight at an International Wonder Waffles in eastern Pennsylvania. It is midnight, quite late for a franchise to be open, but like the obese Austin, Wonder Waffles showeth no mercy. "Adulterated food, chemical additives, rat pellets found in the meat, the exploitation of high school and college youth for less than minimum wages, ruthless union-busting, mindless public relations with clowns and visits to the handicapped to mask the exploitation. The corporate conglomerate machinery of this country is seen at its ugliest in *pseudo-Gemeinschaft*,"

I conclude and offer the cashier a fine view of the Smith & Wesson while otherwise, behind her, the desultory midnight activities of Wonder Waffles go on. "Give me all of your money," I say. "Everything in the till."

The cashier regards me with round and somewhat kindly eyes. "You're crazy," she says, "you have to be crazy."

"I wish that I were," I say sadly. "Unfortunately I am not. I am merely administering the truth."

"Are you some kind of a preacher or something?"

"No. I am an armed robber. Give me all of the money."

"I never knew an armed robber to make a speech like that."

"I have a college degree," I say mindlessly. "I am also the author of certain published works in obscure literary magazines and did a stint as an employee of a cultural commission before I ran out of money and patience. This gun is absolutely functional. Do not force me to use it."

She fumbles in the drawer, comes up with two handfuls of money which hang from her palms like fresh vegetables. "There isn't that much," she says, "receipts are less than you would think and the route manager comes in twice a day to pick up the cash. They control you very tightly if you're a wholly owned franchise which unfortunately we are."

"I sympathize," I say. "Put the money in a bag. I need to keep both hands free for the gun. I won't be distracted."

She produces a bag from underneath the register, deftly pushes the money within. I have the intimation that the franchise book has a procedure for armed robbery as inflexible as for hamburger condiments. "That was very interesting what you said," the cashier says, "I mean the rat pellets and all and conglomeration. You think that this is really a dishonest business?"

"One of the greatest," I say, "one of the real greats," and take the bag. "I am merely showing you the real face of Wonder Waffles which Wonder Waffles would hide from the world. Outright confiscation."

"You certainly are serious, aren't you?" she says. "Something like Robin Hood."

"A discredited myth," I say. "I keep for myself; I facilitate the transfer of goods in only a single direction." I move without haste toward the door. "I'm not rationalizing my crimes, you see. I simply happen to be slightly desperate."

"I know what you mean," she says, "the conditions here aren't what you would think and there are no benefits at all. I could tell you stories—"

"Please do not," I say, "I have heard them all in college and at the foundation," and move through the doors and into the Sedan de Ville, which I start without haste and drive back to Route Eighty without panic. Red warning lights flash ominously but the fan belts appear secure and grumbling the Cadillac moves to fifty-five with the air of a car providing me with one last gift.

I maintain a legal speed of fifty-five miles an hour—there are certain sanctions within which even existentialists must operate—all the way back on eighty to where it intersects with ninety-five and on ninety-five itself I cut back to fifty. Troopers everywhere. The New Jersey Turnpike south leads me with stately ease eventually to the Baltimore-Washington Expressway just past the Chesapeake Memorial Bridge. At a franchised stop I have the car filled with gasoline and replace a badly worn front tire, paying with a flourish. Restored by two cups of Wonder Waffles franchised coffee I return to the car and drive it farther south where in due course I land in the very seat of government. I park the car at a discreet distance from my true destination, take a bus to the Capitol Building, and after inquiries post myself in the Senate Office Building.

I am merely waiting to do to the senator directly what he is doing to all of us less directly, I point out to the security forces when they arrive. I am merely attempting to convert a metaphor into a reality, to deal with circumstances in a direct and circumspect fashion. The security forces, however, are having none of this. "Used-car lots are one thing," they say to me, "and Wonder Waffles are another, and possibly, just possibly, metaphysics are a third, but when you start dealing with power, that is something entirely different, we keep careful tabs on people like you and always, *always* you start off one way and end up another, exceed your limits, there's just no end to what you want, is there?" and so on and so forth *ad infinitum*, as we used to say in the Department of Speech & Communication, and they take me away from there having confiscated the gun, having confiscated the money, but leaving me (very thoughtfully as matters will probably turn out) several fresh napkins from Wonder Waffles with dancing clowns and singing bears with which I can wipe my fevered forehead as I try to figure out whom I can call, how I can raise bail, and if I raise bail exactly where in this world there will ever be another place for me.

April 1978: New Jersey

Afterword to "Varieties of Religious Experience"

Alfred Hitchcock's had a transfer of ownership and editor in 1975 and I was finally able to sell the market; recently I have sold them with fair consistency.* (Nothing doing with the prior administration; between 1967 and 1975 I sent them alone or in collaboration upward of twenty manuscripts and sold them none.) Belatedly I have been able to do for the new editor, Eleanor Sullivan, precisely the kind of work I had wanted to try in the mystery short story: inferential, assaultive of stereotypes, some slight expansion of formula, gentle mockery of that formula, and so on. Since I was unable to sell that kind of work to the mystery market of my early career I took it to science fiction.

Since my so-called career, like that of most commercial writers, is little more than a function of what I could write and where I could sell, I wonder how things would have been different if I had been able to sell *Alfred Hitchcock's* or *Ellery Queen's* magazines from the outset with the relative ease with which I was able to sell the science fiction markets. Perhaps I would have followed a parallel course in another field and become Donald E. Westlake, Brian Garfield, or John T. Lutz, distinguished colleagues all. On the other hand, I never had the feel for the mystery that I did for science fiction and probably belonged in science fiction anyway. Ernest M. Hutter did me a favor: sped me on my way, for which I can say not only to the editors but to the non- or ex-editors, thank you kindly.

---

*And more recently I quit. Ontogeny recapitulates phylogeny—11/79.

Inside Out

I've got to start stacking them in the bedroom, now. The corpses, that is.

The living room, alas, is full. It was bound to happen sooner or later. Still, it is a shock to realize that the day of inevitability has come. There is simply no room anymore. Floor to ceiling, ceiling to floor, in four rows the bodies are stacked except for that little space in the corner I have left for my footrest and chair. Even the television set is gone. It was hard to sacrifice that but business is business. I put it at the foot of the bed, dreading the time when I would have to start putting the bodies where I slept. But I must face reality and the living room is finished. *Fini. Kaput* and *terminus*. Cheerlessly I accept my fate. If I am to go on murdering I will have to bring the bodies, as the abbess said to the bishop, into the boudoir. And I am, of course, going to go on murdering.

You betcha.

When I do away with Brown, the superintendent, tonight then, his corpse will go in the far corner, beside the dresser. Virgin territory so to speak ... not that there is sexual undertone to this matter. None whatsoever. It is what it is. It is not a metaphor. It is not a symbol. It is the pure sad business of murder.

Brown rolls the emptied garbage cans across the lobby, filling my rooms with sounds from hell. He also refuses to clean the steps more than once a week. Time and again, I have asked him to desist from the one and perform the other, but the man is obdurate. He pretends not to learn English. He pretends not to hear and points to his left ear. He indicates other responsibilities. This morning I saw four disgusting orange peels on the third-floor landing, already turned brown. There is no way that a man of my disposition can deal with this anymore, but I am not able to move. For one thing, what would I do with the bodies? It would be *such* a job to transport them all.

Accordingly, Brown or what is left of him will repose in the bedroom tonight. *Au boudoir il couche.*

The murders are imaginary, of course. I am not actually a mass murderer. These are fictive murders, illusory corpses that have slowly filled these quarters since I began my difficult adjustment about a year ago. Abusive peddlers, disgusting street persons, noxious fellow employees in the Division. In my mind I act out intricate murders, in body I pantomime the matter of conveying the corpses, in my heart all of the dead dwell with me, mild and stoic in their condition. It is a fantasy that enables me to go on, just barely, in this disgusting urban existence: if I could not banish those who offend I would be unable to function. It is of course a perilous business, this fantasy, since I might plunge over the fine line someday and *actually* believe I have done away with these people, but it is the only way I can continue in circumstantial balance.

Giving the fantasy credence, however, demands discipline and a lot of so-called scut work. It is with regret that I have yielded all my living room but for chair and footrest, but also out of simple respect for will. If I were not to make reasonable sacrifices in order to propitiate this accord it would be meaningless. One cannot play the violin well (I do not, incidentally) without years of painful work with wrists and fingers, acquiring technique. One cannot be a proper employee of the Division (I am, I am) without careful study of its dismal and destructive procedures. One cannot be an imaginary mass murderer without taking responsibility for imaginary dead.

The derelict who wipes my windshield with a dirty rag at the bridge exit still is there, of course, although I murdered him six months ago. This morning he cursed me when I gave him only fifteen cents through a cautiously opened window. His rag hardly infiltrated my vision, his curses fell upon benign and smiling countenance. How could I tell him after all, "Sir, you no longer exist. Since I did away with you half a year ago your real activities in the real world have made no impression upon me. Your rag is a blur, your curses song. I drove a sharp knife between your sixth and seventh ribs in this very street before witnesses, threw your body into the trunk, and conveyed it bloodless to my apartment where it now reposes. The essential *you* lies sandwiched in my apartment between the waitress from the Forum Diner who spilled a glass of ice water in my lap and the medical social worker from the Division who said I had no grasp whatsoever of the nature of schizoid disassociation. You're finished, right?"

No. Wrong. I do not think he would understand. This miserable creature, along with the waitress, the medical social worker, and so many others, cannot appreciate the metaphysics of the situation.

I did away with Brown in his apartment two hours ago. "Mr. Brown," I said when he opened the door, "I can't take this anymore. You're totally irresponsible. It's not only the orange peels, the hide-and-seek when the toilet will not flush, and the terrible smells of disinfectant when you occasionally wash the lobby. That would be enough, but it is your insolence that degrades my spirit. You do not accept the fact that I am a human being who has a right to simple services. By ignoring my needs, you have denied my humanity."

Ah, well. Then I shot him in the left temple with the delicate point twenty-two I use for such extreme cases. The radio was playing the Symphony Number One Hundred and One in D Major of Franz Joseph Haydn loudly as I dragged him out of there, closing the door firmly behind. I would not have suspected that he had a taste for classical music, but this does not mitigate the situation. Besides, the second violin parts in the Haydn symphonies are monstrous, lacking melody or reason. No wonder I gave up the second violin years ago. Now Brown lies at the foot of my bed. Intermittently he appears to sigh in the perfectitude of his perfect peace.

The medical social worker commented today during conference upon my abstracted attitude and twice tapped me on the hand to make me attentive. I know she feels something has reduced my caseworker's efficacy but how could I possibly explain that the reason my attention lapses is that she was smothered many weeks ago and has not drawn a breath, even in pantomime, since?

Brown's corpse is curiously odorous. Here is a new phenomenon. I am a committed housekeeper and cannot abide smells of any kind in my apartment (other than pipe or rosin) and my corpses are aseptic. Brown's, however, is not. It is increasingly foul. My sleep was disturbed last night. Heavy sprays of the popular kitchen disinfectant do not work. The apartment was even worse when I came home tonight.

I *knew* it was a mistake starting disposal in the bedroom but what were my choices? There is simply no room left outside of here and I will not have corpses in the bathroom. I will absolutely not put them there. There are limits. I will just have to do the best I can. After a while I'll either get used to this or the smell will dissipate on its own.

I should get rid of Brown's body—the smell is impossible—but I am reluctant to do so. It would set a dangerous precedent, it would break a pattern. If I were to dispose of his body he would not then be symbolically dead and if I did it with him might I not be then tempted to do it with one of the others? Or with succeeding victims? My project would become totally self-defeating and I would have accomplished nothing.

It has of course occurred to me to call the real Brown to help me dispose of the imaginary Brown but I am not going to do that either. It would be a pretty irony but one he would not understand. I will have to do the job myself or hold on.

Anyway, I haven't seen him around in days.

It is all too much. Too much, too much. I could not deal with it anymore and accordingly dragged Brown's body to the landing for pickup tomorrow morning. That should solve the problem, although I am concerned at the rupture of my pattern and also by the curious weight of his body as I lumbered with it, fireman-carry fashion, into the stairwell. He is the most unusually corporeal of all my victims. Even in imaginary death this lover of Haydn seems capable, typically, of making me miserable.

Two policemen at the door demand entrance to my apartment. Behind them I can see a circle of tenants.

There seems to be a problem.

At the first opportunity during this interview I intend to distract the police and kill them, thus putting an end to the harassment, but I have a feeling that it won't work.

I should *never* have abandoned the living room as a mausoleum. That was my only mistake. I should have begun disposing of old corpses as they were replaced by the new. It would have been sufficient. It would have been good enough.

But it's too late now, the police say.

I think they're right.

November 1977: New Jersey

Afterword to "Inside Out"

This was a story written off an editorial idea, not too common in that way among the Collected Works (I would have made a very poor man's Garrett or Anvil*) but probably successful, since the idea, that of Eleanor Sullivan of *Alfred Hitchcock's*, was, ah, suited to the writer. "How about a set of imaginary corpses that turns into one real one?" Eleanor offered in November of 1977. How about that indeed? I understand from Bill Pronzini that the editor of *Best Detective Annual*, Ed Hoch, considers the story as of this writing (8/78) one of the very best of the year. Is this a comment upon my proficiency or the level of the American mystery or both or neither? Do not *hasten* to comment.

Many of my characters work in Bureaus of Division & Necessity, strange bureaucratic structures drained of all but procedural obsession, and recently more than a few of them have been violinists (inept) or would-be violinists (unsuccessful). I wonder what this has to do with anything.

---

* Not to derogate these writers or any others. The days of derogation of colleagues are past in the first place, and in the second, in their own way, Garrett and Anvil are better persons and better writers than I. Garrett's "Hunting Lodge" and Anvil's "Mind Partner," which I selected for *Neglected Visions*, co-edited with Martin Greenberg and Joseph D. Olander, are first-rate.

Line of Succession

I am Scoot. The felon. You all know of me, although perhaps until this moment you have not known my name. You still do not: Scoot is a conjuration, it need not concern. It is not really my name but my destiny that engages you so.

I am the recidivist, the bail-jumper, the mugger of old ladies while on parole for assaulting young ones. Because of a failure in the correct reading of my rights under Miranda statute, because of a cop's tainted goods I have stolen with clumsy fingerprints, because the foreman of the jury concealed an indictment of his own, I am returned over and again to the streets to perpetrate my horrid but rewarding existence.

You all know of me from the tabloid press and its editorials: I am the one who slips through the law's interstices ... softheaded judges, cowardly district attorneys, and libertarian court-appointed lawyers ambitious to advance. I strike fear into the heart of the city, ignite finders of rage in the suburbs. I am the subject of angry tenants' meetings and the mumblings of the whiskey sergeants. I am Scoot the defendant; I commit my crimes and slip free, return to my well-appointed home (furnished, of course, with stolen goods) to collect welfare under a false identity. There I plan further outrages.

None of this is easy, you know. It is not. I am dedicated to my calling, which leaves little room for human companionship or avocation. By keeping all of you so very mad at me, I shore up your very sanity.

Otherwise, who might make you mad and what would you do?

I entrap a middle-aged man in an alley. I hit him over the head, seize his wallet and umbrella, and sprint into the night. Halfway through the intersection, however, I catch the attention of a skidding prowl car. Angry police emerge, pin me against a wall, spread-eagle, seize the umbrella roughly and then the wallet. "We've got you now," one of them, an old adversary, says, "this time we've got you."

The victim, however, proves to have disappeared from where I left him and when I am arraigned it is without testimony. The judge and my adversary, the good Patrolman Kelly, get into a furious argument over the worthlessness of the evidence and Kelly is much humiliated. I back courteously from the bench. The judge waves me into the night.

At the door I retrieve the umbrella, a poor return for a night's work but better than nothing for what proves to be a gathering rain. I use the rain to steal hubcaps from cars on the deserted street and add them to my collection. So that the night should end as fully as it began I use the last sleepy half hour to write letters of extortion.

In the morning the papers run headlines on pages three or five: SCOOT ESCAPES JUSTICE AGAIN. There is an unflattering picture of me being escorted from the police car raising a taunting hand to the camera. The editorials in both papers are outraged, pointing out that the law is truly lawless if such as I may use it to be free.

I shrug, toss the papers which I have stolen from a blind news dealer over the curb, littering shamelessly, and walk into the subway to investigate new stations uptown which I have heard are excellent for muggings. I wear my dark glasses and am a little fearful of being recognized (but then, too, I enjoy celebrity; my feelings are classically ambivalent) but most of my fellow passengers are too engrossed in their newspapers to pay attention.

Just to keep in practice I pick their pockets.

The welfare worker visits me as she does once every six months and asks if any details have changed. They never do, of course. I am receiving aid to the disabled as the result of a diagnosis of psycho-neurosis, mixed type, given me by a bleeding-heart department psychiatrist many years ago. My refusal to get a job is in itself, the psychiatrist pointed out cleverly, a symptom of mental illness. The welfare worker asks for rent receipts, medical receipts, transportation receipts, and clothing receipts. I hand her a forged clump which she stuffs into her black book.

Looking at her I think idly of theft or more atrocious crimes but repress the impulse. I am not a psychopath. I am fully dedicated to my work for my own sad reasons. Collecting welfare as I do under several names at many addresses, it would be foolish to antagonize her and set up falling dominoes of closed cases.

In the morning I am very busy. I make my extortion rounds, then visit a schoolyard where I discuss with children the many advantages of starting out life on drugs. Breaking for coffee in a restaurant (and strolling past the cashier nonchalantly without paying), I trot south and steal a 1973 Eldorado cabriolet convertible parked snazzily at the curb, top down. I go joyriding, prior to stripping it of all expensive options.

It is a pleasure to be on the highways again, however, and I madly exceed the speed limit, moving beyond seventy-five, waving cheerfully to businessmen and pedestrians from the center lane as, horn blaring, I move along. They scream curses. A 1971 Caprice station wagon with optional heavy-duty rack overturns.

I drive on laughing, the radar alert in the expensive car protecting me from apprehension. All that I miss is a sixteen-ounce can of beer to consume but I am a teetotaler, soberly committed to the tasks at hand and taking essentially (here is the point of my confession entire) no joy from what I must do but only the weary certitude of necessity.

SCOOT SUSPECTED OF WILD JOYRIDE THROUGH CLIFFS INJURING SIX, the headlines read. In an interview an exasperated assistant DA points out that this could hardly be possible: my license was revoked for hit-and-run many years ago. As an enterprising investigative reporter notes on the adjoining page, however, the revocation was rescinded. I had been denied counsel at the last hearing. I had not been advised of my right to remain silent.

I ransack five apartments on the exclusive West Side and while finding few valuables manage to leave a note in every one of them: SCOOT WAS THE THIEF. They must have me to hate. They must be reminded of my hateful presence at all times.

Otherwise, or at least as headquarters has reminded me, they might get too close to less tolerable truths.

CITY STUNNED UNDER SCOOT REIGN OF TERROR.

My old adversary Patrolman Kelly arrests me in the early hours, without evidence and out of frustration, but he has of course no warrant to enter the apartment, nor evidence of hot pursuit, so his case is again thrown out. As I whisk through the corridors I again hear loud argument and the abuse of the judge. I feel a quiver of sympathy for them both. Sometimes I think that they are as hated as I and I can freelance for a living.

"I'm very sorry," the young headquarters emissary says to me that night. "We're going to have to take you off this assignment." He has appeared in the guise of a thin, nervous man with blotches on his palms and the intensity of a cleric. "We're taking you off immediately."

"I don't understand," I say, surprised. "I can't see why you're doing this. Haven't I performed my job satisfactorily?"

"Better than that. You've been superb."

"So what's wrong?"

"What's wrong is precisely that point," he says. "You've been *too* good, Scoot. You've completely personalized your function. It's Scoot they hate, Scoot who is the object of their rage, Scoot whom they hold responsible for the misery, bankruptcy, and emptiness of their lives. You've overtaken their consciousness."

"But that's what I'm *supposed* to do. The conditions—"

"Ah yes," the cleric says, "but you're too good, Scoot. I told you, you're superb. It isn't the faceless or the multitude they hate now, it's you. You've personalized the issue."

"So what?" I say again. "This is most unfair, to be condemned merely for having done my job so well."

"So this," the emissary says. "Attend to me, please. What happens if you *are* apprehended, if you are read your rights properly, if you are caught at the scene of a crime, if your adversary does not taint evidence or the judge is at last satisfied? What if they do throw your ass in jail?"

"That's very doubtful."

"Of course it's doubtful. But what happens if your ass is in the slammer and they're *still* miserable, eh? Eh? What then, smartass?"

"I don't know," I say. The concept is too sophisticated for me; I am a man of action, not thought. "It never concerned me. It's not my problem."

"No, it isn't. It's ours," the emissary says. "We have to deal with the issue and we will." He removes a large and frightening pistol from his overcoat, one with whose caliber I am unfamiliar. Most of the time I avoid concealed weapons; the laws on these are intrusive. "It's certainly our problem and we're going to have to take you off the assignment."

"But why the gun?" I say.

"You know why."

"No I don't," I lie. "You couldn't mean ..."

"I'm afraid so," he says after a little pause. "We couldn't have you around trying to live a decent life. You make too many angry."

"They'll get you," I say to him, "they'll get you for this. You won't escape. You can't just murder a man for doing his job."

"Ah yes," the emissary says, "yes we *can*." He slips a bullet into the chamber, giving me the slyest and sweetest of smiles. "I'm replacing you, you see, and the first thing the idiots are going to do is to screw up the reading of the rights."

He raises the gun.

"Don't worry about the implications," he adds helpfully. "You can rest assured that I'll call myself Scoot, too. They'll never notice the difference."

They probably won't.

March 1978: New Jersey

Afterword to "Line of Succession"

Stanley Elkin, whose *The Franchiser* (1976) is probably the best novel of the decade thus far* did a savage and unrepentant piece for *Esquire* years ago, "A Requiem for Bullies"; this is in the nature of an affirmation and response. Stanley Elkin is the most gifted stylist of our time, who has written at least two novels and ten short stories that will live; I am to him as is the aphid to the morning light, but one must try. (It is particularly pleasing to try within the genre magazines ... sometimes I feel as those pocket revolutionaries of the thirties, plotting their schemes of bringing down the system from within, must have felt. Of course, most of the time I feel like a fool and remember that most members of the group theater, the YCL, and so on and so forth, changed the system all right, they became it. One cannot do anti-genre work within the genres by definition; it took me years to resolve this for myself but 'tis true, 'tis true.)

Scoot was written on the afternoon of a birthday (not mine) and of a minor auto accident (definitely mine). Both contributed to the, um, subtext. Both are remembered.**

---

* *Revolutionary Road* by Richard Yates wins the Malzberg Award for the sixties, since you ask, and Ralph Ellison's *Invisible Man* for the fifties (Nabokov's *Lolita* would win easy except that the award is for American writers and Nabokov was a figure of world literature). Forties very tough, perhaps *The Naked and the Dead* by Mailer because of a weak field; the thirties, a rank outsider, Daniel Fuchs's *Low Company*. The twenties must go to *Gatsby* and *The Sun Also Rises*, dead heat. The prize consists of one dollar payable on request and my lasting humility.

** But now I have a new car—11/79.

Reaction-Formation

Outrage won't help it. Sulking won't do much. Letters to the editor won't do the trick. The ballot box certainly isn't the answer, the Senator points out, since they're all indistinguishable anyway. Alike as two peas in a pod, as has been pointed out, and so on.

No sir, the Senator concludes, reinforcing my own reluctant conclusion. The only action available to a citizen now is outright murder. Not that I want to advocate overthrow of the government, the Senator chuckles, not that I find violent means anything other than reprehensible. Repre*hen*sible, the Senator says, chewing and spitting tobacco arrhythmically. Still, what are you going to do, son? Sit back and take this the rest of your life? Let them take away your American *rights?* Got to make an example of at least one of them, then they'll get the message.

I have come to agree with the Senator. The Senator is long retired, of course. He represented an unimportant state, one of the Dakotas maybe (I am not too clear on this), briefly some years ago when the governor appointed him to keep the seat for the governor's own campaign. All told, the Senator might have served four months, at the dreary end of a dreary session. "Taught me this, though, son," the Senator says cheerfully, "every single thing you read about them in the papers, that you imagine in your head, is *nothing* to the way they are. It is one of the few things in this country that lives up to every suspicion you have about it. You couldn't buy the experience." Nowadays the Senator lives in retirement with me. We share these furnished rooms together, the Senator and I, splitting rent and food bills, and so on. The Senator, childless, lost his wife many years ago and drifted into the obscurity of urban life; rudderless, he frequented bars, grills, brokerage houses, and the like. Our friendship was, as they say, a natural from the moment we met. For him there is the security of lodgings, companionship, and a willing ear. For me is the honor of living with a once United States Senator, no matter how obscure. And of course the Senator has been a wise counselor. It was he who brought me to my full understanding of the processes of government not so long ago.

"Can't do nothing, *no*how," the Senator concludes, "'less you take a gun and give them a message in the gut," and sadly I concur. This final discussion seems to have cinched matters, as they say; my own political theories have reached sad fruition. I really do not want to be an assassin but then again if the voice of the people is ever going to be heard again in the land it will have to start with me. At the least it will draw attention. I nod grimly and stand, begin to prepare for the journey south.

"Sure wish I could come with you," the Senator says when I have completed my toilet and valise, tucked the pistol away, and phoned the airline for reservations. "Would be real nice to see the Capitol again. Of course," he says, his eyes saddening, "I'm an old man and travel isn't what it used to be for me. Might be a strain upon my heart and digestion just having to go to that horrible place again. Still, I'd give it a try if—"

"Don't think of it," I say. "I wouldn't consider it. Your health, your heart, your life are too important. You just stay here and wait for me."

"Sure will be thinking of you, son. Be with you every minute in spirit, you know that."

"Of course," I say. "I'll give you a call, let you know how it's going."

"Sure would *like* to be down there," the Senator says again. "Cherry blossom time, the monument, all those filibusters, the crisp crackle of bills passing back and forth in the cloakroom, and those secretaries, ah, those secretaries—"

"Not to consider," I say. "I need you here, you're too important to me. What would my life be without you?"

The Senator looks embarrassed. "Ah, you're tickling me, son," he says. "A nice young fellow like you, you don't need a senator in these rooms, you need a nice little girl, a nice little wife—"

"I need you," I say; "who could compare a girl to a senator? The honor, the pride of it—"

"You make too much of me, son," the Senator says and blushes, but does not protest further. I say good-bye to him warmly, gripping his old hands, patting his old, warm, sallow cheeks, then to avoid sentimental overflow move quickly to the door, down the stairs, into the street, toward the airport bus station, toward the airport, etc., etc. The pistol, I realize, will be a problem at airport security; I throw it merrily into a sewer. It is my first experience with airlines; I am happy to have remembered security in time. Interception would be ghastly. Check-in, skycaps, boarding pass, etc. In due course and in unexciting manner I find myself in the Capitol. I procure another point forty-five in one of the shops on the outskirts. The availability of cheap weaponry in the republic is wonderful; everything that the Senator says about our helplessness is right, but we do have that. I take a taxi to the visitors' gallery, wait in shuffling line, eventually am admitted to an excellent front-row seat. Visibility is high, position is just peachy keen. I fondle the pistol inside my clothing.

It is as if I can hear the Senator murmuring to me as I say, "Which one should I take? That young woman from New England looks very interesting."

"Oh no," the Senator says. "The urban centers are the most corrupt. I would say the gentleman there from New York."

"How about the short old man from Wisconsin? You've told me about those Midwesterners."

"True," the Senator says, "true, true, true. They are all an abomination. Still, overall, I'd reckon with the man from the big city. They are really the worst. The drugs, the vice, the corruption."

"Surely," I say. I respect the Senator's judgment. I would not override him for an instant; it is he, after all, who is responsible for where I am today and who has so imbued my life with honor. Accordingly I remove the pistol, focus, and do the necessary. It is an excellent shot and has instant results. Military training is another of the few benefits of this so-called democracy; if you listen to what they are trying to tell you they will teach you how to shoot. Much commotion on the floor, of course.

I arise with superb calm, holding the pistol loosely. There is grandiosity in my stride as I move toward one of the doors. Guards are there, of course, to clap enormous hands upon me, bring me to the floor. I submit to their barbarities and indignities. It will all be over soon enough. "You've done very well, son," the Senator says to me. "That was an excellent shot."

"Thank you, Senator," I say to him. I am yanked upright. The guards pin me against a wall and produce handcuffs. The Senator, who seems to have taken a later flight, stands to their rear, looking upon me, beaming. His old features are suffused with pleasure. I feel as I had always known I would: that I have done something for the Republic.

"Why?" one of the guards asks me as they start to take me out of there. "Why could you possibly have done it?"

"You'll have to ask the Senator," I say. "He can answer far better than I."

"Senator?" the guards say. The others stare at me too. "What senator?"

I look toward the Senator himself, but his eyes have suddenly gone dull and hard. "I'm sorry, son," he says, "but I refuse to take any questions. You're my secretary, you'll have to answer all of them on your own. It's your responsibility. I have nothing to do with any of this."

Those politicians!

You can't trust a one.

July 1978: New Jersey

Afterword to "Reaction-Formation"

Another *Alfred Hitchcock's*—slanted story, "Reaction-Formation" is actually another way of looking at the central material of "Trashing" (included in *Down Here in the Dream Quarter* complete with frustrated afterword). Although we are clearly in the post-assassination era, I am an assassination-era writer; like J. G. Ballard, I am evocative, perhaps, of an older, somewhat more melodramatic time. These assassination stories, mine and Ballard's, may even generate a certain nostalgia today, proving that circumstance has in wait for authors ironies more hideous than even the writers could imagine: J. G. Ballard and the undersigned to bring you again their famous and well-loved late-sixties rags!

Indigestion

Ah well. Then again I sometimes wonder how it might have been if instead of the anonymous and forlorn I had ingested instead the bodies of the famous. The cells of Spinoza swimming to mingle with my own bright and burbling blood, the obsessions of Beethoven, the clear and cunning visions of W. J. Bryan taken unto me and merged with my glutinous bloodstream ... why, I might have been anything. Anything at all! I would have been a congregation, a celebration unto myself, not Henry of this common nature (which for all the ecstasy of my activities is what I am; I know my limitations) but Henry Transmogrified, carrying within himself the seeds and decomposition of hundreds of the best.

If the ingestion of a corpse enables one (as I humbly do believe your honor) to take on many of the intellectual qualities of the deceased, then it is clear that I am limited only by the limitations of those within me. Still, that is absolute.

Still. I frequent bleak graveyards located far from the fashionable suburbs; I content myself with fresh grave sites unattended—which can only mean that the deceased left as little of a mark in the departure from life as in the partaking—I observe the amenities of my cruel and inexplicable trade by working as much as I can on the periphery of feeling. Not for me the leap into the still-open grave surrounded by mourning relatives and creditors, not for me either an attempt to insinuate myself nearer the deceased by obtaining a job in the trade: mortician, laboratory attendant, morgue custodian, and so on. For me there is an appreciation of the amenities of feeling. I observe them. I do what I must not without a bright thread of shame. I admit that I am a fiend.

Spinoza and Beethoven, the Kennedys or the cellular decomposition of Nobel Prize winners revolve with me not; I suit myself with simpler game, not a little of it (I will admit this, too) gathered from the potter's fields. I own a shortwave radio and keep up with the latest police reports; if a derelict is delivered anonymously DOA to a hospital I want to be prepared to call upon him tomorrow. But it is not me, it is Henry no longer, it is (as I have said) a congregation that now takes itself upon these tours; the dead feed upon the dead and all two hundred and fifty-five of us, the original Henry and parts of the two hundred and fifty-four he has consumed, prowl about their obsessive errands. I am more than a congregation, I am a civilization, an urban culture (or at least a medium-sized village) to myself. At the end of all of this, I am sure, lies a knowledge so absolute that only the amorphous outlines of the goal, rosy in their radiance, are there to tantalize me. I do not know what I (what we) am (are), I only know that I must go forward. Besides, the dead are very tasty. Eating parts of decomposed corpses is exciting, not only a bizarre gourmet treat but, as a meal taken on the run, heightened by a sense of mortality, of imminent capture. One can enjoy the task for its own sake. I enjoy eating the dead. (I already warned you that I was a fiend.)

So much for exposition and all of this in the persona of the original Henry, the corpse-eating Henry who began his journey just three and a half years ago. But Henry, now thirty-seven, can hardly be said to exist anymore, his fragile, mean soul has been overtaken by the souls of the two hundred and fifty-four ingested so that the congregation clangs and bangs against itself nervously within the confines of the tenement that is Henry's persona. Each of the two hundred and fifty-four would have its tale to tell; each of them could make its own case. They have found their immortality within Henry; this is firmly believed and each of them (as are all the living, too) is an individual, but the stories would remit to a common banality, a reiteration of the germinal act of *having been eaten*; this would be rather repetitious and thus Henry, the true and final narrator of these adventures, Henry will suppress the other two hundred and fifty-four in the interests of economy and fictional imperative, dealing only with the present instances as they refract into the past, as they summon up the future. It is he, after all, who has devised for the two hundred and fifty-four their immortality.

Into his rooms at some careful hour of the dawn Henry comes, his congregation chanting within him. Fluids roil murkily; Henry has spent the hours of the night at a cemetery in Forest Hills (Forest Hills!) where he has eaten richly of parts of an old woman buried not sixteen hours before. From his careful reading of the obituaries, from his tennis shoes and alert stalk, from his gloved hands, strong shoulders, and wood-cutting devices, from his energy and ambition Henry has derived rich proceeds; not only has he gorged himself with a hand, a foot, and an eyeball but (in a festival of gluttony) Henry has also eaten part of the chin and a weary, crushed-in nose, these last two superfluities sickening him, but Henry could not stop. Sometimes he is unable to control himself. Tossing over the dirt with shaking hands, replacing the marker guiltily, Henry stumbled away from the graveyard and onto a one hundred and two Queens Boulevard bus at the end of the line, his appearance bringing only desultory attention from the three inhabitants of the bus: a workman, a driver, a drug addict who sat nodding secretly in the back. Looking at Henry, it is impossible to know what they might have made of his appearance, the dirt on his shoes, the dirt on his nostrils, his flushed and yet pallid demeanor, but Henry knew what to make of them: looking at them, it was as if he regarded not people but metaphors, metaphors for the corpses that they would be. Shyly and tentatively, yet with increasing boldness, Henry and his congregation regarded these three, wondering what it might be like at some date in the indefinite future to eat them, what their personalities might be like added to the two hundred and fifty-four already in his bloodstream, the two hundred and fifty-fifth making sliding entrance through gullet and bowels, and they in turn looked back. Did they judge his thoughts? Regarding his shovel, the valise in which he held his cutter, did these three have any inkling of that secret buzzing greedily in Henry's brain and throat like a demented insect? Or did they simply think nothing at all; were their minds as clean and darkly paneled as the minds of the dead? Henry looked between his feet and thought nothing at all, afflicted with an indigestion so severe that it drove metaphysical speculation clear from the pulpit of his consciousness, from the church of his interior, from the congregation of his choice. He returned to his rooms.

Not unaware that he was a fiend, Henry took the usual precautions when he had emerged from the one hundred and two Queens Boulevard bus at the intersection of two numbered avenues. At one wastebasket he disposed of his gloves, at another the woolen hat which he had worn for customary disguise and which had become smeared in a somewhat implicatory fashion; at a third (Henry, staggering from his indigestion, reeling down the length of Queens Boulevard, pausing at wastebaskets to hurl objects, might have had a riotous aspect to anyone who was watching; Henry is not unaware of his appearance or how his activities might strike an appalled and unreasoning world; for this reason he takes more than the usual precautions over his activities and tries to write about himself in the third person as much as possible so that anyone stumbling across these well-secreted notes posthumously might well think that I was talking about someone *else*, which in more than a few senses is the case) Henry paused to retch, his insides convulsing as certain displacements took effect (he should not have had that eyeball), and then, somewhat eased in the flesh if not in the murmurings of the spirit, he returned to his rooms where he found the Other waiting for him as the Other so often does after these expeditions.

It might be necessary, by laws of fictional imperative already referred to, to discuss the Other, to talk about the background of the beast, to explain what it was doing in the rooms and why it and Henry have such undue familiarity, but if it is all the same to everyone, Henry will refuse this task. Henry will not discuss this anymore, being quite familiar with the appearance of the Other and the Other's reasons for being there and having discussed this at length in previous narratives. Besides, there are certain things which lie, perhaps, outside of any decent opinion of mankind, outside of any normal range of human behavior, and which, when written about, when even *hinted* about, can cause only the most unusual disgust and revulsion, open up emotions and responses that are archaic and long since buried. Let them stay buried. There will be no discussion of the Other here other than to state that it was there again and that Henry felt the old twisting fear in his vitals. He had never gotten over his terror of the Other. Try as he had to supersede that terror, to realize that much of it was imaginary, that all of it could be overcome, he could not stop that feeling but indeed found himself in its thrall. Very much as did his congregation, which squirmed, trembled in place, murmured warnings and imprecations. Half a congregation, three-quarters Henry, four-fifths what he had most recently consumed, Henry faced the Other as bravely as he could and said, "I thought I told you that I didn't want you here anymore. I thought that we settled that last time. Come on. Get out of here."

The Other took a slightly different posture and said, "Come now, Henry, enough of this." It eyed him, saw the look on his face which must have told him everything, not that a ringing, foaming belch from Henry did not tell him more; small specks of blood that were not his then pouring from Henry's mouth to the corners of his lips. Henry wiped them slowly, trying not to call attention to this disaster, but it was already too late. The face of the Other congealed. It licked its horrid lips.

"You've been doing it again," it said.

"That's none of your business. That's none of your affair."

"But I'm afraid that it is my affair, Henry. It's very much my responsibility; I'm implicated in this up to the hilt. Haven't I warned you?"

"Warn away," Henry said rather sullenly. He was terrified but still sullen; sullen but yet terrified; part of this having to do with the reactions of his congregation. Some of them were sullen but then again others of them were terrified. His reactions were never consistent because his congregation was inconsistent. It involved a cross section. If Henry had partaken of a better class of person, if Henry had determined unto himself that he would seek only the best and the most consistent of personality traits, then things might have been quite different, but then again Henry could not control himself. Gluttony predominated, and the urge to multiply. If one cannot multiply in one way then one must do it in another, but this is a line of speculation that Henry finds very arcane and *he will not pursue it under any circumstances.* "Get out of here," he said again sullenly and with terror. "Get out now."

"You've been eating people," the Other said flatly. "You've been going to graves and tearing them open and you've been taking out corpses and eating them. A finger here, an eyeball there, sometimes a whole hand, occasionally even an arm. I know what you're doing, Henry. Do you think I'm a fool? You've been warned again and again."

"It's none of your business," Henry said. He put down the valise with a clatter, walked then into the second of the two rooms of his two-room furnished apartment, in which second room he walked to the window, looked down the clear pipe of the air shaft to the sheer drop, three stories below, the implacable stones of the courtyard assuming to him, in the first intimations of the dawn, the aspect of a kind of destiny. "None of your business," he repeated, hearing the footsteps of the Other as it came through the doorway and closed distance between them. There was no way to keep the horrid creature out.

"You've been warned and warned, Henry," the Other said, somewhat repetitiously. "You've been warned nicely and you've been warned harshly. You've been begged and you've been threatened. You've been reasoned with and once we even looked at pictures together while I tried to explain to you nicely why you can't go around eating corpses. Every time I thought you got the point but you're hopeless, Henry. You just keep on doing it. It's got to stop."

Henry shook his head, standing against the window. "What I do is my business," he said. "Besides," he added, "I've got not only myself to consider now. I'm eating for two hundred and fifty-six."

"That is lunacy, Henry. There are no two hundred and fifty-six. There is only you. Your personality does not increase through the personalities of those you ingest. The soul is ephemeral; it flies away at the moment of death. There is nothing but flesh. You lust to eat flesh, Henry. There is no congregation. It is only yourself and the rest is rationalization."

"Get out of here," Henry said severely. His stomach roiled at the thought that he might not be two hundred and fifty-six but only himself. Alone, alone: always alone; the suggestion was obscene. It could not be. He knew if nothing else that ingestion had given him *companionship.* He put the thought away. "Get out or I'll strike you."

The Other giggled in a rather feminine way. It has a rather high voice when under stress, very much as Henry does although Henry can control himself better. "Don't be ridiculous," it said, "I can't get out. I won't get out. You can't get rid of me. This has got to stop."

"I mean it," Henry said, turning from the window, raising his hand in a threatening way. "I've had quite enough of this now. Be gone with you."

The Other paused, looming, hanging just beyond Henry's reach. Its horrid little eyes turned meditative, its green scales prickled. It shook its beaked head. "I'm sorry," it said, "I'm sorry, Henry. This has gone too far. You're quite dangerous and you won't be held back. I've tried reasoning and threatening, beggings and explanations. Still you go on looting graves, desecrating the friendless dead. This is hopeless. It has got to stop." It nodded solemnly, in a sudden and decisive way. "Yes," it said, "this has got to stop."

It closed upon Henry and a claw came out; suddenly Henry felt himself held within a tremendous and beckoning claw, yanked up against the scales of the creature. They exuded a foul odor; Henry felt the strength and conviction of the Other pouring into him and regrets suddenly spun the tumblers of his mind. Why hadn't he listened? Why hadn't he heeded the warnings? Why had he not understood that the Other was merely, as it had oft repeated, doing this for his own good in lieu of more horrid actions? But it was too late for any of this, of course. Henry knew how late it was. The Other had indeed threatened him and Henry had not thought that the threats would come to pass but now they had, and as he clung to the horrid green of the creature, a slimy ooze coming from little pores like abscesses in the scales of the Other, Henry's whole life seemed to flick before his eyes, right up to his thirty-fifth year when these activities (and the Other) had entered his life. Why had he done it? Why had he found it necessary to look to the dead for sustenance when there were so many of the living? Insight like a belch exploded and expanded his consciousness, but of course it was too late for any of this. With little peeps and cries his congregation fled the temple of his insides, plunged gabbling into the vestry of his unconscious, and Henry realized that he was indeed alone, always to be alone.

"I'm afraid that I'm going to have to kill you now," the Other said. It inclined its tentacled head in a gesture gracious and somehow touching, something humanoid in the aspect. "It's for your own good, Henry," it pointed out, "this would just go on and on and eventually you'd wind up doing something really dangerous and stupid like frequenting funeral homes, looking around open coffins. This has got to be brought to an end."

And Henry said, "Yes, yes, I see what you mean," his breath cut off by that suffocating embrace, his body arched in a spasm of agreement, for he did see, he truly saw what the Other was saying; he saw too that the Other, all along, had merely been trying to help him, to educate him into a better way of life, and like all of the other opportunities offered him Henry had mocked and lost this last of them but too late, too late for any of this. "I'm sorry," the Other said, "Henry, I'm truly sorry but there must come an end to this," and guided him toward the window, centered Henry against it and then with one terrific thrust sent Henry arching and vaulting through the glass; for one instant hanging high in the air, his skin severed by a thousand cuts, his body at dreadful stillness, looking at the Other, Henry thought that he understood everything up to the Other's identity ... but in the next instant as he began that long, expiring fall to the courtyard beneath he realized that he understood nothing at all and that all of it must be, as it had always been, a mystery.

His last thought before his body explodes is not for himself but his congregation as truly befits the minister he has tried to be ... but his congregation is out of touch, no time for benediction, and all two hundred and fifty-six of them slant to the stones before rebounding, the organs of his dismembered body spokes. The impact fire.

The impact fire.

January 1974: New Jersey

Afterword to "Indigestion"

Written to commission ("How about one in which the narrator eats corpses?") for a Roger Elwood/Curtis book anthology of disgusting stories about disgusting acts (but no sex, please; we have to sell this to the kids) "Indigestion" is probably as literate and erudite a story as could be written on the material. When I reread it once on five ounces of vodka it even assumed a surreal brilliance.

Rachel Cosgrove Payes, a steely-haired and steely-eyed suburban lady who writes science fiction and romantic suspense novels accused me at an SFWA function a year ago or so of "really writing a lot just to suit Elwood, I find it kind of disgusting."* "What can I say to you, Rachel?" the undersigned replied. "I am a full-time writer, a house, a car, a wife, two children—" "It still makes me mad," she said. "Me too," I answered. This is an argument as old as the evolution of the commercial marketplace for American fiction; I doubt if there is any resolution but wish to point out that at least it has been confronted. My career, such as it is or was, can be called a testimony of my ambivalence.

Still, as stories of men who eat corpses go, this is first-rate. Agreed?

---

*Rachel said something a little stronger than that, but she is a good person at heart and anyway I am into mellower retrospective nowadays.

A Clone at Last
(with Bill Pronzini)

"I'm sorry," the lovely blonde said to Lapham, "but I could never invite a man into my Home Complex that I don't really know. But thanks anyway for an interesting evening."
And she shut the door firmly in his face.

Lapham was very tired of women telling him they didn't invite a man into their Home Complex that they didn't really know. He was very tired of having doors shut in his face. It was 2172, a new era in interpersonal communication, wasn't it? And he was actually a fairly decent-looking man, wasn't he? Not to mention being a fairly successful pocket deity to many of the *Aphid chorae* of Ceres, and having a number of good qualities that included but were not limited to earnestness, honesty, punctuality, and never squeezing his pimples in public. Or taking the bandages off his radiation scars.
For some reason, however, women did not seem to like him.
So Lapham, in desperation; finally went to the Cloning Foundation and applied for Opposite-Gender Replication. He would *create* the woman who would understand him. So there. Opposite-Gender Replication was a recent innovation of the Foundation, having been established only within the most recent decade and having been made available at terrific expense to people such as Lapham who had reasons to need an understanding response from those of a different genital persuasion.
Lapham permitted his blood to be typed, his cells to be analyzed, his brain waves to be charted, his persona to be electromagnetically shocked, and his private parts to be fondled in an unseemly fashion. His facial bandages, however, were left respectfully in place by the personnel of the enormously expensive Cloning Foundation. (He had inherited three quarters of the asteroid Ceres, which made his lot somewhat easier.) At the end of this painful and somewhat unprintable exercise, a pure cell was extracted and left to lie in the darkest spaces of the Foundation's nethermost level.
Lapham waited for eighteen years. Eighteen years was then as now the age of legal majority and he did not wish to be indicted for statutory rape of himself. The years sped by. Lapham invented a cheap substitute for the wheel, and after patent rode it all the way to Proxima Centauri and back. Bored, he created sublife in one of the testing arenas and fed

it to the grateful *Aphid chorae*. He waited patiently, amusing himself through all the empty little hours as he aged, not imperceptibly, from twenty-nine to forty-seven.

He did not, through all of this, deal with women at all. He was saving himself for herself.

At precisely oh eight hundred hours on her eighteenth birthday, the pimply blond clone said, "I'm sorry but I never invite a man into my Home Complex that I don't really know. But thanks anyway for an interesting evening."

And Lapham shut the door firmly in Lapham's face.

April 1978: New Jersey

Afterword to "A Clone at Last"

This short-short, as submitted, was dedicated to the memory of Fred Brown, an epigraph removed for publication. The dreadful intimation lurks that Ed Ferman left it out, not through oversight, but because he felt the name of Fredric Brown (1906-72) would mean nothing to contemporary readers. One hopes not.

We thought of doing a series of Lapham stories, did Bill Pronzini and I, and even drafted a sequel to this, but gave it up as a bad idea. There is really nothing left to say about Lapham or his condition.

This story was untitled in draft, by the way; we put our minds independently to the problem and came up with "A Clone at Last" simultaneously. Pronzini/Malzberg may not be the most legendary of collaborations (or then again, what the hell, it may be) but it is distinguished, as is Lapham's fate, by a certain, um, inevitability.

Backing Up

So I show him the gun. This is the great leveler, the great persuader. "I must tell you," I say in my mellow voice, "that we are dissatisfied with the collections over a very long period." The gun is a point forty-five caliber precision job, not that this really matters since it is not the make of guns but their function that interests most laymen. "You are five thousand dollars behind," I add. "Not even allowing for the matter of interest."

He looks at me with calm, sad eyes. His name is Brown, I believe that I have got that right, no need to look on the card to check as I am definitely in the right office, and he says, "I told you, I need more time. I am doing the best I can. Furs is a seasonal business, an erratic business, and this is not our season." It is February, I should point out, although a very mild and springlike February, my forehead in this small room is veritably jeweled with sweat. "Next month," he says, "next month I will have something for you."

"Next month is not sufficient," I say. "My instructions are not to leave without a down payment now. Two thousand dollars is suggested." "I do not have two thousand dollars," he says. He looks down at the floor, then up at me with curious brightness. "Anyway," he says, "I don't think that you have the nerve."

"What?"

"I said I don't think you have the nerve. The guts," Brown says. He puts his palms flat on the desk, raises himself to military posture. "I don't think that you have the guts to blow my head off at high noon on the seventh floor of this building with at least forty people on the same floor right now. The walls are like paper here. Corners are cut in the construction business something awful. The whole place may hear the shot, up to the fortieth story. You wouldn't think of it."

"Don't toy with me, Brown," I say. I focus my mouth into a snarl. "I do not like being toyed with and have a vile temper. To say nothing of a job to do."

Brown shakes his head. "We all have a job to do," he says, "but I don't think that you have the nerve to do yours. The guts." He stares at me from his rigid posture. "Go on," he says, "blow my head off. I don't have five thousand dollars. I don't have two thousand dollars. I have nothing to give you, so you're just going to have to carry through." His eyes glint disturbingly. He is exactly right about the construction business. Roadways, churches, automobiles, nothing is built the way that it used to be. Corruption and the cutting of corners prevail. Even the silencer on the pistol is flimsy; I do not trust it.

"Come on," he challenges. The position he has taken seems to have given him a sense of release. "Come on, do it. I have nothing to give you."

He is quite right. My orders do not provide for the contingency of defiance. Whether I have the nerve is another issue; I do not have to consider that now. Reluctantly I lower the pistol. "I'll be back," I say. "Soon. Maybe today. Certainly tomorrow. You can't run. I know where you live. Your wife, your children."

Brown's face leers with sudden power. "You won't do it to them either," he says. "You won't do it to anyone. You've lost the fire, you see. You've acquired scruple. You're like all the construction people now, all the contractors. You just want an edge without risk."

"I don't have to take this kind of abuse," I say and put away the pistol and leave his office quickly. My footsteps clatter in the hallways; the whisk of elevators is audible at fifty paces.

What is the raw material of these modern office buildings? Chewing gum?

Considering the issue of scruple, I make my way crosstown and find in his accustomed place the bartender whose gambling losses are now in excess of fifteen thousand. He is alone behind the counter at this difficult hour of a February afternoon, but his face does not light with pleasure when he sees me. Quite the opposite. "I told you yesterday," he says, "and I told you the day before that, too. I don't have it. I need time to get it together. At least a month."

"They don't want to wait a month."

"That's their problem," he says. He dries his hands noisily on a towel. "I have to ask you to leave," he says. "Hanging around here, it creates the wrong kind of atmosphere. Customers might be disturbed."

"I'll have a rye and soda."

"No," he says, "I don't want to serve you."

I reach my hand into my pocket in a menacing gesture. "Come on," he says, "this business with guns no longer fascinates. I tell you, I don't have it. I have personal problems, medical bills. Maybe by June I can work something out. Right now I can't do a thing."

"You're in no position to make that statement."

"You're in no position to refuse." He flings the towel down the length of the bar. "Come on," he says, "eighty-six it. I've had enough of this."

Striations and laughter float from the television set. An afternoon program, celebrity quiz or something. The level of television has deteriorated as much as everything else, I think as I back away from the bar. Nothing works quite as it used to. Nothing can quite be trusted. Quality levels go down. Strapped gamblers and bankrupt fur manufacturers take a dictatorial position and there seems no way to deal with them. Nothing is quite as it used to be; none of this would have gone on even five years ago. It is part of urban rot, I think.

"And stay out of here," the bartender says as I go through the door.

Who do these people think they are? Why do they think the world owes them a living?

I phone in to tell them that collections have not gone well. They grumble if the message comes direct but for the fourth day in a row it is the answering service and the answering service, of course, assumes a neutral posture. Sometimes I wonder if the messages are even passed on. Sometimes I wonder if they are out of the office permanently. Sometimes I wonder if I need this job but then common sense prevails; at my age and stage of life there are few new careers open to me. It is one of the hazards of an overly liberal education; I should have learned a trade.

I take the train north and come in at the usual time. Lydia's face is clamped with tension but at least the children are out for the evening, having dinner with their friends, I am told. "Pour your own drink," Lydia says, "I'm not any servant. I've had a bad day myself." I can see from her expression that it is going to be a difficult evening. We will be up until at least midnight and it will be necessary for me once again to explain to her the meaningfulness of life in the suburbs. Since I no longer believe in that, I will find it tedious and agonizing. "If you want dinner you take me out," Lydia says, "I didn't feel like cooking."

"Restaurant food isn't home cooking."

"We can go to the Major."

The Major is the local chain motel. "Franchises are no good," I say. "Franchising has destroyed this nation. Everything the same and nothing very good."

Her eyes, infinitely weary, look up at me. "I don't want to hear that now," she says, "please don't start up on that with me now."

Who does the woman think she is, anyway? What has happened to the social institution of marriage?

May 1978: New Jersey

Afterword to "Backing Up"

Here is another writer's story; the narrator, of course, is dealing not with prospective victims but with publishers, agents, etc. Editors, maybe. In a very early foreword to "Market in Aliens" I shared my astonishment at learning that the piece was really about writers and agents; in a more mature foreword years later I speculated that *all* fiction might be a metaphor for the writer's situation since fiction is, after all, perpetrated by writers who one way or the other will discuss what they know best. This way leads to the slaughterhouse, of course; "Backing Up" was a deft hundred-dollar exercise that fits indistinguishably, I suspect, into the pages of *Hitchcock's*, honest work for reasonable wages and leave the matter there.

September 1958

He was lying on Mars, the dead metallic spheres of Deimos/Phobos overhead, moving silver in the darkness, the density of the sands pressing his gear as slowly he worked the inhalator: *a hundred and two, a hundred and three*. Draw the breath, do not panic. He could see Earth hanging forty million miles close to him, had the sensation that he could touch it if he desired, but that possibility passed. The Martians materialized again beside him.

"Have you decided," the vocal one said, the other standing limply, trustfully to one side, "have you made your decision?" In that moment it could have indeed been a dream, all of this making passage through the web of sleep, but he knew that this was not, he was a spacer, a technician, his subconscious was under control, and this illusion of an illusion passed from him. He turned on the sands, faced them.

"Yes," he said. "I've decided. I've done the only thing that I could do." He blinked, trying to fasten the dark line of sight on the hanging Earth and once again it dropped from consciousness. Some deficiency not of perception but of the atmosphere had taken it from him. "Yes," he said again, "I know what I will do. I will stay. I will resist no more."

"That is a wise decision," the Martian said. "You will pursue enlightenment, then? You will embark upon the course of wisdom?"

"You don't understand," he said. "I am not doing this for the sake of enlightenment but only because I know the fate of Earth itself is at stake."

The Martian shrugged delicately. "Same thing," it said. "Your fate and the fate of your homeland are after all intertwined, a single reality, and in that all flesh, all spirit must gather."

Twice in the cafeteria he told himself that now was the time to speak to her, *now*, there would be no better. She was seated alone, drinking coffee, looking through the window toward the dim intersection of trees on the quadrangle, but twice at the last moment he failed. She intimidated him; his own need was frightening. But finally when he heard the bell for the ten-fifty he knew that he would lose her if he did not speak. He put the magazine at which he had been staring, not really reading, into his briefcase and stood. I must talk to her, he thought, or hate myself through all the nights.

He went over to her, looked down. If there were others he had no awareness. "Hello," he said, "hello, how are you?" She looked up at him, her eyes fuller and more luminescent than he had ever remembered, and then she sighed and he could feel her drifting away. He had her and then he did not and a wrench that might have been pain moved him. I will not be able to bear myself if I do not do this, he thought. "Friday," he said, "do you want to go out with me on Friday night?"

Again she stared at him. "We could go to a movie," he said desperately, "or just sit in your sorority house and talk, or go somewhere and have a cup of coffee. Coffee would be all right or even a drink if you want to. I have nothing against drinking. I go drinking by myself sometimes on Friday nights when I'm not going out with anyone which I hope I will be this time."

Her eyes closed. She seemed to be meditating. Her breasts were small but well shaped as far as he could tell from the way the sweater fell across the tight brassiere. You had to take some things on faith, at least at the beginning. "All right," she said, "all right if you want to, but I've got late minutes. So I'd have to be in on early curfew, maybe nine-thirty."

"Oh, that would be fine," he said, "that would be wonderful," and he had a vision; in that vision they were intertwined, a single reality, all flesh, all spirit gathered.

In the vault he learned the first mysteries of origin, the rituals of connection, the dark and terrible heart of history that lay in their tombs, and as the spirits of the dead Martians, one by one, came through on the hidden tapes he was filled not only with awe but with a dark and congealed sense of shame. They had been such a people as he could never understand. He understood nothing. He had come forty million miles in scout for treasure but the treasure was ash; it was as nothing beside the spirits of this dead race.

He would have to learn why they had willed themselves to die (having everything, they had nonetheless willed themselves to die) and only then would he be able to communicate with them. Across the screen of his heart moved centuries of pain and passion, dense and so near to purpose that he could in this trance almost apprehend, but then it broke from him, it broke as he came weeping from slumber to realize that he did not know the language of their desire. Would never. And so could not touch them or convey their strange and terrible wisdom.

On Friday he put his magazines aside and walked trembling to her sorority wondering that such a girl would have him, but after three cups of coffee in the Varsity he began to understand. She talked of her family and the painful reasons why she could not get along with them and in due course he was able to walk with her past the campus and into the park. At the access leading to the gardens she hesitated for a moment as if his intentions had been written on his forehead and then with a smile that seemed to imply far more than even he had known she moved ahead. He followed her. They sat on a bench in the midst of flowers.

She put her head on his shoulder after a time and leaned against him, breathing quietly, looking at the stars. Very easily against the dark sky they began to kiss then, short contact, then longer, and finally he felt her close to him. I do not understand, he thought, and in that moment she began to drift away. She was there and then not and a wrench that might have been pain moved him, but more likely it was the knowledge of how he would miss her that drove him forward. She backed him away. "I think we should go now," she said.

"All right," he said. He had the sense not to push further. It was, after all, only a first date. Across the screen of his heart he felt warmth moving, pain impacted but so near to purpose with her hand in his that he could almost understand what it might be like if they were close, but later when she left him with a cool kiss he came weeping from slumber to realize that he did not know the language of her desire and so could never touch or convey his own strange and terrible wisdom.

"You must tell," they said to him in the dawn, "you must tell them who we are, what we have become, what will happen to us if they continue this plunder." Alive with the memories on the tapes he nodded and said yes, he would try, but later, when he got on the transistors of the ship alone to somehow communicate what had happened, he found that there was no way in which he could proceed.

There was nothing, really, that he could say. What could he say? If he said that two Martians, one speaking, one silent, had come to him in the long night under the mechanical moons and had shown him the treasure of history in their vaults they would think him mad. They would never believe him and would order him home. Worse would come in his place.

So he said nothing. He said only that the program had gone as planned, without difficulties. He had the proper samples. No signs of alien intelligence or artifacts. They said that they would consequently bring in the larger ships.

He shut off the transistors, weeping. When the two Martians came later to ask him what had been said he told them that headquarters had listened and agreed and had canceled plans for the invasion. Give them a few hours of peace. They nodded gently and left him and it was only then that he could permit the stain of implication to burn, burn within him, and the dark blood of his shame moved within the corridors of his being.

The next morning in the Psych class they shared he knew that something was wrong. She would not look at him, even when he passed over a note. When he caught up with her at the door after class he knew that it was done for. "Why?" he said. He had to be direct. He folded his magazine into the textbook and put both into his briefcase. "What happened? What went wrong?"

She did not stop walking. It was his self-revulsion that sped him after her and finally at an empty space near a door she could not get through the crowd and turned and said, "For God's sake, stop being emotional. We just went for coffee, that was all." Coffee, he wanted to say, coffee, that was my *life*, but he did not say it. It was impossible. He had slept with his failure all during the night and had known it this morning; he felt his spirit leaping with shrieks to absorb the defeat which would join others neatly in the dead chambers of self.

"All right," he said, "all right," and turned, he could at least leave her with dignity, he could get out of this feeling no worse ... but then as a tall fraternity man he recognized waved to her the length of the hall and came toward her confidently he knew that he would be spared nothing.

He would be spared nothing. The stain of his implication burned within him and the dark blood of his shame moved within the corridors of his being.

The great fleet landed in due course and wiped the shit out of the planet, anyway.

October 1974: New Jersey

Afterword to "September 1958"

I've investigated this theme many times—perhaps more than any other science fiction writer—but never with more feeling. It comes from the same emotional milieu and stylistic approach as my "Yearbook" and is probably unsalable in the contemporary science fiction markets. And the quarterlies/*New Yorker* circuit would either not understand what I was doing at all or take it for an attack upon science fiction. They can go, in the words of the sainted John Brunner about another facet of the market, to hell.

Into the Breach

Now. They have managed in this enlightened year of 2147 to give you a second chance at life or Life but you must question whether or not it is truly worth it. On several counts. In the first place you must make it to the government man at six in the A.M. only to wait in sterile abscess for hours until it is your turn to sign the statement admitting that you have destroyed your life and see no possibility of change in your present circumstances and have no hope, etc., only to be taken through interviews in which you must make even more explicit your failure, and in the second place, friends and protectors, Timeback itself is very painful.

There is no reason of course why it should not be: any process that forces you psychokinetically (psychochemically? psychoneurologically? I could never figure out any of this stuff) to coexist at all levels of your chronology before recycling is bound to be pretty agonizing, encompassing the little *b* and the Big *D* as well as all that stuff in between, all those humiliating times when they put it to you or vice versa and you got nailed in an alley by the Keepers. Recapitulation may be a kind of jolt and there are those, perhaps, who even enjoy it and I not to sit in judgment of them but it is not *my* kind of jolt you must understand, nor could it ever be.

Nevertheless and heigh-ho, a memoir. All had gone wrong, all wrong with me: broken union, lost contracts, spoiled vectors, and no seeming possibility of conjoinment. Wish I had those forty-seven to live all over again (but they never give you everything to relive, a smaller piece, a *much* smaller piece has to serve) and so I take me down to the Municipal Building where the government man stalks and go in and find a waiting cubicle. Here I wait and wait and await and await, finally going to the desk to say to the government woman (they come in two sexes here), "Okay, I give up now, my spirit is broken, when will they serve me?" and she gives me a look, I give her a look, I return to the cubicle with the thought in me that her distress is as real as my own. God help me, the government man and the government woman have feelings too. They know pain, they suffer. Who would have dreamed it? There is nothing else to say.

Finally, another one, not the same as the reception government woman but one who looks much like her (in this world in which we now live all is reduced to similarity except the failures, who celebrate individuation) comes in to give me the blessed forms and says, "You must state exactly *why* you want Timeback. Remember that. You cannot equivocate on these forms but must tell the truth," and I say, "You mean, they want me to tell exactly how I failed, how I came to know this pain," and she either shrugs or she does not shrug and says, "If this is the interpretation you want to put on it. That is up to you. You will have to deal with your own hostility," and I say, "Up yours, lady," because of course I *do* have hostility and all comes to focus once more. We hate each other. We always must. We seem to find release in that knowledge which refracted another way could be love and she leaves, I imagine her talking to the receptionist about me; I imagine she *is* the receptionist and take the form already imprinted with my name and social data of course and fill in for AGE REQUESTED that of *46* which is a fine age much unlike my dismal present and for REASON state *I no longer feel capable; I cannot come to terms with this for I am in great pain*, which is not eloquent of course but will serve and in the bargain is stolen from the answer which my good friend Harry Barnes provided on his own successful application for Timeback three years past. (I think of Harry often but it is impossible for us to meet; he asked to be taken almost all the way back to the little *b*.) The non-receptionist comes back and I give her the form not without hatred. All at peace now and in control with my vulnerability spread before her, I wait while she looks at it for a while and then says, "This is highly irregular." They all talk that way. "The age part of it."

"How so?"

"You're forty-seven but according to this you want to be forty-six. Just forty-six?"

"That's right."

"Just a year Timeback?"

"Exactly."

"This enormous dislocation merely for a year? I fail to understand this. You will not be permitted to resume your circumstances, you know."

"I know. I know that well. I want to be forty-six again. Forty-six is my fix; I want the kicks so forty-six." A little carefully evolved insanity never hurts; they like to feel that all who ask for Timeback are mentally ill. "Slick," I added.

"I am empowered to ask you just how deeply you have considered the process or your own condition."

"Oh, very deeply."

"One-year passages are relatively uncommon. Particularly past forty. The psyche freezes. You will be relatively the same person but suffer the same environmental dislocation."

"I know all that garbage," I say. I hate them. How I hate them! But of course they live their own Gehenna: most of them, the stories go, are those who failed in second passage and can never try again.

(Psychochemical factors? Psychoneurological? Psychokinesthetic?) Seeing misery braces them a little. "I am quite prepared."

"You will be the same—"

"It all began to stink for me at forty-seven," I said. I say. I said or say; I live in alternating past and present tense; more and more it is difficult (one of the symptoms of my condition) to determine whether I live in lost or ongoing time. What is there to say? "Some break down in puberty, I know, others around twenty-seven with the first palpitations of age, but that was it for me. I was managing very nicely until I got decategorized."

"Surely you are projecting. Decategorization is a spiritual force—"

"I don't want to discuss it," I said to the non-receptionist. In different circumstances I might have considered attempting to master her sexually but that was before my admission of failure. Simple assault, complex lust will not solve my problems, I now understand. I have gone beyond that. "Put it through. It has to go through, that's my right, you cannot reject a request. I have researched this, you see."

"Of course," she says, "of course you have that right, but then again consultation is mandatory," something gentler flowing from her in thick waves (do I sense her own pain, a flick of comprehension?), and made an initial at the bottom of the page, then waved at the door. "It doesn't make any difference to us here, we merely obey the forms. The spirit killeth but the letter giveth life."

She stands aside then, I pass through the door. At the end of the corridor an attendant waits to guide me toward the machines.

In truth and to explicate my feelings very quickly at this point since a memoir must focus not only on event but ethos, I heard somewhere once, I am feeling very good because not only am I on the way into Timeback, I feel I have also humiliated the government woman and established my fundamental power over her. There are whole gradations of feeling which make life richer than it would be if lived without an interior. Very few realize this nowadays, being fixated on the seemingly easier display of Timeback. Not to complain of *them* of course since I have utterly failed. I have utterly failed. Inside the cove the attendant pulls aside a curtain and I go into the machine which is now mine and he disappears as a minor character from my life playing a role so insignificant that I see no need to delineate the attendant further or ever. I hold the handles for balance, think no more. Push the button. Jump. (Since I am going only a short distance I do not need to denude myself, an absolutely disgusting necessity of the longer flights.)

There is what I take to be the usual grinding prelude, then the psychic shifts and unspeakable horrors to which I have already referred and which I do not want to discuss further except to verify that they were terrible, worse than what I had imagined them to be and I have a lively consciousness ... but in any event they pass as everything must one way or the other and I come back to myself.

I come back to myself. I am perfectly composed albeit forty-six and already feeling nonembittered as would be hoped for. I emerge, nod to whoever might be witnessing and then—before my movement can be anticipated or suitably annulled—I run with purpose down the corridor and out of the center.

They do not expect anything like this of course. They have never had anything like this in history, I suspect, so it is really quite easy to make escape. No new circumstances for me, friends, begone with your warnings: I will take things as they were. As they should be.

As I come onto the street, the shouts already fading behind as I accelerate past the swarming crowds of the Assassination Festival which always takes place outside the government building at midafternoon, I wonder if I have made a large mistake. I am afflicted with an instant of that kind of regret so commonly recalled at key moments in memoirs; doubt, indecision ... but then as the excitement seizes me and forty-six once more in the world of 2147, no longer exactly attuned to the century (which was so much of the trouble; now I no longer need feel the burden of the millennium being carried by me), I return briskly to the Project without further ado or adieu as the expression goes and at the Project I perform the necessary.

I perform the necessary in an almost leisurely fashion, knowing now that I have all the time I need (they may catch me but too late), I do it good and deep and hard with that lack of equivocation for which I was so well celebrated before she got to me last year and ruined my life. Destroyed me. She screams but once in the cavern of the century and then burbles brightly silent.

I await the messengers and bustling minor characters of my tragedy quite patiently, enjoying the patterns her blood makes on the lacquer of the floor.

In the chambers before complete defusion (a mock trial for form has preceded this of course; they observe all of the forms at this time in place of understanding how they were built) they want to know exactly what I hoped to accomplish and how I could have committed such an antisocial act but I stand on my rite of passage and make no comment. I have absolutely nothing to say. They cannot force me to speak. So they mumble and sputter and at last they say they are sorry but the penalties must stand of course (the penalties must always stand) and then they hurl me through Timeback again quite regretfully. It would be nice for rounding effect if the government woman could be there at the trial to observe my destiny but this is impossible of course due to other surrounding unpleasant circumstances and nothing more to be said about that.

Going through Timeback all the way is of course quite horrendous (anyone would suspect this of total wipe) but that is really all I will know of it because when I come out this last time it will be Clean Slate, the bassinet and goo-goo to the government man in the sterile place in the solemn cove in the beating heart in the empty place of the great machine in the gigantic city where Timeback plunges and plunges back finally, a Mrs. Murphy of the Spirit, oh my friends the fire.

March 1976: New Jersey

Afterword to "Into the Breach"

"Into the Breach" is, I think, an *Analog* story* but should have appeared in *Fantastic*, to which it was eventually sold. Like so much of my ambitious work it sold to Ultimate Publications and I have long since been forced to conclude that the outlines of my career might have been significantly different had it not been for Ted White and Sol Cohen, who, whatever their sins, kept those two bimonthlies alive for a decade and deserve better from all of us. White's unfailing openness to new work, Cohen's willingness to let his editor edit, will be worth a chapter in that true, unwritten history of science fiction which obsesses me. My own brief, forgettable tenure as editor of the Ultimate magazines (4/68— 10/68) has put me in awe of what Ted White has been able to do. I hope that he, Sol, and the magazines are still around when this appears, but regardless I hope they read it and know my sense of debt.**

---

* "We're on different world-lines!" Ben Bova said. So much for my shrewd sense of the market.

** Well, they may read this and they may know my sense of debt (hesitant on the former, doubtful on the latter) but they're gone, folks: Cohen sold the properties to his partner, Arthur Bernhard, in late 1979 and White was disaffiliated shortly thereafter; he is at this writing the new editor of *Heavy Metal*. *Amazing* and *Fantastic* as quarterlies continue to gasp along but sans my work; "Into the Breach" as paid-up inventory was nonetheless returned to me in 11/79, appears for the first time in this collection, and in so doing enables me to close the books on yet another aspect of the Exciting Malzberg Story: no more work in *A/F. Hab rachmanos*, saith the preacher—11/79.

On "Revelations" (Essay)

Revelations was the first novel I wrote, in April 1971, after moving to the house in northeast New Jersey that we still occupy. The opening chapters had been written in Manhattan late in 1970 and the contract given before the move, but because I had a pretty fair idea of what this book was about and where I wanted it going, I deliberately held off on the writing until after the move. Fearful of a block in new premises, I wanted to have before me something of which I was certain. Writers are that way. After having written approximately thirty novels in Manhattan, the last ten in a stuffy, odorous, clangorous little maid's room with wall-to-wall fumes (described with vindictive accuracy in *Herovit's World*), I was afraid that I would be unable to function in a clean, well-lighted place immersed in trees and anointed by the cries of birds attempting to clear the vapors of Ridgefield Park's refineries from their tiny throats.

Not to worry. *Revelations* was written in three weeks and probably gave me as little trouble as any novel until 1975 when everything was trouble. I went on to write more than three dozen novels amid trees and birds with backdrip, and when a certain narrowing of intensity, reluctance to continue, loss of facility hit in early 1975 they had little to do with the physical environment in which I was writing. So in one sense *Revelations* is close to my heart; whatever its defects, it proved to me when I was still (despite my proficiency and modestly growing reputation) not quite sure of what I was doing that I was able to write from a level where I was precise indeed.

It is a creditable novel. I read it on original publication and again when reissued with as much pleasure as I can bring to my own work. It freed me from the fear of a block at what might have been a bad time (men may feel this way about otherwise ordinary women whom they have met and been loved by at crucial moments of their lives) and it also strikes me, *pace* Pronzini, as being one of my five most successful novels. It is also one of the few novels I have written about which I have something to say beyond the text and it is in that spirit that I would like to turn to the book itself now, moving from circumstance to interior instead of interior to circumstance which is my more usual writing method—one particularly visible in *Revelations* itself.

Revelations was written just about midway between *The Falling Astronauts* (February 1971) and *Beyond Apollo* (July and August 1971) and shares with them not only certain obsessions and characters representative of that time—mad astronauts; sexual dysfunction as representing the necessary loss of energy of the machine age; the single human voice crying in madness or in truth out through the network of the machines as a last hopeless expression of the idiosyncratic heart before the darkness of the great engines—but a certain similarity in development as well. In all three novels the protagonist has been emotionally devastated by the failure of a space voyage; in all three he is trying to understand the failure in a way that will explain him to himself. The differences among the three novels are at least as crucial, however: in *Falling Astronauts* the protagonist breaks down only at the end of the book; in *Beyond Apollo* he is crazy from the opening lines. *Revelations*, that transitional novel, is equivocal. Hurwitz is mad but then again he is not; he is quite beyond the line but he is the only character on the *Revelations* television program who is trying to establish emotional links to what is going on, the only one who has some sense of responsibility left. He is on the way toward coming apart but he is not precisely there.

At one time I thought that *Falling Astronauts* was a first draft of *Beyond Apollo*, that the latter novel was the former, darker and more compressed, with almost all of the events taken out. Pure state of mind, in fact. When I read *Revelations*, however, I understood that it was not quite as simple as that. This novel is a key step on the way from the rather ambitious but narratively clumsy and lumpish *Falling Astronauts* to the fugal interstices of *Beyond Apollo*, which is as technically seamless as *Falling Astronauts* is technically flawed. In *Revelations* I was beginning to transmute the material and come to grips with it by squeezing the pain out, putting the narrative density in, but I was not quite there yet. Oddly, this may be to the effect that *Revelations* is the best of the three novels. *Beyond Apollo*, which had an audience and is certainly the most commercially successful of my science fiction novels, is perhaps too private, too off-putting and cold, whereas *Falling Astronauts* even in its best scenes lives for me as little more than a competent attempt at a competent commercial novel. It is not fully controlled. *Revelations* may get the best of the two books—the event of *Astronauts*, the rhetoric and dreadful pain of *Apollo*—and in fact may be a terminal treatment of the theme. Perhaps it and not *Apollo* tied off the paranoid astronaut, the terrible strictures of NASA, which so obsessed me from the years 1969 to 1971. (It is true that after *Beyond Apollo* I quit. Barring one short story, "Notes Leading Down to the Disaster" in April 1972, I never touched the theme again. I work my obsessions over endlessly but only to a point and when I am done with them at last they are done. I have not written about horse racing for that matter since the summer of 1970 or institutionalized sex since the beginning of 1974. So there is hope for some new material by the eighties, my friends.)

At the time that I first tied into this theme, just about the time of the Borman moon-circling and Bible-thumping mission of Christmas 1968, I was the only science fiction writer there. Later on there were some, but modesty will never prevent me from saying that in America I was first and that I found at the dying end of the sixties and NASA's heavy-duty program one of the last new directions which science fiction, for so long inventive, has seen since about 1965.*

That direction was the theme of space exploration by bureaucracy as dehumanizing *not* because space had to be that way—because we have never understood what we are; because only in space might we find definition of purpose—but because of the bureaucracy. The fact that NASA and the Johnson/Nixon administrations made space exploration merely an extension of the American corporate state through the federal civil service (a distraction from Vietnam, I called it back then) struck me as despicable and hopeless.

It was despicable because it was despicable—we can barely claim the right to our own hearts; we cannot claim the cosmos—but more to the point it was hopeless because at least nine tenths of Americans loathe, fear, and disbelieve their government. If space was to be perceived as the product of government, then it was only a matter of time (how little! how little!) before the population turned away and the government, finding it no longer useful as dazzlement and otherwise crushingly expensive, would similarly abandon it. I saw all this coming as early as July 21, 1969, when Chappaquiddick was already beginning to crowd the front page for attention, and I knew for sure when Apollo 13 was almost lost in transit that I had been right ... because the reaction of many I knew (and I was close to many among them) was that the disaster had been imagined by NASA and produced by the networks and Nixon to reestablish public interest in the program and to make Nixon, that lost cause, look good.

By 1971, Gardner Dozois reported to me, the news of yet another moon landing announced at a science fiction convention, of all places, attracted no interest whatsoever. In the entertainment culture very little holds past twenty-six or at the most thirty-nine weeks. By 1971 there were

* But consolidation is a form of invention and Ed Bryant, Carter Scholz, Gregory Benford, and Alice Sheldon, to name four, seem to have moved the field and marked it significantly in recent years simply by taking Ballard, Silverberg, and me for granted and incorporating our themes in technological science fiction. The edge of the future is reasonable, not despairing.

new concerns in the government—like putting every American slightly to the left of Mike Mansfield in jail within a few years—and by 1973, of course, several very funny things had happened to all of us on the way to the concentration camps.

I saw it all coming ... the collapse of the space program, that is to say, the collapse of NASA and the Cape and the Houston program. Even as I saw it I cried out in rage because it was never space exploration against which I had taken a position, but merely its capture, in contemporary America, by a repressive government operating through an enormous bureaucracy that was dead of feeling, careless of hope. We deserved better than all of this, I thought; we did indeed deserve—would find it necessary—to continue outward and inward toward the other planets. But the government did not care, could not understand. By the middle of the seventies it had taken not only large pieces of our past from us but almost all of our future.

How right I was in seeing that the structure of the program and its administration would drive many astronauts crazy we have only been intimating in recent years ... because I was right about that. I knew from the beginning that my insights were correct, I knew that the men going into those capsules—ostensibly as operators, actually as cargo—would be forced to come to terms with the devastating fact *that they could serve only by being machinery* and that many of them, sensitive and reflective as all of us in our better moments would wish them to be, could not easily deal with this fact. Only years later did we learn of the divorces, the breakdowns, the lurches into mysticism, the scattered children, the pain that the bureaucracy had inflicted upon some of these astronauts, but by then *Revelations* and *Falling Astronauts* and *Beyond Apollo* (and a good many others) were out of print or nearly so, and even if they had not been it would hardly have mattered. *Nothing* the serious writer of fiction does in America today matters at all.**

There is little personal aggrandizement to be found here in trying to tell the truth, which I was although at the time I was writing these books there was a little diversity awaiting the counterrevolution and I was making a fair living on advances. It was all so long ago. So is *Revelations*. For a futuristic (near-future, granted) novel it seems, like so much science fiction, to be curiously and rapidly dated. Sf, of course, was almost never meant to be about the future, it was merely another category of genre, constructing templates for the momentary diversion ... but certain novels like *More Than Human* and *The Demolished Man*

** Six million published words of fiction and a dozen years as a fully committed quote serious unquote writer stand behind this assertion, gents and fair ladies.

could have been written today whereas others like *A Canticle for Leibowitz* or *Fahrenheit 451* or *Revelations* seem to be very much of a time, already framed in retrospect, when read years later. How nearly quaint all these astronauts, moonshots, endorsements, and *angst* seem! I think that I made only one serious error in the three astronaut books; I knew the program was doomed but did not realize it would be so forgotten, so utterly subsumed by Farrah or "Three's Company" or Jarvis. One learns. If I were to rewrite the novel now—I would not—it would be an emotionless book lurching toward absurdity and Monaghan would have felt no pain. His dialogues with Marvin Martin, like his copulation, would have been obiter dicta. For fun, not for shame.

But no rewrites. Please! It is seven years later now, seven and a half, and I cannot (and this is a blessing) get back to the writer I was any more than we can return to the dimly remembered world of the late sixties of which 1971 was the pale, weak, and final extension. Leave it stand. A novel may be an attempt at art (this one was, anyway) but it is also a work of documentary, witness, testimony. It becomes its own small piece of sacred ground. *Revelations* shows where my heart and fragments of the culture intersected in April 1971. Let it make the record; let us not cheapen the concept of rediscovery by feeling that the past must be sanitized in order to work. The founding fathers, a few of them, were racists with bad teeth. Malzberg in 1971 as now had his flaws as a writer, as a person. Let them speak. To recognize what we have been is to move a little toward knowing what we are. To know what we are is to become human. Which I still take to be a value.

Value, value. The night falling around us, choking like a collar, and oh my dear and darkness, absolutely nothing to be done because the light of revelation is gone.

April 1976: New Jersey

Thirty-six Views of His Dead Majesty

ONE: IN THE COCKPIT

In the cockpit, he conceives that he is drowning in salt water. Water like amniotic fluid rises to his nostrils, his ears, and yet he is still breathing easily, some subterranean creature, amphibious, converted. He draws himself slowly from the dream and watches Neptune riding on the high port, seeing the ruined city. In the ruined city he will reclaim his life although his assignment is simpler: fly over, plot the abscissa, plot the terrain, find where the treasure might lie. Deep in the monitoring instruments he hears the beating of his heart, the stir of his groin, the rhythm of his breath. He thinks of a girl he once touched and his eyes are filled with salt.

TWO: THE LOST GIANT

He is dead, statuary now, extended to enormous size and breadth, his hollow eyes closed against the dark stars of Neptune. The city, reclaimed, has built this monument to his memory and this is the time of celebration. From all the parts of the sterile and gleaming city the inhabitants come, every knee to bend and every tongue to pay homage. Children carry toys mimicking the vessel in which he conducted the survey of the ruined city, elders at the base of the statuary repeat the special oaths and pleadings associated with the recollection of his name. Above all of it, stunned and inert he broods, the lights of the city revealing little crevices within the stone, a lost giant high above the city of his name.

THREE: IT IS NOT MERELY FOR TREASURE

"It is not merely for treasure," the warders had said, just prior to the debarkation. "You must understand this, it is not only for what we may take from the darkened city. The treasure is very important; under the rubble are the artifacts which will give us the solution to the machinery which will save our lives. But it is not merely for that, if you think you are sent for the treasure you are wrong."

He had said nothing. He had found that the best way to deal with the warders was with mild gestures, mild silences, attitudes of reciprocation, flattened palms. To confront would be meaningless. Self-confrontation was the basic transaction.

"We are dealing with lives here. We are dealing with the human spirit."

He had thought of the spirit, the human spirit, beating within his chest like a bird, locked like a stone. Do I have a spirit? he had wondered. The warders had been gentle and not lacking a certain compassion but of course they could not answer this question. Their specialty was the detail work.

FOUR: THE WOMAN, ALL WOMEN, CAPTURED

When he was young he had been fascinated by the dead moons of Mars, Deimos and Phobos. In the colony he had learned their history: the Martians, that perished race, had thrown out these two satellites as beacons in their final time and then, one by one, had slowly perished, gone to their rest, embalmed, in the deep center of the planet. Lying in his bed at night, looking at an angle through the thick pane he could barely see them crossing the angle of his vision, suspended. In sleep the sound of their machinery had consumed him and become mingled with other images, those of women. Someday he would have a woman, he would have all women, he would lie with them in the night, the Deimos and Phobos of his scrotum suspended above them. The woman, all women, captured by the light of his presence he would penetrate deeply and to the limit of his being high above the Martians who lay in frieze, their wide eyes open, their limbs glazed, their passion and terror embalmed forever in the silk of darkness.

FIVE: THE KING OF ALL THE WORLD

Settling into orbit above Neptune he had thought, I am the king of this world. Others will come and some will serve my memory, but this is an abandoned planet: no life, no laughter. Underneath the rubble the artifacts but they do not carry breath. Once there was a great civilization upon Neptune, once there was a great civilization upon Mars, but both of them are gone. On Mars I was not the king because we were the successors but here, here I am—

The tick of the instruments burned imprints, moving flickers of light, gathering the vessel of his soul. He had felt the stigmata, the burning of the flesh, strapped to his throne. The king of all the world.

SIX: ON THE TABLE OF THE NIGHT

In gear he had played upon the sands of Mars. Respirator, cables, emergency cutoffs, monitors, devices. Were support to fail, a light would flicker in the Dome and technicians would dispatch emergency aid. On the sands in his game he had conceived that he had met a Martian, the last representative of that great and awesome civilization which had contributed many wonders to say nothing of artificial satellites, signals of anguish, tossed to the heavens in rage. "Pardon me, sir," he said to the Martian, "I am very young, only twelve, and do not know the various mysteries of your civilization but I would be most anxious to learn. According to all I have read you were very sophisticated and spiritually advanced but you ran out of fuel and other necessities and were unable to replace them or leave your planet so you decided instead to die. Why did you do this? How could you be so advanced and unable to save yourselves?"

"Salvation begins at the interior," the Martian said. He was very tall with delicately molded features, an intricacy of pattern that made him appear simultaneously very old and infantile, little puffs of dust coming from the fine, webbed crevices. "The interior begins at the self. Like a bride death came unto us and we received her."

"I do not understand," he said. "I am only twelve. I do not know why you would call death a bride."

"Remember Neptune," the Martian said. "Remember the great ships between the stars, remember the passage and what you have become now and do not ask then why death is a bride."

He had reached to touch the Martian but the figure vanished. This was reasonable, utterly reasonable; one had no business conversing with a dream image from a dead civilization. "Neptune was not a race, Neptune was a part of us," he had pointed out to the emptiness but there was no reply. The monitors of his support equipment sang, confirming that he was alive, safe, preserved on the planet, but he knew that on the table of the night, staring at the dead moons, he would not be sure of this.

SEVEN: FOR UNTO US A CHILD IS BORN

Many years later he lies in a cubicle on Ganymede, holding the girl who will become his wife. Her hair is the color of ash and in embrace he thinks of the ruins of Neptune, the devastated craters through which he will soon poke and pry, looking for the secret of the machines. "I love you," he says, running his fingers through that hair, but he is not sure of this or much else, there has, after all, been so much damage. He grew up in the colony on Mars staring at dead moons: how far can he possibly travel? Nevertheless, "I love you," he says again and begins to work upon her the slow motions of generation. She thrusts back at him, runs her palm against his forehead. "It's all right," she says, "It's all right," and he feels her moisten to his necessity. It is not the first time that they have had sex but never before with this intensity. Then again it may only be the imagined craters of Neptune.

"It's all right," she says, "it's all right," and rising above her he feels enormously aged, at some great remove from himself, then, coming down, taking her breast in his mouth while he manages perilous connection, he sucks deep to her murmurs. Old, half-abandoned, on his way to the ruins of Neptune he thinks, for unto us a child is born, unto us a son is given.

She touches the back of his neck, arches, gives a little cry. She comes. And the government shall be upon his shoulder.

EIGHT: WHAT TOUCHES ONE TOUCHES ALL

Technical matters must be attended to. He is a great technician. He has been selected for his potential, trained far beyond that, refined to a degree where, under stress, he may become an access to the machinery. He brings the craft in at low angle, searching for the spot on the terrain where he is to land. Perihelion. Two centuries ago the city of Neptune was a great, enclosed place no less grand than all the places of Mars, but when the factions of Neptune first turned upon one another and then threatened the stability of the outer colonies support was withdrawn and all three and a half million of them died. It was stupid for those so dependent upon the outside for their life system to have been aggressive but through all the millennia of his desire man has been perverse. Attitude of longitude. Plans and schemes for the reconstruction of the outer colonies were hidden in the city along with many rare and valuable artifacts and now they are necessary.

Plain of Jove. He takes the craft down.

It bounces, comes to rest. He stays in the cockpit, the beams working, looking at the rubble, then removes the microphone. "Downside," he says, "at eighteen forty-six. No, eighteen forty-seven and twelve." What touches one touches all.

"We reclaim Neptune," he says.

NINE: FINE EYES

In statuary his fine eyes seem to be alive, the stone of his frame poised for motion. Children stare at him in awe beyond the protective barrier; elders whisper small confidences concerning legend to them. Children are children; until recently the time of his ceremony had been an occasion for mockery but legend has solidified into circumstance just as his flesh has solidified to stone and there have not been cheers or taunts for a while. Blind eyes seeking the many suns, he looms immobile. The elders are given the orders of the day.

TEN: AND HE SHALL PURIFY

He looks for the first time at the face of his son. The child is behind glass, the reflection misshapen, and for a moment he thinks that the child might be deformed, that some subtle disorder of his genes or his wife's might have been passed in the blood so that his weakness is now made flesh, but then as he shifts to the right to find a different aspect he discovers the warpage: the child is normal. The features are regular, the aspect clear. Within him I shall live again, he thinks, and he shall purify the sons of Levi, that they may offer unto the Lord an offering in righteousness. In righteousness. The child opens a mouth suddenly cavernous and screams but he hears nothing, the sound protected by the glass, the paneling, and as he stares at his son he thinks for a moment that it is only the source of the scream that he witnesses but then this passes away and he is once again within the cockpit of self.

ELEVEN: THE DEAD MARTIAN

In the hall of the custodians, on exhibit, was the preserved body of a Martian. No one knew the role of this Martian or why he alone had been found aboveground, embalmed upon the sands, but one of the first acts had been to preserve the remains in ice. When the colony opened the museum, the Martian had been its founding object. The Martian lay amid some artifacts of its civilizations: mysterious scrolls and implements surrounding the coffin, indecipherable testimony that even scholars had been unable to unlock. Once, illegally, he had touched the corpse and had found to his horror that the flesh was not stone but resilient instead and his finger had sprung back upon him with the speed of corruption, the energy of life.

TWELVE: THE MAIDEN OF THE SEA

Prowling amid Neptune's ruins he kept the warders apprised of his progress. Here what appeared to have been a cache of weapons, there the remains of an administrative center, over by the far edge the clearly preserved outlines of a palace of pleasure. His reports were terse, accurate, to the point, drained of emotion. They had warned him of the possible effects of the ruins upon his spirit; he had been trained against emotional paralysis. He was not paralyzed. He was in control. Born on Earth, raised on Mars, married and trained on Ganymede, he would not be undone by the wreckage of Neptune. Nonetheless, when the hallucination of the Maiden of the Sea came upon him he did not know in quite what manner to report.

There she was, six feet and staring at him, her eyes luminous and concerned, the planes of her face enveloping shadow, standing against one of the walls of the lost city. From the wall pieces and hollows had been excavated, giving the aspect and texture of shattered teeth, and in the interstices she glowed, beckoning. "This is not easy," she said, matter-of-factly, as if they had been communicating all his life, which in certain essential senses they had, "but you had best accept the matter and go on from there. You had best understand that I make as much reality as any of the aspects of your past which piece by piece confront you as you move through the places of Neptune. Resistance will be quite futile since I am, after all, a projection of your internal conflicts and needs."

Internal conflicts and needs. Yes, she is quite correct: on one level he desires her and on another he does not. On one level he accepts the reality of the Maiden of the Sea and on another he is convinced that she is hallucinatory and he is showing signs of breakdown. On one level he knows he should make a complete report, omitting no details of this encounter, and on another he knows that this would be dangerous and futile: they could only regard him as insane. Stunned, paralyzed, he stares at her luminescence while the slow wheel of his life turns.

THIRTEEN: OUT FROM GANYMEDE

Out from Ganymede men have voyaged to the rim of the solar system and have then paused. The nearest of the Centauris is four point two light years distant and is waste anyway; at the very least only a voyage to Sirius, the dog star, would be productive in terms of cost versus possible return. But neither the blueprints nor the material for a faster-than-light drive exist at the present time. Humanity has become decadent and to a certain degree has lost access to its own history. It is known that the colonies on Neptune were the most technologically sophisticated of all the civilizations and that within the blasted city might well lie intact the data and materials for the star drive, and it is this which has made necessary the selection of the most competent astronaut and engineer for the mission of recovery.

Out from Ganymede he has voyaged on his strange and terrible mission of discovery, but exactly as he has approached Neptune, to that degree has his competence—even motivation—been drained. Now he seems to exist in dreams and mist, some strange collision of all the planes and angles of his life so that he cannot separate recollection from necessity, meaning from dreams. He has dwelt in the corridors of sanity all the years of his life but only as he approached Neptune has he come to understand that these corridors are narrow and contained, small grooves in the large and terrible mystery of circumstance which compose only one colorless and limited means of making way through the interstices. This is very disturbing in one way but in another it is very exciting.

It is exciting to discover that he might have been wrong on everything.

Then again, he might have been *right* about everything. There is no foreclosure of options once the barriers between memory and desire have been destroyed.

FOURTEEN: HIS WIFE'S BREAST, THE WARDER'S SOUL

There was no way that he could tell the warders of his sin. By that time it had been too late, all preparations had been made, he had been committed to the voyage. How could he have said to them, "I am not competent, this competence you admire is a fiction. It is based upon a series of avoidances but in the cockpit, in that long, slow transversal, I will become literally undone. Half-mad I will wander the ruined city, sending back little reports of damage." The warders were not without compassion but how could they have understood? His wife's breast, the warder's soul, they were equally departed from him now. There was nothing that could be done.

Of course he had prepared himself diligently for just this circumstance.

FIFTEEN: THE MARTIAN AND THE MAIDEN

The Martian and the maiden discuss his condition. Patiently he listens; he is witness to important decisions that must be made. But only in a while. "We drowned in ice and fire," the Martian says. "We drowned ten million years before he was born, yet lay underneath the spaces of his youth. Our influence must have been great."

"No greater than mine," the maiden says. She arches, assuming a position of some seductiveness. "I am not hallucinatory. I am the last artifact of the ruined city left to activate should it ever be visited and I have my own purposes. I have my reality. I am not trivial."

"He cannot really deal with much more of this," the Martian points out.

"The tensions are acute. We were underground whereas you are visible to him and speaking. I think that you should understand this."

"I think that you should understand that he will do precisely as he wants," the Maiden of the Sea says. "No more than his destiny was controlled by you is it controlled by me. Always, eternally, he will enact what he must be and you and I come after the fact. This is useless."

"But not hallucinatory," the Martian says judiciously. Last survivor of a judicious race, he has been trained to state all aspects. "The artifacts of Neptune make possible this confrontation."

"The artifacts of Neptune also enjamb his memory," the Maiden of the Sea says, "but ultimately what does this have to do with anything?"

Indeed, he thinks. What does it have to do with anything? He should issue a complete report on these events but he knows that he would only disconcert the warders. They are counting on him. The future of the race may well depend upon the outcome of his mission. The warders would not be interested in his private emotional stress.

SIXTEEN: PAST ALL DESIRE

Transfixed in the cockpit he sees himself as another artifact of the restored city, embalmed in Lucite in a corner exhibit. Past all desire he is surveyed by scholars and tourists who make comments on his aspect. To his left is the dead Martian. To his right is the Maiden of the Sea. At the center he holds forever, his position tentative yet firm, untenable yet lasting, despicable but fair.

SEVENTEEN: A WILD AND BESTIAL RACE

The civilization of Neptune, just prior to the invasion of the Ganymede and Titan colonies, asked for the unconditional surrender of the inner governments. It was a desperate and unrealistic demand but this was a wild and bestial race which saw no limitations to its role of conquest. Five hundred thousand souls on Titan were killed in the first incendiaries and after that there was no decision to be made. The civilization of Neptune would have to be destroyed. Enormous armaments were dispatched and from a distance of several million miles the last, great weapons were utilized.

He has dreamed now and then of the destruction of Neptune. He has taken himself to be on the surface of the planet, turned to the sky, the light blooming in the sky, filling all aspects of his vision, and then at last the pain, the vault which moved past shock to take him to the dead center. At one moment he would be underneath the flames, at the next he would have been overtaken and into that dying core he would descend. He is not sure that on some previous plane of his existence he had not been on that planet, had not been annihilated, but mysticism runs counter to his recent training and it has not been until the reclamation itself that many thoughts like these have occupied him along with those of the dead Martian of his childhood.

EIGHTEEN: THE PEOPLE THAT WALKED IN DARKNESS

He prowls the city. Here a building shattered and spent, there an excavation, over in the distance rubble that might have been an arena or a place of worship. He has been given logarithms that will lead him to the place where the artifacts are thought buried but he has no haste; he will find them in time. Perhaps later. Now it is the city itself that fascinates him.

One hundred and seventeen thousand Martian years ago there were Neptunians in all of these places, going about their tasks, the orders of their day. Their leaders were vicious and venal but how much did their venality really have to do with the common lives of citizens? Very little, he suspects. Here in this building councils might have been held, plans made for deadly attack, but in the arena Neptunians were engaged in simpler delights. Children gamboled. Mechanical animals entertained. The people that walked in darkness did not know of the evil counsels of their leaders but in due course and as an outcome of all of them have seen a great light.

The bulbs of his sustenance turn orange. A slight overload here. The Maiden of the Sea has left him temporarily but he is sure that she will return. Everything will return. Everything that has happened will happen always and unto all the spaces of recorded time.

NINETEEN: HE DREAMS THAT HE IS DYING

Now the maintenance lights are red, indicating some critical overload in the respirators. He dreams accordingly that he is dying, that his oxygen has been cut and here on the surface of Neptune at the very age of thirty-eight the censors of time have *x*'ed him. It is very distressing in one way because the survival instinct has been built into him but in another fashion it is almost sensuous to die. He has, after all, been waiting so long. Life is merely a holding action against the anticipated death, he thinks, and begins to strangle in the respirator. A thick bubble clots his throat, he feels light-headed. Slowly he reaches for the emergency switch that will bring oxygen from a different source. Panic will do him no good. His hand, damp, slides past the lever and he feels consciousness leave him in strips but he will not give into this. Fundamentally he is a technician. He brings his hand back to the switch, unfurls it.

Bright, his lungs fill with air and his staring eyes see renewed the surfaces of Neptune.

TWENTY: IN THE COLONY

He has never returned to Earth. Youth on Mars has destroyed his tolerance for higher gravity, impure atmosphere, the constant, small metabolic adjustments that would enable him to function at one point six. In the colony he had imagined what it would be like as an adult to return to the planet but he had not been far into adolescence when he realized that it was impossible and that if he were ever to leave Mars it would have to be a voyage outward. As he would come closer to the sun, he came to understand, so he would self-destruct. Ganymede had been his decision upon the conclusion of training. He could not imagine a lifetime upon Mars. Ganymede had been as far and wild to him, as great a frontier of possibilities, as much later Neptune had become.

Still, perhaps he should have considered the possibility of returning to Earth. The technological means were there to adjust gradually through simulation. He might have been happier, everything might have been different. Earth was decadence, but this had never disturbed him.

His love of decadence was the reason, perhaps, for his selection to find the artifacts.

TWENTY-ONE: ALONE AT LAST, HIS WIFE

He has not seen his wife or son for some time, nor has he missed them. Alone at last, his wife, he conceives, might have found her identity, an identity which he had long submerged. "You must take your risks; I will take mine," she had said to him, explaining why she would return to Mars rather than remain on Ganymede through the training and the mission. "It cannot go on this way." He had agreed, solemnly. It could not go on this way. They had not been good for each other, the child, wrinkled and shrieking, had seemed to make visible the damages of their connection. "I want to live," she had said, "I am a person also, you have to understand this," and he had agreed with that too. She was a person also.

She was a person and he was a person and somehow it had not quite worked out but that did not have to do so much with the tensions between them as with the fact that they had met, that they had lain on Mars. The first time had been in gear on the sands over the place where he imagined the dead Martian to be buried, and the fact that he had needed the sustaining presence of his old confidant to make the motions of love might have indicated that their relationship, from the start, had been corrupt.

Alone at last, his wife has, perhaps, worked this out and can view him with some compassion. And then again, perhaps, she has not.

TWENTY-TWO: AND WRITE THEM UPON THE DOOR POSTS OF THINE HOUSE

Transfigured he faces Pluto as the Deacons begin the brief, formal ceremony of reaffirmation. There are fewer Elders each time; they too are mortal and are not being replaced. Neptune has become at this time a sophisticated and postmystical culture but there are still more than enough to carry the tradition through. For frontlets between thine eyes. And write them upon the door posts of thine house. That ye may remember. Incense is scattered upon the fabricate altar at his feet and from the machinery comes the simulated cry of the Maiden of the Sea as she pressed upon herself, upon him, offering her perilous and fruitful gifts. And do all my commandments and be holy unto me.

TWENTY-THREE: AND SHAME AND LOSS AND GRIEF

Poised before the enclosure in which, according to the detailed charts, the artifacts lie, he is interrupted in his meditations by the dead Martian who has made special efforts to follow him here, leaving the maiden. "You do not want to do this," the dead Martian says. "You do not want to make recovery of the plans. Humanity will be restored. The great starships will come again. The fabric of the cultures will reunite. Voyage will make possible the institutions. And nothing will come of it."

"That is not for me to say," he says. "I cannot make that judgment."

"We made that judgment. It was our choice twenty-three million years ago not to seek the stars but to turn inward upon ourselves under the sands and die. Nothing will come of all of this but the old trappings: pain and lust, murder and doom. The shriveling of the heart and shame and loss and grief. There will be no outcome other than finally the smudged and blackened memories of prayer. Stand aside. Turn. Return to the craft and say that you were unable to locate the artifacts. Say that they were there but ruined. Do not visit upon your kin what we would not to ours. Let there be an early end. Truncation is all," the Martian says wisely. "Believe me, throughout eternity there is this one truth." He points a shriveled limb at the stars. "Leave the mystery," he says. "Die in mystery, not spoilage."

He thinks of what the dead Martian has said to him for a long time but then he pushes against the place where the wall splits and enters. He goes amid the artifacts, sifts through them for the necessary.

It is, after all, not his decision to make. He is relieved of that responsibility. No one can accuse him. He is merely the instrument of design.

TWENTY-FOUR: IN THE HEART OF ALL DESIGN

Later he lies with the Maiden of the Sea, locked to her condition at the bottom of the reservoir that one by one has disgorged all of the blueprints which he has coldly signaled to the warders. In the heart of all design, wedged tightly, he feels himself gathering. Her palms run across his forehead. He is going to climax, he knows. He is going to climax. It will be the first such time for him that he will do so unaided by the image of the dead Martian.

TWENTY-FIVE: THE SONS OF LEVI

Some of the inhabitants of the Neptune colony are guilty and some of them are not but in the great and perishing light that stretches their heaven from Pluto to the arc of Titan all of them die together. Fate and screams intermingle in that vast explosion of consequence. Brooding in his dream, he watches them perish, thinking that when he too joins the saving darkness he will not have to separate the good from the bad ever again.

All righteous, the sons of Levi.

TWENTY-SIX: IN THE TOWER OF THE WARDERS

In the tower of the warders he tries to explain his position. He has fulfilled all of the schemes of their training; nonetheless he feels desolate. He is not convinced that the retrieval of the artifacts will change the course of humanity, nor, for that matter, his own life. Because he is unsure of the sanity of this view he tries to state it mildly, holding in the true despair that comes from his ambivalence. "I am not sure that anything, will come of this," he says, "but the smudged and blackened memories and the shriveling of the heart. Shame and loss and grief." He notes his tight respiration, the even and deadly flow of the blood. He can say all of these things, yet remain in control. He has always been controlled, even his disintegration, he senses, will be perfectly architectured. "Consider what we do here," he says, "for this is not a contemptible consideration. This is not a contemptible request."

They look at him mildly. It is a decadent, a tolerant age, the warders are not impressed by their role. "We need the artifacts," they say, "this must be the controlling consideration. If you feel un able—"

"I do not know what I feel," he says. This is true. This is the basic statement of his being. He does not know what he feels. He does not know what they feel. In the tower of the warders he comes to understand that motive and circumstance need not be intertwined but exploded, moving at different angles in the empty spaces between the stars, disengaged forever.

TWENTY-SEVEN: FOR ALL REDEMPTION GIVE THANKS

He completes the sexual act with the Maiden of the Sea. It is not all that he might have expected but perhaps better than anything he deserves. Apologetic upon climax, apologetic upon withdrawal, he now stands, brushing little bits of Neptune from his knee. Only his genitalia, in tentative erection, have reached the dangerous atmosphere of the planet, but he will take what measures he can to protect against contamination. "Thank you," he says. He has been trained to be polite. All of his training from the outset has been contrived toward these courtesies. His years on Mars have similarly acquainted him with the need to maintain a mild aspect. "For all redemption give thanks, for all possibilities beyond the absolute know praise." He is thinking of the blueprints which at this very moment are being examined by the warders. "I appreciate this very much," he says.

She does not respond, being of restrained temperament. Then again, she might be imaginary, exactly as has been his qualified success. Her eyes dark, luminous confront him and in those eyes staring he sees the restored cities of Neptune as they will someday be at that time just before the great engines were started that would take cargo beyond the Centauris and toward the heart of Sirius. The dog star. The next outpost of all the known and unknown universe.

TWENTY-EIGHT: TIME IS CIRCUMSTANCE

"Time is circumstance," his old friend, the dead Martian, points out. "It is not linear but a function of event. Return to the cockpit. Return to Ganymede. Enact strict chronology which as we now know is only a symptom of psychosis. Without this, however, you would be even madder.

Accept your condition. Accept all conditions. One by one we returned to the deep sands to die. Your death will not be so easy, but then who is to say that it was not the right choice? Such judgments are beyond me. They are beyond you as well."

The dead Martian's eyes glint fire; he seems profoundly excited. "From such choices you must enact your life. It is sadness but all is sadness. Sadness is not of itself an unhappy condition."

He stumbles over the ruined terrain, looking for the ship. The Martian is quite right, of course. Going back is a madness but if he does not hold on to the progression of visible event he will have had nothing.

Behind, he hears the walls of the city collapse further upon one another. He knows—or he does not know—that he will never see the Maiden of the Sea again. That he will. That he will and will not. Always.

TWENTY-NINE: POISED FOR FLIGHT

Poised for flight, the engines stammering, he is overcome by a fit of weeping. This too will pass, he thinks, this too will pass, but lets the terrible sounds and sobs overtake. There is no shame in it, he thinks. The craft shakes to his cries.

THIRTY: AND DARKNESS MY BRIDE

Lying with his wife on Ganymede, he thinks of the voyage to come. This is their last time together. When the lights come on again she will have returned to Mars. Why prowl the ruined city, he thinks, when comfort lies beside me? His son is already on Mars, all arrangements have been made. "I want you," he says in the darkness, "I want you very much," but she is already asleep. In the destiny of her rest she moans at the sound of his voice, turns from him. He rolls upon his back, discarding the sheets, and clutches himself.

And darkness my bride, he thinks and slowly, as ever, does the necessary.

THIRTY-ONE: WHEN ALL AT LAST IS DONE

The restoration complete, the city rebuilt, the men of Neptune prepare for their race to the stars. Ships are tugged into position, engines moved through the range of strength to test stress. When all at last is done the voyagers will depart but arrangements can be made.

Speeches are given. Testimonies are offered. Ceremonies for the preservation of the voyagers are enacted. The glistening dome of the city is opened so that the ships may pass.

Dead in the cockpit of circumstance he broods over these activities. Scraps of stone adorn his brow. The children are gone although at another cycle and as before they will come to offer prayer.

THIRTY-TWO: YOUR DESTINY IS NOT ORDINARY

"Your destiny is not ordinary," the dead Martian whispers on the sands. "You will do unusual things, you will face massive circumstance. In the end it all might have been for naught but this is not for us to say; there is a spirit through all condition which unifies. You will know pain. You will know laughter. You will know all in between because you have special purchase upon the worlds. "Meanwhile," the Martian offers, "do not ask more of your life than life is prepared to offer."

He runs the sands through the web of his supporting gear, listening. The dead Martian has told him many things through their encounters but never so intensely and in such tones of richness. He knows that he is suited for special things, he knows he will be tested for greatness. He knows that dead he will be statuary.

THIRTY-THREE: AND FISH AND FOWL

The warders on Ganymede offer him congratulations. He has completed his mission. The blueprints are perfect. The transmitted sketches of the artifacts are exact. The lost materials have been recovered. They offer him honor and riches and power and glory. "Consume everything off the face of the earth," they say, "and man and beast and fish and fowl, and still your memory will live. You have given us back the stars. You may have for the rest of your life everything that you want. You have only to make the request and it will be done. You can be the king of the whole world if you will."

He sits before them mildly. He is not pleased but he is not displeased. He is not hopeful but he is not hopeless. He is somewhere in the middle. "Speak to us," they say, "tell us what you want and within all our powers it will be given."

I want to be taken out of time, he thinks, but how could they understand? "I want," he says, "I want the Maiden of the Sea."

"That is impossible," they say, "you cannot possess that which is merely envisioned." They are reasonable. They are reasonable people; this is the source of their power. "You'd better think of something practical," they add. "Technologically relevant, technologically created."

"You are liars," he replies. A feeling of betrayal comes over him and soon enough, he knows, he will begin to sulk.

THIRTY-FOUR: THIS DARK AND MEGALOMANIAC VISION

He dreams that the inhabitants of Neptune have offered him the secret, the secret which will control all existence, but when he awakens from this dark and rather megalomaniacal vision he finds that all is, essentially, as it was. It is very difficult, even for a spaceman, to get a grip on matters.

THIRTY-FIVE: THE POINT COMES CLEAR

He can, however, do as the inhabitants did, he can reconstruct. In reconstruction lies truth, he posits. Or lies. It is all the same, he now understands.

THIRTY-SIX: IN THE COCKPIT

In the cockpit, he conceives that he is drowning in salt water. Water like amniotic fluid rises to his nostrils, his ears, and yet he is still breathing.

January 1978: New Jersey

Afterword to "Thirty-six Views of His Dead Majesty"

Written in 1/78, "Thirty-six Views of His Dead Majesty" proved (for reasons that the story itself makes either clear or Very Clear) hideously difficult to place and finally ended up in Roy Torgeson's original anthology by the skin of its teeth or edge of its 8½ X 11, choose your metaphor. ("This is very strange stuff, Barry.") Grateful as always to have it placed. (Why be ungrateful?) It is not easy to place material like this in science fiction but the consolation is obvious; it would be impossible to place it in a paying market elsewhere and even unto this moment the genre has shown a willingness to accommodate work (at least from one of its minor Brand Names) that no other publishing category, least of all Quality Lit., can today. The meaning of this is obvious. Remorse doth intermingle richly with anger in this best of all impossibilities; science fiction, ladies and gents, is about all we've got left and we'd better take care of it.*

---

*I think it's too late—11/79.

The Trials of Sigmund

Freud's third patient of the morning is a political activist named Schicklgruber. The ex-house painter has been referred by a general practitioner; the complaint is impotence but Freud quickly perceives that the symptom is merely cover for deep inner rage and that Schicklgruber is actually in need of extended therapy which he can neither afford nor understand. The small man has an ordinary mind and little insight. "I am afraid," Freud says, relighting his cigar, "that there is little I can do for you. A little wine before encounters might not hurt." He flicks out the match, puts it into an ashtray, rolls the cigar between his sensitive teeth, noting tiny slivers of pain in the lower right quadrant. Referred, no doubt; the nascent cancer is blooming. Well, there is nothing to be done about that.

"You mean you will not treat me," Schicklgruber says bitterly. He is a bitter man. His mustache twitches. "You have been recommended."

"Not at this time," Freud says. "My casebook is so full, my researches so demanding, and there is the travel—"

"I won't stand for this," Schicklgruber says and yet, ironically, he does just that, twitching in front of Freud. "You deny me help like all the rest of them. I tell you I have plans—"

"We all have plans," Freud says gently, "in this world we consider alternatives right up to the end. It is a necessary delusion." He exhales smoke, spits out bitter tobacco, feeling vibrations beneath his temple. Disgustedly he puts out the cigar. Why must this happen to him? "The consultation is free," he says. "I will not charge for this advice."

"You will pay a terribly penalty," Schicklgruber says unconvincingly and turns, leaves the room. Freud hears him swearing in the corridor and then the outer door is closed roughly. Freud thinks of waste, pain, human folly. Schicklgruber will come to nothing and forty years from now, still impotent, will continue to project his insufficiency on the social condition. Self-delusion is rampant. The times foster self-delusion as an arboretum does plants, Freud thinks wryly and considers his appointment book. His next patient, in Vienna on a quick journalistic tour, is Colonel Robert McCormick, editor in chief and publisher of the Chicago *Tribune*. Freud sighs again and reinserts his cigar. He will die of cancer of the jaw more than a decade from now but what can be done about it? Life, as his own studies have proven, is preordained. At least he will leave a legacy of research.

Freud takes a further moment between patients to rest and freshen himself. He is a contemplative and feeling man; patients tend to overlap in his mind if he does not take the last ten minutes of the hour to restructure. Richard Strauss has reactive depression. Alban Berg, sorrowfully trapped in a terrible marriage, cannot escape his dominant wife to marry the wife of a colleague with whom he is having a tragic affair. William Randolph Hearst has delusions of persecution. Alice B. Toklas is in love with her employer, a stern novelist, but dreads her own lesbian impulses. Warren Gamaliel Harding feels manipulated. And so on and on. Freud is famous. He has founded a new school of mental science. From all over the world the well-known and the obscure come to him seeking help and he can give them so little. Most of them, like Schicklgruber, must be sent on their way at once. Others, like Gertrude Stein's housekeeper, submit to a long and torturous analysis but remain in anguish. A few in negative transference have been exceedingly unpleasant. It is all so painful. Still, one must continue. Freud's researches and profound ruminations on the human condition have given him a tragic sense.

He goes to the door and ushers in Robert McCormick, a florid man in sombrero with large boutonniere. Freud has no secretary. McCormick is known for his bizarre garb and posturing. A secretary would only be distancing and in addition might read his precious, private files. McCormick's self-delusion is unlike Schicklgruber's, Freud senses, it is *apparatchik*. If truth were marketable, McCormick would change his policies and wear simpler garb.

Freud seats himself behind his desk and strokes his beard, waiting for McCormick to speak. More and more his thought patterns break like this; his consciousness flits from topic to topic. Anxiety neurosis to be sure, moderately well compensated, but there is the problem that he might … well, Freud worries about insanity. He knows that his estranged colleague Jung thinks him mad and has been spreading scurrilous allegations, also Alfred Adler. *He* knows that he is not mad but nonetheless—

McCormick says, "I am not here for treatment, Doctor. I know of your wonderful work and have come to make you an offer, a fine offer. I would like you to write an advice column exclusively for our newspaper in which you can give readers practical answers to their problems. Five times a week you can do this and we offer a year's contract. With our syndicate working on this you might double your income immediately … we have quite a large number of newspapers using our columnists, you know, even in your peculiar country."

"I'm sorry," Freud says. "I'm not interested."

"Think of it, Dr. Freed," McCormick says earnestly, "a platform in

America! You are well thought of among foreigners and in the ivory towers, but the man in the street barely knows you. This would make you famous!"

"My name is *Freud*. No, your offer is kind but to accept it would be unprofessional. I am a researcher, a scholar, a doctor. Not an advice columnist."

"Think of the good you might do. You could treat many instead of selected lunatics."

"I'm sorry," Freud says. "You do not understand. Neurosis is not lunacy. Neurosis is a poetic malfunction. Insanity is a language of the heart." He stands to terminate the interview. "I will not."

"You're just another intellectual," McCormick says nastily. "Thinking you're so goddamned superior to those of us who do the real work. Well, the hell with you."

Freud considers the rosy hue, the cast eye, the bigotry. Rank projection, of course, and self-hatred but he has no time for that and McCormick, he perceives, is as essentially untreatable as Schicklgruber. "Please leave," he says.

"I bought a whole hour."

"You bought nothing," Freud says. "I do not wish to speak with you. The consultation is free." His tragic sense, awakened, scuttles like a small animal within his heart. Really, he has made too many sacrifices, he thinks. Pain, torment, misdirection, abuse, martyrdom, and for what? To be a gossip columnist, a gossip columnist for Robert McCormick? "You're like all the rest of them," he says, thinking, oddly, of Carl and Alfred. "Get out."

"Not so whatsoever," Colonel McCormick says oddly. He stands, removes an ancient pistol from his clothing, and aims it shakily. To his horror Freud senses that he is about to be killed. Richard Strauss will continue to shit in fever and Alban Berg will never confront his latent homosexuality. His researches will languish; Jung will pirate all of his insights, obliterate his reputation....

"Please," he says, raising a hand. "I'm going to die anyway of a cancer of the jaw. I've been through all the materials. Don't interfere with the preordained—"

"There is nothing preordained," McCormick says. He shoots Freud in the right eye. Freud collapses. Dying, he notices the rose on McCormick's boutonniere suddenly unfurl, spout water. It is a splendid image and he wonders if it is merely a version of poetic truth or a function of McCormick's own plan.

"I don't have to take this kind of thing," he hears McCormick say. "Not from a lousy shrink." Footsteps recede. Freud supposes that the publisher will now make an offer to Jung. Well, it serves Carl right, he thinks. He has always had, whatever his pretensions, a cheap populist mentality. He will take the offer and it will destroy his academic legitimacy.

May 1979: New Jersey

Afterword to "The Trials of Sigmund"

The late Marianne Moore (Brooklyn Dodger fan and coiner of the name "Utopian Turtletop" for what Ford Motor Company, disregarding her paid advice, stupidly decided instead to call "Edsel") described poetry as the rendering of real toads in imaginary gardens; I think that if she had been familiar with science fiction—Ms. Moore would, I think, have *loved* conventions—she would have applied the same definition to our field. On another level one can simply ask: "What hath Doctorow wrought?" and the answer is as it always is with innovative work, a *hell* of a lot of *obiter dicta* of which I hope "The Trials of Sigmund" is not only a spirited but a useful example, tracking the real toads deeper into that garden than even the toads themselves might have conceived.

On this one, however, my friends, defenders, and editors in science fiction finally balked. There are limits, the ladies and gents seemed to point out, and then there are *limits*. Enough already.

I slide it unostentatiously into the back of the (hardcover) book, however, and grant it the flickering permanence to be found in the basements of libraries, so the hell with it. I would like to feel that it will be read, someday, by a Marianne Moore fan if not (I am not, alas, a true mystic) the redoubtable Ms. Moore herself.

The Man Who Loved the Midnight Lady

So I report for the next sequence and am diverted to the IRT uptown Seventh Avenue from New Lots Avenue to 241st Street White Plains Road. On the midnight run there are only six of us in the second car, two of whom are sleeping. Drunks. The other three comprise two old men with dreaming expressions and a woman with several shopping bags. The train lurches its way out of 72nd and then stalls in the tunnel approaching 79th. The fans shut down along with the bulbs; small emergency lights flick. We sit there for ten to fifteen minutes before the first gentle wisps of smoke. "My God," says the woman with the shopping bags, "there's a fire in the tunnel. We'll all incinerate."

"Not to worry, madam," I say, "it's probably only smoke from debris which has touched the third rail." Historicity has its uses; a fixed past, when relived, can at least quell panic. "We'll be on our way in just a little while, I'm sure."

"We'll never be on our way," she says. She reaches down, clutches two of her bags. "We'd better make a run for it while we still have time. We can't afford to waste a moment."

The two old men stare at her. The sleeping drunks say nothing, of course. Subway drunks are notably quiescent. "My jewels, my life," the woman says. "Also my helpless grandchildren. My chest is tight, I can't breathe. Oh, my God, let's get out of here."

"Everything will be well, madam," I say with superb calm and at that moment the train lurches forward, upsetting the bags still on the floor. Little rags and pieces of paper spill from one of them. The woman stares at it fixedly. The train gathers speed. "As you see," I say, "you had nothing to worry about at all."

"You are crazy," she says, "you are a crazy person," and I think of something to say that will somehow give her as much insult as she has given me but the train is moving furiously past 86th Street now, the stanchions like pinwheels through the dirty windows, and the old men are looking at me intensely and the drunks are twitching in their places and the procedural technicians are notorious for this kind of thing anyway—out of some perversity they squeeze in extraneous matter to taunt subjects—and it is not worth worrying about. We stagger into 96th Street. The woman begins to sing, atonally.

So I come through that unscathed and report for the next reconstruction and go under the receptors and find myself on the

Orient Express or at least it reminds me of an Orient Express for a midnight border crossing. The car is packed with sinister people of all types to say nothing of children who cling to uninterested mothers. Almost everybody looks like a smuggler. I try to look inconspicuous but it is very difficult considering the very simplicity of my costume and manner in a situation where everyone looks exotic. A man with large mustaches across the aisle motions to me, then leans forward and says, "Who are you?"

"I am just a traveler," I say.

"You do not look like a traveler," he says with overtones of menace, "you look like the police."

I look around the car, seeking some sympathy or assistance, but instead find that in the sudden quiet many people are staring at me with dangerous expressions. "That is ridiculous," I say. "I am not the police."

"And if you were, would you admit this? We know how to deal with police on the Orient Express," the man says. He reaches inside his turban and extracts a large knife clotted with stray wisps of hair. "We have our own justice here, rude justice, but it suits all of our purposes." He puts the knife against my forehead and I feel the thin sensation of skin parting. "All of our purposes," he repeats.

It occurs to me that I am being threatened with death. There are rumors that this has happened in the reconstructive process, there are even hints that on occasion death has ensued, hysteric overload being the phrase, but I attempt to hold onto my superb calm. I am being closely observed at all times and it is all part of the examination process. "Do not be ridiculous," I repeat, "there are a hundred witnesses here and I am innocent."

"All of them are my friends," the man with mustaches says, "and your manner is that of the distinctly guilty. Rude interpositions make for extravagant deals," he says and brings the knife slowly down my forehead. Something falls into my eyes that is not sweat. The car is silent and all, particularly the children, lean forward with interested expressions.

I move away from the knife and try to parry it with certain movements I learned in an early orientation center but the edges of my calm have already become ragged and I feel I am on the verge of committing a dangerous *faux pas* which will abort my training or recycle me to a much earlier stage which would be equally disastrous but it is at that instant that the train comes to a screaming halt and with shouts and cries several dozen uniformed men push their way into the already overburdened car, waving dangerous armaments. "We are the Kiev police," one of them cries, "and we have information that there is a smuggler on this train. Everybody will present themselves at once and divest themselves of all of their outer garments."

My assailant moves quickly from me and disappears behind a seat, no small accomplishment considering the degree to which the car is now occupied. I feel an arm around my shoulders and look up into kindly gray features underneath a helmet. "I am the Chief Inspector," the features say, "and I want to thank you for all of your help in preparing for our surprise entrance. Thanks to your courageous efforts, we have already deduced the identity of the smuggler."

I am unable to do anything but nod although pleasure must show clearly on my own kindly features. "If it were not for the efforts of those such as you," the Chief Inspector says, "this dangerous passage would be unchecked and within less than a generation all of the world would be in the snare of that delusory and terrible drug opium."

I nod in acceptance of his praise. My assailant, surrounded by police, is taken off struggling. The Chief Inspector reaches into his pockets and hands me a special award of merit suitable for framing and a badge granting me honorary status with the Kiev police. Nonetheless, even after his presentation and exit, the train does not move and I come to understand that the sudden halt has led to a locking of the brake mechanism which is very common among trains of such ancient vintage as exist on the Orient Express.

So I am brought before the committee which says that I am doing fairly well, nothing extraordinary, *comme ci, comme ça*, as the old expression goes, but that my command of the lexicon of trains is still somewhat shaky. "What is a Pullman?" they ask. "What is a siding? What is a rear compartment, a caboose, a trip signal, a stoking device?" Some of their questions I answer correctly, others I answer incorrectly, a few I cannot answer at all. They remind me that the practicum is necessarily 80 percent of the examinations and that I am right to concentrate upon a good performance but they remind me also that a good performance on the verbal section can often be the difference between failure and passing and I would be well advised to pay some attention to the texts during interim periods. All in all, though, they are not condemnatory and cite my performance under pressure in the Orient Express as being a distinguished example which they will keep on the belts as part of their training classes. "It is an exotic and arcane area of study which you have selected," they conclude, "and certainly singles you out as unusual, but you must understand that the rarity of your goal is not sufficient basis for a passing mark. We certainly do need a new scholar on passenger trains in this section but he must conform to the same rigorous standards as anyone aspiring to be a flotation pilot."

"I understand that," I say. "I'm genuinely interested in the subject or I never would have applied for the training. I have no objection to conforming to a high standard of knowledge; I wish to know it for my own sake." This is a standard reply, of course. They like to hear this kind of thing. In truth I am no more interested in trains than any of my peers but did indeed select them since it is such an unusual area that I felt it would be easy to qualify and obtain permanent status in the research division. Despite their warnings I still believe this to be the case. "I want to know every aspect possible," I conclude.

"Of course," they say, "and by the way there is no such thing as hysteric, suggestion-induced death during training; this is an institutional rumor which we have never been able to quash but it is worthless," and then they send me from there although hardly reassured because it is the material that they take the trouble to deny that more often than not turns out to be the truth.

So I am on the Yankee Clipper, coach car, heading toward Boston and after a while, soothed but bored by the gliding of forest shapes outside, decide to go to the club car for a drink. A porter tells me that all of the tables are occupied but if I desire I may join a young lady in the rear in an empty chair. I say that I will do this and find that she is blond, very young, and very beautiful, with pained eyes, having a soft drink and staring through the windows wistfully. We fall into conversation as usually happens in club cars at night and in the space of less than half an hour fall deeply and truly in love in the manner of men and women who meet on trains. I ask her if she will join me at our mutual destination but her eyes become filmed and she says that she has a dark and terrible secret which forever precludes consummation of our relationship. I do not press her for further details but merely sit there and hold her hand, feeling the warm pressure of her spirit pass into mine. After a time she suggests that we stand on the observation car, which we do, and we stand there embracing and kissing for a long time as the train bears us due east from Albany to the closed spaces of old Boston. "If only it could be," she says, "if only it could be," and leans against me, I feel her body shaking, and then at last the secret comes out; she is not alive, she is merely a ghost, the ghost of a beautiful young woman who threw herself to death from a train forty years ago because of an unhappy romance and is now doomed through eternity to ride the Yankee Clipper and fall into hopeless relationships with young men like myself whose presence can only hurt her over and again. This is her purgatory for the crime of suicide. She is the midnight lady; the specter of passage. Hearing her story quite unmans me, which is to be expected under the circumstances, and I find her suddenly cold within my grasp, then insubstantial, and soon she has faded away. I find myself alone on the observation car. Slowly I return to the club car, which is now almost empty, find a deserted table, and slowly, bleakly, drink myself toward unconsciousness thinking of the midnight lady, as all unconscious of its terrible legacy, the steel of the coffin of my hopes carries me toward Henry James's Boston.

So I am now a public official and hold between my hands the golden spike which will splice one section of rail to another section of rail meaning that trains will now run through all of the wild and beautiful continent. A laborer hands me a hammer; I take it clumsily, the spike almost falling in the grasp of one hand. I steady it, clumsily hit it off-center once to the sound of cheering. The workman takes both spike and hammer from me and I mount a podium and make a short speech.

"Now the continent is joined," I say, "we have the rail link that makes all of us one people, one commerce. The trains will run through the heart of the wilderness and through the canyons of the cities, the blood passage that will keep us vital, and this country will last as long as the trains; only when the last train has gone to the last siding will this country perish." Well, you know political rhetoric of that period. There is more cheering although I can barely hear it; it must be the sound of the hammer blow still filling my ears. "The trains are our lives," I conclude and step down. The workman assists me, wavering, from the podium and in the distance I can hear a horn. The great train: the great train is coming. I lean forward, trying to catch the first vision of its gaunt bulk at the far edge of the tablelands.

So they say that I have done satisfactorily on the practicum, nothing remarkable, but a good command of all the materials if a slight lack of originality, an ease with the material that shows the results of study and application. They are mildly congratulatory. They proceed with the verbal and I tell them what a diesel is and a smokestack and a steel-driving man and old ninety-eight and they ask me to put my helmet and sensors away and leave the room and when I return they tell me that I have been commissioned and then rise, one by one, to solemnly shake my hand and welcome me to the ranks of the Institute. Trained for this by my experiences as a politician to say nothing of the dangers of the Orient Express, I accept their congratulations with humility, with the mildest and least self-important of demeanors. At length they confer upon me a certificate and an oath and then I am escorted from the room and taken to my larger quarters which will be my residence as long as I remain part of the Institute. Quarters are six by eleven and contain a bed, a wooden table, a mirror, and a basin. I am overwhelmed with these amenities and understand for the first time how truly worthwhile all of my endeavors have been and what it will mean to me to be part of the Institute, if only in a forgotten and virtually useless area of history.

So I take myself to the board the next day and am given my second assignment and in due course find myself on the Calais Coach, twirling my mustaches and sipping at a small carafe of wine while thinking about the problems of mushroom cultivation which await me in the south of Belgium, that home to which in retirement I am now returning. "We have a great problem, monsieur," someone says to me and I look up to see an excited steward, "we have deduced your identity and need the assistance of the great and famous Monsieur. One of the passengers in the next car has been murdered in his sleep; there are twelve fellow passengers but no witnesses and it can only be one of them but all of them deny it. We must solve this mystery before we reach the south of Belgium or it will become a serious police matter of much disgrace to the company."

"Yes, yes," I say and move my round little bulk from the seat, hands behind me for purchase, then adjust my mustaches with a flourish and slowly follow the steward into the Calais Coach, catching for just a moment between cars the enormous sense of speed, heat, light, power, and distance from which the trains have so briefly shielded me before I come into the insulated spaces within to face, not for the first time in my illustrious career, the problem of death in the small and perished spaces. And the midnight lady.

And the midnight lady.

September 1976: New Jersey

IN THE
STONE HOUSE

By Barry N. Malzberg

For Joyce, Stephanie Jill & Erika Cornell

Heavy Metal

Let me tell you about Ohio. Ohio is where they did this to me, he said, extending his right hand, showing us the puffiness, the faint red streaks, the stabs of infection. Ohio, he said, fifty thousand, maybe sixty thousand handshakes, dangling my arm past that crowd all the way in from Erie to downtown. They almost tore my arm off in that state, I must have smiled my way through a whole generation of baby Republicans. Look at that, he said, the numbers streaking the screen, making it a big tote board. Thirty-two electoral votes the other way. What did Tricky do to get them? Don't answer that, he said, that fine head tilting upward, the hair flying, the teeth coming from the grayness of his face to dazzle, dazzle. This is not a night for answers, he said, it is a night for questions.

We're going to lose this election, he said. We're going to lose this fucking election, Dave. Oh no, Powers said, clasping his shoulder, winking and squeezing, oh no, Johnny boy, it's not over yet. Wait until Cincinnati comes in, he said, pointing at the figures over Cronkite's shoulder. Oh no, Jack said, *you* wait until Cincinnati comes in and buries us. I'm going to go out for a little walk down the compound.

Old Joe in the corner said, Stay awhile Jack. It's going to be a long night. There's a lot coming in; it's too early to go a-walking, a-walking. Jack stared at him. Take a flying, Dad, he said. No, that is not what he said, I have to retract that, but it is what he thought, I being in a position to tell this from my peculiar and special vantage point. I need to ponder some, Dad, is what he said. He heaved up from the couch. No, don't hold him, Joe said to the boys. He needs to be off to himself a bit, he does. We all need to be by ourselves sometime. A curious, weepy look passed across the old man's features, not characteristic under the circumstances. Such strength he had been, such ungiving optimism. But it was a long night, the edge was off, Ohio was going down and now it turned on the West and then on Daley.

Jack and I left the room quickly. No one noticed my departure. Though I am his most trusted confidant, the true partner in his endeavors, I have never been able to attract much attention or respect from the Circle. Powers explained it to me once, that wild Irish rose, the reasons for this, but I paid them little attention.

Why did we do this? Bobby said. This was after Johnson had said that he would take the nomination. No one thought he would. He would turn it down and we would go to Symington or somebody, no one had quite figured it out yet. But Johnson, shambling and stuttering in his own fatigue, had been pulled into a room by Rayburn and locked up there for a long time and when he came out he said that he would go. I can't believe this, Bobby said. He was frantic, his shirt was open to the waist and his eyes were streaming. This is what comes from staying up all night and not thinking things through. What are we going to do now? Where is Jack? Where is that brother of mine? This is no time for him to go to a room.

But it was such a time. Humping and pumping, showing his blonde campaign worker a New Frontier, locked to high attention on the double bed in room three-zero-three, the one kept in reserve for special use, listed to one D. Smith of Brockport, someone's idea of a pun, the next President of the United States had other things on his mind, heavier considerations of state. It is not necessary to be graphic, I want to be graphic; it would be a pleasure to describe every twist and shout, every bounce and jounce, but this is not really my function and it would be interpreted as an act of betrayal, benign as my purposes might be. It was a riotous and earthy fuck, at least from the point of view of the candidate, who had a tendency to overestimate his performance. Testimony from the blonde was not available. She was yet another in that long, interrupted skein of collisions from here to there and in all of the states of the union, another in that series of mysterious disappearances, sudden abscissa in daylight, strange lateness for appointments. No one except me could bring witness or documentation and I, of course, would never betray confidences or eyesight. Sufficient to say that the candidate had his discretion and his good points, he had a sense of control and an impatience for repetition, meaning that he spread far and wide and interchangeably.

We've got to talk to him, Bobby said. Maybe there's a way out of this. Where is he? As if I didn't know, Bobby said. He thinks I'm stupid, he thinks that none of us know what the hell is really going on. But he's got to stop this. This kind of thing can't go on; it's going to take everything away from us, we aren't talking Hyannis Port now or the Mayfair, this is Municipal Stadium and the Coliseum and prime time. They'll murder us, they'll leave us for dead. I've got to get him, Bobby said. There's got to be a way around this situation. He looked at me and for just a moment I thought our gaze would lock, that my true and secret knowledge would be confronted, but then, of course, his gaze passed through. How could he see me? He couldn't see me, of course. I was in the room with the blonde, the candidate having already left, the blonde slowly and weepily reassembling herself, fumbling for her lipstick, her face streaked in the soft and surprising daylight. Had it really happened? the blonde wondered. A lot of them get to wondering that. This was not the way I thought it would be, if it happened. They think that a lot too. Over the years I have heard a lot of these internal monologues, and it is a depressing thing to witness, I want to tell you, although, of course, they are entitled to no sympathy. I will not allow sentiment to get in the way of my perception: lots of them, almost all of them do it because they want to fuck a senator, maybe someday a president, not a man. The institution, the office, not the person. This is something I would impart to them if I had patience.

No, he said to Bobby, there's nothing that we can do. This was a couple of hours later, holed up in the small suite, Sorenson and O'Donnell trying out the acceptance speech on each other in the next room. A deal's a deal and that's that.

I never thought he'd take it, Bobby said. Two hours of sleep, snatched in the candidate's absence, had made him sullen, meaner, had not relieved him at all. He crossed us up. It was that son of a bitch Rayburn. He was going to shove it back in our faces until Rayburn got him alone in that room.

Mr. Sam is a tough one, Jack said. You don't want to get alone in a room with him, not unless you have a chastity belt.

We're going to have trouble, Bobby said. It's going to be trouble all the way. You think Lyndon Bird is going to shut up and get out of the way? Maybe he'll have another heart attack.

And maybe he won't, Jack said. Take the positive view. We need him. He locks up the South.

He'll be in Lynchburg, talking about nigras. *Nigras, nigras*, he'll be saying. You think that stuff is going to go over? He'll have the New York press on his tail then, they'll print that stuff and we'll get killed.

Jack swatted him on the shoulder. You got something against Lyndon Bird? he said. This was your idea, remember that. This was all your idea. I didn't push nothing on you.

I never thought he'd take it, Bobby said. It was a conciliatory gesture. *Con-cil-ee-a-tory*, get it? Who would think the tall fucker would go for it?

Heart attack, Jack said. He had that whopper four years ago, maybe it's time to slow down. Can't be making deals in the Senate forever. That's what Mr. Sam told him, probably, time to semi-retire, Lyndon. And if the kid's back really goes out or he gets a bullet hole in his forehead, who is to say what the advantages of state might be? Jack giggled. Maybe Mr. Sam measured a rifle or two for him.

Oh, shit on this, Bobby said. Enough of this. We're stuck with it, aren't we? We can't get out.

Call him insurance, Jack said. Who's going to try to scramble my brains with Lyndon Bird in the wings?

Some Southern patriot might want to get real close. They take their politics serious in the South.

Let me tell you something, brother, Jack said, we take our goddamned politics pretty seriously in the North too, you understand? We got reasons for Lyndon Bird on this ticket and we're going to follow through, you understand? He's going to give us Texas for sure and probably the South and we're going to need every vote he can bring in for sure. They're not so crazy about the Pope down there, you may have noticed.

The Pope? Bobby said, you want to talk about the Pope, do you? You'd do better keeping your hands off the blondes for a while, you want to talk issues like that, you hear me? Lyndon Bird isn't going to bring in the adultery vote and that's for sure.

Do I hear you, Bobby? Do I hear you saying what I think you're saying? Is that true?

You hear, Bobby said. You think I'm a fool, he said, you think we're all stupid here. But we can tell a hawk from a handsaw and it's bigger stakes now than we've ever had. I hear you very well. I hope you hear me.

There is more to his discussion, a lot more, but it was at that point that I withdrew. Family matters deserve a certain privacy. Furthermore, I have heard much of it before and there is very little new, it is simply, as Bobby has pointed out, a new venue.

Out on the beach at Hyannis, his hands in his pocket, walking under the cold stars, the hard wedge of sky, the implacable night all around us, Jack said, It's going to come down to Daley, isn't it? Daley's the whole ball game.

I don't know, I said, there's still the whole West. California could go either way. We can sneak by without Illinois, I think.

Forget California, Jack said. California is Tricky's state. They may know him best, but there's pride and tradition. I can't get arrested in that state. I don't understand them. I don't understand the women and I don't like the weather.

There's Texas, I said, we have Texas, we'll get the Southwest too.

No, Jack said, you're missing the point. It's going to come down to Daley. If Daley can hold the count back, then we'll get Illinois. It depends on the downstate totals and whether they can be pried loose before he's ready to let them go. Don't argue with me, I know the setup.

I'm not here to argue with you, I said. I'm here to help.

Yes, he said, all of you are here to help. Sorenson, O'Donnell, Powers, Schlesinger, Lyndon Bird, Bobby, you're all my friends. Symington, Stevenson, my comrades at arms. He stopped, kicked the sand, turned abruptly and headed south, stomping at pebbles, hands in his pocket. Eleven o'clock on election night and the wind socking at his ears like a fist. Everyone is looking out for me, right? But who has to carry this? Who has to carry this through? I'm the train, you're the passengers. I feel like a fucking horse, sometimes. I wish I were a riderless horse.

I said nothing, concentrating on keeping up with him. When he is in one of these moods, Black Irish, a mood he can dive into so breathtakingly as to stun, it is best to say nothing, to cultivate a kind of distance. Maybe Powers knows what to do at times like these but I do not.

Well, there are limits, he said. There are limits to all of us. I gave it all I could and maybe it's not good enough. Bobby is going to blame me, he's going to lay it at my door but that's bullshit, I did everything that I could. There are limits to all of us, he said.

I understand that, I said. How could I argue? No one is more conscious of that limitation than I. You gave it a great run, I said.

I'm not a riderless horse, he said. I'm a forty-three-year-old Irish with a bad back and wife trouble and other troubles you wouldn't know and I have it all to carry on my own. He stopped, bent, grabbed a pebble and from a crouch threw it into the sea, then grabbed his back and slowly came from the crouch. Fucking back, he said. Fucking *back*. It hurts. It hurts all the time. They told me that it would but I never believed them. I thought it would go away. You want to know the truth? he said. Nothing goes away. *Nothing*. You just carry it and you carry it forever.

Maybe we should go back, I said. They're sitting in there, making trouble for themselves, looking at those returns, and maybe they'll get a call in and say something stupid. Bobby's not there, I said, so no one's really in command.

Fuck them, Jack said. But he turned again and started walking slowly toward the houses. The hell with them. Maybe old Harry was right, he said. You know what Harry said before the convention, that I didn't have the experience, that I needed some seasoning.

Truman's an old guy, I said. He's seventy-six. I think he's senile.

Yeah, he said, well me too, maybe. He's gone back, the old guy, he really has. How do you think I liked that? Seasoning! You think old Ave would make a better president. Ave, you can't tell if he's asleep or awake except maybe the size of his cock. It's smaller when he's awake. He spat in the sands. Not that I'd want to check, he said. Seasoning! Well, I've been seasoned now all right. I've been salted and peppered.

There's always next time, I said foolishly. It isn't the last election.

He swatted at the back of his neck as if a bee had hit him, then turned toward me. That's bullshit, he said. Tricky, once he's in, he'll amend the Constitution if he has to. He'll declare martial law. He'll put the troops in the streets. He's *never* going to give up. He paused at the fence, laid his hands on the gate. Well, maybe he'll give it up, he said. He's an old poker player. Tricky, I don't think he'd put his life on the line to stay. But there's no way, he said. It wouldn't work. They'll say it was because of the Catholic issue, not the age or experience, but the religious business. Al Smith queered things for more than thirty years and had to die before someone else got a chance. Thirty years from now I'll be seventy-three. Except I won't be seventy-three, he said. You can bank on it. That's for sure. He trudged through the gate, held it, walked back slowly. No, this is the end for me, one-shot and out. You see this? he said, extending his swollen right hand. That's Ohio, all right, they almost broke it in Ohio and now they're taking me down. So if it happened there it will happen everywhere.

You're just depressed, I said, it's all piling in on you. You're tired. It's a long night. There are a lot of returns coming in. It's not over, not at all. You may not even need Daley.

Yeah, he said, pausing at the door, then pushing through. Right, I may not even need Daley. I didn't need Lyndon Bird either, did I? Everyone knew who I needed or not but we're in this goddamned count for good and I just blew Ohio and that's for sure.

Nothing's for sure.

All right, he said, you have a point there all right. The absolute certainty of uncertainty has always appealed. He almost smiled then but in the diminished and difficult light it was hard to tell. Not that my attention was fixated in that way, of course.

White followed us around, he sensed early the way that it might be going and he knew there was a book in it. Even if Jack lost it would still be a big book, a bestseller, an insider's look at the process. That was what White the old *Times*man called it anyway. You're the right candidate at the right time, he said to Jack, and this is the pivotal election of the American century. He said a lot of things like that, kissing it for all it was worth. Of course in the book he would come off as objective or, if we lost, full of admonition. I think we should get rid of this guy, Powers said, he means us no good, and O'Donnell pretty much felt the same way, but in relation to White only Bobby mattered and Bobby was adamant. He stays, he said, we give him what he wants, he'll give us what we need. What we needed of course was a *Time* endorsement or at least an even shot. We needed Luce to get off our ass. Everyone remembered what he had done to Adlai. We play ball with this guy, Luce will go along, Bobby said. We clam up on him or push him away and we'll get the full treatment in *Time* and that's the end of it. And another thing, Bobby said, for these four months, Jack, you've got to play it straight. There's too much press, too much attention. We can't take the risks.

Jack said, I don't know what you're talking about.

Bullshit, you don't know what I'm talking about. There no secrets and there's no time for that crap now, Jack. For four months you act like Old Joe at a family weekend. Afterwards, we'll talk about it.

They wouldn't print anything, Jack said. They wouldn't touch this.

You don't know *what* they'll do, you get Luce mad enough. Which is why we're letting Teddy White through the door. You let him in, you make the kind of concessions I made here, you let old Lyndon Bird run loose out there in Galveston and New Orleans and talk about the *nigras* in our name, you're not going to screw us up at home. You hear that, Jack? You hear me?

I hear you, he said. I always heard you. You know what it's like? You know what it's like to be out here pushing, pushing? I hurt all the time, Bobby; my back can't take it, there are times I want to cave in.

Pussy won't change it. Doesn't change a goddamned thing. Besides, with back trouble, what are you humping away for? You want to be on a wood board on the floor, reading draft speeches, that's what you want.

You really want this, Jack said. You really want it bad, don't you, Bobby? Sometimes I think you want it worse than I do. And that means a whole hell of a lot.

We're in this to win. No point going into anything as bad as a national campaign and losing. I don't want to lose, Jack.

What if we do, Bobby? What if we lose?

There's something in you that wants to give up, isn't there Jack? I have it too, I know it's in you. But this is the kind of stuff you've got to keep down, it doesn't matter. You understand that, brother?

I understand everything, Bobby. Still, just for the hell of it. It's just the two of us in this room, nobody's listening, nobody's hanging around outside the door at four in the morning. Even Powers said his little prayers and gave it up two hours ago. *What if we lose?*

Well, Bobby said, if that's the case, I'll go to the Teamsters, I guess. Ask Hoffa for a job.

Do that, huh?

He knows I've got the skills, Bobby said. He can't be uncertain on that.

Just so you have a job. The Senate doesn't look so bad to me sometimes, you know?

It's too late, Bobby said. You know why it's too late? Sometimes I think I don't know anything. It's a whole New Frontier out there, remember?

I'll tell you why it's too late. Because you'd have to go back there and serve with Lyndon Bird who will not only remember that he lost to you at the convention, will not only remember that he ran under you for the most useless job in the country, tits on a boar hog, but that because of you he *lost*. He'll blame you. And he'll make your life miserable.

Thanks a lot, Bobby. Why don't you tell that to White, give him a sidebar?

Jack, you'd better tell that to yourself. Because if we lose, we have no future. We're in his sights. And that's why you're going to calm down and hold onto yourself for three months.

There was more of it, a lot more. They would go on this way sometimes all night, would abandon any pretense of sleep and just have at it. They were brothers, they loved each other, that too. But at a certain point, it was all too much for me. I had other things on my mind and I did not have, as they would say, their commitment.

Tricky banged his knee getting out of a limousine in October and got it infected, Tricky's luck. We thought that that would do it, when he had to take to his wretched bed for almost a week and cancel all campaigning. This and the debates seemed to take him down, there was a point in mid-October when it was all crowds and shouting, thunder in the air and the clean, high purpose of victory. The motorcades, the crowded podium downtown, the pumping, prancing bands, the colors of the Fall, all of them seemed to mesh and carry us forward in one vast, surging pennant that swallowed and wrapped us in the history to be made. The Bishop's speech had worked or at least that was what Gallup was saying, and Lyndon Bird was putting out his all, doing what he was supposed to do and apparently keeping it from the Northern papers. In those days, Jack grew larger, redder, firmer, he seemed to shine with power and even the back relented a little, he was able to lean forward in the limousines, wave unsupported, make his way in and out of the banquet halls without stumbling. At the Smith banquet he laid them all out, even made Tricky smile his pained smile when Spellman came over and kissed him.

But Tricky was stubborn, he had a second-stringer's insistence and he got out of bed and came on. Eisenhower, a picture on the wall until then, began to make more noises, coming to understand for the first time perhaps that a man twenty-seven years younger, a junior officer and not a Republican, might come to change the guard and maybe revise a few ranks. We struggled on through the suddenly diminished arc of Fall, the darkness earlier, the flights bumpier, the motorcades ever more arduous and desperate. In New York there was a rally scheduled for five in the evening and a crowd of maybe 20,000, the largest crowd ever to gather for a candidate's rally, we were told, waited in the dusk and chill for three hours but Jack never came, the schedule had come hopelessly askew and he was still in Syracuse, shouting at a banquet of 500 young or younger Democrats until it was too late to get in there. It happened a lot in those gathering days, the sense of slow and careful unraveling and Bobby was helpless to deal with it, was not able to reach the top man here, the top contact there, we were told, picked up one disclaimer after the next. Tricky, undeterred by the Quemoy-Matsu shelling and the missile gap plugged on and on, offering more Republican cloth coats. Daley finally caught up with us in Evanston, very late, after the campaign had gone to bed, after we had nearly canceled Chicago in the torrent of missed connections.

I want to know where your head is, he said, I want to know what the fuck you think you're fucking doing, that's all.

Jack stared at him. Listen, he said, I don't need—

Bobby put a hand on his elbow. That's just this guy's way, the hand pressure said. This is Dick Daley. Hear him out. Do nothing.

Yes you need, Daley said. You need all the help you can fucking get. You're screwing it up. The word is out.

I'm doing all right, Jack said. The polls—

Fuck on the polls, Daley said. He had come in with three silent men, large men, they stood with scarves over their shoulders and one of them rubbed Daley's back like a handler. You take the polls, you can read them in East Sheboygan picking up garbage. You're going to lose this, Daley said, you're on the way.

Now I don't think—

I don't care what you think. What you think is of no interest to me. You want to lose, that's okay, you got a safe seat in Massachusetts and you own half of fucking Hyannis and Boston, anyway. But you take me down in state, that's something else. You can hurt me, you hear that?

No one hurts you, Dick, Bobby said. You're beyond hurting.

Daley gave him a quick, sudden look, all jowls and curiosity. You think so? he said. Old Joe tell you to say that, you think that's the way to handle this? Well it isn't.

What do you want? Bobby said. Just tell me what it is.

Who talks? You talk? The brother is running for president, the wrong brother is making the deals. Who's the show here?

I'm the show, Jack said. He took his arm free from Bobby's grasp. What do you want? he said. You can't come in and shit all over me like this. You don't like me, okay, but I'm your party's nominee—

Ground Adlai, Daley said, that's the first thing you can do. Shut him the fuck up. We've had Adlai twice around the bend, it's enough Adlai. Every time he speaks he loses you five hundred votes. You already got every Jew on the West Side, there's nothing more he can do for you. Shut him up.

Adlai's not so easy to shut up, Bobby said.

You are an inexperienced man, Daley said. You are an inexperienced kid running a goddamned national campaign and you understand nothing. Adlai can be shut up. Anyone can be shut up. Haven't heard much from old Harry recently, have you? Been real quiet since the convention hasn't he? But you got to get to Adlai. Tell him to shitcan it, you hear me?

We'll talk to him, Jack said. What's the other stuff?

You do more than talk to him, Daley said. You don't patronize me, young fellow, I wiped your daddy's ass many a time when he got it out of line. The other thing is I've got some stuff on Tricky you can use. He put a hand out, one of the handlers found an envelope, put it in the palm. Real good stuff, you take a look. You can feed it out.

Feed it out? Bobby said. He shook his head, laughed. To who? Who's going to print whatever you have there? *The Republication National Gazette?* We haven't got a publisher who would touch this.

You feed it out where you can, Daley said. You get it to the reporters and let it leak. Reporters know what to do, how to pass things along. They all hate Tricky, anyway.

Jack looked at the envelope. Do I have to open this? he said. Read it?

Not necessarily. Just pass it along.

Why don't you pass it along?

Because, you shit, Daley said, *I'm* not running for fucking President of the fucking United States, that's why. Because I'm just a wheelhorse, the big boss. You're the one with the credibility. Don't you understand campaigning?

We got pretty far without knowing anything, Bobby said. For a couple of rich kids we did pretty good, don't you think?

Daley shook his head. You fool, he said. You got through because I *let* you through, that's why. You don't get near the gates of the stockyards if I don't open them. And another thing, Jack.

What's that? Jack said. He handed the envelope to Bobby. Bobby opened the envelope and looked at the contents, shaking his head. What crap, Bobby said. Anybody could have known this.

Anybody could but nobody does, Daley said. Another thing, Jack. You quit the fucking around. I have my sources, I know what's going on.

Nothing's going on, Bobby said. We already talked about that.

Your information is wrong, Daley said. Your information is full of shit. You are only the brother, you don't know what the hell is going on. It's going on all the time.

Nothing's going on, I tell you, Bobby said.

Four-fifteen Tuesday, Daley said. At the Holiday Inn, room two-four-one. Seventeen minutes. She cried at the end. Cried at the beginning too, but not in the middle. You must be some guy, Mr. President, Mr. Senator. Got out of the room at four-thirty-two. You think I don't know? We know everything.

Bobby looked at Jack. Tuesday? he said.

Jack shrugged, stared at the wall. The henchmen, all three of them, laughed.

Shit, Bobby said. Shit, I thought we had a deal.

We had a deal, Jack said.

I can't control everything. I can't lead you around, Jack. I'm not Old Joe and you're not fourteen years old.

Okay, Jack said, okay, I hear you. I won't—

More and more, Daley said. You're going to do it more and more. You get elected, you'll think you can take on the world. You'll take on fucking Marilyn Monroe in Madison Square Garden, that's what you'll do.

Bobby said, This is too much, Jack. I don't want to handle this.

Okay, Jack said, okay, Dick. I'll stay clean.

Stay clean! You better get a nun's habit, you son of a bitch. You start screwing around in office, you think the whole country is Massachusetts, the press will cover up for you? You think Sam Rayburn is Joe Kennedy? You think Joe Martin is Dave Powers? They'll crucify you, you horny, tormented son of a bitch, and you'll take us *all* down. You cut it out, do you hear me? He turned, motioned to the henchmen, walked out of the room.

Jack ran after him, brushing Bobby's arm away. Dick! he said, and Daley, already in the hall, turned, looked at him. What is it? Daley said. I've said what I have to, there's nothing else to say. You got the word.

You don't walk out on me, Jack said. I'm running for goddamned president, you show some respect, you understand? I'm forty-three years old, you don't shit on me like this.

Anything else, kid? Daley said. His face was blotched. What else do you have to tell me?

No, Jack said.

Good.

I don't mean no, there's nothing else to tell you. I mean, no, I won't cut it out. I don't take orders from you. I live my own life, you hear me?

Jack, Bobby said, Jack, come back in the room.

I'm forty-three, Jack said, I don't have to listen to your shit. I listened to Old Joe's crap for years, that's enough of it. I hid him away and I'll hide you. I'm living *my* life, my way. You don't tell me what to do, you understand that?

Oh yes, Daley said, I understand. I understand good.

Go away, Jack said, get out of here. Go and play with the fishes, I don't give a fuck for you and your shit. He snatched the papers from Bobby's hands and threw them at Daley. Fuck your crap, he said. See? I can say fuck too. I have a temper too. I got some ideas too. Get out of here, Jack said, go away.

I'll do that, Daley said. He bent, took the papers, put them into his coat pocket. His henchmen wiped invisible spots from his shoulders. He walked away.

Jack stood there, breathing hard, then his respiration slowly faded to normal. Shrugging off Bobby's touch, he walked back to the room. The hell with it, he said. I lose, I lose. I'll live longer, anyway.

Jack—

I mean it, Jack said, *I'll live longer*. How long would I last, listening to guys like Daley, taking orders from them?

Daley's the ball game, Bobby said. He's the ball game.

No, Jack said. He closed the door behind them, walked to the cabinet, took out a bottle and a pack of the cigarettes he never smoked in public. No way, he said, *I'm* the ball game. Win or lose.

We could have used that stuff on Tricky. It was solid stuff.

Fuck it, Jack said. Fuck the solid stuff. Maybe we go for dreams and air now.

Just like Adlai? Bobby said.

I don't care. Just like Adlai.

Powers said, We won't know any more until late morning. Go to bed, Jack. Lie down. It will still be there in the morning.

Illinois is coming in, Jack said. It will come in by dawn's early light. We'll hang around for it.

You never know, Bobby said. You never know. Consider the alternative.

I've considered the alternative, Jack said. All of them. You know what? What I told the son of a bitch that night is true, it's true, that's all. I'll live longer. So I'll give up the Senate seat. I'll write a book or something, one on my own this time. Maybe look for something else out there.

You think there's peace that way, Bobby said, peace for guys like us going that way? Losers? Losing?

Yeah, Jack said. He took a deep breath, blew it out, rubbed his back, showed his right hand to the room. When it comes down, he said, when the swelling goes away, I'll be able to jerk off again, anyway.

We all laughed at that. I laughed too. I had to, even knowing what I knew. He was a scrapper. He was, in or out of it, the toughest guy I knew, tougher than Old Joe could ever have measured. And never said a bad word to those other than what deserved it.

Let's have a drink, Jack said. Let's pray for Tricky.

We had a drink. Daley released the Chicago returns at 6:15 A.M. We lost Illinois by 240,000 votes and with it, the election.

Turpentine

The sociologist was defiant all the way to Kirk's office, but when he saw the scene, when he got what you could call a sociological perspective of the ordnance, his mood changed right quick. What is this? he said. What the fuck is this? Trust a sociologist to toss a *fuck* in when he is talking to the troops. That's what they teach them in the schools now, get down, get right, be *relevant*, talk out of that hip side of your mouth. Saying *fuck* puts everybody at his or her ease, like the sociologist and you, you are on the same side of the party, fighting the *est*ablishment. Except we don't really go along with that shit anymore, there is our side and there is the rest of them and the line is not to be crossed by sociologists, white sociologists from the University of Chicago with a Ph.D. in population, as the catalog we had researched put it. Give us the plans, Richard said, just give us the plans. We know you have them.

The sociologist stared, little guy, maybe five and a half feet, still gripping the satchel he had snatched when we grabbed him from his office. What are you talking about? he said. He took in the scene pretty good; we could see him making sociological calculations behind that forehead of his. I should have gotten out of here, he said. That was my mistake. When the going was good, I should have got. We had trashed Kirk's office pretty good by then, although nothing as to what the press was going to say later. I could figure out what the press would say. By the time the Rosenthals were through with us, they would have the dung piled feet deep; as they say would be talking about the jism on the carpets instead of into the Barnard girls, where it had been properly aimed. But there was no way to put off that kind of crap: as Richard said, you took your shot and you aimed it and the rest of it was establishment blues, that was all. The plans, he said again. The underground reactor, the tunnels, the way in. We know you have them. They were planted in your office a month ago when the stuff started getting serious. I want them now.

The sociologist stared at Richard. You're crazy, he said. You've got to be crazy. What are you talking about, nuclear reactors, tunnels? That's for the Department of Physics, not for me. I'm in the soft sciences.

You in soft sciences, mother, Richard said, going into his deep Panther act. Maybe I should explain that we were a mixed crowd—heavily mixed, as they say, boys and girls, black and white—but Richard in shades and full regalia had asked for the whole show and we had fallen back against the walls. If there was one thing he knew, Richard had said, it was how to put the screws to a white sociologist. Watch me jive, he had said, lean back and learn how we're going to deal with the rest of these mothers from the point of revolution *on*. We had laughed then but it didn't seem so funny now, Richard himself being carried away a bit with the shades and the chain act. But we were deep in by then and no arguing it. You *real* soft, Richard said. Let me explain to you, he said, coming up to the sociologist and giving him the finger in the gut, one, two, three, the rhythm boys. Back when things started moving around here about a month ago, foxy old Administration whose very offices you will note we now *occupy* thought that it would be best to get the plans, the secret plans for the underground tunnels out of the head offices and to some place relatively innocent. *Inno-cent* you get that, you understand the frame? We're just trying to be helpful and refresh your memory.

I don't know what's going on here, the sociologist said. Believe me, you have me at a loss. I am willing to help, but I never heard of anything like this. You have me at at a loss, I told you, I want—

You see my friend Ronald X here? Richard said. Ronald X is my security consultant, my comrade-in-arms, you dig? He is a desperate man.

That is right, I said, I am a desperate man.

He comes from a greatly deprived background, Richard said. You know all about cultural deprivation, they give out Ph.D.'s in that subject. Your guy Alinsky in Chicago, he runs seminars on the streets about people like my friend Ronald X. There is *capital funding* from the government to study the deprivations in the head of this desperate man over here.

The sociologist stared at Richard as if he had never seen anyone like him before. Possibly this is true. It is possible that Richard was a new experience for the sociologist, just as he had been for me back in those times when we were sharing backgrounds down at the Union. You can see what a desperate man he is from the look in his eyes, Richard said. He is from CCNY, which makes him even more frantic because he does not have that fine education and potentially prestigious degree behind him. He is just your basic nigger, Ronald X, and he is very angry.

I want your help, I said, I want you to find me the plans. That is a simple request and then I will not be so desperate. I will leap over my cultural background and be as solid and reasonable as you. But right now I am strictly speaking not civilized.

The sociologist seemed tormented, or perhaps the word was abstract. These shades of meaning are more for Richard than me. Clear to us, though, *no* part of Chicago population studies seemed to have prepared him for this, or at least he had not taken the course. That had been an elective, dealing with mad up-against-the-wall niggers in the president's office at 2:00 A.M. with about twenty-five hundred police ringing the campus and the place going crazy. Maybe if he went back to school for some postpost-graduate work he would remember to take that course next time. But right now he was flat out of luck. That out-of-luck expression seemed to filter through all of his hard little features and then he said, I still don't know what the deal is. But I'll go back with you and look through desk drawers. I don't care.

That is a righteous cooperative attitude, Richard said, we can praise that motherfucking attitude. Richard always leaves the *g* on when he uses the big word. He says that it makes them more terrified, proper grammatical perspective in a brute scheme, something like a doctor explaining the logistics of testicular cords just before he cuts your balls off. Brings it all home. We'll just send you on your way then, Richard said, and soon you'll be back.

I stayed behind to help you, the sociologist said. I didn't want to run out of the buildings, I wanted to show solidarity.

Well, you showing it, Richard said. Ain't he showing it, Ronald? Let's go.

I take the sociologist by the arm in a deep Muslim squeeze and propel him through the door. Some of the brothers separate themselves from the wall and follow us, but this is our party and I know it. Richard has left it all up to me, this part, and I would say I were proud if I did not have so much else on my concentrated and busy mind.

They got reactors, Richard had said to me a few hours earlier, while we were working the plan, this just after we had crashed through into Kirk's office and sent them running. We're going to get hold of them. We're going to get the nukes.

It's a dumb plan, Jonathan said. Look at me. Listen to me. We can't get at reactors.

They got a motherfucking atomic pile under this place, Richard said. Everybody knows that. Had it for years. You can feel the little heat, the explosions bouncing through the grass when you cut across the quad. Once I was taking a leak in the physics building, I could feel *atomic heat* pass through my generous organ.

I didn't say they weren't there, Jonathan said. Everyone knows it, all right. But messing with nukes is high-caliber business. They get wild, we get hold of atomic shit.

Your trouble, Richard said, you a gentle-ass white guy from the suburbs of *Mahopac* or somewhere, you're interested in symbolic gestures, in *radicalization*, in heavy rioting in dress gear. Both me and Ronald, though, we got a different background, we got a somewhat different grasp of the situation. We're here, we're going to take it all the way.

This is not the answer, Jonathan said. He took out a handkerchief, shook it, removed his glasses, began to wipe them. We're doing just what we should. We got the buildings clear, we got the campus secure. The campus is ours tonight. They're afraid to come in, and we can get out anytime we want. Now we press the nonnegotiable demands.

You white boys amuse me, Richard said. He took the glasses from Richard's hand, gave them a few strokes with his fingers. You think this is display, you with your nonnegotiable demands, your symbolic gestures, your *liberating* the president's office. You're full of shit, that's what you are. You're playing and they're playing. But we're not, that's the whole difference. Ronald and I, we're in this for keeps. Wake up in the morning, you can go back to Mahopac. Wake up in the morning, Ronald and I are still black. He's humping for dollars at CCNY, I'm kissing ass down here in the department of stripes and ribbons, but they put the lights on and we're niggers. So we're serious. We got to be serious, that's our condition.

So what are you going to do? Jonathan said. You're going to hold up the university, that's it? You're going to go nuclear on them? That's heavy shit, heavy water down there, you fuck around with it, you'll blow all of us up.

I got techniques, Richard said, I got plans. Me and my ringleader, Ronald, we got big plans. We get access to the atomics, they're not going to be so quick to rush in.

Jonathan put the glasses back on his nose. He looked like what he was going to become, a professor of literature, the glasses flashing clean bright white light now. In that angle I could see Richard's point, finally, and the answer that went through me was as clean as the light. That's about it, I said, the man has just about put it right.

They're not coming in anyway, Jonathan said. They're ringing the buildings but they're not going anywhere. I tell you, it's a triumph, we got them paralyzed. We're getting our story out to the press and they're listening.

You white fool, Richard said, you think they're listening? They're just holding off, letting the little boys and girls play. Three days from now, they can't tear-gas us out, they'll come in with grenades and clean out the place. You're in a playpen, boy, you don't understand anything. But it's a lot more serious for us and that's the fucking truth. The confab is over. Split. We're going to get us a sociologist and some directions.

Jonathan looked at me. Can't you understand? he said. If we go for the reactor, that's a whole different gig. That changes the rules on them and they'll come in and kill us.

You never understood, did you? I said. I grabbed him by neat handfuls of his shirt, pulled him toward me. We not interested in symbolic gestures, I said, we not interested in little white boys' and girls' game, playing around in the toilets, making the nursery school mad. We are in this for *keeps* now and you just opened the door to that. You let us in, you wanted a collaboration, you wanted a multiracial movement, you wanted a national protest—well, that's what you got. And now it's time to stand aside and let the men work this out.

Jonathan looked at me and then away, stared at Richard. The stare was a good preparation for what we would see from the sociologist a little bit later. I can't believe it, he said, you *are* serious. You really think that this is going to work.

We don't care if it works, Richard said, it's just something we do, dig? We go all the way. You want multiracial, you got it. You want up against the wall, this is it. We not talking about humping in the president's chair, leaving Kirk a little white stuff on the walls. We talking about power, about possession. So that's it. You understand the situation?

He surely do, I said to Richard. He surely does. I do not think that it is necessary to discuss it with the stud anymore.

Oh one more thing, Richard said. You staying with us, you understand?

Of course I'm staying with you, Jonathan said. I wouldn't—

You think you sneak out of the building about 4:00 A.M., you turn to white in the morning sun and go back to Mahopac, you got it wrong. You in it all the way, just like us. We got fifteen bloods with carbines and serious intentions, you change your mind on that.

He's not changing his mind, I said. His mind is visibly unchanged.

Richard laughed. I did some laughing, too. Then we went back into the main room and announced that there would be a continuation of the plan, there being no need to tell the boys and girls in the outer echelon anything more at this point, and then we went hunting for a sociology professor. Jonathan had been very good at getting hold of the secret plans and administration fallback positions. We had to give him credit for that. Before our little disagreement, so thoroughly resolved, Jonathan had been a real worker for the cause. Of course, he had had a different name for it.

In the concrete it was just Richard and me, looking at the dials, watching the dials do their little dance, hearing the thunder of the machines, smelling all of those compressors and atom splitters and heavy isotopic remedies. The sociologist had come across like a hooker, and the plans had been airtight. Everything was exactly where it was supposed to be, us and the place together. Now, Richard said, adjusting his weapon and rubbing his hands, now we show them some real nonnegotiable demands. Nonnegotiable isn't a slip of paper and four little white girls screaming and shaking their tits. Nonnegotiable is here it is baby or we blow up Riverside Park and the West End tavern and the place where Kirk's asshole sits, too. How about that? He giggled, higher-pitched than I've ever heard him. Can a CCNY guy dig it? he said.

I can dig it, I said. I can dig a lot. It is heavy business.

I think we can do this, Richard said. I got five, six guys with heavy-tech brains and good mechanical aptitudes, I think they can really twist those dials and make this thing work. I thought it was a wild chance when we started, yes. Wild; I know it, he said, I thought Jonathan was crazy. But now it's not so wild. I think it can work.

What can work? I said. Anything?

Anything at all. We'll put a few demands, we'll test them out. For openers, Richard said, I want New York City.

What's that? I said.

Oh, not all of it, he said. They can keep Harlem. They can even keep Brownsville and Bed-Stuy, they so crazy for it. But they can hand me Park Avenue and Seventy-ninth and the stock exchange and we'll go on from here. He gave me a gleaming smile. That's what I think.

Looking at Richard, it occurred to me—and not for the first time—that the boy was really crazy, that he was as crazy as the sociologist and maybe Jonathan thought he was. But that didn't make him any less lovable, only a hell of a lot more dangerous, I thought. We better rejoin the troops, I said. The troops be getting anxious soon.

Oh, we rejoin, Richard said. We rejoin and then we reup. How would you like Arpels? Me, I'm going to take Tiffany's. We're going to shake things up a little in this city. You know why? he said.

Because we are desperate men, I said. Because we are the underclass, we are the natives right out of Congoland and we got nothing to lose.

That's right, Richard said. Oh, you is a righteous lad, all right.

The white boys and girls aren't going to take that too much to heart, I said.

No, they ain't, Richard said. But they let us in, didn't they? You invite the piper, you buy the meal.

The rumbling goes on and on as we draft our statement and then it is time to get back to the troops. But only for a while, I think. We have our battle plan now. We have our heads toward the situation. Soon enough, maybe, there will be no need for the troops. When they go through the stuff left in Kirk's office, maybe they don't necessarily find our names and pedigrees after all. It depends. It is, as they say, a fluid situation. It is closing in on the end of the sixties and everything is not as it was here in walrusland.

The first communiqué meets silence and the second communiqué gets only a beat from whoever is on the phone at the other end. The third communiqué, however, setting a midnight deadline, does get some response. We'll get back to you, they say. They do not believe it. Obviously they do not believe it. We have to begin reading off some coordinates and serial numbers on isotope containers before the tone of the responses changes.

I think they believe us now, Richard said. I do believe that they believe we got nukes here and we are ready like the boys in Vietnam to die. I think midnight will see some interesting responses.

We have asked them to withdraw all of their troops by midnight and also to issue a statement of capitulation. Otherwise the first reactor goes off. We have guarantees that this can be done although, of course, one can never be sure. The phone, dead for so long, is suddenly lively. They plead for more time, time to work things out. We read them a few more serial numbers. A senior physicist from the State Department, or that is what he says he is, gets on the line and we have to convince him, too. After a while he goes away.

The sociology professor is crashed out on the floor, a couple of ladies around him, rubbing his shoulders. We tell him that we will not necessarily identify him as the collaborator but he will have to stay with us for a while. We will, however, make it as easy and pleasant for him as possible. The white girls are cooperative, as is so often the case with white girls and white men, also black men now that you asked.

We sit and pass the time, Richard and I sharing some old stories. Our backgrounds may be different, me with my gentle middle-class thing and he on the harder rock, but they are also quite similar. We are both niggers, after all. They plead for another twelve hours' extension and Richard gets on the horn this time and tells them this is the commander and they can fuck themselves. Two hours, that is it; 2:00 A.M. and their troops and dogs are off the campus or the first reactor goes on-line. We will talk about Tiffany's later. They say they will get back to us.

Jonathan comes in from the back room, where we have stashed him. After three hours' sleep we would expect him to be more reasonable or at least less wired, but this is not the case. He is more frantic than ever.

I've been thinking this through, he said. Been talking to a few people.

That's good, Richard said. Talk is always good. High communication, that was your original demand, right?

We have to pull back, Jonathan said, this isn't going to work. It won't work with these odds.

It's working fine, Richard says. Don't you think so, Ronald? I shrug. Working okay by me, I say.

This guy, Jonathan said, this LBJ. He just pulled out, you understand? The war did him in, *he* did him in. All he wanted in the world was to be the king and they took it away from him and worst of all he had to sink the knife in himself, you dig that?

I dig that fine, Richard says, it is a satisfying source of pleasure. It is an inspiration. It sends us on our way.

So this guy lost everything, Jonathan says, Old LBJ, he doesn't care anymore, don't you see? The worst that can happen has happened. He won't be president.

Still got the Hump, Richard says. He giggled. The Hump will keep the chair mighty warm, also his mouth, don't you agree?

You don't get it at all, Jonathan says, you really don't get it. He grabs Richard's wrists. You are dealing with a guy who has already lost everything. He has nothing more to lose, not the Hump, not anything. He doesn't care, you're pushing him over the edge. He is leaning over, half-trying to bring Richard up.

Let go of my wrists, white man, Richard says very quietly. Just release your grip.

Damn it, Jonathan says, I worked this out. I may be white but I'm not stupid. You're dealing with a guy who has already lost everything, you're putting him in a box now, don't you see?

See? Richard says. I see everything. I am far-ranging. You are still grasping my wrists. You let them go within the next ten seconds or you see who will lose everything and how.

He hates New York, Jonathan says, letting him go, crouching beside us. He thinks that everything that beat him came out of New York anyway. Now he's got the enemy at home, waving nukes. You know what that means?

I know what it means, I say. It means that we are finally making an impression.

We're making an impression, Jonathan says, we're making a *big* impression. He's going to hit us, that's what's going to happen. He'll send in the Strategic Air Command.

Oh, white boy, Richard says, you have a fertile mind and heart. The Strategic Air Command. He chuckles. You don't understand who has who by the balls here, he says. You don't understand the situation.

I understand the situation, Jonathan says, we are in heavy shit. We are in the heaviest shit. We are dealing with a crazy man by being crazy. You know what happens then?

I don't know, Richard says, help me.

He's just looking for an excuse, Jonathan says. You've given him all the excuse he needs. You've brought Vietnam home.

Time he got to Vietnam, Richard says. Time for sure.

And he's got the provocation now. He'll use the bomb.

Richard says, Jonathan, you losing your cool. Nuke out a bunch of college kids with a reactor? Shit, what you talking about? We can't do *nothing* with that machine, that little bitty old separator. That's the word from the Chemistry Department. We can rattle the bones, Richard says, but we can't pull no action.

LBJ doesn't know that, Jonathan says. LBJ's no nuclear scientist.

Neither are we, Richard says. He's figured that out already. But he's got poor public relations.

You don't get it, Jonathan says. He doesn't know about bitty old separators and radioactivity. Doesn't *care*, either. For him, we've turned into Viet Cong. He thinks he's got the Viet Cong right here at home and he's going to trash us out, that's what I think.

Talk to the Chemistry Department, Richard says. Examine their isotopes, see what they got to say.

LBJ has freaked out, Jonathan says. He's over the line, he doesn't care what we can do, he's got the excuse. I'm telling you, we better back off.

Richard takes Jonathan by the wrist, hauls himself up, gives him a push. *You* back off, he says. You back off all your life, in the morning you're still white. It's a game for you and now the stakes are a little too high. But you can't get out. He points to the sociology professor, the professor hiding between four tits over on the carpet, the little coeds stroking his hair.

You and he are black as us tonight, he says. You going to stay through the end, see this through one time.

We'll see it through, Jonathan says. You fool, there's nowhere to hide. There's no place to go, you think it's any safer on Thirty-fifth Street or up in Inwood than it is right here? We can't get out anywhere, none of us. We're cooked to a circumference of four hundred and fifty miles. Because we're the enemy and now he's got the rationalization he needs.

It's throwdown time, Richard says. That honky, he's not going to throw it down, that's all.

You'll see, Jonathan says. He walks out the open door. It feels as if we have been shouting, but for all the notice our conversation takes, we might have been whispering. Or maybe all the troops, the sociology professor and his companions, they too, are simply asleep. It is deep night, and in the extinguished spaces now I can barely see Richard.

White boy, Richard says. Establishment bitch. Just another one all the time.

What if he's right? I say.

What's that?

I said, What if he's right? What if LBJ doesn't give a shit anymore? What if he just hits us with everything he has? Jonathan's right, he's a dead man anyway. He's out of office. How long is he going to live?

You're as crazy as the rest of them, Richard says. Me, I'm going to get a little sleep, be alert at 2:00 A.M. Need my beautify sleep for some serious negotiating.

He could be right, he says. You just know it.

You, too, Ronald? Richard says. His eyes are round, maybe amused, hard to tell in the dark. You going to go establishment on me, too?

I'm not going anywhere.

That's good. Because it's too late. Richard says, you get that? It's just too goddamned late and we're going to see it through now. We got the plan and the plan is going to work right through to the end and that's the end of the plan. He rambles off toward the couch. Crash me back in half an hour, he says. Stand the sentry. Play watch.

I get up, follow him partway across the room, then lean against the wall to brace myself, feeling unsteady. There is a sudden shift and uneasiness in the room. I can hear the sound of distant humming.

It would happen so fast, I say to Richard, we wouldn't even know it had happened.

He says nothing.

I have read about these things, I say. It is like a head-on automobile crash. If you know it's happened, it hasn't happened. It's so fast you are dead before you know it.

I am already asleep, Richard says, I am finding my righteous moments.

In the dark, I lean against the wall. The professor is muttering something. Maybe other things are going on outside; the lawn seems suddenly close against me and I can smell the stink of the occupiers.

And then there is an amazing light, the light of Calvary.

I see the light; I know it is happening.

Which means then according to Richard that if I see it going on it isn't going on, except it is.

It is and *it is*.

And the screaming, and the fire ...

Quartermain

ALL FLESH IS AS GRASS: "You know how it will be," the modal says. "You will wander upon the desert. You will contest with Satan. You will return to Galilee. You will find yourself riding upon an ass. A few small dazzlements, a few larger enchantments, mobs, publicity, betrayal and vengeance. You will be taken to a high place, lots cast over vestments and etc." Its voice drops to a confidential tone. "It will be extremely painful, Quartermain," it advises. "These things have a certain cheap, dramatic force but there is no way that you can be properly committed to the extreme and, I might add, embarrassing agonies. Are you sure you want to go through with this?"

"Of course I want to go through with it," I say. I should point out that I am at a final briefing, that I have passed the various levels of qualification and that the modal, an intimidating but harmless device, is trying to harass me. "Don't be concerned," I say, "I can handle any of this."

Lights blink across the modal; one gathers that it might shrug if a room-sized cube were capable of gesture. "Very well," it says, "you will do as you will. I must warn you, Quartermain, this is no easy business. A cheap religious fanaticism will carry you only so far. Wait until they drive in the nails."

"Wait until you hear my seven last words," I counter.

"I'm waiting," the modal says. "I'm waiting and waiting. I suspire in conclave after conclave, interview after interview and, Quartermain, I will be waiting yet. I have seen you come and I have seen you go."

"Believe this," I say, "I am different."

"I have heard that before," the modal says. "Truly I have heard that before."

BLESSED ARE THE DEAD: "Your name is Nicholas Quartermain," Satan says with deadly earnestness. For the purposes of our encounter he has assumed the frame of a youngish woman, rather fetchingly attired in scant clothing and equipped with the postures of seduction. I must admit that I do not find him unattractive although, of course, I am not enticed. "You have come to replicate the apocryphal chronicles of Jesus of Nazareth in the hope that a satisfactory crucifixion and a necessary ascension will grant you credibility as a cult head, but I tell you, Nicholas, you are a fool. Better men than you have fallen on the road to Bethlehem, the very best have cursed their Father on the

Cross. No one has emerged from these simulations since they began and you will be no different." Satan reaches into her low-cut dress, takes out a large, well-formed breast, shows it to me. "Why not stop now, save yourself a lot of trouble and have a good time? Better to fail here than in the court of Pilate and besides, I'm getting so *tired* of these encounters, these dialogues. Come on. Be reasonable."

I stare at the old Tempter with disdain. "Never," I say, "I cannot be distracted by such cheap devices."

Satan winks, drops the breast. "Why not be diverted by the fantastic?" She arches a finger; from the dim mist which surrounds us the hundred priests emerge whispering in robes of splendor; great mythic birds enchanting in their plumage and color whirl against the sudden bowl of sky. "You want miracles?" Satan says, "I give you miracles. It surpasses your bread-and-wine tricks any time. You have to understand that you're dealing with a professional here, Quartermain. Dazzlements are my oldest charm."

I watch the chanting priests, the wheeling birds. "This is an impressive demonstration, I agree," I say, "but this is not a matter of display. I am familiar with all of your divertissements."

Satan shakes her splendid head, makes a moue of discontent. "You dislike enchantment?" she asks. "Very well then, settle for rhetoric." She makes a gesture of dismissal, the priests and birds reluctantly dissolve and the sky closes in like a grey collar once again. "I can defeat you with rhetoric of the most rigorous sort since I was, as you know and as any study of the proper texts will reveal, His best loved just before the moments of the Fall. I am that part of Him split off to walk up and down upon the earth and to and fro upon it, to test those for whom conviction is the highest necessity. In fact," Satan says, again with that fetching moue, "you might consider me to be His assistant, Quartermain, and what do you say now to a little wrestling? Forty days and forty nights of wrestling? You'll have a few tales for the boys in the Nazarene, you obsessed little darling!"

I look upon her and I look upon her and after a long time the knowledge of my resistance seems to settle inside and the slow fire of shame bums through her cheekbones, melting the mask of seduction, but as the birds and the beasts of the empty spaces begin to flutter and congregate once more, I understand that this will not be easy. Thirty-nine nights and thirty-eight days to go. I have instructed myself to keep precise records.

THOU SHALT BRUISE HIS HEAD: One must do something in the twenty-second, tra-la, to keep from being poisoned or going mad; my choice was to qualify for a Cult. Access, however, is controlled tightly, as would be expected in this highly alienated and stratified culture, and the simulations are so difficult that only one out of twenty or so, it is rumored, even *qualify*. Beyond qualification the chances are uncertain; Satan's testimony that no one has ever succeeded is—well—Satanic but it cannot be more than one out of a hundred according to the rumors. The only information would be from the cult heads themselves and needless to say they will not talk. The failures will talk and through the Inventories I talked to many of them but the counsel of failure is not to be trusted. "You haven't a chance, Quartermain," my Counselor told me. "For one thing the trials are manipulated, and for another you *believe* in the apocrypha. It is this belief that is going to *undo* you." Then she laughed and laughed, mad laughter from the bitch until I fell upon her and drained her dry but as I rose and fell, rose and fell, her hands tearing at my back like prosthetic claws I could see the defeat in her eyes: I was leaving her after the Simulations, regardless of their outcome, and I would be taken from the Complex forever. This could only depress her since we had, as may be obvious, an active relationship. "Oh you fool," my Counselor screamed in the throes of orgasm (then again it may only have been disappointment), "you fool, this is the twenty-second. Nobody believes in that shit anymore!" But she was wrong, quite wrong: *lots* believed in that shit any more. The cult heads had a splendid and lucrative occupation. I was tired of living in the engines.

I SHALL UTTERLY CONSUME ALL THINGS OFF THE FACE OF THE EARTH: So I wrestle and wrestle with Satan; she assumes many forms and arguments over the endless weeks to follow, a falcon and a sage, a technician and a wild beast, a stone, a bone, a crone. And I come through all of these struggles and impositions with my belief, if not my virtue, intact until finally on the fortieth day (I believe that it is the fortieth but by this time my record-keeping, needless to say, has become somewhat dishevelled) He appears Himself, a special appearance as guaranteed by all the apocrypha and looks at me lying on the desert floor in a rather exhausted condition and says, "Quartermain, what are you doing? Why have you done all of this to yourself?"

"For the splendor," I say. His form is ineffable and I will, hence, not attempt to describe it. "For the sacrifice and for the necessity, to commit myself to You as Your only begotten Son—"

He makes a dismissive gesture. "Do that in the temples," He says. "It's not necessary here, this is a confidential discussion." He squats in clouds of glory, clasps his hands, spits into the sand. "No, really," He says, "the outcome is impossibly humiliating and the question of Resurrection is still being debated. You have no assurance. All that awaits you are heat, dust, lepers, the misbegotten, the legions, the crucifix and a most miserably bleeding and sweaty ordeal. Why not get out now? You can call for an end to this ridiculous simulation and be resting comfortably in the recovery shack in just a few moments."

"It isn't really You," I say grimly. "It's him in another form. You've assumed another shape in order to tempt me. Get thee behind me, Satan."

"Oh come on," He says with a splendidly graceful gesture. "Really Quartermain, if you've gotten to the 39th day of this you ought to have more sophistication than that. We're working together; we're a team."

I lick my burning lips. "Is that supposed to unsettle me?" I say. "I knew that all along and it's merely another aspect of doubt. A Cult Leader must be able to subsume himself in mystery. It doesn't change anything. I'm not unsettled at all."

"Ah well," He says, "ah well," and rises from his crouch. "You are of strong stuff, Quartermain, or at least of stronger stuff than most of them, but if this doesn't unsettle you, the ass certainly will. No creature of the twenty-second century is really equipped to ride upon an ass. For any considerable distance to be sure."

"I'll deal with that when the time comes," I say. "Right now I have another day on this bloody desert."

"And a very good day to you *indeed*," He says, and disappears, leaving me to my various cogitations and moanings which, considering the thirst, heat, starvation, pain, and humility which have been invoked upon me, are considerable. It is very hard to take a sense of dignity from all of this, but astonishments, as I have perhaps brought Him to understand, are few.

COMFORT ME WITH APPLES: Long consultations with my Counselor resonate within memory as I founder in delirium on the desert floor. "You are an ambitious man, Quartermain," she said to me. "There is a core of obsession within you which profoundly fails to intersect with the sense of the times. This is no century for ambition. The machinery, the engines of the night have overtaken us all; it is best perhaps to give one's will to them. There are small escape hatches, possibilities offered: the lotteries, the Slaughtering Docks, the Technician's License and the Cult Leaderships, but they are, as we know, largely illusory, rigged against achievement and functioning largely as safety valves. It would be far easier for you if you were to accept your condition, give up; easier for me too because predictably I have fallen in love with you and your ambition works against the small layers of peace we might create as insulation. Come on, Quartermain," she said, offering me her hand, "come to me and rest. It really isn't that bad once you accept the circumstances. The machines don't want our souls, merely our respect."

I looked upon her, my gentle and wise Counselor, assigned to me many years ago to give comfort to me as I was to give comfort to her, each of us Counselor to the other in a relationship alternately stratified and affectional. It would be easy, I thought, easy to take that acceptance which she offered, to give into the will of the machinery and the dark administrators who controlled the complex. For a passing moment I felt more profound than any I had ever known, but in the next instant I had passed through as I had done so many times, and knew that it was impossible. "It is impossible,"

I said. "I want to be a Cult Leader. I want to have my servitors and the congregation; I have something to say, I want to disseminate that message. I do not want to give in, not when the will exists to be otherwise."

"Vanity of vanities," she said quietly, "all is vanity."

"So true," I said. "To give up is vanity, to struggle is vanity. To struggle is what I have elected."

"You are a fool," she said, "a self-dramatizing fool." Her eyes were moist. "Come here," she said, "look upon the city; all of the greys and greens. The walls of the city were erected to guard us against the monstrous, the truly insane, outside of those walls anything may happen—"

"Vanity of vanities," I said. And thought of the desert outside those walls, the desert upon which, if I were strong enough, I would take the forty and assert the oath and return to toss one by one with casual strength all of the money changers from the temple. "The time, the season."

Her hands upon me insistent, her voice against me insistent. "You are a fool, Quartermain," she said, "and the price of your foolishness will be mightily extracted from you."

"Cult Leaders have their choice of women," I point out.

FOR UNTO US A CHILD IS BORN: The fortieth day expires and, grumbling, Satan releases me; he has, after all, no choice according to the contract. I return to the city where food and water await me along with devotion of my followers, a small and hardy band who seem to have increased in my absence. They look at me with awe. "It wasn't that difficult," I say self-deprecatingly, "I was armored with the strength of my own innocence. Too, you have to consider the benefits." Nonetheless they remain unshaken in their devotion. I have returned gaunt and bearded and it is possible that an aura of the divine clings to me although the secret is that it is not faith but cynicism which has gotten me through the ordeal. "Rabbi," one of them says, "what do we do now?"

"We gather, we formalize, we recruit, we go upon the countryside, perform miracles, raise a dead man or two, redeem a harlot, comfort the sick, give grace to the graceless, find an ass, come into Jerusalem, attract the attention of the legions and so on and so forth," I say. "Eventually, sooner than we would like, we get to the grimmer parts but that does not have to concern us now. In fact," I say rising, "this does not have to concern us at all. Consider it merely as a journey, as a set of tasks to be completed for a preordained goal." For me, if not for you, I think.

"Did you *wrestle* out there, Rabbi?" a boy asks, his eyes round and devoted.

"Like a son of a bitch," I assure him.

UPON THIS ROCK: Peter, Paul, Mark, Simon Peter. Judas is the only problem; eventually I find a thin, sullen youth with a limp whose generalized rage seems easy enough, when the time comes, to direct toward betrayal. Assuming custody of the lot and giving them simple instruction I go upon the countryside. Loaves and fishes are easy, the Magdalene interlude only slightly embarrassing. (She misunderstands my motives initially. It has been so long since Counseling that I almost respond but fortunately hold myself in check and eventually the Magdalene understands.) Lazarus is noisome and disgusting, far fleshier and more odorous than might possible be inferred through the materials but discipline and a visualization of the many rewards of being a Cult Leader squeeze me through the vile episode. Peter follows me into the fields on the evening of this adventure and says, "Are you sure you want to go through with this, Quartermain?"

"Of course I'm sure," I say. I should point out—if it is necessary to point it out—that the disciples, congregation, observers and hangers-on are all professionals from the twenty-second who function in Simulation; they have their own reasons for being on the scene. "That was all settled in the desert."

"You seemed overcome with revulsion back there. And the really difficult stuff is still ahead."

"Nothing to it," I say. I give the trembling youth a clap on the shoulder. "After what I've been through already this is *nothing*."

"Very well," Peter says, "I'm just trying to help. We *are* disciples you know; we have that responsibility."

"Oh I know that," I say with a booming laugh. I am really quite giddy; who would not be, considering the situation? "I know you're there to help. And the best way that you can help is by *staying in place.*"

"Certainly," Peter says, "certainly, Rabbi," but I detect a bit of sullenness in his posture and am given to understand, as I should have understood from the beginning, that my goals and those of the disciples are not necessarily confluent. They are, after all, creatures of the Simulator and hence of the State. One must embrace this understanding and after a time one does.

IN THE BEGINNING WAS THE WORD: The ass, a miserable creature, is taken from pasture and I am lashed on. Somewhat awkwardly I ride into Jerusalem surrounded by my ragged troops. (The texts give no hint of the essential indignity and anonymity of the enterprise; there are *many* riding on asses toward Jerusalem in this time. Only in retrospect did I assume stature.) I find rude quarters; Judas disappears upon predictable, mysterious business. The Magdalene comes to visit me during this interval in my tent, and when she drops her cowl I see to my surprise that she is my Counselor.

"Well, what did you expect?" she says. "There's a long commitment here. I had to come and be with you to see it through. Now come home before it's too late."

"What do you mean?"

"I mean it's time to stop. This is ridiculous, Quartermain. You've done very well up to this point but now the nails and the torment begin. You haven't really begun to suffer."

"Are you working for the Simulators?"

"Don't be ridiculous," she says, tossing her head in a gesture not unlike that of Satan a long time ago although I do not, for an instant, confuse the two. "I'm working for no one. I care for you. I have your interests at heart. Listen, you've shown a lot of courage and you've carried this on far longer than almost anyone. We can have a nice life together. It isn't so hard once you give up and accept the situation. And you've proven a good deal to yourself."

"Leave now," I say. "Leave before I become angry."

"Come on," she says, putting her hands on my shoulders. "Enter me. Let me show you what you'll be missing. Cult leaders must remain chaste you know."

"I must remain chaste," I say. Her breasts suddenly appear. "What are you doing?"

"Trying to help you come to your senses before it's too late, Quartermain. This is insane." She rubs a breast against my nose. "Come on," she says, "it gets much easier once you accept the truth."

I hold her arms tightly, desperately wrench her away from me. She stumbles back. "Get out of here," I shout, "get out of here right now!"

Her eyes are luminescent. "You're really serious about this," she says. "You really *are*. You *believe* in this—"

"Don't you?" I say. "Don't we all?"

"You fool," she says, backing toward the tent flap, "don't you know that no one has ever become a Cult Leader this way? They told me the truth and I'm risking everything by carrying it to you but there's no other way. All of the Cult Leaders are State Employees, the stories of the Simulators are all lies, just to keep the masses in check, to make them believe there's a way out. Now get out of this before it's too late."

"And you too," I say, "you too. And after the life from which I saved you and the immortality you have been given. It is too unkind."

"You're mad, Quartermain," the Magdalene says. "You're filled with madness."

"Get thee behind me," I say and plunge toward her furiously, but the canvas drops and I am alone.

BEFORE THE COCK CROWS: The crowd—much larger than before and more respectably garbed—shouts for Barabbas and Pilate says to me in his heavy accent, "You see, it is quite impossible. I gave you a fair chance, however. You must admit that."

I say nothing to him. There is nothing, after all, to say. I can hear Judas frantically counting his silver somewhere in the background. The crowd murmurs for the next step in the process and I move forward, lift my arms. "To the high place," I say, "to the high place now."

A blush spreads over Pilate's features. He leans toward me and whispers, "I've been authorized to make you a final offer. We can get you out of here quickly. There's no need for this, Quartermain. We're all on your side and really you've done admirably until now, there's no reason to suffer—"

"To the high place!" I scream and the soldiers seize me under the arms and take me away. There is an instant of hesitation as I brush through the crowd and for a harsh, shocking instant I fear that the soldiers too are authorized to make me a compromise but then common, sense reasserts itself along with speed and I am carried away. Huge wooden blocks are fastened in place along my back. The soldiers cannot possibly be part of an authorization. Not *everyone* can be in on this. They could not employ and manipulate thousands simply to divert one Quest. Or could they? The resources of the technicians are awesome. I may have misunderstood the situation.

WHY HAS THOU FORSAKEN ME? The thieves, chatty in their dilemma, toss insults back and forth over me as I hang in difficult posture. Flashes of color below give me hope that the casting of lots has begun. "Ain't it a bitch?" one of the thieves says, "ain't it just a merry bitch? The things a man gets put through," and then he dies or at least he seems to die, his face slackens, drool appears, his body gives out and lies slack. "I had big plans," the other thief confides to me, "I didn't see no way to make it in the armies. But I guess there's just no way for the common folk, eh chief?"

"Before this night is out you shall dwell with me in heaven," I say.

"Ah," the thief says, "the same old bullshit, that's all you get."

FORGIVE THEM! In the blood haze one of the hundred priests in the guise of a bird appears before me. "Quartermain," he says, "I am prepared to make you a final offer. This is the last time. There is no Resurrection. There is no Church. There is nothing; you have been misled by the texts just like so many of them, so it would serve you to attend closely. We can get you out of here and make you a Lecturer in Metaphysics. With a high-level rating and much better domicile. Think of the comforts. Also the Counselor. She's very emotionally tied to you."

"Go away," I say.

"Quartermain, you're not being reasonable."

"Go away." The huge dark bird flutters, inclines. "I mean it," I say. "I'm not going to sell out now. I've gone too far."

"You're crazy. There's nothing beyond. Nothing."

"There's a Leadership."

"You'll be dead."

"In the Simulators?"

"Truth," the bird says. "This is no dream, you fool."

"Go away," I say for the third time. The bird shakes its huge head.

"You're a fool. Quartermain, you could have had it all."

"I have nothing if I yield. Upon this rock I will build my church."

"You were warned," the hundredth priest says and flies. Coma storms and lashed to the wood, I lose count of the breaths of my betrayal.

LIFT UP YOUR HEADS O YE GATES: The stone is rolled away on the third day but I am not there, of course. Nor on the fourth, fifth, or, tenth. On the fortieth they think to search the desert and there they find my bones, thus obviating any necessity for worship.

In the twenty-second you can't take anything seriously.

The Prince of the Steppes

There are those who say Yuri Semeyonvich Tomavechki is in favor of continued entrapment of Western nations, but it is a lie, is a wholesale misrepresentation, is a—I try to put this in your rhetoric—terrible contravention of the truth. Yuri Semeyonvich Tomavechki—difficult name, unassimilable name to be reduced to "Simon" within course of these remarks—is in favor of free nations, free commerce, free exchange of information, materials, goods and goddesses through all the spaces of Western and Eastern culture. With exchange, with free passage of goods, comes comity, comes understanding, comes rapprochement of the nations, not to say era of peace and justice to be ushered at beginning of millennium, thank you very much, good wishes are shared.

Yuri Semeyonvich Tomavechki, known as Simon in memoir, great believer in social justice. Now telepathic spy burrowed deep in regions of Red Hook, Brooklyn, in disguise of wholesale capitalist taxi driver ferrying Western capitalists from one destination to the next, food stamp center to Sparkle City, grand mall to Crossroads of World, Yuri sit down deep in cab, crunch in front seat of medallion #367846 New York Taxi & Limousine Commission, think deep thoughts, carry impressions to heart of secret offices in Moscow where hidden masters transmit Western impulses into code, transfer to office of premier code references to grant insight into decadent practices of long-surpassed West.

Fall of West of no interest to Simon. Simon interested only in fulfilling mission in Flatlands and Red Hook sections of Brooklyn, New York, returning to Moscow, assuming position of quiet, assimilated worker amongst workers of state. Telepathy an unbidden ability, an unshared gift; Simon turn off telepathy upon return to Moscow, live in dignity and simplicity. Simon does not *want* telepathy; does not want to tune into girl companion as put hopeful hand on upper breast, hear girl companion say in mind, "What is this?", or, "I give this five more minutes and then I lie down," or, "How many rubles in long run is worth this?", or, "Simon, he beautiful creature; I transfer hand soon to *lower* breast." Simon, twenty-nine years old, prefer uncertainties, prefer little possibilities and mysterious to evidence given by telepathic gift. Simon long embarrassed by share of consciousness given by gift, embarrassed, too, by unbidden emergence that takes him so conclusively to Brooklyn Western capitalist state. Simon, mind open now, will close mind in Moscow, never open again.

Simon, digressing, drives his cab up and down Flatbush Avenue seeking "fare." "Fare" Simon seeks is specific; this not random chase but specific, known goal, appear for casualness and hope to evade Western police not yet aware (it is hoped) of telepathic spy. "Fare is Elena Wresicwz Theveya—abbreviate in memoir to "Elena"—cousin of famous defected scientist now defected to Los Angeles, defected scientist cousin Nicholas known to be inventor of D-Bomb, dangerous secrets, more dangerous than is ever known. Feared give secret to warmongering Western interests in Los Angeles. Elena, known contact in Red Hook, in Brooklyn, has access to famous Nicholas, knows, it is suspected, of famous Nicholas plans. Short-range telepath Simon (range no good beyond thirty feet—it is unfortunate, it is loss, but such is pathos of Simon range; otherwise, Nicholas be long since investigated) to find Elena as "fare" in Flatbush section, Brooklyn, drive Elena to constant destination, capitalist Wall Street pig place where is junior trainee and plumb unconscious for thoughts. Contact with Nicholas? Possession of plans? Passage of plans from Nicholas to dangerous Western agents ready to employ D-Bomb? Or Nicholas innocent of warlike intention; simply living in Los Angeles, cooperating with cinema to be made of his life, cinema rights purchased by famous director? All to be resolved by Simon, telepathic spy hunched over wheel of defunct Checker 1972 taxi sedan, scanning heart of Brooklyn, looking for "fare." OFF-DUTY sign twinkling above roof. Elena soon to emerge from hovel, to look for taxiist to take to Wall Street pig place, Simon slyly positioned for pickup. Plan worked out with secret office supervisors in Moscow, contact with Elena to be useful—if useful enough, terminate assignment, return small apartment Moscow, pick up worker's life in quiet worker's way, telepathic access closed off. Live quietly once more. Such is plan.

Is big plan, hah. Is demonstration of futility of human effort, just as Western philosophy says. Practical workers philosophy say life is meaningful, is not cluttered with purposes of disaster, but practical workers philosophy in this case wrong; despairing decadent philosophy of West is right.

Big plan, hah! Return to quiet life in Moscow, hah! Learn secrets of Nicholas and repent of admission of telepathy, hah!

Simon learn intricacies of Western thought, Western possibility. Simon to be plunged into world, as is said, of guilt and sorrow like world banishment of which is predicted by Lenin, other grand figures, other figures of belief and subsistence and trust.

Picking up Elena no problem. Cruise back, cruise forth, wait, be waited, show gay, show abandon, be patient. At length, Elena, just like girl in good modern photograph in wallet that have for study, emerge for taxi coming from hovel, stand patient in street. Ignore one waving arm, two buses, three crosswise cyclists with packages, and arrive at curbside, signaling to Elena is available. Is cab at service. Telepathic spy ready to drain mind of all secrets about D-Bomb cousin, Nicholas, report secrets to headquarters, embark upon path of retaliation against decadent culture that would employ such D-Bomb secrets? Of this, Elena knows nothing. Depth of travesty is this: no one knows. To the best knowledge, am only telepathic spy. No other telepath on either side of cold war, not Western or Eastern bloc in all of these centuries. Only telepath to emerge Simon, and he not emerge either if keep big mouth shut when red-cheeked schoolboy in classroom on Lenin Boulevard. Keep big mouth shut is Western expression, if not Western trait; not keeping mouth shut put Simon in cab in Red Hook, Brooklyn, disguised as industrious immigrant taxi driver. Elena, in backseat, looks at back of neck of industrious immigrant and says, "Thirty Pearl, and quickness, please; am late." She had slight and delightful accent, although emigrated many years before Simon. Twelve years in country, for Elena, now twenty-seven, came on special visa with family when just sprouting breasts, as Americans say. "Must get there quickly," Elena says.

Sturdy industrious immigrant shrugs, puts Checker in drive gear, presses on accelerator, and moves past Nevins Street. It is short way to Manhattan Bridge, then short on bridge to Canal, then short again south to capitalist pig district where Pearl located, so must use telepathic gifts, must push hard. Push hard, then, at short, satisfactory range against mind of girl in backseat, plumbing for special news. Traffic, dogs, indigent citizens scatter on Flatbush Avenue before me as I concentrate outer eye on evasion, inner eye on Elena. "Ah," Elena says. "Ah yes." At hint of invasion, mind reflexively contracts, leading often to *ah* sound, sometimes *eeh* sound, even gulp of insult, small, controllable epileptic fit. Is harmless, and amnesia always in wake of probe, so there is no concern. Amnesia will be total. Sturdy immigrant pushes hard against blonde mind of pretty assimilated defector in backseat, and mind rears up in response, one by one disgorges all of its secrets, tilts like cornucopia and tumbles all of secrets into mind of Simon, which eagerly receives. Like sex but reversal, man mind take while female mind give. Simon not obsessed with sex, too much product of controlled environment, telepathic gift, tensions of state to be much concerned with sex, but Simon know value of metaphor, too, as secrets pour in.

Simon, arm on steering wheel, keen Soviet reflexes attendant to twitches in traffic, approaches bridge while fascinated, absorbing information ... mind of Elena slides information *chuck-chuck* into telepathic spy.

D-Bomb not spurious, Simon finds; also, Nicholas releasing plans to chairman Department of Mathematics at state university branch in northern California. Chairman plant of capitalist intelligence agency, who, in guise of friendship and comity, has learned D-Bomb information from Nicholas in guise of salving conscience. Nicholas, racked and tortured by solitariness of possession of absolute weapon, does not know what to do. In seeking advice, confides to chairman, who is conduit to center of capitalist power in Washington.

D-Bomb plans already known to Washington.

All of this apparent, tilted into mind of Simon, because Elena is Washington contact, is in closest collaboration with center of power. is so, this, because Elena is using contact with cousin, confidentiality of correspondence, atmosphere to trust, to cajole uncle to release D-Bomb secret to secret intelligence officer at Department of Mathematics. Reason for this is that Elena has promised, will promise, has had sexual congress with much older cousin (age fifty-four) Nicholas. All of this—images of congress, too—pour into eager but shocked mind of Simon, who almost hits Doberman pinscher and aged owner at Henry Street, inferring this information. Images of congress so bright as to be stunning; Simon no fool, no latecomer to arena of sexual connection, nonetheless shocked, discombobulated by implication. D-Bomb secrets well advanced in quarters capable of rapid and ominous advancement, Simon infers as Doberman drags owner to safety and Elena, grunting *eeh*, falls out of telepathic contact by virtue of fainting, of collapsing to floor of Checker 1972 discontinued model.

Fainted passenger in car, dangerous information in mind, telepathic spy disguised as hardworking, dedicated family-devoted immigrant drives over Manhattan Bridge thinking of dangerous nature of subject and appeal.

Conveyance of information, hah! And yet, hah again! If Simon turns over this information to proper controlling source—who is, forgot to mention, dispatcher in guise of Pole at cab company that Simon serves—return to Moscow will be much accelerated but not in fashion Simon will want. Interrogations, delays, possibilities of angst and anomie will be almost limitless as interrogators, in Soviet style, take appallment at messenger of humble but dangerous news.

At Pearl Street, then, Simon has decision to make. Elena has recovered from aspects of telepathic drain; is sitting poised and uneasy on rear seat of cab, somewhat ill at ease but nonetheless willing to confront training program in debentures and long-term conversion bonds to better of ability, Elena seeking revenge upon difficult childhood and rage at Soviet Union by seeking capitalist skill (telepathy has revealed). She reaches into pocketbook with industrious hands, looking at me appraisingly. Does not see tortured eyes, does not see truly chiseled artistic features or telepath's pain and knowledge, but only hat, clothes, façade of hardworking immigrant. You may keep the change," she says, while fumbling for bill they call *tenner*. "What a speedy trip! I never had such a fast trip. I must have slept. I remember nothing of it."

Flocks of walkers, to say nothing of oppressive sight of tall buildings, have us momentarily pinned, locked in place. "No," I say, "payment is not necessary."

"Not necessary?"

"We have business more urgent," I say, "business that exceeds payment of fare. You must take me at once to your cousin, Nicholas."

She stares at me. It is impossible with limited descriptive powers, power of distraction, to indicate kind of stare or what effect this has had upon her, upon me. This is unexpected speech of strange, industrious immigrant Checker cab driver found on Flatbush Avenue and now on Pearl Street. "Who *are* you?" she says. "Who are—?"

"Is no time," I say. "Is no time for all of that. Must see Nicholas, inventor of D-Bomb, persuade him of error of his ways before all plans released to dangerous chairman and construction of bomb begins, thus ending life for all on planet. To give this information to government at this time utterly disastrous; you and I will be in cell in Moscow in twelve hours with roaches for partners and nothing to discuss. We must go to Los Angeles at once," I say. "At once. There is no time for cajolement, no time for whisperings of credibility and certainty; it is essential you accept. You accept? We take cab to airport of Kennedy right now, purchase budget-buster waitaround standby emergency fare, and we go out to Los Angeles at once."

Of nature of response, I cede moment. Is impossible within compass to explain conversation. Elena stares with wonderment, incites with passion, talks with rage, gasps with shock, but cab already on move from Pearl Street, heading toward airport of Kennedy, secure doors locked from front seat as is provided in special bulletproof vehicle reserved by Pole for Simon his own duties. Conversation does not lead to cooperation, not all the way, but in nature of such conversations assisted by years of experience interrogation at better hands than these, credibility is accomplished.

"Was your mistake leading Nicholas to cooperate," I say. "Was your reason to sit on Nicholas, to refuse. Now you make big problem, you make possible imminence of descent of all civilization if prognosticative powers do not fail." Prognostication is not allied with telepathic gift, but Elena at this point ready to accept that assurance.

Elena, by time of arrival at airport of Kennedy, is ready to accept almost anything at all. Elena's acceptance is no encouragement to Simon's modesty, however. Simon properly, expeditiously, refuses further telepathic investigation of Elena consciousness, Simon believing in essential privacy and integrity of human condition.

Telepathic powers do not assure prognostication is true, but do have mildly telekinetic, transportational, directional powers. Utilized in expeditious way, enable us to: a) leave Checker in inconspicuous place without penalty, b) find a way to budget-buster emergency standby line front at once through exercise of powerful influence and sudden somnolence of those in preceding part of line, c) ensure sufficient sickness on part of booked passengers to guarantee all standby admissions. Soon Elena and I are on Delta Air budget-buster seats flight 807, winging our way to Los Angeles, seated and sipping drinks of various alcoholic content, while Simon, no slave of circumstance he, resolves to tell Elena everything. Reasons for flight. Reasons for assumption of knowledge. Even reason for knowing of sexual contact between fifty-four-year-old cousin and twenty-seven-year-old teenage defector now studying debentures. "How dare you—" Elena says, but then full import of talent—also air pockets—hit her, and turbulence causes sudden cessation of conversation. Would be possible to go on with all further exchanges—shared memories of Moscow, shared memories of childhood of approximately same generation, even beginning of yielding by Elena—but is not necessary under the circumstances. Say that by flight's end—I risk one quick, harmless but revealing probe— Simon has replaced Nicholas, at least in part, as object of sexual fantasy.

We deplane, as expression goes, and find ourselves in airport of L.A.- Extension, even more bewildering than place of Kennedy. We do this, we do that, telekinesis showing itself once again of mild usage. In rental car, Elena's credit information having worked its informational wonders, Simon driving once again but Elena in front seat now, we are soon enough in quiet town of Tarzana, where Nicholas resides with many textbooks and lustful intent. "We must come upon him unwarned," I have said to Elena. "Is vital that there be no prior discussion; we do not have time." After six hours of my suasion and emolumentary discussion, she has agreed. There is no resistance left in sexually fantasizing Elena. We enter upon pink-and-white building of sort clung to by immigrants and actors of Moscow Art Theatre, and on fourth floor—Simon accelerates narrative, but it is important to say end of world looms if experiments not instantly cessation, and acceleration is only comprehensible course—pound on apartment of Nicholas. Elena clings to elbow as Simon heroically pounds. Simon pounds like heroic worker, like troops in *Alexander Nevsky*. Door is suddenly pulled off, rotten on hinges; from door emerges face. Face bright with mustache, with damp sweats.

"This is not Nicholas," Elena says.

I know this already. Nicholas image has been plucked from unconscious of disgorging telepathized Elena. This is something else with face of commissar, face of all faces I have seen in a hundred dreaming nights, face I have always expected

"Come in, Yuri Semeyonvich Tomavechki," face says, and enormous arms, perhaps connected to another body, reach forward, impel humble form into apartment, Elena shambling in thereafter, yank humble form to attentive posture while behind is deadly sound of Elena's laughter, now bubbling as in recollected secret sexual encounter with Nicholas recorded in memories once extracted so recently. Elena laughs and laughs.

"Ah, Yuri Semeyonvich," commissar with face like dreams says, that face enormous, leaning over, "do you think, do you really think, we let telepathic spy alone, uncontrolled, in Red Hook, Brooklyn, to work will without control?"

Laughter and laughter. Simon has nothing to state; stating seems beyond him. Room seems full of laughter; Simon, even in his distress, is convinced that he is not alone.

"*Short range is short fool!*" commissar says; "*D-Bomb is big, big range!*"—and claps Simon on shoulder, drags Simon in nearer and nearer, laughing. Elena laughing, too, all of capitalist and Eastern culture laughing together; while over in corner, Simon sees Nicholas, man he recognizes from Elena unconscious as Nicholas, crouching over plans, rubbing hands on plans, laughing over plans, laughing and laughing, as ever so subtly, ever so suddenly, curtain of civilization seems to come down on scene; and soon enough, Simon, in extreme distress, finds it possible to see no more. Simon feels intense explosive fires building within, feels himself—presence of attractive, seductive Elena not necessity for perpetration of this powerful longing—on verge of explosion of extinguishing force.

Simon observes as if from great distance commissar and Nicholas exchange look of penetrating intelligence, look that Simon seems to recall from Moscow dreams, Moscow nights, Leningrad possibilities and conferences. "Now?" commissar says to Cousin Nicholas. "Right now?"

"Now," Cousin Nicholas says with distinct lilt, lilt to voice resemblance to that in voice of Boris Godunov before deposed czar in famous opera by drunkard Mussorgsky go tumbling down steps to bowels of Hell. "Now," repeats Nicholas.

Simon feels pain that is that of comprehension, feels himself on verge of awful insight, tries to push away, but insight comes nevertheless. Simon understands in a suddenness what has happened to him.

"Is on schedule," Elena says. Her face is masked, traitorous, her voice cool and appraising. Passion seems to be left on budget-buster flight; is no passion in this face. "Arm him now," she says to Cousin Nicholas, who winks at her.

"Is already armed," Nicholas says, to obvious satisfaction of commissar.

Inference not sufficient here; decadent Western literature demands— unlike progressive Soviet worker-oriented literature—that explanations be made, explicitness be accomplished, in last moments before night of many suns, Yuri Semeyonvich Tomavechki—last known as "Simon," herewith to be known as Archangel of Soviet Power—will cause to explain, let reader in on secret, on terrible process.

"Is accomplished well," commissar is saying, "but is not of a certainty yet; produce proof of the arming." Elena reaches forth, grasps invidious infamous telepathic spy Simon in enormous and clutching hold. Explanation to follow.

Here is explanation: is trigger. Is all scheme to trigger. Is gathering of many forces in Los Angeles, is the use of Elena in her hot-bloodedness to entrap the naive and haplessly hot-blooded Simon, is the creation of imposter-Nicholas as necessary third force.

"Boom!" says first agent, pointing.

"Boom!" says second agent.

Third agent, working quickly on Simon, has no time for such mockery or commentary, being busily engaged. "Assembly completed," agent now says, "Like false czar, is waiting."

Simon himself is D-Bomb.

D-Bomb to go off at convenience.

Later, not so much later, bing-bam.

Andante Lugubre

Tchaikovsky lived on, stunk in the wheelchair, broke into the pustules and exploded surfaces of extreme old age, exuded the leprous but alluring perfume of death. How could he have expected this in his tragic and masked 40s when suicide had been his companion, self-immolation the glowing ring of fire at the far end of his spasms and jerky thrusts? But now he lived on and on, surviving the rivalries at the Conservatory, his self-loathing, the scandalous and poorly concealed sex life, the conflicts with his brother Modest, more treacherous than he but long, long dead.

Tchaikovsky aged: he went on and on, lived tremulously past the threats to the czar, the division of the Balkans, the second and successful revolution. He fled Moscow at 77 for a brief stay in Berlin, then inched his way via Paris to the Hollywood Hills where he enjoyed a sinister celebrity as the composer of popular ballet scores and survivor of the Bolsheviks. In his early 90s, discarding flesh like a fungus, no longer composing, not a composer for four decades since the quite shocking unsuccessful attempt at the conservatory to poison him, Tchaikovsky became the recipient of renewed public attention, found indeed a minor revival. His music began to be used as background score for the new talking pictures. He was also a focus for the increasing colony of Russian émigrés and sullen victims of Stalin, who continued to pour into both coasts speaking rumors of insanity as the Soviet Union became less tolerable, Stalin ever more crazy. Wizened, reeking, unable to summon his diminished wits, Tchaikovsky was nonetheless drafted as one of the early opponents of Hitler, was made nominal head of various committees of the entertainment industry which expressed alarm at Hitler's increasingly brutal reign. Tchaikovsky had never had much use for Jews or gypsies himself but seemed to agree, nodding and reeking, that Hitler was certainly a menace.

Ninety-eight years old, blanket across his decomposing knees, trembling hands tucked into one another in some palsied approximation of infantile masturbation, the hands sneaking little touches of his vanished genitals tucked all against one another underneath the worn and faded blanket bearing scenes from the Bolshevik assault upon the Romanoff treasures, Tchaikovsky on one of his bad days was still sumptuously wheeled by Samuel Goldwyn (born *Goldfish*) into Ciro's in Los Angeles where a meeting on behalf of the American-Russo-Jewish alliance had been called to discuss means of opposing Hitler and bringing public attention to *Kristellnacht* and the oncoming mass murders. Sergei Rachmaninoff, now in his late 60s and failing visibly from a multitude of physical insults and exile, sat at the table beside Walt Disney, Darryl Zanuck and other titans and solons of this vanished time. Gershwin was supposed to have been there and in fact was to have chaired the meeting but the treatments for the brain tumor only partially removed in 1937 had reduced him to a shuddering and crazy recluse in his institutionalized holdings and there were rumors that he recognized no one, not even Ira. Upton Sinclair had sent a telegram of regret and regard, as had Norman Thomas. But Arnold Schoenberg and Eric Korngold were there and as a measure of the President's own interest, Harry Hopkins had sent an aide as an unofficial observer. The aide, a shy man named Jacob Javits, would later achieve some minor political office, although he never achieved—due perhaps to his close affiliation with what came to be called the 'Kike Committee'—the Senate or governorship to which he felt entitled.

Tchaikovsky sat through the often contentious meeting in a stuporous and commingled condition. At the age of 99—a remarkable chronology but hardly a time of life which held much sparkle as the grim and devious Rachmaninoff advised the table—he had succumbed progressively to not only the stink but the more terrible organic deterioration of extreme old age and sat shrivelled within his chair, little wisps and patches of his youthful music circulating unsuccessfully within his brain as he tried to pay some minimal attention to the proceedings. Schoenberg was convinced that without petitions, demands, huge rallies and radical demonstrations, the Jews of Germany and perhaps all of Europe were doomed. Rachmaninoff, who had never particularly cared for Jews as a race but was willing to concede their humanity and their very real difficulties at the present time, agreed with this position but suggested that outrage would only generate unpleasant public attention. Korngold, who was trying to manage a very difficult course in motion pictures at this time—his scores were quite successful but he had a reputation as a firebrand and troublemaker, doubtless because of the ardor of his youth—at 42 wanted no more trouble. Unable to convince Goldwyn or Zanuck of this repentance, however, Korngold had little to say, although he whispered agreement with Schoenberg. Goldwyn, ever master of malaprop, suggested that Hitler be sent a series of conditions by the solons of Hollywood with the penalties for his ignorance to reach severity if he did not agree to cease in his persecution.

Zanuck had little to add to this, being concerned largely with the etiquette of the affair and his desire not to give offense or to be too conspicuously Jewish while at the same time offering solidarity. So it was left to Hopkins' assistant, the 35-year-old Javits, a real go-getter it had been rumored, to make some statement, but Jacob fumbled uncomfortably with his hat, said that he was there to be an observer and that the administration while certainly concerned with the plight of the Jewish community could not in these dark and invasive times take a position. Rumors of Poland's imminent fall, Javits added, rendered the Administration's position even more difficult. How could Roosevelt come out strongly for the Jews if war was beckoning? It would be said that the country had entered the war, had declared war on behalf of the Jews and that could lead only to an unpopular verdict and a loss of public support. It was best if the Jewish interests, even those as influential and highly placed as the Hollywood masters, waited and allowed events to overtake Hitler,

"After all," Javits said, "once Hitler goes to war, once he finds himself actively entangled with this country and its allies, he will be far too busy and threatened to murder more Jews. He will have to turn his attention to larger matters." As this seemed horrifyingly on the verge of real tastelessness, Javits smiled painfully and said, "You do understand, do you not, that I am myself Jewish. There is no intent, none whatsoever, to minimize the seriousness of the situation, but strategic considerations do apply."

Coiled within the themes of his First Symphony, the Winter-Dreams now thundering through the bare and shattered panels of his sensibility, Tchaikovsky heard only the word *Jews* and it seemed to bring him to a kind of attention; for the first time on this tortured afternoon, for the first time in many weeks in fact he appeared to focus on the situation. "Jews," Tchaikovsky bellowed. "Let me tell you about Jews. The Czar had a special feeling and their problems in my opinion have long been overrated. Now you have to consider the political situation, to say nothing of their influence upon the Conservatory. My first plan was to continue with opera but Rimsky had some unpleasant things to say about *Onegin* and then again it was never the same after Mme. von Meck died and I lost a charming and willful supporter. And that is all I have to say about that," The composer concluded, "You really do have to watch those Jews, that is very important, because it is clear that the Jews are always watching you."

This effort seemed to exhaust him, the pustules on his fervid skin seemed to open, the bellowing of the old composer having taken him to a thin and perilous intensity which made a knifing stink. Tchaikovsky fell back against his chair. Rachmaninoff, neither Jew lover nor great supporter of Tchaikovsky, muttered in disgust and cast bitter glances at Schoenberg and Korngold who looked at him with an equal loathing. "If there is nothing more to say," Rachmaninoff pointed out, "perhaps we should adjourn this meeting. I have bags to pack, business to attend, I am entraining to conduct the Philadelphia Orchestra next Saturday, also I can contribute nothing more here."

"Essentially" the composer said, "and with apologies to my distinguished colleagues, I think that the Jews must protect themselves. We had to fend for ourselves during our Bolshevik storming, Petyr and I, there was little help coming across the waters or the boundaries for such as we when the Bolsheviks started shooting at us, and similarly, if the Jews are to escape this sodden *fatedness*, they will have to manage on their own. We can offer funds, perhaps, but little public support."

Rachmaninoff's statement incited little opposition although there was sullen grumbling to be heard up and down the corridors of Ciro's back room, then Schoenberg sighed and stood and said, "There has never been any help for the Jews throughout the history of the Diaspora and surely that will not change now. So I move that we give this up and adjourn." There was a general murmur indicating agreement. "I concur," Korngold said, standing in turn, "If we cannot be given help freely then there is no help whatsoever, isn't that clear?" This seemed to have brought the meeting toward a necessary conclusion.

Jacob Javits was the first to leave, closing the notebook into which he had scribbled reflections and odd scraps of dialogue. He wished everyone well. "I wish you all well," said the ambitious 35-year-old, his persona already fixed toward a political career. One by one, making sure that they would not be seen in collusion or friendship, the executives left, Disney last of all, casting veiled glances at Tchaikovsky but offering nothing. There was scuttlebutt that Disney's intelligence was far overrated, that the cartoon man was in over his head, that he was the creation of his assistants and support system but there was no one within or without the Colony who would challenge any of this. Finally only Tchaikovsky, leaking pus and memories, snoozing in his elaborate wheelchair, Rachmaninoff, Korngold and Schoenberg were left, Tchaikovsky's attendant Goldwyn having departed with the executives after pushing the chair with a flourish toward the composers. "So there you have it, gentlemen," Schoenberg said. "As you can see, there is nothing for us, but then again there never was, and we should not have expected otherwise."

Korngold said nothing. Striving for accommodation ever since his exile from Germany, he had through luck and connection found profitable work scoring films but despised himself all the more, and feeling the disapproval of Schoenberg he could hardly reach out in a gesture of agreement. Rachmaninoff said, "You will have to deal with this yourselves, of course. My fate is somewhat different, and I will not pretend that I share destiny with you Jews." Rachmaninoff gestured, the sweep of his hand seeming to include Tchaikovsky as well.

"Well, sure," Tchaikovsky said from the depths of his blanket and sudden, hazy recollection of the apotheosis second act of *The Nutcracker*, emerging from this cloister of dimly regretted music to momentarily engage circumstance in the way that the wry old, the pained, the terminally ill, the humorless old and the senile so often manage. "Of course that is true but up to a point. Jews live on and on just as myself," Tchaikovsky said. "Lenin and Marx themselves knew that there was no end to the problem simply because of their eager and avaricious nature. Does that make any sense? What makes sense? We must consider, we must consider." The odoriferous composer hummed the descending notes of the first big theme of the first movement of his *Pathetique* in a voice so cracked that no one, not even the skilled composers and musicians, could understand what the man was singing. "They just go on and on, those Jews," Tchaikovsky said. "They live on and on and always will."

He began to conduct that first movement from the chair, the violins pounding in his head, the bassi weeping, the waving of his arms seeming epileptic to the unschooled, medically naive observers who stared at him with confusion but without any hope at all.

"So much for petitions, memories, justice or prayer," Tchaikovsky concluded and wrapped his blanket more tightly, muffling in some way the stink of his gangrenous farts. Korngold came forward, gave the chair a sudden push although whether to provide locomotion or show resentment was never made clear. The aged and quivering Tchaikovsky, only 88 pounds including his wounds and excrescence, now fully wracked by the implausibility of his unforeseen condition, fell straight from the chair and onto the floor at Ciro's, exploding the cartilage of his nose and inducing massive bleeding. That bleeding took the composer so close to death that only the heroic efforts of the hastily-summoned ambulance attendants were able to save his life, hold him together to await the final medical disaster which would surely come at some point past the invasion of Poland.

But this did not happen.

Tchaikovsky lived on and on, he superseded his odor and the poisonous corruption of his flesh, he became at last something slender and aseptic, odorless in the chair. He attended Schoenberg's funeral in 1951 hidden under even more blankets and insignia, he lived on to be greeted by Clifford Odets in Hollywood when Tchaikovsky was wheeled into the Un-American Activities Committee hearings. He lived on and on close to the present era, in fact, perhaps beyond. He is a survivor of purges and Bolsheviks, depression and despair, Mme. von Meck and all of the indignities of a buried sexual existence. He is in fact alive today although in ever-worsening health, unable now to even express flatulence. Regrettably, none of the others have survived, nor did the European Jews they sought to protect. What does this mean? It means almost nothing: it is an anomaly which defies the ability of even an ironist to assess.

Standards & Practices

Emily Dickinson could sense her options winding down. The biological clock in the first place, 37 years old now and no child, no husband, not even a man about whom she could fantasize; then too on all other fronts her life seemed to have become sallow, wasted. The City University was cutting back now even on the adjunct positions; the building management had made specious "improvements" to her studio and had socked her with a twenty-eight-dollar-a-month increase. Everywhere she turned this sullen October she felt the sense of her imprisonment ever more palpable. Staring down 85th Street at the Hudson, looking at the fireball sun collapse unevenly behind the monstrous buildings of Fort Lee, New Jersey, Emily felt as if she herself were sinking, as if

> *That enormous ball; unbuckled to its waist*
> *Charmless, the suitor beckoning to his celestial hutch*
> *As if not embrace but the stone grave without haste*
> *Awaited those kissing—beckoning—unguent clutch.*

And the poetry was not doing well either; ever since Howard Moss had died the *New Yorker* had been closed to her. *Epoch*, the *Massachusetts Review* were not even postage money and after the little flurry surrounding her first book, a close runner-up for the Lamont Moss had told her, and a one-thousand-dollar grant from the Academy of Arts & Letters, she had been unable to attract any interest in what she felt was her far stronger second collection, now going the contest circuit after five years of failing to find even Capra or Swallow Press. Of course the poetry had never been anything which she could have taken seriously, it had been as her brother Austin had told her so many years ago "a very nice outlet" and that was about all but it was frustrating to find even this closed off to her now. But the men situation was worse; after the little thing she had had going with Oliver hit or miss for a couple of years, at least he had been predictable and she could count on him to do nothing crazy, after that had come to a quick truncation with Oliver's online management shifting half the company, bang! Like that to Santa Fe, she had had no man in her life at all. Not that she could gird herself to the seeking. Where were they? They were all married or gay or crazy or some combination of the three and then too there was the lurking possibility of AIDS with anyone at any time, that

> *Small bite, the grand and sweeping unbuttoning*
> *In corridors far and dense, the swoon of gluttony*
> *Unappeased by that darker fear; grave to grave*
> *We travel and only that dreaming bite become our nave.*

You perhaps reached that point, close to 40 or a little beyond, where all of your plans and scuttling for possibility seem only to have led to this West Side of replication and loss, the dropping of the sun into the river prefiguring the fall of her own life. And yet Emily was not able to accept this, had not come from Amherst to Mount Holyoke to work-study to her marginal academic career in New York to give it all up at the age of 38. There were possibilities, she had not utterly lost her looks, was this not the age of millennial possibility? Girded by thoughts like this to say nothing of her own determination, Emily Dickinson resolved to find some recovered possibility in her life, to unleash

> *As if in concourse meadow—the touch of the stones*
> *Thunderous in that creating storm—oh with hand*
> *Unbent in the nave, hearing His groans*
> *Thunderous in the surprising concourse of his hand.*

Remembering her unsatisfactory experience in EST, the truly unsettling men she had met and the Saturdays spent in hard chairs listening to the shouting, fighting for control of her bladder, Emily elected to stay away from self-improvement yet could not resist taking a free interview with the Church of Latent Possibility situated at Times Square. Crisp in the denims of the Ocean Going Latitudes, the senior group of the Church, her interviewer efficiently took her biography, nodded sympathetically when Emily confided her unsatisfactory experiences with psychiatry, her sense of betrayal when Oliver had raised himself from the bed after their penultimate coupling to tell her that he was leaving town. "They always wait until after sex," Emily said bitterly, "if they have something awful to tell you. No matter who they are, that's how they handle it."

"Isn't that the truth?" the Ocean Going lieutenant said. Well groomed in her immaculate uniform, she reminded Emily of her mother back in Amherst, warning her that all men were swine, but only in the most sympathetic tones. "Will you want a full reconditioning?" the lieutenant said. "I think that would be best to turn your life around. It would be twenty sessions in ten weeks and then we'll reevaluate." When Emily said nothing, the lieutenant cleared her throat and said, "That would be one thousand dollars for the initial consultation and assignment. Of course we can work out terms."

Ancient Puritan warnings seemed to circulate in the abscess of memory within Emily's consciousness, along with the severe cast of her mother's features when she felt that Emily and Austin were, as her expression were "going off" with her. "I don't think I can afford anything like that," Emily Dickinson said. "I was more or less just looking for some advice, maybe some kind of genial mixer, college graduates, young singles, like that—"

"Well," the lieutenant said and paused. "Well, of course, there are functions such as that. But that must come later. After you're reestablished, after we've had a chance—"

"I'm sorry," Emily said. She pushed the hard chair away, retreated toward the door, trying to appear casual but aware that the lieutenant's features had shifted to a kind of dread and focused attentiveness. "I guess this wasn't for me after all. One thousand dollars for reconditioning. I mean, I don't want to be *reconditioned*, I'd just like a date or maybe a chance at a tenure track somewhere in the city, that's all. I'm afraid you take my ambitions as being too large. I'm 38 years old, it's really too late to be *reconditioned*." Feeling dignity flee along with any intimations of a more positive self-image, Emily stumbled through the door and into Times Square thinking: I have taken my life too seriously, it is time to establish some distance, some space between—

> *The angels and the dust that surely comes for me*
> *Or the darkness and the cast light of lost possibility.*

Emily attends the short-story reading at Symphony Space Theater on Broadway at 95th Street. In a packed theater of white West Siders and upwardly mobile singles or nearly attached she listens to stories of Flannery O'Connor, Woody Allen and Russell Bates as read by several actors, the only one she likes being Frances Sternhagen. The O'Connor strikes her as being needlessly morbid but when the old woman is shot dead the audience breaks into applause and Emily remembers that in modern criticism this act is conceived as being not murderous but sacramental. Repulsive as this may be, she has herself taught that interpretation at Hunter College not so many years ago. Now however she finds it difficult to take such bland assurances into an October night populated by her chattering, contented contemporaries and homeless people who sit on crates and mumble about money or the sonsofbitches. Emily finds herself approached and escorted by the man who had sat at her left during the reading, a short man with assassin's features who had kicked her once by accident and then when he had apologized had given her a longing but ambiguous look. Now he says that he is a clinical psychologist who does adjunct work at Einstein and consultations at Cornell as well as sustaining a small practice and he could see that she hated the O'Connor story as much as he did. He suggests that since they both seem to be unescorted they go to the Library Restaurant and have some dinner.

Emily knows that he is married and probably has at least two children and does not get along badly enough with his wife to make him even the vaguest of prospects. At 38 and in this city, granted her experience and that of her friends, she has all the intelligence and acuity she needs not to be murdered as a result of her own stupidity, but pushing him away now seems to require more energy than simply submitting. She is lonely and perhaps the oceangoers are right; she is in need of a thorough reconditioning. His name is Robert and he was struck right away by the sensitivity and intensity of her features, he would bet that she is creative in some ways, maybe even a writer. Is this true? By this time they are already seated in the restaurant. Emily talks about the City University but does not mention the poetry, that being the most private part of herself and in any event she is barely writing now. They talk amiably enough through and after dinner and now it is time to decide what to do. Not so many years ago, Emily thinks she might have had a somewhat wider series of choices or possibilities but this, of course, is the AIDS era and one does nothing on a first or even a fifteenth encounter until one has thoroughly researched the situation. She asks for Robert's phone number.

"Why don't you give me yours?" he says.

She does so. There is little enough at risk and she has a police lock, a doorman and an answering machine. "Now will you give me your number?" she says.

"It's easier for me to call you," Robert says. "I'm out a lot and having trouble on the line. You can reach me at Einstein on Tuesday afternoons late, usually and at Cornell on Saturday mornings."

Now she knows he is married. The near-disclosure is neither thunderous nor amusing, it is simply part of the landscape like the faded seats in the theater and the imploded sun collapsing into the foul Hudson. "Well," she says, "well, it's been nice talking with you. I have to teach an early class, though, so we'd best go." She puts a twenty-dollar bill on the table. "That should be fair," she says. "Take care of the check. Maybe I'll see you at the next reading. Maybe not." He looks at her silently, his face slightly abashed, a small boy perhaps caught fondling himself in the back of the classroom, under his desk. She walks out of the classroom as she had walked from the church a few days ago, her stride even, her legs curiously shaky, however. She has been walking out of too many places this way recently and for no apparent purpose. There is some air of finality in these places which she would like to think of as millennial but which she suspects has to do with her own age and condition.

Emily finds herself at a sports bar on upper Broadway, surrounded by singles, staring without much interest at a New York Rangers playoff game on five television sets suspended above the bar. Increasingly in these last weeks she has found herself in situations like these, after a long period when she had felt that all of this nonsense was behind her. It must have something to do with the season but then again Oliver's departure and failure to write may have had a greater effect upon her than she could have ever expected. The Rangers score a goal and lead 5-3 but St. Louis gets two late surprise goals to tie and then wins in the third minute of overtime, creating a mood in the sports bar which comes as close to ugly as affluent, cynical West Siders can be in the presence of an impersonal disaster. In all of this time, too, no one has spoken to her; she has sat at the bar invisibly and invisibly now she puts money on the bar. Has the long-feared collapse of all association come to her? Has she lost her looks, her soul or any sense of possibility? She does not know but preparing to leave the bar, Emily has a wild feeling of dislocation, it settles upon her like a cloak and she can feel the uneasy and uneven shifting within her heart. "Excuse me," a man says, brushing past her, waving at his date who seems to glow with necessity, her face suffused with love as she waves back. Emily has always feared her acuity, felt it as a curse but she has never known it to give her the kind of pain which she now feels. She is not a bad-looking woman, is she? Howard Moss had been enamored of her poetry and had actually taken three of her minor poems, then had maneuvered the Viking acceptance of the collection. All of that had been ten years ago, of course. Things change in ten years. In fact, things can become terminal in much less time than this, Emily thinks.

She leaves the bar, cries of revulsion toward the Rangers sounding behind her. She has the odd and irrational thought that perhaps she should call Robert after all, find him at Einstein on Tuesday and say, "All right, I'm not going anywhere either. Who are we kidding? You get a test and I'll have a test and if that works out we can have a wracking, pointless affair." She thinks of this, the thought of it almost palpable as she strides down Broadway, not looking at the beggars, not looking at the homeless clumped like bushes to the sidewalk, thinking that there are certain degrees of insight which are perhaps insupportable. Perhaps this explains why she has more or less ceased to write poetry and has sought advice in places like the Church of Latent Possibility, companionship from men like Robert, communion in spaces like the sports bar. She has become a version of herself she could not have imagined when she was that young woman at Holyoke twenty years ago, a feeling then as if

> *His Features—Tumultuous in the Night*
> *Came and embraced—made my frail gasps Wind—*
> *And in the harshness of the sudden Wind his light*
> *Touch and tumble were not then to Find—*

And then again it may simply be, as her friends in Massachusetts had warned her when she came to take the adjunct post so many years ago, that life in New York would simply be insupportable.

At the end-of-semester party for the English Department staff and their significant others, Emily—who has invited and come with Robert but cannot now see him at the other side of the lounge, so packed is the room—is arguing, quite pointlessly, with a bearded lawyer, the husband of a medievalist, who says that he was never able to bear the work of William Wordsworth. "Or any of those mystic types," he says. "Blake or Donne. Or Edna St. Vincent Millay. There was a woman I could never stand. She was full of fairy tales and cheap gimmicks."

"I'm not sure," Emily says. She impulsively reaches out a soothing hand, strokes his elbow. There is nothing erotic in her touch and with his wife three feet away, no sense of possibility and they both know it. The gesture means nothing and is therefore safe. "I think that *Aria da Capo* is really quite charming," Emily says. "She has a lot to say about the fragility of fantasy, the extinguishment of hope, I think."

"Well," the lawyer says, "that may be what you think." He stares at the place on his jacket Emily had touched as if it were somehow engraved with meaning. "But I don't see it that way. I don't think that Edna St. Vincent Millay has anything to do with the West Side of Manhattan in 1992."

"Oh, I don't know," Emily Dickinson says. She suppresses a wild, a demonic urge to seize the lawyer's private parts and inflict knowledge upon them. "I mean, we can't be sure, can we?" She smiles at him and in the dense spaces of the room feels her heart, thundering and enormous, sway like a fruit in that interior orchard, the wind of knowledge coursing through her.

"I think she might be *very* relevant," Emily Dickinson says and thinks of Robert's helpless touch. "If you look for her, really look for her hard," she says.

Darwinian Pacts

Do you want to hear a story? A story? Of course you do, your curiosity is limitless: here is a story. An assassin, let us call him Gregor Mendel, is summoned on special detail to track and kill an important man. Mendel is frightened by the orders, terrified by necessity, but he has a long history in this trade and is essentially unemployable outside of it; he adapts to the rigors of circumstance and he believes in following orders. Slowly, slowly the assassin narrows the circle of his own evasions, his own reluctance, conceals his dilemma (as everything else) from his wife, circumscribes his own evasions until he is convinced that this is not only an assignment but a great task. Like the alchemy of the Middle Ages, like the summoning of gold to lead, Mendel sees himself as gripped by destiny.

The transition to purpose is not immediate, it takes many months until Mendel can be really brought to the point of action. But at last then, at last, hand on heart, he solemnly nods, accepts the assignment, leaves the room. Heart on trigger, trigger to bolt, knowledge to destiny, Mendel *explodes* his high and perilous deed in a fireball of fond recrimination, tender retribution, and the target is ever so publicly, ever so finally dead. This is the sentimental part of the narrative: Mendel feels badly about this. He adores his wife and infant even though he cannot talk to or touch them; he knows himself to be a profound and feeling man, he is not touched lightly by the wicked temper of his time. Mendel weeps for the widow of his target, for the children of his quarry. Knowing the depths of loss, stunned by his own velocity of mourning, Mendel feels the burden of his duty as he is seized by huge and controlling hands, dragged away. He is entrapped and arrested, of course. Mendel had been assured of success, of an escape route, but they had lied to him as he rapidly discovers, and it is the work of few authorities to truncate his pathetic flight and drag him into custody.

Ah, Mendel! Too late, at last, he discovers that he has not only been a tool, he has acted as the only bridge between those who gave the orders and those who would find the truth. Only Mendel could connect the two. If Mendel is killed, his directors and caretakers will be invulnerable. Bridge, then, cat's-paw, our poor Mendel. Oh how his forehead burns, his eyes dazzle with the tears of his discovery! In the brief span now allotted, what rage and betrayal, what recrimination and pain for him as, carried in custody through the bowels of the police station, he is shot in the stomach.

It does not take him long to die. Even at the moment of death it is possible that Mendel has had little knowledge, although we cannot be sure of this. Ultimately, we can only infer his interior, his processes, we are not privy to them. His wife felt Mendel's engorged, raging tool within her spitting fire and yet he gave *her* no part of knowledge, how much less for the rest of us. Ultimately, layered within himself, Mendel dies, as we all must, some sooner, some much later, some clutching the cloak of judgment, others casting it.

You have heard the story. The essential outlines, anyway. This is the greater and cruder arc of narrative.

But, but, but there is a little more: here is the withheld denouement, the windup, the smash smasheroo, the old surprise end which can of course be no surprise because the least of you must have crafted your credulity toward this end. One more detail, thus, to clinch the matter.

No, I am not Mendel.

Nor the widow, nor his quarry. Mendel is dead and so is the quarry and the others will go on in one way or the other. Some will prosper. Others will change their names, unlearn the place of Mendel's grave. All will be changed in smaller or greater ways, but all will be unchanged in some more fundamental sense.

The ending is this: I am Mendel's assassin. I am the man who killed the man who killed. The hand of his undoing is mine. The betrayer and vindication of the assassin, both of them are mine. That is the story in its center and its arc.

This amazing revelation, none of you could have suspected it, none of you would have known, this astonishing revelation given early rather than late ... even that is not the totality, for here is a story with many, many endings, some of them unrevealed. One closes a box, opens another box; one ends a prayer, begins an imprecation, it is one of those Eastern voyages of discovery and memory which we calculate. The story is diverse, involuted. So here is yet another true conclusion: I have performed under instruction. Removing one bridge, *I* have become the bridge. I know those who created Mendel and sent him on his tasks, I can lead you straight toward them. It is within my power, if I say so, to pledge to you the full and desperate revelation of our time, and that is why I have offered you this story with many endings, a story that only I can transmogrify.

It is abominably cold in this place.

It is cold, I am dying, the freeze not from weather but from the cold and deadly fire with which they beam death into my bones, my burning and insubstantial soul. They have ordered me to death, they hurl cancer at me. Oh my soul, it is cold from my knowledge, their machination. Attend to the rays of death! Consider the condition of the dappled and complaisant Mendel as from his parapet he arches his back to the task, extends his arms, sighs, scratches himself, thinks of women, thinks of the small and florid spaces of his wife's cunt as he waits for the motorcade, the damned motorcade to plummet. Consider Mendel as he belches, squirms, adjusts his rifle, adjusts his underwear, flexes himself for his vault toward immortality, and consider me as well, entombed in this cell, asking only the opportunity to share as one must the source of the commands that so spirited me here.

Oh, Dallas. I thought that Chicago was the center of darkness, that Chicago was the rock of our enchantment and entrapment, that it was at Chicago where the rolling continent ended and began but that was before I trundled south, found quarters in this deadly and constant city. It was in Dallas where I came to understand the true meaning of passage, the sheer weight and force of the continent as it caved toward crushing circumstance here and never got out. In Chicago I could smell the slaughterhouses all the time, the moaning and clatter of the beasts and their stink rose and rose into all of the parlors where I carried out my fate, I smelt the cattle all of the time, but the stockyards were nothing as against the deeper and richer stink of Dallas, not oil, not coastal waters, not the fumes of the derricks and the corruption, but something deeper, ever deeper, that seemed to carry me back further than I had ever before reached.

In Chicago there were summers where I believed that I was on the arc of a death not so existential as personal and final (as some Midwest deaths need not be), the obliteration of all possibility in that most secret and concealed of all places, but oh boy, oh boy, Chicago was toy city, was Gang Expo as against Dallas. It was Dallas who taught me not to live, not to die, not exactly but rather that the two were indistinguishable. That like Mendel one could be placed in a circumstance where they became the same and one did not, ultimately, know in what state one might be. They taught a hard and final school in Dallas and then they locked up the boxes of the Stadium Club and put the real knives to bear. You hang around, you stay around, you place a bet or two, you follow the grind and the knives in your time and you learn a thing or three but you can never, truly learn enough. Murder exceeds knowledge by a sufficient favor, oh Macbeth.

Do you want to hear the domestic story? Do you want to hear the gentler and more sentimental, the linoleumed and porcelained interior of this narrative? Even assassins have home lives, you know, even assassins can cry at the more rending moments of certain films or at home movies of the Presidential candidate holding his daughter on his knee.

So consider this as part of the detritus of a life too, this affecting and personal side. Young Mendel, twenty-four years old and knowing more already than he ever dared to think was possible of pain and implication, young and thin Mendel, with his stunned eyes and rifle case stashed, kisses his young wife and infant daughter, bids them a tender farewell, adjusts his clothing, centers his cap (a recent affectation but one that he thinks makes him look rather dashing), and hugs them as he prepares to desert the apartment for his great task. Perhaps Mendel will never see them again. He has to commit himself to that possibility, certainly he cannot deny it. Not after the degree of obligation they have put upon him. "Goodbye," his young wife says. We will not give her a name just now, it is not necessary. It will make the matter too affecting, will break all of the circumstantial bounds. Call her Mrs. Mendel. That is what wives were called at that innocent time. "Goodbye, goodbye," Mrs. Mendel says. His daughter, too young for speech (as Mendel, stricken by sorrow and destiny, has become too old for speech, knows that not words but tragedy must ensue) waves a speechless little hand. Perhaps the baby gurgles. At such a distance, at such a remove from events, who can be sure. "Goo-by," Mrs. Mendel says, mimicking her daughter's sound. "Goo-by." She knows few words of English but she is capable of assessing moods, she is no fool, not insensitive, merely in over her head as almost everyone at this impossible time was. Gigantic events are created by those who are fundamentally unaware of their own significance. It is most distressing. Much of this gives me more pain than I can possibly say. It is all part of the circumstances in which we are plunged.

Think of Mendel. He is about to leave. He has coffee in his stomach, anticipation as well as dread in his bearing, he has been made sufficiently alert for the duties to come. Mrs. Mendel knows nothing of this assignment, is unaware of Mendel's destination or preparation, really understands only the imperatives of her own appetite, her daughter's appetite, her fear, but she can sense Mendel's tension and perhaps a little whiff of his thrall comes upon her. "Goo-by," she says again. Mendel stands at the door and waves. The M-1 is stashed in the warehouse. Dreaming of the M-1, thinking of this smuggled rifle which he has assembled from the cautious pieces his masters have sent from various widely dispersed military supply depots in this and other countries, Mendel sits at the window of the bus, rocking in the traffic, closing and opening his eyes convulsively. Soon the dreaming M-1 will be in his hand. He thinks of the slide of the barrel in his hand, the feel of his wife's thigh, the rapid swell and rise of her cunt as he slammed inside her, when, two days ago, perhaps three. The cunt and the rifle blend in his consciousness as such things are wont to do. The bus slams to a sickening jolt in heavy traffic, Mendel slides, desperately grips the railing. In his half-dream it is as if he has been shot, as if the jolt were a fatal wound. He thinks of Mrs. Mendel, the slide of her arm, touch of her lips, but the image is replaced by that of the President. Mendel deeply admires the President, envies him, would like to have his life. His assignment is nothing personal, as he keeps on reminding himself; he has a very high opinion of the President, as do many Americans of this time. Certainly nothing will be known of the President for years and years, of his secret life, hidden desire and when—long after the acts I am trying desperately to objectively describe here—it is revealed, it will have no bearing upon that sense of loss and mourning that will soon enough rack the nation. Dallas to Mendel's eyes could now be Chicago, it is indistinguishable from Chicago in his half-doze. These places torn from the continent, taken arbitrarily from the rock and the sluice, called "cities," given spaces where one could prosper, flourish, starve, or die, all at the same time, never knowing one another.

Mendel knows that he may never see his wife and child again. It is difficult, perilous for him to dwell on this, and so, to the best of his ability, he does not.

Here is my own revelation; here is my own detritus and admission: for years I had loved Mrs. Mendel, if only at a great distance and in a yearning and covert way. I loved the *idea* of her before I knew she existed; when I became aware of her reality my excitement quickened to force, to desperation. The love of most women is not for me, I have had my problems, have always had difficulty with the run of women produced by America at this part of the century ... but the youth, vulnerability, lack of language, uncertainty, sheer *ignorance* of Mrs. Mendel inflamed me. Here at last was someone with whom I could deal, someone who I would know as she would know me. Now and then, through the course of my days, dealing with the beaten and insulting women who came to work for me, I would close my eyes and there would be Mrs. Mendel or someone very much like her. I would give her a first name, would characterize her as I must to draw her closer. Grace, I would call her. Oh Grace. "Oh Grace," I wanted to say, even as I took measurements from strippers and made arrangements for liquor deliveries, ignore this heavy and corrupt mask, this sagging tissue, this dispirited crown and sunken face, this is not the man but merely what

Chicago beat into him, this rubble is a concealment of the man inside.

"Oh Grace," I would add to persuade her, "I am not merely a functionary, not a running man for my masters and your husband's: I am a tender and sensitive man, I suffer. Grace, Grace," I would murmur to her, hoping that she would hear and on some level I am sure she did, "touch me and know my yearning, clasp me and know my burning, my yearning and my burning, my lust and my dust, my cry and my sigh," but I did not would not say things like this, I kept them inside.

Much be kept inside; Chicago taught me restraint and the heaviness, the weariness of a burdened body, tossed like a sack into Lake Michigan, sinking without a merry burble. "I am not the sort of man," I did not therefore say to her, "who looks capable of such speech, such yearning, but I know this, I will say this: Mendel cannot give you what you want, what you need. He has a small and crushed soul; he hasn't the breadth of spirit which I can give, don't you see that? Don't you know it?" Oh, I could have said and this much else to her; "I know your life is as stricken for love as mine and that with one another we can find the better parts of ourselves." But I said nothing. Business must prevail and the mask of circumstance.

Said nothing until that day when I was summoned to Carlos's presence and was then for the first time determined to speak my need. "I do love her," I said. "I have seen her picture, I have seen her on the streets. I love Grace Mendel. You must know this."

"It is all right," Carlos said. "You are free to speak. We are beyond love," he said. "We are into action now. You will be celebrated, you will be a national hero, you will be acclaimed and admired if you but do what we ask. You will be jailed, yes, of necessity, will serve a brief sentence and be released, they will strew flowers the day you walk out of the prison. Your memoirs can be sold for enormous sums to *Collier's*. Agents will bid for your likeness and the movie."

"Grace. This is what I want."

"Grace," Carlos said, shaking his head. "So be it then. What do I know? What do I know of women? That too, if you wish. We will arrange everything *por favor* if you insist, if you want. Do you understand?"

I am a fat man but I move with gentility and the arc of a dancer. This is my conception of myself: the dancer's vault. I looked at Carlos, brandished a hand. "They will jail me," I said. "There will be great notoriety, a huge trial. I am not a fool, I am not blinded by love. I know what will become of me. It will not be an easy task, it will not admit of resolution."

"Trust us."

"There is a craziness. There is a craziness in this country, in this time.

You wish to make it worse yet and then you will put me at the center of it."

"You will end it," Carlos said. We were sitting in the nightclub in the afternoon, in the false light and streaming dust. There is nothing like a nightclub with the lights off on a sunny weekday afternoon in a fallen October. "You will be a hero because you will have killed the craziness that killed the craziness. And this woman, she will be yours."

"I don't know. I love her too much and she knows of me too little."

"Love," Carlos said. He spat in the dust, ran his toe on the wet spot. "What you Americans will not do for sense, you will do for love. So be it. Trust us. It will happen. All things will happen."

"I have seen Mendel. He is—"

"We will not talk of Mendel. He means nothing, he is already perished and *morte* in the run of history. It is you upon whom it depends. But you will do us this favor," Carlos said, "for without it nothing can happen at all. You owe us this," he said, "and now it is time for me to ask, to insist. You can refuse," he said. "That refusal is within your right."

I looked in his face and saw cast back to me the light of my own refusal and it was heavy, it was blunt, it was an ax in the darkness. "No," I said, "I will not refuse."

"That is good," he said, "we would be most hurt or disappointed if that were indeed the case. This is a nation that flourishes on its disappointment, on the teasing of expectations. We do not wish to join them. It is this Grace you love? Then there will be an arrangement."

"It is not the woman," I said then. It was not insight but resignation then that leached from the pores of understanding. All of my life had been predicted upon denial, surely nothing now could change. "It is not the woman," I said again, pondering. "It cannot be for her, then. You know it is impossible between us. You know that for all my desire, she is merely a fiction."

In Carlos's presence I mimicked his speech, just as in the presence of masters in Chicago I spoke like Capone. In New Orleans I slid into an almost impenetrable Southern accent. This is one of my traits. There are those who say—do not, do not believe them!—that I am an empty man, that I am a bankrupt man, that there is nothing inside me other than an utter and credulous responsiveness and that I take on the sounds and speech of those whom I address. It is a temptation to think this way, even though I know that is not the case. I have an interior, I suffer, how could I speak to you like this were I not suffering?

"It will destroy us," I said to Carlos.

"Oh, no. You do not understand, still. There is nothing to be destroyed. You cannot abolish a nullity. You cannot eliminate a cipher. By subtraction you are participating in addition."

"I will do it," I said. This was another voice, a Chicago voice, a voice of the north, of stone and concrete, of rifle fire in garages. It was the voice that I had always known would emerge. "I will do it, I will kill the killer. I will destroy Mendel."

"This is good. I hope it is sincerely meant."

"Everything is sincerely meant," I said. There was more conversation to be sure, and I could, if I were to reach back to that time, find and record it, but what is the point? What is the point of any of this? The outlines of the discussion are clear, the difficult rim of necessity, the bowl of recollection filled. "I will do it," I must have added finally, "because I have no choice."

"Surely you do. We all have choice, right up to the lip of the grave."

"That is a Latinism," I said. "I reject that. I make no statement. I understand that there is nothing else to be done. Not for Grace Mendel then, no matter how I love her. Not for the nation. Not even for self or for old debts or for Chicago or fear. But because it must be done."

"As you wish," Carlos said. This must have been the next day. The conversation was spread, I think, over several days, perhaps I mean several months, as negotiations and calculations were made. One compresses for the sake of unity and recall, but nothing was so simple. (Except for Mendel's bus ride; that is exactly how it happened, how it must have happened.) "As you will," Carlos said. "As you want," Carlos added. He said other things as well, made many interesting brisk points and philosophical comments about the collapse of our civilization, but they are not to be reported, nor is the nature of my difficult obligation. That obligation was clear then, clear now, clear for all time, glinting at us through all the tunnels and tents of recall as I try to assure you of the seriousness of my position.

Poor Mendel. Have I constructed him as he has been presented or does he really exist in that way? How much of Mendel can be known outside of these calculations? Thinking of him, thinking of all that has happened, I wonder about this and other things, wonder if this "Mendel" I have created is not merely another aspect of this putrescent and dying self. Struggling to the sixth floor of the warehouse, thinking of his difficult and necessary obligation, did Mendel know what he was doing? Did he ever come to terms with its meaning? Or was it all mindless, circumstantial, arbitrary, operative, the cells moving toward their own completion? Does he do what he must for guile, or out of passion? Is it the President of whom he thinks at this moment? The President has consorted with evil, made perilous arrangements, indulged impossible risk, reparations are due. The "Mendel" I have conceived thinks of this and that as he hunches over his bologna sandwich on rye, his homemade lunch humbly packed by the unthinking Grace and placed in the rifle case, the bread crumbs scattered on the floor for future officers to marvel at. Sooner or later he would have had to die anyway, Mendel thinks or does not think. This is merely a matter of adding purpose, of granting structure, of ordering the mindless and unfiltered events of our lives toward some kind of outcome. And so thinking, he sighs, begins the final assembly, embarks wearily but with much dedication upon the great task. One must have sympathy for him. One must understand Gregor Mendel's position here. Nothing is easy for this tormented young man and matters will become only more difficult as the years go on and on and on.

Dallas was a fresh start, I thought. Dallas would enable me to reconstruct my life. Oh, I was a practical man when I headed for Dallas, truly I thought it would be different. How was I to know? How were any of us to know? Observe the earnestness of my voice, the earnestness of my eyes. I am not casual about this, I am giving you hard and real information here, slabs of life *cut* from the bleeding and necessitous whole.

So one can apprehend this as Mendel himself might have seen it then, peering over the rifle sight after the shot he could see the President's head explode through the force of that bullet, no, there is *another* bullet, that second shot placed with deadly and preventive force which breaks open the slab of skull, the blood leaping in a high, fine, weeping line from the interior of the skull. Mendel can see this (as I can) and he bellows, for all his fear, one astonished *ya-hoo! heigh-ho!* as that second, disappearing supplementary shot struck home, secret help from the secret masters, but no time for Mendel to relish this act of extirpation, no time at all. He must flee. He has been given strict orders, he knows what he must do next.

Ya-hoo! heigh-ho! and squirm on belly to the staircase, rising then only as the door is reached and so, so then the clumsy, shouting, excoriating events of that profound afternoon continue.

"Oh, if you could only know me, Grace," I want to say to her. "I'm a fat blur, a figure in black-and-white fleeing through the bottom of a screen and that is all I will ever be but I loved you, don't you know that? I loved you and what you became in a way that Mendel never could, you must understand, you must accept, you must pledge for my love." But to say this would be a craziness; even now, at this time, it is impossible for me to say this. Of all the things I have done or have not done, this begging, wailing appeal to Grace would be the maddest of all and so I will not, will never do this.

No, it is Carlos's business which I conduct, with more brutality and efficiency perhaps than anyone could have known, than *either* of us at that or any other time would have thought, and the extrapolate dimensions of this horror sprawl ever further. They let me in, they pushed me forward, they slid the little gun in my hand and helped me point it. They were huge and ever helpful as I knew they must be. First the confirming call from Carlos, just before these climactic events. "He is being transferred at eleven," Carlos had said. "He will make transversal through the basement, the information is excellent, be there on time and we will put everything in your hands." They put everything in my hands. "There will be no further instructions." There were no further instructions. "We will allow no margin whatsoever for your failure." There was no failure.

There was no failure; I did what had to be done, overtook with efficacy. Dare I say "overtook with Grace"? So, then I overtook with grace. Falling away from me, falling in that place, that astonished look of recognition in his eyes for all (who could know) to see, Mendel fell and fell (and fell) away, his mouth pursed in an accusatory O you! much like his *ya-hoo! heigh-ho!* as he went down. "You, you have done this," he would have said more mildly, added in a tone shockingly like commendation, but there was no speech, only the withdrawal and the falling. Their hands upon me, the hands of the state were enormous, a deliverance, a speeding toward obsequy and conclusion, a voice in my ear then whispering *say nothing, say nothing* and so I was dragged, complaisant as Mendel, complaisant as the now dead President himself from that public and wretched space.

If I could tell you here and at this place what I wished to become of Grace and myself I would but I cannot; this is not at all possible. She would come, would come to me in love and tender searching, uttering my name, but I cannot divulge this, I cannot bear it, I cannot at the end come to terms with what cannot be but let it be known, let it be known that if it were other than what it must have been ... we might have had that urgent and whispering closure in the dark.

Slowly, methodically, my bones are cooked by their secret and deadly rays into the froth of cancer.

"You fool," Mendel wants to point out, "you were worse than me; I knew that I was wretched and doomed from the beginning but I never thought that there was anything else. But you were like him, like the President, you *believed* everything you were told. You were even worse then: what I did was at least for passion, and history will make of me how and what it will but, *you*, you—"

"I did it for passion," I wanted to say but did not. "My passion exceeded yours, it outgrew the sun, it was larger and burning ever brighter than yours. I am a ridiculous figure, yes, with a cocked hat and a fat belly, but inside I *suffer*, I am a man of some dimension and pity, consider what I have been able to establish for Mendel, how fair I have been."

No Grace, no light, only the cold and deadly force of their beams, burning, burning my bones, my light—

Do you want to hear a story? Everyone wants to hear a story, little children in their beds and grownups by the fire. But I cannot, will not tell you here; you have got to remove me, get me out of here, get me away so that I will tell you all of it, oh so much more than you have yet heard. Describe Carlos, tell you the shape of Grace's tits. What Mendel said to her in the dark. What the President planned for the Republic. Everyone knows me, everyone! *Everyone!*

Allegro Marcato

Sooner or later it had to come down to this confrontation. Art Tosca knew it, had battled it for months as best he could, but the big fellow was outrageous, impossible now, and there was a point past which you could not tolerate this. You would lose support, lose the club all the way down the line. Even Gehrig was giving Tosca strange glances in the dugout now, shaking his head. When Gehrig gave that look, the end was near. *Basta*, Tosca thought. He had not changed his name from Arturo Toscanini to Art Tosca, struggled his way out of Genoa, Parma, taken the long way boat to the docks at California, fought through the wretched years toting fruit and taking shit from longshoremen, spent those endless years in the minors coming in to find curses lettered on his locker and his uniform tied in knots on the floor, so that he could end up like this. There was only one last exit on the hell's express and the big fellow was pushing him there. He motioned Ruth to the footstool in the big tin can that was his office and closed the door. "*Basta*," he said to the big fellow. "That means enough. You know your Italian, George? I've taken as much of your shit as I intend to. You're out of the lineup."

Ruth folded his hands, looked at the floor, gave him that contrite look which, when mixed in with the curses and the humping motions, was supposed to drag everybody back across the line, make you say, *Well, he's just a big kid, and back off*. It had worked every time, up to a point, but now it would not. "You're drinking yourself to fucking death, you're humping everything that doesn't run from you, and you're dropping balls you should get to. I'm not a goddamned preacher," Tosca said. "You want to throw your life away, get yourself a dose of clap that will put you under the infield, blow out your liver, that's up to you—but you're not ready to play anymore. Look at you," he said. "You stink. You stink of cheap wine, your batting average is .275, and you haven't hit a home run in three weeks. You can't even draw a walk." He felt the Italian expletives rising within him, choked them back. "I don't know that Guinea talk," the Babe would say. "Don't give me that Eye-talian shit." Worse yet, Ruppert had said the same thing to him only a few days ago when he had tried to discuss the situation with old Jake. "You hear me?" he said to the big fellow. "I'm not going to put up with this shit. You're on the bench. You got it? I'm sitting you down until you're ready to play. You don't run this club; *I* do."

The Babe shrugged. His cheeks flushed a little, but he took it very nice, very calm. That was the thing, you couldn't really get through to him unless you really did and if that happened, then he could reach out and kill you. A couple of years back, two rookies on the Browns rode him about his dark color and made a few suggestions about racial background and Ruth had taken out after them and caught them under the stands and had almost killed them. Ruppert had had to pull all the weight he had with Landis to get that one dismissed in 1925 and get the big fellow reinstated. But in so doing, Ruppert had said, he had used up all of his clout and the next time would be straight to jail, the owner had said. Of course, this was different. Ruth wasn't threatening to kill Tosca or anyone. He just wasn't playing, was humping and pissing and eating and boozing his way through every road trip and home stand, and taking down the rest of them with him.

"You're sitting," Tosca said. "You got that clear? You're on the pine until you shape up. Get the hell out of here, Babe. Just go and think about it."

"You can't do this to me," Ruth said. "I'll go to the Colonel. He knows all about you. I'll talk to Barrow. You think Barrow will make me take this shit? You think that?" Ruth screamed and reached out a furious hand toward Tosca, who slapped it away and screamed at him in Italian. "*Larghamente!*"

"I don't have to take that from some pissant Guinea son of a bitch," Ruth screamed and came at him again. Tosca turned and picked up the first thing he could get his hands on—the hot water bottle that he took into the dugout—and threw it at the big fellow, hitting him on the forehead. Ruth reeled back, shocked. "Get out!" Tosca said. "Get out of here or I'll fucking call the police, you understand?" Ruth bellowed something and came at him and Tosca dodged back against the wall, thinking: *this guy could kill me as fast as he could fuck a cow*. He prepared to go down screaming and defiant, but the door of the room was yanked open and Gehrig and Koenig were standing there, Koenig looking grim, and just behind them Lazzeri, who, of course, had made sense of the Italian.

"Problems, Chief?" Gehrig asked.

Ruth stopped, backed off, shook his head, and stared at Gehrig. "Lou?" the Babe said, "Lou, he's *benching* me, I can't take that crap." He began to mumble something and Gehrig put an arm around the big fellow's shoulders and guided him from the room.

"Come on, Babe," he said quietly, soothingly, and Ruth quivered against him. "Come on, come on," and Gehrig took him away, looking back over his shoulder, shaking his head at Tosca.

I'm in over my head, Tocsa thought. *I could have been killed there if Larruping Lou hadn't saved my ass. But what could I do? He's putting us all the way down with his shit. If he goes on this way, we'll be invisible by August. And these '27 Yankees could be the greatest club I'll ever manage.*

Now and then, when he could, Tosca would take in a concert, Damrosch and the New York Symphony, or he would go to the Metropolitan Opera House and sit in the Family Circle incognito and listen to Verdi or Wagner, his favorites. Nobody knew the manager of the Yankees at either place. Tosca had always liked music, it meant a lot to him. There was no formal training, of course, after the few cello lessons his parents had scraped together when he was a little boy in Genoa, and through all the years struggling in the ports and then in the minors he had almost forgotten about it, but he guessed that the music had always been there. He still liked it a lot, sometimes would hear it in his head, odd rhythms against the sound of the bats and the crowd, and, of course, Verdi was a man who knew something about what it was like to manage a bunch like this. *Va penserio*, fly thought, that was the right thing, certainly. Fly thought far from all these ramparts; if you thought, you got into trouble. It was a strange thing, a funny thing how a little cello-playing Guinea from Genoa would wind up manager of the Yankees in New York in the '20s, hearing all the sounds of the city and taking shit from the Babe and trying to deal with a bunch of men who, with exceptions like Gehrig or Meusel, were more childish than all the urchins of his home town, but that was America for you. It was a strange and wondrous land, as the Colonel, Jake Ruppert, had pointed out to him in so many of their conversations. Jake Ruppert, a bartender and now a bootlegger, could be the greatest sporting owner in the country, little Arturo Toscanini from Genoa could become Art Tosca and take over the helm of the club which had been called unmanageable. It was a peculiar business, all right.

Tosca thought of things like this all the time, the strange and convoluted nature of his odyssey and the way in which, how peculiarly, it had come to this circumstance. First he had played ball because it was a way to get off the docks and it was something which interested him, the patterns, the rhythm in the hit-and-run, and then there was the opportunity to play in the new Pacific Coast League for a hundred dollars a month and then, when the Seals manager had gone to Tijuana over a Labor Day weekend and never come back, he had found himself suddenly managing and showing, they told him, an aptitude for it. A career utility second baseman had turned out at the age of 50 to have some real talent for managing, or at least for staying out of people's way, and then there had been the sudden late-night visit with Ruppert and

Barrow who had passed through town, they said, especially to see him, and then it was 1922 and he was managing the New York Yankees, the champion New York Yankees just a year after they had won their first pennant and McGraw had dropped them in the Series. McGraw dropped them again, too, and it wasn't until 1923 that they had won the World Championship for the first time, but after that the '26 pennant had come easy and for the first time in his sixty years, coming into that '27 season, Art Tosca had felt set, had felt that there was some permanence in his position, some real control. And then Ruth, forty pounds overweight, fat and stupid from his triumphs in two World Series and the 47-home-run year in '26, had gone haywire over the winter and had reported in '27 crazy and arrogant and convinced that he was running the club, not Ruppert or Tosca or Barrow, not Gehrig or Meusel or Landis but only he, the Babe himself, and the season had fallen apart on him, unraveled from April to August until now they lay ten games back of an old Senators team, just barely over .500 and not able to get anything going while Babe Ruth lurched and belched all over the field and carried bats around the dugout and fell off to .263 before anyone even grasped the seriousness of the situation. Well, it had been building for a long, long time, all right. The confrontation was overdue, maybe things would change now. Either way he would be out: carry this through the season and Barrow's views would prevail and he would be thrown out. Ruppert might be his friend, but Barrow held the money and was the one without the accent and made the contact deals with the politicians. Everyone knew that. I had to deal with it, Tosca thought. *Either way, I was lost.*

Outside of the ballpark, there was not much for Tosca. He had married young, lost his wife and infant daughter in a flu epidemic in the 1890s, thought about marrying again but never got around to it, not with all the business of baseball, the short winters, the long summers, the travel. Like the Babe, he had planted it here and there in his time, had calculated some moves of his own, but when he turned fifty-five and took over the Yankee job, most of that had seemed to pass away from him; he simply had not been that interested anymore. He could look at the men carrying on, or hang out at the bars on the road and see what was going on and what it did to them, but it was something like watching infield practice. It was fascinating and enviable and something which he understood but was not himself able to carry on. It was like the music for him, something which had happened a long time ago but represented something which he was maybe—he hated to think this way but it was possibly the truth—well out of.

Ruth took the benching badly but without further threats, and sulked his way through the doubleheader in Philadelphia during which Grove shut them out in the first game and they got only three hits in the second and fell to eleven games out, the Senators splitting with the Red Sox that day, and Ruth had said nothing at all but later, when the team was running off the field, Meusel and Joe Dugan sprinting by him, Ruth stopped at the end of the bench where Tosca was slowly packing it in and said, "You put me in tomorrow, you son of a bitch, or I'll kill you. You hear me? I mean that," Ruth said and turned away, and Tosca could not believe that he was hearing this except, of course, that it was exactly the kind of thing which he should have expected to hear.

Ruth was walking away from him, just strolling through the dugout and toward the hole leading to the locker room and Tosca ran after him and said to him, "You talk to me that way, you son of a bitch? *Basta*, I say to you, I call upon you curses!" And without thinking anything more about it, he drew back a fist and hit the big fellow under the eye. Ruth staggered back and roared with surprise, and then roared again and came toward him. Tosca stood his ground as Ruth grabbed him by the NY on his uniform front and began shaking. Shaking and shaking, and Tosca, feeling the pure, high arc of rage within him, spat in Ruth's face and said, "You bastard, I'll get you suspended for life!" and Ruth hit him on the forehead, Tosca spinning away from him and back into the damned splinters and it was then that Gehrig and the rest of them, hearing this, came from the locker room and pulled Ruth away, Ruth screaming, the men shaking, Tosca shaking—and Tosca picked up a 36-ounce bat from the rack and came toward Ruth with every intention of killing the man and Gehrig, his highly trained reflexes saving him while at risk, leapt and caught him and grabbed the bat and sat him down hard.

After that much of it passed in a blur. Ruth was screaming over and over that he would kill Tosca, and Tosca was begging them to let him go so that he could try—but he wasn't very clear on this, maybe Ruth had shaken him up more than he had thought, and hours seemed to go by until the two of them were in Ruppert's office, Ruth on the couch, soaking his hand in a pot of water, and Tosca leaning back against the couch, supported by Gehrig, who looked at the two of them silently and seriously while Ruppert leaned forward and said, "I can't have this, do you understand? I cannot have this on my club. If Landis gets hold of this, you'll both be thrown out of baseball for life, do you know that? I have got to control my ball club."

"You tell him to let me play," Ruth said. "I'm here to play, and no helpless Guinea bastard who never played a day in the majors is going to sit me. If I don't play, I don't live, you hear me?"

"This is *my* ball club," Tosca said. "I was given this club to manage. Until the Colonel fires me, it's mine. You are fucking up my ball club," he said to Ruth. "I will not tolerate this."

Ruth screamed something and impossibly stood and seemed about to come at him again, and Ruppert said something terrible in German and took a gun from his desk and held it on Ruth. The big fellow saw it and slowly unraveled, falling back loosely, then heavily in the chair.

"You son of a bitch," Ruth said. "You pulled a gun on me! You pulled a gun on Babe Ruth! Are you crazy? Are you crazy enough to shoot me?"

"I'm crazy enough to shoot anyone if they're crazy enough to kill themselves," Ruppert said. "Listen here," he said to Tosca. "I hired you and I told you to make the orders, but I didn't hire you to kill this guy or to have me kill him. So I'm the owner and I'm going to make an edict, you hear me? He plays. The Babe plays. But I get one more report of fucking or boozing or carrying on in the cat-house, and you're going to be put on the suspended list and I'll have Landis make it stick. You hear me?" Ruppert said. Ruth said nothing. "I said, do you hear me?" Ruppert said.

Ruth shrugged, looked at the wall. "I guess," he said. "I guess I hear you."

"And you, Tosca," Ruppert said. "You're crazy altogether. You're sixty years old, you want to get a heart attack? You want this big stupe to kill you? You get off this case, you leave it to me. You sit on the bench and you manage, you leave the heavy problems here or to the Commissioner. I'm not going to take this anymore," Ruppert said, "I got a goddamned brewery here and a real set of problems. The Yankees were supposed to be for fun. Some fun," Rupert said. "Now shake hands and get the hell out of here."

"I won't shake the bastard's hand," Ruth said, his eyes tight and incurious behind the fat folds of his cheeks, that strange alertness which Tosca had noticed from the first now consuming him. "The son of a bitch is killing me."

"You let him kill you," Ruppert said. "But you shake his hand and you end this or it's the suspended list right now."

That was when Gehrig stood up and hauled the Babe to his feet and dragged him over. "Now," he said, "the two of you make up for the boss. I'm the captain and that's an order."

Ruth shook his head and reached out a hand. Tosca touched it, feeling the burning, feeling the force coming through the man. *If he had been a kettledrum*, Tosca thought, *I would kick him.*

They drove through August, 12 and 2 the rest of the way, and cut five games off the fading Senators and then in September the big fellow went crazy, going for the fences on every pitch and connecting often enough. He hit 17 home runs in September, getting up to 35 for the year and they went 27 and 3, winning the last 25 in a row and putting the rest of the league out of the way. Tosca stayed on one side of the dugout and Ruth on the other, the rest of them sitting in the center, and nothing touched them, nothing at all, not even the Waner boys in the Series which they won four games to none. On the last day, coming into the ninth inning with a safe lead, Ruth came over to Tosca and stuck out his hand and said, "Let's bury it, do you hear me? Let's bury it," and Tosca, too stunned to find any kind of an attitude, put out his own hand and that seemed to be the end of it, at least for then. They were World Champions and they were champions again the next year, over the Cardinals, and then it all seemed to fall apart very quickly. Ruppert got sick, the big fellow began to lose his timing, and the whole nature of the league had changed. Tosca was out of there at the end of '31, after the third Athletic pennant, kicking around San Francisco for one season of coaching before deciding to give it up and get all the way out of baseball; he got so far out of it, working as a road man when Prohibition had entered, that he was barely aware of Ruth's being dumped by the Yankees, the three home runs early in the season at Boston, and then the pitiful end. Tosca had time in the evenings for music lessons and some on the weekends, too, and learned to play the piano, although of course it was too late to be any good at all. In '41 they invited him back for the Gehrig farewell, but the letter never even caught up to Tosca; in '48 he did get the message about Ruth's farewell but decided to skip that, and also ducked seeing the cancer-ridden big fellow in the hospital at the end.

Tosca was 81 then, and it had all seeped into him. He lived in a furnished room not far from the docks he had worked fifty years ago and waited for the end. If being manager of a four-time World Champion ball club meant anything to anyone, they managed to conceal it pretty well, even though baseball after the Second World War was bigger than it ever had been. Tosca managed to keep out of the nursing home until close to the very end but when it all finished for him in January of 1957, just before his 90th birthday, he guessed that he had ended as pitifully as the big fellow, the Colonel, or anyone else. You couldn't hold it off, that was something he had known long ago, although Ruth with his boozing and mad fucking and pissing away had probably come closer than anyone to making a run at it. Tosca died in full lucidity, feeling miserably deprived, feeling as if he had wasted all of his life or at least close to all of it, but he was smart enough to know that he probably would have felt that way in any other condition and for whatever reason. Drifting in and out of coma he dreamed of throwing one bat after the next at Ruth, hurling bats, bats filling the air like musical notes, the thunder of the bats crashing and crashing against the walls, the lockers, the bony forehead of the crazed big fellow, and Tosca wondered if there was any different or better way he might have handled it. There being no satisfactory answer to this, he died to the sound of a great and empty descending cadence which—had he had more training he might have recognized this, and in fact perhaps he did anyway—composed the opening notes over string tremolo of Beethoven's Ninth Symphony. Oh, Beethoven, what a man! Was there ever such a man as Ruth?

Something from the Seventies

But why me? Winogrand said. This was in the interrogation room, a gadget-strewn place which reminded him of the way his industrial-arts classroom had looked in high school. Maybe a little more threatening because the industrial-arts guy was not a spotted alien with what appeared to be a heavy-duty space weapon of an advanced type. I don't remember anything about the seventies, Winogrand said. I slept through the whole decade. The sixties blew me out. It wasn't the drugs, he added, trying a fetching, self-deprecating moue, just the intensity of the time. The assassinations and the sex and all of that stuff. But really most of it's a blur to me.

Strange, the interrogator said, that's what we hear from the rest of you that we've checked out on this. But, really, we can't accept excuses here. We're trying to do some kind of comprehensive history and we can't have a ten-year gap in the Amurrican century. That's what you call it, right? The Amurrican century. That guy, Booth, that was his name for it.

Luce, Winogrand said. Henry Luce, the guy from *Time*. It's not Amurrican, it's American. Actually, United States. America refers to a bigger place. Where do you want me to start? Winogrand said. He peered over to the shadowed corners of the room in which there seemed to be torture devices, strange implements of an alien sort which he was convinced could do terrible things to Amurrican extremities. That was the trouble with alien invasion and interrogation, it seemed like a joke in the abstract but when you got right to circumstances, they weren't so funny at all. One morning a simple account executive for Universal Steel, the next somewhere in the bowels of what he guessed was an alien spaceship, talking to some multi-tentacled creature who wanted to obtain information on a dry, senseless time, a decade during which, as he tried to look back upon it, Winogrand had not had four minutes of continuous pleasure. Strung end to end as moments of pleasure never were, he might have had two hours of fun through the internment of the hostages. How could this make him an expert on the period and why had the alien snatched him of all people and put him to this horrid condition? He looked at the implements in the shadows again and shuddered. It was remarkable how plans seemed to unravel, tiny plans hardly voiced even to the self, and then your life was atomized into the chemical stink of an alien interrogation room. Well, that was the decade for you. There was the malaise speech, Winogrand said, that was in the summer of 1979. Right after the second gas shortage, the first having been in 1973, and just before the hostages got snatched in Iran. Carter said that it was all our fault, that the country had a stalking malaise because of the sixties assassinations and all the cynicism. He said we needed a spiritual revival. It didn't go over too well. You understand, most of us had spent June and July trying to get a tankful of gas, they reran that November and December of 1973 energy scam right past us again. What we didn't need was some guy shouting at us that our lousy lives were all our fault. It cost him the election.

Not the hostages? the alien said. Somewhere, the greenly tentacled creature seemed to have picked up a little history on its own; perhaps this was not a true interrogation but one of those traps which sneaky aliens were likely to pull, Winogrand thought. The papers had been full of sidebar stories after the invasion, dealing with the sneakiness and duplicity of the aliens. They told lies about their planet of origin and loved to load up the fade line at craps in the casinos. Perhaps deception like entropy was interstellar. We thought it was the hostages swept up at the American embassy in Iran who couldn't be rescued which were responsible for the troubles of your president.

Don't think so, Winogrand said. Look, when you've spent all summer trying to get a tank of gas and fighting 20 percent inflation, you don't need to hear some guy in a sweater telling you that it's all your own fault. Of course, that's just my theory, Winogrand said. Nothing is sure with this stuff, you know. Stupid politics, though.

So how did this Carter get to be president in the first place? the alien said. If he was so stupid, how did he become president?

Boy, Winogrand thought hopelessly, these creatures are really out of it, either that or they were faking a consummate stupidity which was hard to believe. Of course it could merely be a display of alien cunning. Watergate, Winogrand said, the presidential resignation in August of 1974. Then Ford pardoned Nixon. You know who these people are? You know what I'm talking about? The alien made quivering motions of agreement. Well, then, the pardon sunk Ford, Winogrand said. That was in September of 1974, exactly one month after Nixon had resigned on August 9 which led people to think that there had been some kind of a strict deal in the first place. Ford never got over the pardon and then in the first debate in October of 1975 he said that a bunch of Communist satellite countries in Eastern Europe were really free. That pretty much did him in since he did not have a major reputation for intellect in the first place. His idea for beating inflation was to make a speech in the summer of 1975 saying that they were going to print up a whole bunch of buttons saying WIN for WHIP INFLATION NOW, you get it? and everyone should wear one. That was his idea of high policy. I don't even want to think of low policy. Do you understand any of this?

More or less, the alien said. Watergate we've learned a lot about already. The question is why when those tapes were found out in July of 1973 which showed your president had taped every word spoken in his offices for four and a half years didn't Nixon at once dispose of them? We have no such parallel in our own history. It seems inexplicable, really.

Oh, it's not so inexplicable, Winogrand said. He was thinking of the pietà at Kent State, that famous photo taken in May 1970 after the Ohio guardsman had shot five students during the campus protests, the girl screaming over the body of the dead boy. The girl it turned out had been a runaway and seeing the picture in the paper was the first the parents had heard of her in a year. She had come home but then there were more troubles with drugs and somehow nothing had worked out for the girl. Nothing had really worked out for any of them, even though Winogrand had put the drugs and the peace signs away, had transferred to a university nearer home and had resolved to get a degree in something not very controversial. It's not inexplicable, Winogrand said, because Nixon had himself on tape probably promising Ford that he would make him vice president in October of 1973 if Ford would agree to a pardon if Nixon got jammed too tight. Ford would have known about that and it would have gotten *him* nailed for obstruction of justice if it had come out. So it was useful, I guess, to have a lot of things on a lot of people. That was the decade, Winogrand said. Everybody had something on everybody else. The FBI broke into the office of the psychiatrist of the guy, Ellsberg, who had stolen the Pentagon Papers to try to get something on him. On Ellsberg. If they could have found some interesting crazy stuff back then in 1971, they figured that they could get even with him for releasing that stuff proving that everyone in the Pentagon had known that Vietnam was a lost cause from the beginning. You get it? Getting something on someone was just an instrument of national policy, then. If everybody was wired, then everybody was protected. The Houston Plan, Winogrand said. The Plumbers. Deep Throat in the bowels of the White House, meeting Woodward and Bernstein at the Lincoln Memorial with fancy, private stuff on Nixon. The whole ten years was tattletale, that's all. If the sixties were the caldron with the lid off, the seventies were in the oven. The Philharmonic had had enough of Leonard Bernstein and his fund-raising for the Black Panthers so it got this real tight French guy, Boulez, in 1968 and until he got fired in 1977 Boulez wired the whole program with pots and pans and electrolysis.

This is very interesting, the alien said. It seemed in the half-light of the interrogation room to be drained now of malice, to be in the same broken, vulnerable, querulous posture that Winogrand had imagined himself occupying for most of that miserable decade. Really a strange, a miserable time, perched on his knees, not always metaphorically, waiting for first one humiliation, then the next to softly descend upon him. Wallace lying in the shopping plaza in Maryland in May 1972, shot by Bremer, paralyzed for life two days before Wallace won the Michigan primary anyway and then had to quit the race due to incontinence, paralysis, pain and an understanding of the mortuary arts. A sinkhole, that was what the seventies had been, Wallace lying on his back on the stones in the same posture as RFK in that kitchen in Los Angeles and the wife, Cornelia, over him screaming. A missed assassination, though, just like the two attempts on Ford, Fromme and Sarah Jane Moore two months apart in 1975. A cold decade, the seventies, but not as efficient for all of its sleekness, as the sixties. In the sixties people got put down, the seventies though were just for hanging around and around, sometimes until the eighties or even nineties. Bush had been chairman of the Republican National Committee during Watergate at Nixon's behest. McGovern had backed Eagleton a thousand percent in August 1972 when word got out about the shock treatments Eagleton had incurred and then three days later had dumped him from the ticket in favor of Shriver. No, it was not an efficient decade.

It had more bark than bite, though, Winogrand said pointlessly. I mean, you could tough it out, you could get through it. Not like the sixties. The sixties could kind of sneak around and sneak around on you and then burn out your brainpan but even though the seventies started out tougher with that failed *Apollo 13* and the secret bombing of Cambodia, they wimped out in the malaise speech. A clear arc toward extinguishment, Winogrand said. Is there anything else you need to know? Can I go now? Are we finished?

It's hard to understand you people, the interrogator said. You take all of your history so *seriously* and yet nothing happens.

I told you that to start, Winogrand said earnestly. I told you that it was a cold gray time. You said you knew, that everyone else had told you that too. Well, that's what it was. It was a cold gray time. The Oakland A's won three world championships in a row from 1972 through 1974 and then Steinbrenner and Martin and Jackson had the New York Yankee follies in the late seventies so it wasn't *all* a matter of recycling at a lower level. A few things changed. Even I changed, Winogrand said. He could feel the slow throb of change moving within him although maybe it was inertia or a kind of moral paralysis. There was no difference amongst all of these—change, fear, moral paralysis, sexual desire, the whole grab bag of virtues and vices—and that was another thing the seventies had taught him.

Believe me, Winogrand said, you don't want this place. The more you learn about it the less you can see, am I right? I'd like to be excused now.

His interrogator bobbed its tentacles in a way which seemed very much like a shrug of assent although of course, anthropomorphizing was pretty much a constant in the alien-human spatial relations which Winogrand had noted. What we can't understand, the interrogator said, taking testimony on this century of yours in decade-long testimony, cutting up the century and trying to get the picture here ... we simply can't understand how and why you cling to any concept of linearity. Don't you see how disjunctive this is? Yet you seek for connections even when there are no connections.

Well, Winogrand said, and felt the full weight of the century coursing thickly through like sludge, like knowledge, like some river of testimony, well, that's how we were framed. We're a linear race. We believe in chronology. We hold to chronology as if it had consequence. Everyone, Winogrand said, but Nixon that is. I don't think that he's linear which is why he is still around. The shadows poked from the corners of the room, seeming to dazzle in the sudden heat and Winogrand felt himself beginning to slide away, toward a lucid and grateful consciousness. Well thank you, he heard the alien say, thank you for your time and trouble. We'll have to consider all of this but I think there's a very good possibility that we want no part of this. None at all. Too much malaise, the alien said. You should talk, Winogrand said and then, sinking into the reconstructed unconsciousness from which time and again they had hauled him, he felt himself on the lip of a profound but casual insight which seemed to wait for him like a net just below that abyss of sleep. *Linear*, he thought, that was the fallacy, and then he was out and the aliens going about their continuing work which consisted of trying to find some way of reordering the century. The trouble was that like a Chinese puzzle, it didn't seem to fit no matter *how* you placed those tubes of the decade. Of their eventual decision, then, the account executive remained blameless.

The High Purpose
with Carter Scholz

Passing Youngstown, Ohio, its steel mills flaming beyond an unseen horizon, Hammett said, "They're behind us." Chandler's reaction, he noted with disgust, was to take his foot off the gas. The Cadillac Sedan de Ville wallowed, began to slide, and Chandler had to fight the wheel to straighten it.

"Son of a bitch," said Chandler. "Dirty son of a bitch."

"Your choice," Hammett said. Chandler had picked out the car in the lot, had even argued for it, until Hammett had reluctantly gone along. What did he know about cars, anyway? The best part of his experience had been on foot, peering into warehouses and protecting scabs. Whereas Chandler was part of the gentry; he went everywhere on wheels, or so he said. Goddamned Englishman.

"How long?" Chandler asked.

"Till what?"

"I mean how long have they been back there, for Christ's sake? And what the hell do they want?"

Hammett hated it when the Englishman cursed. It sounded like something he'd practiced. So he said, "I don't know." He knew all right, or at least had a good idea, but if Chandler couldn't figure it out for himself, Hammett couldn't tell him.

Chandler pressed the accelerator again, and the overpowered car lurched ahead, spilling into the shoulder.

"Take it easy," Hammett said. "Don't let them know we've seen them." He was certain that their pursuers already knew that. If nothing else, Chandler's erratic driving just then had told them. But he wanted to calm Chandler down. He was an inept driver at best. Hammett should have been driving, but there was no time to make the switch, and in any case he hadn't been behind the wheel for six years, since that incident in Juarez. So they were stuck.

"How far back?" said Chandler.

"A mile or more. Don't worry about it." Hammett looked at the gas gauge. They had filled up outside Cleveland, and now there was three-quarters of a tank left. He didn't know if they'd have time to stop again.

Hammett didn't want to think about how they had gotten into it. But retrospection seemed obligatory; the turnpike offered nothing but trucks shuddering past them on both sides, or Chandler occasionally making an insane lunge up between a couple of barreling monsters. If he had been writing this situation instead of living it, this would have been the time to drop in exposition, cast his mind back to reveal the reasons for the flight with Raymond Chandler in a Cadillac from a bunch of professionals who wanted to kill them. But he did not want to think about it. You simply had to keep moving forward, and pick up the pieces later, if at all. This was about the worst time he'd ever had, but then again, it had been bad before and he had gotten out.

At fifty-six your life should have leveled out; the unpredictable or menacing might come from an affair or from bad news at the annual physical, but it should not connect to chases in cars, frantic evasive maneuvers, and a panicky Englishman at the wheel who would rather be sipping tea in La Jolla. I should not have gotten into this, Hammett thought, and he had to smile at that: his whole life was a matter of situations he should not have gotten into.

He leaned back in the seat, closed his eyes. Let Chandler run the car up the tail pipe of a semi. He was so tired of it all. Yet he felt the skittering of his heart, and with one ear kept alert to Chandler's panic. Chandler seemed to be murmuring. Praying, perhaps.

Chandler was not praying. He was recalling when Hammett had proposed the idea to him. Hammett had been reasonable; the idea itself had seemed sensible. They would simply get away. Away from the circumstantial grinding down of their essence that had entrapped them both. Why not? They could afford it. They were not rich, but their work had made them comfortable. Why not use the profits from the work to get away from the work, and the life connected to it?

The difference was that Chandler was still working, and Hammett had given up long ago. He was obviously never going to write again. He made noises about a mainstream novel, and had even told Chandler the title one drunken night in Nebraska—*Tulip*—and when Chandler wrinkled his nose at that, gave the title his professional scorn, Hammett had simply shrugged and upended the bourbon bottle into his mouth. No, the man was burned out, gone. *Tulip* (unbelievable that he was so far gone as to even consider such a title!) would be discovered as a jumble of notes after his death, and Hellman or some other executor would have a hell of a time trying to put it into publishable shape.

But Chandler was working, despite everything. Wasn't he? *The Long Goodbye* no longer seemed like a joke or a mockery. After countless evasions, he had finally sat down to it with some of the old dedication to getting the job done. And the work came. It was good. It would be longer than anything he had done before, and possibly the best thing he had ever done. And despite that, Chandler had not been able to stand up against Hammett when he had proposed the idea.

The two men had met just once before, at a 1936 West Coast get-together for *Black Mask* contributors. Chandler still had the photograph. He was looking across at Hammett with a certain measured resentment in his features, and Hammett was returning the look. He doubted that Dashiell remembered. After all, Hammett was through writing by then, had come just for the booze, and Chandler had scarcely started. He had not seen the man again until he came to Chandler with the idea.

The *high purpose*, Hammett had called it. To Chandler, writing had always been the high purpose: writing against the grain of things, of manners, of the literary snobs, of the genteel English mystery novelists. Death is real, murder is not a hobby of the upper class. The streets are mean, and someone must walk them and say so. But Hammett was persuasive. "Come on, Ray," he had said. "You don't *believe* all that crap, do you?" And for the moment at least, Chandler had to admit, yes, it was crap, it was all made up, he had never even seen a corpse; Marlowe was as estranged from him as Sam Spade was from Dashiell, whose Pinkerton days were spent mostly patrolling warehouses and protecting scabs.

Perhaps it was that Dashiell had been there first. Hammett would always be regarded as his predecessor. It wasn't fair; the man was actually younger than he, had not even much wanted to be a writer— yet in Chandler's mind (and probably Hammett's, though Chandler had never been able to draw him out on this), he was always going to be regarded as an imitator. No, it wasn't fair. Hammett's "experience" as a detective had been of no use to his writing (though it helped his career); of far more use had been his reading of Hemingway. At least Chandler had had the taste not to imitate that. Yet it was true that Chandler had learned from Hammett. And therefore, he had gone along with the scheme. Had even suggested going East, had bought the car, had collaborated in every way. Had put himself in this situation.

Son of a bitch, Chandler thought. Who is there to blame? Hammett seemed to be asleep. If the trucks flanking them moved together, Hammett would not even note the transition from life to death. He had always been that kind of man. And maybe that was the source of his strength; that he did not give a damn, seemed to have internalized death to the point where everything in life came easy. That could be why he had stopped writing. Chandler did not know. His hands were damp on the wheel, and he wished he were back in L.A., bringing Cissy her tea, even working on some piece of shit screenplay, drunk and in despair—anything but this. But there was no way to stop now, no way until the very end.

The kid would occasionally glance up at him, not quite seeing him, a look of puzzlement on his keen face that might have been a recognition of the shifted air in the cheap room, or simply a plot point or adjective that needed work. No way to tell.

The thing was, he could not do it alone. He wrote exclusively about loners, but he was not one. The unfinished *Tulip* proved that, if his "visits" to the kid did not. You are talking to yourself, he wanted to tell the kid, because you want company. It's pathetic.

So he had sought out Chandler.

What a mistake, he thought now.

Perhaps he'd been drunken and sentimental when he made the decision. Wouldn't surprise him. He'd thought of Chandler as a peer because, of all the people who'd written in the genre, they were the two best. How was he to know that Chandler was as troubled as he and even less capable of coping with the paraphernalia of existence? In the clarity of despair, it had seemed easy: get away, just the two of them, abdicate, cultivate some kind of exile, find a new world. Away from the committees, the politicians, the pressures, the scriptwriters, the critics, the Communists, away from everything. Even Lillian. Oh, yes, Lillian was part of it, all right.

He came full awake as the Cadillac's horn bleated faintly against the roar of wind. The speedometer, in green, showed eighty-five. Chandler leaned out the open driver's window to shout at a truck he was passing on the right. At the end of the downgrade, the car bottomed out, and Hammett felt his stomach bounce in sympathy as the machine lazily adjusted on its springs to the accumulated inertia. We have no chance, Hammett thought.

Outside Pittsburgh, two men stretched themselves under the mercury-vapor lamps of a Cities Service gas station while an attendant in a pressed uniform filled the tank of their Ford.

"They're getting ahead, you know," said the man named Smith.

"Let them," said Jones. "Where can they go?"

To Hammett, it had seemed easy at the time. The plan had elegance and economy. When it came to him, its elegance and economy reminded him first of how he felt working on the early stories in San Francisco. And second, of his more recent moments of despair, which were not always drunken. Despair, he wanted to go back and tell the kid on Eddy Street at the borrowed typewriter, has a clarity all its own. What do you think you are after here? Words on paper are not it. You will end up at your destination whether or not you do this.

The pursuers picked them up again slightly past Harrisburg. Hammett was beginning to worry. It was as if they would not wait for the end of the line, would not follow the neat strictures of a well-made plot, would instead blow them off the road in a gesture of anarchy without even the clarity of despair, or the requiem of a curt denouement. He had not expected this, but he felt now, emanating from the headlights behind them, a feral hunger beyond anything in the world he lived in. He recognized it: it was the hunger beneath the surface of what he had written. It was something he had flirted with, in the solipsism of creation, something he had acknowledged without endorsing, something he had denied without mastering. Something real. Something just coming of age now in 1951, something with a face bland as the face of Elisha Cook, who'd played the gunsel in Huston's film of *The Maltese Falcon*, but with a chill scent of machinery beneath it. Something like the screenplay that fellow Shulman had lately told him about, *Rebel Without A Cause*, something new entirely, yet something he could have, should have foreseen.

Chandler felt it, too. His driving improved. He ceased to fiddle with the dash controls, the radio, but put all his attention on the road. Hammett's respect for him renewed somewhat. Yes, Chandler had felt that whiff of the beyond, the thing without a face that lurked at the edge of implication of all their work. He felt it now, and applied himself to the craft of outrunning it. At the wheel, at the typewriter—no difference. The unpredictable line of the road, the unpredictable turns of a plot, the nuance of a curve or a line of dialogue—he was again glad that he had company, and almost glad that it was Chandler. The man was not one of the worst.

"Raymond," said Hammett. How strange: he was feeling loquacious. "It doesn't matter, you know. None of it matters. The work, the money, the critics—nothing. Only this. Keeping ahead of them."

Chandler said nothing. The road unwound beneath the headlights.

Smith said, "What is it about, exactly?"

Jones sighed. It had been a mistake to go with Smith, but that was the best he could do. He had found the man hanging out in the lobby of a hotel. The desk clerk had been eyeing Smith suspiciously. At that point Jones had been none too clear on his own motivations, so he had moved by instinct, had steered Smith outside, and had talked with him.

He must have been persuasive. For Smith had gone along with it. Get a car, find their quarry, follow them, kill them. That simple. For a reason they both somehow understood, but had not yet articulated.

"Go to sleep, Smith," said Jones. "What it's about doesn't matter. If we knew what it was about, *exactly*, would we do it?"

"I know what I want," muttered Smith. "I want them dead."

"Why, *exactly?* Why do you want that, Smith?" He was pressing things. Trying to find a limit. But Smith was not interested in that. Not yet.

Suddenly Hammett said, "Pull off here."

Chandler's hands responded first. His brain was half asleep. "We'll switch now," said Hammett, getting out of the car. Chandler was still sitting slumped at the wheel when Hammett reached the driver's door.

"Give it a rest, Ray. I know this place."

Chandler got out and went around to the passenger side. Hammett drove a leisurely quarter mile, and turned up a smaller road. They followed this in silence for a half hour. Chandler dozed fitfully, could not help himself, and came out of it feeling that he'd fallen asleep at the wheel. Then he'd turn, frantic, to look at the dark void behind him, scanning for the glow of headlights behind the last rise.

They stopped in front of a dark farmhouse.

"Sid Perelman's place," said Hammett. "You know Sid? Pep West's brother-in-law. Pep put me up at the Sutton Club Hotel after I skipped the Pierre in '32. I was broke and I had to finish *Falcon.* Pep moved out here for a while after that."

"Is Perelman here?" Chandler asked.

"I doubt it. I doubt it very much."

Suddenly Hammett put the car in gear and drove it over grass to a spot behind a carriage house. He doused the lights and left the car. He walked briskly back over the grass, scuffing it with his shoes, and bending to brush it with his hand. He looked up. Headlights approached from behind a hill. He returned to the car.

It would be a hell of a way to die. Somehow he *had* expected Sid to be here. The natty attire, the unfailing good humor, the wit that didn't grate on him the way wit usually did. He had even thought Pep might be here. But Pep had been dead for ten years.

He said nothing about the headlights to Chandler. Instead he said, "Christmas 1940 was awfully merry, wasn't it?"

"What's it about?"

"You remember—Scott Fitzgerald, and the day after that Pep West. Two of the best. Dead within a day of each other."

Yes, Chandler remembered. They had all been in Hollywood. He had just finished *Farewell, My Lovely*, and there seemed a chance that the movie rights would go.

Then Chandler heard the motor.

"Don't move," Hammett said. "Don't make a sound." A hell of a way to die. In a car. In a car that he had driven into a blind alley, expecting some sort of supernal grace to descend on him. A last visit to Sid and Pep, to old times, maybe a way out of the whole rotten mess of the past twenty years, a way out of the bad way out he'd talked Chandler into. He had honestly thought that their pursuers would pass the place without a thought. He'd underestimated them. Chandler was panicked again. Hammett wondered if he'd have to slug the Englishman.

The motor stopped. Steps came up the gravel. A flashlight beam played in the grass past where they were parked behind the carriage house. Hammett felt the first tickle of a coughing fit snake up his lungs. He swallowed hard.

Hammett shut his eyes. A few minutes later he heard low voices, the crunch of gravel again. The motor started. The other car drove off.

"Jesus!" Chandler whispered.

Hammett was shaking and did not trust his voice. He got out and let Chandler take the wheel.

Chandler insisted on having literary discussions. Mostly Hammett pretended to be asleep. It was pathetic, the way Chandler harped on what Charles Morton had said about him in the *Atlantic*, and how the English regarded him as a literary writer. Hammett had had far too much of that shit. When he'd first met Lillian, he was a pulp writer. Soon enough he was a celebrity. Gertrude Stein had put him in a novel; he'd met her once at a party in Beverly Hills. Chaplin was there, too; he recalled nothing else except passing out drunk. Lillian's connections. God, it was awful, and to hear Chandler going on about this kind of culture, sometimes in awe, still like a fifth-former who'd once met Yeats, it was nauseous.

Chandler was the older man; that was the odd thing. Not one reader in a hundred knew this, because Chandler had started to write much later in life than Hammett, had started to write in fact after Hammett had finished. And because he had chosen to write in Hammett's genre, inevitably he seemed a follower. Whose fault was that? Hammett wondered. Not his. In a way he was gratified that Chandler had done it. It vindicated him. For one thing, he no longer had to do it himself.

But it also annoyed him. Chandler had seen the strong bones of Hammett's work—give him that—and had known enough to use what was usable. But he had fleshed out the skeleton with his own evasions and preciousness. And that Hammett didn't like. It was theft and fakery. Well, who was he to complain? If he called that theft, then

Hemingway had a case against him.

At least Hemingway and I could tell the real from the literary, he thought. Better than this one, anyway. He glanced over at Chandler's pinched face as a light swept past overhead.

He was tired of thinking. Face it, he couldn't tell the real any better than the rest of them. If he could, he wouldn't be in this situation. He had no right to rag Chandler. Hadn't his own first sale been to Mencken at *Smart Set?* Hadn't he loved the parties Lillian took him to, at first? What crap. And Mencken bought *Black Mask*—slumming, it turned out, just using it and *Saucy Stories* to fund his tony journals. So Hammett had written for *Black Mask*, but by then Mencken was gone and he had "Cap" Shaw to deal with.

But that wasn't quite it. It was more that he had written too well, had gotten close enough to the real to bring things into being. As had Chandler. You were hagridden by the real before you started, and it only got worse and worse. He'd put something into *The Thin Man* (and Jesus, how he hated Nick and Nora by now), a two-thousand-word quote about cannibalism from *Celebrated Criminal Cases In America*, just dropped it into the middle of a scene, wrecking the whole dramatic flow. It was the only thing he still liked about the book.

"Ray," he said, "it is the beginning of the end when you discover you have style."

"If I had been driving, this wouldn't have happened," Smith said. "I could have caught them. I'm a better driver than you. I used to do the Ventura Highway for fun."

Jones had a headache. Ever since they'd lost the pair outside Erwinna, Pennsylvania, Smith had been ragging him. And Smith didn't yet have the faintest idea of what was at stake.

True, Jones had blundered. He should have checked the farm more closely. He hadn't because it had smelled strange. Now he felt certain that they had been there. But it didn't matter. They couldn't get away.

"I mean it, Jones. Once, ten years ago, I drove from Chicago to L.A.— that's over two thousand miles—in a day. No sleep, just stops for gas. And I was still fresh at the end."

"Ten years ago. Good for you, Smith."

"You think I'm some kind of nut," Smith said. "You don't respect me, you think I'm a fool, you think because you can sit there and say nothing, you're somehow stronger or better than I am, but that's not true. You don't know me, Jones. You don't know what I've been through."

"All right," said Jones. He thought: Tell me about it, tell me about what true is.

"Those guys," said Smith. "They know nothing of it. It's dirt, all if it, but bright dirt. They think they know it. They write it up, they sound tough, they make it seem real. But it's just words. They don't know what a heel in the gut feels like. They never got shot." He paused, looked at the gun in his hand. "I want them to know pain. Just once I want them to feel what it's like. Can you understand that, Jones?"

Yes, Jones thought, I can understand that. But he said nothing.

"One shot for each. That's not too much to ask."

That's not what we're here for, Jones thought. You're getting personal again. We're not here to get personal. But he said nothing. There was absolutely nothing to say.

"If we lose them, Jones, if you lose them"—and Smith's voice was slightly different now, as deep and as slow as the voice Jones had tried to cultivate over the years—"if it happens that way, I'm going to kill you. I just want you to know that."

Jones said, "And then what?"

"And then we'll see. But it won't matter to you."

No, it won't, Jones thought. I believe him.

"You still think I'm a clown?"

"No," Jones said, "I don't think you're a clown."

As they passed through the strange dead towns of west Jersey, Chandler tried to imagine what he had ever seen in the plan. He had left his work, just when he was getting back to it; had left Cissy, who needed him now more than ever; had just walked out of his life. It was utterly out of character. He wasn't a roving bum like Hammett. And it was not just the strength of the man's character—true, going along seemed a way to make something up to Hammett, to cancel for once and all the claims of imitation. If he did this for Hammett, he wouldn't owe the man a thing, ever again.

But he had his own reasons for wanting to get away. He was sixty-two now. Cissy, his wife, was eighty, and dying by half-inches. He couldn't stand it. Perhaps it was foolish to have married her, but he'd been only thirty then, and she was beautiful at forty-eight: bright, full of life, a fighter. It tore him up to live with those memories now, day in and out, getting the meals, doing the shopping. He remembered how it had been last year when they'd had to put their black cat, Taki, to sleep. A shot of Nembutal in the leg, and two seconds later she wasn't there. The vet gave another shot straight to the heart to make sure. Why, when you were ready to give up, did it have to be any harder than that?

Oh, yes, he could still see the attraction in the plan. But he had known after an hour on the road that it was impossible. All Hammett wanted to do was drink and abuse Chandler for not really understanding his material, how painful life really was. All he wanted to do, really, was to abuse Chandler, call him an effete Englishman who was slumming by writing for *Black Mask*. Chandler painstakingly pointed out that he was born in Chicago, that his British naturalization had never been legal (he was having tax problems over that one), and that he had never looked down on the mystery, only on bad writing. Hammett said he had never heard such shit. Chandler, driving, had watched Hammett get drunker and drunker and had begun drinking himself, probably just to prove that he could not be intimidated in that way, and after that the trip had become a nightmare, a disaster. He had nearly killed them both outside Chicago. He had cut out the drinking then (Hammett's capacity was unmatchable, in any case), and even Hammett had sobered up slightly.

The two assassins must have picked them up about then, although Hammett thought that it was far earlier. That they had been trailed from the very beginning. Chandler wondered if this was some Communist or FBI scenario that Hammett had perversely involved him in, but in his heart he knew it wasn't. He knew the assassins were after him just as much as Hammett. And for the same reasons.

And he had admired this man. Well, it was over now. Especially after that business at the farm. He was tempted to try something like it himself: cut the engine, pull over, throw the keys, and wait for them to close in. It would be a proper and fitting ending to the whole mess.

But he knew he did not have the courage. So he kept driving, kept on the strange dark west Jersey roads watching for a glimmer of pursuit in the mirror, hating Hammett, hating himself, hating everything that was represented everywhere.

They had turned onto Route 9W in Nyack, New York. The assassins had picked them up again. Hammett risked turning in the seat, saw fog and darkness. Little fumes seemed to be coming up from the center of the road, dark clouds of poison. He had thought California ugly, but this was worse. In the distance behind him he saw the headlights, cutting through the fog.

"Half mile back," he said. "Maybe less."

Chandler nodded grimly, gripping the wheel. His face was twisted in boyish frustration. "It isn't fair," he said. He pounded the wheel once, abruptly, jiggled the gas pedal, then had to brake sharply as the car entered a curve. "Isn't *fair*," he said again. "We can't outrun them."

"You picked the car," said Hammett.

"Damn it!" Chandler said. "I know I picked the car! Why do you have to keep telling me that? It's all my fault, all right? We're going to die on this road, and the last thing I'll hear is you telling me it was my decision."

"All right," Hammett said.

"You went along with it. You—"

"I know that," Hammett said. He turned in the seat again. The lights were the size now of an animal's eyes, brighter now in the fog. "They're gaining on us. You'd better try something."

"Like what? It was your choice, too, your goddamned plan. This is no time to put it all on me—"

"I said it's *all right*," Hammett said sharply. Chandler yanked the wheel left, then right. The car went almost out of control. He's going to kill us, thought Hammett. They won't even have to catch us. "Just drive," he said quietly. "If we can get to the bridge, we have a chance."

"No chance," said Chandler hopelessly. "No chance from the very beginning."

Hammett sighed. The man was right. But at the mention of the bridge, Chandler pumped the gas. Perhaps he could be given hope, Hammett thought. Hold him together somehow. It couldn't be more than five miles now; they were into Jersey again, had just passed Tenafly; if they could get into New York City, they might be able to lose them in the streets.

The assassins, after the almost desultory pursuit from Pennsylvania, seemed to sense this, too. They knew far less about Manhattan than Hammett did, of course; he had only once written about New York, though he had lived there, on and off, for over twenty years. And Chandler had never written about it.

They came from a deep curve on the treacherous highway. Chandler pumped the gas. "Maybe there is a chance," Chandler said.

Hammett said nothing. He watched the road. The poisonous fog whipped past them.

Smith said, "This is it. We've got to catch them soon. We've got to stop them before they carry this on any further."

Jones shrugged, but something in the younger man's tone made him uneasy. "Don't know," he said.

"We can't permit it," Smith looked at the Colt .45 in his hand. "Our mission is clear. Sometimes you have to draw a line."

Jones worked the heater. He didn't like the road, he didn't like the fog, and he increasingly didn't like Smith. He wondered if he had been like this on his first job. Probably; he remembered shooting the middle-aged fat ex-dick who'd been his partner. Left him by the side of a road outside Seattle. Never knew his name.

No, thought Jones. This line of thought is not reassuring.

In the far distance he could see the ghost of the Cadillac's taillights, but Chandler had opened the distance in the past few miles.

"Don't they understand?" said Smith. "It can't go on and on. There had to be an end to it." He looked at the gun. "I don't want to be here. I never wanted to be here. Nobody wants to be here, but there's a job and there has to be a man to do it."

If only the silly son of a bitch would shut up, thought Jones. I don't want to hear the messages he's getting. I've heard them too often. Maybe I've done this too often. What year is it, anyway?

"We're not going to make it, are we?" Smith said.

"I don't know. It's close." Had he ever made it? Had he ever, once, in all the chases, actually made it? He could see Hammett's thin face laughing at the question. He jammed the accelerator to the floor.

"Let me drive," said Smith.

"No. No time to switch."

"They're going to make it, aren't they?" Smith said. "They're going to get over the bridge and into the streets and we'll lose them, and it will all be like this never was. That's what's going to happen, isn't it, Jones?"

"I don't know," Jones said. "It's possible." And went on driving.

With the bridge in sight now, Chandler pulled a maneuver. He hit the brakes and drifted toward a closed Texaco station, its lights out, its pumps covered by cloth.

"No," Hammett said, suddenly going cold. He didn't like the scene, not a bit; it seemed too familiar.

"Don't do it."

"Don't do what?"

"Don't stop."

"Look, Dash, we can wait them out—"

"You stupid bastard," Hammett said, and for the first time on this drive, he felt himself losing his temper, as he had not even at the hotel in Chicago where Chandler had gotten drunk and gone around the dining room telling everyone that they were in the presence of two of the major writers of the century. "We can't wait anybody out. We're running for our lives now. They're not going to make that mistake at the farm twice."

"Listen, Dash …"

"No, *you* listen. It's just words for you. This is not another plot, not some made-up fantasy; those guys are serious, they're here to kill us. And they will if you don't show some control." He kicked Chandler in the calf. "Drive."

They were rolling slowly towards the Texaco's entrance. Chandler pulled back to the left, accelerated past the closed station. "They're coming up on us again," he said.

"Of course they're coming up on us: you lost us time."

"Listen, Dash. This was your idea. Remember that. If we're here at all it's because of you. I didn't start this, you did—"

Always, Hammett thought. It always comes to this. Even at the end he will deny it, will put it all on me. But maybe he is right. It is all my fault. It did originate with me. Even though he brought it to this.

"We have a chance if you push it," Hammett said.

"All my life I pushed it," said Chandler. "Maybe it's time to stop pushing. Maybe I should go back to England. Maybe—"

"Will you shut up." Hammett felt an almost murderous rage.

"I left Cissy back there. I left her." Chandler was almost crying now. "Everything I did or wrote was just a fire for her to warm her hands by."

The miserable fucked-up bastard, Hammett thought. He said, "And I had a dog once, but it died."

Chandler turned to him with the look of a maniac. Behind the round glasses his eyes were berserk. Then he suddenly laughed. The car lurched as it went into the shoulder, and Chandler wrestled it back, breathing through his teeth.

Smith said, "They're going to make it. They're two hundred yards short of the toll booths, that's all."

Jones was not too upset. In the wake of the motels and fast-food joints in the past mile, in the spatter of light from the bridge, he had gained visibility and was closing ground. At the booths it might be a dead heat. It would not be as neat as it would have been if Chandler had pulled off into the Texaco, but he thought he could improvise.

"I won't let them make it," Smith said. "When they stop to pay the toll, I'll shoot them. We'll come up fast behind them and have a shot."

"Sure," Jones said. "And every attendant and Port Authority cop will be on us in thirty seconds. Why not just shoot the both of us and be done with it?"

"They can't get away with this," Smith said. "It's our lives, too."

Jones watched the Cadillac take the last curve, begin to move up the ramp. It was about 4 A.M. There were a few cars scattered in the space between them and the booths, but not enough to make a difference. Jones wondered who they all were, what they were doing out at this hour, at the edge of that great city built of real steel around a core of fantasy. A collaborative fantasy, he realized. Of course. Not just Smith and me out here with our mission; not just the dark roads and the fog and the mean streets and the blood; not just the victims of some arbitrary creation, but collaborators in it. We have collaborated with those two bastards up ahead in our victimization. That's it, he thought. We can't take them because we didn't realize that from the start. We went along with it. How repellent, he thought, and how true.

Smith seemed to have some sense of it, too, as the unreality of the dark roads yielded the day-bright mercury lamps all around them. "We might have another chance yet," Smith said. "We're supposed to get rid of them, remember?" Isn't that what we're supposed to do?"

"I don't know," Jones said. "I honestly don't know."

"Let me take over," Smith begged. "Let me do it."

"I don't know," Jones said. "I don't think I care anymore." And maybe that was it. How could you care? Halfway into the century, knowing what he knew, having lived through what he had done, was it possible to care anymore? He could feel the fog seeping through the windows, getting into his skin. He could feel the future dissolving him.

"Do what you have to," he said to Smith. "It's your life. It's my life. It's their lives, too."

As they neared the booths, Hammett saw Chandler think about running them. He put his hand, holding a quarter, on top of Chandler's right hand on the wheel, squeezing it.

"No," he said. "We don't attract attention. We don't give them a chance at a scene. We pay the toll like good citizens. Roll down the window."

"They're coming up fast, Dash."

"What happened in the last scene of *The Lady in the Lake?*"

Chandler looked over at him. It was the first direct acknowledgment he had that Hammett had read any of his stuff. In that last scene the heavy runs a sentry post on a dam. Shortly after, at the bottom of the dam, is the wreck of a car and something that had been a man.

"You think we have a chance?"

"We pay the toll," said Hammett, withdrawing his hand. Chandler took the quarter and put it between his teeth.

"I wanted to be a serious writer, Dash," said Chandler between his clenched teeth. "I wasn't really writing mysteries, I thought I was writing literature."

"I figured that out," Hammett said, thinking, now he's going to go confessional on me. We're going to make it, and I'm going to end up living with this lunatic.

Chandler took the coin out of his mouth, started to roll down the window. "Maybe I was wrong, maybe I shouldn't have looked down on the mystery. I didn't really...."

Yes, Hammett thought, and maybe you should have thought that a bullet in the heart is a bullet in the heart and not a thing learned out of books. That a corpse is no symbol. Now that they're closing in on you from behind and you're starting to think for the first time, but it's a little goddamned late, isn't it, Ray? A little late in the day for all that to occur to you—and don't tell me better late than never.

Chandler extended his left arm to the attendant. His head lolled back, as if awaiting the bullet.

Now you understand, Hammett thought. Now, when it's too late, as it's too late for all of us, now you finally see what it all really means.

The attendant was ignoring them. "I was wrong, Dash. But that doesn't make it all my fault, does it?"

You poor bastard, Hammett thought. You still don't understand that implication is universal and that we take the shroud the moment we open our eyes.

The attendant looked up, took the toll from Chandler. Directly behind them, almost touching their bumper, was the other car.

Smith sat holding the gun in his lap while Jones idled the engine and then cut it, stopping the car in the far right emergency lane just past the booths.

"I couldn't do it," he said, trembling.

"I know," Jones said.

"Right up to the last minute. But then I couldn't."

"Don't think about it." Jones didn't want to talk. He just wanted to continue over the bridge, then bear left all the way around the terminal and come back out. Back into the darkness.

"Why couldn't I? I know all about them. I knew they had to die. I knew it was up to me. There was no other way. But I couldn't. Why, Jones?"

"You're not the first."

"What?"

"A lot of us find that out. More than you would think. It isn't the same when you have to do it."

"I've killed before. I know what death is."

Jones leaned forward and started the engine. It took awhile. The Ford seemed to have given up also.

"Really," Smith said. "I really have. That's the truth."

"Sure," Jones said. "You know the truth about everything." He got the car moving. He stayed in the far right lane, doing thirty. "I didn't see you pulling any gun."

"I didn't expect to."

"Then why did you tell me—"

"I didn't tell you anything. I didn't tell you anything at all. We each live our own lives within an abyss. That's all I know. That's all the truth there is."

Smith wiped at his eyes. "I hate this," he said, "I *hate* it."

"We all do," Jones said. "But we keep doing it, don't we?"

At the Fifty-sixth Street exit on the West Side Highway, Chandler finally said, "I think we lost them."

"All right," Hammett said.

"I don't think they crossed the bridge."

"I think that's right," said Hammett.

"Why? Why did they give up?"

"I don't know," Hammett said. He thought that he did know, but it was nothing to discuss. "We'll take a room somewhere. The Sutton Club is long gone, but there's a cheap place near Times Square, the Dixie. Jam-packed with hookers. In the morning we'll figure out our next move."

"You think we got away for good?"

"We have to act like we did. Otherwise, what's the point?"

"Why would they let us go like that?"

"I don't know," Hammett said. "Maybe your sensational driving scared them off."

Chandler looked at him sidelong. "You think I'm stupid."

"I didn't say that."

"We were dead meat back there. But they let us go."

"Apparently."

"Why do you think so?"

Hammett shrugged. "Maybe they understood. Maybe it's that."

"Understood what?"

"What they had to. And no more."

First Chandler would unpack the good whiskey he had been saving in his valise since leaving the Coast. Then he would call the bellhop for some ice and have a drink. Then he would have another drink and try to figure his next move. Maybe he would work on *The Long Goodbye*. Maybe he would convince Hammett to do some work, even on that damned *Tulip*, but probably not. It didn't matter now.

"Dash," he would say:

Hammett would look at him. "What now?"

"Do you think it might be any different since we got away? That it might be a fresh start or something?"

"No," Hammett would say. "You never get away."

All Assassins

So I went into the office. Duty calls and calls and calls, of course. No sign of the senator, however, no ruddy Irish features glowing with health and purpose, greeting me with warm and friendly dedication, no handclasp, no (contrarily) sullen and preoccupied glare responding to my benign presence. Only a Scotch-taped note (compulsive is the senator, hold down the note against errant breezes): AT JOINT COMMITTEE HEARING; CLEAR UNTIL FOUR. "Joint committee meetings"—right. More humping and pumping, more sulking and hulking, no jamming and ramming for the public eye, however, and it takes a man of the senator's unusual cunning, not to say ferocity, to treat his own appointments secretary as part of the adversary press. Still, there is no quarreling, absolutely no disputation with success, with the ability to turn a marginal seat into a landslide, a landslide into an annuity, the senator will be president someday if we can keep his joint committee hearings private and of this there is no possible doubt, not any shade of a doubt whatever. I closed the door, left the note, not to say the aspect of the room, to its own devices, and padded back up the hall, waving indolently to Sorenson, shaking my head, then went to my desk where Papa Joe lurked. "No," I said. "He's at a joint committee hearing."

The old man stared at me without much encouragement. His face is unpleasant, all of the senator's features subtly converted against themselves, or so I have theorized. One theorizes a lot in this business; it is as likely a substitute as one can find for vanished conviction. "Says he'll be gone all afternoon."

"The son of the bitch is hiding out," Pa Joe said. "He told you to tell me that. He's in that office, nailing that little twat from Framingham I saw him with yesterday."

"No he's not," I said. "He's really not there. He's not nailing anything." Sometimes Pa Joe is exasperating; it is very difficult to maintain suitable distance, remembering that everything the senator has become he owes to the man. "He's really gone."

"I know the little tail. She's been hanging around for days looking for a spot. I saw her leafleting out at Lenox last month, waving at him. You think I miss something, Oswald? I don't miss anything. Nobody has to make room for me in the motorcades, I can see my own way."

"He's not there," I said again. Up to a point one deals with Pa Joe and then of course one stops. The senator has been very explicit on the issue. "Humor him, we're not looking for trouble," he has told me. "Within limits, jolly him along. But if he gets tight, Lee, pull the plug. Tell him where to go. He's not going to live forever and I've come into my inheritance." Pa Joe must have seen this recollection in my face. Disinterest came over him like a shroud, loathing two or three steps behind that. "I'll talk to him," he said. "I'll straighten him out." He slammed his hat atop his fine, gnarled, ruined Irish head, so much like the senator's, yet so compellingly unlike. Not an electable head. Boston, perhaps, but not a suburb with a per cap income above $10,000 would vote for a head like that. Appointive positions strictly. "That randy son of a bitch is going to go too far," Pa Joe said and strode out, leaving the door open, making little thumping noises deep in the corridor as he disappeared. An adventurous pursuit, political life, family life, the conjoinment of the two; an adventurous and hearty pursuit indeed, but one with humiliations small and large to pursue one through all the spaces of one's life. It is at moments like these, caught between Pa Joe and son John, Ambassador X and Senator Y, that I am apt to feel a flush of resentment which burns, which singes like the darkening pit itself. I remind myself that I could never have found on my own, that, power junkie that I am, I have found myself on the conveyance toward the heights and this mantra soothes, aids, levels me a bit; I find that I can fit myself back into the perspective of the day. "Joint committee hearing." There are times when I think that a man who would lie to his own appointment secretary would lie to the country, but then again, could the senator possibly lie to the country? He would not even lie to the twat from Framingham.

I know. I set it up.

Dave Powers thinks that '72 is the year, that the senator will be making his move then, not waiting until '76. Johnson is weakening, will never endorse him, but the lack of endorsement may be a plus. Symington, Humphrey too old. The war will be a problem, but as Powers says, a war will never hurt a Democrat in office while it is going on; it is after the fact that the Democrats hit the dust. Powers is filled with little speculations and whimsies of this sort; the senator loves him, has carried him through all of the partitions and spaces of his life. I have no opinion on Powers myself. "Lee," Powers says, "you're too intense. You must loosen up, my lad. You think that politics is issues, but politics is really a synthesis of drinking and fucking, in alphabetical order. You have the makings of a spanking lad, but you need perspective. '72 is the year, but if you do not find perspective you'll never last until that golden time."

Powers has a point; I am too intense. Drinking and fucking have always struck me as peripheral activities. (Which is why I think I amuse the senator and why we have gone such a distance together; he measures himself against me, always favorably.) Still, it is intensity that mans the phone lines, keeps the press happy, manages the constituency, negotiates with Pa Joe, and provides twat from Framingham, all of this with the kind of dispatch and efficiency the senator can simulate but not cultivate on his own, and Dave Powers is not to forget it. Or the senator. "'72, my lad," Powers says, passing me in the hall, nodding to me from the back of the cafeteria, nudging me as I scurry toward the cloakroom, papers in hand. "'72, '72!" Keeping me on a leash of possibility, straining against the power of my own disinclination, which, I should remind myself, is occasionally visible; if it can be seen by such as Powers, what then might the senator think?

"So, Lee," the senator said, "what do you think? Cape Cod or Hyannisport? Where should we make the announcement?"

"I can't say." The car slewed under my grip; I felt the rear wheels begin to go, coaxed it back to the road. A jolting announcement. Simply stunning in context; the first indication. "Why not Washington?"

The senator smiled, cuffed me on the elbows, but gently, gently, knowing the thin bond between the car and myself. "This is not the year to announce *anything* in Washington. Except perhaps a resignation. The local constituency is best, man of the soil and sea. Do you think LBJ will make it all the way out? Come on, Lee, ease up a little, you look as if I punched you in the face. It's only rock 'n roll, Lee, it's only a declaration of intent. We have *months* to go before we specify the primaries."

"It's a big responsibility. I don't know." Staring through the heavy windshield, seeing the refractions of all the distant, constituent traffic as we rolled on the strip of 95, I thought, he is not serious. He is an accomplished and charming man and he is right, we have gone a distance together, but in the center of his Irish soul there is frivolity; he is only a man trying to get through. Maybe some tragic sense is missing, or maybe then again there is nothing *but* tragic sense and Joe has forced him to avoid coming to terms too well with what he knows. I cover for him, I drive his car, I give him counsel and caution, but I know him no better than I did eight years ago when all of this began, and if we go another eight years, if we see him in the Oval Office, I will still know him no better.

"I think LBJ will make it through," I said. "He's too mean to die, too mean to let it go."

"He could resign. If he resigns, Hubert is the incumbent. That gives him advantages."

"I don't think he'll let it go," I said. "He couldn't let the war go, he won't let the office."

"I think you're right," the senator said after a long pause. "I think he'll hold on to the end and Hubert is fucked again. Fucked again!" He leaned further in the seat, put a hand over his eyes. "They're all fucked," he said. "Even me. Mostly me. You know what Rochelle from Framingham wanted? A copy of *Profiles in Courage* and a handkerchief." He giggled. "A *handkerchief.*"

"Did you give it to her?"

"Of course I gave it to her. I gave her everything she wanted. Don't you think to ask me why such an unusual request?"

I shrugged. "No, it didn't occur to me."

"So little occurs to you, Lee. You are the most implacable man I know. Hidden depths, that's what you've got, but sometimes I wish you could be a little more forthcoming, don't you? A little straightforwardness in the clinches never hurts. Look at Dave."

"Look at Ted."

"Ted? Ted is a behind-the-scenes man. You, you're up front serving the public, Lee. A little gregariousness. Gregarity? Stop clutching the wheel that way, you're doing fine."

But I wasn't. I wasn't doing fine. Taking little sidelong glances at the senator, measuring him, measuring the road, measuring all of the small and large calculations that had taken him to this moment, it occurred to me in that heavy car, perhaps for the first time, that the war had no bearing, the country had no bearing, not even Papa Joe had the credibility that I thought.... It was the announcement itself, the announcement and the election and the rest of it meant as much to him as the local talent from Framingham. The twat from up north. The quick sidesaddle fuck in the little apartment downtown.

It is a tumultuous and difficult time. Shielded as we are in Washington by prerogative and legislature, adulation and expense account, the smooth and functioning engines of power, it is impossible still not to sense how chaotic the circumstances have become. LBJ's war goes on and on, the draft hurtles to ever higher figures, eighty percent of our male youth are being packed off at least for training, and the convulsions are beginning to move from the campuses to the surrounding towns. LBJ would not be electable even if he were constitutionally able to run. He is no more electable now than Nixon was in '64; it had taken Nixon only three years to dissipate any of the small advantages with which he had been elected, to disgrace himself publicly as he had privately. But the suddenness of Nixon's collapse, the fullness of his capitulation, had made Johnson arrogant. Now it was the war he had chosen to explore which had truly become his; Vietnam was no longer the dead Nixon's but the living Johnson's war, and in the pulse and thunder of that distant news the country was beginning slowly, inexorably, to come apart. We could feel the shock in that slow and evil summer of '71 and on that first swing through the Midwest, after the announcement in Lowell, the Revolutionary statue photogenically in the background, I could begin to measure the dimensions of the dilemma we faced. Because if it was Johnson's war, then it was the party's, and yet the senator could only campaign through the medium of the party, that was clear. Always an insider, he was a systems man, a cool and efficient operator, and it is this which had drawn me to him from the beginning. A lone cat all my life, disenfranchisement my condition, it had been as enormously appealing to work with someone who casually dealt with power as it must have been entrancing to the senator to have a member of the Fair Play for Cuba Committee setting up his engagements and now and then even doing a little procuring, all part of the appointments function.

Looking at the farmland, seeing the broken and empty aspect of the faces lined on the streets waiting for us, I began to feel the weight of the senator's incomprehension, the implacability of his desire.

Caught between Daley and Papa Joe on the senator's night of nights. I felt the thin stab of their teasing; I have never been comfortable with men like this and yet my life, somehow, took me amid them, landed me in that hotel room. "Tell me, Lee," Daley said, "don't you *ever* want to get a little of that?" He pointed at the television set, the woman caught in the box, in frieze, cheering. "Don't you ever think of that stuff hanging around our boy?"

"I think of it," I said. "I don't have to do it, though."

"He doesn't do it," Papa Joe said. "Our boy Lee doesn't do *anything*." He nudged Daley, two rumpled, sweating, scotch-stinking old men on a couch in the largest hotel room I have ever seen. "That's what appeals to the senator; Lee's a look-but-don't-touch, look-but-don't-even-*think* kind of guy. The senator needs that in the house."

"The senator needs almost anything. Ten votes short on the first ballot, you hear that? We're going to get it on the switches."

"Fuck you, Dick," Papa Joe said. "We want to work for it."

They both laughed. The thick and reeking stink of their laughter made me twitch. I moved further back on the chair, saw the round and deadly aspect of their smiles, the further obbligato of their laughter. "Lee's a real fastidious, *correct* kind of guy," Papa Joe said. "I wish I had met him fifty years ago; I would have led a cleaner life."

"Such a clean life," Daley said. "You never would have gotten it out of your pants? No pants, no senator, Ambassador."

They laughed again. And again and again and again, their henchmen on the other side of the room picking up the laughter as if they knew what it was about, and we listened to the call of the roll of the states, Daley suddenly all business with pad and pencil.

Switches and more switches. Connally took Texas away from Humphrey and gave it to the senator on the first ballot, after all. Put him over.

Daley winked. "There's your vice-president," he said.

"But he's for the war," I said. I couldn't help myself. A high bleat, a college sophomore's whine, a little-boy voice. The tinkle of betrayal in that voice. "He's been for the war all along. He won't—"

"A *great* vice president," Daley said.

"And just think of that oil money coming in," Papa Joe said. "Your problem, Lee—I've been thinking about it seriously, now—your problem is that you probably turned it down early, turned it down from something really *good* when you were seventeen or so, and it hurt you so much, made you feel so bad that you decided you'd never be hurt that way again. So you made believe that it didn't exist. You spent the next seventeen years denying pussy."

"Denying pussy," Daley said. "Look at those bastards jumping! Well," he said, "we'd better get down to the floor, do our business. Been fun up here, Joe, but we got to leave our boy and tidy up on the unanimity. Or at least I do. You can stay here and talk pussy with Lee if you want, but I better show my face."

"No, that's all right," Papa Joe said. "I think I can show up now, too. Family is all right after the nomination, right?" I stood. Little waves of nausea battled with the other stuff in me, the nausea winning. The senator was nominated and I was going to throw up. In the small, cold, contracting spaces of the room, now dwindling around me to bind me like a blanket, I began to sense the crux of the betrayal.

But no time, no time for that.

In the small, cluttered room in Dallas, the senator's first major appearance after the convention, Connally's city, Connally's state, Connally's option, hunched with the senator over the table, going over the text of the speech, the correct draft run off frantically on the copier only moments before, I say to him, "You can't say this about the war. Not even in Dallas. Not even here. It will cost you the election."

"No, it won't," the senator says. His eyes are lustrous, convincing. "It won't cost me anything. It's the right statement in the right place. When we get in we can do whatever we want, Lee, but this is Texas; we've got an election here. I'm not going to turn into Nixon, not going to go in for any foolishness. It's the right place, right now, and it will pay dividends." He brushes me idly, absently on the shoulder. "If you're so upset, we'll talk about it later some more."

"I won't have it! You can't do it!"

He stares at me; in his face I can see now what Dave Powers once called *the cleaver*. Others have been looked at that way, I understand that now, but never to this moment me. "Lee," he says, "what is wrong with you?"

"You're the antiwar candidate! Your acceptance speech—"

"Lighten up, Lee," the senator says, "or quit. This is politics. This is a national campaign." He turns, moves toward the door, his gait smooth and casual, brisk and contained. "If you don't want to deal with it," he says, "see Bobby and turn your keys in. I have no time for this crap now, I really don't."

He leaves the room, the door swings behind him, in the distance the dim and convulsive roar of the crowd; and standing there I feel it break over me, all of it, not only these years in his employ but the years before, the wandering, the exploration, the horrors of Moscow. It is betrayal, *that* is what has stalked me all these years just as I have stalked it, betrayal and I meeting at last, all masks off in this room in Dallas, and what I feel like now—and this has been waiting all my life— is like a twat from Framingham. Local talent, regionally wrought. And nationally dismembered.

How could I have known? But I should have known. I *did* know; it was only a matter of placement.

I must make plans, I think. *Plans*. He is a dangerous man, an evil man; he is a man capable of anything. If he will allow the war, then he will allow the demons, the true and terrible burning of justice; he will let through all of the gnomes and fires of the apocalypse, he is a man capable of imprinting the mark of the beast savagely, savagely—

Plans.

I still had my credentials! I had not quit. I was close to him, as close as I had ever been. No one but I knew what must be done.

Old point-thirty-eight Smith & Wesson, a souvenir from the Fair Play Committee upon my departure. Point-thirty-eight Smith & Wesson, close in, close in, a winging shot as he and Connally embrace upon the rostrum, get them both, two shots, get them—

Big plans.

Understanding Entropy

So I go to Martin Donner's bedside in the room they have staked out for him in Florida, and I ask him the crucial question: If you had known? I say, if you had known that it would end this way, that you would be dying of a hundred wounds, of the tuberculosis, the pneumocystitis, of the parasites and the kidney breakdown and the hepatitis, the jaundice, the venereum and the shattering of the pancreas, if you had known that five years after the positive diagnosis and three years after the first episode of the pneumonia you would be lying here, 82 pounds, filled with morphine which does not work anymore—oh, nothing works but that isn't quite the point, is it? they are trying—with your lover and your daughters and your wife and the doctors circling in the outer room and coming in now and then to inspect your reeking corpus, some of them weeping, others taking your pulse and monitoring your breathing: if you had known this 15 years ago, Martin Donner, if you had known everything that would happen to you and that it would end this way, would you have left your wife and children to their lives and your history and gone out to Fire Island, Cherry Groves, the baths and the bathhouses and the quick and the scuffled, the long and the grievous affairs full time, no longer sneaking around? Would you if you had known? Or would you have stayed in your marriage in the suburbs, Martin Donner, and played with your daughters and watched them grow and claimed your wife with closed eyes in the marriage bed and nothing more, nothing more because you would never know when the dogs truly came into the basement and snuffled up the stairs? Oh, maybe once a year you might let some man tend to you with rubber gloves in a bank vault but otherwise nothing, nothing, nothing at all? If you could have seen that it would have ended this way, Martin, what would you have done? Tell me the truth now. Do you know the truth? Is there any such thing as the truth? Because I need, I need, I need to know now, it affects my own situation.

He stares at me. He is relatively lucid now, it come and it goes, in and out, back and forth, the pounding on the chest has loosened the phlegm, the morphine has momentarily quelled the cough, he thinks that he can think, although this is not necessarily the issue and he thinks, of course, that I am a hallucination. Hallucination is common in this late-life condition, although the dementia has not affected him as fully as it might in a few more hours or (if he lasts that long, he probably will not) days. I don't know, he says. His eyes are strangely lustrous, the only motion, the only thing in his face not quiescent, the rest is dead, bland, sunken, a canvas upon which has been embedded the full and perfect features of the dead, the valley of the dead, the shakes and valleys and small tablelands upon which the dead walk until at last they sleep.

Yes, Martin Donner says, yes I do know. I can answer that. He thrashes weakly, the ganglia in his shattered nerves trying to pull into alignment. I wouldn't have done it, he said. I would not have died this way. It is not worth it. I thought it was worth it, that it was worth any price to be what you are, to live expressly and fully but it is not, this is unbearable, I am sinking. I am sinking in disgrace. I wet myself, I humiliate myself, I see visions and dreams of such inextinguishable horror ... no, he says, no, and his voice is momentarily stronger, he screams in the room, no, he says, I would not have left them. I would have stayed there and I would have died, I would have died in a thousand ways, but it is the difference between metaphor and truth, they are not the same, once I thought they were but no, no, no, no, no, he says uncontrollably, the word ratcheting and he sinks into the steaming sheets, his eyes fluttering, closed and the coughing, the moaning, the turgid phlegm passes again through his desiccated and shattered cavities.

No, he says, and no, I think, his answer is no, and momentarily there is a kind of settling; I can feel my own realignment and sense of history colliding with imminence, merging with the steaming and impenetrable future, but of course this fusion cannot last and I am in Martin Donner's bedroom 15 years earlier, the bedroom on the second floor of the suburban colonial in one of the nicest areas of a nicer suburb in these sets of anterooms to the city, and I have put the question again. I have put it to him calmly and without sinister intent and then have used my powers—the powers granted me by the old and terrible antagonist who nonetheless and this is undeniable always plays fair, as fairly as Martin did not with his wife and daughters and friends and family through all of the years up to this point. I show him the bottles, the tubing, the arc and density of the room, the harsh and desperate light and it is uncommonly vivid; I have placed all my powers in the service of this adumbration. Oh yes, Martin says, seeing it all, oh yes, I see it now. Yes, he says, it is worth it. I would do this. I would not have been deterred. It is worth it. It is worth anything to expressly enact what you are, what you must be, the full and alarming necessities of the soul. So I do not care, he says. I am going, I am going to leave, if this is my destiny so be it. His features congeal with conviction, unlike his face in the room of his death they recede and pulsate, project and flutter with light, there is light all through him. Worth it, he says, worth it to be what one is.

How many years until this happens? he says. Not that it matters. But I want to know.

Seventeen, I say. Seventeen years and not all of them will be happy. Your daughters will weep and one of them will hate you, there will be many betrayals, also other illnesses, earlier illnesses, small and large betrayals, a terrible bout with hepatitis. Disgraceful venereal conditions.

I don't care, he says, 17 years is good time. In 17 years, lying here, sneaking, pounding myself into myself, I will be dead, I will have killed myself anyway. No, he says, there is no question, there is no argument, I have made my choice. He closes his eyes, smiles, thinking evidently that he is dreaming. Such dialogues are common inside Martin in this crucial time; he thinks that he is constructing a worst case venue, but is nonetheless being firm. Yes, he says, I will do this. His breathing, irregular, levels. As I withdraw, he thinks that he is making passage into dreamless slumber. As he recedes he feels, I know, some kind of imminence and perhaps it is my question, no less than anything else, which has led him to this resolution. Or perhaps not. It is difficult to work within such difficult and speculative borders without being overwhelmed by my own relative helplessness and stupor.

But of course this is in only partial quest of verification. I move through the channels of recorded (and possible) time, asking Martin Donner this question at various places within the continuum. I discuss this with him at Cherry Grove in 1978 at a tea dance while he is hanging shyly against the walls: yes, he says, of course it is worth it; I ask him this in 1986 when, thunderously the implications of the positive diagnosis begin to come through to him and he closes his eyes as I force the pictures in his head, showing him what it would be like. I don't know, he says, I don't know, I am in shock, I am in agony here, I can't give you a false or a real answer, can take no position: how can I tell? Maybe I shouldn't have done it, I don't know, I don't know.

Take then the question to him in Chicago two years later; he is attending a class reunion with his lover, partial remission, he feels in control of himself, some benignity, perhaps illusory, but the moment can be extended, he feels, as so many other moments have been extended. I would have done it again, he says, knowing what I know; I would have wanted it this way still, I would not have treated it differently. I would not exchange these years for anything.

Ask him and ask him, up and down the line, sometimes an enthusiastic, desperate yes, other times more tentative, a no at the end and tracking back from that no mostly for the six to eight months before this special, spectacularly extended agony, his position is not fixed any more than it might have been when 20, 30 years ago Martin refused to respond to the messages flicking like trap shots from the basement of his sensibility. Nothing is sure, nothing is firm. Mostly yes, an occasional no, more no as the end is approached, but even then at some of the moments in between, the moments of worst anguish, a soft, insistent yes. It is not fixed, nothing is fixed, the human condition is not fixed. The price we will pay for fully expressing what we are does seem indeterminate then. It resonates, this confusion, against my own uncertainty and I understand then, staring at and through all of this, that there can be no answers from Martin, none at all. If Martin is the voice and tensor of all possibility, then there is no possibility, no singularity.

Understanding this does not surprise me but fills me with a desperate and irreparable weakness. I would not have had it this way. I would have wanted surer answers. Everyone wants answers if not the answer, ever.

I return to my old antagonist on the desert at last, confused, and hand him the helmet and the simulating device and the other armaments of our translation, our bargain, our possibility. I have wrestled and wrestled, I say, I have wrestled you through all the avenues of this life and I do not know, I am stunned and pinned, dislocated and shattered. Martin is not the answer, he can provide me with no basis at all.

Of course, my old antagonist says. His ruddy skin glows with sympathy or perhaps it is only health. Or vindication. You see, he says, you are left with it, just as I said, you are left with all of this on your own. You must decide what price to pay and whether that is correct and no one can know. He backs away from me, horns a rapier, fine eyes glints of purpose in the night. Now, he says, now you must decide. You, not Martin Donner who is only a paradox or a metaphor, you must make that decision. It is the 40th day, he says. Soon it will be the 40th night. You must now turn in the way you will and there is no returning.

Yes, I say, yes, I understand that. Before me, closing my eyes like Martin in the hallucinatory daze, I see the traps, the sights, the vision of my own circumstance, the donkey, the cobblestones, the crowds, Pilate's smooth and terrible judgement, the hanging and the darkness. I see and I see and I see and in the iron spikes of the sun of Golgotha, alone and under the darkness, I see too the expanding and necessitous heart of God.

Ship Full of Jews

Cristoforo could hear the moaning from steerage, the Chassids were chanting again, moaning and raving in their strange and steeped tongue, the sounds of the Hebrew emerging cloudily from the deck of the *Pinta*, filling him with some mixture of dread and regard, religiosity and hope, the swells and pitching of the barren seas reminding him of the essential perilousness of his journey. Images of spices, fragrant bouquets from the sullen and mysterious East rose in his nostrils, taunting thoughts of the new and deadly continent opening up before him possessed him with a kind of graciousness. The sounds of the Chassids were overwhelming. Sometimes they would pray for hours, unstopping, one choir beginning when another paused, filling the moist air with imprecations and song, at other times they were silent, pitching and rolling in the deck, the queasiness of their condition doubtless the origin of this strange and necessary silence. Cristoforo did not understand any of it.

Of course the Chassids were not to understand, they were to transport. Isabella had pointed this out to him. "They are none of your concern," she had said, "they are being deported, will keep to themselves under guard, will pray and rave in their strange way, but have nothing to do with your journey." The excitable queen had gazed at him, her eyes full and penetrating in the darkness. There was something very special between her and Cristoforo; that had been his intimation from the start, but of course under Ferdinand's cruel gaze and with the happenstance of the Inquisition, it was impossible to bring this strange and stunned accord to any kind of realization. Cristoforo was a temporal man, his mind was seized by the fragrance of spices, but his imagination remained clear and pristine, somewhere to the side of fantasy. He had an assignment to commit, the Chassids were only the most marginal part. Standing on the deck, swaying, finding purchase on the thin and decaying boards of this wretched ship that was, his great friend, the queen, had insisted, the very best available to him, Cristoforo pondered his fate, considered his condition, swung his keen and penetrating gaze toward *el Norte*, the hidden land beyond the dip of the great horizon. *Santa María*, Cristoforo murmured, and did not know if he was invoking that mother of passage or merely repeating the name of that third and most eccentric ship, filled with roustabouts and assassins, also deported from Spain, a gang so cruel that he had taken Ferdinand's instruction not to deal with that ship at all, even in his capacity as overseer of the voyage. "You will really be much better, my son," Ferdinand had said, "staying with your crew and examining the route with compass and disjunction, allowing the guards to control that hostile ship." Cristoforo had shrugged. Who was he to argue with Ferdinand? A king's reputation stood between him and all desire. Cristoforo lusted hopelessly for the queen, but all proportion was necessary within the arc of condition. Sometimes his thoughts were metaphysical, sometimes they were practical, and at all times the three ships rolled and sculled their way toward the New World. Abolish all desire, Cristoforo thought, and the spices of desire may someday soon be yours.

"Excuse me, master," his yeoman said, approaching with downcast gaze and suitable humility. Everyone knew of Cristoforo's special relationship with Isabella, also his terrible temper and the secret instructions from the queen, which reportedly granted him the right to scuttle any who displeased him. Behind lay the specter of the Inquisition, only for the Jews so far, but who could tell; ahead lay the equally imponderable New World; but somewhere in the middle Cristoforo presided, and his word was terrible, his authority absolute. "The rabbi has requested permission to speak to you. He asked me to carry this message."

Rabbi? What Rabbi? Cristoforo could feel his consciousness swim as he slowly reoriented himself to the possession of a steerage filled not only with chanting but with hierarchy. There was a leader or several leaders of the Chassids, yes, and they obtained not only the spiritual but the temporal title *rebbe*, corrupted by the idiomatic language of his day to this less forbidding form. Jesus had been *rebbe*, too, Cristoforo noted, not a religious man, no longer possessed by any vision other than the spicy and nefarious East toward which they so perilously cruised, he recalled from his childhood pictures of the bearded Master, who had of course emerged from the Pharisees of his day and had been put to torture and death for daring to rival them in popularity. Or was that the story? He was not sure; the Inquisition of course was a final settling of accounts for this ancient injustice, but Cristoforo, concerned with matters of the sea as well as certain entanglements on shore, which even before Isabella had made his life colorful and difficult, had not paid much attention to this. "Master," the yeoman said, "I have brought the Rabbi to the deck. He is insistent over there; he is asking for appearances."

Cristoforo shrugged. A shrug seemed to possess him head to toe, front to back, through all the specious and yet solid aspects of his frame; he had been shrugging, he sometimes thought, all his life. Shrug for the mean-spirited Barcelona of his day, which seemed obsessed with questions of reparation that could not concern a simple master of the seas. A shrug for Isabella, who, after all, was beyond him for all of her flirtatiousness and desirability and would have made much trouble in the possession, a trouble that he suspected, she would have found no less titillating than the specter of his murder. Shrug for the *Santa María* and its decks full of felons who would be the first to grapple with the savages of the New Land if the savages were to show any hostile intention. Shrug for the jewels and fragrances that Ferdinand had promised him if he were successful on this difficult mission. Shrug for this and shrug for that, meet the temper of the world with a certain calculated indifference and ignore the screams and concerns of the Inquisition which, after all, had absolutely nothing to do with him and which would go on its tortuous way whether or not he was present. "So, bring him here," Cristoforo said. "Let me discuss with you later the proper way to deal below deck, do you hear me?"

"Whatever you say, master," the yeoman said, and gestured. The rabbi, a huge bearded man wrapped in vestments of his calling—but they *all* seemed to wear strange and elaborate garb—shuffled toward him downcast, his eyes seeking the deck, then his head tilting upward, the strange, luminous, Israelic eyes locking with Cristoforo's in a way that induced strange sensations, perhaps due to the odors of steerage wafting from the rabbi and the vague screams across the water, which might have been emanating from the *Niña*, just barely visible, or the more distant *Santa María*, which, *Jesus Christo*, he could not and would not want to see in these conditions. "Well, well," he said to the Jew as the yeoman backed away, submission in all of his posture—if nothing else he had established deference in this crew, he had the weight of royalty behind him, and there were rumored special and terrible arrangements that the king could visit even at a distance upon mutineers, spies among the crew. "Tell me what brings you above deck? Yes, what do you want?"

The Jew, still staring at him in that curious and affecting way, said, "My name is Solomon. *Schelemo*, I come to ask you a favor."

"I am not interested in your name," Cristoforo said. "Your names, frankly, mean nothing to me."

"Yes, but—"

"If I wanted to establish special relations with Jews," Cristoforo said, "it would not be through the medium of names. I would request your presence in other ways. You are here, below the decks, on sufferance, through the mercy of Isabella and Ferdinand, our king and queen. I have nothing whatsoever to do with any of this, I am simply under orders."

"That is understood," the Jew said. "The conditions below are impossible. There are five hundred and fifty-two of us, and we are fainting. We are placed one upon another in tight racks and without fresh air, without even the possibility of air. There is much fainting and illness."

"This is not my account," Cristoforo said. "Conditions are difficult for all of us. This is a voyage of privation."

"I beg of you," Solomon said. "Permit us to come above decks. Not all together, but ten or twenty at a time, just to relieve ourselves of this torment, to take the air, to move—"

"Conditions are worse on the *Santa María*," Cristoforo said. "It is a slave ship, filled with the darkest felons of our time. But they do not complain. They drift upon the waters to the New World uncomplainingly, and they hold against the day."

"I know nothing of that," Solomon said. "I know only the conditions below deck. We are perishing. Soon the disease will begin, then the slow and terrible wasting of flesh. Even our most fervent prayers will go unanswered."

Cristoforo shrugged. Another shrug. Shrug at this, turn away from that, consider the Marins, who, it was rumored, had renounced their Judaism to live in secret and had thus evaded the eye of the Inquisition while seeking penalties in other ways. Shrug at the sea, shrug at the New World itself. If it had been left to him, he would have been a merchant at the port of Barcelona and would have left conditions such as these to the more intrepid. How did this happen to him? How had he become the master of such a rude voyage? It was all that Cristoforo could do not to reach out and shake the rabbi, explain that there were many in agony here and that agony was not now only a matter of steerage. But he said nothing of course. The loneliness and fervency of command.

"I am sorry," he said, "I cannot help you. You will have to do what you can down there. It is so decreed. The conditions were made quite explicit to me, surely the same was done for you."

"But how long," Solomon said. "How long will this voyage be?"

Another shrug. Shrug at distance, at lust, at all the complications of empire and design. "I can't answer that," Cristoforo said. "It could be weeks, it could be a matter of days. We have been at sea for almost a month and we are in uncharted waters. When the New World looms over the horizon and not before, then the journey will end. The rest is in hands we cannot understand. Surely you know of imponderables, of fate."

"I know of nothing," Solomon said. "You misjudge us, all of us, clearly.

We are not cattle. We are as you, and we are suffering. Men, women, and little children, some with pets smuggled aboard, all in pain, all of them with special and necessary grace. Do you understand any of this?"

"You are to return below deck at once," Cristoforo said, the dark lash of anger trailing through his bowels. "Now, before this continues. You are insolent and you are exceeding my patience. You were taken aboard by measure of the queen's generosity and because she took a sudden and unaccustomed pity upon you. I know of nothing else."

"They cry," Solomon said. "They pray, and in their prayers is their spirit and their torment." He gestured. "Can't you hear?" Indeed, the keening of the Jews to which Cristoforo had accommodated himself as he had to the stunning curvature of the water struck him suddenly, rose up within him now with the urgency if not the fragrance of those spices he sought. Words seemed to emerge dimly from the groans of insistence, then subsided. "*Adonai*," the Jews cried. "*Elohim, Brich hu omen*." "O countrymen," Solomon said, "my countrymen, my brother—"

"Enough," Cristoforo said. "I am the captain." He turned his back to signal that the interview was over, that the petition had been reviewed and denied, that, no less than Torquemada, he had been forced to obduracy as a means of containing these people. Behind him he could hear grunts, then whimpers as if Solomon were planning some desperate final assault. Cristoforo shook his head, folded his arm, stared grimly at the sea, which heaved from its greenish depths the small mysteries of flotsam, small pieces of debris that assumed vaguely organic shape, then were swallowed by the water. "*V'yisgadal. Shmeh rabo*." The small and diminished sound of Solomon pattering away from him and then the chants rising from the spaces of Neptune, mingling with the sounds of the sea itself, swaddling Cristoforo in the dangerous and terrible sounds that signaled the slow turning of the earth, the emergence of the New World to the starboard. In the distance Cristoforo imagined that he could see mountains, could glimpse the tread of elephants, could see the bangles of princes as they contended with one another for the splendors of their new estate, but he knew the signs of delirium when from a great distance he let it signal him. He was a man of the sea. Cristoforo shrugged again, shrug for the Jews, for Torquemada's insistence, for Torquemada's descent. Shrug for the New World, shrug for the troubles and purchase of five hundred Jews below deck whom he would never see, could never grasp. More was to be done and later. He felt his body lighten as a sense of decision came upon him. This would only last to a certain point, then there would be another circumstance. He was sure of it. Shrug and step, step and shrug, a sudden disturbing intimation of Isabella's swollen and needful breast prodding at him as he signaled the yeoman to take over the helm, however momentarily.

On the *Santa María* Torquemada, enthused, gathered the desperadoes around him. Garbed as they, indistinguishable from them, far departed from the priestly robes of his magnificence, he had become their equal and therefore their superior. The plan was working. The cunning and ingenious plan—worked out in the most sacred places of the Church and then with the king and queen—was working. "O listen to me," Torquemada said. "O listen, friends and companions." They gathered around him, the most desperate men of Spain, men so desperate that on this voyage of desperadoes they had been segregated. Only Torquemada could control them, could understand and apprehend their spirit, and it was for this reason—*to test himself*—that he had embarked upon this exile. Behind him the Jews, who soon enough would be encountered. "The New World beckons," Torquemada said. "A place of justice, light, and peace. Attend to it! Can you not see it?" Unshaven and desperate heads turned, gleaning the new land through the spume of the sea. "Here we will begin afresh," Torquemada said. "That was the plan, the plan for all of us." They murmured in response. "Here," Torquemada said, "we will take the Jews and plant them, rid the world of Israel, depart then for new and better shores. But you must keep your courage up. Must not fail."

"Kill them," one of the men said. "We should go back to the master's ship and kill them now."

Torquemada smiled, thinking of how far he had taken them, how far all of them had come in this one sharp, difficult month of voyage. "Not just yet," he said. "It must be at the right time for the right purpose. Now it would be just slaughter. There was enough slaughter in Spain, here it will be of a different kind. We will seed the ground," Torquemada said. "We will expend their blood in the purposes of consecration, and it will be better."

"You talk like a priest," one of them said. "Are you a priest, then? Or are you one of us."

"I am one of this and one of the other," Torquemada said. "I make faith with you in these spaces as you make faith with me. Soon the mountains, the tablelands of the New World will be upon us and we will turn them holy under the gush of sacrificial blood. But for now," he said, "for now we must once again pray, we must place our knives and ordnance in protected places and pray for a good conclusion to this voyage. Do you hear me? *Ave María*," Torquemada said, and continued with the familiar litany. They settled in with him, attentive as scholars to the rhythm of his words. *I had no choice*, Torquemada thought, looking at the high plumes of the water, the sails glinting against the turbulence. *It was difficult, but the only means to carry forth the Inquisition. One must constantly move outward in order to move inward. We had accomplished our sacred purposes in Madrid. Barcelona had become ours as well. Soon it would have turned within, and by losing everything we would have gone beyond risk. But here, here, by transporting the Jews, by moving forth even as we move back, we have encountered and made ripe the oldest possibilities of all.*

Or am I not sanctified? he thought, a man of doubt as well as of faith, just as the honored Savior himself had been. *It is this or that? Is it one thing or the other? Is that shipful of Jews headed for the Jerusalem of the spirit that we will erect or, aligned in the sign of the cross, will they perish at the bottom of the seas? In Cristoforo's hands,* he thought, *but fortunately I can attend to the matters of transcendence, leave the temporal in the hands of Cristoforo.* "Thy will be done," Torquemada said. They looked at him intently. He raised his hands in the gesture of submission, feeling the terrible power of the water underneath.

In the racks Solomon said, "I did the best I could. I pleaded with him. I asked for air and light."

"But he said no," the three Davids said. "He said no," the Israelites said. "He would not have us," Judith and Rachel said, wiping the foreheads of the children who clustered. "He refused."

"That is right," Solomon said. "He refused. He said that we were steerage, garbage, at the behest of the queen but of no concern to him. I told him that we would die, and he turned away. There is nothing to be done."

"Cristoforo is not a man of mercy," Judith said. "He cares nothing for any of us."

"That is not so," Solomon said. "He is doing what he must, just as we are. He is in the control of larger forces. At least we are on the seas. We have been spared the Inquisition. Maybe it will be different for those of us who live. If they live. If we live. This damnable voyage ..."

"Spared the Inquisition," Ruth said, taking Solomon's hand, "but not the Inquisitor. The Inquisitor is always with us. He comes in the night, he follows on the seas, he screams from the bowels of Neptune. I understand that now."

"Nothing to be done," Solomon said. "We are creatures of their mercy."

"I tell you," Rachel said, "that there is a judgment coming that is beyond all of us. They seek a New World, but it is eternally the old."

The steerage, silent when Solomon had returned, cast down to silence by hope or at least curiosity, resumed, broken fragments of prayers ascending only to the thin bulkheads that made them crouch against the racks, then dispersed. "It will not be long," Solomon said, "we cannot survive this. We are a shipful of Jews, not of mystics or explorers, and in our flight is our guilt and our culpability. Nevertheless—"

"Nevertheless," Judith said, as if she had taken his thought, pressing his hand, "nevertheless we have at least carried ourselves, carried a bit of testimony, moved to some different place through the designs of our own spirit. We are not Marins. We are not apostosaic. Our apostasy is of a different kind."

"All displacement is apostasy," Solomon said, the chanting murmuring about him, the disputation with Judith—*this woman*, to engage not only in prayers but Talmudic disputation with women was their peculiar but necessary fate in these conditions—continuing, all of their strange and strangely confluent anguish melding as the *Pinta* inexorably carried them toward a fate they could not determine, in all faith, in the faith of God, the one God of Israel whose Name was One and whose Oneness was indivisible in the heart of their exile.

Torquemada, seized by a sudden spirit of ecstasy and affirmation, struck as if by a bolt from the brow of the Holy Ghost, began to dance and heave upon the deck of the *Santa María*, incognizant of the stares of the felons, indifferent to the risks that this display of ecstasy might bring upon him, the steps of his dance carrying him from one side of the ship to the next while on the bosom of the ocean the craft lurched and spilled not only its provisions but its prayers in the sullen light of this journey.

And so, and so they came upon the New World then, the slave ship and the master's ship and the ship between, the shipful of Jews and the ship of the Inquisitor, caught their first glimpse of the New World through the mist and fog of their combined prayers, and in that moment, as Torquemada leapt, as the Jews chanted, as a grim and compliant Cristoforo set sextant and compass and shrugged toward this newest part of his destiny, in that moment it was as if all the centuries had slipped by and this strange and mismatched concatenation of spirits and flesh, voyagers and prisoners, repelled and necessitous, were gathered by that bolt that had struck Torquemada and that swept them from the bosom of the ocean to the bowels of the ship, then expelled them to all of the crevices of the twentieth century itself, myths of purgation and collision hastening their way toward the apostasies to come. The shipful of Jews, their captain, their keeper, and their inquisitor joined at last in that voyage of transcendence. Cristoforo dreamed it, dreamed it all, dreamed that he was in the enormous grasp of Isabella herself, her capacious sex absorbing and expelling him as would all of the centuries and scholars to come and the spray of his seed upon the ocean of the queen the plume to drag him past myth and toward that first terrible awareness of his destiny. Cristoforo the Jew. Cristoforo the keeper of souls *V'ysh ka'dash. Shmeh rabbo.*

Brich hu.

Omen.

Amos

Because: Because they spoke of epiphany, but huddled in the crevices of their ignorance, fingers in mouths, palpitating with terror. *Because:* Winogrand thought, because in that insular bowl of millennial history, they spoke of prophecy, of the need for grand and vaulting truths (Wino*grand*, he had named himself, extending by one febrile letter his more modest born moniker, Winograd), but what they were really after was the same old stuff. Daunting angels and the thin strumming of harps, beneficent smiles from the celestial imps, and for thrills, those apples from the Song of Solomon. Winogrand knew the truth: he knew the purchased angles, knew all the hard and soft luck of this dummied-up century; still, he had to maintain a placid exterior, keep the fizz pleasantly inexpressive, one wink to the host before the commercial break. Back with some more prophecies for the new millennium from Don Winogrand, master futurologist. Now a message from the miracle makers who bring it all home to you.

Message from the miracle makers. Don Winogrand, once Wino*grad*, now sent on the road by the Institute to spread comforting intimations of ease and housekeeping convenience, popular science as kitchen aid, government-funded research as light brigade of the mother's helpers; Don Winogrand, that old fraud now forty-seven, smoothed into middle-aged wimpery by the public relations flacks of the Institute, out to do the talk-show circuit to bring a better tomorrow to the assembled; Winogrand, that old thief of the night who in his time had pounded and jazzed with the best of the haymakers and the dissolute; Don Winogrand, now turned roadman for a better tomorrow, had expended his youth and minor gift for paraphrase to this expected end—what he had *not* expected, however, was that in this apparent middle age (what could you call forty-seven?—there was George Blanda, of course, Gaylord Perry, and, for a few bleak moments, Bobby Hull; in the arts, there were guys like Bruckner or Frost who had seemed to find the right notes only when they were past forty, but this was America, dish-towel America, where limpness, limpness was *all*, and Winogrand could no longer sustain the delusion that he was heading up on the arc of his promise, tracking that final, conclusive epiphany with every inch of his aching heart, not with the grim night sweats and the small flickers of depression whisking like silverfish across the screen of his consciousness), he would become—there was no other way to put this, no more fortunate way to phrase the situation—something of a religious fanatic. Acts 22! he wanted to shout before the commercial breaks, while the host was trying to lay a broad beam to a real futurologist. Galatians, verses 6 and 8 from the 2nd chapter! They drew out his bones like sealing wax, cast lots over his vestments! This is not simple stuff, you know. We have passed into a new millennium; Daniel in the Lion's Den was nothing as to Joe America in the year 2002. *Mene, mene* to you, too. But Winogrand had been able, to date, to restrain himself. Such prophecies, such theological outpourings, would have been risky stuff even on high heels in Washington Square Park—try it on the radio, and watch the boards light one, two, three. Winogrand counseled calm to himself, hyped calm the way that Solomon had hawked apples to Bathsheba, soothed himself in the off-camera urgings of the night like a real trouper. Courage, Don; the millennia wait for no man. Courageous Don, the Millennial Man. But this was a guise that he did not think, strictly speaking, would last.

Don Winogrand, spokesman for the Institute of the American Academic Sciences, concealed his burgeoning fanatical instincts under his placid fizz, businesslike demeanor, spoke to himself calmly in the crucial minutes before the breaks when the urge to quote Scripture was at its most intense. Breasts were helpful. Thinking of breasts could level him off, keep him in gear, remind him of hazy days and lost avenues of promise up and down which Winograd (no "n" in those happy days of tumescent insight sudden stabs of really passionate insight) would wander staring at the half-exposed, the semi-exposed, the vaguely intimated, the tautly shaped breasts of women of all ages, thinking about his destiny and investing huge stream-of-consciousness time in what he well knew, if applied differently, might have made him some real money. The concentration of his youth had, at least, given him the trick of breasts; he could evoke them in his head, run them across the panoply of inner sight, inspect them gratuitously from all angles—never touching, of course, never responding with external gesture or evidence. Bathsheba must have used similar devices (in reverse, of course) to calm down David, hold him up, manage him for inspection; the architecture of the space shuttles and satellite dishes of which Winogrand spoke so knowledgeably was breast-like, mammillary in many of its angles as well. The thing to do was to keep panning that camera of attention, focus on the breasts, and try to push the dangerous, fanatical theology far to one side. It would do poorly for the Institute of the American Academic Sciences to have its spokesperson, its radio & media contact man, begin to scream of Galatians or the Great Snake of Saint John the Divine in the middle of an until-then sensible interview about the practicality of the L-5 capsule—or so at least the frantic but leveled-down Winogrand would remind himself in his few private moments. Of course, getting close to the breasts was an entirely different story. Many a slip betwixt, and all of that. His private life was a snare and a trap, something not to think of if he wanted to keep his mind on business, and that was for one sure thing. Prophets weren't supposed to have private lives, anyway. When had Jonah checked in with the wife and kiddies on his shipboard way? Had he thought of preserving the gourd for some sweetie down the pike in Tarshish way? Who was there to smooth down Zephaniah's turgid brow after all that ranting and raving? You stayed in your robes, you never showed them the unprophet, the private side of oneself, and you kept the pressure on, just as the Big Guy with the agenda tended to keep the pressure on you. That was a certainty.

Winogrand kept busy. He kept the faith (not in the theological sense—that was one slip he would not make—but certainly in the academic). He revealed none of his distress, his dualism, his slow, encroaching fanaticism, to his contact points in the American Sciences brigade, trouping instead from one city to the next, coach class, minor upgrading permitted in the absence of a full load, checking in at moderate-priced hotels and launching blissful little projectiles of science and industry on those radio and television talk circuiteers that the Institute's efficient public relations arm had scheduled. The television, much of it cable (but with national access), was filled with makeup, clowns, and jugglers, the thump and sweat of audiences concealed behind the cameras, who applauded news of a more convenient tomorrow, but had specific questions on cost—Winogrand did not like it, but it was controlled, and the backlighting held him in place in a way that the radio did not. The radio: small, odorous studios, headphones, the strange, screened calls clattering in at odd angles ("Mike here from *Eau Claire*. How can you say that there's a better tomorrow, when we can't even make a person-to-person phone call? And is there anything to that stuff about the UFO files being unclassified?") gave Winogrand (oh, that "n" had changed everything for him: he had been a cautious, conservative guy, pledge chairman with the Alpha Eps, and then on a career path with General Socony, with a higher-horizons benefit program and an only mildly adulterous marriage, until they had pulled him from the back room, given him an "n," made him a spokesperson, and sent him on the road on behalf of the Institute) a sense toward the end of the programs that he was coming in close toward some final apprehension of the human condition: the millennial beast—just a little bit late, but that was scheduling for you, and if a crosstown bus could get tied up for half an hour, then certainly a millennial promise could get blocked for a couple of years—was snaffling and snaffling, sometimes at the virtual back of his head. Daniel, Galatians, Zephaniah, the stoning of Saint Paul! Winogrand wanted to shout over the empty, zooming wires of the net, and even the seven-second delay could not have stopped him, but he was able to control himself on the radio for the same reasons that he managed control less perilously on television: what would happen to him if he promised direct evidence of the Second Coming? How long would he last? What would the Institute do with a man of science who shouted that Jesus was definitely, this minute, on the way? For one thing, they would take away his expense account almost immediately, and for another, they would almost certainly remove him from his position of corporate loan—he would have to go back to Socony (whose company psychiatrists would almost certainly disqualify him), and then he would have to make a new kind of life for himself. What kind of new life was possible at forty-seven? At forty-seven Winogrand had had three, maybe four lives—he had had his allotted American share and more; there was simply no possibility of reconstruction, not at this point. Graduate school at his age? Perhaps a law degree? Civil Service, social work with the long-term unemployed and unembarrassable? Even if Jesus *were* to come at some point during these struggles, Winogrand could be sure that it would not be in time to do him any good. The problem was that Winogrand's timing had always been excruciating: nothing had worked out in precisely the right fashion, and now the millennial revolution itself, like the crosstown bus, had failed to show up on time.

Winogrand suffered. There was really nothing to do but suffer; in the night he saw corporate snakes of damnation; in the day he could see personnel psychological profiles that had to do with numbering the beast; in the wondrous kitchens and convenience satellites (a fragment of the refractory Moon in your own refrigerator!) of which he spoke, Winogrand could see the awful sights that had so distressed Lot's wife—but meanwhile, it was absolutely necessary to go on, to maintain the appearance and the demeanor of the proper spokesman for the Age of Science. In that Age of Science: the gleam and glitter of the satellite dishes, the technophile's thin and grateful gaze in the presence of pure machinery; in the clamor and clutter of technology's finest promise, Winogrand sometimes felt hammered to small potatoes; at other times—particularly when the hosts had paid attention to his ariettas on the duality of science and achievement—he felt like Big Onions, Big Casino itself filling miasmically all of the spaces of the ether. I am a spokesman for science who knows that Jesus will come again! Winogrand wanted to whisper to the occasional lady acquaintances he was able to connect with (mostly on the basis of his visual celebrity; don't

I know that fizz?) at the motel bars in their delicate, shell-pink ears. Jesus will taketh all of this away with his right hand and grant us the Rapture with his left! But Winogrand said none of this whatsoever; even on those rare occasions when the ladies might have been listening (or not listening), there were risks one simply did not want to take if one wanted to stay on the payroll. Which was climbing all the time, what with the judgments Ethel's lawyers kept on getting, and the endless arc in the college tuition payments.

Winogrand, released momentarily from the arc and abscissa of his dilemma (he liked to think in those terms: he had a "dilemma"; he was a "spokesperson"; he was "trying to balance between passion and equity"), found himself in a nearly abandoned synagogue on the South Side of Philadelphia, tallith and yarmulke yanked to a fare-thee-well Hasidim in seedy garb staring at him with wonder and vengeance in their eyes as, all out of control now, Winogrand raved and ranted about Jesus. Well, it had seemed like a good idea at the time. Born Jewish, trained in the customs of a religion he had (before his conversion under the influence of science) always found amusing as a young man, Winogrand had been dragged in for *minyan* duty while wandering downtown after a late-night talk show at which he had pledged the secrets of the stars, perhaps immortality itself, to the next generation of call-in listeners. Hysterical with the desire to please the Jews and banish once and for all the image of his long-departed father—who had thought the Holy Days were a bunch of crap just as he plunked down for two seats at Yizkor because you never knew—overtaken by visions of snakes and Redeemers even more intense than that he had suffered on phone duty, Winogrand had begun to speak in tongues at the invocation of the altar, and now the Hasidim were really mad; they were determined; they came upon him with all of the intensity and fervidity with which the king's intelligence officers must have conveyed the handwriting on the wall to the choleric Nabucco. "It's all right; it's all right!" Winogrand shouted; "I was just trying you out, seeing how it would go, a kind of juxtaposition, you know; 'Jesus will come again' was a metaphor!" But this did not seem to discourage the nine Hasidim; rather, it inflamed them. They began to strike at him with prayer books. Winogrand, caught between a dollar and a hard place—as his angry old man had had cause to say before settling in grumbling for his one prayer session of the year—shouted with embarrassment and rigor, trying to distract the Jews, perhaps trying to focus their attention elsewhere, but they were undistractible, as purely focused as any spokesman for the sciences in the new millennium, and Winogrand felt:

his yarmulke being ripped askew, his tallith being seized at off-angles, his phylacterics being unthreaded from his ears (borrowed goods all), and then he was like the lots-casters' object, himself being speeded in high places toward an egress. For a moment, Winogrand thought he caught it, thought he could really see and feel what was going on, a true hypnagogic gratitude flooding his entrails, but then he was soaring over, and then into, the stony, ungrieving pavement of South Philadelphia, and the insight passed. "And don't come back, you *marin!*" someone shouted in Yiddish, a curse that Winogrand was able to dope out thanks to his old man's counsel and the experience of several years of Yiddish in the back room of Socony on his lunch hour during a period of his life when employees were encouraged to seek their past with the help of instruction. A crown of thorns seemed to have replaced the yarmulke on his head, but the distraught Winograd—now Winogrand with an "n," a spokesperson for purposes both grand and mysterious—was unable to focus upon the irony or the necessity, being otherwise occupied. You tried to stay with the essentials, and you see where it got you. Martyrdom wasn't the ticket, though, and Winogrand had never, not even when talking of the flaming deaths of astronauts on launching pads, ever called it a proper substitute for science or religion.

In his last days on the communications circuit, before it became quite evident that he had outlived not only corporate but personal usefulness (they took out the "n," removed his flight privileges, and put him under his real name in a euphemistically titled Happy Home for the To-Be-Rest-Cured and Needful), Winogrand found that he had reached a kind of placidity; he was no longer eager or expostulatory in his moods or responses. If the moderators asked, they got routine answers; if they didn't ask, Winogrand was quite happy to giggle and think silently of the Rapture, the chair that would in just a little while take him straight upward and out to Heaven. Up and out, his yarmulke reattached to his head, the cross angles of his history and his splendid belief lending him comfort, all of the hicker and dicker and thunder and blunder of modern science falling away as Winogrand himself, ever faster, ever higher, in the hands of Jesus himself, would speed to his final destiny. "For the astronauts would have wanted us to do just that," Winogrand would say if he were asked, if the hosts prodded a little, if the callers got nasty, but he was just as happy not to say it; "they knew what it was like to be a little late, just as Peter wandering in the garden, waiting for that rooster to crow; might have missed a point or two? You go and work for the sciences, beat out the one and the two of scientific discourse, you got to expect you'll get rapped in the shins a little." It was decided that

Winogrand was incomprehensible; higher decisions were made at higher levels. In the chair speeding toward Heaven, Winogrand felt disdainful of all of it—the Happy Home, too—the clouds and the blood and the hood and the cross of his blessed destiny were quite enough for him. They never gave him the "n" back; the man was no longer grand, nor was his job. He worked eventually in soup kitchens. There were lots of anticipations of Acts and Galatians and Saint John in the soup kitchens Winograd dished out of, but there was not—discernible to him, anyway—any action.

There is a further part, having to do with his return to the South Philadelphia minyan and the extraordinary, pathetic, embarrassing millennial result, but it has no place in this chronicle.

Improvident Excess

Harmless tracked the candidate from motel to grange hall, from civic auditorium to the review stand in front of City Hall, from Des Moines to St. Pete to North Platte, finally catching up to him in the parking lot of Toys "R" Us in Newton, leveled the rifle for the killing shot, blew off the candidate's head at thirty feet downrange in a crowd, a spectacular shot for an amateur but the same old stuff for Gerald Harmless, skilled assassin and political consultant for hire. He disassembled the Mauser quickly, slipped it under the floorboards of the Blazer wagon they had shipped him, scooted the hell out of there before the ordnance around the candidate had even reacted to the impact. Harmless had great reflexes. Reflexes, of course, were all that you had to count on in this business; everything else was ideology and excuses—crap, that was to say. At the big traffic circle which spun him off to the south Harmless found a covey of police cars spinning out the other way, timed his release carefully, then opened the Blazer to full throttle and barreled off behind a huge truck. A quarter mile down the road he pulled into a diner, locked and abandoned the car, not worrying about the floorboards, and went inside to phone for a cab. Thirty-five minutes later he was at the airport, and the rest of the stuff was easy. The candidate's head, exploded, had been huge, had blown into the air like someone's air ball on a gymnasium floor, had hit the platform with a rotten bump before Harmless had pulled his glance away and had worked on getting out of there. Watching the consequences of his work was along with the money the only compensation he got from his work, reading about this stuff in the newspaper only depressed him, but there was no way that he could hang around and follow through on any of this stuff. You could watch or you could fire, he liked to tell his contracts, and they had nodded understandingly enough at that. Thorough and careful were best every time. There was no substitute for forethought.

On the plane, Gerald Harmless, thirty-eight years old, college dropout (accounting major), man of affairs and projects, hummed an odd little victory tune to himself, a song of accomplishment, of toneless satisfaction while businessmen on the commuter special made a little time with the stewardesses and complained about expense allowances. It all went past Harmless; it represented a view of life which he had put out of his head many, many years ago. Now he was a political consultant, public affairs division, deeply involved in the displacement and management of potential governments. He had a stack of business cards which said that. Left to his own, Harmless would as soon have taken his losses, cashed it in now, spent the remainder of his life considering the rich and mottled past and the consternation which he had so often left behind, but this would have been unwise. Ceaseless motion was the only way to address the current situation, and there were also powerful expenses to meet. Isn't that so? he said to the blond stewardess when she told him to secure his tray, please, and put the notebook underneath the seat. You have to control your situation at all costs. I suppose that's exactly right, sir, the stewardess said. Somewhere back of her blond, vacant eyes shone—Harmless speculated—the pure and awful fear of the disaster which awaited them all underneath, but he would not probe for it. The time for casual relationships had come and gone in his life without ever being exploited; he was a political consultant, not a casual pursuer of stewardesses. Fucking was only a metaphor for purer, deadlier stuff anyway, Harmless speculated. The plane bounced slightly on the landing, and Harmless thought of the scandal which might have ensued if there had been a fatal crash but somehow his diary had been saved. He kept a careful record of his accomplishments; the accounting mentality and need for ledgers persisted. He had had more to do with political life in America, he supposed, than any consultant, newspaper publisher, or ideologue, he supposed. Not that he had gotten into this to effect great changes. He had gotten into this to make a living, no megalomaniac he, and that rather than fantasies of influence was what had kept him in the trade.

Debarking casually at La Guardia, just another squat, slightly defeated thirty-eight-year-old guy among hundreds of voyagers, Harmless enjoyed the somnolent breezes of the city, conveyed his valise to the rental counter, asked for a compact with air-conditioning and signed the necessary pages, drove cautiously into New York, parked freely on West Forty-eighth Street at this late and safe hour, and went directly to the room which he had booked two days earlier at the Hilton, opened it, found his contact sitting in the armchair, waiting for him. It no longer concerned Harmless that these people had no respect for his privacy, that, too, was part of the trade-off, and as they had warned him from the beginning, they got in anywhere. A little late, his contact, a bearded man named Brown said. He looked a little bit like Tchaikovsky, a Slavic-looking fellow with hot eyes and a huge gray beard, a haunted expression in those eyes which might have come from too much *Pathètique* but most likely from the strains of being a political mover and shaker, a whole directorate on his own. You had any trouble?

Harmless shrugged, put down the valise, closed the door quietly. No trouble, he said. Delay on takeoff, a little bit of a rough landing. Traffic might have been a little tricky over the Willets Point Bridge, but nothing spectacular.

It went all right, Brown said. You looked at the papers, listened to the radio?

I never read the papers or listen to the radio, Harmless said. I drive with the windows up and the radio off. I figure if there's any real news, it will get to me, and otherwise it breaks my concentration. There was no trouble, was there?

Well, no, Brown said. Not that kind of trouble. You took his head off. He was dead before he moved, he probably thought that he was having a sudden bad dream, and then he stopped noticing anything. I don't think that there's going to be too much of a vote for him in the primary; of course, you can never tell about protest votes. His handlers seem pretty broken up about it.

That's a shame, Harmless said. What I try to do, I try to keep the handlers happy. I wouldn't want to displease them in any way. Did they really make you drink poison? Harmless said. That's the story I hear, that they made you drink up the poison because you were supposed to be a fag.

What the hell are you talking about?

Tchaikovsky, Harmless said. Don't you know anything about serious music? You look just like Tchaikovsky, a top Russian composer. He died at fifty-three, supposed to be poisoned water in an epidemic, but the word now is that the czar didn't like a fag being his court composer so he got the nobles together and they advised him he'd better check out. That's a kind of humiliating way to go, you know? Socrates this guy wasn't. He should have defied them, made an issue of it. But I guess that they were rough on you if you weren't straight in old Russia. Of course, I don't know anything about it, either straight or bent. I am truly sublimated in my craft.

You talk crazy, Brown said. You always talk crazy. I don't know why they put up with this. He touched his beard. You say I look like this guy Tchaikovsky?

He's dead. You look like pictures of him. I can get you some, you want to look.

I don't think I need to look, Brown said. Now there's another assignment here, and it's a little bit of a tricky one, so I want to put it to you fast and get your reaction if you'll sit down.

Harmless sat on the couch, looked at the floor, then slyly at Brown. There's a matter of five grand on delivery, he said. You got the delivery, the papers make that clear, right? So how about the five grand?

That's coming, Brown said. That's no problem. Now this assignment, we want you to off Curley. We want you to call him and tell him you got to report directly on some business we had down here and you got to meet him someplace private. You take him to the Inn, he won't give you any trouble, he's been taken out there before. Then you do him in close range. Some stuff came up, and we can't carry him no more. Curley is going to have to go.

That's ridiculous, Harmless said. Curley's my contact; he's my setup guy, just like you're my reporting-in guy. I can't kill him. I never heard of anything like that. Who do you think I am?

Well, that's the deal, Brown said. He looked uncomfortable for a moment; then it passed, and he was his bearded, imposing, death-haunted Tchaikovskyan self again. This concerns stuff you don't need to know about anyway, but Curley has got to go. He's made a lot of trouble, never mind what, and it's going to be bad news until we clear the way.

That's crazy, Harmless said. Curley sends me out on these jobs. How do I know this isn't all a trick, a test? You and Curley want to find out if I'm loyal to him, if I can be trusted. If I say no, I won't take him out, then I get good marks, but if I go along with the deal, I get offed. Hey, Harmless said, I got cable and a videotape recorder, I watch the same stuff everybody does in my time off. I've seen the movies; this is a loyalty test. No, I won't play; I can't go along with any of this stuff. Staring at Brown, Harmless succumbed to an old intimation, one that he had recently felt on the plane: He had been in the business too long; it was time to get out. He was being edged that way; there were things about it which more and more were pushing him out of any sense of choice. There were no old hit men and no old political consultants either, and that was a clear truism in the trade, along with the need to clear your path of exit every time, before you got started. I think I'll just be on my way, Harmless said. I'll just go out into the night. I got the car on a week's rental. Maybe I'll go to the mountains or something. I could use some recuperative time. I recuperate, I turn the car in, that's the end of it. There are no hard feelings, you understand? I guess I'm saying that this is my career and retirement plan which is going into effect, my personal pension and higher horizons program, you know what I'm saying? I appreciate the opportunity, but this isn't a career tenure track position, you get the drift. He pulled up his socks, made scrambling motions with his feet, looked poised.

Sit down, Brown said loudly. This is no test, and I'm afraid that your options aren't so good. In fact, they're quite limited. You want to get out, that's your decision, sometimes a guy can't hack it no more, and we don't want to stand in anyone's way. But before that you're going to take care of Curley.

Look here, Brown said, putting a huge, cautionary hand on Harmless's shoulder, his piercing eyes seeming to radiate the same pain and intensity that Tchaikovsky's might have registered as he leaned forward to smell the cholera-loaded water. Maybe this seems a little tough for you, but I'm afraid we've got no alternatives here. Curley has to go, and you're the only guy we know who can get close to him no questions asked, you been carrying his water for quite a while now. So you go into Bensonhurst, you take care of this business, and we're quits, that's all. Later on you can go anywhere you want; we got a nice locker at Grand Central full of stuff you can use, take you on your way. Brown reached into his pocket, extended a key as if it were a baton. It's all yours in locker twenty sixty-five after you take care of this one piece of business. I would suggest that you make this as easy for us as possible, Harmless, because one way or the other you're going to have to do it.

I never wanted to get into intrigue, Harmless said. That was never the deal. Political consultancy, outside work, that was why I hired on. Curley said that I'd never get tied into the inside stuff, and I trusted him.

Well, Brown said, well, yes, that's true. A lot of us trusted him. A lot of us trusted him and found that was a pretty big mistake. He took Harmless's wrist, pulled him near, put the key in the palm, and closed Harmless's fingers one by one around them. Trust me, Brown said. The checkout guy's word is gold even if the check-in guy turned out to be a louse and a double-crosser. You tell Curley you got to give him some important inside information, and then you give him the information deep inside, you know? And that will be the end of it. I know for a fact, Harmless, that you got a very poor personal life, almost no personal life at all, what you find in locker twenty sixty-five could change all of that around. You do us this assignment, then we're quits. Otherwise we're quits in a different way. That's all I have to say, Brown said, towering over the confused and unsettled Harmless with a truly czarist elegance even though the height difference could only have been a couple of inches. The phone is here, the key is there, the ordnance I assume is in the valise, Brown said, so you're all set. You sure don't need any more instructions, do you? So that's it, Brown said. I don't mean to be terse or inconsiderate or anything, really, but that's all I have to say. Brown was at the door, then out of the door quickly, the vastly discombobulated Harmless feeling the heat of the key slowly coiling through his palm, reaching with its tendrils toward that heart of purpose which previously only politics had inflamed.

Harmless thought of the ramifications of American politics, the marvelous possibilities of government by accident or assassination as he rode on the subway into Bensonhurst. The arranged meeting with Curley could not have gone easier: Just meet me at the usual place, the back room, Curley had said when Harmless had said he needed to talk. You did good today, Curley said, I seen all the papers, I read the reports, you cleaned him out of the race. That's one goddamned less problem we got to face in these times. Harmless wondered if the people at the St. Petersburg Conservatory had talked this way when they squeezed the poison into Tchaikovsky: one less fag for whom to apologize, one less set of scandals. Squeezing the pistol in his inner coat pocket, Harmless considered not only government by accident or assassination but his own role in the vast convulsions and eddies of history. Also, the roles of all these people in the subway with him, New Yorkers and urban denizens of various ages, colors, and backgrounds, each of them scrambling around trying to assert some control but knowing at the center that there was no control at all. Everything was beyond them. Find someone who made a little bit too much trouble, and the shot would come from the roof or maybe there would be the sudden revelation from the secret woman, and that would be the end of him. Everything was in the grip of larger forces, not necessarily sinister but certainly insistent, Harmless thought, and that includes me, too. Except that I decided to go to work for them at an earlier age and express political consultancy in a little more direct manner. Also, I have no opinions and get paid for having no opinions; that puts me on the opposite end of almost everyone these days.

Harmless considered the forces and vast convulsions, disguised as accidents, in contemporary America all the way to the Atlantic Avenue stop, made it out into the air, then in a quick, stinking dark of the abandoned railroad yards, took a cab to the bar, no worry about leaving witnesses or identification, no one gave a damn in Brooklyn or anywhere else, and walked through the bar, past the video games and the football replay on the back wall and into the anteroom, where Curley sat alone, a gin in front of him, smoking a cigar and looking at him incuriously. Boy, oh, boy, Gerry, Curley said, you're sure looking terrible for a guy who changed the face of history today. You ought to take a little pleasure in what you're doing; you made a real contribution. Curley shook his head, laughed, banged the seat next to him. So sit down, he said, tell me what you got in mind? What's the problem, Gerry? I hear *agita* on the phone, and *agita* is not my thing. You made a botch? Everything seemed all right on TV; they're already changing the subject back to football. You want more work? We got to wait a little while until this cools. There may be something else later on this year, it's hard to tell. What do you have to say, Gerry? I'm patient, I been waiting, but I got my own exposure on this deal, too.

Feeling the weight of the gun, of all history on him, Harmless felt something else as well; it might have been a disdain so profound that it leached into all the crevices of activity and possibility. I don't want to do this, he said, and Curley stared at him, his brown eyes bright with consternation, a twinkle shading a little toward consternation but ready at any time to go back to merriment. I don't get it, Curley said, what's the deal here now, Gerry? I got no time to play twenty questions with you, and Harmless could feel the disdain emerging, driving him toward a shrug, a shrug of marvelous callousness and ease as he withdrew the gun. I got orders, he said pointlessly. I mean, I got pretty strong orders; I wouldn't do this on my own. He pulled the trigger. Curley's head, Harmless noted did not explode like the candidate's, but rather it *cracked*, split into uneven parts like a rotten cantaloupe, and from the crack at the center the lymph sprang, settling into a thick ooze. Disgusting. That was political consultancy for you. Harmless put the second slug into his contact man's throat and watched the consequences come out, pus and pulp, the American condition itself scrambling its way from the man's head. The enraged heart, still astonished by this immediacy, raced frantically: Curley spewed the colors of the flag into the air. Had to do it, Harmless said, not quite sure whom he was addressing, and backed the chair from the table, stood, held the gun, turned toward the door.

They would be coming in soon; he knew this with that utter precision for which he had already through his deeds become famous. They would be coming in soon, cleaning out the issue, settling things cold. It was like Tchaikovsky, get the situation settled, the embarrassment pushed away with the least amount of trouble. But in that slow and burning instant before Brown and his pals came in to even off the job and close down the curtains, in that uneven and attenuated instant, Harmless said, Let's hear it for the red, white, and blue, three cheers for the grand old flag we all love, and aimed the gun not at his head but at the aperture, waiting for the czar and his minions to come through the door then, waiting in that certainty that no Tchaikovsky he, he would shoot to kill and they would have to take him down screaming. We live here, it's our country, he said to the vomitous, stinking, headless thing spread on the table; we made it, and we can break it. They would have to put the poison in, Harmless thought. He would not do it to himself. He waited in pallid and perfect attention, hearing at last the thunder of the Cossacks.

Hitler at Nuremberg

The humiliation.

Not the incarceration. That I accept. I would have done the same to any of them: Eisenhower, Churchill, that traitor Joe Stalin in the dock, manacles removed only when in full court. One must intern the enemy. The enemy is not there to be humored.

But to be assembled with these lying subordinates, to be enmeshed with them. Himmler, Goering, Streicher, that dog. To take the air, eat the meals, meet the lawyers chained to these fools. A head of state is entitled to be managed with respect, and that I do not forgive them. Also these foul, stinking quarters, the piss-cans, the scraps of uneaten food in the corners, unclean, unclean! *tref* the kikes say, and the sound of the dogs in the courtyard. These are not quarters I would have given them. I would have placed interned enemies in better places, isolated, given Stalin or Truman the respect due a leader. This foul air grips, it clings, I can feel the indelicate heave of the stomach and the need to vomit but no, I am disciplined. I will not give them the satisfaction. I will not show weakness.

My generals, he thinks, my aides, my partners and collaborators in the great adventure of the Reich. Who would have known? he thinks. I had no idea what they were doing in my name. No head of state can be responsible for everything. If there is no delegation of duties, there is only fragmentation and disorder. I permitted them autonomy, I treated them as I would have been. Who was to know? Who could have possibly known what was going on there? The camps, the exterminations, the trains, the mad accountings, the accumulation in the refineries, the crematoria working frantically in the beginning of '45 just before it all fell ... I knew nothing of this. The Russians obsessed me, the failures of the Luftwaffe, the betrayals and incompetence of the generals. The poverty of Dönetz's face when he looked at me and said, "It is all over; I think we should sue for peace." These are the issues which concerned me, great matters of state, of defeat, of the fall of empires, of the final, frozen, perilous march to the abyss. Not the Jews and their Final Solution. I had no position on that at all.

I was sick of Jews, he says in open court. Sick of them, do you hear me! Usurers, thieves, international bankers, Communists and spies, yes, but I could not be concerned with them anymore; if in half a millennium the Inquisition had not been able to bring peace to the continent and disperse them, then my own feeble efforts would be unavailing. I did not want anything more to do with the Jews. Let Eichmann take care of it, I said to Himmler. *Poof!* I clean my hands of this, let Eichmann arrange for their deportation. *Arbeit machen frei*. Keep them at their tasks.

He needs the microphones more as his testimony continues. At the beginning he had entered the dock straight and angry, dark with pride and the consistency of his purpose, he would not bow to them, would need no technology, would not need to resort to machines to make his position felt. But as it went on and on into the week, then stretched past the end of the month, then into the odorous spring, the dampest stink of spring he had ever known, his voice began to fail and they gave him the microphones. In full-throated whisper he explained his position, took them through all of it again and again, hating his weakness, his dependence. Their attention was fixed; not even at the Reichstag had he had a crowd held in such thrall. Yet he could tell that the situation had been poised against him, he was not getting through. He was not making his position clear. They did not believe him. If they had accepted what he had to say, then the full monstrousness of their own deeds would have reared up against them and they would have known that they were worse than he. So from the start it was necessary to target him, make him the assassin at the center of the state. Himmler, Streicher, Goering, and all of the rest of them, and now the Allies, were in their palm. I was not responsible, he said in open court. It was the manufacture of bitter and disloyal aides, Jew-haters and gypsy killers. Regiments of the feeble-minded fell before them like wheat. I was preoccupied with the international situation. I was concerned with great matters of state. What did I care, what do I care about your bunch of Jews and what would you have me do for any of them? He raises his hand in bitter salute in the dank cell of his inquisition and hears the engines of history clattering dimly for him, the voices of the guards riotous in the hall.

He is a small man but filled with self-confidence, dapper and precise, clean and organized. Here in these quarters he holds on to his dignity, gives them a head of state who they will see has not crumbled to circumstance. The thousand-year Reich was not to be, but the Fuehrer remains. In the courtyard when Goering and Himmler approach him, he moves away quickly, making gestures of dismissal. He will not talk to them, not now, not ever again. They have secret microphones on their persons and will broadcast his words to the Allied interrogator, he knows that. They will do anything now to protect themselves, to make a stab at salvation, they will deliver the Fuehrer to these conquerors as if they were gods. Only Streicher has access to him, old Julius who speaks the language of the people and has always had an amusing, peasant insight. "I hear rumors," Julius has said to him, "our armies are still in the field. They are under cover. They are preparing themselves for a final assault. They will storm this place and we will be free. That is what I hear," Julius says. "We must have courage and we must be patient. In the meantime, we eat pork and tell them whatever they want to hear and wait for better times."

Julius is an idiot. His intelligence is borderline at best, worse than that, but he has had his virtues of loyalty, and here in his ragged uniform and ridiculous cap he seems to have been stripped down by the captors and the situation to the schoolboy he once was, the bully with terror lurking at the corners of his being. It is possible to feel pity for Julius if not for his situation. The man is a fool, they are all fools. They should not be here.

In the rooms when Dönetz had brought word of the final assault Eva had said, "Take the poison. I am ready to take the poison," and as he had promised he had counted out the capsules, one, two, three, four for her, the other six for him, he had estimated that he was one and a half times stronger than she and so had saved the larger amount, but after she had downed her share, he found that *he was not able to take them*, something powerful within him denied the capsules and, terrified, he had flung them against the wall. Eva had stared and screamed, staggered to her feet filled with rage at his betrayal, and had made desperate retching motions to try to disgorge her own share, but the retching acted only to weaken a frame already caved in and she had fallen, rolling then into a dull state of inanition and alone in the bunker then he had waited. He could not take the poison, after all. He had had it all planned; the poison surely was the proper fashion, the proper rebuke for these sinister enemies who had infiltrated what he thought were his last loyal troops and had destroyed him, but suicide was a sin, it was an evil, and unlike Hess he would die defiant, would resist them to the end.

So that was the way they had found him then, clutched in the corner, arms in a cross over his chest, hands on his throat, shouting at them, "I will not yield, I will not yield," as they dragged him away. Or was that what he had shouted? He could not remember. Another voice, one from a distance, might have cried "I surrender, I surrender," or "don't kill me," but he is not sure of this. He is not sure of anything, the old certainties seem to have departed. He paces the courtyard, shrugs at the guards, spits at his associates, waves away Julius. "No," he says, "not even you. I do not want to talk to you." In his mind he goes over the testimony again and again. Tomorrow once more he must attempt to explain himself, make clear to them why it could have been no other way and why he had in those last years been turned into the figurehead in whose name mad generals did unspeakable things, but he knows that they will not believe him. None of them will ever believe him again. It is enough to make him weep.

I sent Hess. I detailed Hess to England, I could tell that early how out of control the situation was. They were killing Jews in my name, advancing toward Stalingrad in the worst of winters with orders to sack the capital, and I knew nothing of it until much later. They had sealed me off by then, put me in Berchtesgaden with false information and the dogs running wild and free in the mountains. The dogs, always the dogs, sniffing, poking, ramming their way into everything. "Hess," I said, "sue for peace. Tell them what the situation has become. I would go with you but they watch me every moment. They follow me with their eyes and with their guns. I am a prisoner here. Take the plane and the documents. Tell them that we will capitulate. Tell them that we will admit their entry into Berlin and turn over control if they will allow us a just and generous and honest surrender." His eyes gleamed with assent. Hess was a weak man, but his weakness was all that I could trust. "You have my full and confidential support," I said. "Go on your way."

I detailed Hess. It was all my doing, he went up into the plane, up in the air, over the border, and then into the bizarre, pathetic aftermath. Of which I learned only later. I was always afraid of Eichmann. I knew there was a craziness, an evil in the man. "Jews do not have to be killed," I said to him. "Do not kill the Jews. Intern them if you must and use them as pressure for munitions and cooperation, release them piecemeal for quarter from Roosevelt and Churchill, but do not kill them. The Jews are valuable capital, not to be expended."

"I never had extermination camps in mind," he said to the prosecutor. "*Arbeit machen frei*, they were work camps." Jackson laughed at me, opened his mouth and roared with laughter while the court quaked. I could see then that there was no chance, no chance for me while I was there to act as scapegoat. If I had been dead, if I had taken the poison, they would have said that it was all my orders, that they were just following orders, and even though I had not taken the poison, my presence was only a small inconvenience. "We were just following orders," Goering said. That fat fool sat in court day after day, facing me, his eyes locked to mine as he explained this, and then one by one these men who had seized the government in my name said that they were following orders. If Eichmann had been there, he would have said that it was for the love of Jews that he had taken the job and that he had used the camps as exterminating devices only because I insisted. Eichmann would have said that he was a clerk who went home to his quarters night after night, wretched from a day of following orders, but he had fled. I knew from the start, could not have known otherwise, that it was all fictitious, a dumb show, and that they would destroy me to save themselves. But then such is the obligation of the head of state. I had seen that clearly in '33 and taken upon myself that risk and obligation. I do not complain.

I complain no more, I will resist but not seek pity. It is their dock, their lies, their option. Goering and Himmler will be next, but I will go first with the satisfaction of knowing that hanging me means *nothing*. They have the wrong man, they have the wrong understanding. They cannot hang a country, they cannot hang the world, but only this poor and necessary symbol. I know this. I know that it could not have been otherwise. I am clear and determined, I meet the enemy on his own terms and my own declaration.

Permitted the courtyard no longer after the verdict, he says that he does not mind the confinement in the cell. He monitors the time carefully and listens to the birds in the trees in this damp season. Goering is brought under guard to express his condolences, but he will not listen. Himmler arrives, but he turns away. Streicher comes in sackcloth, the sheen of alcohol on his face and they embrace and he feels the palpating waves of sweat and event coming from Streicher's glands. Good-bye, Julius, he says. Of all of them you were the only one I could trust. Because you were so stupid, he does not add. Julius is taken away. Now, erect in his camouflage, neatly dressed and waiting for the guards, he sits calmly in his cell, thinking of Eva and the long nights now in Berchtesgaden, the dogs clamoring in the hills, the two of them clamoring further, the smell and necessity of the century all around. He had plans, great plans, but they were destroyed by those he trusted and there is nothing to do now but wait for the full and final verdict which he hopes will be somewhat more generous than this. "*Coward*," Eva had shrieked at him, dying. "*You coward!*" No, not exactly. There was something larger at issue. The century knifes through him, the lightning bolt carrying him toward the millennium. The rope is light and amazingly soothing as it is yanked into place. It could have been any of you, any of you.

Any of you.

Concerto Accademico

The first dragon entered Orchestra Hall and moved gracelessly, a three ton package, toward the podium just as the Tarrytown Symphony was beginning the third movement of the Vaughan Williams Ninth Symphony. Glassop, in the third chair of the seconds, on the outside thanks to the old style antiphonal seating that gave the seconds their own arch opposite the firsts, was among the first to see it but he kept very calm, bowing only slightly disturbed by the entrance of the green beast, slithering now down the aisle. Fulkes, the conductor was, of course, unaware of the dragon at this point and Glassop did not see fit to enlighten him. In the dim light the auditorium, no artificial illumination being turned on for a day rehearsal; the beast looked like a floating, cleaned-up crocodile. Glassop had seen pictures in the children's books, knew at least what he was looking at. He was no dummy. The beast was definitely a dragon and it looked most determined, as if it had a mission. Glassop hit the pizzicatos, listening to the theme crawling from the bassoons, tried to concentrate upon the notes. You had to stay calm in this business, if you got caught up in the moment by moment stuff, you could be destroyed like Nikisch throwing the baton on his toe and dying of septicemia in the days before antibiotics. And Toscanini, of course, taking out a violist's eye with a flung baton. "Excuse me," Schmitt, his seatmate said, "but is that a reptile coming down the aisle?" Schmitt had played in the Oslo Philharmonic, second stand firsts he had complained to Glassop, before he had decided to join his daughter and spend his pension in America. He was a dour Scandinavian and not such a good violinist, but Glassop knew that he was observant.

"It's a dragon," Glassop said. "Like in the forest or maybe with the queen."

"I know what it is, dummy," Schmitt said. "But where does it come from?"

Glassop shrugged. Sometimes no answer was the best answer. The dragon paused midway between the back doors and the podium and seemed to paw the ground, fixed the woodwinds on risers of the Tarrytown Symphony with a dim and preoccupied pair of eyes. Fulkes banged the baton on the empty music stand, said "Woodwinds, woodwinds!" until all of them stopped. Glassop rested his violin on his knee, looked at the middle-aged conductor whose life was edged in disappointment, Glassop supposed, married to an heiress and conducting a semi-professional orchestra in Westchester when his real ambitions lay somewhat to the south. Once as an assistant conductor of the New York Philharmonic he had filled in for Boulez at a children's concert, but that was a long time ago.

"*Woodwinds*," Fulkes said, "that is not the way that this very sinister passage is played. You must make legato, must lead the way toward the flugelhorn!"

"Dragons," Schmitt said. "They were rumored to be in the forests of Riga when I was a young man. Of course I am not a young man now, my friend. Do you smell that beast?"

Glassop inhaled delicate draughts of air, thinking of his grandson, Zeke, and what he would make of a dragon in the orchestra hall. Probably the boy would be as matter of fact as Schmitt or perhaps as oblivious as Wilkes. Children nowadays were exposed to too much sensation, murders on the MTV, dragons were nothing to them. The one at issue pawed the tiled floors and then sat gracelessly on its haunches, fixing Fulkes' back with an insistent and compelling expression. It might have been holding an oboe for the degree of attention it now showed.

"This is a most sinister symphony," Fulkes said. "Vaughan Williams composed it in 1958, in the last year of his life. He was 86 years old and not feeling very well and he looked, in the words of Colin Davis, like a sack of bricks. We must acquaint ourselves with a man who thought of himself as being on friendly terms with death, who saw death, so to speak, as a disheveled guest in his own home, perhaps an elderly acquaintance who himself looked like a sack of bricks. Later on it is time for the middle strings to plumb the nature of the north region, but now the woodwinds must gracefully usher the old fellow in. Do you understand?"

Glassop shrugged, and stared over at the fourth stand firsts where, on the inside, sat Gertrude whom he loved. Gertrude had come to the Tarrytown Symphony only as a means, she said, of filling up the hours while her children slowly dismantled her life but Glassop thought that he knew better, that he could look deeply into her very soul. Thirty years younger than he and most of the string section of this orchestra of refugees from Communism or decadence or retirees from capitalism, she had she said a mature and loving heart and no prejudice at all against second violinists or older men. If her husband and children were only to die, she had told Glassop once in the sacramental confines of the rear booth at the college coffee shop, she would genuinely consider his offer, his aching need. Of course this was not likely at any time in the foreseeable, but then again you did not know.

Gertrude looked over at him, said something. *Dra-gon*, Glassop lip-read expertly. *Do you see the dra-gon?* She made a circle of her right thumb and forefinger, gripped the bow, raised it, pointed to the far aisle. *Am I cra-zy?* Glassop lip-read. *Is that a dragon?*

No, Glassop motioned with his head, then nodded yes. No, you are not crazy. Yes, that is a dragon. He did this twice to make sure that the message could not be confused. Gertrude sighed, shrugged, raised the bow again. *Are we the only ones?* she said. *To see it? To see the dra-gon?* Glassop shrugged. Who knew? It was enough to manage your own perceptions, let alone account for those of others. *I don't know*, he mouthed back to her. Now it was her turn to shrug, and then turn a page of the score as if in dismissal. Well, that was what the emotion of pure love got you at 67. If he were lucky he would, with the Greek philosopher, have the beast taken from him soon enough. In the meantime, he had the assurance from Gertrude who was the recipient of his earnest if unavailing passion that he was not mad, that he had indeed glimpsed a dragon in the aisle. Perhaps others had, too. Perhaps the entire orchestra had grasped the situation but was remaining very calm. That was the nature of the Tarrytown Symphony. These were people who had, most of them, been through a great deal, much displacement, the fulcrum of dispossession had had its way with two out of three of them and a dragon in orchestra hall was at this time among the lesser of their concerns.

"That is good enough," Fulkes said. "We try again now. From the beginning of the movement, please. Remember, should we get that far that the last movement is *attaca*, you must make the audience feel the transition rather than see it. Vaughan Williams died just three weeks after the premiere and the night before Boult made the recording. We will endeavor now not to do the same."

Glassop put the fiddle under his chin, listened to Barnett's snare drum, watched Leonard Zeller put the clarinet through the opening phrases. What was it like for Vaughan Williams in that last year? Glassop wondered. Eighty-six years old, still writing symphonies, did he see dragons? English music was full of moats, castles, knights and unicorns, surely there must have been room for a dragon there. The Czechs had goblins and water sprites, dour Scandinavians like Schmitt were concerned largely with dwarfs. But dragons were kind of hard to place, not really nationalized in the way that most myths were. Glassop followed Fulkes' baton, was cued in, played his way through the grim answering theme.

The dragon rose suddenly to all fours and bellowed, then raised its front legs to rear to a surprising height, perhaps half the distance to the roof of the orchestra hall. The sound was surprisingly high, fluted, not what one would associate with a menacing beast. However, it stopped the woodwinds cold and broke down Solomon before he could raise the flugelhorn. There was no question now of the visibility of the dragon or the attention of the Tarrytown Symphony. The players were indeed fixated upon the situation. Fulkes turned, stared into the auditorium, then whirled back and faced them. "Oh, my," he said, "oh, my, it is very large." He grasped his chest, pounded it in an odd rhythm, then dropped the baton. "I think I am going to faint," Fulkes said. "It is a great, a surprising strain."

The dragon wandered toward the edge of the stage, perched on the floor then right under the second violins, closest to Glassop. At the fourth stand on the outside, Glassop had the most privileged of vantage points, he could stare the animal down eye to eye and at the same time maintain some perspective. "Oh, my," Fulkes said, lunging to the right, then the left. "I have never seen anything like this." He fell to his knees, crept around the podium, found the baton and lurching into a half-crouch fled the podium, lunging through the firsts at hobbling speed and exiting behind the curtain. There were sounds of consternation among the bassi and two of the firsts at the rear stand rose to follow Fulkes, possibly to check upon his health, but otherwise all remained calm. Glassop stared at the dragon, an elongated and amiable crocodile with large, fixed eyes and a peculiarly generous expression around the mouth. The beast exhaled and the smell of flowers wafted its way to Glassop, filling his nostrils with sweet and ancient odors.

"Oh, what a grand circumstance," Schmitt said, entranced, holding his violin with two hands against his belly and looking at the engaging beast beneath them. "Magic," Schmitt said as if having returned from the land of the fiords that very morning. "It is magic."

Glassop put his violin slowly, firmly on the floor. Magic, he thought, Schmitt was right. The quality was of magic. Seen from this angle the beast was enormous yet somehow accessible. Peacefully it exuded its floral scent and then Glassop extended his hand to touch a scale, the dragon licked Glassop's hand with the greatest and gentlest of attention. Glassop felt a strange and wondrous peace filling him.

He stood carefully, making sure that he did not bump his violin, a simulated machine-made Amati worth perhaps twelve hundred dollars but of some sentimental meaning and went to the podium, mounted it slowly and stiffly. The Tarrytown Symphony—old men, older men, middle-aged women, a few people of indeterminate age and of course his beloved, harried Gertrude—stared at him. The rear stand first violinists had followed Fulkes and there were a few gaps in the woodwinds and bassi but the body of the 73 member orchestra remained on stage. Glassop found himself filled with an odd and persuasive joy, something unlike anything he had felt in these many years. He looked at the dragon—which was now submitting to Schmitt's scratchings and whispered confidences—for courage and then he looked at Gertrude who gave him her most attentive and dedicated coffee-shop smile and then he addressed the orchestra.

"At eighty-six," Glassop said, "Ralph Vaughan Williams, the great British composer who Colin Davis described as looking in his dotage like a sack of bricks experienced wonders, knew wonders, composed in that eighty-seventh year of his the greatest of his nine symphonies and lived to hear its premiere. He heard wonders, saw dragons, saw lovely and mythical beasts against the screen of his consciousness, wrote a fierce and humorous commentary. Can we do less? In our own near-dotage can we ask less of ourselves than did Ralph Vaughan Williams?

"Come," Glassop said, feeling massive, solid, feeling the full *locality* of himself and basking in the sudden and expanded breath of the dragon, "We will make music together. In E minor we will make such sounds as Ralph Vaughan Williams heard from the fen, as he moved toward the far region. Gertrude," Gloss said, "I truly love you, wreckage that I am, I confer upon you the benison of my understanding and my simple, unadorned, insubstantial passion." He raised the baton. "From the beginning," Glassop said, "we will start the E Minor symphony from the beginning with its earnest, descending theme and we will move on and on through its thirty-seven minutes of steady grandeur. Celli, prepare to lead."

Glassop, no longer a refugee, raised his hands. The music sighed from the celli. Behind him Glassop could hear the sound of the dragon's heart as it opened its joyous mouth to emit fire, the pure fire ascending from its living breath and in the arch of Gertrude's bow Glassop dreamed that he could see the mysterious fen, the walking stick of Ralph Vaughan Williams, the splendid old man himself as riding the fire of the dragon he sped toward eternity.

—in memory of Sir Adrian Boult

The Intransigents

Rifka stared at the director. I don't believe it, he said.

You'd better believe it, the Director said. We've been running the tapes all morning and the words come out the same. She's crying, she's screaming, she's going to call the press. She's got Hopper on the string, Winchell. She's going to let the whole thing out. You shouldn't have pushed her, the Director said. You and that Jeptha, you took her over the line. I warned you, didn't I? I was in the Oval Office with all of the files a year ago and I told you to quit. But would you listen?

Rifka looked at the Director as if for the first time and thought how much he hated him. He really hated the Director, more maybe than anyone else he had found in place when they got there and the Director was an untouchable. He was a son of a bitch, that was all there was to it. Someday the Director would fold up, probably at Pimlico, and keel upside down on the black-eyed Susans, a fat, puffing, ugly man with secrets and coarse arteries. But not in enough time, Rifka knew, for it to help anyone around here. The good ones or those you didn't mind hanging around for a while blew out early but the bastards went on and on and their power never got broke, it just got transferred. Jeptha quit, Rifka said. You have the tapes, you know everything? Then you know he quit. We listened.

The Director looked at his fingernails. Too late, he said. And you didn't quit. So what the hell is the point? Now she's going to take the roof off everything and leave you nowhere to go. Anything you boys look at you feel is yours if you want it. But it doesn't work that way.

It was different with me, Rifka said. He wanted to smash the Director, pound his head into the sleek desk, watch it pulp and explode, watch the blood arc like the files; the tapes, the hidden secrets in the Director's lair would explode if he could only lay a bomb in it. There was no point in thinking that way. The Director was only trying to help. Besides, the Director could destroy them with one phone call, a few careful releases. So what do you want to do? Rifka said.

You learned that from your old man, the Director said. He took a nail buffer from his inside jacket pocket, rubbed it idly over his old nails, then buffed vigorously so that small embers of nail poured into the thin light. But your old man could have learned a thing or two. There were holes in his technique. We go way back, your old man and me. Of course, the Director said, there ain't but a lettuce leaf left there now, is there?

I've had enough of this, Rifka said. The chair squeaked back, he stood. I don't have to listen to this.

Oh yes you do, the Director said, because the way your actress is going, I figure you and your brother and a lot of your friends have maybe forty-eight hours before it's all over. You'd have to go to war with the Commies to push it off the front pages. Sit down, the Director said, I'm not finished talking to you.

I don't have to sit, Rifka said. His voice took on a whining tone, he could hear the pleading within the hollows of his head. I'm your technical superior, he wanted to say, I'm the head of the Justice Department. Don't order me around. Go away. Drop dead. Jeptha will back me up on this. Fuck you, you've terrorized your last politician, you bastard. Rifka said none of this. He sat. The Director worked the buffer on his nails, sighed, leaned toward Rifka. We're going to have to take her out, the Director said. It's the only way. She's hysterical, full of poisons, angry and gut-shot by you boys. It's a bad combination. Don't say anything, you don't have to talk. This is our play. You don't have to order it, you don't even have to not get in the way. But you're going to know beforehand what's happening. That's what is happening.

How do you take her out? Rifka said. It was going too quickly for him, but then all of it had always gone too quickly. Thirty-eight years old, sitting in the Department of Justice, listening to the Director, his nominal subordinate. Two years ago he had been on the road from Los Angeles, spreading the word, ten years before that he and Jeptha had been laughing while the Brahmin staggered around. The Senate seat was theirs. He had had the actress in a hundred ways after Jeptha had gotten rid of her and there had been moments so pure, so vaulting, so pornographic and yet spiritual in their content that he had gasped. People like Rifka grew up thinking about things like this, never getting to do them. But he had gotten to do them. He and Jeptha, standing on the beach together election night, waiting for Daley to report and making their plans. And here he was.

I won't condone it, he said, I won't have a thing to do with it.

No you won't, the Director said. You never did. People like you and Jeptha just powered ahead and figured that people like me would come behind as the clean-up crew. We're going to do it again and we don't even have to ask permission. It won't be too hard.

I don't want to know about it, Rifka said. You don't have to tell me anything.

That's the way you want it, the Director said. Show but don't tell. But it's not going to be that clean. You'll know, all right. We have hold of everything there, it won't be difficult. We're going to save your bacon for the last time, though, Rifka. This is the end. You tell Jeptha that, you hear me?

The Director stood suddenly, wavering in the room. Not a tall man, not imposing, either, but he was threat, pure threat, the secret knife of terror wavering over Rifka in the empty room. He had the files. He had everything, wires running here, wires there, secrets, contents, documents, dossiers. Once with Jeptha a year and a half ago, the Director and the two of them had been laughing over some of the files, the Director's standard greeting, the Director said. Everybody new in office got a good look at them for laughs, could see anything on request. Of course the implication was that your files were back there, too, and could turn up just as quickly. That was a long time ago, before Rifka even knew the actress, before Jeptha had started in with her, before the steel crisis. Before anything. I told him to lay off, the Director said, shouting at Rifka. You get that message back to him. We have cleaned it up for the last time, do you hear? You go and tell your brother that and more. This isn't your playpen and you'd better face that.

Don't ask any questions, the Director said after a pause. The reports will come into you, you just sit and listen. I'd save any official statements of regret, though, for the funeral, you understand? Just some friendly advice. The Director turned and walked slowly out of the office. Rifka looked at him moving through the door, then looked away as the door quietly closed. The insane impulse to call the actress, to warn her, to tell her to leave the house immediately and get out of the country crossed his consciousness, but then whisked away. No line was secure, least of all his. The actress was calling and calling now, he had had everything blocked, he could hardly turn around now and reach out for her. It was the calls that had brought the Director here anyway. Rifka sighed. It really was a mess, he had no idea that it would go this far. That was the thing, matters went out of control. There was no accounting for people, particularly a woman as unstable and pained as the actress. Rifka more than most knew of the pain there.

He called Jeptha instead. Jeptha tried to sound casual but it was obvious that he had been waiting, waiting. Was it fixed? Jeptha wanted to know, was it what he thought it was. Come over and talk to him right now. Rifka said that anything he had to say better be said face-to-face in a secure facility. Was it fixed, was it being worked on? Jeptha shouted. Rifka said he guessed so. That was the problem, they were over their heads, but if they couldn't control this kind of thing, who could?

Rifka had a bad feeling about it. It all had the look of a set-up of some kind. Stevenson had warned how things were down there and Jeptha had seemed to really waver for a little while, but then Johnson and

Yarborough and Connally and the rest of them had become insistent. You've got to go, they said, you'd make fools of us if you don't. Heal the party, Johnson said. Johnson was a big party man as long as it was his party. Rifka had told Jeptha flatly no, don't do it, but Jeptha had after this and that amount of wavering decided that he was committed, he would have to do. There was no way out at this time and there was already the matter of sixty-four. If he were going to dump Lyndon, not going would have been too much of a signal, would have given Lyndon too much lead time to move around and angle. So you had to protect your plans, you had to go. Rifka let himself be persuaded, but he thought the situation was dangerous. Someone could get hurt down there.

They never talked about the actress. After that one conversation in Jeptha's office she had never been mentioned again. There was a big hole in Rifka's life and sometimes when he thought about her he wanted to cry, but of course there was no point to any of that. For Jeptha it seemed to make no difference, Rifka suspected that the actress had been erased from Jeptha's mind months before it happened, leaving the Director—as the Director had rightly said to deal with the situation. That was the point and the Director was right there, too, Jeptha had always had someone to take care of matters for him. Rifka, too, mostly, but sometimes Rifka was doing the taking care. Anyway, there was nothing to be done about it now and talking about her would only have made things more complicated for the two of them. There was some unease, real lacunae between them anyway.

Rifka summoned the Director. It was not the kind of thing which he would have done usually, and there had been no one-on-one contact with the Director since that August afternoon over a year ago, only a few collisions at ceremonial affairs, but he felt now that he had to talk to him. The Director had his secretary put Rifka off several times, but then Rifka, stunned, had lost his temper and used a direct line and told the Director to get the hell over. Which the man had done, looking even older and more corrupt than he had a year and a couple of months ago, but then what would he have expected? Rifka said, I don't like the situation in Dallas. It's an ugly one. I want Jeptha watched and protected at all times.

What the hell you think we're here for? the Director said, and the Secret Service. What kind of shit is this? We protect him all the time, every time, that's our job. That's why we did that little number for you, remember? Well? Do you remember?

Rifka clasped his hands and said, Just shut up. Shut up about that other job, it's all over. This is '63 and we're talking about Dallas. I want

Jeptha protected, you understand? Just make sure that no one gets to him.

This is '62 and it's Los Angeles, the Director said. We worked it then, why shouldn't we work it out now? You're a real shit, the Director said. You go ahead and fire me, you don't like it, Rifka, but that's what you are. You and your protected brother. You leave the stuff lying around and we clean it up. Now you're suddenly afraid for his life. Maybe you should have worried about his life a long time ago? He's got Addison's, the Director said, and he's a self-destructive bastard, too. You don't think we do know that, Rifka? We know everything. You don't like it? Well, what's your suggestion?

There's no suggestion, Rifka said. He could see it now, the swirling, distant chasm, the waters below, he was on the perch, not falling, suspended. He had ventured onto that ledge and that was where he had lived. There was nothing, nothing else to be done, nowhere to go, nowhere to be moved. Just make sure that nothing bad happens, Rifka said. You think I'm a shit, that's on your own time. Civil Service pension rules permit that. Put in for compensated hours.

You're a real funny guy, Rifka, the Director said. Is that all?

That's enough, all right. You heard me. You don't protect him, you'll hear from me. I don't want anyone breaking through the lines.

You liked that stuff, didn't you? the Director said. You Catholic boys with your upbringing, she must have been Gloria Swanson for you. Rockets and pinwheels. You sort of really miss her, don't you?

Rifka stood. He wanted to kill the Director, but then the Director had all of the tapes and files, likewise methods which could be put to any kind of use. The Director knew everyone and everything, had connections at every level, you couldn't fuck with him, that was the sum of it. You just couldn't do that. Maybe you could play him even, but not without terrible risk. Good-bye, he said.

You look real mad, Rifka, the Director said. Real mad and upset. You called me over here, remember? What do you think of that? But don't worry about it, the Director said, swaying upright, stamping his feet on the carpet. We'll take good care of him just like we always did. The office is beyond the man, right? And after I'm gone there will still be an office. The Director walked by Rifka, went to the door, turned, seemed about to say something, said nothing, went out. Rifka unfurled a handkerchief and wiped his forehead. You Catholic boys, right. Yes, that was the way it was for Catholic boys. The Director would know all right.

Much later, almost at the end, Rifka saw how it all came together, saw the way it must have been. The Director had been given a nasty job, he did it like he did all of the others, but this had been personal, difficult in ways which Rifka could not quite fathom but which definitely had been there. Jeptha, after the job was done, had to be taken out of the way because Jeptha had been the real cause of the job in the first place.

So that left Rifka. Rifka was still around, had potential, but he was paralyzed, grief-stricken. Out of power, out of Washington. How much damage could a junior senator do, one with plenty of his own agenda, his own grief, and Lyndon who knew the truth hovering over him?

Rifka could figure all of this out, almost at the very end, too late for it to make any difference. He was no threat, he represented nothing to the Director. But there had been the goddamned excruciating war and the administration had drowned in its blood and then it was Rifka's turn to run, to take Lyndon down. The Director had seen early on, maybe even earlier than Rifka himself that this was a real campaign, a real possibility. Rifka in power without Jeptha to hold him back, Rifka in office with the only real agenda to avenge Jeptha—the war was just an excuse—it would have been dangerous. Very much so to a director who knew too much.

Rifka copped to it all. It came upon him suddenly and in a blaze of clarity exactly what the Director would be bound to do and why. But even as that insight burst upon him with clarity and shimmering force, a force which might have once been his in the actress's arms he was already turning from the podium, moving back toward the kitchen. So it's on to Chicago, he said and waved and turned and then the clattering of the gun and Rifka knew, he knew what had necessarily been planned for him just as the actress must have known in the last minutes before the men came in. Too late, though, for both of them, too late for Jeptha, too. The Director, Rifka thought, he hated women, hated women-fuckers, too, and Rifka in power would have known too much. Too late for America, Rifka thought as his brain burst, his brains pouring out in the kitchen. Well, maybe not for America, but a lousy fucking end to one great doomed ride, he thought and then thought no more of this. *The Director had put it in him.*

Hieractic Realignment

The damaged but still vigorous, ever hopeful Blake felt that he had as good a chance at the job now as anyone. Why not? It was simultaneously highly specialized and general to the extreme. One would have to come to this with open credentials. Very few jobs like this existed, after all. The qualifications were ambiguous and the number of such sects quite limited.

Blake, shiftless in so much of his life's occupation but dedicated to spiritual order and with odd, unpredictable flashes of religiosity, knew that he had the qualifications. Who could make a better case? He was a plucky guy, had survived the schoolyard, almost made it intact through Army Basic in the old days to say nothing of graduate school. The circumstances here were stark, all right, everyone knew that, but he understood the situation. He had researched it assiduously.

Here was the situation: after the death of the childless Grand Rabbi, after the immediate internment of that Rabbi, factionalism had overtaken the order and beneath that factionalism an unswerving, uncancelled doubt. This doubt had afflicted the old members, quite paralyzed them, made them unable to move on a successor.

In fact, these excited disputants were unable to reach any accommodation. The conflicts were evident. Most believed that the Rabbi was, as he had indicated in his last years (with a little terminal encouragement from his supporters), the Messiah and he would therefore be shortly returning for the beginning of the thousand days. All the Biblical and Talmudic evidence had pointed to him, and the Messianic faction had brought the weight of scholarly text to bear, had promulgated their views in bumper stickers and posters hailing the "King Messiah." He was the Grand Rabbi, after all, and whatever he had promised—no matter how ostensibly incongruous—was Truth. Did the Torah itself not contain apparent contradictions? The believer's job was to accept, not necessarily to understand. *Na'aseh v'nishmah* lay at the very foundation of the religion.

But a scholarly minority brought a conflicting set of Biblical and Rabbinic citations. This insistent bunch, no less fanatical than their opposites, held that the Rabbi must have seen something on his deathbed which had catapulted him toward his grievous end. He had been a great man, yes, a teacher and a visionary, but had succumbed to the very human and ordinary fate of delusion and guilt toward the end. Illness besets rich and poor, Rabbi and disciple alike. The sooner, then, that he was dismissed from consideration, the sooner the sect could get started on the selection of a new leader. This would be best for all of them and that new leader, no Messiah at all, would be a practical man willing to sort out financial and geographical obstacles which had never been addressed by the Rabbi for the long final years of his primacy.

For the Rabbi in those last years had made it known that he was wholly uninterested in temporal matters, he simply could not be bothered by such concerns. He muttered about "freedom to oppression" and quoted extensively from Isaiah 53. He dreamed and from his bed would share his powerful dream: the arc of the golden covenant, the bleat of the goat tied with ropes and thrown from the highest terrain in praise of the Lord. Making a great gong of absolute judgement. From this long and inconstant dying he had returned with gasping, jewelled visions for his followers, small and precious glimpses of the times to come. A man would come, a redeemer, different from all they had imagined. A soul concealed by a disguise so powerful, so perverse as to test the faith of the most committed. He had confided these visions in whispers to his followers. Most had clasped hands in trust; but opponents had found that they lacked real assurance, that the visions suffered from a lack of conviction, which could only attack their credibility.

So the anti-Messianists, buttressed by the weight and wisdom of ancient lore and less credulous or more ambitious, felt that the Rabbi was stone or decomposition, ashes or dust but in no case fit for return. The Messianic code which would help the Rabbi move on from the grave to assume a commanding spot seemed to have been exposed as an essential market position and it was time to move on. The factions quarreled, despised one another, deplored their opponents' misguidance, engaged in arguments which occasionally became physical, even brutal although there were no known fatalities. In the meantime, some five perilous and unhappy years after the death of the Rabbi, the order—all of its factions—remained almost wholly paralyzed.

Therefore, Blake thought, stumbling along Eastern Parkway, righting himself with the help of garbage cans, scattering pigeons and memory as he lurched toward Headquarters, therefore here was vacancy without occupation. He was getting right down to the possibilities when he had studied the newspaper stories months ago and had fixed his sights on this beauty spot for an enterprising guy, the kind of situation to which an enterprising man could bring some real clarity. Here was possibility and a clear career path once he had established his redemptive or visionary powers. Of course it would help if he could work a modest miracle or two. The job, once accepted, would embody everything which evolved late century concepts of advancement properly deplored. The sect had no use for women, less for the secular world from which the women could protect them. Also and encouragingly, the sect had little tolerance for premature decisions on the issue of Resurrection or even decisions of any kind.

Reason enough for a more sensible Blake, a Blake transmogrified, to have stayed away. But he had reached that careless and unachieved stage, the resting place after all the caroms of unachievement, when whether they like it or otherwise, you had to take your shot. Blake figured that he was as good as anyone, as likely a candidate. On his side was ignorance both of particular text and sacred order, absence of principle should also count for something. The Rabbi's mutterings had been sufficiently vague to accommodate the least likely candidate— someone of no scholarly or even religious background. Against him of course were those remnants of the order who would take no substitutes, allow for no spare parts, and accept nothing short of another ultra- orthodox Jew of profound Talmudic prowess. It would recognizably be the Rabbi come to part the waters or it would be no one. Blake considered this part of the challenge, the most imposing of the obstacles he would have to overcome. Part of ascension, after all, was the dispersion of obstacles, and nowhere in human history, on Earth as in Heaven, was there a religion without its parables of submersion, loss, suffering and final victory. Blake was in his small way a scholar, he had surveyed the situation carefully.

No, Blake was not a frivolous man. A gravitas pervaded his world-view and appearance. A solemn, joyless cast to his demeanor cast shadows over his five feet six inches, his bald skull, his solemn, stalking demeanor. Once, before he had found the tighter focus of these recent years, he had dreamed of women all the time, had dreamed of women tempting him with their posture and private parts, women pressing against the enthralled Blake organ and bringing it to raging, inconstant life. Blake moaned just thinking about it, remembering those days, that imagined sensation, uttered little carnal cries of submission, each of those cries seeming to drive him more deeply into his own accommodation, his own obsession.

Blake's soul often seemed to be raw with dripping paint, with rediscovery and constancy, but the failed relationships, the miserable and misguided women of a lifetime had brought him to a grim awareness of women's treachery: sex as nature's enormous cheat, carnality's commanding giggle as it overcame the sensibilities of earnest men such as himself. O the prized and unpried practice of celibacy!

Blake had often thought. Possessed of fortune by inheritance, stripped of desire by harsh encounter, granted lifetime security by certain meaningful convulsions in foreign currency, the disenchanted, sex-suspicious but always ambitious Blake had been independently wealthy and unattached for many years, ready to seek a meaningful fulltime position which now, with the controversy over the succession, seemed at least possible, worth pursuit. Blake had ideas. Whispers of the second coming, hints and glimmers of celestial transport had combed his nights since adolescence. Becoming the Messiah was your best bet, overall, to make sense out of this mystery.

The idolatrous Blake took public transportation to the headquarters of the sect, after all this consideration, managed to talk his way past colorfully garbed but otherwise ineffective security personnel and found himself, after some florid dialogue at the entrance to the building. Stern security forces possessed only marginally motivated figures, many of them easily as bitter as he. Eager to find some equilibrium and a sponsor, Blake at last faced representatives of the riven sect. All of them, old and young, flushed or beardless, bearded or decrepit were tensely curled into positions of certain defiance.

Defiance Blake understood. He knew his way around. Without defiance you were back there in your kid's bedroom for the rest of your life, pleading out with small change every now and then to scuttle to a nearby movie before returning to fly under the radar again. Parental warnings, women's threats, the remorseless tears of virgins had given him significant life experience. "Here is why I am ready to assume the vacant position, here is why I am willing to be the Messianic figure to the generations," Blake began and went on from there, a little expressiveness here, some quotations of Isaiah or Jeremiah there, a doctrinal panache which he had accumulated with some difficulty accompanying his presentation. Blares of appeal, one syllable warnings of apocalypse in his absence, a bissel of Zephaniah. "You will excuse me, gentlemen," he said in conclusion, "I'm a trifle unsettled here. Just a little unsettled in the presence of what I know to be a major challenge, a real opportunity. I'm overwhelmed by the ambition to serve, I am doing the best I can."

This was certainly true, Blake had always done the best he could. This was Blake's most profound delusion, that he had fully applied himself, that no failure was from lack of definition. None of the hastily assembled court seemed interested in debating the issue with him; they sat in solemn accord, nodding their heads and looking at one another, this group of bearded men of indeterminate age and ambition, in ways more profound, more searching than the neglectful and largely dispossessed

Blake had suspected in a colorful lifetime. At length, one of them, after what appeared to be a flurry of consultation, spoke to him. "My name is Herschel," the man said irrelevantly. "I am 38 years old and I have been selected as the spokesman for this group. Reluctantly, I might note. This is not a task I would have willed. How did you get into these quarters? How long have you been at this?"

"At what?"

"Conversant with the needs of this sect. Interested in filling what you take to be a vacancy. Filled with ego but with no sense of identity. Angry but at a point of great submissiveness."

"Ah," Blake said, "I do not know."

"Poised at this phalanx of persuasiveness and doom. Have you always been this way? Or is it a recent development?"

"I don't know what you're talking about," Blake said earnestly, "I am concerned only with making a case for myself."

"Case for yourself," the man said. Blake's statement seemed to speak to him in some profound manner. Herschel's beard, a beard remarkably similar to all the other beards behind the raised table before which Blake stood penitent, trembled with knowledge or perhaps simple aggrandizement. "Why would you want to make a case for yourself? What of the Messianic codes, the conflicting views of Maimonides and the Kabbalists? Can you resolve them? And surely you do not think that you supersede them."

"I come not to supersede but to fulfill—"

"Are you Jewish?"

"Of course I'm Jewish," Blake said. "Do you think I'm stupid? Do you think that I'd come and ask for a job as your Messiah if I weren't Jewish? That would be ridiculous."

"But you are already ridiculous," Herschel said. "Of course that is part of your fundamental appeal. I would not deny that in any way. Pardon me for a moment while we consider this." He withdrew, motioned the others to gather. They filed away, sank into deep consultation. Hands fluttered, voices carried. Shouts, words of Yiddish barb. The two factions, he guessed, were battling, vision pitted against vision, and through it all, the solemn and hopeful Blake who waited with what he called in his own internal monologue, "an awful patience." Megillah, someone said. World to Come, said another. Prophetic fulfillment said a third. Embarrassment said fourth. Practical guidance, said someone else.

A vote was taken. "Very well," Herschel said briskly, returning, his features contorted by satisfaction. "Listen here, the Rabbi of blessed memory warned us that there would be conflicts, uncertainties. That rivalry would make it impossible to appoint a successor from within our ranks. That there would come then from the West or perhaps it was the East, an apostate who would seek the crown and that this crown would be given because only he could unite us. The Rabbi was quite definite on this point. Some of us ascribed his insistence upon an apostate, in fact the vision itself, to senility but here you are."

"Here I am," Blake said agreeably, "And here I will always be."

"Indeed," Herschel said. "The Rabbi, of blessed memory, was a *tzaddik*, a saint, a holy man, a worker of miracles, the Messiah himself, but some of us would believe that his visions were no more than senile imaginings, yet even they see the practicality of accepting you as the fulfillment of the great Rabbi's prophecy. What do you think, Blake? Do you truly want to be appointed?"

"What else do I have to do? What else would bring me here?"

"So," Herschel said, "So then, in accordance with the declaration of the Rabbi, you are so appointed. Why not? Why shouldn't you be? It so happens that we have only recently come to the decision that we must fill this appalling vacuum or lose all control of our destiny, not that it doesn't seem pretty well gone already. So this is clearly *hashgacha*, Divine Providence, the Holy One Blessed be His hand in our affairs. And no one else has stepped forward to fill the position."

"I accept," Blake said. The capitulation was so immediate that it shocked him but he managed to conceal that shock from the assembled or hoped that he had. He had never expected the procedure to go so quickly, he had imagined objections, responses, dim concordance in the corridors, the necessity to engage in disputation, examination of his genitalia, perhaps, for signs of the imposter. And here he was, so quickly given what had for so long been unclaimed, his every weakness a strength in the wake of the Rabbi's prophecy. Had the deceased Rabbi himself believed in anything he had ever said, or was it all politics, a way of withholding a planned succession which might have sped the Rabbi too soon on his way? Blake suspected that he would never know. "I'm grateful for that," he said, already considering his next move and finding with some surprise that whatever procedures he might have envisioned had so quickly departed. "Of course, it is going to take a while for me to figure out the best method for—" for what? "—for return."

"No problem," said Herschel.

"No problem," said the elders, all of whom seemed to have gathered voice. "*Iss gornicht*," Herschel said for all of them, "Just as long as you feel that you're doing right," and leaned forward to gather him in, Blake felt himself being gathered, felt something wondrous, felt something arched and poised within his heart that he had never before known to exist. The awful grasp, that enormous comity of the believers.

The gravitas and solemnity of responsibility, the mantle of leadership, gathering him in, swaddling him in its weight.

Well, then, was this what the Rabbi had felt, was this what had killed him? Of course the old man had been in his nineties but that kind of thing could kill a horse. A canyon of horses. All vacancy afforded, all locations dwelt, enfolded in such gigantic clutch, the in-gathered Blake felt himself to have become resplendent.

And in that condition, availing himself of the great privilege of his new position, he looked upon his brothers, those priests, inclined his head toward the beating of wings, the shine of timbrel, the clutched and clutching reach of the lost Rabbi himself. So close that their hands seemed to touch. Forget latter destiny, the Messiah dwelt behind, that had always been the secret, first the Messiah, then the quest for union. All of it simple, then.

Blake thought: I should have grasped this a long time ago. I have become the Rabbi, the Rabbi now me, the two of us so close. The two of us waiting and breathing in the unfurled cloak of the World To Come. Hanging from the great heaven itself.

Is this what the Rabbi felt as he waited for the ancient and repossessed times to begin? Could the Rabbi have known such longing, such posture? He thought of his parents and their endless, bleating call to sheephood, he thought of the women he had loved and lost and knew that their vision for him had been thwarted for this, his destiny. This was it, then, all part of another and greater plan, a magnificent construct to bring him, the suffering and astounded Blake, wholly beyond himself, slammed to his knees in this cavern on Eastern Parkway, waiting for the host of all hosts to thus bind him tightly, toss him to the throbbing and merciless stones below?

Was he Abraham's discovered lamb?

He gathered his people around him, their eyes fixed on him in trust and entreaty, dignity and purpose infusing his words. "It is time for *minyan*. Let us pray."

"*Barechu es Adonai hamevorach.* Come and bless the Lord." And the response: "*Baruch Adonai hamevorach l'olam va'ed.* Blessed is the Lord forever and ever."

—and thought, amid the chanting of Hebrew barely remembered, my oh my: if he had become a believer—in fact, the true believer—was this the only prophecy he would fulfill?

Blake sat contemplating the growing pile of *kvitlach* on the desk before him. The stream had been endless, a veritable Noah's flood of the anguished, the wretched, the riven and the pained. They sent their *kvitlach*, their tear-stained letters, typed, handwritten, scrawled on scraps of loose leaf or paper towel or yellow-legal or stationery, the litany of their woes. They came in person—they came on foot, by bus, by subway, by airplane. The lame and the halt in their multitudes, five years' worth of leaderless, Messiahless followers. With questions, their questions.

A blessing for my daughter, she just became a *kallah*, a bride. The young man, he wants to sit and learn in *yeshiva* and how will they make ends meet when the babies arrive—

My wife, she is staining and we have not touched for three years—

My father, he is terribly ill, can you say a prayer—

My grandson, *oy*, he has become an *apikores*, an apostate, he won't even keep kosher anymore—

My mother, my father, my sister, my brother, my soul, my sins, my *mitzvos*—

And the demands of the group. Decisions. Should the outreach house in Boise open a new branch, or should the money be directed to the new Synagogue in Geneva? Should they continue focusing on Sabbath candles for girls, or should they put a new spin on the campaign—maybe the kneading of *challah* dough or the wearing of longer skirts and sleeves? Leadership. Focus. Vision.

Miracles.

Blake's head was splitting, like the Red Sea, his eyes aflame like Moses' burning bush. The pleas, the hunger calling from the eyes of the disparate visitors, the women with wigs and stockings and squalling infants, the men with yarmulkas and sidelocks and Talmudic tomes, the entreaty through their words, through their prayers: Direction. Redemption.

It was time for a miracle. After all, what were Messiahs for anyway? Just to permit the staining women to touch their sex-starved husbands, to reassure the mother of the intermarried young man that her son had sanctified himself through love and anointed himself with the juices of his Catholic beloved as surely as Mama had anointed herself with the hallowed droplets of the mikvah? To move outreach houses and synagogues around the globe like monopoly pieces? To raise a hand in benediction, with Hebrew words barely remembered from pre-Bar Mitzvah Hebrew school, the slanting sunlight calling to him with the joyous shouts of his public school friends, free to bat the ball after school while he sat struggling with alien letters and ancient sounds?

Already the unrest had begun. New factions had sprung up, as brutal in their fire as the old. He is leading us away from the fold. He is overturning the holy Torah, he is sowing seeds of dissent and destruction. Who had, after all, really *heard* the original Rabbi speak of an apostate as his successor? A teacher who, in those last years, had spoken in riddles more convoluted and florid than the Talmud itself, than the legends of Rabbi Nehuniah ben Hakaneh? What kind of *heilige Yid*, holy Jew, would permit music on Sabbath and have tables overflowing with milk and honey—and meat? There was talk of overthrow, of replacement, a pale young Yeshiva student clamoring to take Blake's place.

But then there were the faithful, the devoted, the grateful, the wives freed of menstrual taint, the young men freed of masturbatory restriction, shyly investigating their circumcised trees of life without the burden of ancient guilt. A tiny but growing nexus of the redeemed.

Was this not enough, thought Blake? One by one, was this not the path of God Himself?

But, gazing at the pile of white and grey and yellow paper, like late winter slush, he knew the answer. He knew.

Being a Messiah meant more, had to mean more, or it was a job as tedious, as dreary, as spiritless, as the nine-to-five that his parents and circumstance had imposed, as the women had imposed, that dreary, blurred succession of breasts and limbs and complaint. Plenty of trouble in the here and now but at least it had raised him to a kind of glorious sufficiency, and Blake felt a kind of assurance which had never before been his.

Because being a Messiah meant grandeur, right? Wasn't that the best part of it? Addressing the masses. Miracles. Transcendence. That light, that aura, that in-gathering of those early moments of his appointment.

Redemption.

It was time to call for a *fabreghen*, a gathering. An assembly of all the faithful to bear witness to the rebirth of the movement.

The word had gone out amongst the faithful. The leader, the new Messiah, was convening the multitudes. There were snickers, guffaws on the part of the anti-Blakers, there were fervent little protests on the part of the Blake devotees, there was a general air of unrest, of curiosity, of excitement and anticipation. They knew, the holy assembly, that they were on the verge of a great and final revelation, a miracle which would vault them beyond the confines and dictates of history to the Land of Promise—not the ersatz and secular Israel, but the true and needful *geulah*, deliverance. Redemption.

The men, black-suited and white-shirted, their hair a tapestry of sidelocks and silken skullcaps, the women behind the tall partition quieting their squalling infants and dangling toys before their uncomprehending, restless toddlers, the masses thronging the assembly hall, waiting for the words, the deeds, that would transform and transmogrify history, destiny, existence itself.

And before them, Blake: five foot six, solemn countenance, yarmulka in adornment, his posture of the utmost gravity, his hands outstretched like the very eagle wings of divine promise.

He considered the situation. The pressing crowds, the multitudes assembled outside, men on one side of the street and women on the other, a few curious reporters from *The New York Times* and *The Daily News*, a scattering of Modern Orthodox with knitted yarmulkas and Reform Jews with no yarmulkas at all, and a Catholic priest for good measure. All eyes, all hearts, all souls fixed upon him. Blake. Blake the Messiah.

"*Shalom Aleichem.*" That much Hebrew he remembered. More, though, he needed more. "*Baruch ata, amen.*" There. That was Hebrew, was it not? Now time for some Yiddish. "*Eppis, shaine bochur, yiddene.*" So far so good.

Or was it? A new restlessness, a murmur as people looked to each other. Blake found himself sweating. They were waiting for inspiration, for guidance, for the promised miracle and all reposed within him, Blake, this ordinary, shiftless, disaffected Jew with no particular credentials. A disappointment to his parents (Papa had died years ago, but was Mama even here today to *shep nachas*, and to *kvell* over the glory of her son's position? Or the troops of women who had toppled his frail entreaties, turned away his fragile attempts, women who knew that he "would never amount to anything." Well, what would they say now?)

Oh ye, yes: the women. Where were they now? They could be here, perhaps they were, he could sense them leaning, peering at him from their position behind the partition. Well, he would give them a better look at what was going on.

"Take it down!" He pointed. "The *mechitzah*." A spectacular word he must have learned someplace after all, the ritual barrier between the sexes.

Pandemonium. What was he saying? Heresy! Promiscuity! *P'ritzus!* Removal of the barrier and what next? *Hefkeirus?* Entropy, chaos?

"Take it down, take it down, smash the false gods as Abraham did with his father's idols, as Moses did with the tablets, as Joshua did with the walls of Jericho."

Now there, at last, was language they understood. A murmur swept the crowd as the walls were disassembled and moved away, the women blinking into the sudden glare of unwonted exposure.

And oh, at this unlikely and sanctified moment, Blake felt it. That organ, that damned vehicle of covenant and inconstancy, suddenly surging to life at the sight of all those women with their hats and their wigs and their stockings and sleeves and infants.

It shook, it rocked with sudden melody, it rose and called and sang and then Blake knew what he must do. The call of the Shofar, the cry of the Rabbi across the barrier, the heat of the male bodies and female bodies and infant bodies crowing and crowding and steaming and praying.

Oh boy, he knew then.

Blake chose to dance. Easy does it. A slow, chanting, swaying at first, then faster, wilder, Elijah's whirlwind, the thunder of Sinai, the fire of the Chariot. The shouting and the stamping of the crowd, the goats unchained, as they, too, began to move. Homage to the Rabbi at last and his prophecy fulfilled, all the dreadful witness to that mystical, final dance: I believe with perfect faith in the coming of the Messiah.

The mountains danced like goats, the valleys leaped like lambs in spring, the earth labored and travailed and from the dervish of coiling bodies, that flaming, shuddering serpent of light.

The Only Thing You Learn
In Memory of Cyril M. Kornbluth

Hello, voyager. You come into the bar cautiously, not looking for trouble but ready for anything that you might find, you tell yourself, the token in your left pocket emitting its precious waves of secret and solace as you squeeze it, then let it go. Your posture is poised toward ruin but ready for flight. You are neat and fleet, ready for anything, but willing to stay and fight it out too if you must. There at the end of your bar is the target, just as they had promised in the dusky half-light of the Seven Moons, your target in sailor cap and shapeless jacket, drinking red top and beer chaser wedged in that corner, his eyes curiously alight. You are drawn to him instinctively, not only by the sense of mission you must undergo, but by that necessity in his eyes, you tell yourself that you have never seen anyone quite as open, as charmed, as *needful* as this man whose glance now passes from you disinterestedly, swinging left to right, then down to the shot-glass as he shrugs and drinks. Three hookers in working garb are scattered on the right side of the bar as you approach, none of them displaying any interest in the target—or in anything else—as you glide past, on the other side there are two drunken bums, their heads in their hands, listening to the private and integral sounds of their consciousness, whiskey glasses drained before them. The bartender looks at you incuriously as you come down the line of stools on the left, past the drunken bums, and take your seat beside the target. His sailor cap is oddly peaked, his brown eyes alight with something other than inebriation, but he does not seem willing to make eye contact and in that furious, broken instant during which you assess the situation, you think that despite the assurances of the ancient ones, their pledge that nothing can possibly go wrong, you might have once again, voyager, taken yourself over your head, entered a situation you cannot resolve. It is difficult to say.

What he's having, you tell the bartender who is looking at you. And buy him a round too.

Money, the bartender says. Joint like this, you put your money on the bar *first*. Rules of the house. In his voice is the stentorian sound of the Reptiles; he seems to be vocalizing in their ancient and frightening tongue. Of course they would have put an agent in here, they would allow no corner of the sector to be unoccupied, undefended against precisely this kind of immersion. You do not let this knowledge frighten you.

Of course, you say. In your right pocket, the strange coins and bills seem to emit a strange warmth, something like that of the token but occupying their own heat and substance. You thrust your palm in there, remove a handful, shake them out on the bar in an indiscriminate outpouring. The bartender retreats a little at the sound of the coins, then fixes you with an unwavering gaze. Beside you, the target sits unmoving.

Is that enough? you say.

The bartender shifts, tilts a hand in an either-or gesture, limps back along the railing, and obtains glasses. You hear for the first time the thin racket from the television set above the bar, a comedy of some kind turned down very low, the old black-and-white television hazed toward a kind of omnipresent blur, the figures of the actors only dimly visible. From the television set comes the quiet sound of shrieking which may be part of the live audience in attendance but then again might be the interior of your own astonished and trapped heart, fluttering against the walls of your being. The hookers glance at the television set now and then, the drunken bums pay no attention whatsoever, being too deeply drawn into their own substance, you think, to be concerned with decor. Beside you, the target raises his glass, drains the last of the beer, shakes his head, then stares at you as the bartender comes banging down the rail, places shot-glasses before you, contemptuously up-ends a bottle and fills them with orange liquid. What do you want? the target says.

Your instructions have been very specific. You adhere to them at all perilous costs. That is up to you, my friend, you say. The bartender goes away, returns with two trembling glasses of beer, places them in front of you, takes coins and bills, moves away. The token sends out odd glares of heat from its hidden place. What do you think I want? you say.

I know who you are, the target says. There is no preamble to this statement, no edging into it, the aspect is one of shocking bluntness. You had been warned that this would probably be the case, the target has been pushed far, far beyond the rim of his patience. You're one of them. You're part of *them*. Another one come to torment me, to haunt.

You say nothing. It is time to drink, to put the liquid and its chaser into you, to obtain as much as possible the riot of their own chemistry. You do this, quickly and solemnly, fixing the target with your hopeful and sparkling gaze as the chill and warmth begin to spread through you and then the target does the same, drinking quickly and convulsively, slamming shot-glass and then beer on the counter.

Lies, he says, it's all lies. It's all part of the same swindle. Give me the feeling that I'm at the center of things but I'm *not*. I'm not. You're just using me for something I can't even understand and I don't know—

He stops. It is as if the speech, extracted from him in wrenching syllables, has astonished not its auditor but the target himself. Your instructions on this possible reaction are also quite clear. You have, within the limits of the situation, been given the most explicit procedures and it is within your responsibility to follow it or to face your own terrible penalty.

I'm not one of them, you say now. I'm from the other side. I've come to offer you surcease. Freedom, possibly. The means of freedom rest within your hands. It is within your means.

You look at the target calmly, seriously, while the target finishes the contents of the shot-glass and the beer, then waves his arms at the bartender. Enough of this, he says. I'm getting out. I'm checking out. I'm in over my head here but I have the sense to know it.

You know nothing, you say. Nothing at all. You don't even have the language to express your lack of knowledge. You feel the rage and disgust coming upon you, just as had been predicted, but still, within you, there is the terrible, serene knowledge with which you carried yourself back across the centuries.

Here, you say. Here.

You reach into your left pocket, remove the token, place it on the gleaming surfaces of the bar. It lies there in its phosphorescent glare, leaking power, hints of the millennia and its wastes glinting from it. Even the hookers seem to be entranced, gaining sudden respect for this colloquy, they stare at you and the target with new interest. The drunken bums, oblivious of this as the Reptiles themselves, continue to brood and nod in their vomitous stupor. The bartender, respectful, flicks a towel at the television set and observes all of this with great patience. It is fortunate that this is a neighborhood bar in a bad area and that incoming traffic is light to nonexistent because it is not clear how the token would deal with new entrants or how, for that matter, they would deal with this unleashed power.

Here, you say. Here it is. The sign of the centuries. Reach out. Take it in your hand.

The target looks at the token with an intensity as to minimize your own attention through all of this. You have never, in all of your experience, seen an attentiveness like this. Are you crazy? the target says. You want me to touch that. He gestures at the token. Touch *that*. He recoils, his arms flailing again. Get out of here, he says. Get out of here now. That thing can explode. It can destroy the world. It can—

Why don't you try it? you say. See what it can do. You put an exploratory finger on the token, push it toward the target. Small rays of power seem to pour from it and strike the target in the eyes although this may be illusory. You have been carefully warned about the phenomena in this place, how the surreal, the imagined, the extant can mingle in dangerous and unpredictable fashion.

Anyway, you say, it's up to you. It's your decision. It rests in your hands. The decision is yours.

You stand, your instructions completed, and adjust your clothing, then move slowly down the arc of the bar, moving without urgency but determination toward the door, the bartender now saying, Hey, mister, come back here. You can't leave that thing here. You *can't*—

Yes I can, you say. I can and I must. Behind you, you hear the target beginning to murmur, then scream as the terrific heat of the token, now unleashed by instruction, absorbs him, but you will have nothing of this. Abandoning caution in the rising clamor behind, you sprint toward the door, then out, the strange, swaddling air of this planet gripping you as you stumble toward the checkpoint. Behind, you hear voices, louder and louder sounds, sudden screams, then the *whump!* of great flame and ignition but you do not turn. Oh, you do not turn. You have absorbed your lessons well, terror of the reptiles no less than dedication to your duties impels you as you sprint toward the rendezvous point. Enormous, transmogrified, the target and his cohorts behind you scream for you to stop but it is too late for them, perhaps too late for you as well as you feel the bowl of circumstance closing tightly around you. Oh, voyager, we had it planned this way from the start. The rendezvous will never occur; here you were detailed, here you stay. Be lost, voyager. You shriek with a rage to match that of your target as now, at last and as predicted, the hundred years of fire begin.

Police Actions

"You countrymen," the general said, "so good-hearted, so sincere, so convinced of your righteousness, so clumsy and devoted in all of your duties and for these reasons the most wicked and dangerous nation who ever worked out a policy." He took a sip of wine, motioned to the waiter for a check, smoothed lint from his fatigues (retired, he still came to our cafe in combat gear, prepared for the destabilization which might occur at any time), sighed. "It is not so much that self-righteousness that makes you such a complicated and mesmerizing factor," he said, "for that, we must address your love of pornography and the censor alike, of damnation and religious revivals, of urban retrieval and urban destruction, those marvelous contradictions embedded in your history and responses that you work out so catastrophically on helpless subjects like ourselves." He sighted an imaginary pistol, pulled the trigger with insouciant grace. *Boom!* "Someday I would like to come to your country, see your enclaves, harass your women," the general said. "Of course someday I would like to ski Switzerland, learn Esperanto, foment a true revolution of the spirit overseas. We do not get what we want, *n'est-ce pas?*" The waiter leaned to whisper confidentially while, politely, we looked away although we could sense the urgent sibilance of information dutifully given. "Of course, of course," the general said, "these warnings are unnecessary. My good friends here know I am merely speculating, talking idly, the ravings of a peculiar old man in the sun-spattered café of an occupied and defeated country. Is that not so?" He grinned. We made conciliatory, noncomplicitous gestures. In the square, the birds lofted as if in response to rifle fire.

It is difficult to sort out matters in the midst of self-protection.

But the general was only one of the many counselors and advisors we met in our wanderings that year. It was a restless time, a time to seek some balance, some vaulting perspective that might protect us against the strange new times at home. It was not that we were in flight, we assured ourselves, not flight so much as a search for accommodation with those urgent, millennial versions of ourselves that were coming. The general was one of the curiosa, one of the exhibits of the tour, and he struck us, as perhaps he knew, as being a kind of bad example, a representation of an embittered general in a defeated country overrun and humiliated by our superior firepower. But unlike most of the defeated, he retained his insouciance, not to say a certain style which we found illuminating.

Afterward, later this was, when we had obtained some kind of control over the situation and our emotions, our waiter recognized us on the street and sprinted over. All those months since he had served us and yet his recall was perfect. Out of uniform, he seemed both taller and undefined, a set of features in search of attitude. "Do let me apologize for the general," he said, seizing one of us by the elbows in a gesture combining obsequiousness and insistence in a peculiar way. He is not himself. He is a poor representation of the man he was; he has not been well for many years. He dreams of the invasion, takes responsibility for its outcome, feels that had he performed differently, commanded firmly, showed determination in the eyes of the enemy there would have been a different outcome. The poor man takes no note of ordnance, of superior firepower. He is quite mad, do you understand? There is no other way to explain this."
Standing there, shouting these explanations so fervently, the waiter-in-mufti seemed to be an emblem of what we must have sought on these tours, some proof then that the world was so disordered, so filled with private grief and misapprehension that we simply were not responsible. We bore no blame for what had happened, let alone for the future. But none of this enabled us to deal better with the waiter, who at last had to be dragged off by security monitors, his voice having become enormous, threatening, appalling. Dragged away at high speed by loyal troops, he gesticulated wildly, gestures oddly those of a man displaying handfuls of silverware, plates of appetizer, he seemed motivated in ways both unique and characteristic. But this of course was not for us to meditate on; darkness came to the city, and instructions were issued that we should be in the hotel long before that hammer of dusk struck. The country is under control and yet there is no way of accounting for the private treacheries of the irresponsible in the unpatrolled corridors of their city.

The "we" is not a narrative device, not a provincialism. It is a literal expression. At this post-millennial time, we had come together in the first true shock of purpose and had come to understand that not only was there preservation in our number but that individual identity was dangerous. Identity, that curious and reflexive advancement of the self, had proved again and again to be the source of so much of our trouble; with the assertion of individual demands came exposure, flight, desire, entrapment and sometimes dreadful retaliation. It was the collective *we* that would bear salvation, and so our little group had massed that spring to bury our histories and idiosyncrasies in a shared, compassionate circumstance. We would go through the continents as a conglomerate and show our enemies that there was a different kind of countryman, a humble and quasi-autonomous collective rather than the prideful and dangerous adventurers cursed by the general. *We* is not to be construed as *I*; there is for the intent of these memoirs no *I* at all, and it is surely this reserve, this calm and dedicated ascendancy of the group that matters. We are not like the others. We are the post-millennial example of the New Country, and it is in that spirit that we went forth, put up with abominable hotels, insolent agents, rifle fire at dusk, obscene and terrifying notes left in our quarters and other paraphernalia and exemplification of the brutal state of our world.

Earlier, before his denunciation, the general had led us on a tour of his beloved city, his own quarters, the markets which until recently had been so colorful and filled with pulsing energy, now closed by the obdurate curfew. "This is what you have done," the general said, "you must take responsibility for this. No one else can be blamed." His gestures were forceful, enormous, determined; this was at a time when we had not yet quite taken him for mad and gave credence to his bearing, his thunderous denunciations. "Some admission, some partial confession might have saved a lot of trouble," he pointed out.

There was nothing to say to this. We had been under strict orders from embarkation. No prolonged contact, no real conversations with the populace. We could not be prevented from traveling nor assuming a collective identity, but we were under close orders. *Do not jeopardize our reputation*. Even among ourselves, conversation was brief, and what relationships we had were furtive, cursed with hostility, impotence and real fear. Meant to cling, we found ourselves atomized at this time, the need for a composite self driving us further into inner cells of necessity.

"You sicken me," the general said. "I dismiss, I denounce, I renounce you utterly." He made a threatening gesture, yet from his eye darted a complicitous wink. "I am only playing," that wink said, "I am acting the role of a disaffected military leader of a defeated country in order to enhance your tour of what you regard as some back lot of reality. At any moment, I am prepared to tell dirty stories of my people."

Or were we reading too much into that tic? It is difficult to tell at such distance. We find our way these days into recollection even more laboriously than we forge for a future; pinned amongst absolutes we become ever more cautious with the accumulation of time. This is my theory.

"And such is my renunciation," the general added. He saluted.

Impelled by some larger perspective of my own, I winked in return. The general appeared startled.

"Come, come," the tour guide said. Our guide, native in all cases and indigenous to the culture, is that anomaly: a credible outsider permitted by agencies to take responsibility for our lives. "Enough of this. Let us go on." We wandered toward the boarded marketplace. There seemed to have been much implied by this exchange, but at such a distance it is hard to sort any of it out.

We must avoid at all costs the delusion that we are the occupying force," I cautioned my companions during one of our few unsupervised moments on tour. "We are not our government, we are not responsible for its acts. In fact, we are in flight from our government, we are a neutral, observing force seeking independence from our leaders. We reject guilt. *We* are not the conquerors. None of this was our decision, none of it was of our making; we have no connection to it at all." I could see their disbelief. The speech was not going over well. In every eye too I could see the image of complicity, in every curious and attending feature, a slash of recrimination. In the hammering of the engines drawing us toward the gate, I could hear grenades. "None of this is our fault," I said, but my voice sounded flat and unconvincing, sounded that shrill and defensive tone which I had heard in official addresses and which made it impossible, no matter how fast and determined our flight, to escape identification.

In the lobby, we gathered around our guide. "I must tell you to watch for ordnance, for sudden attack," he said. "You must keep to yourselves and remain alert at all times. There are threats; I cannot be more specific than that, but you would be advised, *well* advised, to stay indoors. We are arranging for a flight to the capital and from there direct to the southernmost part of the continent; this will be best for you, best for all of us. There are problems," he said, "which cannot be disregarded, and we are trying to save the situation if possible. For the moment, we advise you to stay indoors, although civil authority cannot force you."

There were murmurs not so much of fear but outrage, then the babbling questions. Why, why? Why were they focused upon us? We were, if anything, delegates in contravention of the ugly policies they hated. "I am not authorized to answer," the guide said, "but I can tell you that there are some who have found aspects of your statements to be altogether defensive, and in their defensiveness they confirm a sense of outrage. No one can account for the responses of a large population, a difficult, subordinate and defeated country such as this, but there is,

I must tell you, a good deal of anger and it is felt that it might go out of control."

There might have been a good deal more—our guide was well launched and his pleasant, pedagogical features seemed to be adjusting toward an ever more detailed explanation despite his claimed reluctance to analyze—but it was at that moment that the appalling flashes of heat and light began. The artificial plants in the lobby liquified. This disconcerted the clerks, and the ceiling collapse which followed seemed somehow implied by their disorder; the collapse was of such stunning and flabbergasting force as to make further exchanges, even of the most knowledgeable kind, impossible.

Of the aftermath, of the shocks and disasters that sped some of us more deeply into the times ahead while hastening others so quickly out of the millennium, there is little to report; our own awareness is necessarily dim, comes back only in small fragments and hints of recovery. But it has been handled so well, laid out with such documentary insistence by the journalists that none of this should be at all necessary.

No, none of that. We merely felt that you would appreciate a report from the interior, a report from a survivor who can claim to have tried so fervently—if with so little appreciation—to give a different impression of a country that has been so severely misunderstood and whose latter days I now suspect are going to be filled with such difficulty.

I did the best I could to tell the tale.

II

This was the year of Polar Star.

Polar Star was the emblem under which the divided city would be made whole again, the under- and over-classes stitched into a pleasing tapestry of bright and concordant hue in which the infrastructure would bring its own renewed spaces to bind. Polar Star was the accord toward which all of us had struggled for these decades, and now, at last, the restoration would begin.

Oh yes, this was the year of glowing and ambient parties filled with the sound of theremin, heavy percussion, the whisk of invisible dancers. How we stared from the secluded and heavily guarded roofs of the structures which had been safe, how we stared upon the city! How we watched the stars wink and dazzle, the beams of apparatus casting sullen light into the hidden spaces. How long could this polarization continue? we wondered. Sleek in their hidden places, the breasts of privileged women would bounce and bounce while we turned our tortured, more concernedly academic perspective to the teeming, unknown places beneath and said, "Unless there is some attempt to bind these enclaves, we are doomed. We will no longer be able to afford our lives." That was the year Polar Star was to make its first administrative conceptualizations under the Federal banner.

And was then delayed. The new President announced a "moratorium" to consider all Federal agenda. (Although we knew what he really had in mind, the real focus of the delay.) That was the year that Polar Star was to swing open the gates that partitioned us, but instead the hearings disclosed a massive, almost uncontrollable diversion of funds away from Polar Star and into the tributaries of the contractors. Protection, the integrity of the process demanded that the project be put on hold until all corruption had been isolated and controlled, or so the President announced. This was wise thinking, good politics, and all of us—liberal, conservative, reconstructionist and rebellious alike—could do nothing other than accept the agenda. Some were fervid, others were reluctant. Some were highly qualified. A few abstained, fearing the effects of delay. But our sympathies throughout remained with the aims, the ideal of Polar Star. It was only the practice that had sparked those fires of division.

That was the time in which we at last abandoned the idea of "underclass." The sociology of our generation, the fury and anguish surrounding the millennium had purged us of such stereotypes. "There is no underclass," we said to one another. "The 'underclass' is a myth; the term 'underclass' was invented to rationalize oppression." There were, we agreed, only various versions of ourselves, trapped in contesting versions of our own lives, some of them seemingly with no end of travail, others with means of flight or assimilation. Assimilation was our goal under Polar Star. "There will be no 'underclass,'" the manifestos and curricula had stated. "There will be no 'overclass' either. There will be no 'ruling class.' There will be the leveling of difference, the accession of opportunity."

The plans were elaborate, blueprinted; model cities soared into history at the Exposition under the Polar Star banner. We were committed to that goal. It was only the means that defied us, the means by which the old squalor of corruption and kickback, leverage and connection were influential. Under the circumstances, that moratorium was inevitable. We congratulated ourselves upon our willingness to accept the hard and heavy truths of the situation. After our abandonment of stereotypes, after our willingness to accept shared humanity, renewed responsibility, nothing seemed beyond us. The delay of Polar Star was worrisome. There was no question about this. But that delay was only in the interests of a smooth and proficient, an incorruptible and smoothly functioning operation. We were sure of this. We had confidence in our leaders. Newly elected, newly installed, departing the dock of the millennium into the strange and dangerous waters ahead, the President was our coxswain, his gallant associates, the crew and we, we were the landscape toward which they so energetically moved.

That was the year of the easy lay, the quick seduction, the restoking and reassembly of desire, the quick surfacing of new possibilities. Polar Star had made us fluid, had made us come to understand that soon enough all would be entitled to the pursuit of happiness, that barriers outside would fall and, responsively, the barriers of limitation would fall within. Sexual transmission of disease was no longer a factor: all who were going to die had done so, studies assured us. Would soon enough assure us. Reassured then by the most respectable journals of medicine, we were out for a good time. In that year, bouncing and neatly jouncing at our parties, moving our pieces of paper, assigning LED codes at our functional spaces, we had the feeling of being on the lip of massive resolution, of participating in the last period of human strife before true accord. We held breasts tentatively to our lips and made intelligent, concerned sounds as nipples slowly pursed. Cocks and cunts intertwined gracefully in the arbors patrolled by respectful silent security and automatic dogs. A hundred virgins a night fell to the swords of desire.

That was the year Dora became pregnant as an expression of affirmation, as a statement of hope for the metropolis itself. "I will raise my child in Clifton," she said, "I will put her on hobbyhorses in the playground, nurse her openly in Central Park, teach her to read from the graffiti in public facilities. She will be a child of the city and she will flourish." Dora's husband, a sculptor and solemn bureaucrat in the Western division of Polar Star, grinned. In his little eyes glistened querulousness, then panic, then—as we stared—a kind of numbed assent, this being after all the reaction so many had at that time. Numbed assent was what we felt in that year as we huffed and puffed, humped and jumped, played and wooed at our protected parties, waiting for the walls to come down, waiting for the winds of the metropolis to blow across while knowing at the same time that these enclosures were perhaps the best of all spaces we could inherit and Polar Star, which held such promise, also held a kind of portent with which even the most imaginative of us could barely contend.

That was the year before the full extent of the scandals was known. At that time it seemed they were localized, contained, that Polar Star essentially lay intact and that it was only the modus operandi that corrupt elements had compromised. Little did we know the dimensions of the difficulty, or that in the months following how the extent of debasement and venery would be displayed from every basement, every fax, every sideways ticker. In our essential innocence, and it is important to note that we were innocent, that it was not malevolent, that even our seductions, our sexual pledges, our lies and misgroupings were only a function at worst of immaturity and unwillingness to grasp the consequences, we thought that the structure was reparable, that there were ways in which it could be made to last and that it was possible for the process to work.

We were good people. We were not, we felt, malevolent. If Dora was stupid, she certainly wished the throngs beyond the security gates no harm. If she romanticized what she could not see, she did not have the heart of an assassin. We *all* felt this way, that we were good people, that Polar Star was the expression of our goodness and health and decency. In those months before the full extent of misdeed had been exposed, we still believed in the possibility of concord because it came from that belief in ourselves. We had been born that way, educated toward that end all our lives.

How could we have known otherwise?

And that was the year too of odd premonitions. Gliding against one another in the huge and glowing heart of those parties, listening to the distant sounds, watching the tongues of flame to the north and south of us, we would feel the thickening waters of remorse and morning apprehension, feel that slow, clamping stir in the gut which signaled our mortality. Smile as we might, commit ourselves as we could to the coxswain, there were moments for all of us on those rooftops and later in the thick enclosures of our bedrooms when we saw another vision of the metropolis, when we struggled from dreams in which Polar Star had been obliterated, done in by its own sentimentality and manipulation, and we had nothing, nothing to stand between us and the disaster but the certainty and purity of our hearts. We had good hearts. We had been raised to be good people. We knew we were good. We knew that the others for whom Polar Star had been conceived were good also, and that was why we would no longer use that pejorative term, "underclass." We knew that our motives and theirs were confluent and benign, but we could not nonetheless keep that clamp from the gut, the fold from the unspeaking heart.

For we knew. We must have known. We could not forever shield our plans from our plans. But how we tried! We tried and tried. We were good people. We had the larger interests of the country at heart.

That was the year before the year in which the gunfire and the huge lights winked and blazed, roared and stumbled, the year before that time when parties became hopeless and we were forced to consider the unavailing manner of all options.

It was the time before that clangorous summer when Dora said to any of us who would listen, "We lied and lied, we talked our way around everything. We all knew, but we never said even to ourselves what Polar Star was." How could that be, though? How could we have known what Polar Star was? It was urban retrieval gone wrong, that was all, the best of motives, leading only to the worst of outcome. None of this had been planned. Desperate measures led to desperate responses, but this was not the coxswain's original intention.

"Murderers," Dora said, "we're all killers, we set this up, we pulled this lousy job." But that was after the miscarriage and its pathetic aftermath, and by this time Dora was clearly not sane. It was possible to discount everything she said. It was, in fact, necessary to make that discount.

And so we did. We ignored her. We were polite, tolerant, we did not wish to ostracize, but at the same time we were firm. "Listen," we said, "we are decent, we are good, we are sensible people." Our voices were firm, our faces judicious and tolerant. "We had no choice, no control," we added. "Besides, the word 'underclass' remains out of our lexicon." And so it did. We were not pejorative. We were kind people. We had full awareness.

So we were good to Dora, as good as could be under the circumstances, and we protected her as best we could from her own self-destructiveness. We looked forward to the time when Polar Star would permit us to take down the gates and reclaim all of our city. *Our* city.

"Killers," Dora screamed. But the sculptor had left her, *all* of us, in exhaustion, had left her, really. She was almost impossible to tolerate, and no matter how great our ingestion of palliatives, she still appeared ugly.

Kingfish

Every man a king, every king a saint, each and every one of us on our own piece of holy ground. That's what he said. That's what he said to the little guy in Berlin. I was there at the picture-taking after the private conferences, I could hear what Huey said to him over the sounds of the reporters, the hammer of the flashbulbs. Just look this way, boss. You and me and cousin Henry, Aunt Anna and Moses down the lane, there's a glory for each of us and it can be yours too. The little guy kind of jumped and twitched when Huey squeezed him on the shoulder. The interpreter was yammering away in that German of his, but somehow I think the little guy got the message already. He knew more English than he let on. He knew a lot more stuff than he let on about everything.

What do you say there, Adolf? Huey said, and gave an enormous wink. I could have dropped my teeth on the floor. You think we can get this rolling, just the two of us? Hey John, Huey said, motioning to me, don't stand there like a stupe on the sidelines, join the photo session. This here is my vice president, Huey said to the little guy.

The little guy said something in Huey's ear, up close. That's right, Huey said. That, too. He's everybody's vice president. He is the second in command, isn't that right? He gave me a Louisiana-sized wave, clasped my hand. Holding his hand that way, backing into the Fuhrer, I had the little guy boxed against Huey. We had him in perfect position, trapped. We could have stood and tossed him over the Reichstag. But we didn't, standing there frozen in the eye of the world, the press roaring, the sounds drifting around us and in that small abyss Huey squeezed my hand for attention and gave one perfect, focused wink. *Got him*, the wink said. *Got him, didn't I tell you?*

Got you too.

This was the meeting in the Bayou in November of 1935, the famous secret meeting. Never mind where. Huey's boys got to me and said be in Amarillo at midnight and leave the rest to us. We'll get you past the border and leave the delegation at home. It was easy to get away, I was back home for Christmas then. The president wouldn't even have known I had blown town. It had gotten harder and harder to get Roosevelt's attention; it wasn't even worth trying anymore. Now and then I had fantasies of sneaking behind his wheelchair during the State of the Union and pulling the podium away, showing his shrunken parts to the world. But I never would have done that. Damn near would never have done anything if Huey hadn't gotten in touch. Came into the parish humping my way in a big black car, it could have been Capone's chauffeur up there in front, the guys with me in the back Capone's party boys: But I wasn't scared. Who shoots the vice president? Easier to park him under a rug and let him die. I'm going to go for it, Huey said to me. This isn't to bullshit you, I'm coming straight out. I'm running for president.

That's no surprise, I said. It wasn't. The word had been out for years, this Senator wasn't running around Washington for the graft, filibustering for the sake of opening his yap. *Every man a king*. He wanted to be president, all right. If not Roosevelt, then why not him? But Roosevelt seemed to have the banged-out vote pretty well sewed up. I told Huey that. You can't run as the man of the people against this guy, I said, he knows the people too well. He's a sitting president. You'll just have to wait your turn.

I'm not waiting my turn, Huey said. Up close he was intense, even more so than on the radio. There was something in his eyes, something in the set of his body that made you not want to explore his depths. All of this was in a room one-on-one, he wanted no one in there with us. After I got shot at, Huey said, grabbing his arm, I got this insight. There's no sense waiting. You wait, you're just as likely to die. Two inches either way on the gun hand and the guy wouldn't have gotten me in the shoulder, he would have had me in the heart. I would have died there on the Capitol floor.

I know all about it, I said. I read the papers too.

You read a hell of a lot more than the papers, Huey said. You don't pull that dumb cowboy shit on me, John Nance Garner, you're the Vice President of the United States and no goddamned fool. I was calculating, let him have the two terms and run in 1940. But when I saw the blood spouting out of my arm, heard the screaming, saw that cocksucker lying dead on the floor instead of me, I said what the fuck is this? This is all bullshit. I'm making plans, biding my time, while the man on the plow is dying and I could have been dead. I'm going for it now.

That's your prerogative, I said. You've got a tough one ahead of you. But I can wish you well. I got no quarrel with you.

Maybe you should, Huey said. You Texans, you think we're all a bunch of savages and Cajun voodoo lovers here. Or grave robbers. But if you can take it, I can. I want you to run with me, he said. That's the only way. You run with me, we can split him away.

Run with you? I said. You're crazy. Bolt the party, give up the office?

Who said to give up? Huey said. You're Vice President. You're a constitutionally elected official, you're in as solid as him. He can't impeach you and it's only eleven months until the election anyway.

Instead of running as a Democrat you run with me as an Independent. I don't want to go in the party anyway.

Never heard of anything like it, I said. I have to tell you, I was astounded. Ever since that thirty-hour stem-winder in the Senate when Huey had worked with applejack and a tin can strapped to his leg to stop the government cold while he argued the budget and the Book of Genesis and a hundred other things, I had known he was a man to reckon with, no one to underplay, but this was something entirely new This went outside my experience. Shit, I said, you're crazy.

So I'm crazy, Huey said. You think I'm out of place here? It's all crazy. We got ourselves a country in collapse, we got ourselves a situation that won't quit. Got thirty million men wandering the roads of America, ready to kill for a slice of bread, got thirty million women who would hump for the price of an apple or some clothes for the baby. Think it's going to turn around? Think again. We're in critical times, boy. It's all falling apart on us. It's time for someone to take over who cares for the people.

Frank cares for the people, I said. In his way.

His way, Huey said. He gave me that smile, opened his mouth, showed me all the lovely white and open spaces. Just two guys on the Bayou talking sense, he said. Got all the doors closed. Want some whiskey? I got me a bottle of the finest here. He busted Prohibition, I'll give your guy that.

I don't care, I said. I never turned down any whiskey. Huey took a bottle from inside his coat, opened it, passed it to me. Here, he said. Got compunction? Want a glass?

Never heard of that, I said. I took a swig deep down—not bad stuff— and handed it over. You serious? I said. You really mean it?

Sure I mean it, he said. If you come over, I figure we got this election. It all falls into place. You've made a considered judgment, that's it. You're going with the real man of the people. Franklin will have a fit but what can he do? Maybe he can get Lehman to run with him. Two New York kikes, Huey said, and took a swig and giggled. Not that I got anything against kikes, he said. Kikes and shines and Micks and Polacks, hunkies and Cajuns and Injuns and all the rest of them, they're all the soul of the country. But I want this to be a done deal, I don't want to fool around. I want your commitment *now*, and then we'll go on from there.

And then what? I said. How do I go back to Washington and face the man?

You don't have to face him. You can stay on the ranch. You're constitutionally elected, remember? There's nothing he can do to you. We'll wait a couple of months, then we'll hold a joint press conference and announce.

Not Democrat, I said. You want to go third party.

Right, Huey said. He looked at the bottle, shrugged, took another sip. We could probably beat him in the party if we went out for it but we'd bust it wide open and then he'd probably go third party on *me* and split the thing.

No, we'll do it ourselves. The money is there. Don't worry about the money. Just have my ass there, I said, that's what you're telling me?

That's what I'm telling you, he said. Listen, you don't like this guy anyway. That's no secret. And I'll tell you something, all right? He held the bottle out to me. I shook my head. (They have me down for a drunk but it is all part of their misunderstanding. No one goes as far as John Nance Garner has by being a simple drunk. Of course there are other factors.) Here it is, Huey said. I want to be a one-term president, that's all. I'll step aside in '40. You can have it then.

You got it all figured out, I said. What a generous offer.

I'm serious, he said. If I can't make this thing work in one term, I can't do anything in two. Besides, I don't want to be president all my life. I want to lie down here in the sun, run the dogs, know me another woman or two. But I got a few plans. In '40 I can put you over the top.

I didn't believe a word of it. Up to this point I had pretty well taken what Huey had said as he had presented it, but this part was not to be believed. It didn't bother me, of course. Long view or short, you cultivate the situation more or less as it is found and don't push for explanations. I'll think about it, I said. It's going to be ugly stuff. The Republicans want to be heard from.

Republicans! Huey said. Who they got? Hoover again? Charles Evans Hughes? Maybe Styles Bridges? I say the word *Hoover* three times a day until November, I don't have to say anything else. So much for the Republicans. Franklin will be tough but with his vice president jumping ship and every man a king, I think I got a chance. You think I have a chance, Big John?

Yes, I said, I think so. I want to think on this some.

Don't think on it too long, he said. You're getting first offer and best offer but you aren't the only one, you understand. There are a lot of people outside the parishes who see things the way I do, who would be happy to come along. The next person I ask is Rayburn. You think he'll turn it down?

I don't know, I said.

Well I do, Huey said. He turned it down. Conditional. He said I should ask you first, courtesy of the line of succession and all that. But if you don't want it, he said, I should ask him again. That good enough for you?

I'll have another sip of that whiskey, I said. I do declare that ain't bad whiskey, considering.

Yeah, Huey said. You know, I looked down at that blood on the floor of the Capitol and I said, it could have been *my* blood and no one would ever have known what I could have been. There are moments that change you, Big John. Maybe you've had a few.

I think I've had one just now, I said. I took the whiskey bottle from him and palmed it. It felt like a grenade in my hand. I ran the palm over it, up and down, down and up, then drank deep. I'm tired of this job, I said finally, this is a shitty job. Maybe you can give me something to do besides hold a gavel and wait around for you to drop dead.

We'll have plenty for you to do, Huey said. We're gonna be a goddamned *team*, Big John. And in 1940, things work out the way I hope they will, you can have the whole goddamned thing. We'll probably be in a war by then anyway, ain't doing you no favors.

Landon was a clown. Huey was right, the Republicans had nothing, there was no way that they could campaign, nothing that they could say. That was the summer of the dust bowls, the failed crops, the riots in the Capitol. Roosevelt wanted me to step down when he got the word, and then he threatened to impeach me, and then he said he'd send me out to inspect the goddamned Navy in California for six months if I didn't shut up and get in line, but I just laughed at him. There was absolutely nothing that he could do. He was licked and he knew it. He had a sitting vice president who had shifted to an Independent ticket headed by a better man and there was no provision in the Constitution or in the articles of state that could touch me. He couldn't even say too loud that I was a piece of shit because, after all, he had picked me the first time around and I had enough friends in the party to embarrass him on the renomination. Anyway, the Governor of New Jersey ended up as the fool's candidate for vice president and Huey and I took to the road.

We stirred the pots in Metairie and prayed with the ministers in Dallas; we lit fires on a reservation in Albuquerque and then we went to a meeting with Father Divine in Brooklyn. The Father Divine stunt was a ripper, it looked for a couple of days that it would cost us everything, that we would blow the election on that, but then the East came roaring in with the editorials and Rayburn was able to hold Texas and the rest of the South in line just as I knew he would. Father Coughlin went crazy and the Klan had some mighty doings in Florida and outside Atlanta, but Father Divine stood up in Times Square and on 125th Street and then Independence Square and said, these are good men, these are men who understand, I take the curse of racism and hatred from these men because having come from the fires of Satan, the hardest place in the country, they know the truth that will set us free. The Governor of the State of New York—Franklin's state—met Huey in Grand Central Station and shook his hand. Out in the Midwest, crawling from stop to stop, we saw crowds like I had never seen in a hundred years in politics, and in California the farmers and the soldiers and the old soldiers came in a long line to Huey and shook his hand and wept. We know you got something for us, they said. We think you understand. Grandmas wiped his face with their handkerchiefs and now and then, seeing a hungry baby Huey cried. Landon was flabbergasted, he gave it up in early October and went back to Kansas and just about sat on the front porch. Roosevelt fought and fought—no legs but enough courage, I had never denied that—but it all slipped away from him. As Vice President I slipped off to Washington now and then to preside over the Senate, get my face in the papers and pound the gavel and cloakroom a little.

We got 341 electoral votes. We got New York and Pennsylvania. We got California. We lost Ohio and Illinois and we almost lost Texas too, and we sure as hell lost Georgia and Florida, but we didn't lose too much else and in the early morning Wednesday when it was at last over, Huey turned to me and handed me a bottle, that same bottle I swear, and said, We did it, John. *You* did it and I swear I'll never forget. I want to do good, John, he said. You got to believe that, I've only wanted all my life for the working man to have a break—and the working man in this country, he's been screwed right out of his inheritance and his heart. We're going to set this country aright, John, you hear that? For the first time we're going to do it *his* way. I owe it all to you, John. Rayburn snuck in when it was all over, of course he couldn't do anything officially then or later, but he made his position clear. Huey went out the next day and had the press conference.

It was the goddamnedest thing I had ever seen. I had been Vice President of the United States and now I was going to be Vice President again and it was still the goddamnedest thing that I had ever seen. I guess I knew at the time that nothing could ever touch it again like that but I didn't care. There are only a few moments in life, as Huey himself said, and if you are lucky you know when they are there and you use them and you try to run with them all to—and maybe, if you are very smart and lucky past—the grave.

But it started to go badly, early on. By the time of the Olympics, even before the election, we knew that Adolf was no temporary phenomenon, that he was the real thing and that it was a bad situation. The worst.

Adolf did things with crowds that even Huey couldn't do. We could see that in the clips. And the news drifting out was worse and worse.

We're in trouble, Huey said. This was in spring of '37, only the third time I had gotten in to see him since he had been triumphantly inaugurated. It hadn't taken long for him to turn me back into a vice president. This guy is murder, he said. I don't worry about Mussolini so much, he's an Eye-talian and he goes whichever way the wind goes, but Adolf is a killer. He's a killer boy, do you hear that? He is taking us to war.

So what can we do? I said. I fell into the role easily enough, feeding Huey lines, taking his whiskey—he always had a bottle now—and trying not to think about the times past. What the hell, it wasn't worth a pitcher of warm spit anyway, I had known that before. So I had just switched wives, that was all. It was the same bunch of crap and John Nance Garner knew it. Besides, the only real populist is a dead man, I was smart enough to know that. What are we going to do, take Adolf out?

He's killing Jews and Gypsies, Huey said, and ugly looking types and enemies and a lot of good Germans too. He's killing everything that takes his fancy and he's dead serious about this. He is one out-of-control loon and he is putting us on a war footing, do you understand that?

I understand a lot of things.

I can't go nowhere, I can't do the kind of things that got to be done with one eye on that guy. We're going to go over there and try to reason with him. We're going to set up a run to Berlin.

I think not, I said. I think I'll preside over the Senate.

You too, Huey said. We'll take a slow boat, bring along some good whiskey and maybe a few friends. We'll have a nice cruise and we will try to reason with this gent. Maybe he can be persuaded to try reason. If not, we'll still get some good pictures out of it and they'll see that the President was willing to go a ways trying for peace.

I think this is a big mistake, I said. I think we ought to hunker down and wait this out.

Wait what out? Think he's going to stop? His country is leaking Jews. Soon as he's killed everyone he can there he's going to turn outward, want to go other places. This guy likes killing, you understand? We wait him out, he'll be in California.

What can I say? I said. I had another swallow of whiskey. I was always swallowing whiskey in those days. It's your play, I said. You always wanted it your way, Kingfish, so I'm not going to stop you. You want me to go over on an ocean liner with you, I'll go, I just hope it's not the *Titanic*. What the hell, I said, why don't we go all the way? Smuggle a thirty-eight caliber into a state meeting and shoot the fucker in the throat. You think that would solve the problem?

Huey gave me a long odd look. You think I haven't considered that? he said. I am ahead of all you Democrats. But it is not a wise plan. Not at this time.

You think he's a faster draw?

I think that we're at the Reichstag when we try it, that isn't too smart, Huey said. That's all I think. But it is something to be tabled for future reference.

I should have said something then. But vice presidents are not paid to say things other than *in accordance with the Constitution I cast the tie breaking vote in favor of this resolution. Or, I support our great President. Or it ain't worth a pitcher of warm spit.* Trust a vice president to know protocol.

After Berlin, Huey put the invitation right out. Come to Washington and we'll try to settle this thing. But Adolf had other plans, other stuff on his mind about then, and so for that matter did the Kingfish, things were getting cudgeled about in the provinces and Franklin, no quitter, was rallying the Democrats and talking about a people's coalition in 1940. The basic question, Franklin was saying, had to do with what Huey had *done* since the Inauguration and aside from going to Berlin to have his picture taken and making some good speeches against the Wall Street capitalists, Huey hadn't done much at all. These were powerful points and gave the Kingfish pause, or at least kept him preoccupied. So there were some lively times here and about when the food riots started to occur on a regular basis. Business was reviving a little and Hollywood was telling us that things were great but down on the Great White Way or the places where the Commies dwelt, there was a different cast to the situation. And the Commies were getting stronger; anyone, even the Vice President, could see how much real appeal they were finding in the cities.

But by that time it just didn't matter that much. There comes a time when your destiny confronts you and if you don't accept it, you don't begin to work in accord with that destiny, well then you're just a fool. I wasn't going to be president in 1940. I wasn't even going to be vice president by the end of that year; I had been sucked in and served my little purposes and now I was going to be frozen out. The Kingfish had gobbled me up, just a medium-sized fish in the tank. I would be dumped and Huey would run again, maybe win, maybe lose to Franklin this time, but that was going to be the end of it. And by 1940, it was going to be a changed situation anyway. I just didn't give a damn; I wanted to get back on the ranch, I wanted to see the old times out with as much dignity and as little whiskey as I could manage and the hell with the rest of it. So my accommodation was to simply hang on and go on my way. Huey was going to stay out of local statehouses and he had some pretty good protection. Even Capone or Legs Diamond would have had a hell of a time nailing the Kingfish by that time. No fortunate accidents were going to catapult me to any place that I hadn't already been.

But then, just when it seemed settled, it wasn't settled. After Munich, after he gobbled up the rest of Czechoslovakia, Adolf had Goering pass the word direct to Harry Hopkins. He wanted to take up Huey's invitation. He wanted to come over, explore a few things, do a little business.

Peace in our time, Huey said. He's looking for that now, right? Why should the son of a bitch take us up on this now? He's cleaning out the country, he's ready for war. What the hell does he have in mind?

Why are you asking me? I said. I haven't been in here twice in nine months, Huey, I got nothing to tell you.

Don't sulk, Big John, Huey said. I got you in mind all the time, it's just that I've been preoccupied. This is a big country, you know, and there are lots of problems. Maybe we'll get that redistribution working, maybe all of this stuff will come out in the long run, but it isn't going to be nearly as fast as I thought when I was a young man. Got to cultivate patience, that's all.

I have lots of patience, I said, I had it a long time ago. You were the one who was going to turn things around, make it all different by 1940, remember? I didn't say that it was going to happen.

Huey said, you're taking this too hard, John. You're taking it personally. Sit back and help me through this. I want you to meet the guy when he comes off the boat in New York, I want you to escort him around. The Statue of Liberty, maybe Liberty Square in Philadelphia on a day trip. Then you can bring him here and I'll meet him at the White House and we'll talk over things. But I need your support here, I don't want to go trotting out for him, it doesn't suit my purposes.

I'm not a messenger boy, I said. I'm the Vice President. You got to take the office seriously even if you got no use for me.

Ah, nonsense, John, the Kingfish said. You've said yourself what you think of this job and you were right, all the time. I got a crazy plan, John. I think we're going to save the world twenty years of agony and maybe a few million lives. I think we're going to arrange to plug this guy, if not at the dock then maybe when he's walking down Pennsylvania Avenue.

We'll have an accident arranged for him.

That's crazy, I said. Our own lives won't be worth shit. A head of state killed in our protection? They'll go to war the next day.

Goering and Himmler? Goebbels? You think these guys want war? They just want what we have, John, they just want their part of it, that's all. They won't do a goddamned thing. They'll be relieved, they think this guy is crazy too. Every synagogue in the country will have the lights on all night the day he dies. Even Chamberlain will thank us. We'll be treated like heroes. I think the world will fall down and give us everything we want, we get the deed done. That's what I think and your own part is clear. You're going to help me, John, and that's the end of it.

And then what? I said. It's a crazy plan, Huey. And even if it works, can we deal with the consequences?

Well sure, Huey said. I've been dealing with consequences all my life. I love consequences, they're all we got. We don't know what causes, we only know what happens, you understand? I love these talks, I want you to know that. Just the two of us in a room with a bottle, beautiful, I don't know what I would have done if we hadn't had that. Have a drink, John, it's too late.

Too late for what?

Too late not to have a drink, the Kingfish said. So set them up.

So what was there to say? The rest seems very fast in memory although of course it was agonizingly slow in the development, waiting all through it in a suspended anguish, waiting for that heavy thud that would ejaculate us into the latter part of the century. Meeting the prancing, dancing little dictator and his company right off the boat, doing the ceremonial thing, then whirling them through Jimmy Walker's glittering, poisonous city. The Staten Island Ferry, Radio City Music Hall. Two Rockettes flanked Hitler, put their arms around him at my direction, mimed kissing his cheekbones. He glowed, seemed to expand. There was supposed to be a mistress but there was no woman in the party, no woman close to him. Just Himmler, Goering and the impossibly fat Streicher who always seemed to be confiding something to the Fuhrer. We had a private dinner at the Waldorf, talked through the interpreters of cattle and of conditions in Austria during the World War and of the shadows in Europe. Grover Whalen poured wine. I mentioned the Sudetenland, just to have it on record, but the interpreter frowned and I could see that there was no translation. Later, the dictator wanted to see Harlem at midnight. We drove there quickly in covered cars, then back to the Waldorf. At the corner where Father Divine had embraced the Kingfish, women looked at us indolently, poking knees through their skirts. The Fuhrer rumbled in the car but said nothing. We wheeled down Fifth Avenue until the lights glowed softly again, then back into the underground garage. I felt something like a blow at the back of my neck and the thought *Like the Statehouse.* These were the conditions. If it was going to happen, the place would be here. It would be now.

Seated next to the dictator I leaned over to whisper—what? What would he have understood? I had no German. Nor did I know what I would have said. Dead Jews, Gypsies, burning bodies in their graves, the awful aspects of war. I thought of this and leaned back. There was nothing to say. We stopped, the door came open. I got out first and then the guard in the jump seat and then Streicher from the front, panting in sweat, and then Hitler. Hitler came last of all, straightened, looked at me with those strange, focused eyes, that face like a claw. *Raus*, he said in a high voice, *raus*—

His head exploded. One eye seemed to expectorate, fall to the stones of the garage, then fragments of him were cast upward. In the heavy embrace of someone I could not see, I stumbled back. The grasp was enormous, absolutely enfolding, it felt like swaddling, like death, like ascension. The dictator was floating. The dictator, in pieces, was floating in the air.

Now we can begin the business of living, I thought I heard Huey say, his voice enormous in my head. Except of course, that there was no Huey there, only that stricken embrace, and then the broken screams in the garage, the sound of gabbled German, hysteria—

Hitler sifted over me in the sudden darkness.

Under the silt of Hitler, I fell.

The Kingfish sent shocked condolences and offered to accompany the body back to Berlin. But the party and their coffin were already on their way before the announcement at the press conference and then in the dawn, the first reports came of the attacks upon the Embassy. The declaration of war followed by noon.

Chamberlain was furious with us.

But the Kingfish was at the top of his mood, the happiest I had ever seen him.

I always wanted to be a war president, he said. I guess that this was what I was aiming for from the start. We're going to save them, John, he said excitedly, we're going to get them out, we're going to stop the machine. We're going to save them all, Huey said. We're going to save *them all.*

Salvation from the parish.

Fugato

Copland said that he could have gotten Leonard Bernstein out of it, that he could reach people on the draft board. Or, Copland said, failing that, Koussevitzky could pull some strings. No one messed with Koussevitzky in Massachusetts and Leonard was Sergei's boy that summer. But Leonard had said no, no, damned fool that he was, didn't want word getting around that he had dodged the draft or used influence to get out of any Jewish boy's obligation in these terrible times. Besides, Leonard had what he took to be secret knowledge, there was a punctured eardrum just like Sinatra, and if that didn't do the job there was a long history of back trouble. Oy, your lower back, Sam Bernstein used to say to him, you'll inherit your lower back from my lower back and that will be the end of this conducting for you. Better think of sitting in a nice chair in a stockbroker's office. Punctured eardrum. Lower back trouble. A sure ticket out and no scandal, that's what Leonard had thought, had told Aaron not to be so helpful, had told Jerry Robbins when he had gone off to the draft physical that morning in 1942. And now here he was. Here he was, all right. So much for punctured eardrums and the lower back, so much for disdaining Sergei's close contacts with the gentry in Massachusetts, a long way from Tanglewood, Lenny, and no way back that he knew.

In a farmhouse somewhere near the Ardennes forest, pinned down with the remnants of his company by the snipers' fire being laid down with terrible precision from high ground, rolling somewhere in the mud of that forest now become the floor of that farmhouse, Leonard had no time to reflect upon his destiny or the look on his friends' faces when he had come back from that physical and had said, They found me 1-A. They didn't even want to look at my eardrum, they asked me to jump up and down three times, checked for a hernia, and that was it. Incredulity had sprung from Adolph Green's face. Jerry Robbins had been speechless when Leonard had called him. Seventeen months later now and he was a rifleman, a private first class, part of the massive attempt to liberate France, fighting for the spirit of liberty in the land of Ravel, Charles Munch, Bizet, Hector Berlioz; the screams of the riflemen around him, the terrified, choked cries of men who had lost their way and stumbled into this gloating, final darkness in the farmhouse surrounded him with noise and heat, odd flashes of light which Bernstein had never seen before, a light which seemed to sever him not only from any sense of his past but from the very conditions which he thought had organized his life.

Medic! someone screamed, *I'm hit, I'm hit*, and there was the dull throbbing of the guns then, the sound of demolition inside this wretched place, and it occurred to Leonard as he hunched himself below the eaves, clinging to the side of the fireplace, watching the odd and flickering cast of light through the windows, a light which was neither dawn nor the darkness but composed of the constituent parts of his own death, externalized, that he was facing conditions which were utterly out of his control. He had pushed away that insight, that possibility for all of these months, told himself that it was impossible for Leonard Bernstein to lose that fine sense of propriety and balance which he had always equated with his destiny, but now it had gone from him; with a sudden and awful conviction Bernstein knew that he was going to die in this place, surrounded by sniper fire and the bellowings of animals, alert to the whimpers of men unmanned. *Te deum, laudamus. Dies Irae, dies illae.* The sound of all judgment. Berlioz and Mozart, *tuba mirium.*

In Tanglewood in the summer of 1941 Tallulah Bankhead had stolen him from a rehearsal and they had gone to a curtained bower where one by one she said she would reveal to him all of her great charms and secrets and in that great, damp clutch, her musk and necessity flooding around them, Leonard Bernstein had felt himself as with the deaf and dipsomaniacal Beethoven, hunched over the quartets, hunched over the actress, at some final certainty and apprehension of his life. Berlioz's drug-maddened poet dragged off to the gallows. How far from there to here he could not apprehend, but he could make a guess in the darkness. It was less, far less distance than he might have measured. All of his life this dark and terrible thunder, like Tallulah's gasps and secrets, had been waiting to envelop him. The stunned look on Adolph's face, all teeth and regret. Lenny, Lenny, what's going to happen to us? I don't know, Leonard Bernstein had said. What do you think Adolph, that war is for the dopes, for the guys who can't hear things inside their heads? Because they die too, they die, you die, we all die, even Adolph Green and Jerry Robbins and Betty Comden and Berlioz, Beethoven and Nijinsky. The sound of clattering now and the sound of weapons recocked. The Hun was coming in.

At Tanglewood in that summer of 1941 he had met Britten for the first time. Britten, the British composer and his great friend Peter Pears, draft-dodging it in America and going the concert circuit while cursing Churchill and Hitler and T j and Roosevelt too, all of the war-lovers Britten had said. I'm sitting out the war in Massachusetts and New York and points west, Britten had said. Peter and I aren't going to serve their purposes, give them fodder. It is an abomination, all of it. War is an abomination.

Well, of course it was, Leonard had thought, always was, always would be; World War I had knocked out a generation in Europe and now the same thing was happening again. It was the obligation of the artist to oppose war with all his being, to fight against the mania and the stupidity, there was no disagreement there. Don't go, Koussevitzky had said, Lenny, you do not have to go, something can be done. That had been in 1942, after the draft notice had come in, but back in 1941, Bernstein hadn't thought of anything like that at all, the war had still been at a distance and Britten's prediction that Roosevelt would keep the United States out of it until Germany and Japan had fallen into the pit of their exhaustion and corruption had seemed reasonable. Everything about Britten seemed reasonable even though Leonard could not get around the hard, derogatory feeling that the Brit and his lover were draft dodgers with no other name to put on it. They had had fun that summer though, all of them, they had taken over Tanglewood, he and Jerry Robbins and Copland, who had made Leonard his most honored, his favored pet. He conducted the student orchestra and once the Boston Symphony in the *Eroica* with Koussevitzky sitting out in the audience applauding, and it had all seemed very clear and open to him then; he was twenty-three years old and music was opening to him along with everything else and Sam Bernstein, his father, had been a fool. It *was* possible to make a career; Koussevitzky said that he had everything he needed and had arranged for him to go to New York, meet Rodzinski, apply for the assistant conductor position with the New York Philharmonic. How was he to know that it would lead to this? Schumann had heard that A within his head at the beginning of his final descent, the 440-cycle A sounding all day and night, cleaving his brain to shreds, warning him of the end of all possibility, but Leonard had had no warning at all. There was the chaos about which he read occasionally in the *Globe* and the *Times* and then there was the smooth and certain, sometimes convulsive tread of his own life as whispered by Koussevitzky, murmured by Copland, gasped by Bankhead. How was he to know? How were any of them to know? Europe fell on their heads, Britten had said, talking about Wilfred Owen and the poets of death, and now it has fallen on ours, but we must have the constancy to say no. To say no, to say no. Lying in this rotten shingling, hearing the sure and certain sounds of those coming to end one's life, what was constancy? What was the nature of fortitude? It was one thing to talk about it in an undergraduate seminar or to discuss metaphysics with Britten in the empty tent pitched for the concerts but vacant after rehearsal with the sound of insects murmurous in the air but it was another, it was quite another, to face this disaster five thousand miles from Tanglewood or a century and a half from the spangled and heaving Europe which had made Beethoven a celebrity and had turned to Napoleon as liberator. I didn't want this, Leonard Bernstein said hopelessly, I never wanted to make these choices, never wanted to face any of this, but no one in the platoon was at that moment interested in discussing the issue or even debating with him, the pounding outside, the increasingly desperate and imperious shouts had shed notice now: the Hun was coming in.

You can't do this, Copland had said, you have some misguided air of patriotism, Leonard, but patriotism is not going to sustain you under rifle fire nor feed any of those ambitions and purposes of yours. Aaron of course had been in his early forties so it was easy for him to make abstracted debate, even though to his credit Copland had not—as Britten had—aspired to any moral plane or purpose. If Haydn had enlisted in the barricades in Paris in 1789, Copland had said, and had gotten himself killed for the cause of freedom, we would never had had the London symphonies; if Leopold Mozart had put little Johann Wolfgang into the king's service in 1775, what would have become of him when the tides of revolution came asunder? If you have any obligation, Leonard, Copland had said, it is to survive this war intact and serve your career; you can give something unique to the world like Haydn or Mozart, or you can lie somewhere overseas under a cross and to what benefit? To whose benefit? We know people, Leonard, Copland had said, there are things that can be done, and even if they cannot be done you can play the piano for the USO and direct shows, you don't have to take a rifle and start shooting at strangers, even if you're a good rifleman and I think you're a lousy one. Listen to me, Aaron had said, his face intent, as intense as Koussevitzky's when Sergei had said to him, Lenny, you must not put yourself beyond our reach, let me try to help you. It is not too late for this, not even now.

But it had been. It had already been too late, basic training completed, out on ten-day leave, waiting for the orders that would send him over. Bernstein knew that the infantry would be heading for France, every dogface knew that, there were no secrets. Home on leave with the orders cut and the maws of the ships waiting, he had flirted only briefly with the thought that Copland could save him from this, Sergei, even Sam the industrialist who had fought against his son becoming a musician but now wanted to save Leonard for the cause of music at all costs. But it wasn't possible, he had seen that sometime during the infantry training, staggering through the mud, hearing the curses around him and the screaming of the sergeants, the things that they had said about the Jews in the platoon when they thought that the Jews weren't listening. Or *knew* that they were listening but just didn't give a shit. Don't you understand, Aaron? Leonard had said. I can't dodge out. It's not my option. Maybe it's Ben Britten's, he's got a long history of resistance behind him, and anyway everyone knows about him and Peter, and he could probably get out on that basis. But it's different here. It's different for Jews too, don't you see?

Aaron shook his head. Being Jewish has nothing to do with it, he said. It's irrelevant.

No, it's not irrelevant. I've been training with people who think, a lot of them, that the reason we got into this thing, the reason we're going to get killed is because of the Jews, to defend the Jews. So how would it look if this Jew tried to head out of it now? The only way I've shut them up is to say, well, then I'm going to be killed too. This is one Jew who is going to die because of the Jews. You think I want that?

You're being ridiculous, Copland said. You're making more of this than possibly exists. You're a musician, Leonard, you could be a great conductor, maybe even as good a composer. You think that these are outweighed by the necessity to look good for the Gentiles? The Gentiles are going to hate us whatever we do, getting killed for them will just make them hate more. There's nothing we ever could have done to have pleased them, don't you understand that? But Leonard hadn't understood that, he hadn't understood much of anything, he supposed. He had stopped understanding when the 1-A notice had come through and he had known with an utter sense of conviction and completion, maybe the same sense that had come over Britten's idol, Wilfred Owen, in the foxhole, that he was going to die and that there was nothing personal about it, that his death was a large part of a great historical movement. *Te deum, laudamus.* The *kyrie* of the Mozart Requiem had moved hugely within him at that moment, peering at the glazed surfaces of the draft notice and after that it had been a straight plunge down the tube of circumstance to this moment. No, Aaron, he had said, it's too late. I am going to serve this out because it is beyond us. All of it is beyond me now. *There is no counterpoint, it is all monothematic.* Aaron had stared at him beyond the thick glasses. If it is monothematic, he had said, it is because you want to die. It is in your hands, Leonard. You selected the infantry, you allowed this to happen to you. Don't talk about historical inevitability. They had not discussed it again. Aaron had gone back to New York, talking about getting poor old, sick Charles Ives to try to talk some sense into his head. But old, sick Charlie Ives was too deaf and crazy by then to talk to anyone. Leonard had served out the leave time and had shown up at dockside in full field gear, waiting to ship over. He knew that this had been a small surprise to some in the company, they had expected the Jew to go AWOL or to make some heavy arrangements during the leave. But no, here he was. Not that this made any difference or that any increased respect gave him even two inches more space in the dead cubicle below deck where he sweltered and vomited through the terrible weeks of the voyage.

The fantasy had been that he would get to Salzburg, to Vienna, to the haunts and birthplaces of Beethoven and Mozart, that he would somehow give testimony by his presence to their own transcendent meaning in his life. But that had not been in the plans, there were no communions with dead composers on the slate, no communion with live ones either. Schoenberg and Bartók and Rachmaninoff had had the sense to leave these places of blood and dishonor already, but Bernstein had put a rifle in his hand and had headed, not at all stately, the other way. There was something of cosmic humor in this, something as grotesquely and transcendently humorous as the ghostly shrieks and spasms which Beethoven had put into the Opus 135 quartet, sounds which no violins, viola or cello had ever been meant to play, but he could not see the humor. He could not see Tallulah, either, it had been months since he had been able to summon her image, or Koussevitzky's, or anyone from that vanished part of his life; now it was only the close, dense, dank pallor of the troops and the stink of the countryside and now, coming slowly to a kind of frenzied attention, he could see the Germans pouring through the door, the Hun enormous in his uniform, consequential and brutal in his solidity, the sound and stink of the Hun grandiose as in multiple he poured through the door. They were coming to clean out the farmhouse, coming in fact to clean out the whole of Europe, and Bernstein had only the insufficiency of his corpus and a rifle he could barely fire to stand between them.

He came to firing position then, listening to the bellowing of the servants below or from the sides, the screaming and cursing of the men coming in all directions around him and then as the waves and grinding insistence of the attackers came over him, he felt himself sunk into a moment of fierce and total embrace, a sense of absolute collision with a destiny which always must have been there, waiting for him. Fired once. Fired twice. Shouted with the recoil and heard the bullet over his head, fired again and heard the return fire spaced around him, and then at last, the spasm as the bullet hit him cruelly and precisely in the targeted area. He shrunk over the bullet, scrambling against the wall, then felt himself beginning to fall. *Showed them*, Leonard Bernstein thought. *Showed them that a Jew could take the same shit as the Gentiles, showed them that even the Jewboy musician could take it from his gut.* Whether he survived or not seemed at this moment to be a very small thing, almost incidental, completely incidental to this moment of gigantic enclosure, his body a fist gripped around the bullet. Shouts for the medic. *Medic, medic! I'm dying!* Conduct the Philharmonic, Leonard Bernstein thought. Conduct the Philharmonic in Avery Fisher Hall in May 1962, the last concert of the first season at the new hall, the Berlioz *Symphonie Fantastique*, on a Sunday. March to the scaffold, the drug-wrecked poet dragged to his new destiny, spin and leap on the podium, leap as if all heaven was watching, the snarl and scream of the trombones and hang in the air, hang at the top of the leap, never falling, never falling: it is October 14, 1990, and high in that leap Leonard Bernstein waits with perfect resignation and acceptance to see, beyond the clutch of the respirator tubes running in and out of his shattered lungs, to see where or if he will land. *Te deum, laudamus.*

in his sacred memory

Major League Triceratops
With Joyce Malzberg

In the Gallery

In the dim corridor, the spaces hushed by fog, the dim and dazzling lights of the exposed diorama playing, the paleontologist stared at the great, shrouded skeletons revolving slowly into the light, the huge and vaulting figures of *Struthiomimus* and *Triceratops* and that flaming tower, the *Tyrannosaurus*, emerging into the strobe. Look at those sons of bitches, the paleontologist said. He was old as new scientists go, a late career change had plummeted him into university at forty, out at fifty with a deep and final understanding of mortality. Ever see anything like that? The woman whose hand he was holding shrugged and shook her head. She had learned the virtues of silence with this man early on. He would not listen.

They were killers, the paleontologist said. One kick, you were gone. But now *they* are gone. What do you think of that?

I don't think, the woman said.

This was close to the truth, near enough to pass, anyway. The tyrannosaur's enormous knee bone, the arch of that bone, loomed before them and she looked up, the line of her gaze passing almost indifferently, casually, over the small skull, half-concealed behind the foot of the larger *Triceratops*. The skull was the size of a man's and flayed to an ardent white.

Take *that* one on the ranch, the paleontologist said. He scratched his nose. Ride 'em cowboy, he said. Take that one down the loop of Montana, what do you say?

I don't say anything, the woman said. You have taught me the crest of silence. She squeezed his hand, curled a finger in his palm. Not even a haiku, she said. Not even five by seven by five.

The paleontologist turned, stared at her with full interest, his gaze caught by the fine cheekbones, the intensity of her gaze, something of the prehistoria herself, he thought, in this odd and twisted light. Her father had been Japanese, the mother pure *Norteamericana*, and the Orient had seemed buried in her face until this angle, this moment, now in the spattered light cast by the dinosaur, in the clutch of her hand she seemed, suddenly, to bear all of the wound and stain of her heritage. Five by seven by five, the paleontologist said. *In the light the bird / Caught in Cretaceous flight as the bone talks to us*. What do you think of that?

I think it is very decadent, she said. *De-ca-dent*, like the time travelers going back to shoot them on their ranches, that is what I think.

But not touching?

It is touching, she said. Everything is touching in the gallery at noon in the dark. She pointed at the small, shattered ridges of teeth. It may talk to you, she said. It doesn't talk to me.

I have nothing to do with the ranches, he said. It is unfair of you to discuss the ranches. I am a scientist.

Yes, she said, you are very scientific. She made him feel the pressure then, putting her knee against his. *De-ca-dent*, she said again. A great horned thing charging toward us in the night, yes.

You are strange, Maria, the paleontologist said. I do not understand you.

You are the bone, she said. You are the bone which talks to us. Take me home and show me the bone.

He turned away from her but his other hand was reaching, clutching for her waist. She felt the icy, encircling touch. In old Montana, he said. They must have had a time.

They always had a time. Time was nothing for them. They cruised through the dirt like boats. Take me out of here, she said. I have heard enough of Montana and the ranches and time. I don't want to look at the dead things anymore. Now, she said, or not at all.

Am I too *de-ca-dent* for you, Maria? Is that what you are telling me?

She looked at the spaces up and down, the crucifixes of bone assembled now in small wedges up and down the spines of the reconstructed tyrannosaur. I don't know, she said. Am I supposed to?

Back then, back here, he said. His grasp tightened and they were moving then toward the door, he leading, she guiding, the two of them reaching but at the exit they stood for a while, first one then the other pointing at the creatures looming before them. When they were gone at last, the fog, cleared slightly by their respiration, closed on the emptiness and obscured what neither had seen: the small, round skull, shiny and neat as an ornament, lying at the reconstructed rear left foot of the tyrannosaur, the eye hollows glinting in the received light.

In the light my bird, the paleontologist cried later. But that had nothing to do with the gallery, he insisted. Nothing to do with it at all. Her hands on his head were fire.

The Robles Transcripts

I am going to keep notes on this. Testimony is going to be kept. There will be some records of the disaster, if disaster it will be. Going back to torment *Tyrannosaurus*, shoot *Triceratops*, explore the flora of the Cretaceous and sight the huge, dying beasts. We promised Dix a kill and a kill it is going to be, one saved from paradox by this world. It will change nothing. (Perhaps it will change everything. But we wouldn't know, would we?) Consider the *Triceratops*.

Consider that beast. Weight up to five and a quarter tons, more than four thousand kilos, then. Thirty to thirty-five feet in length full grown, flourished or at least lurked in this latest part of the Cretaceous (Latin derivative, *chalk*). One of the largest and meanest of the horned dinosaurs, not like scuttling *Struthiomimus* or businesslike tyrannosaur but rather this is an animal with its own program. Put it down, give it to Dix tomorrow, the number of the beast. With photographs. Three sharp, pointed horns on that bland, boxy rhinoceros face, the horns measuring more than three feet. The mottled cores encircled by a series of occipital bones. Am I doing this right? Ten species, more or less, slightly varied.

Those bony horn cores survive into our era in the form of rhinoceroses and some of the great horned birds. The Great Montana Dude Ranch. Point the launcher, Dix, and let it fly, *unseat the beast*, make his bones run like water. Perhaps overdramatizing but then again, melodrama is the last connection the servant class can attempt toward a sense of their consequence. I think I just made that up now.

It is cold here, the small arc of light, the pungent blasts of heater do not really help, do not conceal the cold. Dix, the winner of the contest, sleeps quietly, gathering himself against his great opportunity. I gather myself *too*. Gather myself in this prehistoric plunge toward—toward what? Reconception and redevelopment to be sure and all the revisions of time. In latter years the *Triceratops* shot by Dix will decompose along with all this era, the living too, steam slowly into the mists. None of it will remain but that small testimony I can leave or that at least I think is the insistence which drives me forward, drives me back, takes me through this busy and circumstantial time.

Dix, poised on the rim of the impossible, leveling the stick of fire and the great beast, confused, stumbling in the chalk and doom.

Morning Light

The notes locked away, his schedule set, insistent sleep craved, Robles stumbled toward awareness quickly, rising through the flickering levels of illumination, reaching toward the weight of sixty-seven million crushing years and found himself lying tangled on the earth, the ropes of the tent a geometry of madness spattering shadows. Cry of prehistoric birds in the distance, the strange, dry whooping of a beast, then. He reared to a seated position, arched away from the sleeping Muffy, fully clothed yes as he had prepared but with the feeling that he had nonetheless fallen helplessly behind, lost all grip and sense of what he had come to do, knew only the falling sickness. But peering through the tent he could see that the little camp was silent, the other tents undisturbed, Dix's tent falling in even folds, this dense time still wrapped heavily around the sleepers. His terror must have come from dreams, not circumstance, some atavism of displacement, of having been taken by time to this utter and dismaying disconnection.

Back in the tent he struggled to move from dreams of wounded reptiles and death then, suppressed the dream sounds of carnage to come, breathed slowly in the clammy silence, his breath curling before him. Muffy sighed, a pretty woman, a pretty distracted woman, no courtesan but a friend, a part of the tour, yes, but more than that to him now, she insisted, and he looked at her momentarily without desire, without any intimation of need, remembering the places his hands had found in that scurrying time earlier when he had been driven from a need he could no more articulate than he could decipher those dim whoops. Let her sleep, yes, he thought, there was enough and a different aspect of time to come.

Standing there, back to the embankment, he could see the reflection of the floodlights spilling through the protected zone, framing the sleeping Muffy Carter, he could see the Cretaceous refracted as panorama, *dio*rama, hurtled dogwood and the swamp having the aspect of the museum. It was a "natural habitat." Robles thought, and put the quote marks in, the biggest and goddamndest habitat of them all, a Cretaceous replicate and just the most remarkable thing. Scratching his ass in the curling sunlight, trying to bring himself to some kind of accommodation, Robles peered at his strange and attractive partner, then turned to see the mesh fences in the distance, the fences walling off the compound, holding it through paradoxical electrification and wire from the gigantic animals that would otherwise in their ignorance blunder through. Protect the animals, protect the travelers, a mutuality of indifference. That was the point of the tour, wasn't it? But they had promised Dix one kill. A major-league *Triceratops*. That was where the center lay now.

He didn't want to think about it. Killing *Triceratops* was not Robles' ticket, he would direct the fire, whisper words of encouragement to Dix, estimate the windage and the burn ratio and the number of meters toward the beast but the kill was all Dix's responsibility, the Combine had made that quite clear, a line had been drawn (just like that for the dinosaurs) and Robles would not have to cross it. I'm here safe, he said, you hear that Muffy? Muffy sighed, clutched a pink pillow in her pretty hands, rubbed her face in the crease, then gave a long, purling groan. I know you don't want to talk about it, he said. No one wants to talk about it. We all have our jobs, we're all safe, aren't we? Dix is the major-league *Triceratops* hunter while you and I make sweet, sweet love under the dogwoods, isn't that right? He listened, heard the catch in her breath, the tiny acquiescence in her exhalation. Right, he said, that is exactly right.

He strode toward the flat, peered out again. Past the enclosure: past the abyss dug into this hollow by Camp Paradox itself (that was Muffy's name for it, it would stay, it was the right term) was the landscape. The shallow depressions, curved mountains, all of this curiously without color like the beasts themselves; small puffs from hidden volcanoes and buttes, those commas and exclamation points of nature. Later, much later, the strata would accumulate: these would be mines, the strata valleys and mountains, over there perhaps downtown Helena. The volcanoes, attended to, the fix of attention, gurgled like beasts, made little whickering sounds in the darkness, and the beasts hidden by the arc and incline of the landscape gurgled like volcanoes. In and out, that shuddering identity.

Robles shook his head, not in awe, awe was not the proper term for any of this. On your sixth voyage back, now much more than a guide (if less than a hunter), you either internalized some of this and put it away or you perished through the implications of the circumstance, just let it carry you under. No, it was the *lack* of anticipation, his strange indifference in this first dawn which was stunning; never had he felt this way before, now the period had no effect upon him. He was rising to confront fire and the beast but he might as well have been in Brooklyn Complex, working out some kind of appropriations plan. That was how much it meant to him now. Even burrowing within Muffy had had that blandness—her deeps which once had seemed magnificent, arching now gave him back only small and splintering visions of himself, little feathered mysteries in the dark. Here in what would become Helena sometime, the mines were yet to be cast from this crystal unrest, the strata and volcanic ash lay millennia in the future as did his own unspeakable conception. To this place, which should have been sacred— Robles felt that this was the only sanctity which could be grasped, all the rest of it was ritual—had come the crowd of travelers with Dix, host and moderator at their front, to sight the huge beasts for the promised international, televised, major-league kill. What fearful symmetry, Robles said. Who would have dreamt that? Hand or eye? Are you up yet?

Amphibian noises from the pallet, water and earth. She flipped a cover at him. I'm up, she said, thanks. What are you talking about?

Poetry, Robles said. Old poetry.

You mean unwritten poetry, Muffy said. Won't be written for ages.

Camp Paradox, Robles said. Camp out of time.

You said it, she said. I didn't. Why don't you come here and lay with me? Create some more paradox.

He looked at her, the shadows dressing her nakedness, casting arrows and curvatures of shape. Better not, he said, everyone will be up soon. What if they saw us locked to ground, playing the old sniffle-snaffle? What then, Muffy?

She yawned. Part of the tour, she said.

I'm a guide, Robles said. You're a counselor. Not professional, it wouldn't look right at all.

What do you think they're doing? Any different than we?

Dix doesn't, Robles said. He doesn't do anything like that at all, ever. Remember? He said that once. A violation of the temple of the holy spirit. He's a fanatic too, not just a great group mind.

You're too serious for me, Muffy said. You're too much of a speculator. I don't have that kind of stuff going on in my head. To me it's all green thoughts, everywhere. Whatever you say, then.

Robles walked to the pallet, looked down at her, then knelt, touched her elbow gently, felt the yielding of the flesh, watched as her mouth opened slightly for entrance or reproof, it hardly mattered, with Muffy Carter they mingled, they were all the same. Everything mingled and intermixed deep in the sweet probe. Murder coming, yes, anachronism aplenty in the deep Cretaceous, but it was all the same to her and everything would come out even in those dark, sweet depths. No copulation, nothing like that in the sendback, the Administrators had said, but Muffy paid as much attention to that as any guide, which was none at all. With good contraception and a tight, banging constraint, what was the difference? she had asked. A pregnancy would be silly, bad luck for all of them, but really, who was to know? What was the difference? There would be no pregnancy and everything happening here then, even the kill, would be an abstraction. The death of the dinosaurs was as diminished as the pregnancy which would not occur: they became in that cosmic accident fungi, heaps of bone trapped in that fungus, then ash, then fossils, trapped in the clumsy and insistent onrush of time. In the new millennium, only a few bones and suggestions then to mark their passage. Come on, she said, get right aboard. Ride me like a hobby horse, ride me like before. Come, come.

Robles felt himself rolling toward her, then yanked himself away. No, he said, not now. It wouldn't work out, it wouldn't be right.

Then go away, she said. She stared at him. I mean it. Just go. Don't *hover*.

Yes, he said, you're right. He tried to stand, felt his knees lock, sank into the dirt, vertigo pulling at him then. You never get used to it, he said. Do you? I can't take it. But it's never been like this before.

Don't get sentimental on me, Muffy said. I'm just a guide.

Maybe you never get used to it, he said. It's all the cartage outside. Hundreds of thousands of tons. How do you get used to it?

Maybe you should pass me my clothes, let me pull myself together then.

You can be blasé, Robles said. That's because you don't have to think about it. You just point and give figures. But I'm supposed to be able to give *interpretation*. It's the intellectual part of me.

You're a deep fellow, she said. You're beyond me. If fate and circumstance hadn't thrown us together, who knows how we might have been? Is it too late for us now? Will we survive? Time will tell, two hundred million years of it.

I'm afraid of Dix, Robles said. Can you understand that? I don't like him. I don't know what he wants.

He wants to shoot *Triceratops*, dummy. That's why he's here.

Not *Triceratops*, Robles said. That's just a symbol, whatever you call it. He wants something else. I don't know where your clothes are. You're going to have to get them yourself.

You're the one who threw them somewhere.

This isn't a hotel, Robles said fiercely. This isn't a one-night stand. We're buried in this place, now, not in the past, can't you see that? It's no joke.

Sure, she said, you're always so right, I'll find my own clothes. See if I care. You throw, I go. He's just a tourist, she said in a different tone. Maybe a host, maybe a personality with an entourage, but he wants what the rest of them do. A few pictures, a little admiration, a thrill to touch his insulated life.

The others didn't want to kill.

We didn't let them, remember? We changed the rules for Dix, that's all. They wanted to kill, all right. That was the lure all along, don't you know that?

He curled an arm over the floor, found a shirt half crouched beneath the pallet, tossed it to her. You're not all dumb, he said. You play that way but you can figure things out pretty good.

Muffy took the shirt from his hand, ran a hand through her hair, patting it down, then pushed her head through. They're all the same to me, she said. Man with a plan, man on a mission, one way or the other.

In the distance, a tyrannosaur screamed, that odd, trapped sound arcing to penetration, then began to whoop with the regularity of a siren. The sound was bucolic at this moment, fed not his apprehension but what Robles wanted to take as heightened perception. The sound mixed into foliage, became oddly comforting. Trees in the diorama rustled harmlessly. Muffy squeezed his hand, peered over his shoulder. Here he comes, she said, there he comes, for heaven's sake. Look at him break water.

Break water it did. Not a tyrannosaur then but a major-league *Triceratops*. Robles had seen them in the distance many times but this emergent *Triceratops* in the near bog was something different, was a stunning son of a bitch, disproportionate but elegant in the sudden proximity. Thirty feet long, half that high, three discolored horns, greenish at this angle, the huge, comic neck frill, those horns jutting at odd angles above the eye and yet at the center of that movement an odd stillness. The gray-brown mass stolid, almost bovine then as it emerged from a crouch, shoot itself toward land, nuzzled at the ground then closed in on a magnolia so furiously leaved that the trunk was invisible. Began to pull at the discolored flowers.

Cute, isn't he? Muffy said.

Oh yes, Robles said, that's the word.

Makes you want to go over and pet them. Ride the *Triceratops*, Daniel? Want to take another seat? I'm not the only hobbyhorse around.

Go to hell, Robles said without anger. Take it on the tour.

A short-frilled ceratopid, Muffy said in a measured voice, tending to have large, unpaired nose horns. The horns are more defensive than instruments of hostility, however, and to avoid injury resulting from combat, the *Triceratops* relies heavily upon bluff displays and evasive maneuvers.

You do that well.

They pay me in time and experience, Muffy said. It's all hypnotic therapy anyway. All those misspent, unspent nights.

My nights weren't so great either, Robles said. I think we all had a pretty bad time. Why else would we show up at Camp Paradox?

Because it's what we're paid to do. See the mountains and ride the beast. And stay out of the way of anachronism.

Smart, Robles said, you're real smart.

You learn something in the service, Muffy said. They watched the *Triceratops* chew contentedly, leaves and twigs tumbling into its throat, no drop at all. The *Triceratops* ate with great delicacy, stripped the magnolia, then seemed to shrug and sink into the bog again. Shoulder high, it wobbled colorlessly away.

Full of purpose, Robles said. More purpose than we have.

Colbert theorizes, Muffy said professionally, that the horns represent individual, random solutions to a common problem of display and protection, that they may indeed represent selectivity by being a kind of sexual lure. Hey, she said, you're not listening. This is very interesting. You ought to pay attention.

I'm paying attention, Robles said. I paid attention to *Triceratops* and now I'm listening to you. And thinking of Dix. The man is dangerous. He wants more than a kill, he wants the beasts to suffer. I can tell that from his face.

You're a perceptive guy, aren't you? How did you get to know so much? It's just a job. You're not responsible for what goes on here, that decision was made by the administration. I think that Dix just wants a trophy like the rest of us. Maybe *Triceratops* is his hobbyhorse, that's all.

He came out as if on cue, Robles said. That one seemed to be performing *for* us. Did you ever think that maybe they were waiting, that all this is some kind of show they've set up for the tourists and we're the ones being watched?

I think you are showing symptoms of needing a rest, Muffy said. Maybe you can take one. But not until this is finished.

You don't think maybe that all of this is programmed? The dinosaurs too? That we're being watched and observed?

You're too deep for me, Muffy said. She adjusted her shirt, stood gracefully. Halfway there, she said. Now I have to look for some pants.

There's too much going on, Robles said. I never thought it out until now, I just took it for granted. But it's impossible, he thought. It's impossible, that was it. Camp Paradox in fact as well as in name, *none* of this should be happening, not by the rights they had established.

A bell clattered behind them, hardly dinosaur sound, but a technological, post-op summons. In the light they lived by bells and those cruising forms. Turning, Robles peered past Muffy, past the transparent arc of the tent wall, and could see beyond them the low structures of the ranch, the five or six tents which with the Transporter comprised Camp Paradox. Small puffs of smoke vented from those tents, little puffs of light and the suggestion of movement within. Reveille. Inside the domed structure at an oblique angle from the tents, Dix himself would be standing now, pacing on the curved ground, staring through the aperture, looking for his *Triceratops*, measuring for the kill. Well, Robles said when the clattering had ceased, I guess today's the day.

Hunting time, Muffy said. Get a square into the belly and onto the range. Poor little warrior.

Dix? He's a contest winner.

No, Muffy said, not Dix. He's got what he'll be getting. You. You're the one. All suffering because of your rhinoceros out there.

It isn't that, Robles said, it isn't that at all. Can't we forget this? Can't we let it be?

That was your decision all the time. You can come and play inside if you want. It isn't all dead things.

No, Robles said. He shook his head. I told you, I can't. But we're doing something wrong, Muffy. It isn't right, not what we're doing here. This is not the way it was supposed to be. Bringing Dix to Camp Paradox, giving him a gun, setting him loose here.

This is hardly the time, she said. That was all decided a long time ago, worked out by people like you. Let's make reveille and go out on the trails and watch Dix a-hunting go. Then we'll be out of here.

We're never out of here.

You're out of me. Wouldn't you like to get back inside? You can, you know. It's what you want to do. What do you want? She grasped his hand, bent it suddenly at the wrist, sent a splinter of pain up his arm. Robles shrieked. Come *on*, she said. Say it, do it. What do you *want?*

Anachronism, Robles said, rubbing his arm, shaking the wrist. Time out of time. I want it to mesh. I want confluence, can you understand that?

Do business, she said, keep your eye on the sparrow. Go sparrow-hunting, let Dix take primordial rhinoceros over there.

Business, he said. There seemed nothing more to say. Not introspective under the best conditions, the convolutions of the tour had made him utterly unable to cope. Big business.

Not for Dix, Muffy said, taking his hand, rubbing the arm expertly, working blood into the sprain. Not for him though.

Pleasure?

Try again, Muffy said.

Further Observations

Rhinolike as they might have been, *Triceratops* nonetheless dropped eggs. The cutting edge theories had been wrong: they weren't warm-blooded, they did not carry or suckle their young. Robles had taken it badly, seeing his teleology upset. He had envisioned *Triceratops* as a pinnacle: first the fire-breathers, then the vegetarians, then the long, galumphing *Struthiomimus*, big as hangar ports, dense as earth, two brains, one prick. They all laid eggs, Robles believed, except *Triceratops*, the advance model, major-league *Triceratops* had vaulted to the next stage. Except that it hadn't. Like all the rest, it laid its seed in the cold, cold ground, abandoned it there. No home on the range for *Triceratops,* no family life at dusk. They were no different than all of the others. In that first expedition, his fragile hold upon evolution had disintegrated, the *Triceratops* had fallen from its distant height to the deserts of inanition and stupidity with all the rest of them. In a sense, Robles felt he had never survived that knowledge. There was no evolution then, no discrimination, only accident and the huge, dark, scuttling forms.

Robles continued to write: An enlarged fragment of shell mounted in the Crete Musée des Beaux Arts, tyrannosaur suspected as keeper, the outer surface not smooth but stucco-like, brought from the Wyoming wastes, one of eighteen preserved for the new and refurbished Musée. Nothing within, the most sophisticated radiology had indicated, but of course it was early in cycle. What would one do with a tyrannosaur? Lady Carter, I seem to have a tyrannosaur on the premises, he is consuming the wallpaper and has most discomfited the butler. What would we do, Lady Carter? Oh never mind, James, the little creature will find its way back to the nest at last. Let us have some stucco.

He struggled to put it down, relying upon primitive implements and means otherwise unacceptable. Oh, to stroll those wastes, to go egg-gathering in the weak Cretaceous sun, return then to Paradox, on what careful and exquisite omelette we could dine. To dine on unhatched *Triceratops*, essence of *oeuf*, to curl with Muffy amongst the dogwood and magnolia, concealed from the prowlings of Dix, safe from his scatterings, to chow down this thrifty forerunner of our modern rhinoceros and ostrich. This is not merely a prize but an opportunity unafforded by *Triceratops* who granted no such leavings. Joint by joint, inch by inch, one can surely chow down this unspeakable history.

And so he continued—

The Nest

It had been a stunt, in fact. Rig a contest, get someone like Dix to win, bring him to Camp Paradox with appropriate publicity, let equipment film good times here. A television personality, Dix carried his own equipment and crew. It had seemed acceptable at the start, had in fact seemed a brilliant plan. Robles had no objection. Robles, knowledgeable, was all for it. Something had to be done and soon, otherwise they would lose the post.

It was time to alter the situation. Business in Cretaceous Montana had collapsed, Camp Paradox was no longer pulling its new millennial weight. Sour clumps of travelers drifted amongst the chuck wagons and the anachronistically styled riding enclosures, looking grim. The dinosaurs, shy even in better times, could hardly be prevailed upon to circle the ranch and were often unavailable for days while the travelers stared glumly at one another and disdained the holos. Bring back a celebrity to go track the dinosaurs in habitat, it had seemed an audacious conception, yes, but what else was there? There were simply very few new ideas and administration had its own problems, had left them more or less to deal with themselves.

Ultimately, the idea had come from Robles. He could fix responsibility at no other point, it had to be this. What wouldn't work as vista might if it were given some aspect of plot: the quest of a celebrity figure to unravel the secrets of his past. Of course Dix could not be enlisted straight off, that would not work, he would have to be taken in the guise of a contest winner but contests themselves were easy enough to manage. Robles had rigged more than his share in another profession, at another time. And Dix had looked good, he had seemed at the start to be precisely what they had needed, personable, jaunty, a quizzical tilt to the head that bespoke intelligence, irony, and a serious interest in the problem of Camp Paradox. Because it is both there and not there, am I right? Dix had said. Because it exists both in and out of time, the only millionaire tourist trap in Montana that is ecologically sound, is that right? They had laughed. Dix had seemed quite reasonable at the start, it had been a pleasure to tilt the contest toward him, make the business of a celebrity winner credible, test things out then.

Who could have known then how it would turn out? Who knew that Dix had an assassin's eye, a hunter's desire? There was no way to tell, not until the announcement. Not until Dix had started to go public with his plans to land a big one back there and carry it back so that the world could share in the meat of his accomplishment. Grinning, showing sketches of *Triceratops* to the cameras, Dix had been Everyman's version of a winner, smiling at them. We'll bring 'em back alive, Dix said. Oh, not the dinosaurs, he said, winking. They'll be dead as tumbleweed. But the *hunters*, the expeditionaries, we'll be alive and we'll have film the likes of which we'll never have again to play for you.

Let's call it off, Robles had said to Arness, who had played the role of the Committee then. Let's just annul the whole thing. I'll take the blame, we can say that we hadn't calculated the paradoxical effect of a shooting or of transporting someone without special biological delousing. I don't care what we say, we can figure out something.

Can't do it, Arness said, you wanted publicity, we have it now. There's too much. We call it off in public, we look bad.

We can say that there are dinosaur eggs in the machines, that the transporter is clogged. What the hell do I care? Robles had said. He had been eager to concede fault, compelled in fact, the need for self-abnegation had seized him, made him shake. This guy is no good, he said. And no good gets worse.

A contest is a contest, Arness had said. We got too much attention, you did even better than we hoped. We can't break it now without looking even worse.

But killing the beast! Killing a *Triceratops*—

Arness said, We've studied this. There's no anachronism, no risk. If we can go stomping around there sixty-seven million years back, we can kill a *Triceratops*. All of this will be fossilization in no time.

We can't be sure of that, Robles said. We can't be sure of anything. Maybe the *Triceratops* he kills is the grandfather of Gawain. Maybe he misses and kills a tyrannosaur who found Atlantis.

All subsumed, Arness said, all of it eaten up by the million of years. The dinosaurs left no trace, remember. We don't even know what they looked like. We don't know if they had pricks or cunts or how the males sniffed each other out. No trace means no risk. So let him shoot one. It will be good for business and we need business. Private enterprise, remember?

Yes, Robles remembered. He knew everything about private enterprise back then, hadn't he been living it back and forth for all these years? Muffy Carter was private enterprise, so was the transporter, so was all of it. You took your chances, you stayed outside the system and made the best of it you could and the rest of it was bullshit, that was his motto. But this is different, he said to Arness. This is a dangerous guy, someone who thinks that the shadow and the act are the same, like all these communications types. I tell you, I don't like it, Robles said.

We don't like it either, Arness said, but we're into the situation and that's all. It's too late. He'll murder us if we back out now what with the exposure he has. He'll make us the laughing stock of late night. He'll say that the whole thing is a studio job and there's no prehistory there, just some hanging loops and video machines. We can't take it. We can't put up with it. So we go through and hope for the best.

Trusting, Robles said, we've always been so trusting. But it's going to catch up with us. We're going to have real trouble.

You and that little Muffy, Arness said, you can keep an eye on him. Muffy can control him, maybe. He likes women, he likes them small.

He better keep his hands off Muffy, Robles said, surprising himself. He just better leave her alone. To Dix later, at their briefing session, he had said, All right, you got to do it, you go ahead and take care of it. Shoot one, get your pictures. But we're going to be careful, you hear me? We're going to watch this all the way. This isn't a safari, it isn't *The African Queen*. You get into real trouble here and you don't back out.

The transporter's going to fail? Dix said. Is that the deal? And we'll be trapped back there then?

The transporter never fails and we got six backups for any problem. No, Robles said, I mean other stuff. Stuff you better be aware of.

Your stuffed animals going to eat me alive?

No, Robles said, it isn't that. I won't let you bait me, he thought. That is your skill, baiting guests into reactions, but it won't happen to me. I can deal with this, I can control the situation.

You better pay attention, he said. You better watch what's going on there and you'd better listen to me.

I listen to everyone, Dix said. That's my own zone of operations, mister, and you better leave that to me.

Leave that to him. Everything in the end got displaced, then. In the night, the tyrannosaurs ran in spasms, small gasps of effort, ran like horses down the rutted streams of the Cretaceous. The grunts of the *Triceratops*, the glide of *Struthiomimus*, the whine of tyrannosaur splitting the weak sun. He was, he knew then, absolutely dedicated, part of the period, unable to see Dix as the others might. The situation had overtaken them.

Camp Paradox Downrange

Once, Robles had had clearly defined plans, before the ethos of it began to crawl into him. The plans were two years with the dinosaurs, just two years shuttling in the transport, pushing tourists around the swamps and bogs of that impossible, riotous past and then he would be done with it, would have enough in hand to make something of himself in the tried and true third millennium.

He didn't have to be a range bum like some of them turned out to be, those who got prehistoric and future all mixed up and spewed it all in the transporter. No, Robles had had a sense of command, more command than that when Muffy had moved in and had attracted his attention, the third of the hostesses but the one that had fully caught his attention. He knew that he and Muffy had a connection, could amount to something, but only if they kept it in defined context. But it was palpable, the trade was clear, you gave them your skills and risk— and your sense of balance too because who could sup with *Struthiomimus* and return to Texas fully sane?—and tried to hold on and at the other side of the pipeline you had security.

He agreed with Muffy: they all started that way and some of them even held on to it but it was hard. Camp Paradox broadened your perspective, broadened it perhaps too much, showed you the end of things disguised as the beginning. It isn't the anachronism though, Muffy said, or the fear of getting tangled in a branch and lying down for good, it isn't the fear of one of these shy beasts gobbling you down … no, it's something else.

Maybe that we're not supposed to screw here, Robles said. Could that be it?

Yeah, sure, Muffy said, I sure do like to screw and maybe that's it. Celibacy will get you in the midst of rut, right?

But that wasn't it, of course. They both knew that, had agreed not to discuss it. It was the intimation front and back that got you, that poised and terrible certainty as you clutched your way through prehistory, taking the tourists around and showing them this or that out of the guidebook, the sense that you were at all times at some dense and thrilling flashpoint and that everything else, all of it further or later, was of no consequence whatsoever. The beasts were too huge, the tourists too stupid, the thunder of the transporter shattering in its impact. There were only extremes, it would turn a dead man into an ironist. This crawled in, centered you after a while, simply would not go away.

The idea had been—he tried to talk this out with Muffy now and then but somehow he could not make it right, maybe they had never been meant to understand one another—that the dinosaurs would change his life. Not Camp Paradox, not the tours, but the beasts themselves. Wasn't that it? If circumstances, if this malevolent and despairing twenty-first century crowding in on him and his wouldn't do it for him, if he had become misfit amidst the holography and the apocalyptic recreation, then perhaps the Cretaceous would make things different. Here on the trails he could dance with *Triceratops,* leap the fantastic with *Tyrannosaurus*, go trapping for himself in that primeval, casual ooze, learn from the nesting of these peculiar and intransigently shy beasts how he might make his own nest finally.

You don't want to nest, Muffy said. No man does. You want to fly, to scatter, to kick the nests down. Any man who doesn't know that hasn't found himself yet. But that's okay, she said. I have my own troubles too. We're all in flight. You want biography, I've got as much as yours and more disastrous.

What they didn't tell you, he wanted to point out to her but he couldn't, there was simply too much he could not discuss, what you didn't know until you learned it agonizingly yourself, slogging every step of it, was that oldest of truths: that darkness you carried within yourself was your own, *yours*. Wherever you were, there was that prehistoria of the spirit and it was of a numbing equalization. Under that ancient but familiar dark with Muffy, cheating a little (but all of them did, everyone knew that, it was the most laughable rule of the service), soaring and bucking and snaffling like the *Triceratops* which obsessed him, Robles had had his little moments now and then, his flickers of possibility. Certainly in the earlier period when the tourists with money and cameras came to open their eyes to the past and gamble at night it had been kind of fun, before Camp Paradox had begun to dwindle—like its age, like all apocalyptic hobbies—into disuse. That had been fun then, screwing Muffy within hairs-breadth of the tourists when the sun went down, sharing information on the beasts during the day as if none of the other part existed and they were truly in the service of the tourists. But as that and the travelers went-away, as the harder necessities of the doubled advancing time stream (moving one to one, there was no other way that the committee could manage, the situation would have been uncontrollable otherwise) closed in, that feeling of possibility, the sheer illicitness of all connection drained. Robles began to understand why the guides looked as they did and why most of them never got out. It was as dense and troubled, as empty and desperate here as in the twenty-first when you turned inward to the situation and it was impossible to project it upon the beasts as had been managed at the outset.

But you couldn't tell the males or females apart, not at a distance. As Muffy had said, that most central information, at least for the explorers, was a mystery along with the private lives of dinosaurs. All you knew were that they clumped together and that the species did not seem to really intermingle. These animals were helpless to the elements, protected only by their size. Surely the stupidest of all creatures, stupid as the trees they ate, they cruised the landscape like distended toys, parodies of the barnyard. Even if you could ship them back, even if there was a way to risk all the rules of time and circumstances: who would want them? What could they possibly yield?

But that had been earlier. That was when Robles had still been fighting for some sense of possibility, some kind of function, before it had all collapsed and he realized that he was just another staring, stricken guide, nothing else. Those thoughts, that concern for polarities had been before the idea of the contest, before they had rigged it for Dix, before the intrepid Dix had appeared, filled with guns and plans. We'll kill one and film the whole thing. The first prehistoric hunt, Dix had said. It will be a sensation. At last they'll see something so big, such a piece of work that they'll be able to give up their own problems and watch the general collapse. That is *media!* Dix had said, and I am your media star.

Well, he had been through that before. He had given his warnings for all the effect they had, and could do no more. Gonna get me one of those, Dix said, and let the folks at home share it all. Give them a good time, let them follow along. Maybe he was right. Maybe that was the truth and Dix had the final and absolute handle. Maybe so, and it was Robles, trapped with his barnyard and with Muffy's sly anomalies, who was the fool. Maybe it was Robles then who was the guy really out of time, more millennial detritus, that was all.

So there came a time when you had to let go, had to let matters take their course, reasonable or unreasonable, there was no other way. If Dix was right, then all of Camp Paradox from the start had been an entertainment device, a dude ranch set up for home movies. When he said that to Muffy she had been extra calm, another layer of disdain coming over her as if she had been prepared for more of Robles's silliness. Let's see what he gets, she said. Maybe he'll run at the first sign of tyrannosaur. These aren't guys of will and courage, she said, they get off from performing behind glass.

We're all behind glass. They ship us back that way in the transporter.

Don't get sophisticated on me, she said. Let's just see what will happen. It doesn't make any difference any other way, does it? I mean, nothing could be worse for business than what we have. So they would see, that was the arrangement. This will end too, Muffy pointed out, Camp Paradox was a fad, a phase like almost everything else. Dix himself would be back in the studios in just a little time.

Think of the litter here, Robles said. Think of what we're leaving behind. I mean that makes some kind of difference, doesn't it?

No it doesn't, Muffy said. She smiled at him. If the centuries ate the dinosaurs then they'll gobble up even the non-degradables. A sensible woman. But everyone was sensible by this time, fixed on outcome. Matters had counseled rationality, Dix too was a businessman. A *Triceratops* shoot was another diversion, that was all.

It was this reasonableness which had left all of them so unprepared, Robles came to think later. They had watched not only sense but passion leached from them here, had left the passion to the beasts, had identified the beasts then with display and had themselves curled in. By assuming control, they had lost control. Early, early on they had learned to screw quietly, emit no sounds, trouble neither downrange anachronism nor the tourists nor the night, wheezing out perfectly controlled, soundless orgasms, teeth sheathed in the other's neck. Oh Muffy had given acquiescence in that prehistoric night but never voice, there was no voice for any of them and that perhaps was the problem.

Tyrannosaurus had that whine but the others made no sounds, only the clumping and crush of vegetation, the deep well of their impression to mark passage. Not barnyard but dirigible, not dinosaurs but huge, misaligned aircraft, Muffy had said.

But had not said this thrashing beside him; during those times she had—ah, correctness!—said nothing at all.

The Hunt

Oh paradox! Dix thought, paradox, most ingenious paradox; leaving the thin straggle of tourists back at the camps, coming hard on *Triceratops*, his body curled to the stalk. Free, free! free for the moment of those controlling bastards in the tent, free of Robles who wanted to abort everything, he could now and at last concentrate on this dreadful and necessary task.

The Magnum, he knew, would more than distort the hapless rhinoceros before him. No, it would *reassemble* the beast, turn the rhino head to pulp, send those stupid eyes, by globule, to the far distance. Bring a video for this, track it for permanence? Hardly likely, this would destroy his audience and he was not there for that, he was to lend comfort to them. Maybe he should have saved this for his private collection but no, no, he wanted no record of slaughter, simply its evidence. Not too long now, he thought. He had the bastard leveled. It stood downrange fifty or sixty yards, shyly bobbing its head, giving him greedy little glances in the sudden adopted frieze, then poking and snaffling at the flowered branch. Dead meat on the hoof then, waiting for him.

Somewhere behind, in what they called Camp Paradox, Dix supposed that Robles and his Muffy were locked to their own task, thrashing away in the bush. He would never ask them, never say anything about it either, but really, what else could they be doing? What was the point of being a loser and blasted back to this kind of convict's exile unless at least you could hump among the beasts, feel the floor of the forest primeval? At least that was the way that Dix figured it. Think of it, he said, talking for the sake of talking, *Triceratops* did not respond to sound, was probably congenitally deaf, gobbling on the leaves anyway, what if Robles loaded her up, got her pregnant? What if the transport failed, not that such a thing was possible, they said? What if the child could get dropped off here sixty-seven million years or whatever behind the timeline? What about that, folks, hey? he said, practicing a riff which would work sooner or later on the concentrated channel. Would the child become its ancestor? Or would the comet due in pretty swift just wipe them out without sunken trace, just as promised? It was something to investigate, he thought, something that might be worth discussing when he brought his true adventures back for them and as he thought of the two of them humping, the leafy violation amidst the beasts, a splinter of envy torqued Dix, spun him, made him grunt with the savagery, the *bullet* of his own need until he put it behind, focusing then on the more immediate circumstance.

Oh paradox, paradox! That was a major-league *Triceratops* all right and as he laid it out in fire on the hot, grabbing flora of this diminished prehistory, so he would lay out *himself*, justify this trip, his life, his circumstance, his sudden and disgraceful need. Camp Paradox had become a cartoon, a vision of stuffed animals and farmyard greenery but this fucker taking the flowers in the sun, that was not a cartoon, that was a big one, the biggest one he could bag and in so doing, change everything. I want him, Dix thought, I want him badly, don't ask why, that's a different thing but I am going to have him. Somewhere in the distance he could dream that they were nesting, could glimpse the other *Triceratops* this had left behind, a family of *Triceratops*, Muffy had said, gathered together and the hell with that. The vision twinkled, was clear for a moment, even clearer than the beast before him: there were those rhinos massed with one another like Robles and Muffy, blinking and seizing in the light. Dix began to move then with small, persistent steps, focused upon his own rhinoceros in the distance, feeling the morning, the vast Cretaceous now draped on him like a cloak. Oh, those creatures would grunt and mutter from indeterminate distance but here, focused, it would be different. Just him and his rhino then, making that oldest of equations.

The animal stood calmly, poised for him in its careful and sonorous fashion, the weight of the Magnum both jarring and comforting. Prowling through the damp plain, the Magnum against his palm, Dix saw that the low dogwood had already shed its blossoms, was stripped to a bark which had the blandness of an uncovered bog, prowling toward the major-league *Triceratops* downrange, he stepped on pink, white and red petals which marked a path swatched carelessly, almost defiantly. The sassafras trees with their leaves of star or circle stood slender and delicate as the legs of *Struthiomimus*, past the trees and the other foliage Dix could see less trodden paths lead from the compounds.

He wasn't the only one who had been on these trails. But he was the first, he knew, to have the courage of the kill, that was something of which he was convinced. He came to a small rise, casting *Triceratops* slightly to his left and then, in the distance, just past what had been his downrange, he saw the nests.

There they were after all, just as he had always known there would have been. Family life in the rhinos. Of course he had been right. At intervals that seemed to be the length of *Triceratops* itself, maybe thirty feet, were five or six sites and as he peered through the foliage he could see a suggestion of bodies clumped, the animals massed then toward some purpose. Here was a crevice and in the distance another, those crevices nests, all occupied, and Dix felt that if he could focus in the most determined way, could squint, could find some utter concentration he would see friendly *Triceratops* emerge to stare, head bowed, showing the frills. How crazy was he? Was this hallucination or had he merely contrived a story around real nests? It was a serious question, something to consider but only later on. When this was over. He had better do something soon, though, nests or whatever, because his customer down there in the distance was going to get nervous soon, real nervous, and would start charging one way or the other very soon. So that was it then, you had to attack the situation at its source, go back to the tangled roots of your history, sixty-seven million years back there. Get into a machine and go to Camp Paradox, seek it there and if you found it—well, if you found it, what then? What next? That was impossible to judge. There was such indeterminacy of circumstance that you had to *kill* your way out of it, had to hack your way through this and that, simply to render some kind of explanation. Well, so much for that dog in the distance. He crouched, dropped to a hunter's position, alertness, sighted the animal. Oh, this is going to make a good one, he said. This is going to make the best, I'm going to *spatter* the son of a bitch, I'm going—

He hadn't heard Robles or Muffy behind, there was no way from the constancy of his self-absorption that he would have tracked them. He hadn't heard them, they had been cut off suddenly, not only in space but from his mind, a clean sheet dropping between his perception and their actuality but now, suddenly, he was aware of the movement behind him, a clash of figures who in no way belonged (like him) in that landscape. He had forgotten them, had crept out on his own and, locked to himself, had forgotten and now he was going to pay for it. He could see them coming up behind him but at the same time he had to keep the damned beast focused, get it in his sights or lose it altogether, try to defend two opposed sights then. Fascinated by a close-up view of the dead eye of *Triceratops* caught in sudden magnification, Dix could feel all within himself tumbling toward that death, that blind, reaching stupidity. Get back! he shouted. Get back or I'll shoot you first! But that was bluff, he was gripped by that dead eye, felt himself arcing toward the bottom of that sensibility and then slowly the transfer lifted just enough to enable him to flex his finger, lock in the sight. Now, he thought, *now before they catch me, before it's sixty-seven million years later, now* I've got him and began to count out the seconds while trying to calculate windage, calculate the sudden and frantic movement of the beast which at last, possessed by its stupidity, had sensed something going on there, not the gun but Robles thrashing through vegetation, bringing the animal to attention. Too late, almost too late then.

Dix fired.

The beast *exploded*, even as Robles's hands reached him, he could feel *Triceratops* slowly atomizing through the corridors of the trees, liquid and fire dancing away from the shattered bone and then, one horn uptilted as if in salute, the *Triceratops* plunged.

Robles Transmogrified

He did it, Robles said and sprinted away from Muffy, I didn't think the son of a bitch would but he *did*, he said, moving frantically, pushing her away, scuttled then through the mud and greenery, feeling himself moving not toward Dix but at some odd cross-angles to his own purpose. Blood had exploded in geysers from the beast but the *Triceratops* was moving nonetheless, moving with uncommon speed, rushing toward Dix with a determination that Robles could not have calculated. Dix hurled the Magnum, began to scream, words that Robles could not make out. *Get down!* Robles shouted, although he wanted the son of a bitch to die. It was reflexivity, it was the good stuff they had been taught in training. He needed to save Dix if only to protect his own position. *Roll,* he shouted, roll away from it!

But Dix, down and yelling could not move and the *Triceratops* was upon him. Robles scrambled, fell to his knees, lurched toward Dix, was able to get a hand on him, felt their connection in the sucking ooze and as he did so, knew with the absolute and perfect perception he had sought in and out of time all his life that Dix was not going to die, that Dix would get away with this, would live to tell the tale and that it would be *Robles* who was going to perish. Get away, he shouted, this time to Muffy, for God's sake, save *yourself!* knowing that it had all been set from the beginning, their own scuttling copulations too, and then as he tried to raise Dix hopelessly, use the man as a shield, the beast was already on top of him, hurling Dix with its snout to the side, seizing Robles in its huge grasp. There was blood all over him, all over them and then pressure and Robles felt suddenly transcendent, not like the transporter which yanked you here and yanked you there but different, a true conquest, a true sense of control then masked as the greatest pain he had ever known. Dix was screaming something again but it was Muffy's voice to which Robles, dying, felt attuned: she was saying something to him, something which would explain everything and if he could only attend he would understand but she had become very old, she had become older than the pyramids, than the dawn of man, than the ascent of the great beasts, she had receded from him at great and greater speed and he could not hear her, could not reach.

Somehow, it no longer mattered. It didn't matter at all.

After the Gallery

Later, deep in the darkness, the paleontologist asleep beside her, Maria remembered what she had seen in the gallery, that sudden awareness before he had pulled her away. At the skeletal foot, shiny and neat as an ornament (had anyone else seen this?) a cylindrical skull, the eye hollows glinting in the received light.

Now what would that mean? the Japanese wondered and thought of the skull for a moment and the haiku the paleontologist had made for her:

> In the light the bird
> Caught in Cretaceous flight as
> The bone talks to us.

The haiku suddenly in the sleep toward which she descended curling around the skull, a ribbon around the little ornament and she wanted to push that ribbon aside and look more closely, see the final and evident truth she knew was there—but it was impossible, she was too tired, she could not make that separation. Sleep took her, the holovision playing on soundlessly in the room showing described images of the host amidst the dinosaurs.

The bone did not talk to her anymore, then.

In the Stone House

11/22/63 Joe Kennedy, Jr. wipes the stock of the rifle again, his hands shaking, then, dissatisfied, breaks it open for the third time, making sure that the shells are still there, that the trigger is properly positioned. He reassembles the gear slowly, cursing the damned M-1, cursing his own stupidity in putting so much dependency upon a weapon which was no damned good. He should have had better equipment, not relied on the old Army supply service. But then getting better equipment would have brought some attention and he didn't want that. You had to carry this on in secrecy. Joe Kennedy, Jr. knows all about secrecy now, has counted upon it, has made it his mistral and the source of all his splendor. Too late, Jack. Too late for all of this, Joe Kennedy mumbles. He positions the cartons on the floor, peers out the window. A scattering of crowd, good, the street cleared, better, no sign of the motorcade yet in the distance. A little behind schedule but nothing ominous. Jack and the powder puff would be along soon enough.

Joe Kennedy, once President of the United States, now reduced (in his own mind if not quite in the estimation of the press) to sniveling bum, sniveling potential assassin, perches on the sixth floor of the Dallas School Book Depository, waiting for the presidential motorcade. He will sight his rifle on his brother's tousled head, hope for the best, pull the trigger. It is a difficult business, assassinating your younger brother, crazier yet if you are an ex-President of the United States, 1952-1956, which raises fratricide to the level of lunacy but there you are. It is the last great service, Joe knows, which he can perform, not only for patrimony but for the country. Jack is out of control, the arrogant little bastard had never been trustworthy in the first place but to a certain point he had been manipulable, now he was no longer.

You had to save the plan, that was all: the plan was all that mattered and Jack had broken the plan, shattered everything, the bastard. Joe thought of this, thought of that, considered all of the dreadful but necessary implications of his position, watching the sun drop little pools of uneven light on the dusty surfaces of the cartons of books, feeling the old clarity coming back. It had been a long time since he had felt this level of control but here it was, at last he knew what he was after, what had to be done. In the distance, he thought he could hear the sound of shouting, the thin tremor of drums and then as he arched his body, peered awkwardly out the window, he could see the thin movement of the crowd which could only indicate, yes, that the motorcade was coming. His breath was high in his throat, perched there like some enormous bird. Joe felt alive, felt more in possession of himself than he had in this long, dreadful exiled time. Well, he would wait it out, that was all. This was a serious business. There was nothing frivolous about it. The time for frivolity was gone.

11/22/46 I don't want it, Joe Jr. said to Jack, the big strapping jock. I was never cut out for politics. This is ridiculous. Jack laughed at him, winked riotously, hit him on the back. You may not be cut out for it, Jack said, but you got it. Mr. Smith goes to Washington. Shake 'em up good, Joe. You're a fucking war hero.

Going to be a lot of war heroes down there, Bobby said. War heroes are going to be a dime a dozen right through the decade. Sure going to be a shake-up time there, right, Dad?

Oh sure, Joe Sr. said, beaming at the three of them. Joe hadn't seen the old man in this kind of mood on land since before the war. This was what they called a family, the four of them getting together after the election to figure out what the right move would be. But that was all a bunch of crap, Joe knew, all the old man wanted to do was to look at them and gloat. His three sons, the Congressman ready for his first term, everything lining up after the war just as the old man had promised. Feels good, doesn't it? the old man said. Well, it's a way to welcome the boys home, right? I promised you a homecoming.

I didn't want this, Joe Jr. said. Going up against the old man was a losing cause but he had to go on the record, if he had taken bombers out over Germany then he could go up against the Ambassador to the Court of St. James's. Couldn't he? But it was all crap, he couldn't stand up to it. No one could, the old man rode you down one way or the other and you just had to take it. I could get used to it though, he said.

Oh, you can get used to it, the old man said. Power is fun, even if a freshman Congressman hasn't got any. And the living is easy.

Lots of women, Jack said. Don't forget the women.

You never forgot anything, Bobby said. In your whole life you let nothing go by. I think I'll bail out of this, Dad, Bobby said. I have business downtown.

We have business to settle, the old man said. You'll go in a few minutes, when I say you can. Joe, I want a staff put together. You know the names, but I'd like to hear what you have to say if you have any ideas.

Oh, I have ideas, Joe said. I have lots of ideas. You'll never listen to any of them. Hyannisport, Joe thought. It always comes back to Hyannisport. Wherever you go, however hard you fly, whatever risks you take, you wind up in a room in a house on the beach where the old man tells you what to do. Why don't you just go ahead and fix it? he said to the Ambassador. I'm sure anything you want is okay with me.

I'll tell you this right now, Jack said. I don't want any part of it. I don't want to go to Washington and I don't want to be anyone's aide-in-waiting. I'm going to go back to school.

You think so, the Ambassador said. You think that's really the plan?

I'll get a graduate degree, Jack said. I always wanted to teach history. Maybe I'll go to law school. He yawned. No Congress for me, he said, no agenda, no roll calls, no quorums. I had enough of that on the high seas, thank you very much.

I'm too young, Bobby said. Don't look at me, Dad. It may be a young man's country again, but Joe can't have a twenty-two-year-old assistant. Besides, they'll just say that I got put on the payroll to keep me off the streets.

You see? Joe said to the Ambassador, it's a family revolt. Your sons are standing up and being counted. No aide-de-camp in the room, no assistant either. So just go ahead and get the Honey Fitz delegation, because I don't give a shit. It's all the same to me.

You're a defiant prick, the old man said. You know that? I give you everything and you shit on me. You think a few stripes, a couple of bombs, and you're hot shit. Well, you're the same little bum you were before the war, you know? Who do you think pulled you those assignments?

Joe felt the old anger. Hyannisport, Hyannisport, throwing sand at the beach, they could get you every time. That seemed to be part of the deal, you thought you could get away from it but the old man could always get you back.

Leave me alone, Joe said. Just leave me alone. You wanted me to run for Congress, I ran. You wanted me to make speeches; I made war hero speeches. You want a staff, appoint a staff. Just leave me out of it, you know? You don't give a damn anyway, so just have it your way.

Bobby said, Joe, calm down. It's okay.

He's just ragging you, Jack said. That's his way. You know that he means well. He's just kidding you, trying to get you to pay attention, right, Dad? But I think we should ease off, go for a swim or something.

You'll go when I say, the Ambassador said. Jack you're going to Washington with him. There's no time to waste and there's no time to screw around either. Bobby, you can go to law school, we won't need you for a few years but you're going to check in and stay close.

I don't want any part of this, Jack said. I want to study history, be a professor at Wellesley. Maybe Duke. Show the girls the way through the

New Deal or maybe the Middle Ages. I've had all the goddamned politics I'll ever want. Jack paused, looked at the Ambassador, then took out a handkerchief and wiped his forehead slowly. I really am going to Washington, he said. You really mean it, don't you? The academy is just a dream, isn't it?

Just about, the Ambassador said. I told you, we have no time for that. We have to get down to cases. There's a country out there.

Oh, there's a country out there, Joe Jr. thought, it's been out there for a hundred and seventy years now, waiting for us. And now the Ambassador figures it's about time that he took it. The sprawl of the land, the heat of the old man's need, the sense of injustice tilted within him, and for a moment it was as if the walls had come down and he could see everything, could see what was in store for all of them, the poor, foolish damned Ambassador too, but then mercifully the walls went up again and he could see only the bare surfaces of the conference room in Hyannisport. You really do mean it, don't you, he said you meant it all.

From the start, the Ambassador said. Before you were ever born. Before I was ever born, I meant it. And you too, Joe. *You* mean it. Because you'd better.

11/22/63 It wasn't easy, Joe Kennedy, Jr. thinks, to progress from President to one-term President to ex-President to sniveling bum to assassin all in a seven-year period, it was an arc of history which refracted by opposites the old man's journey and might have been thought impossible if he, Joe Kennedy, Jr., hadn't proven that it was possible. But you had to work at it, you really did have to put your best attention to it because the country loved the few ex-Presidents it had so very much and paid such kind attention to them. But it helped if your younger brother had succeeded you as President and had found his own distinction and style in such a way as to absorb your own traces, and it also helped if you really needed to escape, if you needed somehow to sink back into the morass that his life had become since the Ambassador had looked at him in 1956 and had pulled the plug. You're through, laddie, the Ambassador had said, you've gone as far with this as you're going to go. You are not going to run in November, you are going to announce your withdrawal in Jack's favor right now, or things will get very hot for all of us. Do you understand that? Joe had understood it very well.

He had always understood the Ambassador. Maybe that was the problem, his father had been refractory of Joe Jr. from the start; Joe had felt not exactly like an extension of the Ambassador but simply a spare part, something extra that could be screwed in, unstuck, manipulated, it didn't matter, he was always around. Sometimes he had wanted to stand up to the Ambassador, he had given him a mild push in 1946 when he hadn't wanted to run for Congress, but that had collapsed pretty soon and then he had fought a little harder in '48 when the Ambassador had said that now was the time to go for the Governor's chair, a really shitty job then and now. In '51 Governor Joe Kennedy, Jr. had *really* struggled when the Ambassador had said, okay, now is the time, Truman is out of the way and we are going to stick it to this ignorant old general and take the presidency. For a few wild moments Joe had thought that he would beat down the Ambassador through simple expediency, make a speech in the Capitol like Silent Cal had in 1919 and simply pull down the temple, but he hadn't been able to do it then either. There was something very persuasive about the Ambassador, very tough, very ungiving. Ask Rose, ask Kathleen. Well, ask Rose now anyway. Ask Bobby if you could find him. That had been the worst of it, going out for the presidency, going through the worst imaginable campaign and the terrible events of the convention when he had had to break Adlai open right there in front of everyone, but since then it had gotten a little easier. It always got easier when you simply gave up, Jack had warned him and it was true, nothing had been as bad as that struggle in '52 and the convention, even '56 when Joe had had the plug pulled on him was easy in comparison. But once he had broken, once he had come down all the way to sniveling bum territory, it had been as if he had an entirely new perspective on things.

The perspective was new every day. Now Joe Jr. had a real grasp of the situation. More and more he was seeing it the Ambassador's way. Once you gave it up and gave the Ambassador his points, admitted what he was and that he had probably been right all along, everything else fell into line. Still, Joe Jr. knew that he was fucked up in his own mind. He couldn't figure out if he was doing this *for* the Ambassador or against him, whether it was his last great service for his father or a terrible act of defiance. It didn't matter, he supposed. This introspection, this wondering, this internalization, it just got you nowhere in the first place, you had to go on like the Ambassador himself and simply *do* things. The motorcade was in sight now, he thought he could see it, the lead cars of the agents. The crowd was straggling into separate ragged lines on either side of the street, the first advance patrol car came down the empty street between the barricades. It wouldn't be much longer now. Joe Kennedy, Jr. fondled the rifle and thought about this and that, thought about the nature of conditions and the question of his own sacrifice. He wanted one clear shot, that was all. One plug, one bolt of revenge, one pure thunderbolt, as Emily Dickinson said, to scalp his living soul. After that he would take his chances just like the rest of the world; he would come into a cause-and-effect world where things simply happened or failed to happen as a result of consequence. Oh Jack, he thought, it could have been different, but even as he murmured this he knew it was bullshit, it could have been no different at all. The old man had worked it out in his head long before any of them were born, had lain on a thousand pillows of resentment running the pictures through his head over and again, and by the time the four sons came along, they were nothing other than aspects of the plan like angels in the mind of God. The whole thing was determinism, that was all. One pure thunderbolt. To scalp his living soul.

10/22/63 I called you in, JFK said, because whatever has happened to us, whatever you've become, you're still a President and you're my brother. So I want you to know that I'm pulling the plug on all of this. Bobby is not going to get my endorsement. Bobby will never be President.

Joe looked at him. Past security, past the guards, past Salinger and O'Donnell into the Oval Office. Nobody had even looked at him. It had been as if he were dead. Only Caroline had waved at him when she saw her uncle go by. Caroline was probably the last friend Joe Jr. had in the family, now that he thought about it. What are you saying? he said. What does this mean to me?

It means that the dynasty is coming to a roaring halt, JFK said. He smiled at Joe. It means that Bobby is being dismissed from the Cabinet this afternoon. A press release has already been prepared. He is not being allowed to resign, he has been fired as Attorney General, *comprende?* And I will do everything within my power to make sure that he never runs for office again. The line is running out, Joe. There will be no more.

I don't understand, Joe said. I truly do not understand. His mind was as clear, as vacant as it had been the day he had been elected in 1952 and had come to understand that he had no agenda, not the shred of an agenda for the eight years of the presidency which stretched before him, and that the Ambassador had no real agenda either, they had been dumped by the wave of history but they were on the beach. Why are you doing this? he said to JFK. And why did you call me here to tell me that? What did you think I could do?

Well, nothing at all, JFK said. Call it a family courtesy. You can tell it to the Ambassador, that's what you can do for me. Tell it to Old Joe, break the word before he gets it from the radio. No Bobby in his future. The old man will shit a brick, but frankly, that's *his* problem. I have no concern for that now.

But why? Joe said. He seemed to be fixed on this point. He somehow couldn't get beyond it. That was what came from being your old man's first son, you had to take all of the mistakes, make them so that the others could have a smoother deal. Some deal they had. The deal was me, then you, then Bobby, Joe said. Now you're breaking the deal. There seemed to be a whining tone to his voice. In just a few moments he would cry. Then what? What did that mean? The crying Mr. President. I can't tell the Ambassador, Joe Jr. said. He'll go wild. He'll kill me.

You're fifty years old, JFK said. You've been the President of the United States. You're afraid some ancient fart with a cane is going to kill you? Is that what he's done to us? For what? For what purpose?

But why? Joe said again. Bobby was a good Attorney General. He never gave you any trouble. He got rid of Hoffa. He's got Hoover held down, the first guy in thirty years to do that. *I* couldn't do that. He's the next in line. So—

Because the country isn't our playpen, JFK said, because there has to be something else but the Ambassador's craziness and our own knee reflexes twitching away. Because it has to be broken sometime. I'm going to go for Lyndon. He's taken the shit admirably, he's kept out of the way, he's even been as polite as an ignorant Texan can be. Let *him* run the place for a while, I just want to go out and get laid which constitutionally I have to do now anyway. Maybe Lyndon will tame his sex life a little. Whatever he wants, it's okay with me.

It's crazy, Joe Jr. said, I've never heard such craziness. I can't believe that you're telling me this, that I'm here to listen. I wasn't a very good President. I fucked up, I admit it. The old man was right to tell me that I had to go. I admit it now, I never wanted to be there and the country was done a disservice. You did all right, Jack, in your way, up to a point. You kept Nixon out anyway, and that's a fact. But now you're betraying everything. I just don't get it. I don't—

Caroline, the President said. Caroline, honey. He extended his arms and the little girl bolted from the right doorway, ran toward him giggling. JFK leaned over, scooped up the six-year-old, bounced her in the air. Daddy, Caroline said. Joe could see the glint in their eyes, the same eyes really, the communion between the two. But it's best, still, he thought, it's best I didn't get married, didn't have children. It wouldn't have worked out. And I have spared a wife and children the disgrace of my life. I have at least kept the sadness to myself. Say hello to Uncle Joe, JFK said. Your uncle misses you.

I said hello when he came in, Caroline said. She squinted. Uncle Joe is tired, she said. He looks so tired.

We get tired earlier and earlier, honey, JFK said. He put the little girl on his lap, kissed the top of her head, spilled her off. That's enough, he said. We have to talk now. You can come back and play later.

I'll play later, Caroline agreed. She came over and kissed Joe on the cheek. I want to play with you later, she said and ran out. Joe stared at JFK, feeling the imprint of the little girl's lips on him.

It's enormous, he said, I don't believe it. This cannot be. This cannot be happening to us.

It was always meant to happen, JFK said. Now I told you. We can sneak you out the back way so that no one knows you were here.

How is Bobby taking it, Joe said, does he know?

JFK grinned. I guess he would know, the President said. I mean, I fired him face to face. It would be difficult to do that and for him not to *know*, right? Oh, he's in a ruddy gloom, Bobby is. But he'll get over it. We all get over it sooner or later. I've had my heart broken more times than you were up over Germany, Joe, and I've lived to tell the tale. You've lived pretty good yourself, and they could have shot you down anytime. Life goes on as long as you have it, that's all, you know? I'll get you down the back stairs. Anyway, that's the deal. How's your love life? I'll tell you, it's never been the same for me since the blonde did herself in. But that's another story.

Don't talk to me about the blonde, Joe said. How can you talk about the blonde? This is vile, do you hear me? It is enormous. It is impossible, it is the end of all of us, don't you see? You have destroyed us.

No, JFK said. He patted Joe's hand. That's why you're still trapped and I'm free now. Because you don't see it, you never got away, even when he made you quit you were still his property. But I see it and I tell you that this is the making of us. This is the beginning. It is the true beginning of the story. It is the beginning of the Kennedy story and someday you will see that. And now it is time for you to go, brother, but you may take a paperweight from the Oval Office as a reminder of why you no longer miss the place.

10/26/63 He hadn't been able to reach the old man first, of course. That was impossible. He had put in the call to the compound right after the conversation with Jack but no luck, the word was that the old man was getting physical therapy and couldn't be bothered. Not even by his son, the ex-President of the United States. Which meant that the old man was fucking or trying to fuck the nurse again. Half of his brain had been shut down, but the old man was still in there fighting and for all Joe Jr. knew he was having a kind of success. You had to give the old man credit, he was in there fighting until the end. In the second place, no one was really returning his calls or picking him up now, it was amazing how far an ex-President could fall if he had been out of office for almost seven years and if he had a brother-successor who was a real bastard. A real maneuverer, that was JFK. Thinking about it could get Joe sick so he tried not to consider what had happened to him, how quickly it had all unraveled. Throttlebottom, wasn't that the name? the little Vice President in *Of Thee I Sing* who gave guided tours around the White House wearing a uniform and who had lunch with his mother every day. Joe hadn't turned into a Throttlebottom, not quite, he could probably seek paying employment and get it if he wanted (he didn't want it) and probably half the adult population could name his previous occupation, but it was still a hell of a thing.

So he had settled for trying to get through to Bobby. Bobby at least would take his calls, would listen to him, and this time maybe Joe could say a few words to the Attorney General that might be of some comfort. It was a hell of a situation, that was for sure. But Bobby wasn't available, he was locked up incommunicado somewhere in the Justice Department, maybe with Hoover for all Joe knew, and there was no word on whether he would return the call if ever. So Joe had been absolutely at loose ends, the first time it had been that way for him in years. He literally did not know where to go. Surfacing, showing up in public would be suicide now, the press would be all over him, would want quotes, would want to know what Jack had in mind. The city was exploding, absolutely on fire with this, with the unbelievable news that JFK had ditched his younger brother, the Attorney General, and had announced that he was going to back the Vice President for the nomination. The end of the dynasty, it seemed, the planned succession of Kennedys. Ted had been smart, he was hiding out in the Senate well, holding the gavel for the absent LBJ and denying comment of all kind. Besides, what the hell could a freshman Senator have to say about any of this? Teddy was thirty-one years old, he was in the Senate on a family pass, everybody knew that they had used up every bit of credit this time to sneak him in and if there was a next stop for the dynasty it wouldn't be at his house for a long time, maybe never.

So Joe stayed away from Teddy too. He hung out in the secret apartment on K Street, just him and his one Secret Service guy, sharing a bottle and telling stories about the war yet again, they had both been pilots over Dresden and Secret Service had had worse luck than Joe, had had to make an emergency landing and evade capture over land. It was kind of an interesting story, but Joe was sick of it. He was sick of the whole damned thing, that was the truth, the war and the hero stories and the dynasty and the old man's plans, all of it, the whole business.

There was enough of it now, and with JFK pulling this rotten move there would be nothing but a recycling of all that stuff over and again.

There had been a time, just a few moments it seemed, after his discharge, when Joe thought that he might be free of it. Just as JFK had planned to go on and teach history at Harvard or Tufts or Haverford, hang out some place and be an academic, avoid the whole thing, Joe had thought that he might go to law school and then into pro bono work of some kind, maybe go into the down-and-out district around Scully Square and try to pay back some of Honey Fitz's debts. It wouldn't have been a bad life and somewhere along the way there might even have been a woman, one of the succession who would have stuck. He could have gotten a subscription to Friday Symphony, gone to Symphony Hall in the early afternoons and sat in the slant light of that cathedral and listened to Brahms, just Brahms and pro bono and one woman who would listen to him ... but that shimmering little moment had passed when the old man had sat them down early in the year and had laid out the situation. You and you and you. Joe would have tried to balk, but what was the point? No one got anywhere with the old man, Gloria Swanson had been the strongest-willed actress in the world, stronger than Marion Davies had been with the Ambassador's friend Hearst, and where had it gotten her? She was a slut on a boat, just gash for the old man and that's how she stayed. If Gloria Swanson couldn't beat this guy, then Joe who bore his name with the diminishing *Jr.* below didn't have a chance. JFK didn't have a chance, Bobby with his verve and his big eyes was down on the list but he was locked in too. Only Ted among them might have gotten through, he was fourteen years old then and the old man hadn't noticed him yet.

So Joe had capitulated. Run for Congress? All right he would run for Congress. Spring for the Senate because you had to keep on moving or get shot out of the water? That would be okay too. The presidency? Well, that had been a big leap, the biggest, but the Ambassador had put it to him bluntly. No one is going to beat the general unless *we* do it, the Ambassador had said, Truman is finished and the Democrats are done for unless they get a complete overhaul. And then what? Do you want that bastard Nixon just a heartbeat away, waiting for the old general to keel over? You know that the general is a figurehead, it will be Nixon and McCarthy running the show and we don't want that, do we? Joe Jr. had fallen for that, not Nixon so much, a thirty-nine-year-old shit who Joe had gotten to know in the Senate as too much of a nut case to ever be dangerous—but McCarthy in control ... that was another story. (He hadn't known the Ambassador's full cunning, hadn't measured the Ambassador's plans.) So okay, he had run. He shrugged. What the hell? It was the presidency, there were people who had been forced to do far worse, like march to their deaths in gas chambers or take rickety planes high in the air to be open targets for every ground gunner in Dresden. You couldn't complain that being forced to run for the presidency was perdition. All right, Joe had said, all right then. We'll try it. There was the good possibility they would lose, the general had his points, and if he didn't lose, how bad could it be? He already knew that he was just keeping the seat warm for Jack, who the Ambassador was beginning to suspect was the real political guy here, the real son-in-waiting. Joe Jr. didn't care about that either. If they would just leave him alone, he could put it together. Sure he could. That was the plan.

Oddly, it was LBJ who took him out of this recursive brooding, this spiteful hammering at his history, the infinite and repeated measure of the betrayals which had become his post-presidential lot and now seemed in the wake of the Ambassador's unavailability, JFK's implacability, Bobby's invisibility, to be his complete fate. LBJ had turned him up at the secret apartment and had invited him over to Blair House for a confidential talk, just a courtesy he hoped he would get from the ex-President in hope of his continued support. That was LBJ for you, still maneuvering around, even when the maneuvering was unnecessary and made him look silly. But he couldn't get off the can. All right with me, Joe Jr. said. He told his Secret Service to take the afternoon off and went over on his own. No one seemed to care. Security had really been so lax with the ex-President for years that it was almost as if they had wanted him to get taken down, just end the whole problem. LBJ was full of courtesies, of winks and nods, of little pats on the hand and flourishes with the bottle of Jack Daniel's which he insisted Joe Jr. partake. I hope, LBJ said, that I can persuade you to put my name in nomination. It would be a great honor.

I don't know, Joe said, I haven't thought about it.

A *serious* honor, LBJ said. Or you can be a second if that's all you want. Anything you say. It would be a great unifying gesture.

I haven't thought about it, Joe said. I'm still in shock. I just haven't worked this out.

Yes, LBJ said, it is sure a shock. That is a boy of many surprises, our Jack, isn't he? He is one surprising boy in good times and bad. But certainly a good-looking boy and a *great* President. I hope that I can honor him in succession.

That was LBJ. Blair House, the sitting room, no one there, Claudia knocking around somewhere upstairs, the staff dismissed or in hiding for the afternoon, an audience of one, then, and LBJ was still making speeches. You had to give him all kinds of credit, he never stopped. But wasn't that the Ambassador's lesson? You couldn't let go, you couldn't let down, not even once, because then you got led into bad habits and soon it would all unravel. So LBJ was still working the territory, audience of one, audience of a thousand, it was all the same. Still, Joe *was* the ex-President, that should count for something. So maybe he was an audience of a thousand.

Tell me, LBJ said. His cunning features, those of a hound, became even more shrewd, he leaned toward Joe. Fifty-five years old, he had the sudden, frightening ingenuousness of the thirteen-year-old kid in the schoolyard saying to the first grader, I sure could use your lunch money now, so why don't you pass it over? Why did he do it? LBJ said. What does he have up his sleeve?

I don't know, Joe said. I really don't know.

You talked to him. He had you in there the day after he did it, the day after he told me and Bobby what he was going to do. He must have told you something. What is the plan? Is he straight on this?

As far as I know.

Why would he ditch Bobby? Did Bobby do something bad? LBJ said, nudging Joe's elbow. Was that it, was it some kind of get-even, or to protect him? Because I've got to know that. If something comes out when I'm running, in mid-campaign, I ought to know that now. Why would he ditch his own brother?

I can't answer that, Joe said. I don't think there's anything bad, though. I just think maybe that he's had enough.

Who's had enough? The President?

JFK, Joe said. He's had enough of this. Maybe he wants to break the line, you know? My father—

Oh, that Ambassador is something, LBJ said, he is really something: Fighting back from a stroke and all that. Still as stubborn as they come, a real guy. One of my favorite people. He paused. You say Jack has had enough of him?

Maybe, Joe said. Maybe that's it. I can't be sure. You have to draw a line somewhere. Maybe Jack has drawn that line.

I don't know, LBJ said. It's too deep for me, I'm just a simple son of the South, a man's man, a drinking derby of one. He lifted the glass. I sure would appreciate your support though, he said. And that's a fact. Your support would be very important to me. The Kennedys *are* this country, you know that, don't you?

Oh, I hope not, Joe said. I hope that's not the case.

But it's true. Sure you boys are. You put it together. You're in the movie magazines and the newspapers, you're on television and you're a soap opera too. You *are* America. A poor Southern boy like me, he hardly has a chance to get his name in nomination these days. Which is why Jack astounds me, why I can't figure this out.

Don't ask me, Joe said, I am the ex-President. If I could figure things out I would be in a different condition.

LBJ put a hand on his wrist. He wouldn't double-cross me, would he? he said. That's what I want to know. This isn't some slick maneuver, is it, and at the convention Bobby storms it and looks like an opposition candidate when it's really you all the same? That would be a bad business.

Joe shrugged. I don't know, he said, I'm out of all this. It's just headlines and memories to me now.

That stuff with Cuba, LBJ said, that was a pisser. I thought that Bobby was going to shit, I swear. I thought he was going to have a fit right in that office. But the guy went along with the plan in the end, didn't he? He fell into line. You boys, you all fall into line with each other, no matter how it seems. That's family, right?

Joe put down the glass, shook it, watched the ice revolve. Maybe, he said. I tell you, I don't know. You have me up here for a special reason, to pump me for information, and I tell you I can't give you what you want. I'm going to go now, I'm going to pack it in. Maybe you'll hear from me later.

A nomination would be a good thing, LBJ said. And there would be something in it for you. How would you like to be Secretary of State? How about that? or UN ambassador? I've had enough of Adlai, I think, we all have. Or how would you like to be your old man and go to the Court of St. James's? You'd be the first ex-President to do some real government service. Why don't you think about it? You're a young man, younger than I, you still got it all ahead of you. We can work out something.

That was it. That was LBJ. He could always work out something, that was the way he saw life, everyone was stumbling around, looking to have an angle or to enact one, and Joe was just part of the party. Any man could be bought, any man could be sold. By all rights of experience, LBJ was on the ball, that was the way it happened. I don't know, Joe said, I'll think about it. We can talk about it next year. It's a long way to the convention.

It's going to be Atlantic City, LBJ said. That's where I want it. Jack said it was my choice and that's it.

Sure, Joe said, sure. There had to be a way out of Blair House. He had been over when he was in office a few times, Sparkman had shown him the corridors and hallways, he ought to remember. Sparkman was good at getting out of Blair House and so was he. He walked. LBJ sat on the chair at attention, his hands folded, peering at him brightly, letting him go unescorted. That was LBJ. Ferally alert, right through to the very end. It got you a reputation and you had to eat a lot of shit along the way, but at the end you were around all right, and there to pick up the pieces. All of the pieces. So much for the succession. Joe snapped back, came away from the parapet, looked no more at the imponderable, unspeakable future, felt himself hurled again and again into the hard wall of the past. Somewhere back there were the conditions which if only understood could have changed all of this, even yet. Or so he thought. But you never knew. You never knew.

8/28/46 In the stone house at Hyannisport, Joe Jr. had sat with the girl, Rhoda, through the early afternoon and talked, talked through the soft dwindling light curling in the windows and into the early dark. They had made love through the morning, past stupor and into that high, fine, dense place which Joe had known only a few times in his life, most of them at high altitude and in dread of imminent death, but this was different. They had only known each other for three days but the connection was there, even a sense of possibility. The campaign was going all right, it was more than a safe seat, it was so easy that even the old man had slacked off on him and had allowed him to take a few days off for what the old man called with a smile, *rejuvenation*. The big push would begin right after Labor Day, but now there was some time for Rhoda. She was pretty in an unconventional, Wellesley-girl kind of way, the body wasn't much but she knew how to use it, and beyond that there was something else, something which touched Joe and showed him parts of himself which he had never been convinced were quite there. Knowing that they were there would have been too risky, dangerous maybe, but in this late August the Congressman-to-be didn't care. Rhoda was a secretary at the Worcester office, detailed to be on the road, just filling in the summer after college while she made decisions about her life, she said, but Joe suspected that she didn't much care either. Not caring was precious, there was so little of it in life and even then Joe must have known that it would never be happening for him again, that this was a weekend knocked out of eternity.

I don't understand, she said to him, I don't understand what it is with you boys. Young men. The three of you. I mean I haven't met Eddie yet, but it's probably the four of you. What is it with you and your father?

I don't know, Joe said. I don't know what you're asking.

I've seen how you talk about him. I've seen how you act when he comes to headquarters or gets up on that rostrum with you, I've watched Jack's face, and Bobby's too. You're afraid of him, aren't you? He really scares you, all of you, very badly.

This is not the way to make points with the Congressman, Joe said. You are not playing your cards right if you are looking for my heart.

I'm not looking for your heart, Rhoda said. She held his hand, looked at him with much intensity. I'm looking for *you*, don't you know that? I'm trying to find you, Joe, I'm trying to help us both see who you are. You were in the war, you flew planes, dropped bombs, you were a hero. Jack did Navy duty. Bobby didn't do much of anything but that wasn't his fault, the two of you boys though were out there making the world free for democracy. What does he have over you?

It's not fear, exactly, Joe said. It's not that. The Ambassador—He paused. The Ambassador is a very strong man. He is very insistent. He has big plans and has had them for a long time. Sometimes it is just easier to get out of the way and let him have his plans, you know? It is not worth opposing him.

This makes no sense at all, she said. You know that you're not a coward. So why are you acting like one? You saved the world for him, Joe. So why do you want to please him so? What is there about him that he holds over you?

Plans, Joe said. He has large plans. It's hard to explain. It's hard for anyone outside of the family to understand—

That's bullshit, she said and smiled at him when she saw him twitch. Bullshit, she said again. You don't have to be in the family to figure out what he has in mind. He wants you to be President. The first Catholic President. Primogenitor, because you're the oldest. Then Jack. Then Bobby. Then for all I know, Edward. One, two, three, four. Those are his plans. He's always had them, from the time his sons were born. He would have drowned his daughters if Rose hadn't taken on the responsibility for them. Am I shocking you, Joe? You know it's the truth. Anyone can see it. You talk of his big plans as if it's some kind of sacred secret, but the fact is that everyone knows it. So why don't you admit it and decide if you want to play or not? You don't have to play, you know. You can go off and have a nice life. She squeezed his hand. You're good-looking. You've got lots of money, even if he cuts you off you can make your way. You're not dumb. You can go and be a professor of history.

That's Jack's ambition, Joe said. Not mine. But Jack's not going to make that either.

So what's yours? Rhoda said. What do you want, Joe?

Congress, he said, I want to go to Congress.

No you don't.

Sure I do. It will keep me off the streets.

Then the Senate? The Governor's chair? The presidency? You want that, Joe? Is the whole package set with Jack behind you?

He shrugged. I don't want to talk about it anymore, he said. You're supposed to be helping with the campaign, not asking questions. You're very pretty, he said. When the light catches you in a certain way—

Blarney will get you everywhere, she said. But you've already been into the sacred trust. I think you have something to think about, she said. I think that you've got some very serious thoughts ahead of you. Because this isn't what you want, Joe, and it's not too late to pull out.

How do you know what I want?

I don't. But I know what you *don't* want and that's it. Let Jack have it, she said. He'd have taken your place anyway if something had gone wrong. If you had been killed overseas, Jack would have been doing what you are right now. He will anyway. So you can get out of this.

You're persuasive, Joe said, pretty and persuasive. But I don't think you understand. There are centuries of family history here, generations of ignorance and slight, the Ambassador and all his forebears working—

I'm not interested in that, she said. I'm interested in *you*. I haven't been fucking the Ambassador or Jack all night and all morning, it's been you. You're the one I care about and I want you to see, want you to know—

He put a hand on her lips. All right, he said. I understand you. It's enough. I understand what you're trying to say. You don't have to say any more.

But you won't change, she said, will you? One pretty girl in one afternoon isn't going to make any difference at all. All those centuries of family history, generations of ignorance and slight, the Ambassador and his forebears working—

You got me, he said, let's go to bed. Let's make love. I want to see you. I want to enter you, I want to know—

She stared at him, her eyes round and full. In the stone house at Hyannis in that moment, he felt that he could have touched all the deepest parts of her. Maybe, he said. I don't know. I'll think about it. It's too much to think about. Maybe we have a chance, he said. You don't know where you're heading, what this has been, what has become of us. I can only tell you that there's more here than you can know. But we could try—

She put her arms around him. All right, she said, we won't talk any more. We won't say anything more now. I could love you. I don't love you. Maybe I do love you. I just don't know, can you see? We don't know what we are, we have to *dig* for it. You have to go inside, you have to understand.

Yes, he said, yes, we'll try, we'll try to go inside, and in the light and shadow they had come together in that room, not even leaving for the bedroom, and there had been that night and part of the next day too, and then Rhoda had left because her parents would want to know where she had been all these days and she had still been living at home. Then came Worcester and Boston and the tumult of the campaign resumed; it was not as if they simply fell apart, it was not that simple. They saw each other again and they almost came that close again several times, but as October went into November and then past the election and into the plans which had to be made for Washington it became clear to both of them, maybe Rhoda before Joe, that nothing was going to change, that he wasn't going to get out, not then or ever, that he was going to have to follow it through to the end and there was no room for her because she would have been part of the furniture. I think I'll always love you, she said. I don't think I'll ever marry. Me too, he said, me too, Rhoda, but that had all been what she would have called bullshit; Joe was the sincere one, Joe was the one who had never married (he sure had fucked around, though) but Rhoda was hooked up with a professor of economics in less than six months from their parting, went to UCLA with him, had four sons, a nice bit of collusion there, and had died at forty in San Bernardino in a crazy flood that had washed out a campground and drowned her and the oldest boy. So much for that. The stone house at Hyannis, the pinwheels of light, the soft sounds of her against him and the rising too, and then the end of it as they fell and fell and it was not Rhoda but his condition which embraced Joe as he lay there gasping by the cold fireplace, staring at the crazed and absolute configurations of his life. You kept on going, that was all, followed it through, and then on the beach at Hyannis or in the campgrounds at San Bernardino the waters came, the waters always came and they would take you. Take you up, take you down, take you to the castle of your life. Portraits of the Ambassador hung at every angle in every room, glinting, glinting with their spectral knowledge and absolute pity.

11/22/63 Joe checks the stock again of the M-1, feeling it cold and solid in his hands, the trigger a little rigid but it will yield in the clutch, he is sure. The trigger feels a little bit like a clitoris against his index finger, he will jiggle it a little, then take a firm grip and make the rifle come. The thought of this, the analogy, makes Joe giggle a little and there is a strange, whirring moment of descent in which he wonders if he is really losing control, if this act is truly as crazy as it might seem from the outside. All of his life, he now sees, he has been surrounded by ordnance, by gleaming machinery of one description or another, the planes carrying him like an embryo in their thin, shaking, gusty surfaces, then later in the open cars and closed offices of politics, the experiments with hunting and high-caliber bullets which he had carried on at Hyannisport over the weekends, just as a means of getting away, then the years after the Presidency running around the country in high-speed machines, sometimes with the Secret Service in tow, more often not, tracking the highways of his doom, watching America stream by him. In Las Vegas for a while in the late fifties there had been some real peace, hurling himself against the distant totalizers, the green felt of the craps table, the roulette wheel, feeling himself dispersed in these arenas of chance, and in that machinery he had found for the first time since Rhoda the beginnings of a frail if illusory sense of himself ... but that too had ended, Bobby had passed the word, Las Vegas was just too touchy, mob-infested, in the hands of the racketeers and it wouldn't look good if the oldest son and the ex-President were seen at the gaming tables, even if he was surrounded by Federal protection.

Worse if he were surrounded by Federal protection, Bobby had said, because that made the government look like collaborators, made it look as if they were granting special prerogatives to the gangsters. Joe had made something of an issue of it, had even humiliatingly pleaded, but Bobby had been firm, it wouldn't work out. He had to quit. At last the Ambassador himself had brought the word to Joe in a late-night phone call. They weren't talking much in those years, reconciliation had come later if at all, but the Ambassador made the call a special issue. You're entitled to some pleasure, maybe, the Ambassador had said, but you're fucking up things for everybody, Junior. So bury it. Come back East and play the horses at Bowie and Laurel with Hoover, but stay the fuck out of that Mafia trap. And that had been the end for him, he had never gone back since.

But the machinery had persisted, even to this moment when he cradled the M-1 and looked at its dull surfaces, feeling the power humming in the stock, feeling in his wrists the arc of the bullet which would tear off his brother's head. Reconciliation had come later if at all, that was true, but in a way *this* was reconciliation right now, he would be performing the one last great service for the Ambassador that no one else could have conceived, and that service would change everything.

See, you old bastard, I loved you all the time. I gave up everything for you because it was in you that I would find myself and that is what I have, Father, don't you see?

He didn't have to peer into the distance now, the motorcade was visible, clearly within the arc of his vision, it would be only a little while now. In the meantime, Joe Jr. thought, there was absolutely nothing to do but to stay calm, stay crouched amidst the cartons, let it happen. The worst thing would be to lose control now, to become emotional, to begin to think about it. The thinking had all been done. He had blamed the Ambassador for everything back then, had really fixated upon the Ambassador as being—how foolish, how stupid!—the force which destroyed his life, but then he had learned better, had come to understand that he who bore his name was if anything the Ambassador's greatest creation and now he would have to break the President to prove this to all of them. In the end it all came simple, it was far less complex than anyone thought, one fine line carried through it all, and you simply had to follow that arc. The best part of being Throttlebottom was that you could put on a uniform and lead a guided tour and no one would notice, no one at all. Joe Jr. began to hum, hummed a little *marche militaire* in a cracked and insouciant tenor, waiting, waiting now for the cars to come. Getting out quickly, out the back way, that was going to be a tricky business. But he would work on it in due time.

11/22/55 Joe had gone ahead with everything up to that point. The Ambassador wanted to stock the cabinet with Massachusetts pols, that was okay with him; he wanted JFK in at HEW even with the nepotism angle, and that was okay too. He had a certain agenda, the Ambassador, and the best thing to do was to go along with it, otherwise he would take to reminding you of exactly who you were and how you had gotten there and what could be next.

So even putting McCarthy in at State, Joe had gone along with it. That had been the real shocker and he had taken plenty for that; it had looked in the beginning as if it would tear the party apart. But the Ambassador had been insistent. I want this and that's the way it's going to be, he said to Joe. Handle it any way you want, take it to the press, make any goddamned liberal excuse you want, but Tail-Gunner Joe is in there and that's the way it's going to be. What about the eighty-seven Communists he can't produce? Joe had asked mildly. What about that faked Tydings photograph? What about the loyalty oaths and that joke committee? The Ambassador had shrugged. That's all politics, he said, that's for show. The real thing is that I want him in there. He's an old friend and a good guy and we can keep an eye on him better there than in the Senate. Listen here, the Ambassador had said and maybe he was telling the truth, that was the thing about the old man, he could lie and lie and lie and then he'd pull something on you which was absolutely the truth and if you ignored it you could really get in trouble, would you rather have that guy over at State where we can keep an eye on him and control him all the time? Or do you want him in the Senate, skulking around with Nixon, making plans and working against us every minute? You'll see how much sense this makes.

Joe had seen it all right, had known what was going to come on him when he made the announcement, the best thing to do was to announce the Cabinet in a bunch in mid-December right around the tree-lighting ceremonies and kind of *sneak* McCarthy into the back of the pictures and hope that they could get away with it, but that of course wasn't the way it really worked out. The press had been too scared of Tail-Gunner Joe to really make a big issue of it, that had been left for Truman, who went half crazy back in Independence, and to Alger Hiss, but they had certainly made it the story of the day, then the week. Handle it any way you want, the Ambassador had said, so Joe did just that, went on the radio the day after Christmas to talk about the New Unity Coalition which would come out of Tail-Gunner Joe being brought to State, even let the Tail-Gunner join him in the last ten minutes to make his own unity statement, and it seemed for a while as if it actually was going to work out. McCarthy liked his drinks and his boyfriends in secret and his prerogatives and really wasn't as much of a danger as everyone thought, the Ambassador had been quite right there, but then the situation had started to get really nasty when McCarthy all on his own decided to reconvene Un-American Activities and go after a whole flock of homosexuals and Communists who he said had been part of the old China group for years. A hundred were pitched out in October of 1955 in the first wave, and then Tail-Gunner Joe had taken some advice from Nixon and had gone on television, shaking his fists and crying and saying that he was standing up for an administration which was too cowed, just too scared to really face up to the degree of corruption, but the penalties had to be paid. Then McCarthy had spoken about how the H-bomb plans had been shipped out to China and maybe the Soviet satellites by some of these hundred people and it might be too goddamned late to save security, they might have to deal with the possibility of a preventive strike against Peking, and looking at the shouting figure on television, looking at the grays and blues of the Secretary of State who was clearly drunker than he had ever been and absolutely out of control, Joe Jr., the President, had seen that he was going to take whatever risks were entailed, wherever they led, and he had fired the Secretary. Had simply called in Sorenson and told him to get the announcement out immediately and then had phoned the UPI himself at midnight to break the word. This is intolerable, the President had said. McCarthy does not speak for this administration, he speaks for no one. He was an attempt at a coalition which simply went wrong and he is out. Then he had gone to bed, alone as always, with the first solidity of conviction he had felt in more than a decade and had waited for all of it to sweep over him.

It had been even worse than he had thought it might be because McCarthy did not make a frontal attack, he sent up Cohn first and then Harriman (how he got Harriman to front for him was something that Joe could not figure out) and then amazingly Adlai had made a call and said that this was simply too extreme, that perhaps some compromise could be worked out. McCarthy might say that he had overstated the preventive strike issue and felt that the warning alone was sufficient. No, Joe said to the old trimmer, the Governor of Illinois who he had beaten back like a crutch at that rigged 1952 convention, there's no compromise. He's out. He is out as of thirty-six hours ago. He is crazy, Adlai, and I am crazy if I keep him. You don't understand the stakes, Adlai had said, and Joe understood then and only at that moment that Adlai was bought too, that Adlai was bent over and Tail-Gunner Joe had him cold. Adlai was a liberal who had spent his whole life waiting to be buggered and Tail-Gunner Joe had seen it and somehow done the job. It was the first insight the President had ever had which he thought might be worthy of his old man, the Ambassador, which he thought the old man might really have liked and respected, but of course it was too late for gaining respect that way.

At last McCarthy himself had come up alone, his eyes bloodshot, his head tilted, the scent of alcohol and frenzy coming off him, and something else, some deeper odor which Joe could not identify but which he knew was profound. Tail-Gunner Joe had already known that it was over, though. I'm not finished yet, he said. I'm not finished with you yet, Boston. There's plenty more to be said here. You aren't going to fuck with me like this. I came over to your side, gave you the advantage for years because I am a great American, but I see you for what you are now. You're part of them.

A Communist too, Joe said, is that what you're saying?

Never mind what I'm saying, McCarthy had said, you just remember that you're going to go down on this one.

If anyone crosses you he's a Communist, Joe said mildly. It played for a long time and it's probably going to still play, but I can't tolerate it at this level, Senator. The Chinese don't understand our politics, you understand, they don't know that it's all a game you're playing. They and the Russians are likely to do something which might go out of control and that's why you have to go. So you're gone. Except that you won't go easy. So go hard, but go away before I call the Secret Service and have you thrown out by all the powers of the office I have been given. I don't know how deep you're into all of this but I don't think you can compromise the Secret Service, at least not yet. Get out, he had said.

Get out, you stinking, evil son of a bitch, go back to your boys and your press conferences and your glory holes but get the hell out of this White House right now and never come back.

So McCarthy had gone away then, something in Joe's face, certainly not the tone of his voice which was quiet, even choked, must have gotten through to him, but that wasn't the end of it, the Ambassador was up there in two hours, coming right in past Sorenson, past JFK, who was sitting with him, trying to calm Joe down. Get out of here, the Ambassador said to Jack and Jack got up and went, no argument, no response, just cleared out. That was the way it was done. The Ambassador closed the door and turned to the President. Just what the fuck do you think you're doing, he said, what is going on here? I want that man back, you understand. I want him back in office. I don't care how you handle it, a full retraction, a press conference, an arms-around-each-other bit, that's up to you. But you are not going to get this one by me. I have given you a lot of latitude, Junior, but I am not going to give you this one. The Tail-Gunner comes back.

No, Joe said. He's not coming back.

Must I—

No, Joe said. I have given in to you all the way. I have let you have one thing and the other thing, I have gone along with you from the first, I have given you primogeniture and the Presidency and I have not fucked with you, but you are not getting this one. McCarthy is out. He is not coming back. I will stand in the door of State before he ever comes back. I will go to the well of the Senate, I will make a joint session of Congress to hear an address, but he is out. I will get Hoover to release everything from every file on this guy if I have to, but he is *out* and he is not coming back. He will have us all in flames, don't you understand that? He will have a bomb put in Times Square and another in the Rose Garden here. Joe looked at the Ambassador, felt the tears hopelessly come to him. Dad, he said, he's crazy, don't you see that. He had not called the Ambassador Dad in twenty years, it shocked both of them. He wants us all dead for his own advantage, Joe said. That's the truth and you know it. It has to stop.

But it can't, the Ambassador said, it can't because I won't have it. Because I *said* so—

What you say goes almost all the time, Joe said, but it doesn't go this time and that's all. I will be impeached for it if necessary, but it ends here. McCarthy is out. Please, Dad, leave now. I won't throw you out, I can't do this to you, you're my father so I'm begging, but I want you to leave.

All right, the Ambassador said. He sat convulsively, took off his glasses, wiped them, stared at Joe. All right, he said, you'll make it stick. I can see that. You are that serious, you fool. You will stake everything on getting him out.

Yes I will. I must.

Then *you're* finished, the Ambassador said. Don't you understand that? You're all done for. I'll close the books on you. You're a one-term President.

I can't be concerned about that, Dad, Joe said. That's not the issue. The issue is—

The issue is that you can't give me this one. All right then, but it cuts the other way too. *I* can't give you this one either. You're finished, Joe. Jack is the next President. You're getting out. Ill health, inability to govern. You're going to pass it on to your brother, the Secretary of Health, Education and Welfare. You've got enough clout in the party to do it, you're the President. That's what is going to happen.

And if I don't? Joe said, what's going to happen then?

You will, the Ambassador said. He put on his glasses, stared precisely at Joe, rubbed his hands. You can make it hard or you can make it easy, it's up to you. I'll destroy you, Joe. If I have to I'll finish you off. So just get out. Make your announcement tomorrow. Otherwise—

Otherwise what?

Otherwise people are going to start to die, the Ambassador said. Maybe a housewife and college professor in San Bernardino for starters, maybe some other people. I'm not playing around, Joe.

Joe stared at him, swallowed, said nothing at all for a while. He tried to keep his mind blank. That was a trick his father had taught him long, long ago, if they hurt you, if you find yourself really bleeding, just shut up, keep your mind blank as a screen, allow them absolutely nothing. That was the only way to handle it until you got control again.

All right, Joe said, say I do it. Then what? Jack becomes President if he wins the election—

He wins the election, the Ambassador said. Don't you worry about that. He wins the election just like you won the election. We'll make sure of that. That's my department as of right now because *you*, Joe, you are finished. The election will be taken care of.

And so McCarthy gets back in at State, Joe said, so you'll reverse everything I've done here. I can't go along with that. You can take me down but I'll take you down too. Jack as well. You'll all go down, but McCarthy is never going to make a speech about preventive war again.

Okay, the Ambassador said. His glasses glinted, flashed in the light. No McCarthy. That's the deal. He won't be coming back. We'll keep him out.

And you say—

That's my word, the Ambassador said. You'll have to trust me just like I trusted you and got betrayed. Except that I won't betray you. McCarthy won't be Secretary of State.

Or Jenner, Joe said. Or Capehart. Or those swine McCarthy runs around with, I want them out too. That's the deal then. You make that pledge and I'll go quietly. Otherwise—

Otherwise you'll take us all down, the Ambassador said. Except you won't, you won't do that. Because you're a Kennedy, Joe, and that's part of the deal, the family first. He limped toward the door. I want an announcement within forty-eight hours, he said. You can go on television live or call the press or sneak it out to the UPI the way you did the firing. That's up to you. But I want that forty-eight-hour business and that's all there is to it, you hear me? That is very definite.

And if not—?

We've been through that, Joe, the Ambassador said. We don't have to go through it again, do we? He opened the door, nodded at the Secret Service.

I'm your *son!* Joe wanted to shout, I'm your first-born *son*, how can you do this to me? If the door had been closed, if the Ambassador had still been there, he might have done that. But of course the Ambassador was too clever, he was gone already and he knew that the President wasn't going to make that kind of a scene in front of the security. So Joe just sat there, the way the Ambassador had known he must and after a while Jack drifted back in again from the side room where he had heard everything and they just stared at each other. There was absolutely nothing to say. This was another of those times, and there had been plenty in their lives where there was just not one brotherly word that could be passed.

Oh, the Ambassador had been angry at him! Joe had thought that it was irreparable. But of course as the years passed things cooled off. McCarthy died of drink not much later, meaning that he wouldn't have been around much longer anyway, and JFK had turned out in the long run to be an even bigger betrayer in office than Joe had been, in the estimation of the old man. And Joe had come to see after this one great confrontation that the old man had probably been right after all, McCarthy was just red meat for the troops, and backed off China and the Soviet Union with terror so that deals could have been made. Joe in any case never took issue with the Ambassador again; one way or the other that confrontation had been the end for him.

And here in Dallas at last and at least he could come back all the way, perform this one great service for the stricken, nurse fucking, raunchy, devoted old Ambassador who had in the end proven in this circumstance as in so many others to have been absolutely right.

Son of a bitch, JFK had said in the Oval Office that afternoon, son of a bitch, I'm going to be President. Not even a thought of protest or uncertainty, that was how thoroughly the Ambassador had controlled them all. The fucking President, oh my God, I'm the next President.

Well, you'll love it, Joe said, you'll love the perks anyway. There are lots of interesting possibilities in this job.

I wonder if I should get married after all, Jack said, maybe this isn't the time to do it with the campaign coming up and all. Maybe I should wait.

Jackie won't let you wait, Joe had said, she's going to be First Lady now and no one is going to give that up. Except Rhoda, he thought, but that was another wench in another time and so dead, so dead to me. You might as well go ahead and have a big wedding, Joe had said. The voters will love that.

They had, they did, and Jack stormed in over Nixon with 472 electoral votes and Kefauver clinging onto him on the inaugural stand, holding him even tighter than Jackie. Joe Jr.'s instincts had always been good, even if his luck hadn't. One way or the other, the Ambassador had made him a first-class political animal.

A humble one too, and eager to get back under the umbrella. The real betrayal then had been JFK. JFK had broken the line.

11/22/63 The sounds of the motorcade drifting to his high seat in the depository, the sound of the crowd seeming to envelop him, Joe lifts the stock, sets the sight, puts the scope to the curly, tousled head of his brother, seeing the faint pink of Jacqueline's suit refracting an aura, takes off the safety then. With a precision he had never known to be within him, Joe sets the sight, aims the rifle and fires. The first shot is in the throat, Jack falls back, Joe can imagine the look of terror and surprise on his face. Second shot ... he cocks it again. Jackie is starting to scramble, casting wistful, hopeless glances over the back of the limousine. Joe puts the killing shot in, the shot that will come through the Governor's knee, enter Jack's head at a high angle and windage and blow off the skull. Bobby will storm the citadel in a wave of national horror and sympathy which will utterly repudiate the crude, the untalented JFK. For every plan there is another plan. Joe knows this. The Ambassador after all was absolutely right, there was *always* that alternative.

Giggling, Joe Kennedy, Jr. puts down the rifle, lurches for the door, yanks open the door and speeds down the steps toward the open air, leaving the concerns of the motorcade to the Secret Service and to Parkland Hospital. Later that afternoon the ex-President will be found cowering in a movie theater and later yet he will be taken away in what must be the most sensational story in all of American politics, but he will never tell. He will never tell. He will never tell. Only the Ambassador, should the Ambassador come to see him, he will tell the Ambassador everything. Everything. But that is a part of the saga, Joe Jr., assassin of the thirty-fifth President knows, which will have to be told by other than him. His time is done.

He wonders what Rhoda might have known.

The policeman, curious, sees him running and comes toward him. The rifle is back on the sixth floor but Joe still has the .38-caliber Smith & Wesson.

Would Rhoda have made any difference?

Flatly, the policeman comes toward him, then shouting.

Joe reaches for the gun.

THE END

The Sprawl of Intensity; the Intensity of Sprawl

"Publishing short stories in this country is like
tossing feathers down a well."—Donald Barthelme

Henry James defined the successful short story as involving one protagonist, one event, one inevitable (at least in retrospect) outcome. At least that has been my understanding and *The Turn of the Screw* certainly exhibits and elaborates this continuity; there is a minor problem, it is a novella not a short story and the outcome is at best ambiguous, but as Joe E. Brown reminded us, nobody's perfect and *Turn of the Screw* was probably better or at least noisier in Benjamin Britten's adaptation anyway. All generalities are shaky, including this.

It does seem fair to speculate, though, that if James' logging of technique and purpose does hold, then the short story by definition must be a kind of one-off whereas the novel—ah, the novel— "An extended work of fiction that has something wrong with it" is incantatory; it takes a set of characters, a premise or two, a locale or several and it binds them through repetition, through constant revisiting if in a slightly different form, it carries through its material through sheer insistence and it seeks extension of one person, one epiphany through the multiplication of the situation. The novel is a short story with obsessive-compulsive syndrome and from Melville to Wouk to Nabokov to Austen to Grace Metalious it extends its central situation through repetition. The witches in *Macbeth* are chanting arcs and secants which gain their power through citation and re-citation, over and again in the forest of the night; strip *Macbeth* to a single utterance or set of utterances and begins, slowly at first and then with insistence to become an embracing curse. The witches themselves are not principals, they are decor.

This in any event is one way of looking at the situation: the short story not as clipped or truncated narrative but instead another way of looking at the situation; the novel not as an extension or cluttering of the short story but as another version entirely, an Olde Curiosity Shop of accumulated instant.

I originated as a short story writer and was driven to the novel only for market reasons; there was no way—even for Updike, even for Cheever, even for Jack Ritchie—to make a living exclusively through the short story. Left to my own devices and in a different market situation I might never have written a novel. But I was not left to my own devices, very few of us are and gradually through a modicum of wit, a sledgehammer of incantation and a kind of desperation I converted myself into a novelist although never leaving the technique of the short story behind or my preference for it. Over the decades I have published about 500; this is not Bill Ballinger or Edward D. Hoch territory, certainly there were writers active in the 1930's pulp market who ultimately exceeded that total. These writers were in the mass critical mind hacks, a form of android manipulated machinery although they might not have felt of themselves as such. In the so-called literary quarter Updike might have published several hundred, Cheever 160, O'Hara more than that but they paid a certain unhappy price for that level of productivity and only their proficiency in and insistence upon the novel were sufficient to save them from the Stern Decree. Very few writers, "hacks" or "literary," were able to establish lasting critical recognition solely upon the basis of the short story; even the masters of the form like Stanley Ellin, Roald Dahl published novels in some quantity. "Saki" (the British writer Hector H. Munro) was perhaps the only writer who achieved some prominence wholly derivative of command in the short story alone.

Announcing myself at the port of entry as essentially a short story writer was one of many serious mistakes I made in rodomontades attached to my work. Another and even more damaging was to preface my first collection, *Final War and Other Fantasies* published by Ace in 1969 with a flat statement that I was not really a science fiction writer; add to that essentially the same statement preceding my story in Harlan Ellison's 1972 *Again Dangerous Visions* and a certain idiocy and self-destructiveness seems to have been put on the permanent record. Only something like "I really do not like this kind of fiction and disassociate myself from it" could have been more damaging and in fact statements like this trickled from introductions to or commentary on my work for many years. By the time I got wise to the paintbrush I was applying to my work, the damage had been done.

Still, the stories exist even though occasionally I tried to implode them and the two collections preceding are fair examples of how far I attempted to go when I however intermittently abandoned the amusing racket of self-destruction. *Midnight Lady*, published in 1980, is the less ambitious or developed of the two although the Writers Heaven stories strike me—as incestuous or recursive fiction goes—as almost definitive, and there are other stories in that collection which inspired the manager of a Berkeley science fiction shop to put a sign on the table which bore a dozen new copies of the collection: "Really, this is a pretty good book, not as bad as you might think: try it!" "On The Air," my Pacifica Radio story and tribute to the late Steve Post is perhaps the second best of all talk radio stories (the best is "Caius," with Bill Pronzini) and the reprints from *Alfred Hitchcock's Magazine* show me cleverly trying to replicate my career in science fiction (unsuitable stories for suitable markets) before I became wise to my own agenda and cut it out.

Stone House which is the last or penultimate publication of the once revered Arkham House is incontestably my best collection and there are five or six stories which simply represent the best of which I was capable unto this moment; they are stronger than I thought I could ever be. The Huey Long story "Kingfish," the Kennedy title story and maybe above all "Heavy Metal" are entirely beyond my means and I am grateful to have done them.

As I wrote the long-suffering publisher, describing the Afterword which I planned, I would limn an odyssey through which I could publish 500 stories, most of them in respectable or at least paying markets, and be totally unknown. That does not make me—is the line from *Seinfeld*—a bad person.

—New Jersey 31 May 2021

ACKNOWLEDGMENTS

THE MAN WHO LOVED THE MIDNIGHT LADY

"Introduction" copyright © 1980 by Barry N. Malzberg.

"On the Air" copyright © 1976 by Robert Silverberg. Appeared in *New Dimensions 6*.

"Here, Just for a While" copyright © 1977 by Ultimate Publications, Inc. Appeared in *Fantastic*.

"In the Stocks" copyright © 1977 by Robert Silverberg. Appeared in *New Dimensions 7*.

"The Fifties" copyright © 1978 by Conde Nast Publications, Inc. Appeared in the *Analog Yearbook*.

"The Man Who Married a Beagle" copyright © 1977 by Ultimate Publications, Inc. Appeared in *Fantastic*.

"Big Ernie, the Royal Russian, and the Big Trapdoor" copyright © 1978 by Mercury Press, Inc. Appeared in *The Magazine of Fantasy and Science Fiction*.

"Ring, the Brass Ring, the Royal Russian, and I" copyright © 1978 by Mercury Press, Inc. Appeared in *The Magazine of Fantasy and Science Fiction*.

"Of Ladies' Night Out and Otherwise" copyright © 1980 by Barry N. Malzberg.

"The Annual Once-a-Year Bash and Circumstance Party" copyright © 1979 by Mercury Press, Inc. Appeared in *The Magazine of Fantasy and Science Fiction*.

"The Appeal" copyright © 1979 by Davis Publications, Inc. Appeared in *Alfred Hitchcock's Mystery Magazine*.

"Yahrzeit" copyright © 1973 by Fawcett Publications, Inc. Appeared in *Ten Tomorrows*.

"Another Burnt-Out Case" copyright © 1978 by Ultimate Publications, Inc. Appeared in *Fantastic*.

"I'm Going Through the Door" copyright © 1976 by Universal Publishing & Distributing Corp. Appeared in *Galaxy*.

"Cornell" copyright © 1972 by Davis Publications, Inc. Appeared in *Ellery Queen's Mystery Magazine*.

"On Account of Darkness" copyright © 1977 by Mercury Press, Inc. Appeared in *The Magazine of Fantasy and Science Fiction*. Impasse, copyright © 1976 by Web Offset & Lithography, Inc. Appeared in *Odyssey*.

"Varieties of Technological Experience" copyright © 1978 by Conde Nast Publications, Inc. Appeared in *Analog*.

"Varieties of Religious Experience" copyright © 1979 by Davis Publications, Inc. Appeared in *Alfred Hitchcock's Mystery Magazine*. "Inside

Out" copyright © 1978 by Davis Publications, Inc. Appeared in *Alfred Hitchcock's Mystery Magazine*.

"Line of Succession" copyright © 1978 by Davis Publications, Inc. Appeared in *Alfred Hitchcock's Mystery Magazine*. "Reaction-Formation" copyright © 1979 by Davis Publications, Inc. Appeared in *Alfred Hitchcock's Mystery Magazine*.

"Indigestion" copyright © 1977 by Ultimate Publications, Inc. Appeared in *Fantastic*.

"A Clone at Last" copyright © 1978 by Mercury Press, Inc. Appeared in *The Magazine of Fantasy and Science Fiction*.

"Backing Up" copyright © 1978 by Davis Publications, Inc. Appeared in *Alfred Hitchcock's Mystery Magazine*.

"September 1958" copyright © 1980 by Barry N. Malzberg.

"Into the Breach" copyright © 1980 by Barry N. Malzberg.

"On 'Revelations'" copyright © 1976 by Ultimate Publications, Inc. Appeared in *Amazing*.

"Thirty-Six Views of His Dead Majesty" copyright © 1979 by Roy Torgeson. Appeared in *Chrysalis 6*.

"The Trials of Sigmund" copyright © 1980 by Barry N. Malzberg. "The Man Who Loved the Midnight Lady" copyright © 1977 by Bill Pronzini. Appeared in *Midnight Specials*.

Story afterwords copyright © 1980 by Barry N. Malzberg.

IN THE STONE HOUSE

"Heavy Metal" copyright © 1992 by Mike Resnick & Martin H. Greenberg. Appeared in *Alternate Presidents*.

"Turpentine" copyright © 1992 by Martin Greenberg & Gregory Benford. Appeared in *What Might Have Been*.

"Quartermain" copyright © 1984 by Davis Publications. Appeared in *Isaac Asimov's SF Magazine*, January 1985.

"The Prince of the Steppes" copyright © 1988 by Mercury Press, Inc. Appeared in *The Magazine of Fantasy & Science Fiction*, June 1988.

"Andante Lugubre" copyright © 1993 by Sovereign Media, Inc. Appeared in *Science Fiction Age*, July 1993.

"Standards & Practices" copyright © 1993 by Mercury Press, Inc. Appeared in *The Magazine of Fantasy & Science Fiction*, May 1993.

"Darwinian Facts" copyright © 1989 by Ed Gorman & Martin H. Greenberg. Appeared in *Stalkers*.

"Allegro Marcato" copyright © 1993 by Mike Resnick & Martin H. Greenberg. Appeared in *By Any Other Name*.

"Something From the Seventies" copyright © 1993 by Mercury Press, Inc. Appeared in *The Magazine of Fantasy & Science Fiction*, April 1993.

"The High Purpose" copyright © 1985 by Mercury Press, Inc. Appeared in *The Magazine of Fantasy & Science Fiction*, November 1985.

"All Assassins" copyright © 1992 by Martin H. Greenberg & Gregory Benford. Appeared in *What Might Have Been*.

"Understanding Entropy" copyright © 1994 by Sovereign Media, Inc. Appeared in *Science Fiction Age*, July 1994.

"Ship Full of Jews" copyright © 1992 by Omni Publications, Inc. Appeared in *Omni*, April 1992.

"Amos" copyright © 1992 by Mercury Press, Inc. Appeared in *The Magazine of Fantasy & Science Fiction*, July 1992.

"Improvident Excess" copyright © 1992 by Martin H. Greenberg & Max Allan Collins. Appeared in *Murder Is My Business*.

"Hitler At Nuremberg" copyright © 1992 by Mike Resnick & Martin H. Greenberg. Appeared in *By Any Other Name*.

"Concerto Accademico" copyright © 1991 by Martin H. Greenberg. Appeared in *Dinosaur Fantastic*.

"The Intrasigents" copyright © 1993 by Ed Gorman and Martin H. Greenberg. Appeared in *Solved!*

"Hieractic Realignment" copyright © 1999 by Wizards of the Coast. Appeared in *Amazing Stories*.

"The Only Thing You Learn" copyright © 1994 by Robert Silverberg and Karen Haber. Appeared in *Universe 3*.

"Police Actions" copyright © 1992 by Bantam Books. Appeared in *Full Spectrum 3*.

"Kingfish" copyright © 1992 by Mike Resnick & Martin H. Greenberg. Appeared in *Alternate Presidents*. Appears in this edition for the first time.

"Fugato" copyright © 1994 by Mike Resnick & Martin H. Greenberg. Appeared in *Alternate Warriors*.

"Major League Triceratops" copyright © 1992 by Byron Press Associates. Appeared in *The Ultimate Dinosaur*.

"In the Stone House" copyright © 1992 by Mike Resnick & Martin H. Greenberg. Appeared in *Alternate Kennedys*.

Barry N. Malzberg Bibliography

FICTION (as either Barry or Barry N. Malzberg)
Oracle of the Thousand Hands (1968)
Screen (1968)
Confessions of Westchester County (1970)
The Spread (1971)
In My Parents' Bedroom (1971)
The Falling Astronauts (1971)
The Masochist (1972, reprinted as Everything Happened
  to Susan, 1975)
Horizontal Woman (1972; reprinted as The Social Worker, 1973)
Beyond Apollo (1972)
Overlay (1972)
Revelations (1972)
Herovit's World (1973)
In the Enclosure (1973)
The Men Inside (1973)
Phase IV (1973; novelization based on a story
  & screenplay by Mayo Simon)
The Day of the Burning (1974)
The Tactics of Conquest (1974)
Underlay (1974)
The Destruction of the Temple (1974)
Guernica Night (1974)
On a Planet Alien (1974)
Out from Ganymede (1974; stories)
The Sodom and Gomorrah Business (1974)
The Best of Barry N. Malzberg (1975; stories)
The Many Worlds of Barry Malzberg (1975; stories)
Galaxies (1975)
The Gamesman (1975)
Down Here in the Dream Quarter (1976; stories)
Scop (1976)
The Last Transaction (1977)
Chorale (1978)
Malzberg at Large (1979; stories)
The Man Who Loved the Midnight Lady (1980; stories)
The Cross of Fire (1982)
The Remaking of Sigmund Freud (1985)
In the Stone House (2000; stories)
Shiva and Other Stories (2001; stories)

The Passage of the Light: The Recursive Science Fiction of Barry N.
   Malzberg (2004; ed. by Tony Lewis & Mike Resnick; stories)
The Very Best of Barry N. Malzberg (2013; stories)

With Bill Pronzini
The Running of the Beasts (1976)
Acts of Mercy (1977)
Prose Bowl (1980)
Night Screams (1981)
Problems Solved (2003; stories)
On Account of Darkness and Other SF Stories (2004; stories)

As Mike Barry
Lone Wolf series:
Night Raider (1973)
Bay Prowler (1973)
Boston Avenger (1973)
Desert Stalker (1974)
Havana Hit (1974)
Chicago Slaughter (1974)
Peruvian Nightmare (1974)
Los Angeles Holocaust (1974)
Miami Marauder (1974)
Harlem Showdown (1975)
Detroit Massacre (1975)
Phoenix Inferno (1975)
The Killing Run (1975)
Philadelphia Blow-Up (1975)

As Francine di Natale
The Circle (1969)

As Claudine Dumas
The Confessions of a Parisian Chambermaid (1969)

As Mel Johnson/M. L. Johnson
Love Doll (1967; with The Sex Pros by Orrie Hitt)
I, Lesbian (1968)
Just Ask (1968; with Playgirl by Lou Craig)
Instant Sex (1968)
Chained (1968; with Master of Women by March Hastings
   & Love Captive by Dallas Mayo)
Kiss and Run (1968)
Nympho Nurse (1969; with Young and Eager by Jim Conroy & Quickie by
   Gene Evans)

The Sadist (1969)
The Box (1969)
Do It To Me (1969)
Born to Give (1969; with Swap Club by Greg Hamilton & Wild in Bed by
   Dirk Malloy)
Campus Doll (1969; with High School Stud by Robert Hadley)
A Way With All Maidens (1969)

As Howard Lee
Kung Fu #1: The Way of the Tiger, the Sign of the Dragon

As Lee W. Mason
Lady of a Thousand Sorrows (1977)

As K. M. O'Donnell
Empty People (1969)
The Final War and Other Fantasies (1969; stories)
Dwellers of the Deep (1970)
Gather at the Hall of the Planets (1971)
In the Pocket and Other S-F Stories (1971; stories)
Universe Day (1971; stories)

As Elliot B. Reston
The Womanizer (1972)

As Gerrold Watkins
Southern Comfort (1969)
A Bed of Money (1970)
A Satyr's Romance (1970)
Giving It Away (1970)
Art of the Fugue (1970)

NON-FICTION/ESSAYS
The Engines of the Night: Science Fiction in the Eighties
   (1982; essays)
Breakfast in the Ruins (2007; essays: expansion of Engines of the Night)
The Business of Science Fiction: Two Insiders Discuss Writing and
   Publishing (2010; with Mike Resnick)
The Bend at the End of the Road (2018; essays)

EDITED ANTHOLOGIES
Final Stage (1974; with Edward L. Ferman)
Arena (1976; with Edward L. Ferman)
Graven Images (1977; with Edward L. Ferman)
Dark Sins, Dark Dreams (1978; with Bill Pronzini)

The End of Summer: SF in the Fifties (1979; with Bill Pronzini)
Shared Tomorrows: Science Fiction in Collaboration (1979; with Bill Pronzini)
Neglected Visions (1979; with Martin H. Greenberg & Joseph D. Olander)
Bug-Eyed Monsters (1980; with Bill Pronzini)
The Science Fiction of Mark Clifton (1980; with Martin H. Greenberg)
The Arbor House Treasury of Horror & the Supernatural (1981; with Bill Pronzini & Martin H. Greenberg)
The Science Fiction of Kris Neville (1984; with Martin H. Greenberg)
Mystery in the Mainstream (1986; with Bill Pronzini & Martin H. Greenberg)
Uncollected Stars (1986; with Piers Anthony, Martin H. Greenberg & Charles G. Waugh)
The Best Time Travel Stories of All Time (2003)